The yellowbacks... classics of popular fiction

The yellowjackets or yellowbacks were a great series of bestselling adventure and crime thrillers that had its origins in the mid to late 19th century following on from the 'penny dreadfuls'. They virtually began the mass market revolution of the early 20th century with a clear standard format and imprint/series livery (what would today be called branding). Hodder & Stoughton published the yellowjackets in two main series with series run dates of: 1923-1939 and later 1949-1957.

As the tagline ('where thrillers really began') on the back cover implies, the imprint and series focused on thrillers that were the bestsellers of their time. This current reissue or retro revival if you will, brings back many of these masterpieces, now classics in their own way and extends it further by including key titles from that period that were either great crime or thriller or even general commercial fiction (including sub-genres of noir, horror, gothic, romance, westerns, etc.) influences of their time. There are some perennial favourites and many rarities either lost or not easily available being revived in the current series. Writers and characters ranged from adventure heroes like Bulldog Drummond, Allan Quatermain, Richard Hannay, or the Saint through thriller grandmasters Edgar Wallace and E. Phillips Oppenheim, crime and mystery maestros like Patricia Wentworth, GK Chesterton, Agatha Christie, and the Detection club, to western and swashbucklers like Zane Grey, Max Brand, Captain Blood, and even romance or general fiction classics like Hermina Black, Denise Robins, Marie Corelli, or Stella Morton. These were books that had storytelling at their heart and always entertained.

The yellowbacks had both hardback (with varying design elements) and paperback (which built the series look) versions with the latter still carrying the imprint 'yellowjacket'. The current reissues pay tribute to both and use an amalgam of elements from both editions while retaining the complete yellow (or 'mustard-plaster') livery with the author's name in blue beveled type with a 'simulated emboss' effect and a white outer 'outline', and the book title in black. These reissues retain the distinctive size of the original mass market paperback and follow the three main category variations—the thrillers (crime, westerns, mystery, adventure) had blue lettering for the author's name, while Romance and 'softer general fiction had red; and other categories like humour had green.

For more detail and a full list of titles visit https://www.hachetteindia.com/home/yellowbacks

THE SEXTON BLAKE COLLECTION

VOLUME 1

THE SEXTON BLAKE COLLECTION

Sexton Blake is a fictional detective who has been featured in many British comic strips, novels, and dramatic productions since 1893. He began following the Sherlock Holmes trope as is evident even by the Illustrations but later morphed into an adventurer-sleuth rather than just a conventional detective. Blake was featured in various publications from 1893 to 1978 in a variety of formats: single-issue adventures, short stories, serials, and comic strips. In all, Blake appeared in over 4,000 stories by more than 200 different authors. During its heyday (1920s-1940s), Blake's adventures were widely read and translated into at least twenty different languages, including Swedish, Norwegian, Finnish, Dutch, Spanish, German, Portuguese, Italian, French, Arabic, Hindi, and Afrikaans.

The first Sexton Blake story was "The Missing Millionaire" (featured here in this edition). Written by Harry Blyth (using the pseudonym Hal Meredeth), it was published in *The Halfpenny Marvel* number 6, on 20 December 1893, a story paper owned by the Amalgamated Press. Blyth wrote six more Sexton Blake tales, three for the Marvel and three for The Union Jack a story paper launched in April 1894. The Amalgamated Press purchased the rights to Blake along with the first story Blyth had submitted and from 1895 onwards several authors began to pen Blake tales beginning a very profitable syndicate structure. From August 1905 Blake became the resident character in *The Union Jack*, appearing in every issue until its transformation into the *Detective Weekly* in 1933.

Blake's popularity began to grow the early twentieth century, and he was syndicated in several different story papers. These ranged from serials in the tabloid sized *Boys' Friend*, complete tales in the compact *Penny Pictorial*, and short stores in *Answers*, one of the Amalgamated Press' most popular papers. Longer tales over 50,000 words appeared in *The Boys' Friend Library* and the success of these led to the creation of *The Sexton Blake Library* in 1915. This digest-sized publication specialized in longer tales, and at the height of its popularity was published 5 times a month. It ran for almost 50 years.

In 1959 Fleetway Publications acquired the rights to Sexton Blake adventures and published *The Sexton Blake Library* until the title's demise. The final tale, 'The Last Tiger', was published in June 1963. In 1965, Blake editor William Howard Baker licensed the rights of the Sexton Blake character. He published the fifth series of *The Sexton Blake Library* independently via Mayflower-Dell Books, which ran until 1968. He then issued a final series of four Sexton Blake novels, using his Howard Baker Books imprint, in 1969. From 1968 to 1971 Valiant published new comic strips in the style of the Knockout strips from decades earlier. Blake's last original appearance was in *Sexton Blake and the Demon God* "a period thriller with ancient curses and cliff-hanger endings" in 1978.

There are several classic characters from great thriller writers and this first volume introduces some of them.

THE SEXTON BLAKE COLLECTION

Hal Meredeth, Cecil Hayter,
Ernest Sempill, William Murray Graydon,
G.H. Teed, Robert Murray Graydon

VOLUME 1

The Sexton Blake Collection
Sexton Blake's First appearance with 'The Missing Millionaire' was in *The Halfpenny Marvel,* The Amalgamated Press, London, 13 December 1893, and then went to appear in magazines all the way down to 1978. 'The Slave Market' from *The Union Jack* (2nd Series) No 171 in 1907. 'The Man From Scotland Yard' first appeared in *The Boys' Realm* No 266 in 1907. 'The Law of the Sea' first appeared in *The Union Jack* (2nd Series) issue 464 in 1912. 'The Brotherhood of the Yellow Beetle' first appeared in *The Union Jack* issue 507 in 1913. 'A Case of Arson' first appeared in The Union Jack (2nd Series) issue 698 in 1917. 'The Black Eagle' first appeared in *The Union Jack* (2nd Series) issue 1068 in 1923.

1

The texts in these editions in most cases have been reprinted as is, with minimal editorial changes and by and large no bowdlerizing for political correctness; though in some editions, a few words and phrases considered archaic, or those considered offensive now, along with archaic punctuation may have been modified in places to make the text more accessible to today's readers. The narratives, language, beliefs, social mores and/or cultural depictions, in these volumes are a reflection of their times and must be viewed as such. They may also contain certain cultural, racial and gender prejudices and stereotypes that may be outdated or clearly wrong then and wrong today; but their removal would be tantamount to claiming these prejudices never existed. The Publisher does not endorse or support those depictions or stereotypes; and these books have been made available for a discerning audience that will read it for entertainment value and a chronicle/record of popular fiction of past times.

Cover design by Priya Singh adapted from the original classic yellowjacket by Hodder & Stoughton.

Cover illustration: Hodder original.

Series note: Some of the books in the series (unless otherwise credited) may have cover or inside illustrations from the original yellowbacks or early editions, and while full restoration has been attempted, some images may be grainy or faded due to the condition of the original material. The end notes or bonus material or blurb details may have been sourced from the public domain or free use publications such as Wikipedia and attribution is hereby made also allowing similar free use reproduction from here. Sources requiring further specific attribution may write in and further detailing and/or corrections shall be made in subsequent printings/editions.

Reprint specifications may be subject to change including but not limited to finishes, paper, colour sections.

ISBN: 978-93-5731-228-8

Hachette Book Publishing India Pvt. Ltd.
4th & 5th Floors, Corporate Centre,
Plot No. 94, Sector 44, Gurugram - 122 003, India

Typeset in Electra LT STD 10/12.5 pt by Manipal Technologies Limited, Manipal

Printed and bound in India by Manipal Technologies Limited, Manipal

CONTENTS

THE MISSING MILLIONAIRE

Hal Meredeth

THE FIRST CHAPTER

The Detective and His Visitor—A Strange Story of Treachery—The Missing Millionaire.

"Mr. Frank Ellaby wishes to see you, sir."

"Good!" answered Mr. Sexton Blake. "Let him come up, and at once."

The clerk withdrew, and his master gazed thoughtfully at the grimy window of his office in New Inn Chambers.

"So," he muttered, "my wealthy client has come at last, thanks to the influence of my friend Gervaise, of Paris. I wonder what kind of mission it is he has in hand that is to bring me in such high rewards? Gervaise says it may keep me busy for a year or two."

Sexton Blake belonged to the new order of detectives. He possessed a highly-cultivated mind which helped to support his active courage. His refined, clean-shaven face readily lent itself to any disguise, and his mobile features assisted to clinch any facial illusion he desired to produce.

The door again opened, and a tall, handsome man, whose cheeks were bronzed by travel, and whose grey eyes were large and prominent, entered.

"Mr. Blake, I believe?" he said, as he paused on the threshold.

"Very much at your service, Mr. Frank Ellaby. Pray take a seat, and let me hear what I can do for you. Mr. Gervaise prepared me for a visit from you. But I am quite in the dark as to the nature of the business you desire me to undertake."

"It will prove more troublesome than dangerous," said the visitor, with a slight smile. "I will tell you my story, and then you will understand exactly what I want.

"My sister and myself were left orphans before we had finished our schooling. Some friends sent her out to Australia, where I believe she obtained a comfortable situation. It is unnecessary for me to bore you with a description of my struggles for existence. When I was about twenty I, like thousands of other men, old and young, took a severe attack of gold fever. I was determined to get to the Antipodes by hook or by crook, and try my luck at the diggings. If I came across my sister, well and good, although I did not start with any design of finding her. I had one object in view, and one only—that was wealth!

"I have obtained my desire," he added, with a heavy sigh, "But my heart is empty, and my life desolate!

"Out in Australia I met a man and his wife, with whom I became so friendly that he and I became partners in a claim, at which we toiled for months without finding one grain of gold. He was some years older than myself, and he went by the name of Calder Dulk. I don't suppose it was his real title, for I know now that there was nothing true about him.

"In those days I would have trusted him with my life. He, again, was younger than his wife, who was a tall, majestic woman, of French extraction wonderfully accomplished, fiercely ambitious, and altogether unscrupulous.

"I always mistrusted her, and, unfortunately, I had not the art to conceal my dislike.

"Just when we were despairing of ever having any luck, and were thinking of seeking our fortune in some other part, we struck a rich vein of the precious ore, and found ourselves wealthy.

"Like many before us, this sudden success turned our heads. Nothing would do but we must hasten to Melbourne and enjoy ourselves.

"A few days after we arrived there I accidentally found the house where my sister lived. I got there just in time to bid her goodbye forever. She was dying. A beautiful, golden-haired girl of perhaps four years of age was playing in the room.

"'Frank,' gasped my sister, 'I swore to the mother of little Rose there, when she lay on her deathbed, that I would protect her child until she came of age. Take the same oath to me, Frank, so that I may die in peace.'

"There was, of course, no refusing this request at that awful moment, so I most solemnly took the vow she wished.

"'In that cabinet, standing in the corner over there, you will find some papers which will explain who her parents were,' my sister continued, speaking with great difficulty, for life's lamp was at its last flicker. 'When you have perused them you will understand how precious she is, and how important it is that she is well guarded till she becomes a woman and can claim her own!'

"As she ceased speaking she pressed my hand in hers. Smiling on me, she passed into the eternal sleep.

"This sad event so distressed me that I could do nothing in connection with the child or anything just then. Calder Dulk led me away from the place to the hotel where we were staying. He advised me to remain alone and keep quiet until the morning, which I did.

"When the morrow came both he and his wife had disappeared, and they had taken every ounce of gold I possessed with them! Nor was this all. They had run off with the child, too, not forgetting to secure the papers relating to her birth, to which my sister attached so much importance.

"I need not tell you what my emotions were under this stinging reversal of my fortune, at this horrible breach of faith, and at my inability to keep the oath I had so recently made to my dying sister.

"I was powerless to follow them, for I had not sufficient money even to pay the hotel bill. There was nothing I could do but return to the diggings, and by hard labour again woo the favour of the goddess of chance.

"I swore then in my heart that, if I ever did attain wealth, I would spend every farthing of it, if necessary, in hunting down the traitor who had betrayed me, and in finding the child who was so infamously stolen from my protection! So, Mr. Sexton Blake, I am here to obtain your co-operation in this search, which must never cease till my end is attained!"

"How long is it since this double robbery was committed?" asked the detective.

"Fourteen years."

"Whew! That's a long time. Dulk and his wife may be dead; the girl has become a woman."

"And a beautiful one, too, I am sure. You see," Mr Ellaby explained, "for a long, long time my luck was so bad that I scarcely succeeded in keeping body and soul together. It is only recently that the wheel of fortune has taken a turn. Then, as always happens, gold poured in on me till I was tired of gathering it."

"Have you heard anything of these people since?'"

"Absolutely nothing. But your friend, Gervaise, of Paris, believes that Madame Dulk has visited the French capital quite recently. While there she plundered the aristocracy in a most grand and daring manner. No one answering the description of her husband was seen to visit her. As she has undoubtedly left France, it is surmised that she is either in England or America."

"A very wide address," said Blake, with a smile. "If she is a high-toned adventuress, and is in London, she will be easily found. But you are giving me a tall order. When Stanley was sent to Africa to find Livingstone, his search was at least limited to one continent. The whole world is before me. But I will do my best."

"Do that, and whether you fail or succeed, you shall have your own reward. Day and night I shall be at your service to aid you, and you may direct me as you choose."

"We will work together, and I can promise you heartiness on my part. But, I fear if we find Calder Dulk that I shall have helped to bring about a murder."

It was the detective who spoke.

"What do you mean?" demanded Ellaby.

"Simply this: you wish to meet him, *so that you kill him!*"

"When I get him will be time enough for me to decide what I shall do with him," replied the other. "I know you cannot give me any useful advice off-hand. I must let you have a little time to digest my story. Meanwhile, will you lunch with me? I have been away from England so long that it will be safer for both of us if I trust to you to select the restaurant."

"With pleasure," said Blake. "Let us stroll as far as Charing Cross. I think best when I am walking. Come round this way," he added, when they stood in Wych Street, and he pointed to St. Clement's Danes. "I must give a minute's call in Arundel Street."

Two other men were watching them from a neighbouring doorway. They took great care not to be seen.

"That's our man," said one to the other, indicating Frank Ellaby. "Once we secure him we shall be as well off as anyone need ever want to be. He's worth millions! You shadow him, Scooter, and make no mistake about it. If you let him give you the slip it will be as much as your skin is worth."

"No, thanks," laughed the first speaker. "That job is not in my way at all."

In the narrowest part of the Strand, between the two churches, the detective and Frank Ellaby became separated in the roadway, and by some evil chance to latter was knocked down and run over by a carelessly-driven hansom cab.

He was carried to the opposite pavement in an insensible condition. Mr. Sexton Blake feared that he was killed outright.

A tall, handsome woman pressed her way through the crowd, which at once surrounded the injured man.

Her hair was as white as snow, and her eyes were coal-black in colour. It was a face time had treated tenderly. It was determined and commanding, too.

"Let your friend be brought to my house," she said to Blake. "It is close here—only round the corner in Norfolk Street. He may die before he can be taken to the hospital. A doctor lives opposite to where I reside."

Gratefully indeed did the detective accept this opportune proposal. Apart altogether from the common sympathies of humanity, which were strongly developed in Blake, he had selfish reasons for desiring to keep this exceedingly wealthy client alive.

It happed, fortunately, that the front apartment leading off the hall, in the Norfolk Street house, was a bedroom, and here they laid the unconscious man.

In a few minutes Dr. Tuppy, from opposite, was by his side making a careful examination of his injuries.

"One rib fractured," he said. "Severe scalp wounds. No danger. Quiet, good nursing, and my advice will soon put him on his feet again. He must not, on any account be removed for some days. I don't know, madame—"

He paused to be supplied with the name of the lady who had called him in.

"Vulpino," she said, in a musical voice.

"Well, I don't know, Madame Vulpino, whether you can possibly allow the gentleman to stay in your rooms, but I can assure you that he can only be conveyed out of them, at present, at the risk of his life."

"I would not turn an injured dog from my roof," said madame, with a touch of emotion. "He shall stay here till he can be taken away with safety. I have an elderly woman with me who will nurse him."

"Excellent," said the doctor.

"Believe me, he shall want for nothing."

"You are indeed a good Samaritan, madame," declared Blake. "My friend is a man of means, and any expenses you may be put to—"

She closed his speech with a proud wave of her hand, which clearly indicated that she would not accept any money recompense for the inconvenience she was putting herself to.

"Now, my dear sir," said Dr. Tuppy, "*you* can do nothing more for your friend. He is in excellent hands. I will see the nurse, and give her my instructions. He will soon recover consciousness, and then he must have absolute quietness. Of course, you may come round in the morning and see how he is."

Blake, quite easy in his mind, left his new client in the house in Norfolk Street, and set about a careful consideration of the problem which had been put before him, and attending to such other matters as he had in hand.

The next day, at ten o'clock, he called to see how Ellaby was progressing.

The door was opened by a typical specimen of the London lodging-house "slavey."

"Well," he said, good humouredly, "how is my friend this morning?"

"Wot friend? Oh, the gent as was ill yesterday. He's gone."

"Gone? Impossible! How did he go?"

"That's just what missis says when a lodger gets out without paying what he owes. Why sir, how can I tell you how they goes?"

"Madame Vulpino is in, I suppose?" said the detective, as he tried to persuade himself that the girl was talking foolishly, and at random.

"She has gone, too," was the answer. "That was her room he was taken into. Her time was up last night, and she went, and paid up, too. She gave me half-a-crown, and told me not to bother her when she was getting her luggage into the cab. So I didn't. I just went to sleep in the kitchen. My misses was out at the time."

"Will you let me look into Madame Vulpino's room?" said Blake, more perplexed than ever detective was yet.

"Why, of course I will, sir," laughed the girl. "You can come and live in it if you like to pay the rent regular, and gas, and coals, and boots is extra, and I does the boots."

There was no doubt about it. Frank Ellaby was not in that house, nor could any information be obtained as to how he had left it. To make matters worse, no one knew anything about Madame Vulpino.

As for Dr. Tuppy, he simply shrugged his shoulders.

"You are all strangers to me," he said, "and I only know three things about you. First, you call me from my lunch in a dreadful hurry. Second, the removal of the patient last night was quite against my instructions, and will probably kill him. Third, I have received no fee!"

"Frank Ellaby has fallen into bad hands," thought Sexton Blake, as he made his way to his office, feeling very vexed with himself. "Not only into bad hands, but, I fear, powerful ones. I must try and rescue him, whatever it costs me. There can be little doubt that he has been followed from Australia by some desperate gang, who know how wealthy he is. They have succeeded in capturing him in the simplest way possible. They have him in their power, while he is quite helpless. It means a race now between my brains and another London mystery, and I'll back myself to win!"

THE SECOND CHAPTER

Frank Ellaby Finds Himself Bound and Helpless in a Cab—At the Old Water Mill.

To keep the events in this remarkable history abreast of one another as much as possible, we will leave the detective to take his own way of discovering the whereabouts of his rich client, and concern ourselves with Mr Frank Ellaby's own movements.

When he regained his senses he found that he was gagged, and bound hand and foot.

He was in some kind of vehicle which carried no lights. As it jolted along a rough, dark road, it rattled like a ramshackle old four-wheeler. He was stretched along it from the back to the front seat. A piece of plank covered the space between, and gave him additional support.

His injuries occasioned him great pain. At present his senses were numbed, as though the effects of some powerful drug were still clinging to him. He dimly recalled the accident which had befallen him. From then to now was a blank.

He consoled himself at first with the thought that he was being conveyed to some infirmary where he would find ease, and receive kind treatment. But if this was the intention of those who had placed him in the cab, why was he gagged and bound?

The air grew keener, and the part through which they passed more and more silent, till Frank judged that they must now be in the open country. Suddenly the vehicle pulled up with a jerk, which nearly sent the injured man to its other side.

"Wake up, my beauty," said a rough voice.

The door of the cab opened, and Frank's body was prodded playfully with a heavy bludgeon.

"We have reached our destination. You must try and walk into our picturesque country retreat, for you are a bit too heavy for me to carry."

By the aid of the bright moon, Ellaby saw that the gaunt, spectral building which stood before him and back from the road in murky ugliness had been a watermill.

The big wheel was there yet, dripping with slimy weeds. The moon's rays made the still water look green and murderous. The house itself was as forbidding a structure as it is easy to imagine.

The door of the evil place opened. A man carrying a lantern emerged and came towards them. He wore a mask. His voice appeared familiar to Frank, though, at that moment, he could not identify it.

"Is it all right, Bill Bender?" he asked, addressing the rough driver.

"Quite right. Now, my young swell, I'll just undo the strap which holds your legs, and with a little support from me, you will be able to walk inside. Why, bless me, if you haven't got a lovely gold lever, as big as a turnip, and a chain strong enough to hold a horse. I'll take care of these trifles for you, and if you want any civility from me, you had better make no fuss about this little incident.

"You see," continued the ruffian, "if I have any of your nonsense I can give you a touch with *this*"—he tapped the prisoner's head with a life-preserver—"or you can have a dose of *this*."

He produced a pistol, and the barrel gleamed in the moonlight.

"But there," he added, with a coarse laugh, "it won't be any good for you to try on anything. We are a thousand miles from everywhere, as the saying is, and if you try to escape, all you will find will be a watery grave."

They had removed Frank's gag now. Although he was in great pain he addressed them with the utmost coolness and assurance.

"I am too ill and weak to make any attempt to escape, especially from any place which promises warmth, rest, and shelter. Pray help me in, and let me lie down."

"We have ventured to take a few liberties with you tonight," said the man who wore the mask, "but we do not contemplate treating you with violence. Tomorrow, however, will show us whether you are a reasonable, or an unreasonable, man—whether we must resort to force or not."

"Tomorrow will be time enough for that or any other discussion. Tonight my pain is so great I can hardly stand. I beg of you to take me indoors. The man who guards me tonight will have an easy task."

"I am glad to see you take matters so coolly. You shall have all the attention this place affords. Let me warn you. You are as far from human aid here as though you were in your tomb."

THE THIRD CHAPTER

A Threat of Torture—Left to Starve to Death.

"How is your patient getting on now?" The man who had worn the mask asked this question of the ruffian he had called "Bill Bender."

The former was sitting before a well-spread table, enjoying a hearty meal, and the latter had just returned from the room which was to prove Frank Ellaby's prison.

"Beautiful!" was the answer. "I never saw a man in his position take things so cool and comfortable. He could not be more contented in his own hotel."

"I'd rather he made a fuss. He'll prove all the more troublesome to us in the end. These calm, determined men are more difficult to deal with than excitable people."

"We can soon knock the nonsense out of him. What made you cover up your face with that mask tonight, Mr. Calder Dulk?"

"Why, you see," came the slow answer, "after he has paid his ransom, I don't want it to be in his power to take proceedings against me when he is once more free."

"When he is once more free?" repeated Bender, with a low chuckle. "You don't mean that he ever shall get free? One you have got his money, he will only be a danger to you alive. *He'll have to go where the rest have gone.*"

"I neither contemplate, nor do I recommend, violence," said Dulk, with a queer look in his eyes; "when we obtain possession of the cash, I shall leave him here, and you can do what you like with him."

"Thanks; and I shan't forget to keep my eyes on you, either," muttered the rascal.

Frank was put into a comfortable bed, in a warm room, and he was well supplied with everything in the way of nourishment he could desire.

He felt that whoever had bandaged his injuries had done the work with some skill.

There was no window to the apartment, and all escape from it was prevented by a iron-bound oaken door, which was secured by bolts and an iron bar on the outside.

Except for the fact that he was a prisoner in that sinister building, and probably in imminent peril of his life, he might have felt as contented there as in any other place he could have been taken to.

After a long and grave consideration of his present position, he came to the unjust conclusion that Mr. Sexton Blake had proved a scoundrel, and for his own ends had made him a prisoner.

"Yes," thought Frank, "it must be Blake. Not another soul in London knows who I am, or what I am worth! I wonder how much he will want to set me free? I wonder whether I shall ever yield to his infamous demands? I think not. He has played a dangerous game, and he shall suffer for it, Unless they kill me outright. He could not have planned the accident which befell me, but my helplessness may have suggested this cunning plot. Opportunity is the great tempter. I suppose tomorrow my gaolers will tell me their intentions."

When he awoke on the following day, he felt refreshed, and so hungry, that he looked forward eagerly for the appearance of breakfast.

Frank had a remarkably strong constitution, which travel, hardship, and exposure had hardened, and not shattered.

In spite of Doctor Tuppy's prognostication, his sudden and queer removal had not retarded his recovery. He felt in himself that a few days would see him on his feet again, and in fair health. His only visitor the next day was "Bill Bender."

He brought a jug of coffee and a couple of slices of bread and butter.

"We are not going to feed you up with high-class food," said the man, "because it might fire your blood, and we mean to keep you nice and cool." This fare, rough as it proved, was very welcome to Frank.

"Now," continued the ruffian, drawing a packet of papers from his pocket, "I'm going to leave these things with you for your careful and best consideration. One is a cheque on the London Joint Stock Bank for twenty thousand pounds. Oh, my fine millionaire! We've got friends in Paris, who told us which was your London bank."

"Gervaise, of course," Frank thought; "he has planned this with Sexton Blake. I have plunged my head right into the hornets' nest."

"All you have to do," continued "Bill Bender," with a grin, "is to sign this cheque, and then, in case you should not have so much cash as that at the bank, here's a little power of attorney for you to put your name to. It authorised Mr. Cornelius Brown to realise on any stocks or shares, bonds or certificates, personal or real estate, you may possess. Once you have signed these different documents, and we have secured what we have justly earned, you will be free to leave this place and enjoy yourself as you may think best. So it just rests with you, Mr. Frank Ellaby, how long you remain here. We can wait for years, if necessary. *You have not one living person on earth likely to trouble themselves whether you are alive or dead!*"

How true this was Frank knew only too well, and to his sorrow.

"I can't prevent you from leaving the papers here," he said quietly; "but I will never sign one of them as long as I live!"

"That's what you think now, but we will make you change your mind soon."

"I should be a fool to sing."

Frank spoke carelessly. "So long as you want my authorisation to those papers, you will keep me alive for the gratification of your own greed; but once that is satisfied, it will not matter to you whether I am alive or dead. While I am alive I have hope."

"Well, I never thought of that! How clever you are! But, look here; this matter has been put into my hands, and I am going to work it off quick. I don't suppose you are a bit more frightened of death than I am; but there's something worse than that, and it's *torture*. If you won't come to any reasonable terms, *I'll starve you into submission!* Do you hear?"

"You cur!" said Frank, contemptuously. "Why, you would run a mile from me, if I had my strength, and we were on equal terms. As it is, I'll bring you to the earth!"

On the little table by the bedside the man had placed a metal ink-pot and a pen, with the papers to which he wished Frank to put his signature.

The prisoner seized this pewter inkstand, and hurled it, with all the force he could command, full in the face of his brutal custodian.

The blow was unexpected, and Bill dropped to the ground like a log of wood.

Frank thought that the moment for his escape had come, and he tried to struggle into his clothes.

Alas! he was so weak that he had to sink on to the bed, and cling to it, trembling from the effects of his recent exertions.

This gave "Bill Bender" time to regain his feet, and he soon had his prisoner back again between the sheets.

"So that's a sample of temper, is it?" snarled Bill. "I shall look our for you in future. You take my advice. Sign those papers while you have a chance. I'm a bit rough to deal with when

I'm put out, and you have marked my figurehead for life. Until those papers are signed you don't get bit nor sup from me."

With a curse Bill left Frank Ellaby to recover from his prostration as best he could. For two days Frank had neither food nor drink given him.

In one way he suffered terribly, but this heroic treatment helped his injuries to heal up in a miraculously short space of time.

He then began to consider whether, after all, he had not better attach his signature to the documents which were still at the side of his bed.

If he did not do the bidding of these wretches, it was certain they would starve him to death!

Circumstanced as he was he could lose nothing by agreeing to their terms. If he ever did get free he promised himself that he would punish Mr. Gervaise, of Paris, and Mr. Sexton Blake, of London, most severely for their villainy. He hoped, too, that he would be able to make them disgorge the money they had wrenched from him.

Little did he imagine that both these wrongly suspected gentlemen were at that very moment doing all they could to find and rescue him!

The next time "Bill Bender" put his head into the room, with the question whether his prisoner had come to his senses yet, Frank Ellaby said—

"I have signed all you wished me to. Bring me something to eat and to drink. When you have got your money I suppose you will see that I am released from here?"

"Not much," said Bill, with a coarse laugh, as he thrust the papers into the breast pocket of his heavy overcoat "Now, listen to me. If you had not been so obstinate, I would have done fair and honest by you. But you've bee pig-headed, and you've kept me from my pleasures and enjoyments. More than that, you have marked my face. The consequence of which is that *I'm going to leave you here to starve. You can't escape. No one can come to you. Here you shall remain and slowly starve to death.*"

With this speech the ruffian left the room, bolting and barring the door behind him. "He tells the truth for once," groaned Frank, "there is no help of hope for me. I see nothing before me but a dragging out of an existence which will be torture till the end of its last thread!"

THE FOURTH CHAPTER

Gervaise, of Paris, Appears on the Scene—The "Red Lights" of London—The Newspaper Boy's Story—Finding the Old Mill—Dragging the Pool—Discovery of a Body.

"So far all my searchings have been in vain. I have failed to find any trace of Mr. Frank Ellaby."

So said Sexton Blake to his fellow-worker, Detective Gervaise, of Paris, to whom he had telegraphed directly it became known that the millionaire had disappeared.

"I blame myself very much for this catastrophe," said Gervaise, gloomily. "I should have described that woman to you, and have put you on your guard against her. She was as anxious to secure Ellaby as he was to find and punish her. She wanted me to shadow him before he called on me to get information concerning her. I intended coming to England, to put on her track, and I calculated that your speedy discovery of her would bring a substantial reward from our wealthy friend. You have already guessed that this Madame Vulpino and Mrs. Calder Dulk is one person. This unfortunate accident has played havoc with my plans. Fate seems to have worked altogether in favour of Ellaby's enemies."

"On the night of his disappearance," said Blake, "the woman, accompanied by a shabbily-dressed man, drove from Norfolk Street to Charing Cross Station, where she took two tickets for Paris. She and her companion both entered the Continental train, but it is quite certain they never went by it. They must have left it when it was on the point of starting."

"The booking to France was a mere blind—to lead you on to a false scent. There can be no doubt that the woman is still in London, and probably not far off. Very likely the man who accompanied her was Dulk himself. Within a day or so someone will turn up at the London Joint Stock Bank with a cheque signed by the missing man. As we have warned the authorities at the bank to detain any such messenger, I hope to reach the conspirators through that means. There can be no doubt that their object is to extort money from their prisoner—"

"And when they have succeeded what will become of him?" suggested Blake.

"Ah, that is just where all the danger comes in," said Gervaise gravely.

"I wonder if the 'Red Lights,' have any hand in this kidnapping?"

"Who and what are the 'Red Lights,' my friend?"

"It is a new and formidable society of professional lawbreakers of every class. Its conception was due to the fertile brain of a young, well-educated fellow named Leon Polti. It was his idea to join together into one powerful association the most expert operators in all branches of crime. The cleverest burglar throws in his lot with the most accomplished forger, and so on through the whole list of police offences. The notion is a brotherhood of crime, with meeting places, and correspondents all over the country, working for the common good of their own combination, and to the hurt of honest people.

"If Polti could realise his highest ideal and conduct such a gigantic organisation, on strictly business principles, and with keen method, I fear the police would be beaten at every turn, and crime would be triumphant in the land! Luckily, rogues never do agree together for long.

"They will observe no laws—not even their own. So Polti's vast scheme will remain a dream, and nothing else, to the end of time. This case we have in hand looks something like the work of his gang. Watching and waiting for the rich man coming from Australia, and sending the woman over to Paris to shadow him, suggests his methods. I daresay I can find him. He knows me. We will see if we can discover anything of his doings."

At this point their conversation was interrupted by the appearance of a shaggy, flaming head of red hair, which thrust itself into the office through the half-opened doorway.

"Well," interrogated Blake, "what do you want?"

"Please, governor, I'm the boy wot stands about the top of Essex Street, selling papers, and you've given me many a 'brown,' you has."

A body followed the head, and there stood disclosed to the two detectives, a short, bright-faced boy, who looked like nothing so much as an animated bundle of rags. His tattered trousers barely touched his knees, and strips of time-eaten cloth fluttered round his thin, discoloured arm.

"I've got no 'browns' for you today," said Blake, waving his hand impatiently.

"Oh yes, you has, sir," the street boy answered, with a knowing shake of his glowing locks. "Wait till you 'ear wot 'ive got to tell yer, and then I think you'll be good for a 'bob.' It's like this 'ere. Tommy Roundhead says as 'ow you want to find out about a 'toff as was taken out of a house in Arundel Street, late Thursday night. Well, I can tell you all about that 'ere. 'Cos, why? I helped in the job myself."

"If you can help me to find that gentleman," said Blake, with sudden energy, "I'll make a man of you! We won't trouble about shillings. Pounds and pounds shall be spent on you."

"We can decide what to do when we have hear his tale," said Gervaise, with more caution.

"It's like this, governor. I was walking down Arundel Street, wondering where I should pitch myself for the night, when a four-wheeler drives up, and stops at that house. The driver jumps off the box, and I see, at once, that he weren't a reg'lar cabby. 'Ere young Vesuvius!' 'e cries,' 'old the 'osse's ead.' The door of the 'ouse opens without him knocking or ringing. I sees that there's a sort of bed made up in the cab. In a minute or two the driver comes out with another man. Between them they carries a third man, who, if he ain't dead, 'as lost 'is senses. They puts this helpless chap inside, and the coachman, springs on to his box again. 'I shall be there before you,' says the man who is standing on the pavement. He puts 'is 'and in 'is pocket, and, after fumbling about a bit, he pulls out 'arf a sovereign.' "Take that,' he says to me, 'I ain't got noffink smaller.' He walks away quick.

"'Well,' thinks I,' if I gets 'arf a quid for 'olding the 'oss while they puts the swell *into* the cab, perhaps I shall get a bit more if I'm there to 'old it when they take 'im *hout*. So I gets up on the back of the cab, and clings on. But, bless you! I was taken right away to Barking. I didn't get off because I made sure the cab would be coming back again. At last we stops before a tumble-down old watermill. Then the driver brings out a blunderbuss, or sumfink deadly, and a reg'lar hold-fashioned life-preserver. I take to me 'eels in case they should want to give me one on the 'ead. I waits about hoping to see the cab go back. But they puts in the stable there, and I 'as to walk. I falls in with a tramp, and he sneaks my half sovereign. Then the police collars me for being a vagabond, and that's how it is I ain't been at my hold pitch the last day or two."

"This is new indeed!" exclaimed Gervaise. "Can you lead us to this old mill?"

"It's a hawful lonely place," said the boy, "but I think I can find it again."

"Let us go at once," suggested Gervaise.

"We must lose no time," agreed Blake, meditatively, "but we need to go to work with extreme caution. I don't like that remote watermill. It looks murderous in my eyes. If our man is still there, and alive, his gaolers may offer a desperate resistance. The quickest way will be to take the train to Barking."

"Can't do it, governor," declared the lad; "I shall never find the place if I don't go the same way as that four-wheeler did."

So they hired a hansom, and it took half a day to light on the spot where "Bill Bender" had threatened Frank Ellaby with bludgeon and pistol.

"The place is deserted," said Blake. "I fear the worst."

"We shall have no difficulty in getting in," said Gervaise, as he threw the weight of his body against a rotten and ill-secured back-door, which at once flew open.

The rats infesting the place scampered before them as they walked through the musty passages and gloomy rooms.

Upstairs they came on a heavy door, barred and bolted on the outside. Their hearts beat high as they undid these fastenings.

They felt sure they were on the point of entering the room where Mr. Ellaby had been kept prisoner. Would they find him there now, was the question which trembled on the lips of both, but neither spoke.

They were not hopeful of discovering him alive, for he had not answered the shouts they had raised on entering the building. Was his murdered body to meet their horrified gaze?

"Empty, as I expected," said Gervaise. "What a strong room it is? It might have been built for a prison cell. He has been here, that is quite clear. There is his bed, his writing materials—"

"And," said Blake, "an absence of water and of other food!"

"They left him to starve to death!" Gervaise added excitedly, "but he has escaped by tearing the fire-grate from its settings. See how loose the bricks behind are. He could not have had great difficulty in making the hole through which he must have crawled. There is a room beyond—long, narrow. We must follow his example, and see where it leads to."

"His footprints on the dusty floor can still be traced," said Blake. "The open window at the end shows he escaped that way. Why has he not communicated with me?"

"Because," answered Gervaise impressively, "his body lies at the bottom of that still, black-looking pool. You observe, this window is exactly over the old wheel of the watermill. He must have stepped on to it. His weight would make it revolve; he would be hurled into the water. Probably one of the flanges would strike his head, and render him insensible. Then the weeds would catch him in their deadly embrace.

"See! There is his hat floating on the green scum! We must have this water dragged!" As soon as they could procure drags and other aids, the pond was most effectually dragged. After some hours' work, and with much difficulty, they brought a corpse to the bank, about which lank weeds still clung.

"Unhappily, we are too late to preserve the life of Frank Ellaby, for here his body undoubtedly lies. The one thing left for us is to make our very best effort to bring his murderers to justice." It was Gervaise who spoke.

"And that we will do as certainly as we stand here," answered Sexton Blake.

THE FIFTH CHAPTER

The Vicar's Secret—A True Lover—The Cheque for £20,000—Arrested.

In this chapter we must take the reader to the old-fashioned Sussex village of Downslow, and to the ivy-clad rectory there, in the library of which sat the Rev. Frederick Briarton, in grave conversation with Ernest Truelove, a farmer's son, who was on the eve of leaving his old home for London, with the intention of entering one of its medical schools and winning a surgeon's diploma.

"I will not conceal from you my satisfaction at knowing that you have won the love of my dear Rose," said the clergyman, "for I have confidence in your high regard for truth and honour. I am old, and it is idle for me to hope that I can be much longer in this world. I shall die the happier for knowing that Rose has linked her life with one who will do his utmost to shield her from its storms. But, my dear boy, I have a secret to confide to your keeping, which may make you desire to withdraw from the engagement you have entered into."

"Nothing can possibly happen to make me do that," said Ernest fervently.

"Prepare yourself for a shock, my friend. *Rose is not a daughter of mine!* I do not even know who her parents are."

"You have succeeded in surprising me," said young Truelove. "I love Rose for herself alone, and I care not whose child she is!"

"She is the essence of goodness and purity. Many years ago I was chaplain to one of Her Majesty's prisons. A few days before I resigned that appointment to commence duties at a small living in Yorkshire, which had been presented to me, one of the female convicts, a handsome and accomplished woman, sent for me, and, upon her knees, implored me to protect a little girl her arrest and sentence had compelled her to leave in the care of some rough, illiterate people living at Hammersmith. She said that the child was not her own, that it had a great future before it, and that when she was released she would repay me for my trouble, and restore the child to its proper sphere. As I had not been blessed with any children of my own, I was ready enough to adopt Rose. My poor dead wife grew devotedly attached to her, and she was brought up as our own daughter. The time soon came when I began to feel terror lest her convict guardian should appear at our home, and blight its happiness by claiming our darling Rose.

"By the will of an uncle I was practically compelled to change my old name of Sparrow to the one I now bear—Briarton. I have moved about a good deal, too, and perhaps that is why the woman has not found me. I am glad to have eluded her. I would go very much against my moral grain to have to deliver up so pure and gentle a girl to a woman who has once worn a convict's dress. I have never had the courage to tell Rose the truth. She firmly believes herself to be my child."

"Let her die in that faith," said Truelove, promptly.

"It would be cruel to her to tell her the truth now, and no useful purpose would be served. She herself is too good for me to believe that her parents were bad. I will work hard, and in a little over three years I shall secure my diploma; then I can give her a name which shall be her very own, and she can defy anyone who may wish to claim her."

After this, Ernest spent a long time with Rose herself, till the hour came when he had to drive to the station and catch his train. They had repeated their mutual vows over and over again.

When evening prayers were said in the vicarage, the rector introduced a fervent one for the safety and prosperity of

Ernest Truelove, amid the pitfalls and temptations of the huge metropolis.

Meanwhile this young gentleman, having spent an hour or so in Brighton, was dashing on to London at express speed, his regrets at leaving his old friends and the scenes of his youth lightened by this sense of the vivid change which was now to colour the daily routine of his life.

His only fellow-passenger was a young fellow who looked about his own age, but he might have been older. Slight in build, with a creamy skin, and large dark, fascinating eyes, a round smooth chin, and a delicate mouth, he was decidedly effeminate in appearance, and yet there lurked in his every graceful movement a suspicion of sinewy and uncommon strength.

The two had easily fallen into conversation, and this had led to an exchange of cards.

The stranger's bore the name of—

"Leon Polti."

"So," said the latter, to whom the innocent Ernest had confided much of his past history and many of his plans for the future, "you want comfortable lodgings in the centre of London? Ah! Now I don't think you can do better than take up your quarters at the house where my sister and I are temporarily located—99, Bernard Street, Russell Square. It's no distance from Charing Cross Hospital. The landlady is the most obliging creature I ever met with, and the cooking is capital. I know she has a bed and sitting-room to let. Probably you don't mind if they are a bit high up. You can drive home with me tonight. There will be no harm in seeing the place, even if you should elect not to take the apartments."

"I am very much obliged to you," said Ernest. "I have no doubt the place will suit me very well indeed. I suppose, though, I shall have to go to an hotel tonight?"

"Not a bit of it! If you like the accommodations, Madame Dulk, the landlady, will make you perfectly comfortable at once."

Ernest was charmed with the house and with his new friends.

The same evening he dined with Mr Polti, and he saw that this gentleman lived in quite high style. The table was spread with delicacies, in and out of season, and there were famous wines.

"My sister is out of town tonight," said his host. "I hope to introduce you to her tomorrow."

On the following morning he encountered a dark young lady on the stairs. The likeness to Leon Polti was so striking that he could not doubt her near relationship to that gentleman, so he ventured to address her.

"Oh, yes," said, with a laugh, which disclosed a set of brilliant teeth, "I am Nizza Polti. My brother has told me so much about you. I hope we shall be great friends. Some business has called him away; he will not be back for a few days. But," she added, "Madame Dulk generally sits with me in the evening, and any time you like we shall be glad if you will join us."

The days passed very pleasantly with Ernest. Some evenings he saw Nizza, and on others Leon. Their own affairs so fell out that they were never able to be together when young Truelove was in the house.

One evening as Leon was sitting with the medical student in the latter's room, Madame Dulk tapped at the door, and brought word that a gentleman waited below to see Mr. Polti on most urgent business. "Bother him!" said Leon. "Can't he come in the morning?"

"No. He says it is imperative that you see him now."

"He shall wait till I have finished this cigar, at any rate. Tell him so, whoever he may be. I hate these inquisitive people," he added, with a yawn, to Ernest.

When he did at last deign to descend the stairs he found Calder Dulk waiting for him. He took him into another room.

"You have an odd way of disturbing one at most inconvenient moments," said Leon. "Well, what is it you want me for?"

"The rat in his cage has eaten his cheese," replied Dulk, harshly, annoyed at the other's assumption of cool indifference. "In other words, Mr. Frank Ellaby has signed all the papers you made out for him to put his signature to. I've got them with me. It's for you to turn them into good current gold. Our part of the business is finished, and that has been the roughest and the worst section of it. Now you can put in some of your 'fine' work, as you call it."

"I'm afraid you have come in a sneering mood, Dulk." Polti drawled his words out lazily. "And really it does not become so jovial a fellow as yourself. *What has been done with Ellaby?*"

"I left him to 'Bill Bender.' *You* know what he generally does with them."

"It's always force, and never persuasion, with you people," said Leon contemptuously.

"These papers seem to be all right," he continued. "They shall have my attention as soon as possible, and you will all know the result."

"That won't do for me," said Dulk fiercely. "I mean having the lion's share of this plunder. Why, if it hadn't been for me you would not have known of the existence of this Frank Ellaby. But for my wife's promptitude it might have taken you months to capture him. Those papers represent an actual little gold mine. It is through our work, and through the work of no one else, that they have been obtained, and we mean being *paid in full*! You talk about us all being equal. You are like the man in the play. He wanted *his* followers to be equal so long as he was chief. No doubt you would like to be crowned 'Monarch of Criminals,' and 'King of Crime,' and all that kind of thing; but we are not quite such fools as to give way to you."

"You amuse me, Dulk," said Leon, throwing himself back in his chair, and smiling dangerously. "Perhaps you will condescend to remember that, but for me, there would have been no house in Arundel Street to take your victim to—the man you have twice plundered. But for me there would have been no old mill in which to torture him into subjection. But for me you would not now have good broadcloth on your back. But for me the only possible roof for you would be the strong one of the gaol. You want the lion's share of this money? You shall have it all, my friend. Take back your papers; do what you will with them. I wash my hands of the affair, of you, of your wife. You cannot play either the role of knave or honest man. Well, I am better without you. Goodnight."

"Leon, Leon," pleaded Dulk, with a white, anxious face, "don't talk like that! You know I dare not work those papers! Come, come; forgive me! I spoke hastily; I did not mean what I said. Take the papers again. Work as you choose with them; I make no conditions."

"Make conditions!" repeated Leon. "The world must turn inside out before *you* will ever be able to dictate to *me*. Leave those documents. Go away. I will see what can be done. It is a risky business, and I know the hazard better than any of you. If a hitch occurs, there must be instant flight from here."

"Yes," said Polti himself, when he was alone; "I see that I am in most danger from my own followers. They would kill me to gain possession of Frank Ellaby's money. Dulk is the most likely man to strike the first blow. Knowing where my peril lies I can evade it. Extreme caution and swift flight will save me, and nothing else. I thank thee, Fate, for throwing that innocent youth Ernest Truelove in my way!"

On the following morning the student again met Nizza Polti on the stairs.

"My brother has been unexpectedly called away this morning before you were awake," she said in her pretty way, shedding the full light of her eyes on his face. "He wants you to do a small favour for him, and I am sure you will. It is only to get a cheque cashed at the London Joint Stock Bank, and meet him tonight at Charing Cross Railway Station with the money. He is going to Paris with it."

"I shall be delighted to be of any service to him, *and to you,*" said Ernest. "Why! this cheque is for £20,000! Quite a fabulous amount!"

"My brother's transactions often run into five figures." she answered, with a smile. "If the cheque were for a small sum, I could do the business myself. He prefers to trust it to you, because you are stronger and cleverer than I am."

"Directly I have had my breakfast I will go to the bank," declared Ernest, in his impulsive way.

"There is not such a great hurry. So long as you are at the bank by eleven o'clock, that will do."

Just as Ernest was leaving the house a cab drew up at the door. To his great surprise, it contained Rose and the Rev. Frederick Briarton.

It chanced that just as these two reached the house, Madame Dulk was standing at the dining-room window, and she had a clear view of them.

She drew back hastily. Gleams of satisfaction shot from her eyes.

"At last I have found him!" she said to herself. "The clergyman to whom I confided the child. Doubtless that is Rose herself, grown into a beautiful woman. I will lose no time in regaining my prize. My husband and Polti and the rest may have *their* big hauls, but I shall now be better off than any of them!"

"Dad had to come up to London by the very first train on some business in the City," Rose explained.

She was flushed with excitement, and with the delight she felt at seeing her lover again. "So I coaxed him to let me come, too."

"We thought we would give you a surprise," laughed the vicar, "and join you in a little lunch, if you have such a handy thing in the house."

"Only too delighted to see you," said Ernest; "but I must go to the City myself. We can all go together in the cab you have come by, and talk as we go.

"My business is with the Joint Stock Bank," he added, "and it won't occupy many minutes. After that I shall be entirely at your service. What do you think, Mr. Briarton? I'm going to change a cheque for twenty thousand pounds!"

The figures were sufficiently large to impress the rural clergyman, and to awe Rose.

Ernest briefly explained how he chanced to be in possession of so valuable a piece of paper.

They watched him, as he, with a great air if importance (which he could not resist), entered the bank. They saw him emerge from its portals, and then a dreadful thing happened.

A tall, broad man tapped him on the shoulder.

Before he could say a word a pair of handcuffs were thrust on his wrists. Two other men came from across the road with a seeming air of authority. They were seized, too, and treated in the same way.

The police had taken Ernest Truelove into custody. They had also arrested Mr. Gervaise, of Paris, and Mr. Sexton Blake, very much to the complete dismay of both these notable detectives.

Calder Dulk and Leon Polti watched these proceedings from a safe corner, and then made off with all the speed possible.

Poor Rose uttered a cry of distress, and the Reverend Mr. Briarton sprang on to the pavement and was at once in the midst of the excited group, standing shoulder to shoulder with Mr. Frank Ellaby!

THE SIXTH CHAPTER

The Release of the Prisoners—Flying from Justice— "I Will Kill You Both."

"So I have made a good haul, and caught you all at once," said Ellaby, with a grim smile. "I am sorry you have turned out a rogue, Gervaise, for I had formed another opinion of you. I did hope that you, Sexton Blake, were honest, yet you have joined in as vile a conspiracy against my life and fortune as man could devise. As for you," he added, addressing Ernest Truelove, "you have a noble, manly face, which makes me sorry to see you associated with these rascals."

"I do not know what all this means," declared the Rev. Frederick Briarton, "but I do aver that this young gentleman never did a dishonourable action in his life, and, if you dare to detain him, it will be at your own peril. He was simply asked to get this cheque cashed by people who lodge in the house where he has apartments."

"It was Leon Polti's sister," Ernest commenced.

"Ah!" Blake interrupted, "this, as I guessed, is the work of the 'Red Light,' and I hope we shall be able to capture and convict the whole gang. I forgive you, Mr. Ellaby, for thinking I had something to do with your kidnapping; but had you gone to Scotland Yard, instead of to the City Police, you would have heard that Gervaise and myself have toiled day and night to rescue you. Only yesterday we discovered an old mill. We had the pond dragged, and we found one body which, at first, we thought was yours—"

"No, I am still alive," said Frank, "though I did get a ducking there. I hope, Blake, your tale is true."

"If we all drive to Scotland Yard, you will soon be satisfied on that point. It's my opinion, Mr. Ellaby, that this young man has simply been the dupe of the daring Polti crowd."

"I am a clergyman of the Church of England," said Mr. Briarton; "and I have known Ernest Truelove for many years. I am convinced he is incapable of committing a criminal action. I must insist on his immediate release from custody."

"Oh, Rose, Rose!" said Ernest, as his *fiance* joined the throng. "I do wish you had been spared the pain of seeing me so disgraced."

"So your name is Rose?" questioned Frank Ellaby, regarding her fair, fresh young face with interest. "Many years ago I had a little girl stolen from me bearing that name. She must be about your age now. I would give much to find her."

"That is a matter we can discuss some other time," declared the rector, and with such significance that a sudden hope sprung up in Frank's heart. "Ernest Truelove must be released!"

It took very little time to prove how far from the truth was the charge against Messrs. Sexton Blake and Gervaise, to whom Mr. Ellaby made a most handsome apology.

Nor was it long before this gentleman was persuaded to withdraw every imputation against Ernest Truelove; and later, when he knew more of him, he decided to make him reparation for the wrong to which he had been subjected.

They all journeyed to Bernard Street, hoping to effect the capture of Madame Dulk and Nizza Polti, if not of Polti himself.

No one answered their repeated knocks or continuous ringing of the bell.

"The birds have flown," said Blake. "No doubt Mr. Truelove was shadowed to the bank. When he was seen to be taken into custody the warning note was sounded, and the ducks have taken unto themselves wings and vanished. Gervaise and I will see that the railway stations and the wharves are watched.

Every effort shall be made to prevent the escape of the culprits. Now we know them there should not be any difficulty about this. You gentlemen had best make yourselves comfortable at some good family hotel where I can visit you later on, and report progress. Say the Silver Bell, at Charing Cross. I really don't think you can help us now in any way. Too many cooks, you know, spoil even good broth."

"All my personal belongings are in that house," said Ernest, ruefully looking up at its windows.

"I daresay you will get your luggage all right," returned Gervaise, with a smile, "but that is a department of our business which can well afford to wait. We haven't got a moment to lose, so farewell, my friends!"

Gervaise was right. Every second was precious. Already much valuable time had been squandered.

Even as he spoke, Calder Dulk and Nizza Polti stood on the platform of King's Cross Station ready to step into a fast train soon to start for one of the Northern centres.

The appearance of Mr. Frank Ellaby outside the bank had filled Dulk with the direst consternation. He judged there could be no safety for him in England now, especially as Ernest was in custody, and could put them on the track of Madame Dulk, who had gone he knew not where.

"Ah!" he said, when he and Nizza had settled themselves in the carriage, and the train was almost on the move, "we shall get out of London all right, and then entire escape won't be so very difficult."

The whistle sounded, and the great engine gave on mighty gasp of relief.

They were on the move, when the door was torn open, and a man threw himself into the carriage. "Keep still," he yelled, placing himself opposite them. "If you move an inch I'll shoot you both like the dogs you are." He pointed a pistol at each head.

"So," he continued, "you've got possession of the plunder, and you mean to cheat me out of my share—me, who has done all the work, too! It isn't the first time you have tried on that game; but it shall be the last. You look very pretty in that woman's disguise, Leon Polti; but it won't work with me, because I know it. I always swore if a pal played me false that I would kill him. *I mean to kill you both!*"

They knew that their first stoppage was Peterborough, and that they were completely at the mercy of this desperate man, who was none other than Bill Bender, and who laughed to scorn the terrors of the law.

THE SEVENTH CHAPTER

A Struggle for Life—Thrown from the Train.

It was some time before the two men recovered from their surprise. "Don't be a fool, Bill Bender. We have not got a farthing of Frank Ellaby's money. The game is up; the detectives are after a lot of us. We are flying out of London, and mean to lie quiet in the country for a time; that's why we are in this train."

It was Calder Dulk who spoke, half pleadingly, and with somewhat of a reassuring tone to Bill Bender, who still covered him and Nizza Polti with his pistols.

Dulk looked very helpless with the muzzle of the deadly weapon pointed straight at his heart.

"You always were an idiot, Bender," said Nizza, talking in his natural voice—for Nizza and Leon were one.

The disguise was so perfect that only very few of his own followers knew that he did not possess a sister. By the aid of this change of costume he had more than once deceived his confederates, and passed freely out from among them, when very little would have made them tear him to pieces. "Put those silly things down. They are more likely to hurt you than me."

"I am glad you have turned up," Leon added in his cool, business way. "I wanted to see you. I fancy we may yet get hold of that money, and want *your* help, my friend Bender."

They had emerged from King's Cross tunnel now, and were beginning to whiz along at a rate which soon promised exciting speed.

"None of that for me," said Bill. "I've had lots of it from you, and I know you. Now then, young gentleman in the skirts, tumble up the gold. You had the cheque right enough, and you've got the money."

"Certainly I had the cheque," acknowledged Leon quietly, "but you don't suppose I was going to be so foolish as to present it myself?"

"No," growled Bill, "you've all been clever enough to leave me to be the only one who can be identified as being connected with this job. One wears a mask and the other hides himself. Then you try to do me out of the money and leave me to swing, while you enjoy yourselves with wine and other luxuries."

"I sent a young country friend of mine to the bank to get Frank Ellaby's cheque cashed," Leon spoke impressively, "and I suppose he got the money. Dulk and I watched from a safe distance to see if things were all right. All we know is, that when our young friend left the bank he was taken in charge by the police. Just pay particular attention to this, Bill—*Frank Ellaby was there, too, waiting for him!*"

"What!" exclaimed Bill, so astonished at the news that he relaxed a trifle of his vigilance.

"How could he have escaped from the mill? I made sure he was a corpse by this time. He won't rest till he finds me. Yah!" he exclaimed, with a sudden change of demeanour, "you think I am a kid, and you are trying to put me off with those fairy tales till we stop somewhere, where you think you can get help. Come on, pay up, or I'll fire."

"Don't be so thick-headed, Bill; I tell you we have not got the money. Besides, I should never think of swindling *you;* you are too useful to us. Why don't you search us? Perhaps that will satisfy you. You can commence with me."

"So I will," said the thoughtless ruffian, laying his pistols by his side.

Leon was full of tricks. This proposal was only a ruse to put Bill Bender off his guard, and to enable them to deprive him of his weapons. It would have succeeded admirably had not Leon been *too* quick.

He stretched his white hand over to secure the deadly weapons before Bill had half risen from his seat.

The burly bully saw what was intended, and Leon was felled to the floor of the carriage, rendered insensible, and his body kicked under a seat in less time than it takes to write these lines.

Thinking *his* opportunity had come, Calder Dulk now sprung on Bill Bender, to be received by him in his powerful grip.

Dulk was a man of weight and muscle.

Knowing the one he had to deal with, he was sure this must prove a struggle for very life.

Nothing would ever now persuade Bill that there had been no intention to deprive him of his share in the cheque obtained by such desperate means. His teeth were set. His eyes stood out of his head. His whole system throbbed with one idea, and it was a fierce one—to crush Dulk.

This so absorbed his every faculty that he did not hear the rush through the air of the train, the rattle of the carriages, or the frequent wild shrieks of the engine.

No pleadings for mercy from human tongue could touch him!

Dulk's veins rose up his forehead, knotted and black. His face was horror-stricken. He knew that a relentless demon was grappling with him, and it could only be by a superhuman effort that he could escape the death sentence written on that implacable face.

Strive his utmost he did, straining every muscle and nerve.

At one moment the two stood silent, and looking as firm as a pair of Roman wrestlers cut in marble. When the train gave a lurch they were thrown heavily with it. Then came a fierce, panting struggle on the floor. Some seconds one had the advantage, to be quickly wrenched from him by the other.

As they managed at last to struggle to their feet, they never for an instant released their hold on each other.

A thick hot breath fanned their cheeks as a blast from a furnace all the time. The solid seating on each side of them in the narrow passage of that compartment made it difficult for either to throw the other. So each strove with slow, persistent effort to reach the pulsating throat of the other. Bill Bender was the first to win in his deadly effort.

As his thumb and finger closed on Calder Dulk's throat, a groan of triumph escaped him. Now he could throw his whole weight against his victim, for with the latter's lack of breath the muscles of his arms and legs relaxed.

The two fell against the carriage door. A third of Dulk's body was already out of the open window, which had no protecting rail in the middle of it. Just then they were entering a tunnel.

"You are best out altogether!" growled Bill, lifting up the legs of the man, and letting him drop out into the darkness.

A crimson flash of light from the fire of the engine illuminated his ghastly white face as he was swallowed up by the relentless black of that stifling excavation.

"It's Leon Polti who has the money; that's certain, or he would not be got up like a girl," muttered Bill, and he at once commenced to roughly search that gentleman.

"The other has got it after all!" he cried, in disgust. "There all that money lies on the line for any navvy or porter, or anyone to have for the finding. I *must* have a try for it."

The signal towards the exit of the tunnel was against the train, and it slowed.

Bill took advantage of this opportunity, and he dropped gently off the footboard into the gloom.

Leon, now he was lone, sprang to his feet, and, taking down a small bag from the luggage-rail, he quickly made a complete transformation in his dress.

When the train stopped at Peterborough, and he stepped gingerly from his carriage, he appeared in such attire as would have befitted the most exacting up-to-date Bond Street swell.

"I am glad Bill and Dulk have both gone *that* way," he reflected, with an amiable smile. "It is an experience they are not likely to recover from, and they were beginning to get troublesome."

THE EIGHTH CHAPTER

The Drugged Coffee—Coronet or Grave?

While the detectives were pursuing their investigations, Frank Ellaby's party engaged quarters at that cosy and eminently respectable hostelry, the Silver Bell.

Here it naturally followed that Ernest should seek the companionship of Rose, and that Mr. Briarton and Frank Ellaby should exchange confidences one with another.

"From what you have told me," said the latter, "I have little doubt, in my own mind, that your Rose and the little girl my dying sister entrusted to my care are one and the same.

"The woman from whom you received her said no idle words when she declared that the child had a great future before her, for I can give her much wealth.

"Though I never liked Calder Dulk's wife, I did not regard her as a criminal. Though, seeing that she robbed me, the news need not surprise me. Odd, indeed, it is that I should once more be thrown into her clutches.

"Someone has truly said that we all live our lives twice over. Certainly, our experiences have a way of repeating themselves in the strangest manner.

"I quite agree with you, that it would be unwise to say anything to the young lady at present touching her real identity, which I fear we shall never discover, unless we can force that woman Dulk to give up the papers she stole from my sister's escritoire.

"If we once catch her, a promise to withdraw my prosecution against her may work wonders."

"I trust that she and her evil companions may soon be brought to justice," said the clergyman. "They might have ruined my friend, Ernest Truelove, who is so honest himself that he suspects no one. I will remain in London a few days, and see how the search progresses."

"Dad," cried Rose, entering the apartment at that moment, "there is to be a splendid concert at St. James's Hall tonight. Do, please, let us go."

"Certainly. We will all go," laughed Frank. "I will send round to the box-office and secure seats at once. Should Blake want us, we can leave word where we are to be found."

The concert-room was crowded, and on leaving it they became involved in the whirl of a fashionable crush.

Frank Ellaby had called for a cab. While they waited for it a rush from behind separated Rose from her friends.

"This way, miss," said a man to her; "the cab is waiting for you."

She followed the fellow in all simplicity, and soon she was sitting inside a soft, delicately-perfumed vehicle, which drove off at a furious rate before she realised what she had done. A lady, beautifully dressed, sat facing her. She smiled kindly on the young and agitated girl.

"There is some mistake. I have lost my friends. Oh, pray forgive me for getting into your carriage instead of into our cab. Please tell your coachman to stop," cried Rose in alarm.

"I saw your mistake, and it amused me," said the lady, "I dearly love a little joke. Tell me where you wish to go to. My man shall drive us there."

"But my friends—" Rose commenced.

"You will be home before them, and will have the laugh against them. That is all. They deserve a taste of anxiety for losing you. The Silver Bell Hotel? I know it quite well. My house lies the same way, but it comes first.

"We will pause there for a moment, if you don't mind, and then I will take you to your own people."

The splendour of the equipage in which she found herself, and the aristocratic bearing of the white-haired lady, who patronised her with such an easy grace, were sufficient to lull all suspicion of foul play in Rose's mind.

"Indeed, she felt that she was an intruder there, and she considered her hostess very gracious in treating her with such good humour. They pulled up outside a large but dismal-looking house.

"Here we are at my home," said the lady. "Come in with me, if only for a minute. Nay, I insist. You are too nervous to be left alone. Come! we shall yet reach the Silver Bell before your folks get there."

The door of the building opened, and without hands it seemed. Silently it closed behind them, leaving them in a dark passage.

"Take my hand," said her conductress in a more commanding voice.

"I will lead you to the light?"

Rose began to feel frightened now, but she had no choice but to follow her guide along the black corridor, down a number of steps, then to the still open air, again into another building, and up a high flight of stairs.

"Open for us, Belus—open!" said the woman.

Rose was now conscious that some creature was walking in front of them.

She could hear its breath coming and going quickly, but its footfall made no sound, and she wondered whether it was a monkey or a human being. Suddenly her eyes were blinded by a great flood of light.

She stood in one of the most lavishly-furnished rooms her imagination could conceive.

She saw that "Belus" was a dreadfully attenuated man. His skin was dry and yellow, and his flesh all withered up like that of a mummy, to which he bore a strong resemblance.

The horribleness of his appearance was increased by the fact that he had lost one eye, and one arm was gone.

These injuries were all on his left side, and they suggested that he had at some period of his existence been involved in a terrible accident. "Belus has been with me many years," said the strange lady, "and he is very faithful."

"Unto death," declared the ghastly-looking Belus.

"It is well said," laughed his mistress. "Unto death! Get us coffee," she added.

"Indeed, indeed," protested Rose, "I must not stay. Do, please, let me go to my friends. They will be quite upset at my disappearance."

"We will leave here within ten minutes," said the lady, smilingly. "The coffee will revive you. I shall feel hurt if you do not take it."

It proved a delicious decoction of the glorious Arabian berry, and it was served in tiny gold cups chased in a most elegant way; but it had not the effect of stimulating Rose. On the contrary, it made her so drowsy that in a couple of minutes she was sound asleep on the luxurious sofa on which she had been induced to sit!

Her hostess stood over her, and regarded her prostrate figure with an expression of evil triumph.

"What is this?" asked Belus, creeping to her side, "revenge or merely simply villainy?"

"Greed," answered the woman shortly. "This girl is worth much money to me.

"Hark! That is the duke's knock. Take care he does not enter here. Nor must he know of this girl's presence in this house. The time is not yet ripe for the disclosure I have to make. Go to him. You may tell him that I am here, and would see him on a matter of grave importance.

"Do my bidding well, my faithful Belus, and I will reward thee."

"Yes," muttered the man, as he seemed to melt from the room, "as you did before, with the loss of an arm and an eye. Your rewards are perfect, and so shall be my revenge!"

"Ah! my beautiful Rose," reflected the woman, unable to take her eyes off her prisoner.

"What is to be your fate? Are you destined for an early grave, or will you soon wear one of England's noblest coronets?"

THE NINTH CHAPTER

One Thousand Pounds Reward—The Duke of Fenton—A Sudden Death.

"Where is Rose?" demanded Ernest, as the three men clustered round the cab. "She was by my side a second ago," said Frank Ellaby.

"It is but this moment that I spoke to her," declared Mr. Briarton. "It is ridiculous to suppose she has lost us."

They looked around in every direction. They waited till the crush had spent itself, and the pavement was pretty clear, and to their confusion they could see nothing of her. They returned to the hall; she was not there.

The neighbourhood was searched, police and cabmen questioned, and they could gain no tidings of the missing lady.

The extraordinary mystery of her disappearance appalled them. It was as though she had been suddenly swept off the face of the earth.

They made haste back to the hotel, hoping against hope, that, by some possibility, she might have reached it first. Only disappointment awaited them.

The clergyman and Ernest Truelove were both plunged into the deepest distress and consternation.

Frank Ellaby, too, was gravely concerned. It seemed absurd that he should no sooner find the girl he had been searching for all these years than he should allow her to be snatched from him again.

"It is past all comprehension," he said, "that with three of us to guard her, she should be taken from us in this miraculous way. It makes one believe in the supernatural. If money will bring her back she will soon be with us again. I will offer a thousand pounds reward for her recovery. The advertisements shall be sent tonight to all the daily papers."

"I thank you heartily for that generous decision," said Ernest, "but we must strain every nerve to find her ourselves."

"And pray fervently to the One above to bless and protect her," said Mr. Briarton.

Before the missives to the newspapers could be dispatched, Sexton Blake called on them to report such progress as he had made in the hunting down of the 'Red Lights.'

The discovery of the body of a murdered man in the pool by the old mill had made this a police business.

Mr. Blake's efforts were confined solely to the interests of Frank Ellaby, who had now greater reason than ever for desiring to secure Calder Dulk and his desperate wife.

The detective listened to the story of Rose's disappearance with some surprise.

"I can only suppose," he said, "that this is the work of the daring woman who stole the young lady before. How she managed to accomplish her purpose so easily, and in the full blaze of Piccadilly, I do not know.

"Doubtless her object is extortion. She is determined not to let you escape her, Mr. Ellaby. If the young lady is in her power, I can promise you that I will soon bring about her release. Now that I know this woman Dulk, it will not be long before I find her.

"They are an exceedingly slippery gang to deal with. For instance, I have absolute proof that Calder Dulk and Nizza Polti left King's Cross this morning by the North express, which makes its first stoppage at Peterborough.

"I wired to that old cathedral city to have these two people detained until I arrived there, and formally charged them. No one answered their descriptions was to be found in the whole train!

"Indeed, it chanced that there was only one lady 'on board,' and she is the daughter of a well-known clergyman.

"The train goes at a break-neck speed all the way, the guard is certain that no one left it *en route*, and that Nizza Polti and her male companion were in their carriage when it started from King's Cross. They have managed to do the vanishing trick to perfection."

"If that gang have succeeded in capturing poor Rose, they hold a trump card. I shall not dare to proceed against them for fear of imperilling her life. They are quite capable of using her as a shield to protect them from my vengeance."

It was Ellaby who spoke.

"That is true," Blake allowed ruefully. "But if they escape your active hostility, they have still to reckon with the police.

"The offer of a thousand pounds reward will bring a communication from some of them, I'm sure."

While this conversation was taking place in the Silver Bell Hotel, another, and even more important one, was being carried on in the strange house whither Rose had been so cleverly conveyed.

Madame Dulk had left her beautiful and unconscious prisoner still reclining on the luxurious couch.

Entering another apartment, more superbly furnished than the first, Madame found a tall, stoutly-built, aristocratic gentleman waiting for her.

He had keen, grey eyes, which glittered under his grey, heavy eyebrows. His white hair was clipped short to his military-looking head, and his moustache was well trimmed and intensely black.

"I received your message," he said in a cold haughty tone, "and I have come. What have you to tell me now?"

"Will your Grace not deign to take a seat?" said Madame, humbly. "The missing child is again found. Of course she has grown to be a woman now. She is beautiful, and would ornament the highest station in the land."

"Tut!" he spoke impatiently; "what an old story this is! Woman, if you are in difficulties and want money, why not tell me so, and take you chance whether I give it you or not? Why do you always try to touch my purse by some untruthful story?"

"Never, your Grace, never in my life!" protested Madame. "I have been mistaken before—that is all. I have never wilfully deceived you. This time I have made no error. I have seen the minister who took possession of her when I was in prison. She is with him now.

"But the danger which threatens you is to be found in the fact that the brother of the woman who had her as a baby in Australia is here, and with her. He came over expressly to find her, and to vindicate her rights.

"He is enormously rich, and he will spend all he is worth in striving to establish her true identity. With my assistance he might learn this in half-an-hour.

"Now it is for your Grace's consideration whether you will submit to be compelled by law to accept this young lady as the daughter of your late elder brother, and allow her to take over the estates you now posses.

"You can arrange matters with me so that the proof of Lady Rose Fenton's existence can be forever destroyed, and she herself be removed to some safe place abroad.

"As she has never known the joys of the position she is legally entitled to, she can never miss them."

The Duke of Fenton, resting his head on his hand, sat for some minutes without speaking.

"It is a hard problem to solve," he muttered. "If I had only myself to consider, this girl might take her place in our family without hindrance from me. I doubt whether it would be good for her. One has to be bred up to a coronet to wear it with ease.

"But my son, my dear and only son! The sudden appearance of this cousin of his would play sad havoc with his financial position!

"What do you propose, Madame?" he added in a louder tone, and looking up sharply at her.

"I propose that you should have a few days to prosecute your own inquiries about the Rev. Briarton and his so-called daughter," was the woman's prompt reply.

"While you are thus engaged, I undertake to get possession of the young lady, and have her snugly housed at the big place in Bedfordshire.

"Then I will hand her over to you with all the proofs as to her birth, parentage, and so on.

"Then it will be for you to decide what to do with her. You are already satisfied that such a lady does exist."

"Your terms?"

"The difficulties are great; the dangers not to be despised—"

"Your terms?" he repeated, waving his hand impatiently.

"Two thousand pounds!"

"Set about your business," he said. As he rose he allowed a deep sigh to escape him. "Remember, not a hair of her head must be injured; not a cruel word must be said to her. Do not forget that the blood of the Fentons flows in her veins. Woe betide you if you do not pay it proper respect!"

He strode from the room, and out of the house, with a grand, haughty air.

At his carriage door his valet waited for him. The man had made such haste to get there that he was out of breath.

The few words he did utter were sufficient to send the proud nobleman reeling into his equipage as though he had been stabbed to the heart.

"What can have happened?" asked Madame, nervously. She had followed "his Grace" to the door.

"His son is dead," said Belus, who was by her side. "His only son has been struck down suddenly in the billiard-room of his club; heart disease, they say.

"So much for pride of birth and the joy of riches! These aristocrats despise us and trample on us, but they all have to die—oh, yes, they all have to die!"

THE TENTH CHAPTER

Rose Awakes—A Long Ride—The Country House—Leon Polti's New Plot.

When Rose did at last recovered her senses her brain was dizzy and numbed, and her muscles felt sore, as though she had been bruised. Heavy curtains were drawn across the windows, the lights were still burning, so she did not know whether it was night or morning.

She felt as though she had been unconscious for a long, long time. Her recollection returned slowly, and in a blurred, indistinct form.

"Thank goodness, you are once more in possession of your faculties," said Madame, who was sitting by her side. She spoke with great fervour.

"Your papa has only just gone away. Do you know you have lain there like one in a trance for two days?

"The doctor says it is one of the most singular cases he has met with in the whole of his professional experience. He fancies that a small clot of blood must have gone into one of the minute blood-vessels of the brain, and pressing on that important organ, rendered you insensible.

"He advised us that directly consciousness returned to you all danger was passed, and that you would be your old self again, as by a miracle. So you must rise now, and take some sustenance.

"Then I will convey you to a pretty place in the country, which your friends have taken for you, and where they are waiting you."

The poor girl, still suffering from the effects of the powerful drug which had been administered to her, listened to these words in hopeless bewilderment.

Judging from her own feelings, had she been told that she had lain there a week, she would have believed the tale. At any rate, she could do nothing now but obey her hostess. What little strength she had was swallowed up in wonder.

An appetising meal was put before her. She partook sparingly of it, yet it revived her. She was soon ready, and anxious to leave that place, hoping most devoutly that she was really to be taken to her father—or rather to the good old man she had all these years regarded as being her parent.

But for the fact that as she passed out of the front door she saw a patch of blue sky above her, walking into the vehicle which was waiting was like stepping from one room into another.

The fact was, a large "pantechnicon" had been backed close up to the entrance to the house, and its folding doors at its end being opened, made a closed-in passage from the hall of the dwelling to the interior of the van.

So no strange, curious eyes could see Rose leave that residence, and all view of the street she was in was shut out from her.

A swing lamp hanging from the roof diffused a pleasant light through the interior. The floor was heavily carpeted.

There was a comfortable sofa, some easy chairs; a good solid table stood towards the far end, and handy to it were lockers containing crystal, cutlery, wines, and food. An old stove made cooking possible, and a speaking tube rendered instructions to the driver easy. It was certainly the warmest way of travelling by road that could well be devised. There were many conspicuous evidences to prove that Rose was not its first passenger.

When Madame and her prisoner had once entered the van, the man, who was to drive them, closed the doors sharply, and barred them. The horses started off at a sharp trot.

"Now, my dear," said Madame, decisively, "make yourself comfortable, and don't attempt any fuss, or bother me with stupid questions. You are with friends, and that is quite enough for you to know. Later on you shall be told all the fine things that are in store for you!"

"But," faltered poor Rose, "am I not to be taken to my father?"

"Why, of course you are! Have I not told you so? There now, amuse yourself with some of these books while I read the paper."

It was, perhaps, as well for Rose that she was too dazed just then to feel any particular alarm. It all felt like a dream, and not an entirely unpleasant one.

She attempted to read, but drowsiness assailed her, and she continued to drop into short, fitful sleeps, which seemed to tire her more than refresh her.

They had a comfortable lunch, for which she had but small desire, and then came a cup of tea, which failed to refresh her.

On, still on they went, keeping up a round pace all the time. They had four good horses, and Rose fancied that these were changed at least once during one of their many short stoppages.

It must have been towards evening when Madame herself dropped into a doze. The atmosphere of that van was close, and conducive to sleep.

Rose languidly picked the newspaper off this lady's lap.

For some reason, which she herself could not have explained, she was rejoined to see that its date was the one following the night she visited the St. James's Hall. So she had *not* been unconscious for two days, as she had been told.

Then her eyes caught sight of the advertisement, offering one thousand pounds reward for her safe recovery.

Her friends were on the alert, and she felt sure that she would soon be free.

She did not think it possible that in law-abiding England anyone could be long detained against his will, except in a prison or a lunatic asylum.

For her own safety's sake, she determined to take things quite calmly, to show no excitement, and to obey any reasonable command she might receive.

It would require an effort to hide her anxiety, and some courage to affect cheerfulness, when she was all terror in her uncertainty as to what designs her captors had on her.

She felt strong and brave enough to play the difficult part she had set before herself, and by enacting it well she hoped to soon effect her own escape, even if Mr. Briarton failed to find her.

The moon showered its light on them, and the stars twinkled with a frosty brightness when they at last drew up before a large, old-fashioned, substantial country house, which stood in the midst of thickly-timbered grounds.

The hall door was open, and in the yellow glow of the gas was seen the form of Leon Polti.

"You here?" cried Madame, in a tone of distinct anger. "Why have you come to this place?"

"I expect for the same reason as yourself!" he answered, lightly. "For safety. Everything has failed—all has gone wrong. We are all scattered like chaff before the four winds!"

"Enough!" said the woman, curtly. "You and I will discuss business matters later. This way, my dear Rose. You will find your room has been made very comfortable for you."

"I wonder who her pretty friend is?" muttered Leon, as he threw himself on a sofa before a bright fire in one of the sitting-rooms.

"The conditions of our confederation compel me to make you welcome, Leon Polti, anywhere and at any time. But I am sorry you are here tonight. I wish you had not come.

"Besides, I have done with the 'Red Lights' forever! Some of you are clever enough men, and you do great things when you work alone. When together, all you seem to do is to get in each other's way.

"I, at any rate, can afford to do without you."

The was what Madame said when she rejoined him.

"Ah," said Leon, with a cynical smile. "You have thought so before tonight. I have some news for you—your husband is dead!"

"Dead?" she echoed, starting to her feet. Then she fell back in her chair, and again repeated the dread words, "Calder Dulk dead?"

"Well, I saw Bill Bender throw him out of a quick-going train on to the rails and in a tunnel. He seemed half dead before he left us. I don't think he can possibly be alive."

"You saw this, and raised no hand to protect him?"

"I was almost insensible myself. It's a miracle I escaped the same fate. Bender believes that we played him false. He'll do his best to kill me if he ever catches me. As for being here, I won't trouble you for long. All I want is to hide for a few days. By the way, who is your young friend?"

"That, Leon Polti, is my own particular business. She is worth more to me than all your abortive schemes put together would have been, even had you brought them to a successful issue. And I share with no one!"

"Don't you," Leon muttered, after Madame had left him to his own reflections.

"Let me look at that advertisement again. 'One thousand pounds reward.' Ah! A nice little sum.

"Yes, as far as I can judge, the description of the missing lady tallies with that of the one who has just arrived. What an odd thing they don't give her name? Some reason for it, I suppose. 'Clothes marked, R. B.—Apply Proprietor, Silver Hall Hotel.'

"It would be rather amusing were I to snatch this pleasant little prize from your grasp, Madame Dulk? I want a thousand pounds quite as much as you do.

"Nothing can be done till the morning, when I will contrive to get a look at the stolen beauty."

THE ELEVENTH CHAPTER

Sexton Blake has News—The Last of Calder Dulk—A Duke's Repentance—Baffled by Suicide—A Message from Rose.

A few days had passed, and to the surprise of Sexton Blake no one had yet made any serious application for the thousand pounds reward so widely advertised.

Suggestions, descriptions, and offers of help they had from all parts of the country, but nothing that promised the quick return of Rose.

As Mr. Briarton and Frank Ellaby were discussing one of their gloomy breakfasts, Mr. Sexton Blake entered the coffee-room, and took a chair at their table.

"I have some news," he said disconsolately. "I have found Calder Dulk."

"Good!" cried Frank, "through him we may get Rose, if his wife has had anything to do with the dear girl's disappearance."

"I fear he is past giving help to us, or to anyone. Someone has been before you with his vengeance. Dulk is dead!"

"How did it come about?" asked Ellaby, in a low tone.

"His body was found in a tunnel, on the Great Northern Railway. It must have dropped from the North express I told you he and Nizza Polti took tickets by.

"He might have fallen out by accident, or he might have committed suicide; but both these theories are negatived by the fact that his throat, even yet, bears the impress of a powerful thumb and finger, which must have exercised sufficient pressure there to throttle him."

"Surely Nizza Polti had not enough strength—"

"Dear me, no. Indeed, it seems pretty clear that there never was any sister, and that is how I and Scotland Yard have been so often tricked on to wrong scents. Leon and Nizza are one.

"I managed at Peterborough to get permission to examine all the luggage that had come by that particular train, and which had been left in the cloak-room.

"This chanced to consist of one petite portmanteau. It contained a regularly built-up woman's costume, such as are used by female impersonators on the stage, only more delicately manufactured, to suit a drawing-room. The wig was a work of art. *Now* I understood why no Nizza could be found in that train. Leon had entered it at King's Cross as a girl, and had left it at Peterborough in his proper male attire.

"It turns out, too, that a man answering the description of the fellow who left you to starve at the watermill, jumped into the carriage in which Polti and Dulk were, just as the train was on the move.

"Bill Bender, they call him. There is not a worse ruffian unhanged. I suppose he and Dulk quarrelled—quarrelling is the one great characteristic of the criminal character—and Bill Bender strangled him, and then threw him on the line.

"So far the murderer has made good his escape. But the police are keen after him all over the country, and after the whole gang.

"I think we shall see a quick extinction of the 'Red Lights of London.'"

Ernest Truelove just then returned from an early lecture at his college. Truth to tell, his mind was too much stirred with anxiety for the safety of Rose to benefit from the learning which had been poured into it.

"I suppose you have no news of Miss Briarton!" His tone was one of reproach and hopelessness.

The grief which he could never escape from had made its impress on his face.

"You are wrong, Mr. Truelove, this time," said the detective, with a faint smile, "I bring you great news. No less a personage than the Duke of Fenton himself shall restore Miss Rose

Briarton to you. Perhaps, my dear sir, you will read that letter, and aloud."

He handed an envelope to the astonished clergyman, who opened it and repeated its contents, which ran as follows:—

"REV. AND DEAR SIR,

"We, as solicitors to the Duke of Fenton, are instructed by his Grace to ease your anxiety as to the welfare of the young lady to whom you have so kindly acted as guardian for some years past.

"He believes that it is within his power to bring about her return to you with little or no delay. With this view he desires that you meet him at our offices today at 12 o'clock, when he trusts to be in a position to discuss with you this young lady's real position in society, and her prospects, with more freedom than is consistent with such a purely professional communication as this.

"We are, Rev. and Dear Sir
"Your obedient Servants,
"Martindale & Co."

"What does this mean?" asked Mr. Briarton, wonderingly, "and what *can* the Duke of Fenton have to do with my Rose?"

"Simply and briefly," and Sexton Blake, "the facts seem to be these. Martindale and I were schoolboys together at Winchester, and knowing I had this matter in hand, he confided the true state of affairs to me last night.

"It is clear that the late Duke of Fenton (the present Duke's elder brother), was a somewhat adventuresome young man, and that during his travels in Australia he fell in love with, and married, a lady who had everything to recommend her except birth and fortune.

"He persuaded her to keep the union a secret until he had at least seen his parents, and had endeavoured to win their countenance to this wedding of wealth with poverty. The ship he sailed in from Melbourne unhappily sank, and he, with many others, was drowned.

"His wife lodged with your sister, Mr. Ellaby, and in her house she died suddenly, before she could know her husband's sad fate.

"I need not tell you how Miss Ellaby left the child to your care, or how the papers establishing her right to the title of Lady Fenton excited the cupidity of the Dulks. I have ascertained that during their voyage home husband and wife quarrelled.

"It was the present duke who got Madame Dulk sentenced to imprisonment for endeavouring to obtain money under false pretences.

"She produced the child, but at the critical moment her husband went off with the documents necessary to establish its identity. In fact, it was the usual criminal bungle.

"But though the duke, for his own protection, sent this woman to gaol, he quite believed her tale, and when she was released, he had some other transactions with her, for she was then able to produce the documents she had so much wanted before.

"She and her husband had now come to some sort of agreement again.

"When the duke heard that Rose had really been found again, he did not forbid this woman to secure her. He wavered between his good impulses and his bad ones.

"He had not made up his mind what to do about his niece, when his only son was struck down with awful suddenness. The duke has taken this catastrophe as a warning from above, and he has now resolved to freely recognise Lady Rose Fenton, and to accord her the revenues and privileges which are her due.

"So, if you please, we will hasten on to Hanover Square, and keep this appointment with Messrs. Martindale and Co. Why, gentlemen, you don't look just as delighted as you should with my great news."

"It seems," said Mr. Briarton, "that if we recover Rose it will be but to lose her at once in the turmoil of fashionable life."

"A medical student can scarcely aspire to the hand of a duke's daughter," said Ernest, in a crestfallen way.

"I could have given her as much money as she could ever reasonably spend," muttered Frank Ellaby.

"Nonsense!" cried Sexton Blake. "If the young lady is worth troubling about at all she will be just as good, and as lovable, bearing a title as if she remained a simple miss.

"I can't understand how it is," the detective grumbled, "but I get more dismayed when I give people good news than when I have to take them bad. It is the detective's lot to always be received in the opposite way from that which he has a right to expect."

Shortly afterwards they left the house but did not go far in a westwardly direction. They were soon stopped by the hoarse cries of newspaper vendors, who were already abroad with the ghastly tidings of—

"SUICIDE OF THE DUKE OF FENTON!"

It was too true. The untimely cutting off of his much-loved son had driven the nobleman to this rash act.

"We are as far from finding Rose as ever," groaned Mr. Briarton.

"I fear so," said Mr. Blake, "his lawyers know nothing at all concerning her whereabouts."

On their return to the hotel, Mr. Briarton was informed that a rough-looking man was waiting in the minister's sitting-room to see him, and that he had some very important information for them

They all went up, but it chanced that Frank Ellaby was the first to enter the apartment.

"What!" he cried, recognising the burly figure standing defiantly with his back to the window. "I'm glad I have you at last, Bill Bender!"

He would have made a spring on to his old gaoler, but Bill Bender seized a heavy cut-glass water-bottle which was near at hand, and raising it high above his head, cried—

"Move a step, and I'll brain you!"

Sexton Blake, who had followed Frank in, caught the situation with half a glance.

He made a dart round through another room on to the balcony outside. Springing through the window of Mr. Briarton's room, he caught Bill from behind, and had him on the floor before that powerful gentleman was aware of his presence.

At the same moment Ernest Truelove sprang to the detective's help.

"Don't kill me!" gasped Bill, "you'll never forgive yourselves if you do. I've got a message—a message from the young lady—from Miss Rose Briarton!"

THE TWELFTH CHAPTER

The Discovery of Rose—An Awful Tragedy—The End.

Leon Polti's amiable intention of delivering Rose up to the people of the Silver Bell Hotel, receiving the reward for her restoration, and so baulking Madame Dulk's well-laid plans, would have taken very quick effect but for the fact that during his morning ramble through the grounds he detected the form of Bill Bender skulking among the trees.

A feeling of cold terror struck him, for he knew that this desperate character had only one purpose in being there—it was to kill Leon. The latter was sure that so far Bill had not seen him—had, indeed, only guessed that he might be at this rendezvous. So he crept quickly back to the house, resolved to remain in hiding until his enemy should grow tired of watching.

He had one consolation, and it was that while Bill lay waiting for them outside, Madame Dulk would not dare to venture out to set her schemes in motion either.

"It's a bitter reflection that I should be caged up here and powerless to denounce the murderer of my husband, when he might be so easily taken," declared that lady angrily.

"All might have gone well had we left this Frank Ellaby alone. The unlucky plot emanated from you and your husband. Now the hue and cry is out after us hot and active," said Leon.

"Bah! I have no fear of that. What can they prove against me?"

"Sufficient to send you into penal servitude for life. The sooner we are both out of the country the better."

"True. But your way shall not be my way. I have some little business to settle, and that accomplished I shall be able to take care of myself in future."

"That is exactly my case," muttered Leon to himself, "and both our interests revolve round that young girl."

Aloud he added. "So long as Bill remains on guard outside we are powerless to do anything."

"If you were a man, you would go out and kill him," said Madame contemptuously.

"And attract the attention of the police to this only remaining refuge? No, thanks, all we can do is to wait."

Polti was not the only one who had seen Bill Bender lurking in those woods. Rose, at first much to her alarm, had encountered him in one of her brief walks, and promising him rich rewards, had persuaded him to take her message to Mr. Briarton, at the Silver Bell Hotel. Bill had means of scaling the high walls which surrounded the grounds, but it was impossible for her to do so.

Bill's surprise at finding himself face to face with Frank Ellaby can well be imagined. It is not surprising that he blamed himself for having walked into a trap so simply laid for him.

"Now, look here," said the desperado, when they allowed him to regain his feet, though they had securely bound his hands. "If you want to rescue that young lady, I know where she is, and I will take you to her. But you'll have to let me go scot-free afterwards. If you can't agree to those terms, my lips remain closed forever—you may all perish before I'll give you any help."

"Remember, Bill," said Blake, "we are not the police, and we can't control them. Take us to where Miss Rose Briarton is confined, and we will give you your freedom right enough; but you will have to take your chance as to whether the police get you or not."

"That's a chance I take everyday," growled the ruffian. "Come on, I'm your man. Not one of you must leave my sight. I'm not going to have you giving information. The places lies between Bedford and St. Neots. It don't take very long to get there!"

They reached their destination in due course.

As they stood in front of the park-like gates of the principal drive they opened, and Polti, closely muffled up, emerged into the high road. He was alone, and in a smart gig, to which was harnessed a strong, spirited horse.

At sight of Bill he uttered a cry of dismay, and slashed the beast in front of him unmercifully. But there was no escape for him!

With a roar like that of a tiger Bill sprang on to the back of the vehicle. By sheer muscular strength he dragged his heavy body up on to the seat by the side of the driver. Here commenced a fierce and awful struggle for life!

The tugging and jerking of the reins, the swaying of the gig, the dreadful mutterings of the combatants, maddened the high-spirited horse.

Getting the bit between its teeth, it tore madly forward, blind to all before it!

"See!" cried Ernest, in a tone of horror, "where the road takes a sudden bend it skirts a cutting, which makes a sheer drop of forty feet into that turbulent stream. Will that excited animal hold to the highway, or go over?"

Not until the horse reached the edge of the cutting did it realise its danger. With a sudden jerk it turned, as if to get back to the highway and safety once more.

As if by a miracle, the sudden jerk caused the shafts to snap off short, and the traces, which held the horse, were torn in two. The animal retained its footing, but the gig, with the two men, went over the awful height.

And still they struggled, though they were descending to their doom!

They disappeared down the deadly chasm into the deep, fast-running water!

When they were found it was seen that, in its descent, the gig had turned completely over, and had buried Leon and Bill under it at the bottom of the stream, so they had no chance of swimming for their lives, even if they were conscious when they reached the water.

This dreadful tragedy had been witnessed from one of the upper windows of the mansion by Madame Dulk. Except that the horror of it fascinated her for a moment, it occasioned her no regret. She turned away with a shrug of her shoulders.

The telegram she held in her hand concerned her more deeply. It told her of the suicide of the Duke of Fenton. It urged her to meet the sender of it at St. Neots that night.

It was signed "Belus."

"So the duke has gone," she murmured, "and with him my last hope of immediate wealth and safety. The documents proving the legitimacy of Rose are still in my possession, and should be valuable. But I dare not offer them to Frank Ellaby and to Mr. Briarton. It would be one more crime to the list they have against me.

"They had best be destroyed. They shall never benefit any person but myself, for I have gone through much to secure and retain them."

From her travelling bag she withdrew a packet of papers. In the act of casting them into the fire, she paused.

"Even yet they may be of service," she reflected.

At that moment she heard the voice of Frank Ellaby and the others, as they ascended the principal stairs. "The end has come! They are here to take me!" she ejaculated in terror. "But they shall never have these precious proofs."

The documents she had sinned so deeply to obtain she cast on to the burning coals, and the flames greedily devoured them.

The voices came nearer and nearer. They passed her room, and next she heard a joyous cry from Rose, as she was once again in the clergyman's embrace, and in the sunshine of her lover's glad welcome.

Quickly and silently Madame ran into her bedroom. Seizing her cloak and hat, and securing her valuables, she crept down the back staircase, out of the house on to the free, wide road.

She met Belus at St. Neots that evening. To her dismay he was accompanied by a couple of the London police inspectors, who very adroitly decorated her wrists with a pair of handcuffs, and conveyed her straight to the London train, which was already in the station, impatient to commence its rush to the Metropolis.

The two officers from Scotland Yard informed her that they had secured sufficient evidence against her to warrant any judge in sending her to prison for fifteen years.

"When you in your fury threw that lamp at me, and burned half my body away, I swore to be revenged on you," cried Belus, thrusting his malicious, evil face into the carriage window.

"And my time has come now. Take her away, gentlemen—take her away to her righteous doom!"

With a scream of satisfaction the engine dashed forward, and was soon lost in the darkness of the night.

* * *

Frank Ellaby, being in doubt as to what he should do with his wealth, has showered most of it on Rose and Ernest, those fortunate young people who in a few months' time are to be made man and wife.

Sexton Blake has been well rewarded, and he and Mr. Gervaise, of Paris, are partners.

"I did the best I could for you in the matter," he once said to Ellaby; "but it was not so much as I wished."

"Thank goodness!" said the Rev. Fred Briarton, "we have been the means of suppressing those terrible people, the 'Red Lights of London.'"

"Yes," agreed Frank; "we have managed to clear away four desperate criminals at least."

THE SLAVE MARKET!

Cecil Hayter

THE FIRST CHAPTER

Tinker Does Scouting Duty – The Cyclone – The Plunge in the Dark – Tinker in the Hands of the Slave-Dealer

The night was black as pitch, and a heavy, driving, tropical rain was sluicing down in sheets, keeping up a continuous rattling roar which drowned all other sounds into insignificance.

Trees were crashing down in all directions, and the air was filled with flying fragments of splintered timber.

Crouched close to the earth amongst the sodden undergrowth a dark-skinned figure, clad only in a few tattered rags, was crawling slowly and painfully along, pausing now and again to gasp for breath, or to dodge a broken branch hurtling overhead; yet always heading due westward, and peering through the gloom at every chance. During one such pause the figure's outstretched right hand pressed on something cold and slimy – the body of a snake, coiled up in such poor refuge as it could find for itself. The hand was withdrawn with, most remarkable, the crouching form expressed its feelings in fluent, forcible English.

The African explorer of the delta of the Rio de Oro scarcely expects to meet gentlemen with dark skins crawling through thorn-bush of extreme prickliness, and at the same time abusing his position, the weather, the darkness, and all classes of snakes and other reptiles in terse and vigorous Saxon.

Yet the words themselves were clear enough in spite of the moaning of the wind and the lashing of the rain.

'Get out, you brute! Go and roost in a mangrove, you shiny, lopsided, black-nosed worm, or I'll knock your silly head off! Git, confound you! I don't want you sampling the calf of my leg with your fish-hook fangs!'

The last remark was accompanied by a vicious slash with a piece of broken branch, which sent the snake, in the act of striking, hurtling away into the darkness, squirming and writhing with a broken back.

'It may be an excellent night for the job,' went on the prostrate figure grumblingly. 'I don't say it isn't, if you happen to be wearing the cast-off armour of a Harvard forward; but when you're almost in birthday-dress – a couple of handkerchiefs and an ounce or so of stain – all I can say is –'

Crash! came a sixty-foot tree-trunk not three paces ahead, and the grumbler dodged backwards, crab-fashion.

'Oh, my aunt – my dear, respected aunt – that was a close call! Shall I never see my wooden hut again? Next time the boss has a picnic of this kind on I shall ask for a holiday or a week off to wash and groom Pedro. If this rain doesn't wash the stain out of my skin I'll be black all the rest of my life!'

Tinker – for Tinker it was – dodged the fallen tree, skirted round another which was whipping in the wind like a bamboo cane, and came to a halt under a dense bush of mimosa scrub. He was scratched and bleeding from head to foot, the scanty rags on his body were soaked through and through, and though he was on the borders of the equatorial forest belt, he shivered in the chill of the storm.

Somewhere out in the dense blackness on his right Sexton Blake was also making his way as best he could through the undergrowth – so much Tinker knew. But barring that fact, and that vaguely ahead across the swamps lay an Arab slave compound, reputed to be strongly fortified, and astern a comfortable tent, with a couple of months' tinned rations, done up in neat, forty-pound loads, the situation was momentarily, at any rate, uninteresting.

His immediate business was to work his way through a couple of miles of storm-beaten forest in the teeth of a forty-mile-an-hour seaward gale. Having done this, the rest of his instructions were simplicity itself. He had merely to find a track across a trackless swamp, and locate the sentries stationed on that side of the Arab encampment, taking note of their disposition and the weak points of the stockade.

Sexton Blake had assured him that the night was an ideal one for the purpose, as the storm would not only drown any chance snapping of twigs, or slip of foot or hand, but would put the outposts off their guard, and as like as not drive them to cover.

They had, in fact, waited in camp five whole days and nights for just such a chance.

Tinker at this particular moment was beginning to regret that they had not waited fifteen, or fifty, or five hundred.

By the most sanguine of calculations a good half-mile of forest land lay before him, and every yard of that half-mile was fraught with its own peculiar and very realistic trouble. Deadwood falls were not the least of these, to say nothing of snakes, panthers, and a leopard or so, driven half mad with fear.

Once clear of the tree-belt, the swamp had special annoyances of its own, and the sentries, picked from half the blackguards of Africa and the Levant, with a backbone of Soudanese, were likely to prove prickly to handle should he be caught – a by no means unlikely event.

He sat up during a lull in the gale and strained his ears, on the chance of hearing Blake moving; but his master had been trained in the hard school of the border Indian, and knew the trick of crawling through eighteen-inch grass without so much as making the tops quiver. He might as well have listened for the sound of a mole working a field away.

Swish! swish! came the sound of the storm again, and a dazzling crackle of light – vivid blue light – shone on his immediate surroundings.

Vivid and brief as the flash of magnesium powder in the hands of an expert photographer, yet it showed up every detail around, and Tinker was not slow to take advantage of it.

He marked a tree a couple of hundred yards away – a big, stout fellow, standing out conspicuous amongst his comrades – and had time, though barely, to note its direction. Just as he reached it, panting and breathless, another flash spat out of the stormy sky overhead, and glistened on an alligator's snout exactly five feet from Tinker's own nose.

Now, Tinker flattered himself he knew all about alligators. He knew exactly the difference between 'gator and crocodile. He also knew that an alligator will always run from a man if he has a chance. He was very well up in the theory of the creature's habits. But the pace at which he rounded that tree would have earned him a nice brand-new silver cup with a suitable inscription at Lillie Bridge, or any other athletic meeting.

Having reached the lee side, he assured himself that he didn't care tuppence for any 'gator alive, but at the same time it would be more comfortable to attempt the swamp passage a couple of hundred yards further round to the left, and – Well, anyway, he never could stand the smell of musk.

He slid off at a right angle, leaving the alligator in undisputed possession of the shelter of the tree, and kept his knife, his only weapon, clenched in his right fist. He felt healthier like that, though he jabbed his knee badly once.

Another flash and a rumble of thunder – farther off this time – showed him that he was on the outer edge of the tree-belt. It also showed him a dismal stretch of swamp and saw-grass, intersected by slimy reaches of stagnant water, with here and there an artificial canal; and last, but not least, it showed him the bristling ridge of a stout palisade standing out black against a sky of livid steel. Then the light snapped out again, leaving him dazzled and half blinded with his first glimpse of the stronghold of the White Death, as it was called, dancing confusedly before his closed eyes.

Gradually he became accustomed to the darkness once more, and his sight became normal.

The swamp he estimated at five hundred yards broad. On the far side was the palisade, and between, if native reports were to be relied on, lay a triple line of sentries, whose duty it was to guard the palisaded stronghold from attack from without, and to prevent all possibility of escape of the slaves within – at that moment, if rumour was true, numbering no less than five hundred.

He was a man without further use for life who, having drifted into the service of the White Death, presumed to neglect an order. There would be the usual sentries, whether the sun shone with tropical fierceness, or a forty-mile-an-hour gale whipped up the forest giants by the roots.

But Tinker argued shrewdly enough that human nature has much the same weaknesses, whether hidden under a black, brown, or white skin, and that on such a wild night the sentries were likely to have closed in on one another, neglecting their usual patrols, secure in the knowledge that the White Death and his fellow traders in black ivory were little likely to forsake their warm huts and the orgy which was in progress to visit the outposts.

Such being the case, Tinker reluctantly acknowledged that his master was right and that the opportunity was one not to be neglected.

'Sitting here thinking won't make matters any more pleasant,' he muttered to himself, 'and the boss is fit to bust himself with impatience as it is, so here goes!'

He peered round him to try and fix a line of advance – his momentary glimpse had given him an idea of the general direction – and plunged forward into the swamp.

The storm-whipped saw-grass cut his legs and chest badly, and every second he expected to feel a squirming body underfoot. Still he pressed on, knife ready in one hand, with the other prodding in front of him with a forked stick. The lights of the bonfires and the traders' huts began to glimmer fitfully ahead, and after skirting a large lagoon he found himself quite unexpectedly at the brink of the outer of the three surrounding moats. So far, at any rate, he had been unhampered by over-vigilant sentries, no alarm had been sounded; but, for all he knew, watchful eyes might be peering out of the darkness ahead, and a sudden lightning flash would inevitably betray him. At the thought he dropped to cover, and not a moment too soon, for hardly had he flattened himself down in a stagnant puddle amongst the grass-roots than a whole series of crackling zigzagging streams of light split the sky in all directions. So light was it that for the next half-minute he could have read the finest print of a newspaper with ease; but, so far from reading papers, his heart suddenly seemed to leap into his throat, for exactly opposite to him, not twenty feet away, stood a huge Nubian sentry, leaning on a broad-bladed and peculiarly vicious-looking stabbing spear, whilst at his thigh was a heavy machete without a sheath. The water was streaming from his broad shoulders, and his skin shone and glistened with wet, but he took no heed.

Tinker could hear the thump-thump of his own heart; for an instant he was sure the man had seen or heard him. The next this was changed to certainty, for, noiseless as an otter, with one quick glance over his shoulder, the big black dived into the moat.

Tinker grabbed his knife and gathered himself for a spring when the man should reappear. He saw the ripples spread and vanish; a bubble or two rose half-way across, and at that very second the lightning fizzled out, and was succeeded by a heavy, rolling clap of thunder.

Tinker was as plucky as any lad alive, but just then he felt a sickly, chill fear creep over him. The man must have been close on twice his weight, and the thought of that ugly stabbing spear made him choke. This was succeeded by a feeling of dull rage as long-drawn seconds passed, and neither sight nor sound of the man could he get.

If he was to fight for his life, even against such odds, he wished to fight then, that very instant, whilst his blood was up.

Suddenly, after what seemed an interminable interval, his quick ears caught a faint noise of scrambling and splashing – so faint as to be almost indistinguishable above the storm. It was, he judged, twenty yards or more away on his left. Then there came a trampling of the tall grass as some big body forged a way through it with stealthy movements. Fainter and fainter yet grew the sound; then, save for the moaning of the wind, all was silent. Tinker could hardly believe his senses, but, nevertheless, the fact was indisputable – so far from the man being after him, he was clearly as desirous of getting away from the slave-camp unobserved as Tinker was of getting into it – or, at any rate, up to it.

He guessed at once that the man was a deserter and had no intention of returning, for if found absent from his post, and he should fall again into the hands of the White Death, a quick ending would be the greatest mercy he could hope for.

Hearing no sound of pursuit. Tinker clambered out of his pool and reconsidered matters. He had, he reckoned, at least five hours more of total darkness, though when day broke it would break with most surprising suddenness, and practically without warning.

Blake was presumably in a similar position to his own on the far side of the stockade, in the vicinity of the main entrance. It seemed to Tinker that the best thing he could do was to take a leaf out of the deserter's book, and swim for it.

The man had made for the left after diving. Obviously, then, the far bank was less likely to be patrolled at that point, and equally obviously the guard-house and drawbridge must be somewhere on his right.

Tinker edged cautiously to the left, slid noiselessly into the water, and struck out, carrying his knife in his teeth. It was warmer than he had expected, and a few strokes sufficed to take him across. The bank on the far side was steep, and he made some little noise scrambling out; but as luck would have it the gale just at the moment had increased to almost hurricane strength, and no one would have heard him had they been within gripping distance.

He found himself now on a flat stretch of hard, trodden ground, ten paces or so broad, with rifle-pits dug round the outer edge at short intervals. He discovered the first of these by falling headlong into it and giving himself a severe shaking up, to say nothing of nearly sitting on the blade of his knife, which he had dropped in falling.

The outer moat was behind him, immediately in front was the second; beyond lay another strip of ground, the inner moat, and a loopholed stockade of enormous strength.

Native rumour had it that, in addition to these defences, there were three machine-guns mounted at the most vulnerable points – mounted on swivels, so that in the case of an emergency – a sudden mutiny or an out-break amongst the slaves – their fire could be turned inwards, and concentrated on the lines of slave huts, where the poor wretches lay manacled in rows.

On the seaward side, where the treacherous swamp ended, shallow, intricate creeks, securely hidden, afforded sheltered anchorage to the slaving vessels, which, under captains of every conceivable nationality, dodged up and down the coast distributing their cargoes.

Some of the poor wretches, after being transhipped, were only set ashore to toil in long, painful marches, till such as were left alive were resold in the slave markets of the far-away Soudan, or to wealthy sheiks of the fierce Tawarek and Imoshagh Arabs, whitening the caravan routes of the dreaded Igdi desert with the bones of their fallen comrades in misfortune.

The White Death, as the cowering natives named him, the terror of the coast, was cunning as he was treacherous, and had chosen his nest well and hidden it securely. Nothing short of shell-fire from heavy guns could storm the place with any hope of success, and to get them up within range was a physical impossibility.

The White Death, snugly ensconced in his stronghold, raided and harried, traded and slaughtered, as he pleased.

Yet Tinker and Blake, two men – or, to be accurate, a man and a boy – against two hundred of the most unscrupulous sweepings of three continents, were pledged to snatch a prize from the White Death's avaricious claws, from the very heart of this almost impregnable position. And that prize was none other than Sir Richard Losely, Governor of Musardu and the Bambarra hinterlands.

Three months previously news had been flashed home to England from the ivory coast that the White Death and a raiding party of Arabs of the Ulad Bu had swept down south, killing, burning, harrying all in their path, and had overrun the small settlement at Musardu. The handful of black troops had been butchered after a desperate resistance, and Sir Richard Losely, his Majesty's governor, had been carried off badly wounded to the slavers' stronghold, located by rumour vaguely in the region of the delta of the Rio de Oro, on the coast of unknown Tiris.

Tinker, prone on his stomach amongst the now deserted rifle-pits between the outer moats, peered through the darkness at the strong palisade, and wondered where behind it the poor gallant Britisher lay shackled, amidst a horde of black-skinned fellow-sufferers, an object for insult, abuse, and inconceivable cruelty, wounded in defence of his charge, and in the power of the brutal and merciless White Death.

A sudden shift of wind bore down to him a sound of drunken shouting and quarrelling, followed by the snap of a revolver and a ringing scream. The sounds came from where the glare of lights showed strongest over the bristling palisades, marking the chief house, where the White Death himself and his boon companions held high carnival.

There was a momentary interval, then an uproarious shout of laughter, the bawling of hoarse orders, and a sharp, swishing thud; horrible, catlike screams rang out above the wailing of the wind, and Tinker's blood ran cold, then rushed hotly through his veins beneath his stained skin as he realised that some poor wretch of a slave was being flogged, tortured to provide amusement for the White Death and his guests.

The screams died down into a pitiful moaning and became inaudible as Tinker, in a sudden access of rage, throwing caution to the winds, dived once more, and swam till his outstretched fingers grabbed at the second strip of earth separating the moats. He pulled himself up, head and shoulders clear, his right knee was already firmly wedged in an unevenness of the bank, when his neck was seized violently from behind in an iron grip and his face pressed down into the mud, effectually preventing any outcry; a second pair of hands wrenched away his knife with a jerk which nearly dislocated his shoulder, and a heavy foot kicked him brutally in the ribs.

He struggled desperately, squirming like an eel, but without success. The grip on his neck tightened till he felt that in another second it must finish him.

A hoarse voice, speaking out of the darkness above him in mongrel Spanish, bade his captor desist.

'Gently, you fool, gently! It's not so often a bird flies into the trap of its own accord. Catch him alive, and it's two good ounces of gold for us from El Blanco; dead, he's not worth the ash of yesterday's cigarillo. And we're like enough to feel a touch of the bastinado for bungling the business. So now clap a cloth round his head, and give him half an inch of steel under the shoulder-blade as a hint to keep quiet!'

In spite of himself Tinker leapt convulsively as the knife-point drove in; cry out he could not even if he had wanted to, for his mouth was caked with mud under the tight-drawn handkerchief, and unwillingly enough he allowed himself to be hustled along, a fresh jab from the knife following quickly on the slightest attempt to struggle.

He had come to find the White Death's sentries, and he had certainly found them; yet he felt far from pleased, and inwardly he raged at his helplessness.

Then came a peculiar whistle – a signal evidently – the creaking of a windlass as a drawbridge was let down, and, with a final jab, he was jerked through an opening of the palisade into the den of the White Death.

THE SECOND CHAPTER

Blake's Midnight Adventure – In El Blanco's Nest – Face to Face

At the moment of Tinker's passing the palisade Sexton Blake also entered the White Death's stronghold, but from a different point, and in a different fashion.

Chilled with long immersion in the water, clad no more extravagantly than Tinker, cut in a hundred places by the cruel saw-grass, his fingers torn and bleeding, Sexton Blake had, nevertheless, worked on doggedly for three long hours at the very foot of the palisades.

He had found a path across the swamps, not without difficulty, and, abandoning his original plan of reconnoitring the main gate as hopelessly impracticable, had turned aside, crawling Apache fashion through the sentries, just when the storm was at its height, and dived noiselessly into the innermost of the three moats.

This flowed right up to the foot of the palisade itself, and there, hanging by one hand, he had employed the other in hacking savagely with his knife at the stout timbers, with short intervals of rest for three mortal hours.

The wood was sodden and hard to work through, so hard that, had it not been for a piece of unexpected luck, he would have been compelled to desist. One of the timbers, however, had been partially sawn through, owing probably to some mismeasurement when it was originally built, and a careless overseer or a slave, cunning enough to dodge work wherever possible and risk the chances, had allowed the timber to pass as sound, instead of cutting a new one.

Blake hacked away as soon as he discovered this piece of good fortune, and at the end of the first hour was able to wrench that particular piece clear, thereby easing his work on the other. At the end of the third hour he had contrived for himself a hole just large enough to squeeze through, and incidentally snapped his knife short at the haft with the very last bit of prising.

Weaponless and worked to a standstill, he never hesitated, but wriggled through, and cast himself panting on the ground to rest a while. The air struck several degrees colder than the water, and he dared not rest long for fear of getting cramped.

He rose with a shiver and looked about him. Little though he guessed it at the time, one of the first things to catch his eye was a small procession of four some distance away, standing out for an instant in bold relief against a camp-fire glow. The centre figure in that small group was Tinker.

A brief survey of his surroundings sufficed to enable him to make a map of the place in his mind's eye. On his left, somewhere out of sight, was the main gate; opposite him, on the far side of the enclosure, and again on the right hand, small red points of light told him that there lay guardhouses and smaller gates for use in times of emergency, each provided with its own series of drawbridges.

Near at hand, the back of it towards him, was a big, massively-built blockhouse far superior to all the rest; from its size, and the sound of coarse revelry coming from it, it was easy to guess that it was the house of the White Death himself. Beyond, but hidden from his view, on the near side by the blockhouse, was a large open space, lit by fires and surrounded by low shelters, open in front – the market-place, with the magazine at the north-west corner.

Further away, in a semi-circle, the barracks of the fighting men and those in the White Death's service; whilst beyond, lost in the darkness, or, at most, barely visible in the light of the camp-fires, the slave lines, patrolled on every side by sentries and ringed in with a double fence of spiked bamboos, their sharp points hardened in the fire till they were as impassable as steel.

Blake looked at it and shuddered. Somewhere down there amidst an inferno of indescribable squalor and filth, tortured by hope deferred again and again, lay an English gentleman at the mercy of one of the biggest ruffians, if not the biggest, in all Africa – and that means in all the known world.

He moved cautiously forward, keeping a sharp lookout lest he should stumble up against someone unexpectedly in the darkness, and being careful to keep well out of the glow of the fires; and it was well he did so, for before he had taken twenty steps he almost tripped over a recumbent figure, which lay sprawling on its back on the bare ground, breathing stertorously and oblivious of the pelting rain.

Blake bent down, his hands ready to grip and throttle if need be, but the fellow never moved. Liberal doses of coast gin and rum had done their work thoroughly. It would have taken a cannon to wake him.

A big knife, with a carved ivory handle and a heavy blade, was in his belt; an old-fashioned revolver slung on the other side, and he wore a long, loose, woollen robe with a hood which had slipped awry. With deft, skilful fingers Blake relieved the man of his weapons, his embroidered girdle, sandals, and finally of his loose robe, rolling him out of it with no little ceremony, as if he had been a sack of mealies.

An instant later the robe was round his own shoulders, and glad enough he was of the warmth of it. He slipped his feet into the sandals, pulled the hood well over his face, and, thrusting the weapons into his belt, went boldly forward. His one chance, he felt, lay in taking risks with a light heart.

As he drew near the circle, standing under shelter, facing the main building, he drew the hood still closer, and assured himself that both knife and revolver were ready for immediate use.

Other men were there, dressed after a similar fashion, and he watched their movements carefully to try and discover if they were followers of any particular sheik or slave-trader, though without success. At the moment all eyes were concentrated on a scene which was being enacted in front of the blockhouse. On a sheltered verandah sat a dozen or so men round a big table littered with the remnants of a feast. Broken and empty bottles lay everywhere on floor and table, and even on the steps of the verandah itself.

All of them were flushed with wine and spirits; some hopelessly fuddled. Most of them were swarthy or black-skinned men, but two, at least, were pure Arab, handsome but with cruel, evil faces; and there were half-caste Portugee, and Spaniards, and mulattoes. But, above all, one central figure stood out, and it was on him that Blake riveted his attention. He was seated in a heavily-carved armchair in the middle of the table. He had drunk as much, if not more, than any of the others, yet, beyond a flush of red on either cheek and an unnatural brightness of eye, he showed no signs of his debauch. He was an Arab, yet different from other Arabs; his skin was as fair as any Englishman's.

It was said of him that his mother was a Frenchwoman, which may in part have accounted for his light colouring. Certainly he spoke French fluently, and with a pure accent; but then he spoke half a dozen other languages as well. His face expressed little but cold, relentless cruelty and an iron will.

He spoke slowly and but little, yet whenever his thin lips opened, even the hardiest scoundrel present shuddered in his shoes. He was a big man, but comparatively small of bone, and not ungracefully formed. Few Arabs are. It was his fancy on all occasions to dress after the Arab fashion, and entirely in white.

His hair was white, as was his close-cropped beard and moustache; his very lips were colourless. The only thing about him which was a relieving note was a magnificent ruby, which he wore in his turban. It was uncut and only partly polished, but it was worth a fortune in itself, being of a wonderful deep blood-red, emblematical perhaps of the thousands of men, women, and children who had found death at his hands.

As he sat there looking at the scene before him, with fierce, moody eyes, he looked like some death's-head at the feast. In front of the raised daïs or platform of the verandah stood a group of four men.

One was held fast on either side by two of his comrades. He was a heavy-built mulatto, but his face was grey with fear. In front of him, and slightly to one side, stood the fourth man – a full-blooded negro, armed with a gigantic spear.

Though Blake did not know it, and could not guess it, the centre man was sentry of the outer drawbridge, which Tinker had managed to avoid. Five minutes before Tinker himself had stood on that very spot face to face with the White Death. Now the sentry whom he had eluded was to pay the penalty. The man cowered beneath the cold, remorseless eyes of the White Death. Even those who sat at table – such of them as retained their senses – were hushed momentarily into silence; whilst the group with which Blake had ventured to mingle were motionless and awe-stricken, fascinated by the sight, and, luckily for him, heedless of his presence.

Suddenly one of the men at the table raised his glass with a drunken laugh.

'I'll buy him off you, El Blanco! An ounce of gold – two ounces! 'Tis a thousand pities to waste such good material. Give him a round score of dozen at the flogging-post, and I'll buy him for two ounces of good red gold. Some salt in his cuts and a month or so under me will make the brute docile enough!'

El Blanco, the White Death, turned his head slowly towards the speaker.

'Peace, fool!' he said, as though he were speaking to a dog; and the man subsided abjectly. Then to the negro he spat out one word: 'Strike!'

The negro bunched his shoulder-muscles, struck, and the spear stood out a couple of handbreadths clear of the fellow's back.

The White Death regarded the prostrate form with cynical curiosity.

'A good stroke!' he said at length, with a nod. 'Take him away!' And, losing all interest, he drained his flagon at a draught, and sat as before, staring moodily in front of him, paying no heed either to his companions or the rabble collected on the far side of the open space.

Sexton Blake, iron-nerved though he was, shuddered, and as he did so noticed out of the corner of his eye that two men dressed as he was were making towards him. They were pretty far gone in liquor, and he immediately decided that his best chance lay in feigning to be in the same plight.

Turning, he staggered towards them with a lurching step.

'Hola, Pietro!' cried the nearest, with a hoarse laugh, clutching at him. 'The rum sings as merrily in your legs as it does in my head – a pest on it! El Blanco will have us triced up to the post for it if he finds us as far gone the day after tomorrow. He's in a sour mood, too, or he'd have spared the black fellow there.'

Blake clutched at him in turn uncertainly, and mumbled out an unintelligible sentence in coast Portuguese.

The other man laughed, swayed, and nearly fell.

'To the pit with the rounds!' he grumbled huskily. 'For my part, I shall be glad enough when we get the auction over and are well rid of the vermin. Only two more days of rounds and locking and unlocking, and enough, too. There'll be fun when the Inglese is put up to the bidders, the stiff-necked brute!'

Again Blake mumbled out an incoherent answer in a sleepy tone, but every nerve in his body was quivering with excitement. There was to be an auction of slaves in two days' time, that was clear, and Sir Richard was to be sold with the rest. He had only two days, then, in which to do his work.

And then 'the rounds' – what did the drunken brute mean if not that they were to go the rounds of the slave lines and see that all was secure for the night? If that was so, it would be strange if he could not get some word or message to the unfortunate prisoner unobserved – even if it were only a whispered word of help to come. He staggered along with his new-found and unsuspecting comrades, and saw with joy that they were making a line, if a somewhat deviating one, towards the slave huts.

All of a sudden, however, one of them sat down heavily and pulled a half-empty bottle from under his robe.

'Rot the slaves!' he said thickly. 'I'll go no further! El Blanco may see to his vermin himself! Success to our next venture, and let the brutes squeal!'

His fellow made a grab for the bottle, and the pair of them went rolling over and over in the mud, till they subsided under the overhanging eaves of a hut.

Blake went lurching on a step or two. One of them laughed, and the other shouted after him. Sexton Blake, fearful lest their cries should call up a patrol or some of their fellows, pretended to trip up, and rolled over and lay still. Another laugh greeted the action, and they left him in peace.

All hope of getting into the slave camp was gone, for with the bridge up, no password, and without the keys, which dangled from the belt of him with the bottle, the thing was an utter impossibility.

A mad thought flashed across him of stealing the keys of the sheds and making a dash for it, only to be dismissed after an instant's reflection. Having come so far, however, he determined to risk a little more, and have a closer view of the slave lines if he could.

With this end in view, he crept noiselessly to his feet, and, bending low, vanished into the darkness. Twenty minutes later he was back again, having found out all he could, and cast about for the best way to regain his loophole, which he had cut with such pains and care.

Skirting the open space, he rounded the log-house at a respectful distance, moving noiselessly and swiftly. The fires had burnt low and dull by now, and there was a chill of dawn in the dying wind, for the gale had nearly blown itself out; only the three lights of the guardhouses still shone brightly, the log-house itself was in utter darkness. He stole quickly round a large mound of earth which was one of his landmarks, for it was by that that he had found the sleeping man and deprived him of his robe and weapons. Curving sharply to the right, he turned for the palisade, and found himself face to face with the White Death.

THE THIRD CHAPTER

Tracked Down – Blake's Strategy – A Message from the Dead

Blake's hand flew swiftly but unostentatiously to the revolver in his girdle. If the worst came to the worst, he would shoot from the hip and dive for his hole in the palisade.

The White Death scowled at him sullenly.

'You walk late!' he said curtly.

'I come for my comrade, Pietro; he should be here-about,' answered Blake, in a surly tone, imitating as near as he could the guttural accent of his late companions, and replying in low-caste Portuguese.

'Take your hand from your belt!' hissed the White Death, whose keen eyes had noticed the threatening movement. Blake did so, knowing his own powers for quick shooting, and noting that the White Death was unarmed, save for a jewel-hilted stiletto. The sinister, white-robed figure eyed him for a moment, then turned to where the real Pietro lay snoring stertorously, still on his back. 'Throw that pig over the palisade to cool his sodden brain in the moat!'

Blake chuckled inwardly. There was a certain ironical humour in the situation, and he obeyed the order willingly, though with no little difficulty, for Pietro was a heavy brute, and the palisades were high. He managed, however, to get the upper part of his unwieldy burden on to the edge of the stout piles, and a lusty upward jerk of the dangling legs did the rest. The unlucky Pietro fell outwards with a heavy thud and a dull splash as he struck the water. Instantly there came a challenge from a few yard further along.

'Halt! Who goes there?' rang the cry, accompanied by the ready click of a Winchester.

'Peace, fool! It is I! Are you blind as a mole?' gibed El Blanco.

The man murmured something by way of apology, and retired to the far end of his beat.

'Tomorrow I will inspect the kennels at two hours after dawn. See that the gangs under your charge look sleek and well fed, or you shall feel the weight of the lash. You may go!'

Blake turned to leave, but he had not taken three paces, when a stinging blow from a knotty bamboo cane caught him across the back.

'To your den, you knave!' said the White Death. 'Do you think I want such scum as you prowling round the camp to disturb me? To your den!' And in a sudden access of fury he pointed with the stick he carried.

Blake registered the blow in his mind, to be returned with interest at some future date. Meanwhile, he was thankful enough for the anger which had prompted it, for had not El Blanco pointed the way to him he would have had no idea as to where his own particular lodgings were supposed to be, and gone blundering off in the wrong direction.

With a smarting back and in an ugly humour, he followed along the path pointed out till El Blanco was lost in the darkness. Then, kicking off his sandals, he doubled back close under the palisade and searched for his hole. Twice he passed a sentry within a few paces; but one had his back turned, and was leaning on his rifle, and the second was staring out eastward over the swamp, looking for the coming of the dawn which would bring him his relief.

At last, just as there was a suspicion of grey in the sky, he found what he sought. Wrapping his robe into a bundle, with the weapons in the midst, he plunged into the stagnant waters, replacing the cutout fragments of pile behind him, and plastering them thickly with mud. He knew now with a fair amount of accuracy the position of the sentries on the other moats, and evaded them with comparative ease. Once in the swamp-grass, he wriggled his way along, secure from observation, and gained the tree-belt just as the red dawn showed low down on the sky.

A bugle rang out behind him – the slaver's reveille – and across the mist-wreaths overhanging the morass came the sounds of the White Death's nest awakening to a new day of evil activity – a new day, it might be, of torture and degradation for the man whom he had come so far to rescue from the shame of slavery.

In the nest itself that same man woke with a groan in a low-roofed, squalid den, chained ninth in a row of twelve, his eyes filled with dull despair, his throat parched with thirst, and glanced at the grey, pinched faces around him. The man next him – the tenth – was dead. Sir Richard Losely regarded him with something like a sigh of envy. An hour – two hours – and men would come and knock the shackles off the corpse, and so an end. There had been a time when he had regarded such a scene and the men's brutal callousness with horror, and had protested in no measured terms; but his protests had been met with coarse laughs and jests and a spell at the flogging-post, till he, in turn, had become callous and indifferent, with the indifference of despair, looking on death as the least of evils to be expected.

Blake, having gained the forest, made straight for camp, which he reached, thoroughly worn out, as the sun topped the trees on the far bank of the Oro, a mile distant.

The camp itself was snugly hidden in a declivity of a jutting cape or promontory, which had many natural advantages. In the first place, it was well above flood-mark, and at one point was so narrow that two men with rifles could have held it against a hundred. Also it commanded a view of ten or twelve miles both up and down the main stream.

They had been there some nine or ten days in all, their bearers having deserted them many miles upstream, neither promises of liberal 'dashes' of brass rod and beads, nor threats of no payment at all, having the slightest effect when balanced against the terror of possible capture by the dreaded White Death and his satellites.

Consequently, scanty though their stores were, it had taken the pair of them three long days' hard work to fetch them down river in batches, for the current ran swiftly, and was full of dangerous rocks and overfalls, and what took them a matter of a couple of hours to come down on the stream with a full load, plus the risk of capsizing every now and again, necessitated half a day's hard and incessant paddling and tracking to recover. Once, in fact, when a sudden rain had flooded the stream, they had worked like galley-slaves at the paddles for ten consecutive hours, and gained the opposite bank exactly two miles above their starting-point.

Their equipment consisted of a double-roped, green, rot-proof canvas tent, already sadly the worse for wear, a scanty supply of camp furniture, a lamp, chart, compass, and chronometer – of which the chart was hopelessly inaccurate, and the chronometer suffered from a four hours' rest at the bottom of the river – four sound repeating Martin expresses, the same number of revolvers, carrying a short cartridge of similar calibre, a good supply of ammunition, and two months' rations, in neat, forty-pound loads, for the convenience of quick travelling.

This, with a few other necessaries, such as a pressure-filter, a small medicine-chest, and a heavily-built but stiff dugout, formed their outfit, over which, for the last sixteen hours, Pedro had kept watch and ward faithfully, though driven nearly mad by the never-ceasing attacks of mosquito and sandfly.

Blake was so utterly bone-weary on reaching camp that he gave up all idea of food, and, seeing that Tinker had not yet returned, flung himself down on the folding-bed and went fast asleep.

He was awakened by a low, rumbling growl, which brought him to his elbow instantly, listening intently. The sun was high up in the sky; well past midday he judged it to be. He reached out an arm without moving off the bed and grabbed his Martini, which was ready loaded, as always, and listened again, motioning to Pedro to be silent.

The big dog glanced at him reproachfully, but the low rumbling ceased. Blake could hear nothing, but he was too old a campaigner to be caught by so simple a trick. He knew full well that as likely as not somewhere outside the canvas an enemy might be crouching, stealthily watching and waiting for some hasty or chance movement which might show him where to strike.

Fully five minutes passed thus in intolerable suspense; then, inch by inch, Blake slid sideways off the bed and lay prone on the floor. Again he listened, yet not so much as a leaf stirred. Like a snake he wriggled across the floor, his rifle thrust forward, till he reached the flap door of the tent. Stretching out sideways, he managed to get his fingers round the edge of Tinker's pith helmet, eased it noiselessly from the top of the box on which it lay, and, placing it on the muzzle of his rifle, held aslant, pushed it partially through the flap at about a man's chest height from the ground.

Natives and undisciplined men are apt to snap off quickly at anything they see in moments of excitement, and Blake was pretty sure that he would draw the fire of anyone who happened to catch sight of the helmet.

No report of gun or rifle, no swishing shower of throwing-spears followed, however, and after another pause he ventured to withdraw the helmet and crawl through the opening himself. No one was visible on that side, at any rate, and he crawled round the angle of the tent, his keen eyes searching every foot of ground, ready to drop to cover on the slightest warning, his trigger finger ready for instant action.

Not a blade of grass stirred, not a thing moved. There was nothing but the luxuriant tropical verdure, the blazing sun overhead, and the monotonous hum of myriads of insects. The heat seared the marrow in his backbone, the air quivered in dazzling layers behind him, the broad flood of the Oro was like a stream of molten metal; yet, for all its peacefulness, Blake instinctively felt that somewhere in the densely-grown scene around him someone lay lurking; he felt the presence of an unseen, strange body.

He raised his head an inch or so and sniffed cautiously. His nose was keen as any bushman's. At the first he could detect nothing but the sickly smell of the river mud and dank, decaying vegetable matter. Presently, however, a little draft of air floated towards him from inland, and he sniffed again. His eyes hardened, for to his acute senses had been wafted that peculiar musty odour which is a sure sign of the presence of a dark-skinned man.

Not that the dark-skinned people are uncleanly; as a rule the case is very much to the contrary; but the fact remains that between the light races and the dark there always exists that peculiar difference of scent.

And to the dark man, the European or American is just as much an object of aversion as regards the olfactory sense as he himself is to the white.

Sexton Blake snuffed up wind again, dropped flat on his stomach, and advanced to the far corner of the tent. Presently, some fifteen yards away, the tops of the grass moved ever so faintly.

That was enough for him. He glided off at right angles, where the bush was thickest, described a semi-circular curve under cover, and came out again behind his man.

The fellow was almost completely hidden, but he could just glimpse a bronzed side, the haft of a spear, and part of a black head. The man, whoever he was, was evidently watching the camp intently. He crawled up till he was ten feet away, then, rising to his feet, he covered the man with his rifle. The black was clearly alone, or some of his fellows would by now have crept up and rushed the tent from several sides at once.

'Well,' said Blake, in Masangi dialect, for such he imagined the man's tribe to be, 'what does the black dog want that he hides in the grass like a snake?'

'Wow!' cried the astonished man, starting to a crouching position on the first word. 'Wow Inkoos! Silent as the ghosts art thou – a great chief! The little part of an hour gone thou wast there' – and he pointed to the tent – 'for I heard thee go so, as the white men do when they sleep heavily after meat' – and he made a very passable imitation of a snore. 'Also, there was one within who rumbled deep in his throat. Yet now thou art here, and I have heard no sound – not so much as the whisper of a dead leaf – yet my ears are keen! It is magic! Wow, but thou art a great chief and a mighty hunter!' And, dropping his big spear, he sprang to his feet and saluted, eyeing Blake squarely in the face.

He was a man of magnificent physique, the great shoulder muscles rippling as he moved his arm, and his legs, straight as an arrow, terminating in small, beautifully formed feet, with a good arch and gripping power, gave a suggestion of great pace.

'What knowest thou of white men and the ways of white men?' demanded Blake.

'Inkoos, baas. For many moons I served a white man – a man amongst men – down there in the kaffir people's country. Wow, but we hunted and fought and made merry! Twice I saved him from the spears of the Matabele, who are no poor fighters, and twice he also plucked me from the very jaws of death. We were even as blood brothers. Then Inkoos, the baas – my baas – grew weak of a fever in the low countries. Three days and three nights he lay ill. On the fourth I buried him at noon, under a pile of great stones, for the jackals were many, and he had died at dawn. Then my heart was heavy within me, and I travelled blindly, not heeding whither, till I fell in with the soldiers of him whom men call the White Death, in whose kraals I tarried awhile. Now am I here.'

'A tale for children!' said Blake contemptuously, wishing to goad the man on to say more. 'Why should a dog in the service of the White Death come creeping through the grass to disturb my sleep, and why, being found, should not the dog die? If one sees an adder in the path, the wise man sets his heel on it, and so an end.'

'Nay, Inkoos, not if perchance the adder bear a message from the wise man's friend.'

'He who bears a message comes straight to the main gate of the kraal, making the peace sign, that his errand may be quickly accomplished. If one bearing a message lie hid in the thicket, his words are like to be tipped with steel.' And he nodded significantly towards the big spear at the man's feet.

'Maybe, Inkoos,' replied the big man coolly; 'yet I have it in my mind that it is ill work waking a white man suddenly, especially when he sleeps so' – and he imitated a snore. 'For when freshly awakened the white Inkoos are quick to wrath, and quick to strike a blow. Then blood may flow freely without reason, seeing that the waker came in peace. Wherefore I said to myself, "I will wait awhile and rest till the Inkoos awakens and pours water over himself. Then, but not before, he will be safe to approach, and I will come out into the open, laying down my spear in token that there is no enmity betwixt us." '

In spite of himself, Blake had much ado to prevent bursting out laughing. His visitor's graphic and shrewd description of the ordinary Britisher's early morning surliness was distinctly funny. Moreover, it went far to convince Blake that the fellow was speaking the truth.

'Tell me your tale,' he answered, unconcernedly. He was itching to know what the message might be. Already he had a strong suspicion. Yet to show curiosity, even of the faintest, would have meant loss of dignity, and he would have fallen considerably in his self-invited guest's estimation.

'Inkoos, three moons ago there came to the kraal of the White Death, who is a son of the pit – may the jackals devour his bones – a white Inkoos, a fine man, very strong – stronger even than I. But he was badly wounded from a thrust in the side. Moreover, he was chained, as were the other slaves. His eye was fierce, and he was very proud – so proud that not even the White Death himself could tame him. Word went about the camp that he was a great chief set over the peoples of the Bambarra country.

'For three whole moons he has endured like a man. Were he unchained, with nothing but his bare hands, none durst go near him; therefore he is chained all times, even when at work under the slave-drivers. But he is strong as an ox, so strong that, in spite of stripes and blows, the wound in his side has come whole again, and the flesh is clean.

'Inkoos, when I saw him I was minded of my baas down there beneath the big rocks, and my heart grew warm, for he is brave, and I did what little I could for him. So it chanced that the half of a moon ago I gave him food that he might keep his strength, and the White Death saw me giving. He dared not touch me then, not even he, for I was armed, being about to go on duty at the gates. Later, though, he had me taken unawares. There were eight of them, but, even so, three never moved again when I let them go. He had me chained to the flogging-post – me, Lobangu, of the reigning house of the Etbaia, who never felt fetters heavier than those of an enemy in his death-grip.

'Wow, but my spirit burned within me! Little I recked of their stripes as they bit into my flesh, or the jeers of the base-born crowd. But in that hour, chained to the post, I vowed the blood-vow of my people. Not lightly should they offer indignity to a prince and chief of the Etbaia!

'Then, when they released me, I formed a plan, and cringed and fawned, for by cunning alone could I obtain my ends. Moreover, I was of use to the White Death, and, seeing me cringe, his heart was glad, and I was restored to my place amongst those who guard the gates.

'Again a second time I sought out the white Inkoos by stealth, and to him I told the half of my plan, offering to bear messages from him to his friends; then, if all else failed, I would return to him secretly, bearing weapons and the wherewithal to free him of his fetters; and we two, by reason of my knowledge of the camp, would fall upon the White Death and kill him before we ourselves died. How say you, Inkoos – will you bear the message to his friends, and give me for him one rifle such as that you hold in your hands, and also one of the shorter guns with the many chambers, such as I used to oil and clean for my baas who is gone? Or will you perchance strike a good blow yourself for one of your own tribe? For methinks there is the glitter of the true fighting-man in your eye, and he who can move through the undergrowth so that not even I, Lobangu, may hear, must be in very truth a mighty hunter. Say, Inkoos, which shall it be?'

'Does the dog question its master, saying "Whither shall we go"?' replied Blake curtly. 'If this be a true tale, and no child's talk, show me if you can where the White Death brushed flies from your back yonder.'

'Wow!' grunted the big man indignantly, not liking to be reminded of the indignity he had undergone. Nevertheless, he stripped off the loose shirt he was wearing, cut low and wide at the neck, and girt round the middle with a sash, in which was a huge knife. Having done so, he turned his back for Sexton Blake's inspection.

It was a terrible sight, torn and lacerated across and across by the heavy, weighted lashes. Lightly though the man had spoken of the pain, he must have undergone the most exquisite agony – such agony that none but a man of his enormous physique could have retained their senses under the blows. Blake shuddered with disgust to think that such a brutal thing could have been done with impunity. Flogging in moderation, when necessary, is all very well, but here the flesh had been ripped from the man's back.

The wounds corroborated the fellow's story, for as near as Blake could judge they were scarcely a fortnight old, and but partially healed.

'It is good,' he said abruptly. 'Later I will give you medicines for your scratches. What of the message you bear? Give it me and leave me a while – I would think. There is food yonder, but beware of him who guards it.'

Lobangu fumbled in his thick hair and produced a small roll of paper, which he handed over whilst Blake whistled to Pedro. The Nubian's eyes grew wide with astonishment as the big hound came out of the tent, stretching and yawning.

'Wow!' he cried, drawing himself up to the salute. 'Hail, Inkoos, for of a truth thou art a king of beasts, mighty of limb and strong of jaw! Was it thy spoor I struck yonder amongst the trees? Surely I had thought it the passing of a great panther, save that he walks not so – two and two. Hail to thee, Inkoos, king of all dogs of the earth!'

Blake smiled as his strange visitor addressed Pedro; but he said no word, nor did he interfere as the two stood eyeing one another. He had great faith in Pedro's instinctive likes and dislikes, and wished to see what the animal would do.

Pedro sniffed once – twice, and then, without more ado, stalked up and thrust his great muzzle into Lobangu's big brown hand.

'Very much my way of thinking, old man,' muttered Blake to himself. Then aloud: 'There are mealies in the sack, and bananas, likewise black tobacco of the strongest on the ammunition-case. Eat and rest, for I would be alone.'

'Inkoos,' said Lobangu; and strolled off to the tent, accompanied by Pedro.

Blake sat on a rock, his rifle across his knees, and unrolled the paper.

> This [it began] is written from the fortified stronghold of the slave-dealer known along the coast as El Blanco, or the White Death, situated on the northern edge of the delta of the Rio de Oro, on the Tiris littoral, by me, Sir Richard Losely, probably the last words I shall ever write, having been held captive here for nearly three months. The exact date I do not know, having lost count under stress of great misery and hardship.
>
> On July 16th last I was seated in my private office at the Residency at Musardu, going through a batch of official documents to be despatched by runner to the coast, when I heard a great uproar, the rattle of rifle-fire, and screams from the natives under my charge. The garrison consisted of a mere handful of Hausas, the main body having been detached for special service on the frontier under Captain Ellison. This was done by my order, and I wish to exonerate him from all blame. There were not, I fancy, more than ten men under arms in the whole settlement, and so quickly did things occur that by the time I reached the open drill-ground in front of the Residency verandah every man of them had been killed or disabled. I had that morning been holding a court, and had my full dress sword by my side, otherwise I was weaponless. In under two minutes I was wounded in the side and in the hands of the slavers. Of my poor people but few escaped, and at least a hundred were killed on the spot.

> We reached here in fetters after a march of forty-three days, during which the daily average of deaths amongst the slaves from wounds or exhaustion was at least five. I write this as a semi-official report, lest the news of the massacre may only reach the coast in a distorted form, and in the hopes that the bearer, Lobangu, a Nubian tribesman, who has shown me much kindness, and who is about to escape from this den of iniquity, may be able by chance to deliver it to some white hunter or trader. In such case I would ask him three favours, to be granted as favours to a man already on his death-bed. First, a substantial reward to Lobangu himself, for he not only procured me the materials with which to write, but has shown me many kindnesses in a hundred ways, even to sharing his food with me by stealth.

'Good for Lobangu!' muttered Blake. 'He never let on to poor Losely that he had been flogged for it. Pedro was right – the man's a trump!'

> This reward will be recoverable from my family, also any expenses incurred [he continued reading]. Secondly, I would ask that the news be broken to my dear wife as gently and as quickly as possible, suppressing all unpleasant detail, and conveying to her my dying message, which is that my last thoughts will be of her. And I pray that our son Leonard be brought up true to the traditions of the Loselys, that he may serve his King and country faithfully, in however humble a capacity. I should prefer him, when the time comes, to be commissioned by some Border regiment, where he may see active service and prove his mettle, rather than to a home battalion and the dull routine of garrison life. My other affairs are in the hands of the family solicitors. Everything is to go to my dear wife,

with remainder to our son, the estates to be used entirely at her discretion until his coming of age.

Thirdly, I would most earnestly request that in the event of this coming to the hands of the proper authorities, no punitive expedition be organised on my account. The country is difficult, and the expense entailed by such an expedition would be enormous. It would be unfair to embarrass a young country such as the Bambarra district, till lately under my charge, with such a debt. The natives are docile and industrious, and the region has a future before it which I should be sorry to see checked.

I therefore most earnestly urge that no expedition, punitive or otherwise, be undertaken on my account at the expense of a country which, till recently, I had the honour to govern. Lobangu also I believe cherishes some mad scheme of returning at the risk of his life to endeavour to rescue me, or, at least, give me a fighting chance. From this I beg the reader to dissuade him by every means in his power, for in all probability I shall be dead before he can return, and he would be throwing away the life of a brave and honest man to no purpose.

Time grows short, and I lack space; yet this much I will add: There can be no permanent peace and security in the hinterlands of the West Coast and the tribes there located until the White Death and his raiders are dispersed, tried, and hanged. His field of operation, I have learnt, extends from Southern Morocco down to the hinterland of Dahomey. His headquarters, from which I send this by bearer, are, I have stated, on the northern edge of the Oro delta, and very strongly fortified.

To north, east, and south lie swamps impassable to troops almost, absolutely impractical for even light fieldguns. It is surrounded by a high stockade, well-built and loopholed, three moats, and is garrisoned by, as near as I can estimate, two hundred and fifty rifles – Winchester repeaters. The men, though roughly disciplined, are of undoubted bravery, and good shots. Moreover, they have abundance of ammunition. There are three gates in the palisade, each covered by, I think, a Colt quick-firing gun on a swivel mounting; but I have been unable to approach close enough to make certain.

The key to the position is by way of a tortuous maze of uncharted creeks, up which the slaving vessels creep in safely from the westward. When the time is ripe for exterminating this nest of villainy the rainy season should be chosen, the creeks then affording water for vessels of moderate draught. A gunboat or a couple of river boats might then find their way up and shell the place, after which a landing-party of a hundred should suffice.

The water-gate making the objective, as the piles are rotting there to a considerable extent.

There are at present over five hundred poor wretches of slaves here, of whom I am not the least miserable. Above all, send my messages to my wife. Captain Ellison is free from all shadow of blame. Goodbye, and farewell.

RICHARD LOSELY

Hardened though he was to scenes of misery and the tragedies of life, Sexton Blake's eyes were dim, and his throat ached as he read the closing words.

'What a man,' he muttered – 'what a man to be left to rot in this beastly place! Even in his extremity he puts everything before himself. Brave, unselfish, thinking only of others. Hallo, what's this? I thought I had finished.'

He had turned over the last page of the paper, and there, scribbled on the back, was a short note.

Since being here in captivity I have heard a strange tale, so circumstantial that I am convinced there must be some truth in it. It was told me by a fellow-captive, a full-blooded negro, who has been here many years, and is now a kind of attendant on us others. According to him, a peculiarly fine ruby, which the White Death wears in his turban – I myself have seen it – was stolen from the negro when he was captured, and is only one of many such quarried out by a primitive, and, to me, unknown race of dwarf stature, whom he calls by an utterly unpronounceable name, and who inhabit, according to his account, a range of mountains in the far north-east hinterland of the Bambarra territory – a region which we have so far left undisturbed.

I write this because it may be the means of rewarding the white man who shall read this despatch, supposing Lobangu makes good his escape. Or should the reader find the journey too rough to venture, of enriching the exports from Bambarra, and to this end I would recommend my successor to send a small exploring party, under escort and accompanied by an expert, to prospect the region. I can give no further information than that the district lies to the extreme north-east from Musardu, where, according to the account, there is a waterless tract of desert, three days' journey across, beyond which may be seen three high, snow-covered peaks, and that the ruby-mines, if existent, are situated somewhere amongst the lower slopes of those peaks. I can add one fact which may or may not tend to bear out the truth of the story, and that is that when his Majesty's Government assumed the protectorate of Bambarra, amongst the deceased ruler's effects was found a very handsome uncut ruby of fine colour, since loaned, I believe, to the gem collection of the British Museum.

I am empowered by virtue of the office I still nominally hold to offer to any private explorer the half of his findings, and a claim measuring half a mile in each direction, to be chosen at his option, any find outside that claim to be the property of the Bambarra state, and to be devoted to the increase of its revenue.

R. L.

Blake folded up the pages slowly and put them in an inner pocket. As he did so he was suddenly aware that the sun was already sinking behind him, and with a start he realised that Tinker was still absent from camp. Judging from the difficulties and fatigue of his own reconnaissance, he had hardly expected Tinker before noon, but now noon had come and gone these six hours past, and with a sudden sense of misgiving he sprang to his feet and called Lobangu.

THE FOURTH CHAPTER

The Escape – News of Sir Richard – The Struggle by the Dyke – Tinker Sends Word

'Lobangu,' he said quickly, as the big Nubian came striding up and saluted, 'your talk was true talk. I have read the words of the Inkoos who is in the hands of the White Death, and he bids me see that you have your reward. Here I have no gold nor ivory, but later you shall have that which will buy you a kraal and wives and cattle, if such be your wish.'

'Inkoos!'

'Speak on!'

'The reward I would have is the weapons of which I spoke but a little while since, and a double handful of shiny cartridges, both long and short; then I will ask your leave to go.'

'Whither!'

'Back over the swamps to the baas who lies in chains, who speaks to my heart as my own baas spoke in the days that are gone. A double handful only I ask, and may be one or two more for such rabble as we may reach. There shall be some bite the dust before the end. And so an end to all, for I would follow the baas into the dark places, to be his dog, and serve him, and oil his guns, letting none other touch them, for there perhaps I may meet again him who was as my blood brother, and whom I buried beneath the rocks at the coming of the moon. I have spoken. If it is written that reward be due to me, such is the reward I claim. Have I the permission of the Inkoos, for I am a-weary to make a finish?'

Sexton Blake laughed inwardly. The stalwart black savage was just such a man as he could respect, which is more than could be said of many knock-kneed dwellers in town, whose sole aim was to heap up gold by force, fraud, or trickery; though it is true Lobangu's notions of an after-life were somewhat unconventional. One hardly associates Martin repeaters and a burly black Nubian to oil their lock actions with a future state.

'Listen thou, Lobangu, Prince of the Etbaia,' he replied gravely. 'Last night I also was in the nest of the White Death – ay, and met and spoke with El Blanco face to face. I also was struck across the back; yet, even as thou, I took no heed of the blow, for only by cunning, even as thou, might I attain my end, and that end is to rescue the Baas Losely, a very great chief, for which purpose and no other have I crossed the black water. Therefore shalt thou and I go and do such deeds as two men may without fear.'

Lobangu drew himself to his full height and raised his spear till it flashed blood red in the light of the dying sun.

'Men do they breed across the black water! Lions for strength, yet serpents for cunning! Hail, Inkoos! Hail, my father! Wow! But the red blood shall run, and I, Lobangu, my father's jackal, shall drink my fill! I, the follower of him who moves without sound, the stealthy one, the crafty, before whom the grass-tops part yet move not, whose coming and going is silent as the breath of the dawn, whose eye is keen, and whose hand is as a rock of strength! Wow, for the death charge! The spear shall be reddened! Deep shall it drink lives of the enemy –'

'Peace! Be silent!' interrupted Blake, holding up his hand. 'This is no time for empty words. Tomorrow at sun-setting there is to be a selling of slaves to the traders, and amongst others Baas Losely is to be sold – so much I learnt whilst I was in the nest, having entered by means of a hole cut in the foot of the stockade on the eastern wall. That we must prevent, having carefully made a plan. Yet, first, there is another thing to do. Last night another beside myself attempted to enter the nest – a white man, even as I, though his skin was stained dark as thine, and he was clad only in a moocha, with the tribal mark of the Ubangi on his forehead; also he has knowledge of the ways of the Ubangi people, and can speak their tongue. Cunning he is, and brave; yet he has not returned, and much I fear that some evil has befallen him. How say you, Lobangu, did you hear aught of such a one before you escaped from camp, or see aught of a trail through the forest? Surely, though, that last must be so! How else are you come here?'

The Nubian paused a minute, reflecting.

'Look you, Inkoos, so it happened last night, during the great storm, I and another – a fool – were guardians of the middle gate on the south. He, misliking the darkness and the rain, cowered in the shelter. Then I, seeing that the chance was come, walked away some little distance, as if to patrol the bank; there I stood a while listening, and plunged into the moat. Yet now I mind me that at the very instant of my diving I heard something move in the grass on the opposite bank, and, thinking it might be an alligator on his journey across the swamp, and wishing to avoid all noise, I kept beneath the waters, swimming like an otter, and came up twenty yards to one side.

'Then I set my face to the swamp and plunged forward. The Inkoos will remember that the night was very dark, so I saw no trail; yet once or twice I came upon places where the grass had been beat aside, as I then fancied by some huge animal, yet it may have been that the friend of the Inkoos had passed that way.

'I hid in the forest till the coming of the dawn, and there, a little way away, I saw the pug-marks of the king of beasts, which I followed, thinking they would lead to water, for I was athirst, and found both water and the camp. So runs the tale, Inkoos. If it be as I think, the white man must have crossed the outer moat – ay, and it may be the second also, seeing that there was but one to guard it at that point. Ah, no; it would be the hour of the passing of the patrol. If luck were against him, it was there that he would be taken or killed.'

Sexton Blake frowned. This was indeed an added difficulty, for Lobangu's forecast was probably correct. He did not for an instant believe that Tinker would be killed; but it was pretty certain that he was either hurt or captured, just when Blake needed his services most.

'We will eat and rest,' he said, 'till the darkness has quite gathered; then we will go – you and I – following up the trail, and see what may be done.'

'Inkoos!' replied Lobangu, and turned to prepare a meal, proving himself, much to Blake's surprise, a very excellent cook – a most unusual thing in a man of his rank, for, as a rule, a fighting man of a fighting tribe would not demean himself by such menial work.

Not only that, but he took complete charge of the camp, and especially of the rifles, which he cleaned industriously, chewing a great plug of tobacco the while.

An hour after dark they set out. Blake took Pedro on a leash to the far edge of the forest belt, to ensure their striking the swamp at the right point, then sent him back to guard the camp and outfit.

They followed up the swamp trail easily enough to the edge of the outer moat, and found the spot where Tinker had lain hidden, and the marks where he had scrambled up the opposite bank; but there a difficulty arose, for on the bank of the second or middle moat they could hear, though they could not see, a sentry passing up and down.

Blake knew the necessity of getting across if they were to come to the end of the trail, yet in the face of the redoubled vigilance, caused, no doubt, by Tinker's escapade of the previous night, the thing seemed impossible without running the risk of almost certain detection. Lobangu, however, solved the problem.

'Look you, Inkoos,' he whispered, laying down his big spear, 'I can read a trail in the dark by touch only, also I can swim like an otter, as you shall see, keeping always below the surface; so will I cross directly the sentry has passed, and see what may be seen. Should he return unawares, do you just, as he comes up to me, click the lock of your rifle once – so! Then will he pause and gaze out into the darkness; so shall I take him before he can raise an outcry, or, failing that, lie hid in a rifle-pit till he moves on again.'

'Good; so be it!' said Blake reluctantly. For although he was a strong swimmer himself, he shrewdly suspected that Lobangu would be far better than any European.

The Nubian stripped himself to his waistcloth, took a deep breath, and almost before Blake could see what had become of him, he had slipped below the surface of the water, leaving scarcely so much as a bubble to mark where he had dived.

Five minutes passed, yet not a sound could Blake hear anywhere. Then came the soft, monotonous pad of the bare-footed sentry returning on his round.

Blake waited until, as near as he could judge, the fellow was five or six yards from where Lobangu should be, and placed his rifle at half-cock. The sound, faint though it was, caused the man to check instantly, and for a full half-minute he stared out in the direction from which the sound had come. Then Blake heard him grumble something to himself and resume his patrol.

Another five minutes dragged wearily away, and he was beginning to believe, in spite of himself, that Lobangu was a fraud, a well-devised trap to lure him also into the hands of the White Death. The thought made him tighten his lips, and his face grew hard. Should it be so, he registered a vow that, at any rate, the Nubian should not live to gloat over the success of his scheme, if he – Blake – could possibly help it.

He heard the sentry returning once more from the opposite direction, but apparently the man was content to cover only a portion of his original beat, for the steps ceased well away to the right.

Still there was no sign of Lobangu, and Blake reflecting that, in his present position on the brink of the moat, he was exposed to treachery from all quarters, began to think of either pushing on himself or returning to the far side of the outer moat.

A sudden movement of the water's surface, unheard, almost unseen, though just at his feet, placed him on the alert, and, noiseless as an eel, a huge mass began to emerge and finally landed on the bank.

Blake stretched out a hand only to draw it back quickly, for the arm he touched in the darkness was heavy and limp.

'Inkoos,' whispered a voice in his ear, 'I have found that which we sought, ay, and more also. Let us get away to a place where we may make a light in safety. Will the baas deign to carry his jackals' spears and robe, for this man is heavy; but he must leave no track.'

'What have you there, Lobangu?' whispered Blake in return, a sudden chill at his heart.

The next words reassured him, however.

'The pig of a sentry, Inkoos! I followed him in his tramping up and down, having heard the clicking of your rifle-lock, and as he turned my arm slid round his neck – so! He struggled a little, a very little only, and it was over. Then, having accomplished that which was to be done, I returned, bringing him with me, for so the White Death will think he deserted of his own free will even as I did. Had I not done so, perchance they might have chained him to the flogging-post,' he added, with grim humour.

'Of what nationality is he?' asked Blake, in a low tone, picking up the big spear and the robe.

'From the Armoimi, Inkoos. He was one of those who made the marks on my back which you wot of, otherwise I might have spared him. He was El Blanco's head man, having served him many and many moons. Wow! But there will be doings in the camp when he is nowhere to be found, for found he will not be unless, perchance, they find him floating in the Oro's mouth, where the water runs salt to the taste.'

They plodded warily along for a couple of miles, following a single track, in case the White Death might think it worth while to send out a search-party, and heading well to the right of the direct route to the camp.

'Now,' said Blake, signing for a halt, 'what of my white friend, him for whom we seek?'

'Have you fire-sticks, Inkoos; those that strike zzp – so! You have; then I will show you. First of all, I found where he had reached the far bank of the second moat. With my fingers I felt where his knee had pressed deeply in the mud as he raised himself up out of the water, also the marks of his hands gripping, and then all around were signs of struggling. Some of the men – two, I should say, for in the dark it is hard to be sure – wore shoes on their feet; but he and one other went barefoot.

'They did not kill him, Inkoos – no; for I followed the trail for a little way amongst the rifle-pits towards the gates, and he walked amongst the others on his feet. Then I dared venture no further, for there were men by the gate – three of them, laughing and talking amongst themselves – so I slipped into the water again – into the inner of the three moats this time, being minded to take a look at the palisades; and there, just opposite the point of the struggling, I espied a tiny piece of something which glimmered whitely, thrust through the chink of the woodwork, and brought it with me. It was folded carefully, and crackled beneath the fingers, wherefore I guessed it contained a written message for the Inkoos; and here it is as I found it.'

He fumbled in his hair, which seemed to be his favourite storing-place for small articles, and produced a slip of paper, folded roughly into a cocked-hat shape and almost perfectly dry.

Blake took it and glanced at it by the light of a match screened in the palm of his hand. It was thickly covered with writing, in Tinker's hand, and in cipher.

'We must get back to camp, Lobangu,' he said. 'The writing will take time to unravel, and we have no light.'

'Inkoos,' replied Lobangu; and shouldered his grisly burden.

They made direct for the river-bank, and there disposed of the sentry's body by flinging it into the current which flowed swiftly thereabouts, after which they made their way upstream to the tent, and lit the swinging lantern.

Blake began to read anxiously enough and with some difficulty, for the paper was soiled and dirty, and the writing had evidently been done with a stump of pencil sorely in need of sharpening.

I was taken on the second moat [it began abruptly, in the ordinary cipher they used for private messages]. They had collared me and rammed my nose in the mud before I had a chance to make a fight for it. I have seen the White Death. They think I am from the upper reaches of the Ubangi, a half-caste of some sort, who tried to steal into camp after an imaginary relation who had been captured. They haven't bothered about me, except the chaps who collared me, and they get a commission on my price. They just clinked me into the slave-lines, and didn't even trouble to fetter me.

I have found Sir Richard and spoken to him. On the other side I have drawn a rough map of the encampment, having helped myself to a bit of pencil and some paper from the guardhouse of the slaves' enclosure. Escape either over or through the palisade is impossible – at any rate, for Sir Richard, who is strongly chained. I doubt even if I could get away alone, as, for some reason which I cannot ascertain, a much stricter lookout than usual is being kept.

But tomorrow night there is to be a big sale. Already there are a dozen or more vessels lying in the creeks. We can see the masts of the nearest from here over the palisade. Our best chance would be if you could manage to join in with the crowd at the water-gate when the sale begins, pretending to belong to one of the traders' retinue. There will be many newcomers – strangers – I have learnt from the talk of the sentries, so the risk won't be so very great. They say, too, that this is the biggest and last sale there will be till after next rains, as the White Death and his men are off raiding.

If you can get in, bringing us a revolver apiece and a knife, and, above all, the file from the ammunition chest; it will be hard if we can't cut and run during the confusion of the sale, or whilst the feasting is going on afterwards.

I am to be put to work with a gang of others on some rifle-pits close to the palisade, just by where I was captured, and shall try and slip this between the piles when I get a chance. I am pretty sure that you will follow up my trail and find it all right.

P.S. – I wonder what price I shall fetch. I ought to be valuable. We've all had double rations served out today to make us plump.

Blake read the closely-written lines to the end, and smiled grimly at the postscript, which was tucked away in one corner, which was torn and mud-stained. Then he turned the paper over and looked at the sketch-map. So far as the main construction of the fort was concerned, he knew pretty well all he wanted to; but Tinker, having seen the place by daylight, was able to mark the position of the water-gate, and indicate the general lie of the creek beyond, which had been hidden from Blake in the storm and darkness.

'Be they good words, Inkoos?' asked Lobangu, when he had finished.

'Both good and bad,' replied Blake; and gave him a brief outline of Tinker's plan.

Lobangu nodded his black head slowly.

'He is cunning, Inkoos. For so shall we gain an entry without difficulty or questioning, for I have been at the gate at the time of the great sale, and all who come may enter, also there is much tramping to and fro, and quarrelling and confusion; but the going out is a different matter, for then the gates are closed, and a strong guard set, and a count is made of each dealer's slaves as he passes out – ay, and of their attendants and servants also; for the White Death will allow no slave to pass the gate, save such as have been paid for at the table of scales. And before now men have wrapped robes round slaves not rightly theirs, trying to pass them off as attendants, and compelling them to accompany them at the knife's point.'

Sexton Blake's eyes glittered, for Lobangu's words gave him the germ of an idea. He thought for a while in silence, then laid his plan before Lobangu, for he was beginning to have a considerable respect for that worthy's judgment.

'Now, so should it go to my thinking,' he said. 'When tomorrow's sun is low in the sky to the westward, thou and I will lie snugly hidden by the creeks leading out to the black water, yet keeping an eye on the vessels moored there. Then, when those on board depart eager for the sale, we will make our way to one of them, swimming, if need be, and, climbing on board, overpower silently a watch, if they should leave one. So we shall get clothes such as the traders wear, and beneath them we can conceal our weapons, the spare ones for the Inkoos and my friend. This must be done very swiftly, so that we may join the throng clamouring at the Watergate, and gain the inside of the compound. For what shall come afterwards I have not yet fully thought out, yet some sort of a plan I have which I will tell thee later. Does this seem good to thee, Lobangu, of the peoples of the Etbaia?'

'Inkoos,' growled the big Nubian; 'in thy plan all is good, save that there is no word of the White Death, or of the killing, yet I bear the marks of his treatment on me.'

'Peace!' said Blake curtly. 'Go slowly, Hlala gahle, thou Lobangu. A little while ago – perchance I dreamed; yet I thought I heard big words of what thou wouldst do for the sake of the big Inkoos yonder.

'It is to save him and that other that we go to get them alive and safe out of the clutches of the White Death, not to bring a hornets' nest about our ears for the sake of a few scratches on thy tough hide. That once done, we shall be four instead of two, and four men, well armed, resolute, and unafraid, may do much. Then, in our own time, we will go up and speak with the White Death face to face, perchance, when he is busy on his own affairs.'

'Wise words, my father. In truth, I spoke like an untrained boy not fit to have a seat at the council. Meantime, I have that that shall remind me of the day which is to come. It is good.'

And, with a grunt and a salute, he picked up his blanket and curled himself up at the door of the tent.

THE FIFTH CHAPTER

The Slave Market – Tinker Goes Cheap – The Alarm – Broke Away

The last rays of the setting sun shed an intense lurid glow over the bays and creeks and on the upper half of the masts and spars of as nondescript a collection of vessels as could well be imagined – the fleet of the slavers.

Dhows from the Morocco coast, with the huge, tapering spars of their lateen sails; three ancient barques of British build, which half a century before had plied an honest trade out of Bristol or Hull; cutters, yawls, a brig, and schooners innumerable.

From their hiding-place, amidst the dense foliage of the banks, Blake and Lobangu counted no less than seventeen vessels of various tonnage, for the sale about to be held was a record one, and, though this they did not know, a big additional detachment of slaves had been marched into the compound from the North early that morning, bringing up the total to close on twelve hundred head. Thus the slave-lines were packed to suffocation, and the additional confusion and crowding were all in favour of their plans.

They themselves, earlier in the day, had struck camp, and tent and stores had been neatly stowed in the canoe, which was itself snugly hidden under the mangroves, in Pedro's charge, ready for instant use, for when the time came Blake had decided to make a dash for the river, and escape by water.

They had already selected the boat which they intended to board – a small dhow, moored so close to the shore that a gang-plank had been run out from her side to the bank.

For the past hour Blake had been watching her carefully, and had come to the conclusion that there were but seven men aboard her. Being of lighter draught, too, she lay some distance from the rest of the fleet and higher up the creek.

Just as the sun sank, a hubbub arose on the various craft – men shouting, boats being lowered overside, and riding-lights glimmering like fireflies in the swift-falling darkness. Boat after boat shot away, dashing up to the creek head, the crews urged on by their officers, and the slaves in the stern sheets racing against one another for the stage by the water-gate. For it was a case of first come, first served, and he whose crew reached the gate first was entitled to a choice of place at the auction.

The men on the dhow, having no need of a boat, came swarming out along the gang-plank. In the darkness, however, it was almost impossible to see how many came overside, and hearing was out of the question, for the din and racket all around was quite deafening.

In Sexton Blake's judgment five only had left the vessel. Lobangu, however, who, like most natives, could see in anything short of absolute darkness, maintained that only one had been left on board.

They waited a few moments to let the shore-party get a good start: then, leaving their hiding-place, they darted swiftly and silently to the gang-plank, and in a couple of seconds they were on board.

Amidships the empty hold was in readiness to receive its cargo of unfortunate wretches. An ill-kempt riding-light cast a faint glow for'ard; aft, where the cabin was, everything was in darkness.

Hardly had they gained the deck, however, than they heard someone stumbling up the narrow little companion. Blake signed to Lobangu to take cover behind the mast, whilst he himself crouched under the low bulwark just as a gigantic negro came out on deck. He was a repulsive, misshapen-looking brute, but evidently of herculean strength; and Blake had misgivings whether even the pair of them would be able to secure the man without noise. They could have killed him easily enough, but, except in a last extremity, Blake disliked the idea of allowing the man to be stabbed unawares in cold blood.

The fellow was grumbling to himself, evidently in a sour, black temper at not being able to get ashore and join in the orgies which would follow the auction. He stood for a while at the head of the gangway, looking upstream at the bonfire lights which were beginning to glow in the circle of the palisades. Then, apparently, he came to a sudden decision. With a grunt and a heave of his big shoulders, he seized the heavy gangway, and jerked it on board with a single movement.

Blake fancied he heard a muttered 'Wow!' of astonishment from the darkness behind him; indeed, he himself was astounded, for the weight of the thing would have given three ordinary men no little trouble to lift. Then, having taken this rough-and-ready precaution for security of his charge, the negro mounted on to the sail, steadying himself for an instant by a stay, and sprang to the bank, a clear fifteen feet away. He was evidently determined not to be done out of his share of the fun, for, without so much as a look behind him, he went off at a jog-trot in the direction of the gate.

'Wow, Inkoos!' whispered Lobangu, sliding out from behind the mast. 'The man is as strong as a black bull. There would have been a pretty fight here had he waited but a little longer,' he added regretfully.

'Quick!' said Blake. 'We haven't a moment to lose, or we shall not pass in with the crowd.'

They dived down below, and ransacked the stuffy cabin, pitching things this way and that, till at last they found what they were after – an Arab trader's dress, for Blake, with soft sandals and a hood concealing the face; a formidable-looking dagger with an ornate handle he stuck in the girdle, and a similar outfit for Lobangu, with the only difference that the latter's was of plainer stuff and without embroidery work of any kind.

Donning these as quickly as they could, they followed the negro's example, and sprang for the bank, which, encumbered as they were with their robes, proved no easy jump.

The passing of the gate proved easier than even Lobangu had fancied, for, owing to the enormous crowd, no watch of any sort was attempted, and they slipped through amidst a stream of jostling, struggling men, jabbering and shouting in every conceivable dialect and tongue, no one bothering to question them, or even notice them.

The sale had already commenced when they finally got inside the enclosure. On the verandah of the house was seated the White Death at a large table. One end of this was occupied by a pair of gold scales, and two men, who kept the reckoning in a large ledger, for the White Death was nothing if not businesslike.

Round this end of the table, and in a double row behind El Blanco himself, were drawn up the men of his bodyguard, armed with repeating-rifles and murderous-looking machetes.

The centre portion of the table was filled with flasks of wine and spirits, with valuable cut-glass drinking flagons, and boxes of cigars and cigarettes. El Blanco himself was a great smoker, and he was no niggard with either liquor or cigars as regards his guests.

Some ten or a dozen of the principal slavers were allowed seats at this table of honour. The next grade were given places in the open shelters which surrounded the square in front of the house, whilst the smaller fry and the retainers gathered in a big semi-circular crowd at the lower end of the square facing the house.

The whole scene was lit up with big flares and bonfires. It was towards this latter group that Blake and Lobangu made their way. They joined them unhindered, and Blake began to look anxiously around for signs of Tinker and Sir Richard. A big batch of a couple of score of slaves were just being offered.

They were brought round in a gang, each chained to the one in front in a long line, and goaded on by overseers with whips, at intervals along the line.

On first entering the open space, they were driven to the verandah for the inspection of the chief slavers, and the salesman cried aloud their merits. Now and again an individual was unshackled from the line and brought up for closer inspection by one or other of the dealers. Then they were bargained for, and the pick of them bought and paid for in ounces of raw metal – gold or silver, according to price.

One dealer, an Arab, and apparently a great friend of El Blanco, did his bidding in a lordly fashion, naming a price for a batch at a time, irrespective of quality.

Whilst Blake stood watching keenly, he bought in this fashion five lots of two score each, then suddenly dropped out of the bidding, and took to his flagon, whilst an attendant counted out the money.

Having passed the verandah, those who remained unbought were paraded before the second-grade merchants, and the residue – the weaklings of the batch – were in turn brought to the crowd amongst which Blake was standing, and bid for singly or in twos and threes.

Those left over after this third market – and they were very few, for El Blanco's wares were well chosen – were either driven back to the slave lines, or, if suffering from some physical defect, speared ruthlessly and tossed aside; also a certain number of these last were set aside to afford amusement to the inhuman wretches who trafficked in them when the feasting should be ended.

Suddenly Lobangu touched Blake's arm from behind.

'Wow! Inkoos, there – there, on your left! See, he is about to be offered for sale!'

Blake turned in the direction indicated, and there, sure enough, was the big, stalwart form of Sir Richard Losely.

At first, because of the glare of the fire, it was hard to see him, for the blaze which lit the central space was directly between them; but as he was dragged forward by the attendants Sexton Blake gave a half-suppressed gasp of astonishment. Accustomed as he was to a study of physical perfections and an appreciation of muscular force, the figure he saw before him was fairly astounding. Sir Richard, who was stripped, with the exception of a few rags, stood a good six-foot-four on his bare soles; yet, unlike most men of great stature, he was neither weedy nor awkward.

His build was magnificent, and the great muscles rippled and crept under his skin, plain to see even in that dim light. He was cruelly scarred in many places, but he held himself erect, carrying his head proudly, and glancing keenly to right and left with the air of a brave man, desperate, yet calculating his chances even in the face of death.

Blake, having obtained this his first glance of him, and seen what manner of man it was he had set himself the task of rescuing, did some rapid thinking, for such plans as he could make depended necessarily on the changing conditions of the moment, and he must be ready to act instantly – the second an opportunity, however faint, might occur.

Presently his attention was attracted by the peculiar hang-dog walk of a man far down the same line of slaves as that which Sir Richard headed. He was comparatively small and unchained, evidently regarded as of no importance except by one or other of two men who constantly kept an eye on him. Blake understood the situation at once, and, in spite of the vexation it caused him, he could hardly refrain from laughing. The hang-dog slave was Tinker; he realised that the instant he saw him. But Tinker's captors, having a monetary interest in his sale, and mistrusting both the possible purchaser and each other, fearful of being cheated out of their commission, watched him as a cat watches a mouse.

Sir Richard, meanwhile, had been dragged forward alone to the edge of El Blanco's table, too proud to resist where resistance was worse than useless; but in his eye there gleamed a light which boded ill for El Blanco if that worthy should trust himself within springing distance.

'That man means mischief,' Blake commented to himself under his breath. 'If he once gets to handgrips, chained and ill though he is, there'll be no need to send a gunboat to shell this den of iniquity, for El Blanco will be dead. Sir Richard will never leave his hold so long as there's life in either of them. Ah! the White Death is going to do a bit of auctioneering in person, I fancy.'

The tall, white-robed figure rose slowly, the big ruby glistening in the snowy turban, and glanced round the table.

'Gentlemen,' he said to the pack of ruffians round him, 'it is not my habit, as you know, to concern myself with the details of our business, as a rule. But on this particular occasion I have a special lot to offer you. There he is; you can see him for yourself. Strong as an ox. An infernal Britisher – one of those who by their impertinent meddling have done so much to hamper our trade. Now, you can see for yourselves that he is a slave whom, properly handled, a lot of work could be got out of, and that he is of exceptional value and interest; it is for this reason that I put him up by himself as a single lot. But I make this one stipulation – that whoever purchases him shall make sure that he is thoroughly driven.

'He is an obstinate, sullen dog, and I have had to spoil his skin a little myself. It's no good tickling him to keep the flies off; kindness of that sort has no effect. What he needs is half flaying and working till he drops. Apart from that fault, he is a bargain. And, gentlemen, I need hardly say that, after the hint I have given you, the lucky purchaser will see to it that the brute is well broken. He is British, remember, and I don't think that this fraternity is likely to have any little weakness for one of that twice accursed, meddling race. The bidding, to simplify matters, had better be in ounces – gold ounces. We will start the price at twenty7, as time is short and there is much to be done.'

The White Death sat down and eyed the group round him with a savage, dominating sneer of satisfaction, for he could read the hatred and cruelty of the men sitting around him as they scowled at the prospective bargain, and realised that there was not a man there whose fingers didn't itch to make the Englishman's life one long inferno of torture.

Suddenly there came an unlooked-for interruption. Sir Richard's guards had grown momentarily careless of their charge. With a quick jerk and a shrug of his enormous shoulders, he shook himself free of their slackened grip and strode forward a pace.

Betwixt him and the White Death lay the full breadth of the table – an impossible barrier to him, fettered as he was; but those nearest him shrank convulsively, seeing the red battle-light in his eyes.

'Wait!' he cried in a loud, authoritative voice, and speaking in the best coast Arabic, so that all could understand. 'I wish to give you all fair warning that I am Sir Richard Losely, Governor of Musardu, under his Britannic Majesty, and that even now an expedition is approaching – a British expedition – which will wipe you and your crowd of scavenging vermin off the coast! Your men will be shot or hung, your slaves taken from you, and your ships burnt. As for that man there' – and he pointed across the table with outflung arm – 'that vulture whom you call the White Death – I intend to have him taken down to Musardu, tried, and hung in the open market-place, so that all may see, and this, his nest, shall be burnt to the ground.

'You may not believe in this expedition; you doubt. See, here in my hand is a letter from the British.' He suddenly thrust out almost under their noses a piece of white paper, crumpled and written on. 'I received that in the slave lines yesterday, and yet you presume to consider yourselves secure in this foul hole, with your trumpery sentries and dykes!'

Then, without another word, before any of them could recover from their astonishment, he leapt back and thrust the letter into the heart of the bonfire and folded his arms. The letter was indeed from the British. It contained two lines of pencil scrawl from Tinker. But this only one man out of the whole crowd guessed, and that was Blake, who watched the proceedings with a grim smile.

'A very neat and carefully-thought-out piece of bluff,' he muttered under his breath. 'It's told, too. Some of those brutes are feeling scary; though how Tinker, I, and friend Lobangu are to perform the functions of an "expedition" on the scale indicated is a bit hard to say. I fancy Losely will have to tone down the incidental a bit when it comes to bedrock facts.'

The White Death alone of all the traders sat still and unmoved. For an instant, when Sir Richard had thrust out the letter and boldly proclaimed that he had received it in the slave lines, his face had become convulsed with passion, but he instantly recovered his self-command.

'Seize that noisy dog and strike him on the mouth!' he said coldly. 'If you let him slip again there will be work for the whip! The sale will now proceed!'

But Sir Richard's threats had had more effect than even the White Death had calculated on, and bidders who a few moments before would have run the price up merrily with bids of five ounces at a time now hung back, or bid tentatively in single ounces; and even that was more because they were under the eye of the White Death than because they wished to be burdened with so dangerous a purchase.

Slowly the price rose to thirty – to thirty-five – to forty, and there stopped. El Blanco looked round savagely.

'You chicken-hearted curs!' he said, in a low voice. 'You who came here swaggering and blustering about what you will do, lying about what you have done, you are shaking in your shoes just because the white dog snarled at you! You dare not pay a price for him, lest he turn and bite you!'

'Well, I will show you that the White Death is no flincher, and can live up to the reputation which has given him the rule of the coast since some of you were clinging to your mothers' aprons! I will show you how a gentleman adventurer should back his fancy! I bid seventy gold ounces, and buy the dog myself; and, lest you should think I do it for gain, I will prove to you that I choose to pay the money for my pleasure – the pleasure sweetest of all, the pleasure of revenge! For when the sales are over we will have him out here before us, and the drivers, who know their business, shall see if they can't wring a screech or two out of him to sweeten our wine-cups! There are ways – little devices of my own – which will perhaps suffice, yet keep him alive for a merry hour or two, and give us something to grow merry over. Now, you, take the dog away, but keep him nearby, and bid them hurry with the remaining batches of slaves.'

Sir Richard drew himself stiffly up, as if about to risk all on a rush for El Blanco; but his guards, trembling with fear for themselves, clung to him too tightly, and he was led away. He had not gone many steps, however, before he gave a convulsive start, checked in his stride, and pretended to stumble, lest the movement should have aroused suspicion, for Blake and Lobangu, who had been gradually working their way round the square, had managed to join the crowd where he must pass, and Blake contrived to whisper in French – a language none of his guards could understand: 'All right, Losely! Wait! Feign sleepiness!'

The condemned man and his guards moved on. Blake gave them twenty yards' law, and then, silent as two ghosts, stole after them with Lobangu.

The men acted strictly on the letter of their instructions – that is to say, they took Sir Richard round the corner of the house, and no further, for they wished to see as much of what was going on as possible, and once out of eyeshot of the dreaded White Death, they lost their fearfulness.

Blake, watching them carefully, saw Sir Richard sign to them that he wished to rest, and they, regarding him as a man already dead, complied willingly enough, for it saved them trouble.

Blake was still without a definite plan as regards detail, but he was intensely on the alert, and nothing escaped him. He watched, frowning heavily, and Lobangu, motionless as a statue, stood in the deep shadows beside him. One of the guards lit a match, his cigarette having gone out. The flame flickered redly on his features for an instant as he shaded it with curved palms, then, puffing deeply in satisfaction, he threw the still burning end of the match away.

A deep, guttural growl of remonstrance followed swiftly on the action. One of the others sprang up and set his foot on the flame, calling the fellow a fool.

''Tis just such a careless woodhead as thou set fire to this same store three years ago, and got a dozen of us flogged because a score or so of slaves were burnt,' he grumbled; and returned once more to his seat.

Blake gripped Lobangu's arm in an instant; the whole plan had leapt into his mind complete. Sir Richard's words had given him the first glimmering of it; now he saw it settled to the minutest detail.

'See thou, Lobangu,' he whispered, 'when the time is just ripe, but not before, when the last batch of the slaves have passed the auction-tables, thou and I, moving very quickly, must steal on those three men there and overpower them without sound or cry. One at least we must kill. Then, whilst thou workest for thy life on the fetters of the white Inkoos, I will break into the shed at the corner of the house, for there is stored tins of oil to make a great flame, and also, as thou seest, a pile of firewood.

'I will pour the kerosene – the oil that is in the tins – on to the wood, and at the moment the Inkoos is free to move, set light to it. Then shalt thou and the Inkoos, each armed with a revolver, dash for the hole in the palisade which I told thee of, and which lies yonder beneath the big post which sticks up against the skyline, and make for the swamp.'

'Inkoos,' whispered Lobangu, 'I understand.'

'Once on the swamp, bid the white Inkoos race for the camp, and as he goes, bid him fire quickly with the revolver, making as much noise as possible. Then do thou, moving very swiftly, rush to the water-gate and batter on it as one clamouring for entry, shouting that the British warships are come, and that even now the boats are pulling up the creeks. What with the firing from the swamps, the blazing of the house, and the clamouring at the gate, there will be a great rushing hither and thither, and I and the other white Inkoos will pass out unheeded with the crowd pressing through the water-gate to get to their ships and fight the British boats, or rescue their goods.

'There, then, we will meet, and race for our lives for the camp. Even if we are seen they will think us some of themselves running away for fear of the British. And mind that as thou runnest to the water-gate thou dost also fire as much and as often as possible, to give the idea of a ring of scouts thrown forward by the British warships' landing-parties. Now wait and watch, for I have to speak with my friend the other Inkoos.'

Lobangu grunted acquiescence, and Blake glided back to his place by the fire in the big square.

The sales were being pushed along briskly, for all were eager to see the Britisher tortured and to have a relaxation from business.

The slaves being offered, too, were a comparatively poor lot, and many found their way in batches of twos or threes to the smaller dealers. The one plan in Blake's scheme was the difficulty of approaching Tinker, for though unfettered, his captors kept near him, and made constant offers of him to the crowd of buyers, speaking loudly of his good points. According to them he was a very pearl of slaves, a rare bargain – a great maker of coffee and a teller of wonderful, strange tales – the sort of slave, in fact, that any gentleman's house would be incomplete without.

In spite of the critical seriousness of the situation, Blake found it hard to keep a straight face, especially as dealer after dealer dismissed the unfortunate Tinker with a sniff of contempt. His hang-dog air, and the limping slouch with which he saw fit to walk, may have been against him from a selling point of view. Anyway, there is no blinking the fact that poor Tinker had little or no marketable value. Not a single one of the higher class dealers would so much as look at him a second time. They had no use for him. Yet the two gentlemen trying to deal in Tinker shares on a commission vaunted his praises in a way that would have made even an American company-promoter blush. Finally, the last of a straggly lot, he was hawked round amongst the smaller fry, amongst whom stood Blake.

One or two men bid seven or eight ounces in silver for him, but his promoters, intent on their own interests, refused such a price indignantly. The fellow next to Sexton Blake, a low-caste Arab trader, who, so far, had only made three purchases, went as high as ten ounces in a rash moment. This was refused, and he was offered to Blake. Quick as lightning, a look of intelligence passed between bidder and slave; then Tinker, seeing the laughter in Blake's eyes, scowled. His pride was hurt.

Blake, turning to the seller, shrugged his shoulders contemptuously.

'Bah!' he said. 'The fellow is hump-backed and knock-kneed! Look at the way he stands. I don't buy curs of that breed. Why, I'd bet you an ounce that he couldn't stand straight and run from here to the water-gate in an emergency without tripping over himself, the shiftless ape!'

Tinker's eye signalled that he understood, but at the same time Blake's keen ears caught an incautiously muttered sentence in English: 'I'll pay you out for that some day! Knock-kneed, indeed!' And Tinker scowled again more fiercely than ever – so fiercely, indeed, that Blake, choking back a well-night irresistible desire to laugh, hurried on into a stream of abuse lest anyone should grow suspicious. In answer to a further demand for an offer, he bade them roughly take their wares away.

'Bring me a dozen likely-looking ones and I'll buy,' he said to them. 'I can place them – ay, and a dozen more to boot; but that bag of bones, give it to the alligators of the water-gate.'

He laid an emphasis on the last word, and turned away, as if the matter no longer interested him. Tinker shares were distinctly flat, for in the end he was knocked down to a squint-eyed little man a few yards from Sexton Blake, who had already bought some 'job lots', for eleven and a half ounces in silver, for which payment was made with grudging reluctance.

Having watched the transaction completed, Blake hurried back to join Lobangu, and found him keeping a keen eye on Sir Richard.

'Quick, Inkoos,' he whispered, as Blake crouched down beside him. 'Already they are clearing the scales from the tables, and counting the money. As soon as they have been stowed away the feasting will begin in earnest.'

'As quickly as you please,' replied Blake grimly. 'I'll take that big chap nearest us with his shoulder turned, if you can manage the other two. They're lighter built, and should be easy to tackle.'

'Wow! The thing is done, baas,' grunted Lobangu. 'See, I will creep around and come upon them from behind, whilst thou, feigning an excuse, dost walk straight up to them as though in curiosity. They will take no heed, and then, at a signal, the raising of your hand – thus – we will fall on them and make an end.'

'It is good,' said Blake. And Lobangu crept off into the darkness like a snake.

Sexton Blake allowed him five minutes' grace, then he, too, rose and sauntered towards the group, heedless whether they saw him or not, as they would only take him for a trader strolling about, having completed his business.

When he was within three paces of the man he had marked down, he gave the agreed signal. He caught a glimpse of the flash of Lobangu's spear, a gleam in the eyes of Sir Richard, who, lying on his side, had been watching the approach, whilst pretending to doze, and then, springing clear from the ground, he hurled himself on the unsuspecting guard and grabbed him by the throat. Even as he did so, he heard a dull thud and a gasping sigh as Lobangu's steel drove hard under the ribs of the second man, and had a vague impression that Sir Richard had flung his manacled arms over the head and shoulders of the third, and was crushing the life out of him.

What followed was a matter of seconds and fractions of seconds. Lobangu's man jerked and writhed twice – once as the steel went in, once as it was drawn out – and then lay still. Sir Richard's powerful arms locked round the other. The mere touch of the man who had for weeks been his torturer filled him with a berserker rage, and he went mad for the instant. His powerful muscles rippled and twitched, his huge shoulders bunched and contracted; there was a sighing gurgle, like the sigh of an exhausted syphon, then a grisly, muffled cracking and rending of bone and tissue. No human frame could withstand that awful pressure, and his victim dropped, without so much as a groan, crushed into a shapeless mass, his ribs driven inwards like an eggshell stamped on. Sir Richard jerked his arms free.

Blake's impressions, however, were fleeting, for he had his hands full with his own adversary, by far the most powerful of the three. He had taken the man unawares, true, and, to prevent his crying out, had gripped him by the throat; but, as luck would have it, the fellow was sitting with his rifle across his knees, and as soon as he found himself held, naturally tried to fire it and give the alarm.

For the life of him Blake daren't release his throat-grip, yet he could feel the man fumbling for the trigger. He tightened his hold, and then, cautiously drawing up his leg, got his foot across the barrel and kicked for all he was worth. One of the man's hands slipped its grasp, but the other still clutched desperately to the muzzle end of the rifle by the foresight. Blake's hope had been merely to stun the fellow, or, at worst, to choke him into insensibility for the time being. But the rifle was threshing and banging about his ears, liable to go off at any moment, and though it was a hundred to one the bullet would hit no one, it would give the alarm most effectually. It was this man's life or their's, and Blake was not long making his choice. Putting out every pound of strength and weight he possessed, he slipped his right hand round and pressed with all his might. There was a click, like the snapping of a stick, and the body beneath him grew suddenly limp. The rifle dropped with a dull clatter.

A Japanese had shown Blake that trick in a seaman's tea-house on the Hokodate wharf. It had cost Blake three dollars, and as he struggled to his feet, sweating with the strain, he considered the money uncommonly well spent.

Lobangu glanced at him over his shoulder. He was working away with the file for dear life.

'Wow, Inkoos, some day thou shalt show me that trick of the twist! It was bravely done, yet now we shall win through barely. See! Already they make lights, and this chain is but a quarter through!'

Blake, still panting, glanced behind him. The big square space was becoming a mass of lights, and from the shouting and noise the feast had clearly begun already. Any second they might come for their victim. And, sure enough, as he looked he saw a slave coming hurrying round the corner of the house towards them.

'Snap it, Lobangu, snap it!' he cried hoarsely, indifferent now as to whether he was heard or not. 'If you can't, run for it, both of you, and leave the rest to me. Here, Losely, there's a gun for you, if the worst comes to the worst!'

Lobangu threw away the file with a voluble malediction, calling it every name he could think of, and seizing the chain midway plucked at it with all his force. Once, twice, thrice, he wrenched, and then the filed link gave with a snap.

Sir Richard snatched the revolver which the jerk had sent flying from his grasp, and in response to Lobangu's imperative 'Come, baas!' sped after him into the darkness beyond. He would have preferred to stay by Blake, but was too well disciplined to disobey orders, and rightly judged that a man who could do what Blake had done was very capable of looking after himself.

The instant they had vanished, Sexton Blake darted to the store-hut, burst in the flimsy door with a heave of his shoulder, and kicked over the kerosene cans this way and that. Three he flung bodily on the wood pile, and upset the contents of two more, by which time the hurrying messenger was upon him. He hurled another full can full in the astonished man's face, sending him down like a ninepin, with half his teeth loose, yelling like fury.

Blake didn't mind that. The more the fellow yelled the better for his plans. Now he dropped a lighted match here, another there, and half a dozen more at different points of the pile. With a roar a sheet of flame shot skyward, and Blake, hidden from sight by it, picked up his long robes and ran round the back of the house.

So quickly did the blaze flare up that it was level with the top of the big house before he turned the first corner; and the messenger was roaring like a bull, and spitting out teeth to prevent himself from choking. For a couple of minutes, however, so great was the uproar and merriment everywhere that no alarm was taken, no one even seemed to heed the man's cries, till one, more sharp-eared than the rest, caught the word 'Fire!'

Instantly every man – every sober man, that is – was on his feet, and the White Death himself was issuing crisp, sharp orders. The houses were isolated, but a fire might mean a panic, and must be checked.

Suddenly a shot rang out above the tumult, and another and another. There came a scream from one sentry, who dropped, shot at random in the abdomen, and a hoarse challenge from another, followed by what sounded like a scattered, rippling volley. Lobangu and Sir Richard were doing their share right nobly, with a lavish disregard for precious ammunition.

Blake, panting and breathless, reached the opposite side of the crowd from which he had started, having made a complete circuit of the back of the house, which was now partially in flames.

No one had noticed him, all being intent on the far side of the palisade, from whence the sound of firing came.

Sexton Blake saw that the critical moment had come, and, raising his voice, shouted: 'The British – the British upon us! The white prisoner spoke truly! To the water-gate, comrades!'

The cry was instantly caught up, and as though in answer to it, there came the sound of heavy blows on the gate itself, a renewed crackle of firing, and a voice yelling in stentorian tones: 'Quick! Quick, you fools, the British are on the creeks! Open – open, or we are lost! We shall lose our ships!'

Of all the crowd, only El Blanco himself remained cool. His bodyguard round him, he was issuing quick, sharp orders in hissing undertone – sending certain men here, posting others there. The machine-guns were manned, and slaves sent to bring up boxes of ammunition. Others, again, were turned loose to contend with the fire, which had begun to reach dangerous proportions, handing in buckets in long lines from the inner moat, and shovelling earth on to the flames.

But the visiting traders and their men were panic-stricken. There was the sound of a dropping fire from the water-gate now – men blazing into nothingness – and, above all, the shouts of Lobangu from without, imploring admittance in all the tongues and dialects he could command.

He was a wily old savage, and played his part well. From the bellowing uproar, one would have thought that not one man, but a score, were bawling to be let in.

The scared traders, especially the ship-owners, were terrified for their property. The gates were flung open, and they rushed out in a headlong stampede for the boats. Many of the slavers carried a smuggled quick-firer in the captain's cabin, or carefully housed on deck, and with these and their amply-armed crews, they expected little difficulty in beating off the imaginary cruiser's boats by sheer weight of numbers.

Yet each man being anxious to get to his vessel first, they fought and struggled for right of egress, and he who had the biggest following took precedence of his weaker neighbours.

The White Death's trained men, on the other hand, were making for the walls and guard-houses, searching in vain for the hidden enemy in the swamps, whilst others herded in the almost distracted slaves.

Sexton Blake, gliding easily through the turmoil, made his way to the gate, and by free use of elbow, fist, and revolver-butt, fought his way through amidst the foremost, stepped quickly aside to let the throng sweep by, and waited for Tinker.

Lobangu, borne back by the first rush, had also struggled free, and made his way to Blake's side.

'It goes well, baas, it goes well! The white Inkoos is by now halfway across the swamp and none in pursuit. Two sentries on the outer dyke we killed, and many cartridges we fired in the air from the short guns. See how the rats scamper, and yet we are but four, and one recently in chains. Man is foolish as a fat-tailed sheep, Inkoos; where one runs bleating there the others follow! But the White Death runs not. See, he has his own men well in hand. My snake tells me that already he begins to suspect that there is something amiss. See you, he is sending runners here and there amongst the crowd. He smells it out – he smells it out! Inkoos, 'tis well we were going. Having stirred up a hornets' nest, he is a fool indeed who stays to watch their flighting. Wow! see how the messengers are beating back the crowd. Where now is thy friend, the other white Inkoos, for if we tarry we shall be caught as birds on a limed twig; yet even if so, I shall not sorrow much, for my fingers itch for the White Death's throat, and there may be a merry rattle of steel on steel before the end. How say you, baas?'

'Peace, chatterer!' said Blake curtly, watching the crowds struggling in the gate, whilst yet another crowd of El Blanco's following were trying to force them back with threats, blows, and argument, and to close the gates; and this second crowd was ever increasing in numbers.

Suddenly amongst this second lot Blake saw a slim figure diving, twisting, and turning this way and that, shouting meanwhile at the top of his voice: 'Make way – make way there! A message for the outer guard – a message, comrades! Fools and pigs and sons of pigs, make way, I say!'

Some gave way, fearing to brook El Blanco's wrath should they stand in the light of his messenger. Some were shoved or prodded aside by skilful use of knee, elbow, fist, and foot – ay, and head, too, for Tinker's bullet-proof head drove its way into more than one fat trader's stomach in his mad rush for safety.

'My friend comes, Lobangu,' he said quietly, pointing.

The big Nubian gave vent to a guttural: 'Wow! So have I seen a young goat coming down the slopes of the Intambele mountains. Ha, there goes another fat yellow-skin on his back! Thy friend is as an eel, Inkoos – nay, he is more like the big snakes which drive with their heads and break a man's chest-bone. Ah, see the cunning one! He is through; he is past the gate! He is free! Wow! But he is a great, great one! "The slippery one" I shall call him, for he is hard to hold and cunning and brave, yet, above all, he moves like the lightning, sideways and anyways, yet in the end he arrives; for, see, he is past the outermost fringe! Wow! Inkoos, but who are these that follow, shouting? See, most surely they pursue the eel; slowly, it is true, but they will set the dogs on his heels!'

Far away, struggling, yelling, mouthing strange oaths, the two directors of the Tinker syndicate – the two men who had a vested interest in his sale – were charging madly along, whilst, further in the rear still, Tinker's purchaser was labouring at their heels, all yelling at the top of their voices.

'Stop him – stop him! A slave escapes – a slave escapes!'

Tinker, short of breath, gasping, scratched and torn by a score of hands, raced up to them.

'Come on; they're after me! The White Death has already guessed the trick, and is ordering men out to search the swamp!'

Blake and Lobangu formed up behind him, so as momentarily to shield him from view. The pursuers were close behind, and Blake, realising that Tinker was nearly done and sadly needed a breathing space, whispered the one word 'Camp!' Then, raising a yell, darted off at right angles, with a cry of 'There he goes! Stop him, you knaves!' and dashed away into the gloom, Lobangu after him, and a knot of others, amongst the foremost being the two interested and sorrowing commission-agents, with the trader far in the rear.

'Catch him! Trip him!' yelled Blake, slackening speed gradually to allow the others to come up.

The first of Tinker's captors shot by. Blake, darting out a heel, and at the same time making a half turn, tripped him up, and hit out. The blow caught the man squarely on the ear, and he dropped like a log.

Lobangu's method was even more thorough. He collared his man low, and using the fellow's own impetus, swung him clear over his left shoulder into the creek. Then, with a wild laugh and a wave of his arm, he darted after Blake into the long grass as the rush of the crowd bore past, unable to check even if they had wished to.

THE SIXTH CHAPTER

The Chase – In the Grip of the Current –
Quick Shooting – El Blanco Checked

After a sharp burst of a quarter of a mile they came up with Tinker, who had had time to recover his wind, and was, in fact, in a better state than they were themselves, for they had forced the pace to get a good start ere the crowd realised that they had been fooled, and the going was heavy to a degree.

Tinker greeted them with a grin.

'Knock-kneed ape!' he said, under his breath. 'Can't run a yard without tripping himself up. Can't I? I'll bet you I reach the camp with a quarter of a mile lead, sir! How's that for a knock-kneed ape?'

'Oh, get on, and be hanged to you!' said Blake, too breathless to laugh. 'I'll attend to you and your failings when there's time! Bustle, you young vagabond! They're not a hundred miles away, and we must shake 'em off!'

'Very well, sir!' said Tinker, jogging alongside. 'But who in the name of all that's wonderful is our black friend? Mind that hole!'

Blake skirted a shiny-looking patch of water, his feet squelching in the edge of it, and joined up again.

'You've met him before! Pal o' mine! Came out of camp same time you got your nose rubbed in the mud! Heap good sort! Tell you later!' he panted.

They jogged on as best they could in silence. Pursuit was inevitable, but the pursuers had a difficult task, and were rapidly dropping behind for the time being.

They themselves, however, were far from fresh, and the pace soon lagged into a go-as-you-can kind of pace over swamp and dead falls, till they reached the camp – or, rather, the narrow neck of land beyond which the camp had stood.

The dawn was breaking as they got there, and the sight which greeted them was so funny that, in spite of the imminent danger at their heels and their own exhaustion, they were instantly in fits of laughter.

The canoe, with all its equipment, had been hidden amongst the mangroves before Blake and Lobangu started out, and Sir Richard had received careful directions from the Nubian as to how to reach the spot. Being an expert woodsman and big game hunter, he had done this easily enough, even in the darkness, and had found his way to the rocky neck, not twenty yards from the old camping-ground; but there he had met with an entirely unexpected difficulty. In the hurry of the moment, Blake had not unnaturally forgotten to mention that he had left Pedro in charge of the outfit, and Pedro and Sir Richard not having been formally introduced, complications had arisen.

The scene which the three came on in the greying dawn was a strip of rocky, boulder-strewn land, with his Majesty's governor Sir Richard Losely, gracefully attired in some dirty rags, perched on one boulder, and sheltering himself as best he could from the dawn chill, whilst he thoughtfully regarded Pedro, who, with absurdly solemn dignity, was perched on another boulder five paces away, looking at Sir Richard more in sorrow than in anger, but positively refusing to allow him to advance a single step without risking a battle to the death.

Sir Richard heard them coming, and turned round.

'That's no end of a good dog of yours, Mr Blake,' he said, smiling, though his face was grey with pain and fatigue. 'We very nearly had a misunderstanding, because, unfortunately, I have no pockets in my present suit, and was compelled to leave my card-case and letter of introduction behind. He likes me, and I like him; but duty is duty, and I'm hanged if he'll let me pass that white stone there. On the other hand, having a weakness for keeping such skin as I have whole, I've given him to understand that he's not to pass it, either, or there'd be trouble; so here we are. But he's a No. 1 heap good dog, and if I owned a bone that wasn't part of my personal anatomy I'd like to give it him. Meanwhile, I fancy I owe you a good deal more than a man can talk about in my present condition. To put it bluntly, I'm starving, and maybe a little light-headed. You must excuse me. But my lodgings for the past few weeks – or is it years? – have been – er – unusual.'

Sexton Blake glanced at him, and saw that the man's iron frame was on the verge of collapse. His back was wealed and scored with half-healed sores, and the fetters which still dangled from his wrists, though broken asunder, had chafed his flesh to the bone – indeed, only a glance was necessary to show him that there was danger of gangrene.

Lobangu lifted his head suddenly and snuffed up wind.

'They're coming, Inkoos! Already they're in the forest belt.'

Blake nodded.

'Come on, Sir Richard! We must leave the introduction till later. Down, Pedro, old man!'

He thrust a supporting arm under Sir Richard's shoulder and hurried him down to the canoe. In less than a couple of minutes they were out in the swirling eddies of the stream, the dank mist of morning all about them, enveloping them like a thick blanket, dropping down with the current, Lobangu steering skilfully with the paddle.

Just as the shore receded from sight they heard through the mist the yelping and snarling of the slave dogs – curs with keen noses, which the White Death kept for emergencies – and for the first time in his life Pedro, keyed up to battle pitch, forgot himself, for, throwing back his head, he answered the challenge with a deep-throated bay which rang out across the still waters.

'Quiet, you old fool!' whispered Blake, smacking his head. 'Lie down, you idiot!'

And Pedro, full of penitence, obeyed meekly, crouching at the bottom of the canoe. But the mischief had been done. The slave dogs yapped and squealed in answer to the challenge, and their yappings were followed by the shouts of those who had them in leash, and a shot or two fired at random into the mist.

But meanwhile, the canoe was dropping swiftly down in the grip of the current – too swiftly for Blake's liking, for, travelling at such a pace, they would soon be amongst the outer creeks, and with the full light of day the White Death's men and the boats from the various ships would be out searching in every direction, whilst yet others would be exploring the upper river; and so the small party of refugees would be cut off both from before and behind – caught like rats in a trap – for the White Death, as he knew well, would leave no stone unturned to recapture Sir Richard, partly from motives of revenge, but chiefly because his recapture and death were of vital importance to his – El Blanco's – very existence. Should Sir Richard and his allies manage to reach civilisation alive with a tale such as they could tell, it would be a mere matter of days before grapnel and quick-firer shell was pouring into the Nest, sweeping it and its occupants into oblivion.

The White Death was no puffed-up fool to underestimate the gravity of the situation. He knew the British and their ways; he knew the name and armament of every British war-vessel on the coast, and her appearance, too. His spies, moreover, from time to time gave him accurate information as to their whereabouts, and when it was safe to run a cargo or two. Had it not been so, he could never have thrived and prospered as he had done year after year without being caught.

He knew that Sir Richard's escape must mean for him flight, the abandonment of the Nest, and a doubtful final escape even then, for on the coast and in the slave-raiding districts he stood pre-eminent, a man to be feared and conciliated. But up-country, far away on the desert edges, there was many a fierce sheik or Bachaw ready and eager for a chance to cry quits with him.

Therefore he pressed on the pursuit methodically, but with a truly savage vindictiveness.

Blake, sitting in the stern of the canoe next to Lobangu, and peering round him into the swirl of white mist, realised all this as keenly as the White Death himself. The grip of the current still whirled them steadily seaward. Their one chance of safety was to gain the far bank unperceived, and then work upstream in the dark hours, camping at daytime; but the stream here was nearly two miles broad, and in the middle it ran like a mill-race, as he knew from bitter experience.

The crossing would take three or four hours of bitter, hard paddling, and they would be lucky if they could effect a landing on the other side anywhere within six miles below their present position.

He thought hard for a minute. The choice lay between shoving the canoe into the bank under some mangrove branches and chancing discovery by shore search-parties, or trusting to the mist to hold and making a bold push for it at once instead of waiting till dark.

He looked about him anxiously. He had studied the river carefully during the long days he had been waiting his chance to get word to the captive governor, and knew that it was no uncommon thing for the mist to hold till midday, or even later; but then, a sudden draught of wind up or downstream would roll it up as quickly as a man can roll a blanket.

It was a gamble. He bent and whispered a few words to Lobangu, and the latter nodded his black head and took a firmer grip of his paddle. Blake threw off the upper half of his encumbering robes and seized another paddle. Then he leant down and spoke to Sir Richard.

'I am going to risk making a crossing before the mists rise,' he whispered. 'Do you and Pedro lie still in the middle, where you are. There's a rifle by your side, and if we are discovered and pursued you must make the best shooting you can. They will have canoes manned by twenty or thirty slaves apiece. If they come, and you get a chance, always go for the chap with the steering paddle. Pass the word on to Tinker – the chap for'ard – will you, and tell him when I whistle once very low he's to paddle on the bow side and keep on paddling till he drops.'

'Can't I help?' asked Sir Richard. 'I'm feeling ever so much better now, and I'm used to the work.'

'You'll help more by keeping ready to shoot, if need be. Besides, you forget the chains, though broken, are still on your wrists, and the jangle of them would carry for miles along the water. Ready, Lobangu?'

'Inkoos!'

'Round with her head, then! Sit tightly, Losely!' And he gave a low, soft whistle as the canoe shot out broadside on to the stream, heeling over dangerously and increasing her pace as she felt the rush of the water.

'Round again! Head her up sharp!' gasped Blake. And Lobangu's huge shoulders bent and heaved as the canoe turned bow upstream at a slightly inclined angle and began slowly to leave the shore behind her, the three men paddling rhythmically with desperate energy. Only those who have experienced it can realise the dreadful strain and tedium of paddling hour after hour against a bad stretch of one of the African rivers. It is no uncommon thing for a big canoe of forty paddlers to take eight hours' killing work in the attempt to cross a three-mile stretch on their way upstream. Hour after hour they creep along, now gaining a foot or two, now losing yards in a few seconds where the water is worst. The point behind never seems to budge; the point ahead seems constantly receding, and, to make matters worse, all the time the paddlers keep up a deafening shouting and banging. And at the end of the day's journey they have reached the other bank, it is true, but in actual distance they have gained perhaps a bare couple of miles.

Of course, for Blake and his small party a gain of any sort was quite out of the question; their only hope was to gain the far bank, and gain it with a minimum of lost ground, for the further down they drifted the nearer they would be to the boats of the slavers and El Blanco, who would be out searching every creek and cut-off.

Blake's estimate was that the least they could expect to lose was six miles, and it was but eleven or twelve to the river's mouth.

They paddled like demons, keeping the bow of the canoe just on the outward slant upstream, and taking advantage of every yard of slack water. Once, however, Tinker's paddle slipped, the canoe's nose swung outward, and before Blake and Lobangu could steady her, the stream caught her fiercely and spun her twice round like a top. Then Tinker managed to bring her up with a jerk, and they plugged away once more. Now and again a sudden sluice of water through and over sunken rocks caught them and swept them back with a rush for fifty yards or more, all of which had to be struggled for over again foot by foot.

However, there were compensations. The mist held – it even seemed inclined to thicken – and for this they were duly grateful. Moreover, when they had been panting, sweating, and struggling for a couple of hours, as near as they could guess, a dog yapped somewhere behind them. Sir, Richard sat up cautiously and listened with the trained ear of a big game hunter.

'That came from quite a mile way, and we've lost precious little ground, considering,' he said, in low tones. 'We must be close on half-way over, and I fancy the current is setting a bit in our favour hereabouts.'

Blake nodded in response, too blown to waste breath in mere words, and Sir Richard, peering through the fog reek, could see his face, neck, and shoulders glistening with moisture.

Without a word to anyone he sat back in his seat and began rubbing and tearing away at the broken chains of his fetters – cautiously at first, then more roughly; the movement and jerking caused his wrists exquisite pain, but he persisted grimly with his task.

One was off at last, and the other, nearly worn through, came away with a final wrench, just as a sharp gasping exclamation from Blake made him glance up. The mist was lifting.

In his absorption, he had not noticed the faint, chill wind which fanned the side of his cheek, but on Blake, bedewed with perspiration, it struck with an icy chill. Back rolled the white vapour with incredible swiftness, hurrying seaward. Now they could see ahead of them the oily, swirling, leaden-coloured waters, and now, a bare third of a mile away, they could see the long, green line of the opposite bank – their goal – nearer, much nearer than they had dared to hope, yet still far away, for between them and it at one point the oily surface was darkened, showing that there, for a breadth of fifty yards, the current ran between some submerged cleft of rock like a sluice.

The other bank which they had left behind them was still providentially mist-swathed, the fleecy swirls of vapour lingering over the swampy ground of its banks.

The paddlers' backs were aching till they felt as though they were being drilled with hot wires and their muscles were cracking.

'Easy, Inkoos – easy!' gasped Lobangu, who had been casting quick, anxious glances at the water overside. 'Here we may rest a little and rinse our mouths, for, see, we are in dead water, and shall move hardly at all. Then, when we are rested, we can go at that fellow yonder' – pointing to the sluice – 'with the strength of new men.'

Blake, too, glanced at the water, and realised that Lobangu was right. They were just in the centre of backwash or eddy between two strips of swirling current which joined each other farther down, the force of their meeting causing what in those rivers is known as a 'dead water', in which there is practically no stream, what little there is having an upward tendency.

Blake dropped his paddle inboard with a sobbing gasp of relief, and, scooping up some water in his palm, washed his mouth out again and again – an example the others followed. Drink they dare not, for if once they were to start they knew that they would never stop till they had ruined their wind for the final struggle, but lay back against the wooden stays with faces upturned, filling their lungs with great draughts of air; whilst Sir Richard, picking up a fallen paddle, just steadied the canoe where she was with an occasional deft stroke.

But they dare not prolong their rest long, for the mist was rolling off the lower reaches. They could see clearly for a couple of miles already, and somewhere, still hidden in the fog-bank, the White Death's canoes and boats would be out searching for them eagle-eyed.

'I wish you'd let me take your place, Blake,' said Sir Richard, 'or one of the other chaps. I've worked off my infernal irons all but the wrist-bands, and I'm as fresh as a horse.'

Blake shook his head.

'You stick to the shooting, Losely; we shall need it, I can assure you, and not one of us could hit a haystack at present, with our pulses throbbing and our arms aching as they are now. Hark! By Jove, what was that? There it is again! Hear the beggars shouting and yelling and banging their infernal gongs and tom-toms? They'll sight us in the next ten minutes, for certain. Losely, get plenty of cartridges handy. There's a second rifle loaded up just behind you. The steersman, mind; let the rest go hang! Come on, Lobangu – come on, Tinker! Drive her into it, and then make a spurt across the bad bit. It'll sweep us down half a mile at least, but there's easy water beyond.'

From far away, still hidden in the curling mist-banks, came the hoarse, rhythmical shouts of the paddlers of at least two big canoes, for the sounds came from different quarters.

Lobangu turned the canoe's head nearly right upstream to the top of the easy water, so as to get every yard of advantage, and then edged out towards the race. Just as their boat danced and shivered a little on the outer fringe of it, Sir Richard, who, with a rifle across his knees, was gazing astern, gave a cry. The mist had cleared as by magic, and between three and four miles downstream a big forty-paddle war canoe was creeping and nosing her way slowly up the slack water under either bank; while a couple of miles lower down a whole flotilla of boats lay dotted across the slacker estuary waters, to intercept the fugitives should they have made for the open sea. These last were from the slavers' dhows and other vessels in the creek. But the big war canoes were the White Death's own, manned by his picked men, and in the stern of the one on the far bank was the White Death himself, conspicuous by his robes.

Almost simultaneous with Sir Richard's cry came a hoarse shout from the two pursuers, whilst a rifle-shot conveyed the news to those further downstream.

'Shove her into it!' yelled Blake. 'It's just a race now! We'll best the brutes yet!' he added cheerily, though inwardly he wouldn't have given a brass rod for their chances.

The small canoe swung to the rush of the current, and was hurled back a couple of hundred yards on a slant, but she had gained the centre of the worst part as they checked her frantically.

Then began the most terrific struggle of all, Lobangu and Blake throwing every ounce of weight which they possessed into driving her foot by foot against the rush, whilst Tinker, paddling like a demon possessed, kept her nose just at the required angle. They gained a yard – five yards – ten, edging nearer and nearer the slack water, so temptingly close; and then, at the critical instant, Tinker's paddle snapped short off just above the blade. Before he could grab a spare one from behind him the canoe whizzed round, bows downstream, heeling over as she did so till the water poured overside and shot away like an arrow straight for the oncoming war canoe.

Lobangu saw their danger, and that everything depended on him, for Blake was on the wrong side to be of any service. With one dexterous sweep of his paddle he forced her round again, flinging his whole weight to the left to prevent her swamping, and, with a wrench, she shot clear into slack water, where Blake caught her and held her. But the accident had cost them a quarter of a mile, and the big war canoe was closing up fast, barely two thousand yards away.

'This is where you come in, Losely!' said Blake quietly, bending closely to his paddle and keeping time with the others. 'We shall have to rely on you. Three men – and those three pretty well pumped – can't hope to hold forty native paddlers; the handicap is too much. We'll keep plugging away, and give you as much time for fancy shooting as may be. What do you say to taking a sighter?'

Sir Richard nodded.

'Do the best I can. Just before I fire bring her round ever so little, and easy for a stroke.'

He ran up the sights and nestled down to the rifle. There was a crack and a whining drone, then far away a tiny spirt of water, followed by a thud, and a man at one of the bow paddles flung up his arms and fell overside.

'Luck, but a bad shot,' said Sir Richard. 'That was a ricochet; I fired much too low. We'll give 'em a rest till they come to the twelve-hundred mark. If I can't pick my man at that, at any rate I can put an unpleasant sensation into the thick heads of the paddlers.'

The three at the paddles toiled away manfully. Meanwhile, the White Death's own canoe was drawing up gradually on the far side of the stream, evidently meaning to go right up above, and then come down on them in a long, swooping slant.

'Twelve hundred, I think,' said Sir Richard presently, 'as near as no matter. I'll give 'em half a magazine full to worry them.'

The first shot was wide, for the canoe was dancing a little on rippling water; but it had a most fortunate result. It missed the canoe by an inch or two, grazed the foremost man's paddle, knocking it clean out of his hand, and smashed the next three in line; whilst from the yells and screams that arose it had evidently hit the lower hands of two or more of the paddlers.

Sir Richard was quick to follow up his advantage. Jerking another cartridge into the chamber, he fired at the waist of the canoe, and two more men dropped, one springing overboard and swimming in a way which suggested a broken arm, the other dropping where he knelt, and causing no little confusion amongst the other paddlers.

'Sorry, Blake, for disobeying orders,' he said, 'but for the life of me I can't get a bead on the villain with the steering-paddle; the head of the canoe itself comes right in the way – unless you could slant in towards shore a little.'

'Wait until they come to the bend there, the water passes that small headland at a good brisk pace. If we can get them into difficulties just there, it's a hundred to one she broaches to and goes scurrying away into the thick of the current.'

'In that case, I'd stop padding for a bit; it will give all of you chaps a rest and me a better chance of a shot.

'Wow!' said Lobangu, with a grin. 'The flies begin to buzz, Inkoos! Listen to that!'

From the stern of the canoe puffs of white smoke like balls of cotton-wool spirted out, and the air became filled with a droning, whining noise, succeeded a second or two later by the crackling of rifle-fire. But the White Death's men, though good enough shots at point-blank range when dealing with refractory natives, were poor marksmen when elevation was required, or a wind allowance. Moreover, the deadly accuracy of Sir Richard's shooting unnerved them. They had no use for a man who could find his range with a sighting shot at fifteen hundred yards and over, and having found it, keep it.

The pace at the paddles slackened perceptibly, and the shooting grew, if anything, wilder. Now and again a bullet flicked up the water near them, but most fell hopelessly short or droned overhead. Their real danger lay chiefly in a chance ricochet. Sir Richard gave them a couple more shots, both of which took deadly effect in that crowded space, and then waited patiently, cool as ice, yet alert to seize his chance when it came.

'Now!' said Blake tersely: and with a touch of the paddle brought the canoe nearly broadside on.

Sir Richard nestled down to his rifle, whilst the other three kept breathlessly still, lest they should disturb his aim.

The big war canoe was just feeling the bite of the stream, and the man at the steering oar was straining, with his full weight flung on to his work, endeavouring to keep his craft head on – no easy task with half his crew demoralised or out of action.

To those watching it seemed ages whilst the skin tightened and whitened on the knuckles of Sir Richard's gripping hand, the foresight slid up through the minutest fraction of an inch, quivered, became steady as a rock, and an almost invisible pencil of pale flame spat out. So intense was their excitement that they never heeded the report; all their eyes were on the straining figure far astern.

Suddenly the handle of the paddle, jerked free from his loosening grip, sprang upwards like a released spring, and disappeared in the racing waters. The steersman himself slipped backwards, flung out his arms to clutch, turned half over, and fell sideways into the current, shot through the ribs. So far as they could see, he never rose again.

But the great canoe, released from control, darted out into the stream, turned round and round, and, as the rapids caught her, went racing away broadside on, with every now and again a half turn this way or that on the edge of an eddy, whilst the men tried frantically to regain command of her, and could not, for their steering paddle was drifting about no man knew where, and the helmsman with it.

A shout of triumph went up from the four. A single shot had rid them of half their pursuers, and, tired though they were, the thought braced them to meet the remaining canoe.

The odds, however, were still gigantic, and they now had to tackle men under the direct guidance of one of the most cunning, treacherous brains in all Africa, for El Blanco in person was in command. Yet, by a strange irony of Fate, it was due to an over-eagerness on El Blanco's own part – a feeling of contempt for the small force which he regarded as at his mercy – that they came off so well in the end.

Immediately after the defeat of the first canoe, they had held a short council of war, and decided unanimously to make straight for the wooded bank, now quite close to them. There they could not only conceal their canoe, but fight from under cover, and this they did, the three resting from their exertions, whilst Sir Richard kept watch on El Blanco's movements.

Seeing this, El Blanco's obvious course was to go upstream three or four, or even five, miles, cross as directly as he could, land a shore-party a mile or so above them to scour the woods and cut off their retreat by land, whilst the rest came down in the war-canoe and caught them between two fires. In this way their chance of ultimate escape would have been reduced to practically nothing.

But El Blanco was in a cold, bitter rage, and could not wait for that. Having made his way up to a spot half a mile above, he bade his men row like fiends for the point at which the four had landed, and by so doing did what many another before him has done, came to grief by making too much haste.

The White Death had forty paddles at his command; they had had but three. But the extra bulk of the big war-canoe felt the pressure of the water badly. Moreover, the White Death tried to head her across pretty well broadside on, and she began to be swept downstream at a terrific rate, in spite of all their efforts.

They could see the captains walking up and down a central plank, lashing at the paddlers furiously with their great raw-hide whips till the canoe fairly flew through the water, yet still the current swept her downwards.

El Blanco, motionless in the stern beneath the steersman, with a rifle crooked across his arm, scowled at the crew, and bade his captains flog harder.

Yet by the time she touched the stretch where the worst current ran, and was within easy range, she was barely abreast of them, and being driven to leeward yard by yard.

'Now!' said Blake to Sir Richard.

And the latter repeated his tactics. The very first shot sent the helmsman overboard; but, in this case, the big steering-paddle of the canoe was lashed to the stern-post, and another man instantly leapt to it. He dropped, badly wounded, before ever his fingertips reached it, but a third took his place, and, being partially protected by some woodwork as the boat swung, stuck to it.

Blake, Lobangu, Tinker, and Sir Richard promptly blazed into the midst of the crew, with the result that some of the paddlers were thrown into a muddle, and again the boat slewed, but she was fast dropping beyond the range of accurate shooting; and Blake in despair tried a snapshot at El Blanco himself.

It was a near thing, but his muscles were still twitching from his recent exertion, and the bullet merely chipped away some splinters a couple of feet from the slaver's arm. He turned and shook his fist in defiance, and a harsh, sneering laugh of rage floated back over the waters.

Just at that moment, as the refugees were in despair of rendering the vessel helpless, a sudden frothing and turmoil of the stream broke all round the canoe's sides and stern.

'Wow!' cried Lobangu. 'See, Inkoos, see! The river-horses they are driving through them. Now, indeed, my snake tells me that there will be a sight worth beholding, for if a man strike one with his paddle in anger, or through sheer folly, there will be an end of all!'

It was as Lobangu had said. The lashing of the paddles as the boat's crew strove to turn under a hail of blows from the captains had disturbed a school of hippopotami. The great, lumbering brutes, placid and harmless enough, as a rule, if left undisturbed, were scared by the shouting and the noise, yet even then they would have swum away, or sunk out of sight. But the sharp prow of the canoe dashed straight into the back of a great bull, the leader of the herd. He turned at once, with the quickness of an eel, for all his enormous bulk, grunting and bellowing and showing the pink cavern of his great mouth.

Blake saw his chance, and sent a bullet skipping and ricochetting over the water, near enough to annoy the animal still further, and, as if that were not sufficient, a frightened paddler aimed a savage blow at the tender part of the animal's snout, just above the nostrils.

The hard edge of the paddle caught the hippo fair and square, with a resounding thwack, which they could hear even at that distance, two full seconds after the man's arm had fallen.

He backed swiftly, and then, with a swirling rush, dashed straight at the fated boat, jaws open, bellowing hoarsely, whilst the cows and smaller males rose above the surface on all sides, like so many glistening rocks half submerged.

The infuriated brute charged and gripped the vessel amidships with his jaws. There was a crunching, rending sound, and half the starboard side came away in a splintering mass as if it had been as frail as an eggshell.

They, watching breathless, heard the scream of a man caught amongst the wreckage – heard a hoarse growl of inarticulate rage from the White Death, and then a whole chorus of yells as boys, captains, fighting men, and the dreaded slaver himself sprang overboard in all directions, and deserted the sinking boat.

All were strong swimmers, and without a doubt the majority kept afloat till the current swept them down, to be picked up by the boats from the dhows. But even for the strongest swimmer to reach either bank in the teeth of the stream was an impossibility, and since the dhow's boats could not hope to leave the estuary, by reason of their build, the pursuit – momentarily, at any rate – was ended.

THE SEVENTH CHAPTER

Lobangu Goes on an Errand – Blake's Scheme – The Tale of the Rubies

Thoroughly worn out, with strained muscles, powder-scorched faces, and a fatigue so great that they were unconscious even of hunger, the four stretched themselves out, and slept where they lay, secure in the fact that Pedro was more than an adequate guard, and that there was no pressing danger for the next few hours, at any rate.

When they awoke the sun was beginning to sink towards the west, and their first care was to 'kill a tin' of food, for they were ravenous, wash themselves at the stream edge, and then file off the remains of Sir Richard's fetters, whilst Blake prepared some healing disinfectant from the medicine-chest, for the sores on Sir Richard's back – but more especially those round his wrists, where the iron had eaten its way in – were in a most unhealthy state. They were well bathed first, and then bandaged to stop any discharge, the cooling qualities of the lotion giving him much relief.

'Now,' said Blake at last, puffing his pipe gratefully, 'we must hold a palaver. I think we can spare another hour, at least, before there is any risk of further pursuit, and I should like to hear what all of you have to propose.'

Sir Richard, now clothed – somewhat inadequately, it must be confessed – in a spare suit of Blake's, with a broad sash to make up deficiencies where the garments would not join, puffed luxuriously at one of his host and rescuer's small stock of cigars.

'It's good – oh, by Jove, it's good!' he said. 'My dear man, do you realise that I've been without a smoke now for weeks, months, and with food that I could not give my poor old terrier without blushing, yet that infernal brute El Blanco used to come up to me when I was lashed to the flogging-post and puff his cigar-smoke in my face. Jolly good weeds they were, too! I really believe that the thought of enjoying one once more, one of my very own, went far to keep me alive, that and the pleasure of getting my fingers round his throat.

'By the way, you fellows, I'm no speechifier, and there are things so – so – I don't know how to put it – but things it's almost impossible for decent, grown men to talk about and not get idiotic. It's just impossible for me to put my gratitude into words. It wouldn't be any use if I did; but I think you understand, and – well, if I can show you in any way how more than infernally grateful I am, my heartfelt wish is that the chance'll come along. You do understand, don't you? I hate talking, and all that; it seems so futile.'

Blake looked up with one of his quizzical smiles.

'I fancy,' he said, 'that once upon a time Dicky Losely did a very good turn to a small fag who was in trouble at St Ermin's. He was a very small boy and peculiar, and an upper school chap called Dicky Losely, otherwise Spots, pulled him through it; isn't that so?'

Sir Richard stared.

'Spots – St Ermin's. By Jove, I'm hanged if it isn't the same Blake! "Blackamoor", we used to call you. Old man, I am glad! Your pal there, whom Lobangu calls the "Slippery One", hadn't time to fix me up in detail much, so I never connected Sexton Blake and "Blacky". I am glad, old chap! Now, tell me, how on earth did you happen on my track?'

Blake smiled again and shrugged his shoulders.

'I saw an account in the papers, a brief telegram. I'm a detective now by trade, and make it my business to know things. I remembered the name, recognised the fact that Dicky Losely had been made Sir Richard and a D.S.O., and sat down to write to the Colonial Office volunteering, remembering that little episode which we hinted at just now.

'Half way through the letter came a message from them – "would I go down at once" – and I did. Twenty-four hours later I left England. There you have it in a nutshell. I got on your track as far back as Musardu itself, and followed up till I found out that the White Death had a finger in the pie; then I knew where to look for you. But as regards our plans?'

Sir Richard's mouth snapped to like a rat-trap in the twinkling of an eye. He had become once more the stern official, the responsible agent of his Majesty's Government.

'Before and above all there are two things to be done,' he said. 'The first and most important of these is to exterminate the White Death and his nest. The second, which is almost equally important, from the point of view of my people, is to locate those ruby-mines. Mind you, I put the matter very tersely in my note, because it was written under difficulties; but as far as I am concerned, there is very little doubt that the story is absolutely true in every detail – details which I will give you later.'

Blake smiled slowly.

'Ever the same Dicky,' he said; 'a martinet before all things, irrespective of circumstance. Now, if you were talking snugly in your official residence, with a couple of companies of Hausas and a budding sub waiting to do what you told them, it would undoubtedly be a great scheme. You would wire to the next port, and request the assistance of a couple of river gunboats, and a destroyer or two to join in the fun. Then you would organise a neat expedition, most carefully planned and thought out, and wipe our friend El Blanco off the face of the earth. You know you would.

'When you were in his power and felt yourself a solitary prisoner, you had scruples, and did not wish that anything should be done, for fear it was done on your behalf simply and solely; and therefore you wrote that note. But I read between the lines; you knew that it was a positive necessity to exterminate our friend El Blanco, otherwise you would not have given those details about the palisades, their weak points, and so on. Yet you were terrified lest you should be made an excuse. You didn't want any fuss made about you, in fact.

'Now, to come down to bedrock before we deal with your exterminating policy, we have got to get away, and that pretty soon. We've got a deuce of a lot of stuff, which is necessary to our very existence, and not a single bearer. We can't portage it ourselves, and we can't do without it, therefore we must move by water as far as possible. I think that's obvious.

'Now, as regards El Blanco and the possibility of the ruby-mines, I heard a few words from my fellow scoundrels in the compound over there which set me thinking. According to you, these same mines are in the north-east Bambarra country, three days' march over a waterless desert. I know for a fact that our white blackguard's next raid is to follow that very course. A pal of mine, a fellow trader, explained that El Blanco had on his last raid pretty well drained the usual sources, and was looking out for fresh ground. He also has heard the story of the rubies, and is as keen as mustard after them. I can promise you that if we can break away and head off for the Bambarra, it will be a race between us and him. He is due to set out within the week.

'Our escape will throw him back a day or two, and he will expect us to head straight for the nearest settlement. Now, there is a good deal in doing the absolutely unexpected. Therefore, if we break clear and head for the Bambarra, we shall do the last thing in the whole of this small world which he will be on the lookout for. If we get on the track quickly, we shall have at least forty-eight hours' start – probably more – and shall have all the more chance of catching him when he isn't looking; and last, but not least, we shall be able to kill two birds with one stone.

'The main point is to get away now, at once, and secure all the advantage we can. I propose that we light a fire, a roaring big one, fifty yards or so below the canoe, and give his scouts every opportunity of seeing us from the far bank. Having lit it good and strong, we will pile up some more wood, and pretend to go to sleep. You can bet that after today's experience his men will be lynx-eyed, and watch our every move; but at that distance they can't see over well, and we will crawl away from the fire, keeping well out of the light, and make for the canoe through the undergrowth.

'At the outside they will begin to attack at daybreak, and by that time, choosing the slack water inshore, we ought to be twenty miles away, for we've rested and freshened up, and there are four of us to man the paddles.'

Sir Richard nodded.

'Capital!' he said. 'What do you say, slippery one?' he asked, turning to Tinker and calling him by the name Lobangu had given him.

'I don't think we could do better, sir,' answered Tinker.

'Well, then, Blake, old man, whilst we're waiting for a start I'll just tell you what little I know. First, after the raid on Musardu, on our way up, of course, we followed the line at the back of the hinterlands, and so left the north-eastern Bambarra country a couple of hundred miles or so to the eastward. Yet even so, I remember that for quite four days' march, far, far away in the distance, just at dawn and sundown, when the light caught them, I caught sight of snow mountains; and, miserable though I was, I puzzled over what they might be, finally concluding that they must be giants of the ranges through which flow some of the tributaries of the Upper Niger, a region which is practically unknown even by the natives. We on the south left it alone, because there is a wide tract of unfertile desert land betwixt us at Musardu and the ranges; and I think the same thing must be the case to the north and west. You will remember my negro friend mentions a three days' desert march; that desert, I take it, must be on the fringe of Senegal, the El Hodhu.

'After I wrote that note and gave it to Lobangu, he also told me that the stones are found in an old river-bed high up the mountain-side, and that the dwarf tribe who inhabit the caves thereabouts use them chiefly as offerings to a Ju-ju idol, which they think no end of. The stones themselves are regarded merely as tokens, and not particularly valued. The main kraal of the tribe is in a big valley in the centre of the three mountains, and almost inaccessible except by one pass, which, from his accounts, needs a deuce of a lot of climbing.

'Now, if those mountains which I saw and those which he means are the same, we've a deuce of a long journey before us; but we can do a deal of it by water, for this river Oro I have found out trends to the south and east, and is navigable for something like a couple of hundred miles, with a portage here and there. If we can canoe up to its source, it will be hard if we can't get a bearer or two on the way, and tramp it to the mountains. If we have luck there, our best move would be to hit off the nearest tributary of the Niger – there must be one or more within a few days' march – hire canoes, and work downstream to Timbuktu, where we shall be in comparative civilisation, and can get help from the French resident and the merchants, for there are both English, French, and German traders in the town; in fact, I believe that by now they run a service of small and extremely dirty steamers from there right down to the coast. Blackamoor, my son, I have spoken.'

'So I hear,' said Blake drily; 'and since I last knew you, you have learnt to speak considerably more to the purpose than you used in olden times. That's a very nice tuppenny coloured, gilt-edged plan of yours, and it's perfect barring one factor.'

'And that is?'

'I had the honour to inform your Excellency, D.S.O., and half the rest of the alphabet, that our mutual friend El Blanco was perpetrating a giddy little picnic-party of his own in that direction. He, with every facility in the way of bearers, will be able to travel two miles to our one, pretty well, and we shall probably arrive too late for the dance.'

'Then the sooner we're off the better.'

' "Hlala gahle", Spots, as our friend Lobangu is always saying. By the way, Lobangu, what in the deuce are you doing?'

'Inkoos!' grunted Lobangu gravely; and rose with a half-empty tin in his hand.

'Well, I'll be hanged!' said Blake. 'You black scoundrel, you! Who told you to feed Pedro on our Sunday-go-to-meeting corned beef? Do you think you're living in the lap of luxury at the Savoy?'

'The king of beasts was hungry, Inkoos,' said Lobangu stolidly. 'I only gave him a mouthful.'

'A mouthful! Ye gods and little fishes, the old brute has gulped half the tin! Better give him the rest now. I'm very fond of the king of beasts, but I'm blest if I care about canned horse á la Pedro. Come here, you greedy old pig!'

Pedro came up guiltily licking his lips, with an apologetic wag of the tail. Blake tapped him on the nose with a forefinger.

'Look here, you ill-conditioned thief, next time you feel hungry, kindly fill your old carcase with your own proper food. If you want delicacies, you can go and seek 'em out for yourself. Lobangu, that tin was part of your rations, like the parson's sister's cracked egg.'

'Come on, Blake,' cried Sir Richard, 'and let my respected friend Pedro finish his lunch in peace. You were saying –'

'Does the White Death understand English – enough to read it, I mean?'

'He does; speaks it pretty near as well as you or I. Used to jeer at me in it when he felt dull, and I had made an abortive grab at him, the brute.'

'Ah,' said Blake thoughtfully, 'that simplifies matters. I fancy that just now he places more value on you than all the problematical rubies going, for you spell life or death to him and his trade. Now, it's beyond all question that he can travel nearly twice as fast as we can with our stores; but he can't travel a quarter the pace that one of us could go singly, carrying only arms, ammunition, and stores for, say, a week. And if we can get him started off on a hot scent in the wrong direction, I see no reason why we shouldn't be able to steal a march on him. Lobangu' – he broke off suddenly – 'you have told me big tales about your swimming. Indeed, I have seen that you are by no means a helpless log in the water. Would it be possible for you, with a small gun, those that speak six times, and a week's food, to make your way across there?' And he pointed to the far bank.

The big Nubian looked carefully across the waters, sullen and yellow, leaden in the fading light.

'Inkoos, as an otter am I in the water, and few can swim so fast and far. I am ready to try if my father wills. Myself? Yes; I could get across, but only by diving under the topmost rush of the current, and so the little gun and the cartridges would get wet. Moreover, I could not carry with me my big spear, which is my weapon. Yet I think I read the thoughts in thy head aright – to lay a clear, false spoor. Inkoos, five miles above here the river broadens out into a great lake, shallow in parts, yet the stream runs mildly, so that a boy might swim it.'

Blake nodded.

'Then thus shall it be done. By tomorrow's dawn the White Death and his men will be here searching for us, beyond all doubt. Within the hour, therefore, we move; we three in the canoe, but thou, Lobangu, shalt pass along the river's edge through the undergrowth, leaving a well-broken trail easy to read. When we are come to the place thou speakest of – not before – thou shalt take to the water, breaking down branches and treading well the bark edge, we waiting for you amongst the shadows. Then we will paddle; then the greater part of the distance across the rest thou must swim, again making a clear trail on landing, so that El Blanco's men may find the spot easily. After which, travel northward swiftly for two days, lighting little fires by the way, as though a camp had been there, and, having fed, dropping the empty tins which I shall give thee. So shall one day's travel appear as two, and El Blanco and his following keep hot on the scent. Two days more thou shalt go, heading a little east of north, as one uncertain of his direction; but the intervals between the camp-fires shall be greater, and the tins emptied of food scarcer, as it would be with a man fearing to starve with a long journey before him. And at certain points thou shalt leave pieces of paper written upon in cleft sticks by the camping-places which I will give thee. So El Blanco shall persevere on the trail. But on the fifth day, where the ground is rocky or easy to blind the trail, thou shalt leap aside like a stricken buck, and hurry at the top of thy powers southward and eastward, striking the river again three days' march from here; and there we will wait for thee, and the signal of waiting shall be the call of the chirra bird twice repeated.

'On the eighth day thou shalt be there without fail. Yet, in case of an evil mishap, from sunrise on the eighth till sunset on the tenth day we will wait and watch for thee. Is it good talk, Lobangu, prince of the Etbaia?'

'It is good, Inkoos, for surely I listen to the words of the fox, of the chief of the ghost peoples, he who moves silently through the grasses, leaving no trace, the silent one, the crafty, swift and noiseless as the breath of dawn. Wow! Inkoos, my father, the black dog's pads itch for the trail!'

'So it is good, Lobangu; and no harm shalt come to thee, for swift of foot thou art, and canst laugh at the stumbling chase of the slavers. Yet I would have thee be careful, running no hazard. For it is in my mind that El Blanco, hot with rage, shall press on and on even when the trail ends, searching to recover the scent which is lost; so on thy return see that thy tracks are well covered. In such wise El Blanco must lose seven or eight days on the outgoing journey, for he will not be able to move over-swiftly; three days for the searching – believing you always to be the big white Inkoos there, by reason of the messages and the canned foods such as white men use – and again seven or eight days for the return. So shall we gain many days' start, and the white Inkoos will have time to rest and let his wounds heal. Now, it is time to build the fire and depart. A brave man thou art, Lobangu, a man after my own heart, and the white Inkoos and M'lolo, the slippery one, as thou dost name him, you and I, who bid you go forth, will rejoice once more to welcome thee, and it may be to stand shoulder to shoulder again in the warm, quick fight.'

Lobangu sprang to his feet and raised his spear in salute.

'As the wind I go, my father, and as the wind do I return, swift and noiseless. A sighing of the tree-tops, a waving of the grasses, and it is passed by, no man knowing whither. So shall I move, speeding back like an arrow, and the White Death shall eat out his heart whilst his slaves try to read the riddle my feet have set. It is good.'

Whilst the others made up a fire a little further down, Blake wrote three pencil messages, wording them carefully, so that El Blanco, reading them, would think them letters from Losely to his friends, and hinting at the Morocco boundary as a meeting-place.

An hour later the three were paddling up the easy water under the bank, whilst Lobangu made his way through the undergrowth.

A couple of hours brought them to a lagoonlike stretch where the current ran sluggishly, and Lobangu waded into it and clambered on board the canoe. In silence they paddled him as near as they dared venture to the further shore; right in they dare not go, for fear the swish of the paddles might be heard by some chance outpost.

Softly they crept in to within half a mile of the bank, then Lobangu held up his hand, motioning to them to stop, and slid noiselessly over the side.

Blake handed him out a small case of tins, which, being water-tight, would float just clear of the water, on which he laid the revolver and a packet of fifty cartridges. The notes Lobangu stowed in his hair; also matches. His big spear he held in front of him, with one arm pushing the case gently forward.

'Fare thou well, Lobangu!' whispered Blake.

'Farewell, my father! On the eighth day. And fare thou well, king of beasts, to whom I may not give the food in the tins!' he added, chuckling, as with a couple of long, slow strokes he vanished into the night.

THE EIGHTH CHAPTER

Lobangu's Tale – The Emu Hunters – A New Plan – In the El Hodhu Desert

The sun rose clear above the river-mist on the eighth morning, and found Blake, Sir Richard, Pedro and Tinker, enjoying a frugal breakfast. The tent was pitched in a small, natural clearing on the same bank to which Lobangu had swum three days' march lower down. The rest had done them all good, especially Sir Richard; and fish being plentiful, they had been able, much to their delight, to economise stores.

They had seen no human being in all those eight days, for the river tribes of that part had long ago been driven away by the White Death's raiders.

From sun-up onwards they kept a strict watch, yet there was no sign of Lobangu; and towards dusk they began to feel a little anxious.

'I shall never forgive myself if anything happens to him,' said Blake, returning from a reconnoitring expedition for the third time since noon. 'I wouldn't have sent him had I thought there had been any real risk. But he can run like a hare, and he's a match for any two men if he should have fallen into a trap accidentally. Eight days, though, should have been more than an ample allowance. I fully expected him to turn up last night.'

Sir Richard, too, looked gloomy.

'I owe the beggar my life, and a hundred and one kindnesses beside. I'd rather risk the White Death's clutches again than have him fall into them. I do hope he'll pull through. His skin may be black, but he's one of the finest men I ever clapped eyes on.'

'Tinker,' said Blake abruptly, 'shin up that old cabbage palm again, will you? You can see the ground for a couple of miles or so clear from there.'

Tinker leapt up, but before he could take a couple of paces, from far away in the bush came the low, mournful whistle of the chirra calling to his mate. Blake sprang to his feet and gave the answering call; and Pedro, lifting his head, sniffed, rumbled in his throat, and sniffed again.

Presently there came to them the sound of a deep voice chanting a war song – a song of triumph – and in a short time there was a rustling of grass, and Lobangu appeared, grinning as broadly as his dignity would permit.

'Inkoos!' he growled; and up flashed the great spear.

'How fares it, Lobangu?' asked Blake, though he knew by the man's bearing that all was well.

'Good, my father of the ghosts; my snake was with me and kept watch.'

'Your snake didn't manage to guard your arm, anyhow,' said Blake sharply; for on the upper muscle of the left arm was a newly-healed, jagged gash.

Lobangu waved his hand with a gesture of indifference.

'A dog snarled at me, my father. Thus it was. Some time after landing I heard men talking amongst themselves in the wood. They were of El Blanco's bodyguard, and had been searching through the swamps. I listened; then suddenly my snake told me that since I was playing the part of the white Inkoos there, and was a very great chief, it was not fit that I should be disturbed, but should bid them rest in peace, even as he would have done. So I came upon them suddenly and spoke to them with this' – brandishing his big spear. 'Two remained quiet enough; the first was a pretty stroke. Wow! Even I have rarely seen a cleaner thrust. But the third was a big man and a keen fighter; moreover, I was hampered by the body of the second when he came to me. It took some little pains to impress peace on him, though in the end he lay quiet enough; yet not until he had given me this scratch.

'Then, Inkoos, I pressed on, doing in all things as thou didst order; and on the fifth day at dusk I turned aside from the trail amidst rocky ground along a water-course nearly dried, hiding my trail carefully, and headed for the river, leaving El Blanco and his men the better part of two marches behind, as I could see from a high place of stones. Yet in my journey here I struck the river-bank too high, and wasted the half of a day in working down looking for thee.'

'Good for you, Lobangu!' said Sir Richard. 'Now you take a spell, and we'll be off at sunrise.'

For the next week they journeyed upstream, keeping always to the dead waters. The monotony of work at the paddles varied now and again when they had to make a portage over some bad rapids. The country was as green and peaceful as an English park, entirely unpopulated; and game abounded, enabling them to reserve their stores.

At the end of that time the stream narrowed sharply, and the rapids became more numerous, compelling them to load and unload over and over again – a most tedious job.

Just as they were in despair, and were thinking that they would be obliged to abandon a good portion of the stores, pressing on with what little they could carry, they had a tremendous piece of good fortune, falling in with a hunting-party of a tribe from the head of the river who had come down after game.

At first these fellows – strong, active-looking men, with most elaborate topknots tied up with brass and copper wire – were afraid to come near, and bolted for the woods, thinking that they were slavers.

Blake, however, followed them, alone and unarmed, carrying only a handful of brass rods, taken from a trading case, and valued above gold or ivory throughout equatorial Africa. These he deposited on the ground and walked away. One of the headmen came out of the wood cautiously and inspected them, and in twenty minutes the whole party were round the camp clamouring for more, offering to barter ivory and skins in exchange.

Blake explained their wants as best he could in a variety of dialects, and as soon as the men understood they cheerfully bargained to portage all the stores, and to guide them by forest paths to the edge of the desert, which they visited from time to time hunting for emu. The price agreed on was the old and now useless canoe – ten brass rods apiece, and an extra 'dash' or present of five more rods and a piece of cloth to each headman.

Blake had seven or eight cases of trade goods, which he had brought for the sole purpose of bribing natives, and so was only too glad to pay such a very moderate price to willing helpers.

The men proved not only willing and cheerful, as they swung along through the forest tracks, each with his forty-pound load, but they possessed much information of value to the party, when a kind of mixed dialect had been established as a means of communication.

They, too, during their expeditions after emu across the desert, had heard of the dwarf people, whom they called Marani or Nkwandlhu indifferently. They were a mountain tribe, dwelling amidst the 'White Mountains' – the only name they had for the range – were stunted of stature, but very strong, and a very old tribe, not warlike, for no one had ever attacked them; but the hunters of the two had met at times peaceably at an old rancid well half-way across the desert, where once there had been a long-deserted caravan route.

The Marani were fine hunters themselves, and wonderful shots with their long bows and arrows, which, according to the porters, could carry and kill at four hundred paces. None of the hunting-party, nor, so far as they knew, any of their tribe, had ever ventured into the Marani country, for, though peaceable enough, they resented intrusion, and had a heap big Ju-ju of black stone to which they made offerings and once a year a human sacrifice, in order to propitiate him to keep off the storms, which were frequent amidst the mountains, and which destroyed the crops and the cattle; also, they had a place where they hunted for red stones, which they gave to the Ju-ju when they had a particular request to make.

At this Sir Richard pricked up his ears. A ruby-mine in his protectorate meant great things for the whole colony, and for two whole days' march he went along hardly speaking, but pensively figuring out imaginary revenues, modified hut-taxes, and glowing reports to the home authorities.

'I tell you what it is, Blacky,' he said to Sexton Blake; 'those beggars are in the region of my protectorate. They've got the rubies, and I shall see that they're fairly done by. I won't have any swindling company-promoters messing about. Everything's got to be square and above board. As to all the Ju-ju racket and the sacrifices, I shall have to put my foot down. I don't mind them keeping their old idol; it pleases them and don't hurt anyone else. It's no use trying to interfere with tribal customs all in a hurry; but they'll have to compromise on a few fowls or a goat or two, as far as the sacrifice goes, and marry off the girl to the head priest, or something. I say, you might let me overhaul the trade-cases at the next halt; I've got an idea.'

'Right you are, old man!' answered Blake, with a quiet laugh. 'But don't start counting your chickens before they're hatched. For all you know, these amiable gentry may be wanting to sacrifice us when we turn up; and, anyway, the White Death can't be more than a few marches behind at best.'

On the tenth day they reached the edge of the El Hodhu desert, and staring out across it, saw in the distance the three gigantic snow-peaks of the White Mountains towering up against a sunset sky, and looked at them in silent bewilderment, so majestic did they appear, their bases lost in the gathering haze, only the upper glaciers and beetling crags standing out clear-cut and sharp.

They made camp, and after the evening meal Blake sent word for the bearers to be assembled as he wished to speak to them.

On a trade box neatly laid out in front of them were their wages as agreed upon, with an extra dash to each man. These he handed to them in turn.

'Now, my men, you've served us well and faithfully,' he said, speaking slowly, 'and in turn I wish to do you a service – at least, that's the way I look upon it. Your homes, I understand, are far away over there, therefore I imagine that for the moment, at any rate, they will be safe; but you have all of you heard of the White Death, the terror of the coast, the slaver who has spread the fear of worse than death amongst the tribes of the great river.'

The headmen murmured assent.

'Well, less than a moon ago I and these here, the big chief, the slippery one – he whom men call Lobangu – and myself were in the White Death's kraal – two of us prisoners. We escaped, though hardly, but whilst there we learnt many things. First of all, the White Death, having spread terror through many lands and tribes, now purposes to raid the tribes out yonder amongst the White Mountains, after which I have little doubt that, unless he is fought and killed, also those with him, he will in turn raid your kraals also on his return to the coast.

'Moreover, he is very savage, because he fears the white chief here beside me, who is a very great chief indeed, commanding many men, all armed with such weapons as we here carry, though now he is alone but for us, and far from his home, having been taken by stealth by the hands of El Blanco and his men and shamefully used.

'Yet, having escaped El Blanco, the slaver is doubly enraged and afraid of him lest he should return to his own peoples, and, telling them the tale of his wrong, bring with him an army and eat up the kraal of El Blanco, so that there be nothing left of it any more.

'This, then, is that which I have in my mind, whereby both we and you and your womenkind and your old men and children may be served.

'Leave us here, after good service gladly rendered and gladly paid, and look you what happens. We lose our stores and our cases of food for the guns which speak. Crossing the desert, we find the dwarf men, or, perchance, before we are come to the Marani kraals, the White Death will eat us up, for we are few, and then the Marani themselves, after which be assured that El Blanco, glutted with victory, will also return and eat up your tribe, killing and burning and taking all such as are left alive to be sold as slaves.

'These be true words I speak. Here, also, are more words of truth. Do ye all of ye stay by us, acting as guides for the desert and bearers – by doing which ye shall earn many more brass rods of high price; yes, and a dash of cloths to each man – a bright-coloured cloth and the half of a handful of beads of coloured glass, such as your womenfolk love – till we come to the place where we may meet the emu hunters, with whom for generations ye have dwelt in peace. Then shall they and you and we ourselves act in common cause against them, we four being your leaders; and so shall the White Death be wiped out, and you and they dwell in peace. For this much is clear – until that deed is done, neither you nor your people may fish the streams and hunt the game without fear. It is spoken!'

Blake leant back on the ammunition-case which served him as a seat, and puffed thoughtfully at his pipe, eyeing the headmen.

One of them stepped forward, but Blake waved him back.

'Nay; go apart and speak of the matter amongst yourselves. Then, when ye have decided, choose one, and let him speak for the rest. Yet, remember, a march or so in the bush back yonder comes El Blanco and his men with guns and dogs. I tell you a true tale, as ye will shortly find.'

The men withdrew, and Blake puffed away at his pipe.

'They will come, Inkoos,' said Lobangu, in a low tone – 'assuredly they will come. Something of this sort I let fall in the ear of the headman a march or two back. They know of El Blanco; they are brave men, and they will come with us and fight. It will be a good fight, too, for if I read Inkoos's mind aright, we shall fall on them when they are tired and worn out with the desert march; is it not so?'

Blake nodded absent-mindedly, watching Sir Richard out of the corner of his eye. At every halt for the past two or three marches, so soon as the meal was over the Governor of Musardu had retired to the back of the tent with the only pair of scissors, a needle, and thread and several bits of coloured cloth. Nor would he interrupt his task for anything that was not of the most vital importance.

After a short palaver by themselves the men came back, and their leader stepped forward with a salute.

'You have my leave to speak,' said Blake shortly, eyeing them keenly to see if he had judged them aright.

'Aka'hlano' (white captain), began the leader, 'we have taken counsel amongst ourselves as you bade us, and all are of the same mind but one, an "utwano", a mere boy, a person of no account, and we have decided to cast in our lot with yours, and act under your guidance, for alone we could prevail not at all against the White Death and his men with the fire-tubes, such as you have at your side, nor can our best bowmen shoot as the Marani shoot – no, not by four score paces, though we are swifter of foot and better with the spear, both stabbing and throwing. Therefore we will despatch a swift runner backwards along the trail to bring us news of El Blanco and how many men he brings in his train; the utwano we will send to our own kraals to give them warning, and tell them what it is we do, so that they may escape to safe places amongst the foothills, should we fail. 'Twere well to start tomorrow, two hours before sunrise, if we would reach the water before the camping-hour, for the sand is bad at this season, and the going both difficult and heavy. Have I the white chief's permission?'

'You have my leave to go,' said Blake; 'for the runner, he should overtake us the half of a march beyond the wells. Therefore, bid him be both swift and cautious.'

THE NINTH CHAPTER

The Marani Ruby Workers – The Fight in the Gorge – The Death of El Blanco – The Emblem of Empire

They reached the pool of brackish water without incident, rested there for the night, and by noon the next day the runner overtook them, much exhausted, with his right calf muscle ripped by a bullet. He reported that he had sighted El Blanco's camp, which consisted of sixty armed men, together with a score of slaves, evidently recently captured, and forced to act as bearers to the party. Approaching too closely, a sentry had fired a random shot into the bush, grazing his leg; but he had escaped unseen. By his calculation they would reach the wells not later than the next night, for they were travelling fast and in light order. Amongst them was El Blanco in person. He had recognised him by his white robes and the ruby in his turban.

Towards the end of the afternoon, the heat being terrific, they espied some small black dots moving afar off over the desert. These, on closer inspection, proved to be emu, and beyond them, spread out in a long, semicircular line, were some of the dwarfed Marani tribesmen, trying to herd them together in a bunch before closing in.

Two of the headmen left their loads and ran forward, spreading out to right and left, until they were fairly close to the birds, and then, by shouts and cries, driving the flock down on the Marani lines, where they were made short work of, the bag being six full-grown birds and a couple of females. One youngster was taken alive by a couple of the dwarfs, and pinioned with shouts of delight. They hailed the headmen who had so unexpectedly come to their assistance, and the latter, stalking up, explained the situation.

The Marani were at first dubious, and hung back; but Sir Richard went forward alone and spoke to them in the Musarda tongue, which they understood fairly well, though their pronunciation was different. They were hospitable enough, but the fire-sticks – that is, the rifles – they obviously looked on as frankly a fairy-tale, never having even heard of such a weapon; and as the whole point lay in convincing them of the superiority of a modern rifle over their own bows and arrows, conversation for the moment came to a deadlock.

At last a happy thought came to Sir Richard. He bade them let the young emu go, offering them liberal payment if it should finally escape. Before it was released he bade them pick six of their best men to be ready to fire when he gave the word.

'If,' said he, 'your men cannot touch it or wound it sufficiently when I give the word, I will wait whilst a man may count ten, then I will try with my fire-stick. The range will then be double; and if I kill it, then you promise to take us over to the mountains yonder and obey us so long as we fight against the enemy who are coming.'

'Yes, that was true talk,' said the younger bowmen, smiling a little superciliously. 'If.' And they restrung their bows, each selecting his best-feathered arrow.

Sir Richard made them toe the line in a row, and ordered the others to loose the bird. The latter gave a puzzled squawk, looked round him, and was off like the wind. At two hundred paces he gave the word to let fly, and half a dozen arrows flickered and whinnied through the air. Not one touched the bird, but not one missed him by more than six feet, which for bow and arrow at that range, at an object moving like a miniature cyclone, it was marvellous marksmanship. The instant the last arrow sped he began to count, and on the word ten raised his rifle.

It was a difficult shot at the best of times, and his pulses were hammering like mad; but the sun was behind him, and he got a clear sight. Three hundred yards – four hundred – the bird was travelling like an express train. Four-fifty – the rifle twitched; then crack, crack! The first shot a clean miss; the second took it fairly through the chest, just in front of the shoulder bone, and it went over, kicking, and lay still.

A cry of astonishment went up from the Marani hunters, and with one accord they crowded round, laying down their bows.

Sir Richard did his best to look as if he was accustomed to do a little thing of that sort every day before breakfast, though, as a matter of fact, he was wanting to howl with delight at what was really a little bit better than a fluke; but he had had to take the risk, and he took it with luck on his side. The Marani needed no more persuasion. A man who could do a thing like that – just stand up and say 'Bang!' yet kill an emu at close on five hundred paces – could do anything. One of them deferentially squeezed the barrel of the rifle and squinted down it, whilst another equally deferentially began fumbling with the lock action. To save unpleasantness, Sir Richard removed the first by the scruff of the neck, and bowled over the other with a turn of his foot. They both grinned cheerfully. If the man who said 'Bang!' chose to do little things of that sort, surely he was to be given way to and appeased, just as the big black Ju-ju who kept away the storms must be appeased with red stones.

Sir Richard beckoned, and the two parties closed up and foregathered, and, after a short palaver, moved off across the plain to the foothills. This was a small incident, but it was the initial step towards adding several thousand square miles of territory and a tribe of clever and useful natives to one of his Majesty's colonies, to say nothing of adding close on half a million sterling a year to the national treasury.

Hitherto the Bambarra hinterland had been an unknown region, an outlying portion of an ill-defined protectorate. The shooting of the emu was the first step to making it part of the colony, and the Marani hunters – trained shots every one with their own weapons – are learning to handle the Service rifle, and becoming the backbone of some of our picked native levies. That by the way, though.

When Sir Richard fluked his shot, the question was a much more immediate one of life or death, and the annihilation of the White Death himself.

They halted for the night amongst the lower foothills of the great mountain range, and from afar across the Hodhu desert when it grew dark they could see red flickering lights reflected in the sky – the lights of El Blanco's camp-fires. Then the moon rose bright and silvery and blotted them out.

At dawn the hunters led them to the foot of the pass, a narrow rock-bound gorge, with beetling cliffs which overhung on either side. This, so they said, was the only known path to the valley on that side. It led upward at a steep slant for a couple of miles, narrowed into a bottle-shaped neck hardly ten yards wide; then came a green grass plot, a rough circle, surrounded on all sides by craggy cliffs; and again beyond a narrow track, with scarcely room for three men to scramble abreast. This track led sharply up to the snowline high above; and from thence to the valley was, so their guides told them, the better part of a hard day's march.

Blake and Sir Richard surveyed the position carefully, and finally called old Lobangu into consultation.

'See, now, Lobangu,' said Blake, 'tonight El Blanco and his men will be at our last evening's camp. They will see the tramping of feet and the ashes of the fires still warm, and may press on; but they will be tired and footsore from the heat of the desert sands; also they will be hungry, and he is a fool who leads his men to battle on an empty stomach. Therefore, they will wait till the sun is just above the line of the desert, and rest and eat. Now, of these Marani there are some four hundred trained fighting men, armed with bows and arrows and some spears; but to send and summon them and bring them back will take the time of two marches, by which time the White Death will have passed this place. For if we send for reinforcements, then must we also push on and meet them. Yet to me this is surely the place to fight. See here, in this narrow crack in the cliff four or five might hold the passage against ten times their number. Yet we are not four or five, but twenty-five; for of the Marani there be ten, of our bearers eleven, and we four. And El Blanco marches with but sixty rifles and a score of slaves not worth the counting. How sayest thou? Shall we meet them here, or go crying for help to these Marani? Surely it were better to risk the issue here, and soon, for then great will be our fame amongst the tribe we go to.'

'Inkoos, many fights have I seen – some good, some bad – but ever it was the brain that won the issue. Here, if ever, is a spot where generalship means more than numbers. We be four rifles, they sixty, yet under cover and at short range the Marani bows will kill as well as the rifle; and the spear is a useful weapon, too, at a pinch,' he added longingly. 'I am but my father's black dog, yet it would seem to me that –'

'Hold on, Lobangu!' said Blake. 'Here, Spots – Tinker – come here!'

For Sir Richard had wandered off, and was talking to the Marani headman.

'Well, what is it?' he asked, sauntering up with Tinker and Pedro.

'Lobangu has a plan. Fire ahead, you black ruffian; I know you're spoiling for a fight!'

'Wow! Inkoos,' grinned the big Nubian, 'you ask me how it shall go, and I say thus. At dawn a bearer shall be placed as a lookout on either side of the ravine, two bow-shots down, to give notice of the White Death's coming; and yet a third shall take his stand in the pass itself below. Then those above, running swiftly and keeping well below the skyline, shall bear word when El Blanco enters the ravine. But the third shall remain until the foremost of El Blanco's men sight him and give chase.

'Then, and not till then, he also shall turn and run, dodging from side to side to avoid the bullets and to lead them on. Nor must he run over swiftly and outpace them. Then, again, when he comes here where the path grows very narrow, he shall leap the boulders and take cover, El Blanco and his men racing at his heels.

'Thou, Inkoos, M'lolo, the slippery one, and the great white Inkoos lying in wait for them behind these stones with rifles, and meeting them with a crashing volley of lead; the king of beasts being safely bestowed elsewhere, lest he get hurt by a chance shot.

'El Blanco and his slavers, being thrown into confusion by the firing, will throng thickly into the open space here, where the grass grows green and smooth. Those in front will cry back, and those behind will cry on. When that is so – not before – the Marani bowmen and the bearers snugly hidden amongst the cliffs above can rain down flights of arrows and spears into the herding mass of them from behind and from either side, being themselves out of range of your fire. And I, having lured them into the trap, can work my way round over the cliffs, taking two or three with me, including the bearers' headman, who is quick with the spear, and, taking them in the rear, cut down the stragglers and those who flee.'

Blake chuckled.

'An extremely able plan, Lobangu of the Etbaia. And I see that you propose that you should play the part of the running deer, and then work round behind in the hopes of having a slap at El Blanco himself, you old rogue.'

Lobangu's eyes glistened.

'I am my father's dog; yet a little while back my father and the great Inkoos spoke big words of a certain reward. If those words meant nothing, the dog is silent. If, however, they were the words of the white man, which are a bond, then that I claim as my reward, and naught else.'

Blake became grave instantly. He saw the man's blood was up, and that he was in deadly earnest.

'It is good; the word was passed. So shall it be, Lobangu of the house of Etbaia. Yet the risk will be great that you run, and I would rather that you stood with us in the narrow way. El Blanco's men are no bunglers at so short a range as you must run the risk of.'

He paused, but Lobangu's face never moved a muscle. Blake watched him keenly for a moment, standing there like an immovable statue of bronze; then he flung up his hand, to show that the interview was at an end.

'You have claimed the reward; so be it,' he said curtly; and turned away.

Sir Richard said nothing for a moment or two, then he strode up and grasped Lobangu's big paw in a grip which made even that worthy stare.

'You're a brick, old man,' he said huskily, in English – 'a real brick, and grit all through! I'd like to change places, but I suppose I mustn't. That's the worst of being handy with a rifle.'

Lobangu understood, perhaps, a quarter of the words, for his English was limited; but he stared grimly at his fingers where they had been gripped, shook them once or twice, and strolled away, humming a little song to himself which he improvised as he went along about a great white chief whose muscles were of forged steel, and whose touch was as the touch of an elephant in his wrath, and seemed quite pleased.

Meanwhile, Blake had told the plan to the Marani and his own tribesmen, and seen to the setting of the outposts, who were to be relieved in four hours' time. The others were to have a good meal and rest themselves, so as to be thoroughly fresh when the time came.

That night the scouts reported that El Blanco's fires were at the foot of the pass, barely two miles off.

At ten Blake and Tinker went the rounds. Double sentries were thrown out, with orders to relieve each other every two hours, one man sleeping whilst the other watched, for he was anxious that every man should be as fresh as possible when the pinch came.

Before he turned in every preparation was complete to the last detail, and every man knew his post.

The morning's sun rose redly through the haze, and before it was half an hour high an outpost came running in, dodging from cover to cover, to report that the enemy were on the move.

Blake rose, made a hasty toilet by sluicing himself in a pool nearby, and overhauled the lock action of his rifle. As he did so he saw the tall form of Lobangu stalking down the pass through the mist, armed only with his favourite big spear and the machete at his waist. When it came to real fighting Mr Lobangu had a decided preference for cold steel.

The Marani and the other tribesmen were all at their posts, and from the lower end of the gorge even the keenest eye could have detected no sign of their presence.

The White Death's company came along slowly, in any sort of order, a hideous bloodthirsty rabble, shouting and singing, and occasionally letting off their firearms in sheer wantonness.

They were within four hundred yards of the lower and of the arena-like grass space when Lobangu darted into full view, not eighty yards from their leaders, behind whom rode El Blanco in person on a mule, grim, silent, and forbidding-looking.

So surprised were they at the sight of this solitary figure, that a man might have drawn three deep breaths before one of them so much as thought of action. Then, with a yell and a hoarse laugh, they began firing helter-skelter.

But now Lobangu was running, stooping swiftly, and dodging from boulder to boulder uncertainly, as a man desperate and in the grip of a deadly fear. The pursuers seeing this, laughed and shouted again, and, slackening their fire, raced after him, thinking, perhaps, to catch him alive, for Lobangu ran cunningly, not putting out the half of his power, and, gasping and staggering a little, feigning exhaustion.

They gained on him fast, yet he would not increase his pace; and now he was in the open space beneath the hidden spears and arrows of the Marani, and now his pursuers, close at his heels, were in the space also, and the main body of El Blanco's men were entering the trap, El Blanco himself in their midst.

A bullet whistled by, grazing a dull red gash in Lobangu's side; another flicked away, burring and buzzing, having struck the handle of his machete, but he was almost beneath the boulders, behind which lay Tinker, Blake, and Sir Richard.

Suddenly he turned, swiftly as a swallow, with a roar and a laugh of defiance, and circled round into the foremost ranks of his amazed pursuers. The great spear flashed once, twice, and again, and three men dropped before their astonished comrades could fire.

'Come in, Lobangu – come in!' yelled Blake.

'I come, Inkoos!' was the answer.

Once more he circled swiftly, this time at the very top of his speed, and with a mighty leap cleared the stone barrier amidst a hail of bullets, two more of which grazed him. Then, from in front of the slavers, came a crashing volley, and another and another from behind the rocks.

The bullets did terrible work in that densely-packed mass. Men dropped, men fired at random into space, seeing no foe, men turned to flee, to scale the cliffs; and now from either side came clouds of long-shafted flying arrows, which pierced through neck or shoulder downwards till only the feathers remained visible, and after the arrows, throwing-spears.

It was mercifully short, sharp work, and in those brief minutes the countless wrongs and cruelties of a quarter of a century were avenged; those sixty paid the penalty for the death, and worse than death, of countless thousands whom they had driven to the slaver's hold or the torture, the flogging-post, and the alligator-pool.

A small – a very small – remnant turned to flee, hoping to regain the open, but here Lobangu, who had worked round over the cliff, met them with five of the bearers and the headman, armed with spears.

'They must be stamped out!' Sir Richard Losely had said, and they were stamped out, though not before they had shot two of the bearers – the only casualties on Blake's side.

In less than seven minutes from the firing of the first shot not one was left alive, save El Blanco himself. He had pressed forward wherever the fight was thickest, encouraging his men; he had tried again and again to force the passage over the boulders – mounted on his mule, a mark for every weapon round – yet he alone was untouched, for so Sir Richard and Blake had ordered.

Not a bullet nor arrow nor spear had touched him, save a graze below the knee caused by a light-casting spear glancing from a rock.

Sir Richard, Blake, and Tinker rose, their smoking rifles still in their hands.

El Blanco looked round him, grim and undaunted. The cliffs on either side were dotted here and there with dark-skinned bodies. He glanced behind him. Lobangu and his spearmen barred the way. Then he sat quite still in his saddle, waiting.

Sir Richard advanced alone.

'El Blanco,' he said sternly, 'your men are dead. Before long your encampment by the mouth of the Oro will be razed to the ground, and you yourself are captive. Not long ago, when you offered me up for sale and flogged me and tortured me,

I warned you. I told you the day would come – was coming – when your evil rule should be abolished, stamped out, and that I would take you captive to the coast, and have you tried and hung. The time has come. Many bitter memories of wrongs have I scored up against you; yet we British do not gibe at a fallen man. Moreover, you are brave, in spite of all your cruelty. For that reason I offer you one of two alternatives. I don't know that I have any right to do so, but I take the responsibility on my own shoulders. Either you throw down your weapons and come with me as a prisoner to the coast to be tried at Musardu, or you fight me here and now hand to hand with what weapons you please, and the winner shall be free to go unmolested. I give you three minutes to choose.'

Still El Blanco sat motionless, staring fiercely at his questioner, the same grim, fixed look on his colourless features.

Then, without a word, he swung out of the saddle, took from it an Arab praying-mat of rich design and spread it on the grass. He drew his sword, and with the flat of the blade struck the mule across the flank and sent it galloping away. Then he stood on the mat.

A grim smile flickered round Sir Richard's mouth, for he knew that now, at any rate, true to the tradition of the Arab blood in him, El Blanco would fight to the death.

'Do you keep your revolver?' he asked, pointing to El Blanco's girdle.

Still without a spoken word, the White Death plucked the weapon out, and flung it from him.

Sir Richard did the same with his, and handed his rifle to Tinker. 'Lend me a sword, someone,' he said.

A bearer came forward and picked a weapon similar to El Blanco's own from the scabbard of a fallen man, whilst all around looked on in breathless expectancy.

'Are you ready:' asked Sir Richard again.

El Blanco raised his blade, and steel rang against steel. Both fought warily at first – El Blanco to try his antagonist, Sir Richard to try his weapon, for he knew the White Death's reputation as a swordsman.

But he himself had been accounted one of the finest swordsmen in the Army before he left the Service, and had no fear.

The blades ripped and hacked at one another in cut and guard. El Blanco, fighting with growing fury, attacked so savagely that for the first couple of minutes Sir Richard was put to it to defend himself. The blows rained like lightning, now here now there; but always, if only just in time, Sir Richard's blade slid down or across and deflected the blows, till it seemed to the onlookers as though he must be cased in steel, so difficult were the movements to follow.

Gradually, however, the attack slackened in vigour; even El Blanco's iron wrist was unequal to the strain.

Sir Richard saw this, and, brushing aside a rather wild thrust, called sharply: 'Halt!'

El Blanco dropped his point.

'You grow weary,' said Sir Richard. 'Rest a while; then, when you are rested, we will make an end. Bring us water, someone, that we may rinse our mouths.'

Lobangu came forward, bringing a half-gourdful of cool spring water, and offered it to Sir Richard. The latter impatiently motioned him to carry it to El Blanco first, which he did, scowling. Lobangu was a hearty fighter and cheerful, but he did not appreciate such 'woman's ways' as this.

El Blanco drank a mouthful, and pushed the bowl away. Sir Richard did the same; then both men stood a while, resting on their swords. At length the White Death raised his blade again, with a gesture of invitation, and again the steel clashed. But now it was he who fought on the defensive, and Sir Richard who pressed the attack. Once, indeed, his foot slipping, El

Blanco gashed his shoulder a little; but it was more by luck than skill, and the White Death realised it, for he returned to his defence.

Sir Richard was growing impatient to make a finish. Feinting at El Blanco's left leg, he made a terrific slashing backhanded cut at the right shoulder, just where the neck joins. The White Death parried, but too widely. Sir Richard saw his chance. Round came his blade in a swift upward, swooping curve, and then down with terrific force on the unguarded left shoulder.

'Wow!' said Lobangu, staring open-mouthed; and all around the circle ran a little sighing whisper of astonishment.

El Blanco's swordhand relaxed its grip. He swayed heavily once forward, once back, then his knees gave under him, and he dropped, nearly wrenching the blade from Sir Richard's hand. The blow had shorn through bone and muscle and sinew, right down to the heart.

Sir Richard flung down the sword, and walked away all by himself for a little space.

They covered up the face of the dead, and left it till a burial-party could be sent down from the settlement the next day.

It was on the third day after their arrival at the chief Marani kraal that Sir Richard, with Blake, Tinker, and Pedro, sat in state in front of their tent. Before them were spread out all the trade cases. Lobangu, with his great spear, performed the function of orderly; and just beside the camp Sir Richard had had a pole erected, about which he was very mysterious.

On three sides of a square round them the Marani were formed up in triple ranks, leaving an open space in the middle for the headmen, who sat on mats in front of and facing Sir Richard. The bearer tribesmen were in a group a little way apart by themselves.

Sir Richard, knowing the importance of a little display, and lacking a uniform, or, indeed, any respectable dress, had wound a length of red trade calico round his waist, borrowed Blake's pith helmet, which was two sizes too small, and was armed with an Arab sword and a couple of revolvers for show. Pedro had a rosette of red tied on to his collar – that was Tinker's work, and worried Pedro considerably.

On an upturned case was a wooden gourd bowl filled with magnificent uncut rubies.

Sir Richard rose and surveyed the crowd – cheery, sturdy little men, born hunters, and rich in cattle.

'Men of the Marani,' he began, in his deep voice, 'ye have seen the power of the white man, how he is able to say "Bang!" and slay at a great distance; ye have seen how he and some of your bravest hunters, and those men there, overcame the slavers who would have trampled flat your kraal and dragged your women and your young men away in chains to a far country; and ye have said to yourselves, "This is good palaver. The white man and the Marani are heap good friends." Is that not so?'

A low hum of assent went up on all sides, for the small party had become tremendously popular, and the Marani were quite shrewd enough to see the advantage of having the white man on their side.

'Look you, then, men of the Marani,' he continued, 'across the black waters lives a heap big chief ruling wisely over many tribes of many countries and owning countless fighting men, so that when a tribe comes to him saying, "Great chief, we are sore pressed by enemies, give us aid," he sends fighting men with the "bang-sticks" and wipes out the enemy. More, he teaches the chiefs of the tribe to use the bang-sticks themselves, and for this they pay him dues, yet wax fat, because they live without fear.

'I am a very small emir of that great chief, and I hereby offer you his protection. You have there a big black idol, a Ju-ju – a good Ju-ju, yet not altogether good. Now this is the word – that no more shall ye offer up live people to that Ju-ju. If so, and the great chief hear it, or I, his very small emir, then that Ju-ju he lib or die heap quick. But fowls ye may offer, and, twice a year, the blood of a goat. Say, people of Marani, will ye come under the shelter of the white chief's wing?'

Again a low hum of approval signified assent.

'It is good talk,' said Sir Richard. 'Then shall ye become rich and possess bang-sticks and many brass rods and much beads and cattle; for, look you, these red stones, which ye prize not at all, are much prized by the white man; yet, the stones being yours, they shall be bought at a price, not taken from you; yet some of your men shall work for the stones as before, and some – those to whom bang-sticks are given – shall, if they choose, join the ranks of the fighting men of the white chief, receiving pay and also a heap big number one dress. Now, here be presents for your headmen to distribute amongst you' – pointing to the cases. 'And these stones, which are of value, I take that I may show and send word to the wise men of the great chief; payment shall be made for them also later at an agreed price. One case, though, is reserved for those brave men there who came with us from far beyond the desert, with whose tribe I would have you live always in peace. Be these good words?'

The headsmen rubbed their foreheads in the dust in token of agreement; and Sir Richard handed to each a Brummagem-made looking-glass and a handsome dash of brass rod, by way of sealing the bargain.

'Now,' said he, in his most impressive style, 'the people of the Marani are taken under the wing of the great white chief, and in due course all things shall be settled betwixt me and their chiefs, and, as a token, see here the Ju-ju of the white chief's people.'

And he waved his hand towards the pole.

'Run it up, you black fool – run it up!' This was a fierce whispered aside to Lobangu.

'Inkoos!' grinned Lobangu; and hauled on a piece of pack-line.

Slowly there fluttered up into the breeze before the astonished Marani the most curious specimen of the Union Jack probably ever seen. It had been cut out and stitched from trade calicoes by Sir Richard himself, and – well, it could hardly have been worse done. But Sir Richard was immensely proud of it, and, leaping to his feet, he whipped off his, or rather Blake's, helmet, and cheered frantically, Blake and Tinker doing the same, with a curious choky feeling in the throat; whilst Lobangu stood stiffly at the salute, and the Marani shouted in response.

Just as the cheering died away, and the flag, already showing signs of weakness at the seams, fluttered in the breeze, a sudden piercing, yet mellow, sound rang out from far, far away down the valley – a bugle-call!

Blake and Sir Richard stared at one another in astonishment. Suddenly Sir Richard sat back with a roar of laughter.

'I'll be hanged, Blacky, if that isn't young Ellison and some of his Hausas come rushing up the country for news. Won't he be jolly sold when he finds we're here first, and have annexed the whole blessed show? Pedro, I dash you two biscuits and a smoked sausage! You number one heap good dog!'

THE MAN FROM SCOTLAND YARD

Ernest Sempill [a.k.a. *Michael Storm*]

THE FIRST CHAPTER

A Mysterious Searcher of Titles

No. 13, Rail Street, enjoyed a unique reputation. It had excited, but never satisfied, the curiosity of its neighbours.

House-agents called it a villa. People without the same gilt-edged reasons for pretentiousness referred to it as a cottage. It was, none the less, pleasantly situated, standing well back from the road, with its handsomely verandahed gable end giving on to the canal that cuts the Borough of Paddington. It was, moreover, surrounded by a pleasant garden, screened from the street by high green palings and a well-trimmed hedge of privet, and rejoicing in a wealth of roses and tiny lawns.

Mr Marsden, the tenant of No. 13, was a man of such marked reticence that people dubbed him rude. He kept no servant, whose friendly gossip might have revealed those intimate features of his life so dear to neighbourly ears. A charwoman of withered years, of gaunt and aggressive appearance, vanished each morning between eight and ten behind the high, close-panelled gate, which she was always careful to lock after her.

What or where Mr Marsden ate, no one knew. During the eight months he had been there, no local tradesman had ever been called upon to cater for his needs. It was whispered that he was a student, a hunter of ancient and forgotten records; but no one could say on what authority the legend was based. But it seemed to suit him. It fitted his benevolent and venerable aspect. He might have been sixty; or, again, he mightn't.

'Old' Marsden they called him. None knew or cared what his Christian name was. He wore a long, grey beard and a large grey suit. His hat was grey, and so were his smoked spectacles. There was an air of quite insufferable greyness about him altogether. But, beyond the fact that he had paid his rent in advance, and shut the door on the nose of a subscription-seeking evangelist, gossips learnt nothing, and, after the fashion of their kind, relegated him to the oblivion he obviously desired, with the cryptic remark that 'he was probably no better than he ought to be.'

Had the gossips been able to penetrate into a cosy library in the cottage on the sunny September morning on which this story opens, their curiosity would only have been confirmed; for they would have found there Old Marsden peering in lazy content over an open 'Peerage', around which, on the plain oak desk, lay various papers and letters. He looked very bland, very benevolent, and no one gazing at the horn-rimmed, simple spectacles would have even ventured to guess that they concealed a pair of eyes glittering, alert, hard as steel, and a-reek with greed and resolve.

For some minutes Mr Marsden lay back in his chair, his long, firm fingertips pressed together, his gaze fixed on the ceiling, his lips making a cold, thin line level as the edge of a chisel. Then he sat erect, drew the papers and documents on the table towards him, and slowly, deliberately, as if expounding their purport to a hearer unblessed by a surfeit of intelligence, recited their contents.

'We will observe, first,' he said, addressing the patch of sunlit garden opposite him, 'that Allan Audley, Earl of Sevenoaks, succeeded his father, deceased 1872, has remained unmarried, is now fifty-six years of age, is likely to leave his disposable property to his adopted daughter Helen.'

'Secondly, according to Debrett, the heir to the title and entailed property, with its sixty thousand a year rent-roll, is Horace, second son of the late earl, or his heirs, if any; and his whereabouts are unknown.

'Now, here' – he lifted up a document – 'is the marriage-certificate of Horace Audley, son of Allan, Earl of Sevenoaks, with Maria, only daughter of Jim Jenkins, of the Eagle Arms, Windsor.

'And here' – lifting up a second document – 'is a letter, dated April 16th, 1871, from Sevenoaks, to his son Horace, repudiating him and his barmaid wife; and' – exchanging the document for another – 'a further letter, from Horace to his father, evidently returned unopened, in which the Honourable Horace repudiates his father, and affirms his intention of henceforth living under the name of Jenkins, and earning his bread by the sweat of his noble brow.

'The effort evidently killed him' – there was a note of curious malice in his voice as he lifted up two other papers – 'for here is our poor friend Horace's death-certificate, within a month of the date of the birth-certificate of his son Horace, who, according to this *Naval Gazette* – his long fingers smoothed out the sheet – 'is posted under date March 12th, 1904, as coastguard to Fairlight Coastguard Station, Hastings, under the name of Horace Jenkins.

'Wherefore, you will observe, my excellent bluebottle' – he grabbed at, caught, and slowly nipped the fly to death as he spoke – 'that if Allan, the present earl, dies, Horace Jenkins, coastguard, with a romantic attachment to Helen, adopted daughter of the present earl, comes into the title and property.'

He put the papers in order, placed them in a large envelope, and, taking off his spectacles, stared out of the window.

It was curious how the revelation of those hard, gleaming, implacable eyes rendered indescribably malignant the illusion of venerableness that had distinguished his face the moment before. He sat silent for some minutes, watching a spider outside the window, hovering by an invisible thread over a silver sheen of net, where two flies were squirming. The spider dropped, pouncing; and Mr Marsden laughed aloud, rose, and, crossing to a safe, took out a long envelope, and again seated himself at the desk.

From the envelope he drew a single sheet of paper, and again read aloud.

'Listen, O fly, before Mr Spider has finished with your neighbour!' he said, eyeing with malicious appreciation the struggles of the fly in the enmeshing net. 'Listen, then die! In the year of grace 1850, George Audley, cousin to the late Earl of Sevenoaks, landed at Sydney, in Australia; was engaged as cowboy by one Plummer, married Plummer's daughter, and, taking Plummer's name, took with it Plummer's estates, and duly dies in 1871.

'Now, hearken, fly, and learn how capricious is Fate. George Audley – or, George Plummer, as he called himself – has but one son – George – and he, the spendthrift, makes ducks-and-drakes of his heritage, marries, begets a son, whom he also calls George, and who, born in 1875, accompanies his widowed mother to England, and settles in Dawlish.

'And now, O fly, that Mr Spider is preparing for you, listen and learn the malignancy of Fate! George Plummer, in 1893, enters the police force, all ignorant of his wealthy relatives – as ignorant, in fact, as is Horace Jenkins. In 1900, George Plummer is promoted as a very intelligent officer – very intelligent, mark you, O fly! – to Exeter. And in 1903, proving still more intelligent, he is appointed as detective-sergeant at Scotland Yard.

'Hence, O fly, mark the irony of circumstance! Between George Plummer, detective-sergeant at Scotland Yard, and an earldom, with a rent-roll of sixty thousand a year, there stand but two simple lives – simple as yours and your brother's were ten minutes ago; and, fly, as frail. Yes. If Allan, Earl of Sevenoaks, dies, and if Horace Jenkins dies, George Plummer becomes earl, with sixty thousand sovereigns a year, paid quarterly! And to think, O fly, that they might die, just as suddenly and unexpectedly as your brother did, as you are going to do! Ah, would you?'

He darted his long hand through the window, grabbing at the fly, who had succeeded at last in breaking free of the net. But the fly dropped among the rose-branches, and Mr Marsden cursed it viciously, as his clawing hand encountered a particularly curved thorn.

He laughed spitefully as he realised how unaccountably the episode had had power to irritate him. Then, sweeping all his papers into one bundle, he tied them together, and replaced them in the safe, and stood for a moment swaying the heavy door.

'"Plummer" will do,' he muttered, with a grin; and, setting the combination-letter-lock to 'Plummer', he swung the door to.

He took up that morning's *Daily Mail*, and turned to the weather report.

'English Channel and North Sea. Smooth; heavy fog,' he read.

Next he turned to a rack, and took down an 'ABC' and a *Bradshaw*; studied these for a few minutes, then crossed the room, and entered a bedroom communicating.

Some twenty minutes later a side door in No. 13 opened, and there stepped into the garden an alert-looking man, with close-cropped, black hair, and a close-trimmed, pointed, black beard. Over his arm was a light-grey waterproof coat, and he was carrying a small kit-bag. He passed the front gate, walked to the bottom of the garden, and halted at an angle of the high green palings that hid the junction of Rail and Grave Streets.

Through holes in the panelling he scanned each of the streets, and, waiting a few minutes, till Grave Street was empty, he pressed a button in the panelling of the fence. A door opened noiselessly. He slipped through, drawing the door to after him; and a few seconds later, hailing a hansom, entered it, and bade the driver take him to Charing Cross Station.

'Return, sir?' said the clerk at the station, as the man with the pointed beard demanded a first-class ticket for Hastings.

'No,' was the reply, after a moment's hesitation. 'Single.'

And as, seated in the 11.15 for Hastings, he reviewed his morning's work, he chuckled to himself.

'Even their blessed Sexton Blake,' he thought, 'if he had second sight chucked in, would never be able to put his finger on me in the little events that are going to happen.'

Yet, carefully as he had arranged his plans, and despite the diabolical deliberation with which he had weighed and reviewed each detail, it never occurred to him that his reply to the ticket-clerk was the little shuttle in which destiny had caught up the woof of his fate.

THE SECOND CHAPTER

Two Fateful Interviews

When Mr Marsden stepped on to the Hastings platform, no one would have recognised in him either the benevolent recluse of No. 13, Rail Street, or the alert man with the pointed beard of Charing Cross Station. A pair of heavily-smoked pince-nez now adorned his nose, a tawny golden beard swept majestically on his breast, a squash 'topper' covered a wealth of curly auburn hair, and, buttoned up in a loose light-grey coat that enveloped him from chin to toes, he looked, as he bustled through the gate, as if he had stepped from the frame of some ancient canvas depicting the family solicitor.

Mr Marsden had a large share of the artistic and histrionic sense which is instinct to all genius, and whatever part he assumed he acted up to it with all his might. The colossal vanity of the master criminal is insatiate and exacting; and Mr Marsden, as he handed up his ticket, took care that the porter should observe the sheaf of legal-looking documents, and point him respectfully to the street leading to the court-house.

'Some bloomin' lawyer toff from London!' surmised the porter, as Marsden had intended.

Marsden continued on the road to the police-station, asked the road to Fairlight from two policemen, chatted on the foggy weather just long enough to give them time to swear to his personal appearance, then walked off rapidly to a cab-rank, and bade a man drive him to the road above the coastguard station at Fairlight.

Half an hour later he stood looking down on the neat row of white-washed cottages that, perched on a shoulder of the cliff, hung between the wide sweep of common and a dainty cove, from which floated up the soft lap of the full tide. The mist, white and blankety, lay over all the scene, and Mr Marsden, realising that it was impossible to see twenty yards in front, softly clenched his hand in a gesture curiously laden with menace; and then, climbing down the steps cut in the cliff, made his way to the cottages.

A moment later he was accosted by a young man wearing the uniform of the coastguards, and asked what he wanted.

'I am the London representative of Messrs Haggis & Trawl, Solicitors,' he replied urbanely. 'I have come to seek a young man named Jenkins – Horace Jenkins. Is he at the station?'

'He stands before you,' answered the coastguard, with a smile. 'I am Horace Jenkins. What might your business be with me, sir?'

Mr Marsden eyed him keenly. He saw before him a young man of some twenty-six or twenty-seven years of age, with a bright, frank face, eyes grey and keen as his own, and a laughing mouth. He was as tall as Mr Marsden himself, being about five feet ten, and with the alert carriage and easy air of stored force that spoke of trained muscles and tough strength.

'I should like a little conversation with you,' answered Marsden. 'Can we have a private room for a few minutes?'

'I'm afraid not at the moment, sir,' said Jenkins. 'I'm just detailed to take a message into Hastings. But if it wouldn't inconvenience you, I'd ask you to walk on a little of the way –'

'Excellent! Excellent!' interrupted Mr Marsden. 'It was my intention to walk back. We can discuss my business on the way.'

He followed the young coastguard up the steps, noting, with a critical, almost an anxious eye, his lithe play of limb, the ripple of muscle at the swarthy, open neck. Over the common, their path lay on the level for some five hundred yards, to descend then by a long slope, and, clinging to the very edge of the cliff, mount the incline opposite.

'The London representative of Messrs Haggis & Trawl' did not beat about the bush, but proceeded to relate to the astonished coastguard that his name was not really Jenkins, but Audley, and that he was in good truth the heir to an earldom and sixty thousand a year.

'I can scarcely believe it can be true!' cried Jenkins, as they reached the bottom of the dip and began to ascend on the other side. 'Take care here, sir,' he went on. 'I'll go in front, and you'll do well to keep in my footsteps, as the cliff is none too safe in parts.'

Half-way up he paused on a level sward, flanked on one side by a coppice, and on the other jutting out clear above the sea.

'That's a bit that will go one of these days,' he said, as, standing almost at the edge, he pointed to a great crack in the mist-drenched soil. 'This what you've been telling me, sir,' he resumed, 'will make a sight of difference. It's a curious coincidence that the Earl of Sevenoaks is not unknown to me. He has a young lady living with him who's his adopted daughter. I saved her from drowning two years ago, and saw a lot of her, till the earl took her away and forbade her to have anything more to do with me. It'll be a different tale now, I'm thinking.'

'One never knows,' said Mr Marsden; and there was something so curiously triumphant, so occultly sinister in the tone, that the young coastguard stared at him in surprise.

Mr Marsden had come up quite close, and now, as Jenkins looked at him, he began fumbling in the inside pocket of his capacious waterproof, apparently not noticing that he had dropped his glove. Jenkins instinctively stooped to pick it up, and at that instant reeled wildly beneath a violent blow on the ear levelled at him by Mr Marsden's left. Before he knew what had happened, his feet were sprawling over the sheer brink, and another second would have seen him gone into the void, when one of his hands, wildly thrown outward, clutched and held one of the great pearl buttons on Mr Marsden's coat. For a moment he hung there, clawing at the grass with one hand, and trying to get a foothold on the crumbling face of the cliff.

Then, suddenly Mr Marsden's hand glided from his coat, and he poised a short, murderous-looking staff. A shrill cry of 'Help!' burst from the coastguard's lips, Mr Marsden tore loose the clutching hand, and next moment as the cry shrilled forth again the bludgeon fell with a sickening thud on Jenkins' temple, and, with his hands flung wildly up, he toppled backwards and disappeared.

Mr Marsden wiped the sweat from his brow, gave one swift glance round, making sure that he was unobserved, then darted into the coppice. The fog was thickening, and when an hour later a man with close-cropped, black hair, wearing a neatly-trimmed, black, pointed beard, and dressed in a blue lounge suit, a yachting cap, and, carrying a bag, boarded the 5.10 train at St Leonard's after taking a ticket for Sevenoaks, not a soul could have testified to having seen him descend from the cliff, or pass through the town.

From the same train, an hour and a half later, there descended at Sevenoaks an old and infirm-looking gentleman, with white hair and white beard, and large horn spectacles. He was enveloped in a dark overcoat, and was carrying a kit-bag, and he claimed the aid of a porter's arm to escort him to a fly, whose driver he bade to take him to Audley Hall.

The Hall is some distance from the station, and it was nearly eight o'clock when the stranger, descending at the gates and dismissing the fly, walked up the long drive, after assuring himself at the lodge that the Earl of Sevenoaks was at home.

The footman who answered the door eyed him dubiously. He was loth to deny so venerable-looking a gentleman; yet the earl was at dinner, and it was more than his place was worth to disturb him.

The stranger solved the difficulty by quietly entering, slipping half a sovereign in the footman's ready palm, and saying:

'I will wait. Show me into the library, and when your master has finished his dinner tell him that Lord Digby's secretary is here with an important message.'

The footman's doubts faded away, for Lord Digby was one of his master's most intimate friends. He showed the old man into the library – a long, lofty room, the French windows of which overlooked the drive up which *the soi-disant* secretary had just walked.

It was some ten minutes later when the door opened again and admitted the Earl in person. He was a fine, soldierly-looking man, clean-shaven, with hair slightly grizzled, with the stamp of race-pride graven as obviously on the cold, delicate features, as in the poise of head and the commanding, intolerant gaze of his blue eyes.

He closed the door after him, and advanced into the room to the figure standing with back towards him by the window.

'Ah, Frobisher,' he said, 'what can I do for you? I'm sorry – er – what the deuce –'

Five minutes later the stranger opened the window and stepped out on to the lawn. He walked on his heels till he reached the gravel path of the drive, down which he continued leisurely. Near the lodge he encountered a groom, gave him 'Goodnight!' and, passing out of the gates, sauntered off down the road to the station.

It was an hour later that the butler, surprised at the long interview, asked Miss Helen, as the earl's adopted daughter was known to the household, if the stranger had gone.

'I will go and see,' she said.

She went to the library and tapped on the door. Receiving no answer, she tried the handle, only to find the door locked. Becoming alarmed at the continued silence, she called on the butler and footman to force the door. This was a matter of little difficulty to their combined weight, and at the second lunge the staple gave and they were precipitated into the room.

'Heaven save us – it's black murder!' cried the butler as he knelt at his master's side.

In a few minutes the whole household was in confusion, grooms galloping for doctors and the police, and servants huddled together in frightened, whispering groups. Helen, the dead man's adopted daughter, was the only one who kept her head. Despite her blanched cheeks, and the haunting terror in her eyes, she remained calm and grave, and it was she who, when the doctor had pronounced the earl dead, bade the body be left as it was, and locking the room, pocketed the key, and ordered a carriage to take her to the town.

There, after a little delay, she got on the telephone to Scotland Yard, detailed the facts, and asked for their smartest man to be sent down at once.

'We'll send a man down immediately,' said the superintendent in charge at the other end of the line. 'Hold the wire a minute, please.'

'Is Plummer in?' she heard him ask; and the reply in another voice: 'Just come in, sir.'

'Then send him here at once. Are you there? Yes? I am sending you down Detective-Sergeant Plummer. He'll leave by the 11.15. Please have nothing touched till he comes.'

THE THIRD CHAPTER

Fate Cogs the Wheel

At the moment when Mr Marsden had been asking the way to Fairlight from the two policemen in Hastings, a small steam-yacht was creeping through the fog about two miles in the offing from Fairlight. The captain was on the bridge, peering anxiously into the impenetrable mist, and by him there stood a man, a youth, and a huge dog.

'It's getting thicker,' said the man.

'You're right, Mr Blake,' replied the captain.

Sexton Blake, with Tinker and Pedro, had left Greenwich for a weekend rest the previous night on board the *Stella*, the 300-ton yacht of Sir Lorrie Ogden, a man who had a boundless admiration for the great detective, and was forever devising new means to illustrate it.

'I can't come myself,' had said Sir Lorrie, 'but I'll send old Fleming with you. He's a humorous dog for all his silence, and will keep you from boring yourself.'

So Dr Fleming, the great brain specialist, had picked them up at Greenwich, and had fled below when, at eleven that morning, they had run into the fog-bank.

'I'm hanged if I know where we are!' muttered the captain uneasily.

'Better heave to and wait for the fog to lift,' suggested Blake.

'I think I will, sir,' answered the captain. 'There's a lot of currents and nasty shoals along this coast.'

He rang down to the engine-room, and two minutes later the cable rattled out, and the *Stella* lay motionless on the leaden waters. At that moment a gust of wind ploughed a channel through the fog, and revealed for the passing of an instant a span of white cliff, about two miles ahead on their port how.

'Lucky we stopped, captain,' said Blake. 'Did you spot where it was?'

The captain shook his head.

'Hastings Cliffs, I should think,' he said.

'Well, suppose we take a boat's crew and go and see?' said Blake.

'Um! How about picking up the *Stella* again?' protested the captain.

'Oh, if you keep your siren going, we shall do it! We can't go far wrong, and, anyhow, it will be more exciting than standing in this bath.'

Five minutes after the boat was got away, with a couple of men at the oars, and Sexton Blake and Tinker in the stern. Dr Fleming preferred not to quit the comfort of the cabin.

'A bit ghostlike, ain't it?' said Tinker cheerfully, as the *Stella* seemed to be sucked up bodily into the mist.

They pulled on steadily for half an hour, when one of the sailors, jerking his head sideways, drew their attention to the white gleam of houses, that seemed to hang like pebbles between sea and sky.

'Them's Fairlight coastguard station,' said the sailor, 'three miles east o' 'Astings.'

'Then we'll get back and nose into Hastings,' said Blake, as he put the tiller hard down, and brought the cottages on his other beam.

Suddenly he bent forward listening, and, as if moved by a common impulse, the sailors lay on their oars, following his action. Again over the water, indescribably muffled and weird, there wailed a shrill and unmistakable cry for help, and at the same minute, as if the mist had been rent by the agonised appeal, the fog lifted.

'Great heavens!' gasped Blake, one hand pointing upwards to the cliff, the other clenching fiercely on Tinker's arm. For the space of a second they could see the figure of a man, hanging in mid-air, wildly fighting a dim shape, lost in cloud above. Then something seemed to leap through the mist, the fog rolled down again, and, tense with bated breath, they strained forward, listening. A dull, sullen plash came faintly to their ears, galvanising the occupants of the boat into sudden life. Sexton Blake had no need to tell the *Stella* men to put their backs to it. The boat simply flew over the water. Blake measured the distance carefully. They had not been fifty yards from that overhanging cliff against which the full tide was lapping.

'Steady! Hold her!' he cried. 'It must be about here. Keep your eyes skinned. He would sink like a stone.'

'There he is!' cried Tinker, who had already kicked off his boots; and before Blake could stop him he was over the side, and plunging down and down under the water, where his sharp eyes had seen a sudden spray of bubbles.

In a minute he bobbed up, five yards away, with one hand grabbing the collar of an apparently lifeless body. It was the work of seconds to haul them in.

'Why, it's a coastguard,' cried one of the sailors, as his eyes fell on the uniform.

Blake meanwhile was busy examining the inert form. His acquaintance with blows of all sorts had been considerable, and as he saw the livid dent on the coastguard's temple, his face grew very grave.

'This is murder!' he whispered, half to himself.

'What's he got in his fist, guv'nor?' asked Tinker suddenly.

Sexton Blake looked at the man's hands. They were tight clenched, and it was with some difficulty that the detective forced open the rigid fingers. A smile almost of ferocity quivered into his face, and he shook a menacing hand at the cliff above.

'A button torn off a coat, off a light grey waterproof, and a Dent's glove, size seven-and-a-half. Many a man has been hanged for a clue less than this, and as sure as my name is

Sexton Blake, the man to whom this glove and button belong shall hang for this infamous work, if I have to track him over the four quarters of the globe!'

Tinker had rarely seen the great detective so moved. His eyes, brilliant and hard as the gleam of crystal, were fixed in the direction of the cliff, as if by sheer will-power he would drag the mystery out of that enveiling cloud of fog.

Suddenly his teeth snapped together, and he turned to the boatmen. 'Lay to, and pull as you never pulled before,' he said. 'I was nearly forgetting,' he went on, turning to Tinker, 'that the one man in the world who may be able to save this poor fellow is on board the *Stella*.'

'Save him!' echoed Tinker. 'Why, ain't he dead, guv'nor?'

Sexton Blake shook his head.

'I think not,' he said. 'There was just enough flutter at the heart a minute ago to swear by; and if anyone can pull him through, it's Fleming.'

But when Fleming examined his patient, he pulled a long face and shook his head.

'He must have as many lives as nine cats,' he said grimly. 'That smack would have killed most mules even, without counting on the fall. The skull is badly punctured. The frontal bone is simply pulverised. I doubt if he'll survive the operation.'

'We must risk that,' said Blake, who was busily engaged in turning the saloon table into an operating couch. 'It's lucky you have your tools.'

'Never travel without them,' said Fleming lovingly, as he peeled his coat and rolled up his sleeves.

It was a strange sight that ensued. The ship, lying like a dead thing, swathed in mist, silent as the tomb. Men forward gathered in groups, not daring to even whisper. And in the cabin, aglow with electric light, the keen, cool, measured movements of the great scientist and the great detective, fighting death at close quarters, and second by second driving him back.

'He will do,' said Fleming, when the last bandage had been stitched, and he watched the rose-tint warm on the waxlike pallor of the coastguard's face. 'We'll get him into bed, and let Nature do the rest. He'll probably not recover consciousness for some time; but we can do nothing more now. What do you mean to do? Warn the police, I suppose?'

'I think not,' said Blake. 'Not for the present, at least. I shall take up the matter myself. We'll nose through the fog into Hastings. I suppose this poor fellow can't be moved?'

'Impossible!' snapped Fleming. 'He's there for two weeks, at least.'

'Well, we must lie up at Hastings or Newhaven,' said Blake. 'I shall wire for nurses. I suppose you can't stay yourself?'

'For a day or two, yes,' replied Fleming. 'Long enough to see he keeps the right way. The rest will be nursing. I don't follow your idea of not informing the police.'

Sexton Blake smiled grimly.

'I shall keep the matter a dead secret, and swear the crew and all concerned to secrecy for the present,' he said. 'Whoever meant to slaughter that poor young chap is under the impression he succeeded. What his motive may have been I shall have to find out. But having, as he thinks, succeeded, he will act as if our friend here no longer existed, and we shall then see what we shall see.'

'I understand,' said Fleming. 'Give him rope enough –'

'And let him hang himself. Exactly!' assented Blake; and, leaving the cabin, he went in search of the captain.

Half an hour later, a boat containing Sexton Blake, Tinker, and Pedro, pushed off from the *Stella*, and landed at Hastings beach. The boat then put back, and Blake watched it taken aboard, and the steamer nose its way into the fog again, bound for the more sheltered harbour of Newhaven.

Blake was keen to get to work. He knew every inch of the coast, and he was well aware that in such a fog the cliffs would be virtually deserted, and that any trail the assassin might have left would be little likely to be covered. He had spotted the locality when they had witnessed the fall, and in less than an hour after landing he topped the slope overlooking it.

The fog had cleared considerably, and as they came round the coppice, and approached the spot they were seeking, they saw two coastguards examining the ground.

'Anything wrong?' queried Blake, as he came up to them.

'That's as it may be,' was the gruff reply. 'One of our fellows 'as been gone two hours or more, and the chief officer sent us along to find him, as 'e ought to have been back sharp. We ain't seen 'im; but this 'ere' – he lifted up a stout, spiked walking-stick – 'was 'is, and from the ground it looks uncommon like as if he'd stepped over in the fog.'

'How do you know it is his stick?' asked Blake.

'Cos there's 'is initials,' was the answer. '"H.J." – Horace Jenkins, and as decent a young chap as is in the Service. It'll be a terrible blow to 'is mother.'

'I think I should make certain before saying anything that he won't turn up all right,' said Blake.

The coastguards shook their heads and went off, bearing the stick with them. Sexton Blake watched them till they disappeared beyond the rise, and then casting backwards and forwards, for all the world like a setter, he began to examine the ground below and above the plateau where the stick had been found. The merest tyro at the craft could not have failed to distinguish the two sets of tracks, one of two pairs of square-toed flat-heeled Service boots, coming and going, the other of one similar pair, ending at the torn pass at the edge of the cliff, and with it another track, sometimes following, sometimes alongside, likewise stopping at the plateau, but also vanishing into the coppice; and this track was not at all of Service boots, but of the light, high-heeled, pointed-toed order, common enough for town wear.

Sexton Blake took a graduated rule from his pocket, measured the footprints, and made an entry of the details in his memo. book. Then producing a mould he took an impression of each foot.

'See that, Tinker!' he said, his eyes gleaming. 'The third nail in the heel of the left foot has a broken head. Now, before the scent gets cold, let us find out where our quarry's footsteps lead. Put Pedro on the leash, my boy.'

Tinker obeyed him, and the detective, producing the glove and button taken from the coastguard's hand, gave them to the dog to appreciate, and then, with hand and voice, encouraged him to pick up the trail. Pedro was on it in less than a minute, and with tail stiff and neck straining, headed straight along the tracks leading into the coppice. In the centre of this, Pedro began to get excited, and, giving tongue in a clear silver note that woke the echoes, he flung himself into a thorn copse, and started snapping frantically at the roots of a half-dead tree.

'Good dog! Find him!' urged Tinker, almost as excited as the bloodhound.

'Ah!' said Blake, suddenly darting forward and pulling off Pedro, who, having unearthed what looked at first view like a human head, was about to shake it. Blake thrust his hand in among the rotten roots, seized the hair, and produced a fine, but sadly crumpled auburn wig, in which was wrapped an equally fine golden beard. He turned them over and over, examining them. But no mark was there to indicate either maker or owner. The detective stuffed them into his pocket, and urged Pedro forward again. The bloodhound ran straight on now, out across the common, through the town by a perfect maze of side streets and circuitous routes, till he came to the West Marina Station, and whined at fault. A brief calculation of the time it had taken to come from the scene of the murder, showed that the quarry might have taken the 5.10 train up, and as the next train was not due for ten minutes, it seemed justifiable to assume that the assassin had travelled on the 5.10. Blake inquired at the ticket-office, and learnt that only seven tickets had been issued by that train, six being to ladies for London, and one for a slight, dark stranger, with a pointed beard, for Sevenoaks.

'Which may or may not help us,' said Blake to Tinker, 'since the man we want may have had a return ticket.'

'Where away, then, guv'nor?' asked Tinker. 'Shall we try if Pedro can pick up the trail again at Sevenoaks. It would be a bit of a chance, I know; but it's worth it.'

Sexton Blake thought a minute.

'I think we'll chance our luck and go,' he said. 'We're up against no apprentice, Tinker, this time. The fellow who has done this business is no vulgar footpad. He's thought it all out – chosen a foggy day, covered his tracks, and don't mean to make any little slips.

'We'll find him all right, though,' said Tinker. 'Why, you'd smell him out, guv'nor, with all that stuff of his we got!'

'Yes; boots, wig, button, and glove, seems a pocketful, doesn't it?' admitted the detective. 'And if we can get one of them fitted, the rest will hang him.'

It was nearly nine o'clock when they descended at Sevenoaks. Yes, the ticket-collector perfectly well remembered a gentleman who came from St. Leonard's. He was the only one who got out at Sevenoaks. The ticket was in the office now; it was issued that day. No, the gentleman was neither alert nor dark, nor did he wear a black, pointed beard. He was old and infirm, and had driven to Audley Hall. He'd taken a fly from the rank – Bill Poster's fly. Bill was not there. He'd gone back to his stables. They could find him there, behind the second inn on their left going down the street.

Tinker cast a glance of inquiry at Sexton Blake, as they hurried down the street. The detective's eyes were shining, and his lips working.

'On the trail, guv'nor?' he queried, in a whisper.

'We shall see presently,' Blake answered.

In a few minutes they found Bill Poster in person, just about to turn the hose on to a muddy landau, that was standing in the middle of the yard.

Blake stepped quickly up to him and stopped him.

'You drove a stranger up to Audley Hall today from the seven-o'clock train?' he asked.

'An' if I did, what then?' said Bill Poster gruffly.

'Is that the carriage he used?' asked Blake.

'Why, he don't pretend as he left anything in it, do he?' queried Bill, in an aggrieved tone. "Cos if he does, he's a blessed liar!'

Blake grinned, drew out the glove from his pocket, and urged it on Pedro's attention.

'Seek him, old boy!' he whispered.

The dog ran whimpering to and fro, while Bill looked on in wonder and some little alarm. Presently, as Pedro came to the carriage, he gave tongue again, and with one bound was over the door and nosing the cushions.

Blake made a sign to Tinker to haul him off, and asked Poster if he had driven the stranger back from the Hall.

'No, I hain't!' said Poster, beginning to lose his temper under this cross-examination. 'And, what's more, you clear out. I don't want folk poking about my yard.'

'I want to go up to the Hall,' said Blake. 'Will you take me?'

'I ain't had my dinner yet, and I ain't goin' out tonight, even when I 'ave 'ad it,' said Bill; and, turning his back on them, proceeded to souse down the landau.

'We'll go into the inn, and get a bite of something ourselves, Tinker,' said Blake; 'and while we eat, we'll send for a trap.'

'It's going to be something out of the ordinary, my boy,' said Blake gravely. 'Pedro's never at fault. And if there's one thing you can swear to, it is, that the man who tried to murder that coastguard is also the man who drove in Bill Poster's carriage, apparently to stay at the house of the Earl of Sevenoaks.'

'What's the matter with that image?' said Tinker, indicating a pasty-cheeked and trembling-lipped waiter who was sidling towards their table and wringing his hands.

Blake looked inquiringly at him, and his fork stopped on the way to his mouth, as the waiter leant forward and hissed across the table: 'Murder!'

'He's mad!' whispered Tinker; but Blake silenced him with a look.

'Who is murdered?' he asked.

'The hearl!' hissed back the waiter. 'Killed on 'is hown 'earth!'

'The Earl of Sevenoaks? Murdered? When? How?' cried Blake, his eyes ablaze with excitement.

But the waiter, called from the kitchen, sidled away. Sexton Blake leapt to his feet.

'Eat up sharp, Tinker,' he said. 'This is more than coincidence. It is Destiny, or Providence!'

Then he hurried from the room to seek the landlord.

THE FOURTH CHAPTER

A Tangled Skein

When the great detective arrived in the hall, it was to see the landlord handing into her brougham a lady, heavily veiled and closely wrapped in furs, and evidently agitated.

'Ah, Mr Blake!' cried the landlord, as he turned back after watching the brougham drive away. 'Why didn't I know that you were here before Miss Helen Lennox went off? Yes,' he went on, in answer to Sexton Blake's look of query, 'that's the adopted daughter of the earl. Of course, you've heard that he was found murdered in his own library?'

'I heard something,' said the detective. 'I should be glad to know the exact facts.'

'They don't amount to much,' answered the landlord, hugely flattered at having the attention of the great detective. 'It appears that, about eight o'clock, an old gent drives up to the Hall, gives to the footman the name of Frobisher, Lord Digby's private secretary, and is shown in to the library to wait the earl, who hadn't finished dinner. Presently the earl goes in. At the end of an hour Miss Helen goes to see if he's still engaged, as Mr Frobisher hadn't been seen to leave. The door is found locked. No answer is made to Miss Helen's repeated knocking, so the young lady has the door forced, and there lies the earl – dead, with –'

'His temple smashed in by a life-preserver?' suggested Blake softly.

'Exactly,' answered the landlord; 'though how you should know that –'

'And, of course, the window was locked and the curtains drawn?'

The landlord nodded, gaping.

'And between ten and fifteen minutes past eight Mr Frobisher paused at the gate, and said goodnight to the lodge-keeper, and sauntered off down the road, probably towards the station.'

The landlord shrank back a step.

'It wasn't the lodge-keeper. It was a groom, Henry Jostle by name.'

'A detail,' smiled the great detective. 'Landlord, I must have a trap at once, and go up to the Hall. Why was that young lady down here?'

'To 'phone the Yard, sir,' answered the landlord, as he rang up the stables.

'Ah, the Yard are sending!' said Blake, in a disappointed tone. His relations with the Official Criminal Investigation Department were, as the reader knows, of the most cordial kind, but he hated to cross trails. He was sure that he had the case in his grip; that the man who had committed the attempt on Jenkins was the author of this later crime. And he regarded him as his own especial prey. Sexton Blake had no cheap vanities. But the very essence of tenacity is a proper self-respect, and the great detective had no intention of sharing this proper quarry of his own with anyone else. 'Do you know who they are sending?' he asked, as the landlord finished his order to the stables.

'Yes, sir. Miss Lennox mentioned that it's Detective-Sergeant Plummer.'

'Ah!' said Sexton Blake shortly.

'Plummer's that new man, isn't he, guv'nor,' asked Tinker, as they rattled along in a cab towards Audley Hall – 'the one who got in before us, and collared the gang in the Calthrop affair?'

'That's the man,' answered Blake. One of the smartest men in the Yard, if not far and away the smartest. He was only an hour before us in the Calthrop business, Tinker. But I shall be surprised if we don't get back our laurels on this affair weeks before he's in sight of the man.'

'I don't see, sir,' said Tinker, 'how you guessed just what happened up at the Hall. It staggered the landlord fairly.'

Sexton Blake smiled.

'You are not usually so slow-witted, my lad,' he said. 'Ask yourself this: if it is the man we think, how would he be likely to act? Would he not be disguised? Would he not hit with a life-preserver? Would he not cover his tracks and delay pursuit, and therefore close curtains and windows, and equally, therefore, find opportunity of meeting someone with whom to say "Goodnight!" – someone who could testify to his collectedness and benevolent air?'

'Yes, exactly,' replied Tinker; 'but – '

'Well, we surmise this,' went on Blake dreamily, as if to himself. 'We find all these things were done. Therefore, there is a strong probability that it is our man.'

'What a juggins I am!' sighed Tinker. 'It's simple as ABC.

'And though we are not at Z yet,' smiled Blake, 'here, if I mistake not, we are at the Hall.' He signalled the driver to stop some yards before the gate was reached, dismissed him, and watched him return down the road. 'With any other man than Plummer,' he said to Tinker, 'I should not stand on ceremony; but I can't let him think I'm stealing a march on him, so I shall not go near the Hall.'

'Then what are we here for, sir?' asked Tinker.

'You see the roads, my boy. They are like putty after the mist. They'd keep a trail for twenty-four hours, and a print, too. I wish I could get near the library window.' He thought for a moment, reflecting. 'By Jove, I'll risk it!' he said.

'But how will you know it?' asked Tinker.

'Oh, I know the house well enough!' replied Blake. 'I was here some years ago, to look up a jewel robbery. Stay here, Tinker, and keep Pedro.'

Sexton Blake went away from the gates another twenty yards, to where the branch of a tree hung over the railings which surmounted the low stone wall enclosing the garden. It was a risky venture, but his knowledge of men in moments of the great emotion caused by so startling and mysterious a crime made him sure that, whether in the house or the stables, the personnel would be gathered in groups, and that the inspector and police in charge would be inside rather than outside the house.

In two minutes he had located the library window, dashed across the gravel path, and, producing his electric lamp, scanned eagerly the border of grass beneath the window. He gave a little gasp of satisfaction. There, dug deep into the soft turf, was the mark of a left heel, in which the third nail had a broken head. He whipped out his mould, and took an impression, smiling at the irony of Fate which had led the criminal, in his excess of cleverness, to use his heels instead of his toes; for the heel is, of course, much less distinctive than the toe impressions, and also much more broken.

He had just finished, and slipped back his lamp, when he was startled by the opening of the front door. He bolted back to cover only just in time to avoid detection by the inspector, who, coming round to the library window, placed there two policemen, and instructed them neither to walk on the grass nor let anyone approach.

Two minutes later Sexton Blake, with his eyes aglow, was standing by Tinker's side.

'Put Pedro on the leash, my boy.'

Again he made the hound nose the glove; and Pedro, now intimate with the scent, picked it up at once; following it at a sound pace, they left the road half a mile before reaching the village, bore away to the right, scaled the railway embankment, and, following it to a siding, suddenly lost scent.

'That'll do,' said Blake. 'He's boarded a goods train.'

They made their way rapidly to the station, and after some inquiry discovered that a goods express had left that siding for

Charing Cross shortly after mine, and was due at its destination at ten o'clock.

'I've only one thing more to do here, Tinker, and then we'll get back to Hastings,' said Sexton Blake, 'But I must have the ticket given up by the stranger who took the cab for Audley Hall.'

This they had no difficulty in obtaining from the stationmaster; and as they reached the platform, the 11.15 from Charing Cross for Hastings came to a standstill almost in front of them. They boarded an empty carriage, and sat at the windows, watching the passengers stream past them towards the ticket-gate.

'Look, Tinker,' said Blake quietly; 'there's Plummer! Smart work to be here so soon.'

'He looks a regular toff, don't he, guv'nor?' said Tinker, as his shrewd, sharp eyes took in, with a glance that a trained sculptor might have envied him, the form of a quietly-dressed man of some five-feet-ten in height, who, garbed in silk hat and a well-cut Melton overcoat, was standing a little apart, waiting for the crush to get past.

The lamplight fell full on him, revealing a face powerful, quiet, inscrutable, with lips well curved, but of a chisel-edge thinness; with a chin that yielded nothing to Sexton Blake's; with a nose broad at the butt, well shaped, and moulded at the nostrils to those alert curves one only sees in hunting dogs, anxious wives, chemists, and great detectives – that is, in intelligences inured to watching.

His form was alert, his shoulders square and open, his arms with the easy carriage that comes of drill. His waist was overbuckled in the tight long coat, thought Tinker, for anyone but a Piccadilly lounger; and his hips too slight, though the lad recognised that, despite their slightness, they carried a lazy sweep of assured strength in them – the kind of sweep one sees in the haunches of a panther sleepily stretching.

'A regular toff,' Tinker muttered again; then, with a grin, added, 'but for his boots. Do you see his boots, guv'nor?'

Sexton Blake made no answer. He had been watching Plummer's eyes – cold, tranquil, scrutinising, obviously losing no import of the faces thronging past him; yet, thought Blake strangely, curiously, so exaggeratedly intent as to be at variance with the careless set of his face and pose. As he in turn swung round and passed out among the last, Sexton Blake sank back in his seat.

'Yes,' he answered; 'I saw his boots. Regulation pattern. Curious enough, with such a get-up. But he probably had a scramble for the train.'

Yet, as they rolled down to Hastings, Sexton Blake could not help recurring again and again to the inexplicable contradiction offered by Plummer's eyes and Plummer's boots to the rest of Plummer's person. He felt, somehow, that both were a weakness. He had no grudge against Plummer for having wrested a victory from him in the Calthorp affair, but he was determined to score back on this occasion; and if Plummer had a weakness, it was as well to be forewarned of it.

On arriving at Hastings, he sent Tinker off to bed, and, taking the dog, himself set off to the coastguard-station, anxious to interview at the earliest possible moment the mother of Horace Jenkins.

It was nearly four o'clock when he got there, to find, to his bitter disappointment, that his desired interview could never take place. Against his advice, the coastguards had communicated the result of their search and their fears to Mrs Jenkins, and the shock had overwhelmed her.

She had fallen from collapse into syncope, and half an hour before the detective had arrived she had passed away, after murmuring, said the chief officer, 'some unintelligible words like "The earl must know".'

It was in vain that Sexton Blake, revealing his identity, searched the dead woman's effects. Not a paper could he find to give the slightest clue to her identity.

'She was always a very retiring woman,' explained the chief officer, 'and she never said a word about herself, or where she came from. She's been worse the last two years, since a lawyer-fellow from London came down one day when her son was away with the Fleet for the usual sea-service. Plausible fellow, he was, with golden beard and long, auburn 'air. She saw 'im a good two hours, and I know as she 'anded 'im a pile of papers, which he pocketed, for I was passin' her window at the moment. And it's a curious circumstance, sir, now as I comes to take note of it, that once, soon after young Jenkins returned from sea, I was near at 'and, when I hears Mrs Jenkins say to 'im, "Now, Horace, boy, you will be careful. Promise me you will." And young Jenkins laughs, and says, "Of course. But that feller was gammonin' of yer, mother. Who'd have a interest in putting away a 'onest coastguard?" '

'Ah,' said Blake shortly, 'I would like to see the poor woman's body!'

Sexton Blake stared at the dead woman's face intently; but it conveyed no recollection. As he turned to leave the room he caught sight of a photograph of her, and with a deftness that defied the chief officer's detection calmly pocketed it.

He took his way back to Hastings, fatigued, yet buoyed up by the growing, invincible conviction that he was at grips with an intelligence worthy of his utmost effort – an intelligence that had matured its plans year by year, and carried them out at a measured moment with a decision and ingenuity which would be just as prompt to weigh and provide for every slip incidental to circumstance.

It was the kind of case that electrified every drop of blood in his body, and gave to fibre and nerve the tirelessness of steel. He knew that he had been wonderfully quick on the trail, that he held a dozen links beautifully dovetailed; yet he laughed grimly as he had to confess that neither links nor dovetailing gave him a clue to the identity or to the motive of the criminal.

But they gave him only one side of a triangle on which to construct the whole figure, save for the one wide or narrow angle that gave him his direction for motive. That motive must evidently be sought in the relation which had caused the murder by the same hand in the same day of two people so wide apart in station as the Earl of Sevenoaks and Horace Jenkins, coastguard.

And Plummer, then at Sevenoaks, probably had the missing clues under his very nose, and he would not miss their import. Was he not the one man in the Yard who, starting even with himself, had got home first, and on a slenderer trail?

For a moment Sexton Blake wondered if his powers were diminishing, if his intellect was growing less acute, his instinct less sure.

'We shall see!' he said to himself savagely, as he turned in to the telegraph-office in Hastings, and sent to Dr Fleming the following telegram.

WANT TWO GOOD PHOTOGRAPHS OF PATIENT SENT BAKER STREET.

As he passed the police-station he paused.

'Wonder if our friend is a stickler for method?' he said to himself.

He entered, to come out a few minutes later with a thoughtful brow, and a jaw tight-set. He had learnt that two constables had talked with a golden-bearded stranger, and directed him to Fairlight Glen C. G. Station the previous afternoon. They had noticed him, and could describe him to his very boots, and both were prepared to swear on oath that the stranger, who was enveloped in a long, grey water-proof with white buttons, who carried a small kit-bag in his hand, who wore brown gloves, and looked in every respect a private citizen, was wearing regulation Service boots, such as are served to every police-officer in the force.

'Tinker,' said Sexton Blake five minutes later, as he shook the sleeping lad's shoulder – 'Tinker, just time for a tub and breakfast, and then we're off to Sevenoaks.'

THE FIFTH CHAPTER

A Contest in Wits

Tinker found Sexton Blake waiting for him at the breakfast-table above the morning papers. The tragedy at Audley Hall occupied many columns, in the glare of which few would have noticed a paragraph to the effect that 'yesterday a coastguard, Horace Jenkins, slipped over the cliffs above Hastings during the fog. His body, not yet recovered, is supposed to have been washed out to sea.'

Far more was the comment provoked by an announcement in the Agony Column stating that Messrs Small and Fry, solicitors, Bedford Row, London, desired information as to the whereabouts of Horace Audley, brother of the late Earl of Sevenoaks, or of his heirs.

Sexton Blake took note of the address, and ate his breakfast in silence. Tinker knew better than to chatter when he saw the mask down on the great detective's face. Once or twice Blake's eyes gleamed like the flash of summer lightning on a dark night. He maintained the same demeanour all the way to Sevenoaks, and even on the road to the Hall he only broke the silence once to say to Tinker: 'Be on your guard not to let Plummer get on to any clue of ours.'

'As if I should!' said Tinker indignantly.

'Well, then, don't,' retorted the detective drily.

Detective-Sergeant Plummer met them at the gate of the Hall with a pleasant smile.

'Ah, Blake,' he said genially. 'I'm glad you're not bearing ill-will, and have come back. I was afraid that you intended to chuck it when I heard you had gone away last night.'

'Oh, I don't bear malice,' replied Blake easily. It had never occurred to him for a moment that so smart a man as Plummer would fail to hear that he had come and gone. 'But I didn't care to appear to be prowling round and taking advantage of my chance presence here by getting on to your case before you possibly could. Besides, you know, I'm not even retained for it.'

'You haven't got my wire, then?' asked Plummer. 'I telegraphed you to Baker Street first thing.'

'The deuce you did!' said Blake, honestly surprised. 'I didn't get it, for the simple reason I haven't been at Baker Street. I'm down here on another matter, and thought that I'd spend an hour in looking you up and hear the news.'

'I'm much obliged to you.' laughed Plummer. 'But, I say, old man, I wish you'd keep this blessed dog of yours from inquiring round my boots.'

The remark was called forth by the conduct of Pedro, who ever since Plummer had greeted them had been straining on his leash, his ruff distinctly excited, and his nostrils sniffing suspiciously round the sergeant.

'He's quite harmless,' laughed Blake, 'though curious with strangers. What he's not seen before he likes to get once for all the distinctive smell of.'

For a second – or, rather, the fraction of a second – as the laughing eyes of Sexton Blake encountered levelly Plummer's cold, somewhat hard gaze, a thrill like an electric shock ran up the great detective's spine, for at the back of Plummer's eyes there had glimmered that indefinable vibration distinctive of horror, of dread. But it had passed swifter than thought, and as Sexton Blake dragged the dog to the other side, Plummer laughed.

'Oh, I'm not afraid of him,' he said. 'Yes,' he went on, his tone now sharp and official, 'I wired you because I'm honestly baffled. And that amazing instinct of yours is able perhaps to divine what I cannot deduce.'

'I'm sorry,' said Sexton Blake, 'but I'm quite unable to take up this matter. I'm on a case that is absorbing all my time; but I can give you an hour, look round, and offer you what may occur to me, if you like.'

'Um!' grunted Plummer. 'Half an apple's better than no pie, so I must be content. Will you come up to the house, and I'll put the facts before you on the way?'

As he led the way to the library, Plummer recounted nothing beyond what the other already knew, and the interest to Sexton Blake only began as he reached the library, and, looking on the dead man's face, saw at a glance that the fatal blow had been identical with that which had so nearly slain Jenkins.

He bent over it and examined it closely. There could be no doubt that it was made by the same instrument. The wound was in the full light, and as he rose Sexton Blake coolly took a snapshot of it from the button-camera he often wore.

Plummer did not appear to notice it, being intent on explaining how the library windows could be shut from the outside with ease, as they locked automatically as soon as closed.

'Have you found any trace of this impersonator of Mr Frobisher?' asked Sexton Blake.

'Not a trace,' answered Plummer. 'He has engaged no motor, no cab, no train, no room, nor has he even been seen since he said "Goodbye!" to Jostle, the groom. Nor does anyone seem to have seen him in the house, save Jostle's brother, the footman. But for the testimony of the fly-driver and a porter, one would imagine him a creation of Jostle's.'

'Left nothing behind him, I suppose?' asked Blake negligently.

'Not a fingermark,' answered Plummer. 'Not so much as a chair moved.'

'Um!' said Sexton Blake. 'You interest me. Of course, the key was on the inside?'

'There was no key,' answered Plummer; 'only a simple bolt.'

'Then he must have gone through this window, and on to the turf there,' said Blake, pointing to the four-foot border of grass beneath the window.

'No other way,' assented Plummer.

'And last night being foggy and damp,' went on Blake, 'the turf would have retained well the impressions of the feet. Have you got them?'

'There are none,' was Plummer's startling reply.

Sexton Blake never budged a muscle. He knew that there had been a very distinctive footprint, and he wondered if Plummer, believing that he, Blake, was really trying to outvie him, was lying to draw him.

'Extraordinary,' he murmured, in an incredulous tone. 'Yet a man, were he eight feet high, could not have jumped from this window and turned to close it after him without standing on that turf.'

'My reflection entirely,' said Plummer.

'And you verified it?' asked Blake, in an ironic accent.

'Twice,' said Plummer. 'There's no trace of a footprint. But there is a very peculiar trace, namely, a sod, cut entirely out.'

'Ah!' said Blake. 'This really is interesting. You ascertained that point, I suppose, on your arrival last night?'

'There was,' said Plummer, with a slight air of embarrassment, 'I must confess, a grave lapse. On arriving, the inspector assured me the window had been guarded ever since his arrival. I left the constable still on guard, and it was not till after I had exhausted my examination in the house, that I gave a thought to the possibility of the footprints. When I went out, I found the constable on that bench opposite, nodding. He said he had not been to sleep. Anyhow, on examining the ground, I found a sod lately cut out, but no print, no trace of one.'

'Assuming the constable to have slept,' said Blake, 'and I suppose I may presume the gardener or others can swear the turf was intact in the evening, what is your theory?'

'The constable and the inspector,' said Plummer, 'are sure the sod was not cut out when the guard was placed. Therefore, the assassin must either have returned, or have an accomplice in the grounds.'

'Evidently,' said Blake. 'Anything missing?'

'It is not sure,' answered Plummer. 'Miss Lennox, the earl's adopted daughter thinks, is in fact sure, that the earl had a pocket-book, for she saw him transfer the visitor's card to it on quitting the table. That pocket-book is the only thing missing, so far as can be ascertained. What do you make of it?'

Sexton Blake shook his head.

'It is interesting,' he said. 'I wish I could take it up. I think I should go for this pocket-book. I don't think the sod was removed by anyone but the actual murderer. You are up against a longheaded, cool, and resourceful criminal, Plummer. And that kind does not deal with accomplices. Anything audaciously compromising, he would do himself or leave alone.'

'Then in my case you would go for the pocket-book as the final test?' asked Plummer.

'Decidedly,' answered Blake. 'Find the man who took the pocket-book, and you find the assassin. Well, I must be off. Goodday, Plummer, and good luck!'

Plummer insisted on accompanying them down the drive, and bidding them goodbye at the gate.

He stood there a minute, looking after their retreating forms. Then a derisive smile curled his lips.

'Ah, Sexton Blake,' he murmured, 'you want to get back on Sergeant Plummer for the Calthrop affair, do you? Yet after that, you should have known not to leave the trace of your footsteps from the place where you left Mr Tinker, and your brute of a dog, to bang opposite the library window, and back, nor the mark of a mould-rim on that curious impression in the missing sod. However, we shall show you, Sexton Blake, that Sergeant Plummer can get ahead of you again, by arresting the assassin, or at least his accomplice, before even you get to the station.'

He turned and walked up the path leading to the stables, and, asking for the groom, Henry Jostle, sent him up to the house to bring the inspector. On the left of the stables were the groom's quarters, and Plummer, walking across to the door from which Jostle had answered his summons, looked casually into the groom's room. From the stables opposite rose the clatter of the morning cleaning. The yard was deserted, a fact Plummer noticed as he withdrew his head from the half-open door, and walked leisurely to and fro, waiting for the inspector.

It was about five minutes before he came, and Sergeant Plummer whiled away the time by chatting casually to the coachman about Jostle's manner of life. He seemed satisfied by what he had learned, and as the inspector hurried up, he turned quietly to Jostle.

'I want to examine your room, my man,' he said.

'My room! What for? I ain't done nothink,' said Jostle.

'Come along, now, none of your nonsense,' said the inspector roughly. 'Which is your room?'

'That 'un in the middle!' cried the coachman, all agog with interest.

Jostle was half-led, half-dragged across the yard, and pushed through the door.

'Ha!' said Plummer quietly, as he rummaged in a corner. 'This is very interesting.' And, bending down, he lifted from a litter of boots and harness, a piece of sod, about six inches square, on the grass side of which he pointed out to the inspector the imprint of a heel.

'Where did you get this from, my man?' he asked.

'Never seed it afore,' Jostle answered.

'Dropped from heaven right through his ceiling,' said the inspector, with a facetious grin.

The search went on thoroughly. Plummer was an adept at it, and, as if feeling the inspector's eye admiringly on him, he did it thoroughly. At last everything appeared to have been overhauled, and Plummer looked round disappointed.

'There's them half-tops, Mr Plummer,' said the inspector, pointing to the tops hanging on the wall just inside the door.

'And I just cleaned 'em to a fair mirror!' groaned Jostle. 'I'll have enough to do to set this straight, without you mucking them up.'

'Just turn them out carefully, inspector, will you?' said Plummer. 'Your hands are cleaner than mine, you see.'

The inspector grinned, and, lifting the tops down, turned them one after the other upside down, when, to the evident utter consternation of Henry Jostle, there tumbled from the second a pocket-book in morocco leather, with embossed arms in silver.

'Hallo!' said the inspector aghast, standing back.

'The missing pocket-book,' said Sergeant-Detective Plummer, in a cold, convicting tone.

'Gentlemen, I hain't done it,' said Jostle, suddenly standing erect. 'I swear as I never set heyes on it afore.'

'You can tell that to the magistrate,' said Plummer. 'Click the irons on him, inspector, and take him away. Charge him as accessory, and with receiving. He's not the chief. But with this' – he held up the sod – 'I hope to get face to face with the principal before I'm a week older.'

Detective-Sergeant Plummer watched the inspector lead off the protesting Jostle, and then, smiling and self-possessed, he took the way to the station.

THE SIXTH CHAPTER

A Fair Visitor and an Inspiration

It was nearly ten before Sexton Blake finished his breakfast and opened his mail the following morning. He had spent the night, since arriving at Baker Street, a prey to more mental agitation than he had known for some time. The evening papers had acquainted him with Plummer's discovery of the cut sod and the missing pocket-book, and his arrest of the groom, and the news had seemed to him to leave the puzzle in a more tangled state than ever. Pipe after pipe he had smoked as the night gave in to day, lying back in his chair with half-closed eyes, waiting, waiting for that hovering, exasperating, evading touch of coherence, which should put into shape and order the confused tendrils of thought that seemed to be beckoning to his insight now this way, now that, only to baffle him in each.

'With sleep comes counsel,' he quoted at last, and went to bed, resolved to put the problem from him till after breakfast. It asserted itself then in the shape of the photographs of Horace Jenkins, which were sent to Dr Fleming, who reported that his patient, though still unconscious, was doing well, and in all probability would pull through.

'Now for the problem,' he said, slowly loading a briar.

'A lady to see you, sir,' interrupted Tinker, putting his head in at the door.

'Oh, bother! I won't see anyone. Say I'm out,' said Blake.

'But you are not, Mr Blake,' came in a low, sweet voice from beyond Tinker's head, which, under the pressure of a small gloved hand, preceded its owner and its holder into the room.

'Really!' protested Sexton Blake, as Tinker, violently blushing, withdrew hurriedly and left him facing the intruder.

'Don't be angry, Mr Blake,' pleaded the lady. 'I had to see you. And I wasn't going to take no. I am Helen Lennox, the adopted daughter of the Earl of Sevenoaks.'

Her voice broke a little, and Blake, all his resentment vanished, hastened to offer her a chair.

'My dear lady,' he said, in the voice that could be so extraordinarily gentle, 'please do not distress yourself. Sit down, and tell me what I can do for you.'

'Thank you,' Miss Lennox replied, and, drawing back her veil, she lifted to his a countenance that, despite its obvious distress, was winsomely sweet and womanly. Eyes blue and candid as a child's, a mouth generous and tender, a rounded, dimpled chin instinct with determination, a brow broad and transparently white, surmounted by straying locks of gold that nestled beneath a toque of white fur – it was a picture that Sexton Blake, all unsusceptible as he was, could not resist. Its extraordinary combination of simplicity and strength appealed to that fibre of chivalry which was so strong in him. He took a chair opposite her, and waited for her to continue.

'Please go on smoking,' she said, smiling. 'I always let Horace, and his tobacco was dreadfully strong.'

'And may one ask who is Horace?' smiled Blake, as he took advantage of the permission.

'Horace Jenkins, my fiance,' she answered.

The pipe fell from Blake's lips as he sprang to his feet, for once startled out of his adamantine control. 'Horace Jenkins, your fiance!' he echoed.

Miss Lennox rose also, her face suddenly white and frightened.

'You know something!' she cried. 'Oh, I'm sure you do!' And as she noticed Blake's face resume its cold, professional air, she gripped his hands fiercely. 'You shall tell me. You shall tell me, whatever you hide from others. I must know, or I shall die. And I promise you – oh, I promise you that I will not breathe a word of what you tell me to anyone – not even to that detestable Mr Plummer.'

Blake's eyes rested on her tenderly.

'Why "that detestable Mr Plummer"?' he asked softly.

'Because he seemed to be almost glad when I showed him the paragraph in the paper about Horace, and rudely said he could not snatch back what the sea had taken.'

'Sit down, Miss Lennox, and tell me your history,' said Sexton Blake.

'But you do know something,' she persisted. 'You will tell me?'

'Yes, if you are good and calm, I will tell you,' said Blake. He needed no assurance to convince him that those lips and eyes could never belie a promise given. 'And, to set your fears at rest at once, I will tell you now that he is alive, and in my care.'

'Thank God!' she murmured. 'Oh, you do not know what I have suffered! If you had only told me – published it!'

'That would have been,' said Blake very gravely, 'the one sure means to destroy him.' Then, briefly, he related to the breathless girl how he had been enabled to save Jenkins.

She rose as he finished.

'I must go to him,' she said – 'I must go and nurse him.'

Blake smiled.

'Not yet,' he said. 'You have not told me your history.'

'It is scarcely worth the name,' she answered. 'I was left an orphan at five, and Lord Audley, who was third cousin on the maternal side to my mother, adopted me and brought me up. Then, two years ago, I was carried out to sea while bathing, and Horace rescued me; and afterwards I used to go up to the Lovers' Seat at Fairlight, and I saw him many times, and learnt to love him. I told papa – the earl, you know – and he was very angry, refused to see Horace, and forbade me ever to speak to him again. That was two months ago. And I had no news of him at all till I read that dreadful paragraph.'

Blake had listened very carefully.

'Did you know his mother?' he said.

'No,' she answered. 'Horace told me she would never hear of meeting any strangers.'

'You do not know what her husband was?'

'No. Horace told me his father had long been dead.'

'So you know literally nothing of their parentage – where they came from, where Horace was brought up?'

Miss Lennox drew her pretty brow into a frown.

'I have some recollection of Horace saying that he was born near Windsor, but I really cannot be sure.'

Blake sighed and rose.

'Thank you. Miss Lennox!' he said. 'If you will return to Audley Hall, I will let you know the very first minute that Dr Fleming thinks advisable when you can join Horace's nurses. At present only the highest skill can save him. Love must wait for convalescence to do its restorative work. Be brave and silent. And, above all, let no one know that you are in communication with me.'

He bowed her out; and, returning to his room, picked up his briar, and lit it, staring the while into the fire.

'Tinker!' he called. And Tinker, fearing a wigging, came in with even more than ordinary despatch. 'Tinker,' went on Sexton Blake, 'we have come to a high wall made of nothing but clues. I can't see for clues. Let us spade up the wall together, and see how it tumbles.

'First, an unknown being we will call Smith, for convenience, arrives in Hastings the day before yesterday, makes himself conspicuous to the railway-porter and two policemen. He is carrying a kit-bag, wears a grey mackintosh with pearl buttons, has golden hair and beard, and wears regulation police boots.

'We may take it that Mr Smith changes his boots in the carriage that takes him to Fairlight, for it is certainly Mr

Smith of the light waterproof and brown gloves, and burned wig, but with pointed-toe boots, who attempts to murder Horace Jenkins.

'Secondly, Mr Smith, in a pointed beard and dark hair, and Chesterfield coat, makes himself observed by the ticket-clerk in taking the 5.10 train to Sevenoaks.

'Thirdly – as you ascertained yesterday at Charing Cross – a Mr Smith, of similar appearance, made himself similarly observed by a ticket-clerk in taking the morning train to Hastings, single ticket, on the same day. Make a special note of that point, Tinker.

'Next, we find a Mr Smith of the grey and infirm aspect, leaves the 5.10 train from Hastings at Sevenoaks, takes a cab, murders Lord Audley, leaves the impression of his heel outside the library window, and vanishes into a goods-train-siding just as the 9 o'clock goods express would be starting for its destination.

'We are up against a man of parts, Tinker. For all he leaves us of real knowledge is that he has a skill in disguises, and that he pursues identical methods. See how careful he is to identify himself at Hastings as golden-beard, at Sevenoaks as grey-beard.

'But in between times we hear nothing of black-beard, except for identity at the stations. We may, therefore, assume that black-beard desired to be identified only at the stations, and that the black beard is as much a disguise as any of the others.

'Therefore, all we have, in sum, is that Mr Smith is a clean-shaven man, about five feet ten in height, who, the day before yesterday, was absent from London between 11 and 10 at night.'

'You forget Pedro, sir,' suggested Tinker.

'I reserve Pedro,' answered Blake. After a pause, he resumed: 'Of course, it goes without saying that if we find the man to fit one of these facts to, we shall fit all of them, and they will hang him. But he knows that as well as we, and he is strong, my lad. He has only made one mistake. Do you see what it is?'

'He didn't reckon,' said Tinker, 'that only one passenger might get out at Sevenoaks.'

'Good man!' said Blake, with a smile. 'For that is why he had to take the goods train back, for he dare not try another disguise. He had to vanish; but in vanishing he forgot Pedro.'

'I don't see much light come through the spading, sir,' said Tinker.

'Let us finish first,' said Blake. 'We now come to the arrest of Jostle. It is possible that Jostle is an accomplice; that he saw more than he says; that the cut sod is the value of which the pocket-book is the price. But I do not think so.'

'No more do I,' said Tinker stubbornly. 'I'd swear to it! You were talking of identical methods, sir, just now, and something's struck me, struck me hard.'

'Well?' queried Blake.

'I don't like that there Plummer,' said Tinker. 'And no more did Pedro.'

'Is that the identity, Tinker?' said Blake, laughing outright.

'No, it isn't!' growled Tinker, who had his little vanities. 'Pedro didn't like his boots, either,' he went on – 'the regulation police-boots he was wearing, same as golden-beard, who was also got up as a bit of a toff, was wearing, regulation police-boots. And' – the boy bent forward with shining eyes – 'Pedro knew the scent of golden-hair's boots, and couldn't stop sniffing Plummer's. That's my identity.'

Again into Sexton Blake's eyes came that strange amber flicker of light like the flash of summer lightning on a dark sky. He lay back on his chair, his long fingers pointed together, the smoke wreathing past his half-closed eyelids.

'Do you think it possible?' he said very softly at last.

'It's got to be explained,' said Tinker stubbornly, for the lad would have suspected an archangel on a sniff from Pedro.

Sexton Blake stood-up, his jaw set in the iron grip that always delighted Tinker, and foretold action.

'Very well,' said Blake. 'We are treading on high explosives, but we shall tread very softly. We have two objectives now, Tinker. To find out what connection there is between Horace Jenkins and the heir to Sevenoaks; which means to discover the past history of the Jenkins family. And to find out what interest, if any, Mr Smith – we'll still call him Smith – can have in the death of the heir to Sevenoaks, as well as in the death of the earl. It is the only theory to which the fasts can square.'

'Now I must go out to Small & Fry,' went on Sexton Blake. 'I want you, Tinker, to get me some piece of Serge—of – er – Mr Smith's personal clothing. Do you think you can manage it without betraying your identity? You might deceive me. I wouldn't swear you could deceive him!'

'Leave it to me, guv'nor,' said Tinker, delighted.

THE SEVENTH CHAPTER

On the Horns of a Dilemma

As Sexton Blake had indicated to Tinker, his first visit was to the Audley's family lawyers, Messrs Small & Fry, of Bedford Row. Mr Small was a parchment-looking individual of some six foot three; but if he belied his name in inches he lived up to it in minor details. His punctiliousness was a proverb, his prosiness a byword, and his capacity for multiplying unimportant interviews beyond the definition of any taxing master.

Blake, who knew his man, squirmed through an hour to learn what five minutes could tell him – to wit, that Mr Small knew nothing of the missing heir – Horace – save that he had contracted some disgraceful marriage, had been cut off by the family, and never since heard of. It was in his – Mr Small's – 'lamented' father's time, and he had not heard the particulars, nor had his search at Audley Hall been productive of any trace of the certificate or other details. No, Mr Small did not know of any other branch of the family, save that such did exist – that is, if it were not deceased. There had been some remote ancestor who had gone to Australia in the early days of that – er – settlement, and had never since been heard of.

Blake descended the dark staircase in a reverie, so deeply in a reverie that, when he cannoned into a man coming up, he passed him with never a glance, and a mere 'sorry'.

Yet that slight encounter was to have issues much more pregnant than Blake dreamed, issues that were to bring him, and Tinker too, nearer to death than even they, in all their most perilous days, had ever yet been.

For the man going up the stairs had been Detective-Sergeant Plummer, and if Blake had not recognised him, he had recognised Blake, as his first question to Mr Small testified.

'Blake a client of yours?' he asked that gentleman point-blank.

Mr Small regarded Scotland Yard as an institution, and he rather posed before its representatives as a safe man and alert, with whom it was wise to drop frills.

'Dear me, no,' he replied. 'I was really just wondering why he came, or what interest he could have in tracing the Audley heirs. But a clever man, they say!'

'A most capable man,' assented Plummer, and drifted over the same ground as had Blake, and with the same result.

Plummer also descended the stairs in a reverie as deep as had Blake, and his reverie lasted him all the way to Craven Street, Strand, till it was disturbed quite effectively by the landlady of his rooms there, who met him as he opened the street door.

'I hopes as you got your gloves, sir?' she asked.

'What gloves?' snapped Plummer.

'Why, them as you sent for!' bridled the landlady.

Plummer was, in an instant, the widest-awake man in London.

'Ah,' he queried very softly, 'the gloves I sent for?'

'Yes, sir,' babbled on the landlady; 'and I must say as them there messenger boys his himproving in their manners. As nice a spoken boy, he was, as if I'd a brought 'im up myself. Says 'e, "Please, lydy, I'm to take Mr Plummer the gloves what 'e left on 'is table; and, if it ain't a-troublin' yer too much, lydy, I'm to be smart about it, 'cos he's waiting." So smart I was, and I gives 'im the brown pair a-lyin' on your table. "Right-ho!" says 'e. "You're a lydy, you is!" And off he goes, straight down towards the Yard.'

'Quite right, Mrs Jones,' said Plummer gently. 'I had to leave before I got them; but I'll get them at the Yard.'

Then Mr Plummer went into his room, shut and locked the door, and stood for a minute so still that one would have thought he had been suddenly petrified before his own image in the glass. He shook his head slowly; then he addressed his reflection.

'If it's that boy of Blake's, it's that dog. If it's that, Blake is trying to draw my hand. Let us determine if Blake is trying to draw my hand.'

Meanwhile, Blake, after sending various messages and despatching various agents, hurried to Baker Street, to find that Tinker had not only arrived before him, but had apparently turned his own bedroom into an emporium for a rag-shop.

'I've got 'em!' said Tinker triumphantly.

'You seem to have got brain-fever as well,' said Blake, eyeing with disgust the litter of boots and clothes, rags, and every kind of quick-change vestment his disguise-wardrobe contained.

'How did you get them?' he went on.

'Did a messenger-boy – District. Blarney'd the old landlady. D'ye know, guv'nor, it's the old un' that you saved from getting mixed up in that Dalton case?'

And he related to the detective what Mrs Jones had already related to Sergeant Plummer.

'I see,' said Blake thoughtfully. 'I'm afraid, Tinker, that your success, my boy, is likely to cost us trouble. Plummer isn't a man to waste conjectures. He'll divine us; and, if I know my man, he'll be here in half an hour's time.'

'Then he'll be our man!' said Tinker triumphantly.

'We shall not be nearer proving it for that,' said Blake sombrely. 'We shall only be nearer sudden death.'

'I like to be near old friends,' grinned Tinker. 'Here are the gloves, sir. Same mark, same make, same size as the one Jenkins held, sir. Three more identities. If you'll hide them separately, I'll bring up Pedro.'

Two minutes later Blake had handed Pedro not the old familiar glove, but the golden wig and beard to nose, and then turned him loose among the wardrobe.

Five minutes later the gloves that Tinker had brought from Detective-Sergeant Plummer's were lying at Blake's feet.

Blake's face was even more pale than usual, as he picked up the gloves and locked them in his safe with the other clues.

'Another identity, sir!' said Tinker, with a chuckle.

Blake was silent for a moment.

'That decides it,' he said. 'It is war to the death – war without quarter.'

At that moment the bell rang.

'That is Plummer,' said Blake coolly. 'Get into the bedroom again with Pedro, Tinker. Lock the door on the inside, in case Plummer should mistake his way out.'

He slipped a revolver into his pocket, cast a keen, searching glance round the room, then, strolling with leisurely tread to the outer office, threw open the door.

'Ah, Plummer,' he said, 'I was expecting to see you.'

'I thought you might be,' returned Plummer, with the same easy air, 'so I strolled round.'

'The fact is,' went on Blake, 'that I looked on that arrest of Jostle as almost sure to lead to something a bit more sensational, and when nothing came out this morning, I made sure you would come and have a chat with me about it.'

'You are looking up the case, then?' laughed Plummer.

'Neither professionally, nor in any interest,' answered Blake; 'but the scientific spirit is a task-master, I need hardly tell you, Plummer; and the affair certainly has unique points. It simply smells of a master-mind directing it.'

It was a curious scene, poignant with all life's tragedy, as terrible as the second of hush that precedes the devastation of an earthquake, the sight of those two men sitting at their ease in armchairs before a bright fire, each lazily curling the blue tobacco-smoke from their briars, each wearing the inscrutable mask of polite attention, the eyes of each never flickering from that steady, frank regard of a mutual confidence, yet the brains of each governing words that rang letter to letter, question to response, in as deadly, tight a grip as ever was made by sword enveloping sword in a combat to death.

'Unique points, indeed!' murmured Plummer reflectively.

Each was fencing for the other's lead; each desired the revealing thrust that should show the measure of strength. Sexton Blake had the advantage, for he knew what he awaited, and had no reason to press his play. But Plummer's attack was tentative; he did not know what he awaited; he only wanted to know.

Blake felt the sparkle in the electric burden of the atmosphere, as the silence grew around Plummer's last remark. He let it sparkle for two minutes, then rose, brought out a whisky-bottle and syphon, and, pushing a glass over to Plummer, took one himself, and, silent still, mixed a brew.

'Anything fresh?' he asked negligently, as he resumed his seat.

'Yes,' said Plummer, with the air of a man who has taken at last a resolve. 'It's that brings me here. You know, Blake, in all good part, I must say that I'm a bit jealous of your pre-eminent success. I might have been more frank with you at Audley Hall; but I felt that you were playing dark horse. The fact is, the assassin left behind him one glove. I have kept this detail to myself. But this morning a boy came to my rooms and asked, in my name, for a pair of gloves I had forgotten to take out with me. My landlady gave him them. The curious point is that the one odd glove is safe in my pocket at the present moment, and that I never sent anyone to my landlady for any gloves. What do you make of that?'

Plummer leant back in his chair, with a composure that thrilled Blake to admiration. Plummer, marking the effect, leisurely thrust his hand into his pocket and, drawing out an odd glove, handed it across the table.

'That's the one the assassin left behind,' said he.

Sexton Blake, like a man fascinated, looked on it, dumb with amazement at the stupendous, magnificent effrontery of the man.

In a flash the very core of the other's thought was revealed to him. Plummer feared lest he – Blake – should have a doubt of him, should be on a trail, and he was trying not only to bluff him out of it, in case he had nothing more than a suspicion, but to make him declare himself if he had. For the glove Plummer had handed to him was the fellow to that found in the hand of Jenkins. The finesse and the audacity of the dilemma provoked brought Sexton Blake to the keenest grip of himself he had ever been conscious of.

For the dilemma was obvious. If Blake had by any means the other glove, and by it traced the identity of the assassin of the unnamed Jenkins to that of the murderer of Lord Audley, then Blake must attach inevitably such immense importance to this fellow-glove as to betray his knowledge in some shade of emotion. Then Plummer would know. But if Blake attached no importance to this odd glove, then Blake knew nothing, and Plummer's game was safe.

To the reader an explanation, all this to Sexton Blake was as a picture seen by flashlight. He lifted the glove carelessly, examined it, threw it back, and remarked: 'You have, of course, not been able to trace it?'

Plummer shrugged his shoulders.

'It's not the time,' he said. 'I must get nearer the man. And,' he added, with a sibilant viciousness that sounded very like a direct menace, 'the man has given himself into my hands in sending a District messenger-boy for those gloves. It will not take long to find that out.'

'No,' laughed Sexton Blake, drawing out his watch. 'Well, I must apologise, Plummer, but work is work. I don't see that I can offer you any points you don't see as quick or quicker than I do. But,' he added, with a genial tone, as if perforce he must carry their occult courtesy to the exaltation of a direct challenge – 'but if I do hear of anything that puts me on a trail, and will enable me to produce the assassin, I promise you that you shall be the first to hear of it. This way,' he said, laughing as Plummer innocently turned towards the wrong door, leading to the bedroom. 'Goodbye! Let me hear how you get on.'

'I will,' said Plummer, in a tone whose genuineness did not escape Blake's ears.

Plummer was not half-way down the stairs, before Sexton Blake had sprung to the door concealing Tinker.

'Quick, my boy!' he said. 'Shadow him, and report each hour!'

'He's a mug,' said Tinker to himself, as, reaching the street, he saw Plummer strolling leisurely along towards Oxford Street. He loitered on behind; but Plummer never turned his head, and kept straight on, apparently the most unconcerned and aimless pedestrian in London.

Yet Plummer's heart was seething through a torture of emotions into an appalling fixity of purpose, for Plummer was no mean psychologist. He came of a race that had ruled.

His instinct was as fine as Blake's for the value of a pause, of an eyelash flicker. Blake had met him at every point, had made no slip, had so perfectly evaded all device to make him show his suspicion. Therefore, Blake ought to have no suspicion, no clue.

Yct Plummer would have staked his life that the other had a suspicion based on a clue. He smiled as he thought of the final test he was now elaborating. If Blake were satisfied, Blake would not shadow him. If Blake were shadowing him, then all that had just gone by showed that not only had Blake a suspicion, but a case. And whether Blake was shadowing him or not, he – Plummer – would know in two minutes.

He crossed George Street, keeping still his way to Oxford Street, with Tinker hanging some thirty yards behind.

At Seymour Street he turned sharp to the left, and walked straight into a cab that was waiting with open door on the kerb, the cabby standing by the door. He drew to the door, and, as if having received his instructions in advance, the cabby mounted the steps of the house opposite, and rang the bell.

A minute later Tinker lounged round the corner. A glance sufficed to show him that his quarry had vanished. He gave a shrewd glance into the standing cab, but saw only a woman in a grey shawl dangling a long-clothed baby in front of her face.

'He's twigged me, and bolted down the mews,' thought Tinker, hot with shame, and, taking to his heels, bolted down the street, and dived into the first turning.

The cabman descended leisurely from the bell he had not rung, mounted the box, and, wheeling round his steed, turned into Orchard Street, nearly colliding with an automobile that was gently moving across from the opposite side, just as Plummer, inside the cab, was putting the doll and shawl under the opposite seat.

The cabman drove on, and Sexton Blake, in the hooded seat of the automobile, followed it.

'That absolutely settles it!' was the simultaneous reflection of both these unique men, as the one followed the other.

The cab drove straight to Scotland Yard

Sexton Blake waited some forty minutes, scanning the faces that passed out, and was somewhat diverted to see a quarrelsome sea captain being unceremoniously hauled forth and bundled into a cab that was told to drive for Bow Street. Another forty minutes passed, and still Plummer did not appear. Blake entered the office, and asked if he could see him. The inspector, an old friend of the great detective's, winked pleasantly.

'He was taken an hour ago to Bow Street, in charge of two constables, for mutiny on the high seas and conspiracy,' said the inspector.

'What!' cried Blake. 'The drunken captain?'

The inspector chuckled.

'He's one of the smartest,' he said. 'No use waiting for him, Mr Blake. He's two weeks special leave on the Audley case.'

'Thanks,' said Blake, and regained his motor, feeling not only mortified, but sincerely assured that with Plummer on the loose, and thoroughly awake to his danger, his own life and that of Tinker were not worth the purchase of any one hour in any twenty-four.

THE EIGHTH CHAPTER

Crossed Trails

Sexton Blake had too often known humiliation and disaster as the handmaids to victory, to feel abashed by the evidence of another's superior cunning. The failure that crushes the man conscious of the evil of his intent, braces to its last fibre the soul of the man strong in the justice of his cause.

Tinker's sorry face on his arrival at Baker Street acted as a further tonic. The unconquerable detective was never so much at his best as when the fire and glow of final issues lay bare and declared. It was then that his incisiveness, his subtlety, his resource, his audacity made feel their real worth against the spurious values that stalked in their cloaks.

'Recover your laurels, boy,' he said. 'Sling some things into your bag. You go to Exeter and Dawlish by the 3.30 from Paddington. I've no need to teach you how to make inquiries. Dive, burrow, ferret into George Plummer's life, his companions, his antecedents, his parents – in short, make a record of him. There's money, and to spare. Wire all reports essential at once. Goodbye! Trot!'

Tinker went. It took him five minutes to get from his master's table into the cab; but as he bowled along towards Paddington, he took with him a very clear idea of what he had to do.

Sexton Blake faced the emptiness of his outer room, and chafed under the sense of impotence.

'Three days! Three days!'

It was the outside limit that he could allow for his clever young assistant to fulfil his task in time for the dénouement he was preparing. He knew that he could rely on Tinker. He often, in moments of difficulty, spaded over facts in his mind, like a gardener spades over ground he knows; and often he had found it of great use to get back a little from the clods of fact, and watch the way Tinker handled them. More than once he had owed his life, and its great value to the public he loved – the great public that was his only child – to the reckless resource of the boy whose natty and quick intelligence always responded as truly to the motion of service as a good soldier springs to the bugle-call. For Tinker had initiative, and if sometimes the exercise of it took him into danger, he always got out of the scramble with the knowledge he had gone to get.

Sexton Blake, feeling the place rather empty without Tinker, loaded his pipe, lit it, puffed at it, then forgot it.

Between the faint blue curls of smoke, a face had risen to his view – a face that would not be refused.

Sexton Blake fidgeted.

But the face persisted.

'Why should I worry because she was pretty, and taking and convincing?' the great detective murmured to himself.

His reverie galloped away with him. The face of Miss Lennox, as he had last seen her, seemed to rise in front of him and claim his attention.

'Convincing!' he murmured, reflectively regarding the picture of her his mind was conjuring up. 'A good girl. A true woman. That brow affronting Destiny with a clean query. Not often seen, but always desired, in any woman. And the child-eyes of her! A true woman. A woman who ought to be the mother of a great man! The liquid crystal of that gaze is haunting! Candour. Simplicity. Trust.

'Trust! She trusted me. She loves that man who fell over the cliff into my hands. And Miss Helen Lennox's waiting news of him. And Fleming's wire "Let her come!" is seven hours old. Poor girl! Love! What a power it is! It's God's seal on life's promise!'

Sexton Blake relit his pipe, slewed his chair round, and, with a firm grasp, took a sheaf of telegram-forms from the table.

'Miss Lennox, Audley Hall, Sevenoaks. You can leave by the 6.50 for Newhaven!'

He wrote the telegram, and stared at it.

It seemed innocent enough. Yet at the back of his brain he felt that Miss Lennox ought to have someone going down with her.

'I'll wire Fleming to meet her at Lewes,' he muttered.

He took up the telegram-form again, and added the words: 'Dr Fleming will meet you at Lewes, in my name.'

Then he wrote out another wire, addressed it to Dr Fleming, on the *Stella*, asking him to meet Miss Helen Lennox.

> FIANCÉE OF OUR PATIENT, HORACE, IS GOING FROM SEVENOAKS BY 6.50. PLEASE MEET HER AT LEWES. MAKE HER FEEL AT HOME. GIVE HER FULL CHARGE OF NURSES, IN YOUR JUDGMENT. SEXTON BLAKE.

'Curious,' he said to himself, as he eyed and reread for the third time the two telegrams – 'curious! I can't see any accident that can be provoked by these two wires. Yet I feel that I am provoking Fate to do me a shot in the eye. Well, I must risk it!'

He crossed over to the telephone, and asked for a District Messenger.

Four minutes later a boy from the D. M. Service presented himself.

Sexton Blake handed him the two telegrams, commended him for his promptitude, dismissed him, and, crossing to the window, idly wondered what Tinker was doing in his railway carriage.

'There isn't another boy like him!' he murmured to himself, as he gazed down on the busy roll of life beneath.

Baker Street has always got more or less of a hum about it. As Sexton Blake looked down on it, in the grey light that belongs to a February four o'clock in our beloved village of London, he whistled quietly the popular song:

'O, 'Awkins! Dear little 'Awkins!'

He drummed the tune out with his fingers on the windowsill, as one does unconsciously drum out tunes when one is worried and watching for something one does not even know is going to happen.

The D. M. boy seemed to get down the steps to the roll of the song that Sexton Blake was making into the established ghost of a whistle.

Sexton Blake idly followed the boy's casual course. The great detective had the capacity of following the course of a fox in a field of corn. He threaded his eyes into the needle of vision, blindfolded.

Wherefore, when the boy, twenty yards down the street, was brought up sharp by a policeman, Sexton Blake remarked it, and was interested.

He grabbed a pair of field-glasses to see better. And what he saw, interested him more.

The constable stopped the District Messenger Boy with an authoritative touch on the elbow. Sexton Blake, watching through the glasses, was impressed by his air of authority. So, evidently, was the boy. To the alert intelligence of the detective, the quiet movement of the constable's lips seemed almost to echo on the outside rim of his glasses.

The constable pointed towards Regent's Park.

The District Messenger Boy looked that way.

The constable took the telegrams. The boy set off as hard as he could pelt towards Regent's Park.

The constable strolled off on his stolid pace towards the post-office, waving the forms in his hand.

It was that waving that got home on the shore of Blake's mind, and made the pebbles of suspicion rattle, rattle, and seam into a thought.

The constable vanished across the road. A block of motor-buses shoved him into a big obscurity.

'Curious,' he said to himself, as he eyed and re-read for a moment. 'Why should a good policeman take a messenger boy's duty on himself? Is there anything at the back of that?'

He stared down the street.

'No,' he reflected. 'If there was anything in it, it would have been done more neatly. However, I'll see Fleming myself at Lewes.'

A ring at his bell broke into his reverie.

The visitor was Mr Small. He had evidently come on a courtesy visit, and he made it discourteously long. In his office, in Bedford Street, he was a being of a dreary length in sentences. In anyone else's office he was appallingly verbose. He had nothing to say, of any worth, and he said it slowly, in two hours.

When at last he left, Sexton Blake opened the window, and gasped into the fog. Then he took an ABC, gave one glance at it, whistled a hansom, and bolted downstairs.

At Victoria, he arrived to see the end of the train he wanted to take. It was a two hours wait to the next train to Lewes, and as he paced up and down, he asked himself if he was justified in giving eight hours of his time, simply because a P.C. had taken a telegram from a District Messenger Boy. He recognised the obviousness of the answer.

But when Sexton Blake was in the way of letting himself out to follow the mandate of his instinct, he allowed to reason only its place as anchor. Even so, in a running tide, he had to let reason ride. But he had the trust, or the proved instinct, of doing simply what he had set out to do. So he foot-slogged the pavement of the platform, waiting his train, and sure that at the end of the journey there was something for him to do.

How much there was to do, and how true his instinct was, the morrow had to prove to him. Not that he looked often to the morrow to vindicate his attitude in front of a moment.

If anyone had asked him – even if Tinker had asked him – why he was measuring yards with foot-slog on the pavement of that station platform, he would have said: 'I want to see.'

See what? Sexton Blake didn't know.

But he felt that Lewes was his place. He felt that his telegram was an assurance that Miss Lennox might trust in his guidance. And somehow, in the soles of his boots, he trod on the toes of that police-constable who had been somewhat too obviously on the spot to take on a duty that did not belong to him.

Chafe as he might, Sexton Blake could not make the clock work the train. But his instinct of desire to be at Lewes was a true premonition.

He was not a man to be taken by a pretty face, however convincing it might be. His sympathy for Helen Lennox rose in, and was buckled into, Tinker's dive into the running, sullen tide off Fairlight, to save Horace Jenkins. The interest in Sexton Blake's mental outlook was tentative. He felt that she was a woman good and true, for whom a true man might and ought to do good work, must, because she was all that.

He walked about, saying polite things to the platform, to the porters, to the roof, asking nothing but to get down to Lewes on the fool's errand that he wanted to fulfil, simply because, leaning out of a window in a fog, he had not been able to class a police-constable's act in the obvious way of his duty.

And Sexton Blake's instinct was true! For while he was pacing the platform, Miss Lennox was in the train, blessing Sexton Blake for the telegram that was taking her to the man she loved, yet quite unconscious of the deadly peril she was travelling towards.

When the train drew up at Lewes, there was just that little atmosphere of fog that makes stations always obscure.

Miss Helen Lennox clasped her bag, and put her pretty, fresh face out of the window, challenging fog and time. She did not know Dr Fleming, but she had the profoundest trust in Sexton Blake. She had his telegram in her hand as she leant out of the window.

And presently, towards the engaging, frank face, with its evident search in the questioning, blue eyes, there advanced a man. He came along the platform, peering into every face he passed. Twice he looked at Miss Helen Lennox in passing, and she noticed that he had the air of a doctor, and wondered if he was looking for her. She did not like the look of him. His beard was grey. His 'get up' was indiscussably good. His pince-nez were gold-rimmed. His hair was black; so also was his pointed beard. When he passed her the third time he paused.

'Excuse me,' he said, in the kind of silken tone that Miss Lennox recognised as belonging to Harley Street – 'excuse me! Sexton Blake wired me –'

'Oh, then you must be Dr Fleming?' said Miss Helen Lennox. 'Tell me, how is Horace?'

'He is getting on nicely,' replied the man; 'but we must have patience and calm. No excitement. Horace must not be fevered by any kind of emotion. Blake told you that, didn't he?'

'You are going to take me to see Horace, aren't you?' said the girl innocently.

'That is why I am here, my dear young lady,' replied the doctor. 'My motor-car is outside, and there is a porter who will take your valise.'

He handed her down to the platform with the florid kind of gesture that suited him, and led her to the exit.

THE NINTH CHAPTER

The Play of Two Shadows

Detective-Sergeant Plummer had none of the littleness that lends itself to belittling a great foe. He believed in making a big fall for a big man. And his view of Sexton Blake made him feel quite sure that the great detective would never dream of putting his head out of a window to look after a District Messenger Boy to whom he had entrusted telegrams, unless he was very much counting on the telegrams achieving something of importance.

For Plummer had eyes that a lynx might envy. And if Sexton Blake could see out of one corner of a closed eyelid, Plummer had a faculty for rapid judgment based on the half of a glance, that was quite worth a pair of field-glasses.

It is the aptitude for making decisive resolutions on the spur of a minute that has characterised the Nelsons and Napoleons of history. When Plummer felt Sexton Blake's mentality analysing and weighing-up his act in hypothecating the telegrams, it took him but the fraction of a second to realise that the incident might be developed to an end that would surprise Blake most disagreeably.

It was extremely improbable, argued the sergeant, that Blake would guess that his act of spying had been duly appreciated by the object of it. It would, therefore, be highly probable that Sexton Blake would follow him, and walk innocently into any trap prepared for him.

And the trap was there, ready to his hand, in those two telegrams. If Mr Plummer became Dr Fleming, and calmly decoyed Miss Helen Lennox from the train at Lewes, Sexton Blake would be sure to follow her, and in walking into the trap would never walk out.

For if there was one thing of which Detective-Sergeant Plummer was more sure than of any other, it was that the same planet could not any longer conveniently hold himself and Sexton Blake. One had to go, and Plummer meant to stay.

Moreover, Plummer's instinct was as true to criminality as Blake's was to honesty. He felt that if he could solve the riddle of Blake's dictate of a destination for Helen Lennox, he would fathom the causes that had first provoked the great detective to suspect him. He knew that Helen Lennox had had some love passages with Horace Jenkins. For a moment the thought crossed his mind that the coastguard might still be alive, and that *there* was the interpretation of all his trouble; but he put the thought away with a smile of disdain. The blow had been too sure: the sea too blanketed in fog to give up anything unconscious that it had gripped.

Yet, to solve Helen Lennox's destination, and her connection with Blake, appeared to him more and more as a mandate, the nearer he approached the post-office. Once there, he quickly passed the wire for Miss Lennox over the counter, and pocketed the other. Even if he learned nothing from Helen Lennox, he might learn a lot from Blake's method of acting when he found his purpose foiled. And the more he spoiled Blake's interest, the better he would be pleased. If Blake happened to 'die' in a quiet little cottage Plummer knew of near Lewes, the police might settle matters with Dr Fleming and Miss Lennox; and, whatever the police learned, Detective-Sergeant Plummer would have no difficulty in gathering up the threads of.

Plummer was never timorous of his own audacity. As, two hours after delivering Blake's telegram, he paced the platform at Victoria, and twice heard himself addressed as Dr Fleming, he grinned sardonically to himself, thinking how easy it was to impose a counterfeit presentiment on people by an air of likeness and manner, for he knew that Dr Fleming was at least two inches shorter and two inches broader than himself.

He scrutinised, with an eye alert as a hungry hawk's, every face that passed. It was with a sense of keen disappointment that he failed to remark anyone like Sexton Blake. The great detective's tall form was not easily lent to a disguise that would deceive the trained eyes looking out for it. But the only thing on the platform in any way out of the ordinary was a phenomenally stout and seedy parson, who seemed distinctly the worse for drink. He approached Mr Plummer once, and hiccoughed an interrogation at him.

'Doc-tor Fl-flem-ing, n'est-ce-pas?' he said.

The spurious Dr Fleming brushed him aside, with the large authoritative gesture of a man who had studied the complaint his interlocutor was obviously suffering from.

'That fellow was genuine enough to be Blake himself,' ruminated the sergeant as, suddenly swinging round, he noted the drunken one tenderly but firmly buttonholing the stationmaster. 'And,' he went on as he passed him again, with a sharp, piercing glance, 'his stomach is lopsided, and his nose is paste. It's Blake, for a ducat!'

Mr Plummer strolled up to the station-constable, and engaged him in earnest conversation. The constable, with a compeer in plain clothes, gently approached the garrulous parson, just as the eminent doctor was getting into his carriage, and the doors were being slammed to.

The garrulous one lurched against a constable, and reeled into the carriage after 'Dr Fleming'.

The bell for departure rang, and the 'doctor' made an imperceptible sign.

A minute later Mr Plummer had the satisfaction of seeing the man he believed to be Sexton Blake hauled from the carriage and taken into charge for being without a ticket. He leaned through the carriage window as the train glided past the platform, and watched the burly police-constable hustling the garrulous one garrulously along.

'It was overdone,' said the sergeant to himself, as he sank back in his seat. 'I should have thought Blake would have been finer than that. Anyhow, he'll be three or four hours later than I at Lewes, and that will enable me to prepare my little trap.'

Like all Mr Plummer's arrangements, his plan for disposing of Sexton Blake was distinguished by the kind of simplicity which, in avoiding any and every complex detail, makes detection a task of vanity led astray. With Miss Helen Lennox safely locked in Myrtle Cottage, five miles out of Lewes; with 'Dr Fleming' waiting quietly with his experienced bludgeon at the entry Sexton Blake would naturally choose after he had run down the trail (not too carefully to be covered), it would be curious if anything could stay the silent, swift, deadly blow. And when 'Dr Fleming' disappeared, and people found Miss Lennox alone in the house with the corpse of a seedy parson, Mr Plummer could await the results with equanimity, and even with interest.

Miss Lennox, looking out from the train at Lewes, knew, almost before he spoke, that the man in the fur coat, silk hat, and square-toed boots, with an open telegram in his hand, and peering through gold-rimmed glasses into each carriage, must be the Dr Fleming of Sexton Blake's telegram.

Moreover, he was as discreet as he was paternally urbane. For, after introducing himself, with the great detective's telegram for a card, he was quite particular about seeing the telegram Miss Lennox ought to have received.

A smart porter received Miss Lennox's luggage, at the 'doctor's' direction, and conveyed it to the motor-car waiting outside the station.

'But I thought he was at Newhaven?' protested Helen Lennox.

'So he was, my dear young lady,' the 'doctor' reassured her; 'but, in the interests you know of, we thought it better to transport him here.'

'Have we far to go?' asked Miss Lennox, as she followed the 'doctor' out of the station.

The 'doctor' observed that the porter was standing by the open car. He gave him a handsome tip.

'A mere five miles,' he said distinctly, 'along the road to Seaford.'

The porter, handing Miss Lennox into the tonneau, stood by while the 'doctor' mounted the driver's seat and started the machine. And there was certainly something like a grin on his face as the 'doctor' rapped out a quite unmedical expression when, in the first revolution of the wheels, there was a swift hiss, a sudden report, and the car lurched and came to a standstill.

Detective-Sergeant Plummer, descending from the car to examine the wheel, stared at the tyre like a man who had suddenly received a violent and painful blow. He knew the tyres had been all right five minutes before the train bringing Miss Lennox had arrived.

He had hired the machine from a good shop in Lewes about an hour and a half prior to Miss Lennox's arrival, and had taken it a spin to test it.

Yet now, in the fore nearside wheel was a puncture that could only have been made deliberately by a knife.

It was just the kind of accident he would have expected to occur had Sexton Blake been in Lewes.

Sergeant Plummer had no belief in miracles. And as he looked at the tyre, and the more he looked at it, the more conscious he became of the convincing sense of fear. An expert in make-up himself, he was more than adept in identifying it in anyone else. And he was intimately sure that neither at Victoria nor at Lewes had there been anyone who could have been Sexton Blake.

Yet he felt just as sure that the puncture in that wheel was the work of Sexton Blake as if he had seen him do it.

He turned to the porter.

'Has there been any tramp hanging, about here?' he asked. 'This tyre has been wilfully cut.'

'There was a lean-faced fellow, with a jaw like a rock, leaning against the machine as I put the luggage on,' answered the porter: 'but he cleared out as soon as he saw he wasn't wanted.'

'Ah!' sighed Plummer, and looked more thoughtful.

'Are there no cabs here?' he asked sharply, as he noted Miss Lennox had descended from the tonneau, and was looking at him with just the air of deliberate curiosity he did not wish to provoke.

'I dare say I can get you one,' said the porter, and he set off at a smart run, and vanished into a stable-yard two hundred yards down the street.

'A most extraordinary contretemps,' said the doctor, turning to Miss Lennox. 'A mean act of deliberate spite by someone who objects to people who use automobiles.'

'It does certainly seem like that,' said Miss Lennox, a little coldly. 'I wonder why it was done? The porter's description was so identifying, don't you think? "A lean-faced fellow, with a jaw like a rock" – that's what he said, isn't it? Well, do you know, it made me think at once of Mr Sexton Blake.'

'Yes, it would answer to him, now you mention it,' said the 'doctor', with superb assurance.

He was beginning to have a great respect for Miss Lennox.

'Don't you think,' she went on, with as level a look as ever Mr Plummer had had in his life, 'that it would be a good idea, since Mr Blake is to join us, to wait at a hotel till he comes?'

'By all means, if you like!' said Mr Plummer, with disarming promptitude.

He had eyelids like steel door-locks himself, and not a muscle of them so much as flickered as he confronted the girl's clear, unquestioning gaze.

Miss Lennox felt reassured, and a little bit conscious of appearing ungrateful. With the infernal artistry that was his, Mr Plummer was quick to divine it.

'Shall we telegraph to Blake that you have arrived, and prefer to remain at a hotel till he comes?' he said.

'Telegraph that I have arrived – yes,' she said, with her most gracious air. 'But I'll go straight out to see – er – your patient at once. Mr Blake will know the address, of course, so he can follow on there.'

They went on to the telegraph-office, and Miss Lennox wrote out the wire. The porter met them as they came out.

'I've got the cab, lady,' he said

He led them out to the landau, and again pocketed a handsome tip, as he handed them in. There was a waggon piled with bales on the other side of the landau, blocking the view from the window.

'Tell him to go to Myrtle Villa, the Seaford Road,' said the 'doctor', and look here, my dear fellow, just wheel up that motor-car into the yard, and let Refton – you know Refton's shop – know that it is here. Tell him, Dr Fleming will be obliged if he will have the tyre looked to, and the car ready this evening.'

'I'll see to it at once, doctor,' said the porter.

He passed round the back of the cab, to the other side of the waggon, and next minute a man with a great overcoat, a bowler hat, and a flowing black beard put his face in at the window.

'Where did you say to go, guv'nor?' he asked.

'Myrtle Villa!' shouted Plummer, feeling that these repeated delays were getting on his nerves.

'All right! I ain't deaf!' growled the driver, and proceeded to hoist himself on to the box.

As the landau drew out of the yard, the 'doctor', looking out of the window, noticed the porter, with his broad back towards him, stolidly wheeling the motor-car past the waggon, towards the station-sheds.

He suppressed a sigh of relief, and turned to Miss Lennox.

It never occurred to him for a single second that as the train by which he had come had been switched into a siding to let pass the royal special, the fact could possibly have anything to do with the man on the box now in front of him. He thought he had sidetracked, at any rate for a few hours, the ingenuity of the great detective he was fighting. Keen and logical though he was, his science was not so foreseeing as that of Sexton Blake. And though he had divined his enemy at the station, it did not strike him that it was because his enemy wished to be divined, wished to be given in charge, wished 'Dr Fleming' to think him safe out of the way, when he should swing past him in the royal express, in order to arrive an hour before him at Lewes, and, dressed as a porter, open the door for 'Dr Fleming', open the door for Miss Lennox two hours later, and with one clean, quick dig of the knife, render useless the motor-car, and make necessary the cab and its quick-change driver.

There were things not dreamed of in Detective-Sergeant Plummer's scheme of philosophy, that came into Sexton Blake's as a simple illustration of instinct. Which was why the great detective was on the box of the cab, in whose inside was Mr Plummer. Sexton Blake felt that he had the whip hand.

THE TENTH CHAPTER

A Startling Surprise for the Sergeant

Myrtle Villa was charmingly situated for the purpose to which Plummer intended to put it.

It was slightly back from the road, on the outskirts of a long limb of the downs, sufficiently protected in its isolation by an agreeable garden, and safeguarded from loneliness by the view of two red-roofed farms.

Yet the aspect of it was just too completely suited to the sergeant's perspective, to supply a kindred liking to anyone not having the same point of view. It was a noticeable point in the mentality of Plummer, that though he allowed, in his plans, the possibility of others having the cunning to appreciate his wickedness, he himself was incapable of correctly gauging or providing against the power that reposes in the serene gaze of innocence.

It was this lack in him that made Sexton Blake the stronger man. Had Blake been pledged to crime, he would never have dreamed of decoying such a woman as Helen Lennox into a place that could disturb the tranquillity of her outlook.

Miss Lennox, as she stepped from the cab, felt a distinct aversion to entering the remote pretty villa. No one could have been more paternal, genial, and correct than her companion. Yet the glance she gave at him through her eyelashes, did not reassure her. She wished she had stopped at Lewes till Sexton Blake had arrived. But she was a girl of spirit, and she resented the effect of alarm a mere impression could impose.

She signed to the driver to bring in her valises, and followed the 'doctor' through the gate and up the gravel path to the house.

The door was open. The sergeant had seen to external appearances before he had met his guest at the station.

'We are not afraid of wandering tramps here,' he said urbanely. 'There is always someone about the farms to right and left.'

He turned to the driver, who had placed the two portmanteaux in the hall.

'You had better wait, my man,' he said; 'I have a visit to make in the neighbourhood.'

'Now, Miss Lennox,' he went on cheerily, as the driver slouched down to the gate, 'if you will come upstairs, I will show you your room, and send a nurse to bring you to our patient. But I must see him first.'

He preceded her up the stairs, never noticing that his gloved hand was wiping a continuous little train of dust off the banisters.

But Miss Lennox noticed it. She had hardly crossed the threshold, before her woman-sense told her that she was not in a house where a sick man was being attended by two trained nurses.

Detective-Sergeant Plummer was a very capable opponent to anything in the shape of a fellow criminal or a great detective. But he had never had the opportunity of studying what a good woman either thought about her house or expected other people to think about it. His acquaintance with Rail Street had made him somewhat careless about dust. That Miss Lennox should find reason to suspect him because the house was undusted, would have struck him at once as unreasonable, if it had occurred to him. But it had not. He was simply unaware that the house was remarkable from that point of view.

Yet to Miss Lennox the fact was at once elemental and clinching. If her companion was Dr Fleming, and this villa contained two trained nurses and a patient, there would not have been a speck of dust on the banister, the hall would have been brushed, and the mirror in the hat-rack, as the knob of the hall-door, would have been shiningly innocent of all reproach.

But since none of these things were, therefore –

The 'doctor' was standing at an open door, bowing Miss Lennox into the room beyond.

'Why, the windows are all barred!' cried Miss Lennox, as acknowledging the 'doctor's' courtesy with a pleasant smile, she passed into the room, her hand obviously seeking something in the reticule hanging at her wrist.

Detective-Sergeant Plummer had meant to simply and unassumingly lock the door on Miss Lennox the moment she entered, and to leave her there till cold and hunger should make her an amenable witness. But he was feeling so pleased with his characterisation of Dr Fleming that he could not refrain from the pleasure of standing near Miss Lennox for another moment and receiving another bright smile from her for his reassuring words.

As he looked at her erect, graceful figure, set off so daintily in furs, and thought of that chin with its tilt of serene power, and the flashing graciousness of lips and eyes, George Plummer felt that he might do worse than console Helen Lennox for the loss of Horace Jenkins.

He glided towards the window with all the ingratiating assurance of a cobra.

Then – he never could recollect afterwards how it had happened – he was standing alone by the window, with Miss Lennox between him and the door. But a Miss Lennox of quite a different order in the scheme of dream-beings. A Miss Lennox, mocking and glacial in eye and lip, tense in figure, but tense with the drawn-back, held-up muscles of a lioness crouching to spring. And in Miss Lennox's right hand, Detective-Sergeant Plummer noticed the mother-of-pearl butt of a silver-plated revolver. He also noticed the free, businesslike fashion of a Texan cowboy which distinguished the easy grace and alertness of the carelessly-hanging arm. None knew better than the sergeant how to distinguish between the carelessness which betrays ignorance, and the carelessness which illustrates the quiet confidence in proved strength.

Miss Lennox moved quietly backwards to the door.

'I would let your pockets alone,' she said, in a cold, metallic note; and the sergeant, feeling rather than seeing that that infernal little silver-plated toy was pointing directly at his stomach, let his hand glide back to 'attention'.

Miss Lennox smiled, and, leaning against the edge of the half-closed door, looked the 'doctor' up and down, with eyes into whose scrutiny a puzzled look of reminiscence dawned strugglingly.

'Who are you?' she said, at the end of a minute. 'I'm sure I've seen you before.'

'You passed me on the steps the day you visited Sexton Blake,' said the sergeant, with an aplomb that did him credit, considering that every emotion in him was asnarl with rage, and every fibre in his brain ajar with speculating how he might circumvent that confounded toy, and make the she-thing holding it pay for the lesson she was administering his vanity.

'Ah,' sighed Miss Lennox, 'then since you are Dr Fleming, perhaps you will reassure me by telling me the name of your patient, and the conditions under which you received him?'

'I must really protest against the prolongation of this comedy!' cried the doctor, with an air that many a man, even in Harley Street, would have given his carriage for.

He took a step forward, but paused irresolutely as the fair wrist almost imperceptibly was lifted an inch.

'You see,' said Miss Lennox, with a fine smile, 'you forget that a châtelaine so accustomed to governing a house as myself would remark that the stair-rails had not been dusted for at least three months. Perhaps, Dr Fleming' – she emphasised the words with a subtle maliciousness that made the sergeant squirm – 'you will be good enough to give two vigorous peals at that bell by the fireplace on your right. It should surely bring at least one of the trained nurses here.'

'My dear lady,' said the 'doctor,' with a sublime air of patience, 'do consider the patient!'

Miss Lennox laughed – quite a pleasant little tinkling laugh of sheer amusement.

'You are very superb,' she said, in an airy bantering tone, that, despite his control, brought a sudden scowl of rage to the sergeant's face.

'I will go and call the nurse,' he said, recovering himself on the instant, and taking a hasty stride forward.

Miss Lennox's revolver flashed suddenly into full view – level, deadly still, a pretty and most precise argument.

'You will ring that bell. Dr Fleming,' she cooed, 'or I shall reluctantly be compelled to spoil the beautiful make-up of that nose.'

The 'doctor' shrugged his shoulders, simulated a sudden attitude of listening, and as equally a sudden assurance of vindication.

'Ah, at last!' he laughed. 'Sexton Blake will answer for me in person!'

He waved his hand pleasantly towards the door.

Miss Helen Lennox might not, despite the inimitable force of the acting, have been taken in, had her quick ears not perceived what sounded like a smothered chuckle outside the door.

A wild suspicion invaded her that she was making a fool of herself. The little details that a moment ago seemed such a mass of evidence suddenly became little details again, incoherent, and provocative of that chuckle from behind the door.

For a moment she wavered. Her hand fell to her side, and her eyes glanced through the half open door on to the landing.

In the same moment Plummer sprang on her, snatched her revolver from her grasp, and, seizing her waist, dragged her into the room.

'Ha, ha!' he mocked. 'Sexton Blake shall answer for me in person!'

'With pleasure!' said a voice, that the sergeant knew; and, to his amazement, the cabman put his head round the door.

'Sexton Blake!' cried Helen Lennox; and, quick as thought, flung herself on her revolver, now pointed from the 'doctor's' hand at that unexpected head. Her action sent the toy spinning into the fireplace.

'Hands up!' cried Sexton Blake, springing into the room, and tearing off his beard and wig with one hand, while with the other he presented a Service revolver at the sergeant's head.

But the sergeant was a man of resource when on his mettle. And, in answer to the challenge, he simply picked up Miss Lennox, and flung her full into Sexton Blake's arms, and dived for the door.

Before the impact of so fair a burden, the great detective reeled backwards, his revolver cracked, and a bullet whizzing past Plummer's ear splashed a mirror opposite with a thousand stars.

The sergeant raced for the door, but Blake's long leg shot out in a cunning crook, mingled with the 'doctor's' long fur-coat, and Plummer went headlong on his face. Before he could move, the heavy butt of Blake's revolver fell with a tap on his temple that reduced him to a sudden stillness.

Then a pair of bracelets were snapped round his swiftly upturned wrists, and Sergeant Plummer, dazed and almost stupefied with rage, found himself dragged into the room, and planted with a jerk against the wall.

'There, my dear Miss Lennox, it's all over, and you must not distress yourself!' said Sexton Blake consolingly, as he looked to the fair girl, who, in the moment of reaction, stood trembling at his side.

'I heard all that passed,' he went on. 'You behaved with a tact and a force that filled me with admiration. I knew from my messenger that someone had intercepted my telegram, so I took the precaution of arriving on the scene myself.'

'Do you know,' said Miss Lennox, with a laugh that was a trifle hysterical, 'it was because I thought I recognised you in the railway porter, that my suspicions were first aroused. Then, when you vanished, it never struck me that you could have been clever enough to so suddenly reappear as the cabman, especially as I thought I saw you wheeling away the motor-car.'

'Ah,' laughed Blake, 'you don't do yourself justice. If you had not observed the incident of the dust, you would now be locked in this room, and our bungler here – for, after all, he has bungled shockingly – would be probably lying in wait for me with his pet bludgeon.'

'His pet bludgeon!' echoed Miss Lennox, turning pale. 'Do you mean he is the assassin of –'

'That is about his measure,' said Blake. 'We shall establish his identity presently, when he is safe under lock and key. You see, the window is barred,' he went on, drawing her over to the other side of the room. 'Not a word of Horace's name,' he whispered. 'Ah, what was that?' This last, as a sudden sharp 'click!' resounded through the room.

He whipped round in time to see the 'doctor' on his feet, with his hands free.

For the sergeant was a man of no common force. The moment Blake's back was turned, he had knitted his elbows into his ribs, and, with a sudden sharp jerk of his wrists, broken the linking bracelets.

Blake had not the time to take a stride before the sergeant was outside the door, had slammed it to, and locked it on his prisoners.

It was in vain that Blake sprang at it and shook it. The door was solid, the lock also, and the bolts, top and bottom, had been carefully placed there by Plummer's own hands.

It was characteristic of the sergeant that, during the struggle and after it, he had uttered no word. Nor did he do so now. He sat on the stairs, calmly produced his police key, and unlocked the broken steel cuffs from his wrists.

Then, immovable as the Sphinx, he reflected for a full five minutes.

He had not set out with any intention of wreaking hurt on Helen Lennox; at least, not more than would suffice to unlock her secrets. But, after his late experience, he felt against the young girl a bitter and unassuageable venom. He wanted to repay her for all the humiliation she had brought on him, and especially for his fall at Blake's hands. He strolled round the furnished villa, appreciating the flimsy character of the furniture.

Then leisurely he proceeded to pile up outside the door various articles, such as mattresses, light chairs, and other easily combustible material.

He repeated the process in the hall immediately below the staircase.

Then going upstairs, he shut all the windows, and turned on all the gas pipes, and retired to the first landing till the intruding odour of gas warned him that the rooms above were well filled.

He withdrew to the hall, placed a match to the pile below the staircase, assured himself that the flame had well caught, then as leisurely and unconcernedly as if he had been going on a holiday, he made his way through the front door, and locking it behind him, pocketed the key.

Then he mounted the box of the waiting cab, turned the horse's head towards Seaford, and drove away at an easy pace.

It was an hour later, that, on boarding the London express at the little seaside town, he heard that the fire-engines had been called out half an hour previously to a cottage that was ablaze from top to bottom, three miles down the Lewes Road.

He seemed to derive considerable relish from the view of the flames, as he leant out of his speeding carriage, and grinned sardonically on the ruined villa.

'Now for the brat and his dog,' he muttered, as he leant back behind his paper; 'and then my tracks are clear.'

But he was counting without destiny, and the force of his own spite, overreaching himself in his malignant joy, as he had done in his fiendish work. Had he simply left the house to burn, it is probable that Sexton Blake and Miss Lennox must have perished in the flames.

For when the great detective, having exhausted, in vain, every effort to force the door, had turned to the window, it was to find as little hope of escape that way as the other. Not only was the frame solidly nailed down, but even when Blake had wrecked that with an iron rod, torn from the bedstead, he was confronted by seven steel bars, closely clamped into the masonry, and yielding not the fraction of an inch to his frenzied attack on them.

At the end of ten minutes, he leant against the wall, with face pale and rigid, torn between grief for Miss Lennox, and great wrath with himself; for he felt convinced, had felt convinced all along, that Plummer was preparing some trap for him to fall into; and now, by sheer resource and audacity, the sergeant had wrested victory out of defeat, and trapped him, Sexton Blake, as he might have trapped any boy from the school.

'Don't trouble so, Mr Blake,' said Miss Lennox, coming to him, and placing her hands on his. 'Someone is sure to be passing whose attention we can attract.'

'You don't know him,' said Blake sombrely.

He had divined well enough the devilish plan of the sergeant, and it scarcely needed the confirmation of the gas now assailing his nostrils to assure him that Plummer meant neither of them to have a loophole of escape.

Miss Lennox smelt it, too, and her face grew singularly calm, as she fronted the detective with serene, shining eyes.

'I understand,' she said simply. 'But I do not think that bad man counts on what Heaven may do.'

She had hardly spoken, when a roar of exploding gas deafened their ears for a moment.

'The house will be an oven in five minutes,' said Blake, in a tone of despair.

'See,' said Miss Lennox, 'the explosion has broken down the wall there by the window-corner!'

Sexton Blake sprang at it. It was true. In a corner of the room by the window, a great rent showed in the parting wall. He seized the iron rod he had already used to wreck the window-frame, and attacked the gap frenziedly. The cheap brick and plaster fell about him like gravel, and in three minutes he had pierced a way large enough to admit a passage into the adjoining room.

Plummer's excess of caution to ensure the burning of the staircase had stripped the room of anything burnable but the bare walls, and these the fire had not yet achieved sufficient volume to attack seriously. He forced a way through, and handed Miss Lennox after him. In a couple of strides he was at the window. Fifteen feet below was a flower-bed. On the landing without the flames were rising in an ever-increasing roar.

Sexton Blake tore off his long overcoat, slashed it into strips, knotted them together, and in two seconds was lowering Miss Lennox out of the window. As she reached the ground the flames came with a rush, leaping through the door behind him. There was no time for finding anything to which to attach his rope.

Sexton Blake shinned out on to the window-sill, gathered himself together, and leapt clear out into the air. He landed, light as a cat, in the centre of the flower-bed.

'Bravo!' cried Miss Lennox, clapping her hands.

'Come!' said Blake shortly. 'We've got to follow our friend the doctor, or at least forestall him, for if he sets foot on board the *Stella* –'

'But he doesn't know Horace is there,' protested Miss Lennox, panting along at his side.

'There is no telling what he knows,' answered Blake, as he hurried towards the farm, where people were already gathering, viewing the burning villa.

It was two hours later that Sexton Blake handed Miss Lennox on board the *Stella*, and gave her into charge of the genuine Dr Fleming. And though the shining in her eyes as she looked on Horace was some consolation for the man in him, it left the great detective sore and mortified.

And as he got into the special prepared for him at Newhaven, he said to himself: 'Mr Plummer commences to annoy me. It has become a personal question.'

Then he lit his pipe, leaned back, closed his eyes, and, as the train raced through the night, Sexton Blake set himself quietly to find the solution of the personal question.

THE ELEVENTH CHAPTER

A Straight Lead and a Foul Blow

Sexton Blake was not the man to let grass grow under his feet when he meant to march. He had not digested his breakfast the following morning before there emerged from the alley-way giving from his rooms into Baker Street, a ruddy-faced stooping cab-driver.

It was a disguise that had often served him a good turn, and one which he did and lived up to as one likes hot muffins done and lived up to.

For two days he prowled round from mews to mews, from rank to rank, asking the same unvarying question.

'Have any of you chaps taken on a fellow with black hair, small, pointed black beard, carrying a small kit-bag and a coat, who lately went to Charing-Cross Station at eleven in the morning? Bilked me, 'e did!' Sexton Blake would wind up.

And at last he was rewarded by the information that such a man had been taken at a corresponding hour from Bloomfield Road, W.

Then the slouching cab-driver vanished, and Sexton Blake, sitting again in his room at Baker Street, listened with a peaceful smile to the report of Slim, his trusty searcher of ancient registers and other public documents. A quarter of an hour later the detective was on his way to Paddington, where he boarded a train for Windsor. Arrived there, he went straight for the parish church, sought the sacristan, and obtained the registers of marriages for the year 1871, and turning to the month of April, ran his finger down the columns.

'By Jove,' he murmured, as he came to a vacant place, 'old Slim is right!' There the thing faced him – a space for an entry vacant, with filled spaces above and below. He took out his lens and examined it.

'Chemically washed out!' he murmured. 'I wonder – I wonder! It was smart of Slim to spot it!'

The old sacristan had hobbled near him and was watching him with interest.

'Hope there's nothing wrong, sir?' he said. 'There was a gent here two days ago who brought the parson's permission to see the register, and I don't say as I didn't leave him a minute. Most benevolent old gent, 'e was, too, for sure.'

'Have you been here long?' asked Sexton Blake.

'All my life, sir,' was the answer. 'And I be fifty-eight now. Jenkins is my name, sir, son of Jenkins, of the Eagle Arms.'

'Indeed,' said Blake carelessly, although he felt to his fingertips the sudden thrill, the rush of blood the words evoked. 'Well,' he went on, 'you must have been here when this entry was made, between April 18th and April 20th, 1871.'

'Eighteen seventy-one?' echoed Jenkins. 'That was the year my sister Maria was married, sir! Pretty girl she was, too. Married a young spark, name of Audley – 'Orace Audley, if I rec'lect right. But he weren't no good, sir, and he died young. I did 'ear tell as a boy was born to 'em. But they left these parts, and never came back. And where they be now, I couldn't tell.'

'Is that your sister Maria?' asked Blake, suddenly thrusting under the old man's eyes the photograph of Mrs Jenkins he had hypothecated at Fairlight.

'Well, now, I do declare!' said the sacristan. 'That be 'er, sure enough, master. A bit aged, mebbe, but 'er. Oh, my, yes – it's 'er! Where might she be now, sir?'

'I'll let you know about that presently,' said Sexton Blake, as he returned the photo to his pocket, and glanced at his watch. 'I've got to get the next up-train, and have only just time.'

He pressed a coin into the old fellow's hand, and hurried out, while the sacristan busied himself in putting away the registers. They neither of them had noticed that a sandy-haired man had been standing in the shadow of the doorway while they spoke, and that as Blake declared he must catch his train, he had hurried away in the direction of the station.

Pedro, left to himself 'on trust', outside the church, had noticed it, and Blake, as he called him to heel, wondered vaguely what made his ruff so bristly. But he hardly gave it a thought, for his mind was dancing to one refrain.

'At last – at last!' The baffling clue was linked up. Horace Jenkins was Horace Audley, son of the brother of the murdered earl. The two men whose death had been engineered for the same day, had been destined to leave open the earldom. For whom – for whom?

Suddenly the detective stopped dead in the road, his eyes agleam.

He pulled from his pocket-book the enlarged photograph of the dead earl and scanned its features, side by side with those of Horace 'Jenkins'. As one in a dream, he remembered the scene as Plummer had stood with his back to him in that chamber of death, and his vague wonder, ever present, as to where he had seen Plummer's face before. Could Plummer be the representative of that Australian branch lost so long ago? The thought galvanised him into action, and he raced to the station, threw himself into the telegraph-office, and wrote the following telegram.

PLEASE TRACE ME DESCENT OF ONE AUDLEY, LANDING AUSTRALIA PROBABLY BEFORE 1860. LATER PROBABLY CONNECTED WITH ONE PLUMMER. UTMOST URGENCY. – SEXTON BLAKE.

This he copied on two different forms, and sent one to each of the chief of the police in Sydney, Melbourne, and Adelaide. Then he strolled into the station, selected a carriage in the waiting train, threw in his coat and rug, and walked to the bookstall to take a paper.

He was hardly gone a minute, but it was time for the sandy-haired man who had been standing in the church to pass his carriage-door, dexterously insert something between the seat and the cushion where Blake's coat lay, and pass unconcernedly on.

Next moment the train whistled, and Sexton Blake jumped into his carriage, with Pedro at heel.

As the train went out, some sense of magnetism drew the detective's eyes to a stranger standing stock still on the platform. Their gazes crossed, and it did not need the malicious triumph in the eyes of the sandy-haired man to tell Sexton Blake that he was gazing on Detective-Sergeant Plummer.

But that look puzzled him. It had been so malevolently sure. It was clear enough that Plummer had been shadowing him. Why was he not shadowing him still? He could have nothing to triumph over in the former. Was he anticipating some triumph by remaining behind?

'Shut up, Pedro! You're a nuisance!' – this to the dog, who was obstinately butting his nose at his master's thigh, trying to worm his way beneath. To Sexton Blake's surprise Pedro paid no attention to the command, but, with a distinct growl, and with his ruff now erect, redoubled his efforts.

A cold chill, as of death, suddenly ran through Sexton Blake's veins as the significance of that smile and the dog's action linked themselves together. He flung Pedro to the end of the carriage, and gingerly lifted the seat.

There, slender, not three inches long, but sinister beyond expression, lay a small time-fuse dynamite cartridge.

He took the thing of death in his fingers – with a shudder to think what might have happened to the whole train had Pedro taken it in his strong teeth – and, opening the window, waited; then, as the bridge flew under them, hurled it far into mid-stream.

He was conscious as he did so that on the road-bridge opposite, a large automobile was amusing its owner by racing the train. He watched it idly, vaguely, till it drew away in advance, and was lost in a curve of the road.

'At any rate,' he murmured, 'I have the start of him now.'

Then he drew Pedro's head on to his knee, and thanked the dog in that mute way of touch and glance that needs no words. As Paddington drew near, he grew possessed of an insatiate anxiety to get at the next news from Tinker. The boy had telegraphed the night before, 'Trailing', and Sexton Blake knew that once on the scent, Tinker was hard to beat, and impossible to throw off.

The train was hardly at the platform before he was out of it, and in a hansom and bowling along to Baker Street. He paused a moment before mounting to his rooms to turn Pedro in to his quarters and his dinner; then, running upstairs, he saw the desired yellow envelope on his table and tore it open.

GREAT WESTERN – 8.30 – ARRIVAL TONIGHT. COMPLETE CONFIRMATION AND HISTORY. [he read aloud]

In his eagerness, he had not noticed that a motor-car had drawn up behind as his hansom stopped, nor noticed either that as he sprang up the stairs a foot as swift as his own, but noiseless as a cat's, came up in his rear.

But now that the relaxation from the tense, cruel tension of six days had come, there came with it that strange acuteness of hearing which is the concomitant of sudden relief. A divination of a hostile presence was on him, and with a swift gesture he turned.

But even as he turned he saw swinging down on him a curious, flexible life-preserver. He ducked his head, but he was too late. The blow fell with a slogging, mortal weight, crushing him to earth, whirling him into illimitable abysses of blackness, through which as he tumbled there peered the malevolent eyes and devilish, triumphant smile of the yellow-haired man of Windsor. Then everything went out suddenly.

Plummer snatched the telegram and pocketed it, then bent over the prostrate man.

But a puffing as of many grampuses drew his attention to the door, through which Sexton Blake's landlady was panting her way to demand the meaning of the stranger's intrusion. But before she could say a word, the cloth was whipped off the table and thrown over her head, she was bundled into a corner, and Plummer, after a moment's hesitation, turned and darted down the stairs, slamming to the street door behind him, just as Pedro, down below, lifted his nose and gave vent to a long, melancholy howl.

THE TWELFTH CHAPTER

A Crafty Capture

As the Western express drew up punctually to its billed 8.30, at Paddington, Tinker's eager face would assuredly have been a mark that Sexton Blake would not have missed.

Nor did it escape the attention of a gentleman who had been solemnly pacing the platform for some ten minutes before the arrival of the train – a gentleman dressed in immaculate broadcloth, with fur overcoat thrown open to reveal a large wealth of watchchain, and a chest whose sustained throw forward simply hummed with consequential self-esteem. If more than that, coupled with the silk-hat and the deliberate strut of a turkey-cock, were needed to convince the casual observer that he were privileged to gaze on one of the bigwigs of Harley Street, one need only to seek verification in the face.

There, trained benevolence met the eyes. From gold-rimmed pince-nez to tilted chin effulged the self-assurance of an indestructible arrogance, enframed in side-whiskers. Decidedly a very eminent specialist.

Tinker took him in with one flash of the eyes, as the crowd, separating before his stately march, brought him into the lad's vision. It had not required more than one glance up the platform and one down to assure Tinker that his friend and master was not there.

The lad was not going to waste time by waiting. He argued immediately that had Sexton Blake wanted to be there, he would have been there on the tick of the half-hour.

He was therefore swinging away, when a hand, ponderous, fraternal, fell on his shoulder.

Tinker turned to look into the face of what he had mentally classed as a Harley Street goldbug. His heart went like a stone into his boots, and that strange chill of premonition, which is at once so imperious and so inexplicable, held him for a second in its grip.

'You are Mr Tinker?' asked the voice of the stranger huskily – the eminent specialist was evidently suffering from a post-nasal catarrh.

'What's up?' said Tinker, coming to the point, and bracing tight the small of that young back of his, which had already sustained so many disagreeable surprises.

'This is your telegram, I believe?' queried the 'doctor', unfolding the flimsy sheet before the lad's eyes, which gathered in the words he had sent, so full of hope, a few hours ago.

'Yes,' said Tinker, becoming more laconic. 'What's wrong with the guv'nor?'

'You have evidently not seen the evening papers,' pursued the doctor, in an unctuously soothing tone. 'But you look a brave boy.'

'Look here, guv'nor,' said Tinker, stirred to brutality, 'stow bedside manners! I ain't accustomed to them, and they make me ill. What's wrong with Sexton Blake, and why are you here?'

For answer, the doctor, with a majestic air of injured dignity, silently handed Tinker a copy of an evening paper, folded down to bring into relief but the one column. Tinker cast his eyes on it, and his lips shut like a vice.

'Attempted assassination of Mr Sexton Blake!' ran the headline, heavily leaded.

His gaze devoured line after line, taking in the landlady's account of seeing a stranger follow Mr Blake cautiously upstairs, of going up after him, of finding her master prone on the floor, of her indignation at being enveloped by the cloth, of how she escaped and sent at once for a doctor, and so on.

He read on, his breath suspended, till his eyes riveted on the last paragraph.

'Unfortunately, the doctor can hold out no hope of his recovery; nor, alas! can one desire it, for, if he live, that mighty intellect which so long has been the terror of criminals must ever remain useless, senile, imbecile. We understand the patient has been removed to the house of the surgeon who is to perform the operation of trepanning...'

Sexton Blake an imbecile! The station platform seemed to Tinker to suddenly stand on end and hit out at him. He reeled, and as the platform subsided into its familiar attitude, Tinker found himself in the refreshment-room, and the doctor, like a benignant genius, bending over him and urging him to take a drink of the coffee.

'We will add a little restorative,' said the doctor, as the crowd looked on, feeling how nice it must be to be in such eminent hands.

The doctor selected from a small case a tiny, silver-topped bottle, and measured some five or six drops carefully into the coffee.

'Now, my boy, take this. Your friend has need of you,' said the doctor, in his impressive tones.

The words acted on Tinker like a whip. Here he was fainting like a woman, while Sexton Blake was still unavenged. He almost snatched the cup from the doctor's hand, gulped down its contents with a wry face, and, unresistingly yielding himself to the firm, friendly pressure on his arm, allowed himself to be conducted to the private electric motor-car standing against the platform kerb. The doctor insisted on him taking a seat in the covered back.

'I could not wait for my chauffeur,' he said, 'and it seemed so urgent that you should come at once to your friend, that I brought the car myself.'

Tinker felt himself pushed in, and next moment the car, guided by the doctor's hands, was gliding through a sympathetic murmur out of the station yard.

It went slowly at first, hooting its way through the fogbound night till it got into Edgware Road, and turning suddenly to the left, glided at growing speed full north.

Then, and not till then, did the slightest doubt assail Tinker's mind. He had been as a man who, having walked a road a hundred times, one day, in a reverie, strays unconsciously homewards along a parallel route, and only finds his mistake when he discovers that he is trying to open a strange door with his latchkey.

'Harley Street goldbug', Tinker had sized the platform stranger to be. When the stranger introduced himself he had only confirmed Tinker's pre-estimation of him; and, since of all deception self-deception, especially when innocent, is the most obdurate and blinding, all that had since occurred but served to add testimony to the first impression. So Tinker had mounted the car, in the tranquil conviction that the Harley Street goldbug was naturally going to take him to Harley Street.

But when the Harley Street goldbug turned from his natural route, and suddenly raced north instead of east, Tinker felt as if he had been plunged into an iced bath and plucked out by his hair.

He had a rapidity in inference and deduction, a lucidity in grouping, weighing, and judging details that was as remarkable as Sexton Blake's.

The doctor hadn't given a name; he had produced no authority; he had given him medicated coffee, and had simply carried him off on the top of his natural emotions.

Was he a doctor at all? Wasn't the part acted – or obviously acted – unless the man were pompous-mad? Was he not Sexton Blake's assailant? Was he not Plummer?

In thirty seconds Tinker had put Plummer and the doctor side by side in his mental vision, stripped the disguise, and established the identity.

He looked out of the car. They were whirling down Maida Vale at twenty miles an hour amid curses and cries that were swallowed up in the dense white mist.

It was impossible to jump; but it was possible to climb round to the driving-seat, blow out Plummer's brains, and take charge of the car.

He gripped the edge of the front panel, and paused. A sudden surge of sleepiness had welled up on his brain. The medicated coffee! He was drugged. The thought flashed through his brain like a sword-point cutting through the maze of the intolerable drowsiness.

The next moment Tinker had bent forward, and two minutes later the doctor's rug was dropped silently out into the flying night.

But the remedy was later than the effect, and, despite all effort, the doctor's drug gained more and more on the lad's control, and by the time the car, circling round Elgin Avenue, dropped its speed and drew into Castellan Road, Tinker was lying back, deprived of all sense of consciousness as of surroundings.

The car drew along gently, noiseless as a cat, through the muffled streets; and, turning out of Grave Street, stopped at the gate of No. 13, Rail Street. Not a soul was in sight, as the doctor opened the folding gates, wheeled the car in, shut to the gates, and, mounting the seat again, guided the car into a coach-house hollowed out of the building immediately underneath his own bedroom.

Then lifting Tinker out, he bore him through a side door into the house, passed through the room where we first saw Mr Marsden, into a room overlooking the canal, and laid the boy on a sofa. With movements at once easily deliberate and methodical, he took a stout though thin cord, bound Tinker's ankles tightly together, then in and through the binding cord he lashed another cord, to the end of which was attached an 80-lb. weight.

It was characteristic of the man that during the whole time he had not even removed his hat or gloves, and that to anyone entering, he would have presented the same tranquil appearance of pomposity as he had done on the platform at Paddington. His task completed, he looked down on the unconscious Tinker reflectively.

'With Blake a drivelling imbecile for life, and you, my lad, reposing in canal slime, I think that George Marsden Plummer may congratulate himself on having done a good day's work.'

He drew off his gloves, and, throwing them aside, went through Tinker's pockets, till they were bare of everything. He piled the result on a small table, and proceeded to scrutinise them till he came to a small memorandum-book. Running his eyes through this, he suddenly laughed, softly, sardonically, as he realised how very nearly he had been too late. For the book contained his full record, the family history with dates which established a convincing and damning argument for showing George Marsden Plummer as the one person who could benefit by the disappearance of the Earl of Sevenoaks and his heir Horace Jenkins.

He left the other details on the table, and, taking the memorandum book, passed into his study, opened his safe, and threw it in. He regarded the contents for a moment doubtfully, shrugged his shoulders, and closed the safe with the cryptic remark: 'Time to make a bonfire of that when I add to it the clues Sexton Blake has in his safe.'

He laughed softly, the same quiet, devilish, sardonic laugh, as he proceeded to divest himself of his disguise, and check off, aloud, the clues Blake might have.

'Discounting the tide, and admitting the sagacity of the dog,' he said, 'he has a glove, a button, the golden beard, a boot-heel mould, two railway tickets, a pair of my gloves, and – I wonder what he did with that time-fuse cartridge? Ah, of course, heaved it into the river! That would be the flashing-point in mid-air that puzzled me as I motored over the Windsor bridge. Well, now to return to duty.

'Let me check the points,' he went on. 'First to Scotland Yard to get permission to link up Blake's case with the Audley case. They will give me charge all right, which will put me in possession of poor, drivelling Blake's rooms, and safe. Second, to verify, by a personal visit, Blake's condition. Third, to put in formal claim with proofs from Mr Marsden to Silas and Fry, for discovering the heir to the Sevenoaks title. Formal recognition will follow as a matter of course. Fourth, to attend the day after tomorrow the remand appearance of Jostle before the Sevenoaks Bench. Fifth, to close my professional career by proving the assassin of Sevenoaks, Jenkins, Blake, and his brat, to be Mr Marsden, of Rail Street – disappeared. That, I think, will make a sensation. Well, I have worked hard. But an earldom with sixty thousand a year is worth all that.'

By this time he stood dressed as his unconscious associates at Scotland Yard knew him.

He entered the room where Tinker lay, and examined him closely.

'He'll keep till I come back,' he muttered. 'The drug will work for at least ten hours.'

Then he passed out, and, locking all the doors behind him, crossed the garden to the corner giving on Grave and Rail Streets, and pressing the button in the panel, glided through into the fog-bound night.

Quarter of an hour later he was seated in a cab crawling towards Scotland Yard.

It was four hours later that he returned, not too well content with himself. The chief at Scotland Yard had, in fact, seemed distinctly cold, and had not received his proposition to take on the Blake case with the ardour he had anticipated.

'We have other men, Plummer,' he had said, 'and we have given you a free hand in the Audley affair; yet hitherto you have not thought fit to confide in me what you are doing. However, I will leave the matter open for two days. If, in that time, before Jostle appears, in fact, you can satisfy me that the two cases are really connected, as you state, I shall, of course, be pleased to turn it over to you. Meanwhile, it is in Martin's hands, and will rest there.'

It was an authoritative setback in the little scheme he had monologued over. And it jarred him.

As he passed into the room where Tinker lay, he was vindictively ripe for that part of his task which, he was sure, would not miscarry.

He glanced at the boy, carelessly enough, convinced of the efficacy of his drug, and, turning off the light, opened softly the window overlooking the canal five feet below. The fog was blankety. He attached a long rope to a hook in the window, and made a running noose at the other end, then returned to the room.

He had not the slightest notion that Tinker's eyes had never quitted him. He was ignorant of the lad's heroic remedy during the journey there, ignorant, therefore, also, that for the last hour Tinker had been in full possession of his senses, and that concealed in his breast was the long-bladed clasp-knife he had left lying on the table. Tinker had had thoughts of cutting free his legs, and bolting. But he feared lest there might be eyes watching or ears listening in rooms beyond, and he was waiting an occasion.

He lay inert and as if lifeless as Plummer returned, slipped the noose over his head, and ran it tight under his armpits, and, lifting him up, let him gently, hand by hand, through the window down towards the canal. A yard from the window the two were invisible to each other, and Tinker, bending down, caught the weight in one hand, and slashed through the lashings with the other, till a kick would suffice to set his legs free.

As soon as the cold of the water touched him he immersed the weight, letting it sink noiselessly, kicked free the lashings, and, hanging deadweight with held breath, sank to the bottom.

Twice he felt the cord gently tugged, and grinned in his heart with joy to think how truly he had divined Plummer's nefarious scheme for assuring himself of his victim's death. Then the rope gradually paid out, there was a plash of metal striking the water, and Tinker, cutting himself free of the noose, rose to the top, swam with noiseless strokes through the icy water for some hundred yards, then, crossing to the opposite bank, hauled himself out on to the towpath. He shook himself like a young terrier, gained the road, and, pacing the distances till he came to a lamp-post at a street corner, shinned up it, and waited till a drift of the fog showed him that he was at the corner of Bloomfield Road and Lester Street. Then getting back to earth, he set off at a smart trot towards Baker Street.

THE THIRTEENTH CHAPTER

The Drivel of an Imbecile

At nine o'clock the following morning, in a room in Cavendish Square, Dr Fleming sat at breakfast opposite his guest and patient, Sexton Blake.

'It's a marvel to me how a man with such a thick head and a like appetite,' the doctor was saying, 'can possibly be associated with so many brains.'

'It was a squeak, though, doc, eh?' said Blake.

'You may thank your hat and your involuntary movement,' replied Dr Fleming, 'for your life. As it is, it's a marvel there was no bone-crushing.'

'Have you read the papers?' asked Blake, with one of his rare smiles.

'They make me ill,' returned Fleming. 'It's a form of laudatory nausea that is always and only post-mortem. But it was a brilliant idea of yours, that, Blake. It ought to turn your enemy's movements into your very hand. And he seems to be a person whom it's more healthy to be dead to than not at home to.'

'I'll bet you,' said Blake, 'that he will be here by ten o'clock to see me.'

'Well, he can't. You are not fit,' said Fleming.

'On the contrary, I must. He, of all people, must believe that once and for all I am a confirmed and drivelling imbecile. I don't like worrying the public. All the Press chatter was for him and him alone. And if it had not been that he has learnt to trust his bludgeon work, I should have doubted whether this would have taken him in. And even though it was up to his expectation, he won't let it pass without verifying.'

'Detective-Sergeant Plummer is in the waiting-room, sir, and would like to see you' – thus the maid, entering with a card.

'Off you get to bed,' said Fleming. 'Your skull cap is all ready; nurses shall be there in a moment.'

Five minutes later Plummer, with Dr Fleming close at his side, stood looking down at his victim with an air of commiseration.

'I suppose he doesn't know me?' asked Plummer, in a whisper.

'He's a new-born babe, and will never grow older,' lied the doctor hardily.

The great detective's head was enveloped in a skull-cap built of sticking-plaster and lint; his face was livid under a thick coat of delicate green flesh powder; a senile smile flickered round his dribbling lips, which a nurse at his side kept incessantly dabbing; his hands were lying listless, though the fingers from time to time picked idly at the counterpane; a shaded lamp threw a decent gloom over the chastened squalor of so piteous a wreck. A second nurse, moving from a far table, approached the patient, and, lifting his head, poured a teaspoonful of fresh water down his poor, parched throat. Not a detail did Plummer lose, but as he turned away, his only reflection was: 'Well, it gives 'em some work to do; but I'm sorry I left it them!'

Outside the door, he turned suddenly on Fleming, halting him with his face in the full light of the window.

'A dreadful disaster, Dr Fleming,' he said.

'Crime,' corrected the doctor, in his best professional manner.

'Oh, the crime!' said Plummer. 'It's lost sight of in the consequences.'

'Ay, the consequences are the thing to consider!' said Fleming cryptically. His very boot was itching to kick the man hurtfully. In a crime he saw the individual. He was not like Blake, who had ever something of the divine instinct, which, while pitiless in pursuing the crime, almost ignores the personal equation of the individual.

'But can nothing be done with him?' pursued Plummer. 'Is he absolutely incurable?'

Dr Fleming felt the man's eyes burning their devil's point of interrogation into him. He met the gaze candidly, and replied with simplicity: 'Man, if he lives to a hundred, I'll stake my reputation that he'll never, never, never be better than the thing you saw two minutes ago!'

'He's gone away more fooled, more content than any fool I ever saw content with the results of his folly!' reported Dr Fleming, as Blake emerged from the sick-room and joined him, on hearing the front door close.

'Good!' said Blake. 'We'll give him ten minutes, then I must be off. I'm in a fever about that boy Tinker. That brute Plummer got the telegram, for it wasn't there when I came to. I fear lest he met Tinker and decoyed him. Did they bring my wardrobe from Baker Street?'

'Second door to the right on the landing upstairs,' said Dr Fleming. 'And now, man, go and take care of yourself. Yes, yes! I understand. If anyone calls for you, you're in a high fever, and can't and shan't be seen. But if you don't leave me to get into my work, man, I shall be in a delirium.'

Sexton Blake went off chuckling. For all Fleming's crusty manner, he know the value of that great heart and ardent brain, and he knew he could rely on him.

The two had plotted the great detective's public disappearance an hour after Sexton Blake had recovered consciousness from his five minutes swoon. And it had been Fleming who had 'phoned for the reporters, and to Scotland Yard, and who, guarding his door like a vigilant watchdog, interviewed all and arranged all, even to his transport in an ambulance amid the murmurs of the throng that choked the traffic in Baker Street for over two hours.

It was half an hour later that an elderly and fussy old gentleman, with fierce, white moustache and Empire beard, was to be seen inquiring at Paddington from all and everyone for news of a boy arriving by the 8.30 the previous evening. It was Blake.

Information there was, and to spare, and though it confirmed Sexton Blake's fears, it gave him no indication by which he might get on the trail. But he was tenacious as Pedro himself, and step by step, the whole day long, he circled round, tracing the description of the car, till it got him to Edgware Road, and thence, by dint of sheer instinct, hearing of that mad race of an unseeable car through the fog, he followed the trail of report till it ceased at Elgin Avenue. Hour after hour he kept on, till still, aimlessly almost now, casting for scent, he came to the corner of Rail Street and Grave Street, just as an automobile of the given description was gliding out of the gate of 13, Rail Street, engineered by a trim, dark man wearing a pointed black beard.

Sexton Blake drew back, and walked down Grave Street, and the car rolled on. For once, Plummer, sure that his enemies were disposed off, was off his guard, and, full of his visit as Mr Marsden to Messrs Small & Fry, was careless of who might see him.

It took Blake less than five minutes to make an entry to No. 13. His heart sank as, on the table in the room overhanging the canal, he saw a collection of articles he at once identified as Tinker's. The boy had been lured here and done to death. He gnashed his teeth on his lips in rage and grief, feverishly racing from room to room. When at last he was certain that Tinker was neither in nor about the premises, a great revulsion of feeling came on him, and, collapsing into a chair, he abandoned himself to despair and grief.

A kind of stupor fell on him, and for long he sat gazing into vacancy, unconscious of anything but the appalling, overwhelming sense of loss and desolation.

He never noticed, he whose ears were ordinarily as keen as a fox's – he never noticed the stealthy uplifting of a window, the cat-like creeping of footsteps cautiously planted. He sat where Marsden had sat the day of fate, in the same high-backed chair, looking out of the same window. Little was visible of him, save the voluminous whiskers and moustachios and the soft felt hat.

The footsteps were in the room now. A moment later they paused behind his chair.

Then, before he could move, before he could realise where he was, or what had happened, a noose had run tight round his neck, a couple of half turns held his arms powerless, while again and again the quick lashing was whipped round, till he sat trussed up like any fowl in Farringdon Street – he, the greatest detective the world had ever known.

'It was well,' he sighed. 'I shall find Tinker after all.'

He was conscious of a form that passed round the edge of his chair and seated itself nonchalantly on the table in front of him. Then a voice, hoarse with triumph, and fibred with justice, said: 'Now, Mr Man of Many Disguises, Mr George Marsden Plummer, we, you and I, will talk of vengeance!'

Something in the voice caused Sexton Blake to lift his head, and stare.

He saw a man, old as his own appearance, almost so similar, in fact, that he might have been looking at his reflection.

'I don't know you,' he said, in a voice still laden with his burden of despair. 'Who are you?'

'Can't you guess?' was the answer, in tones, which, for all their jeering vindictiveness, were so strangely familiar that his eyes devoured the face in front in an agony of doubt and wonder. 'Can't you guess, Mr Sergeant Plummer? I'm the avenger of Sexton Blake!'

'Tinker!' yelled Sexton Blake, straining like a caged lion at his bonds.

'The guv'nor!' gasped Tinker.

THE FOURTEENTH CHAPTER

A Bolt from the Blue

While Sexton Blake and Tinker were mutually explaining to each other their separate adventures, Mr Marsden was occupied in laying before Messrs Small & Fry the proofs of claim of one 'to rest unnamed pending negotiations' to the title and estates of the Earl of Sevenoaks.

He was received by the partners in company, and they were inclined to be supercilious, until Mr Marsden claimed their promise for the sum of £40,000, 'in consideration of services rendered', the day he should produce to them in person the veritable heir, and the established proofs of his identity and claim.

It took Mr Marsden three and a half hours to convince Messrs Small & Fry, but he did convince them, and he got his written guarantee, 'subject to the endorsement of the heir'. He left, promising them that the following morning he would call on them with the heir and his proofs. And as he left, he cursed them for meticulous, prosy, posing, long-winded images of vanity, for he was already half an hour late in keeping the appointment his chief had imposed on him for six o'clock that evening.

He selected a four-wheeler, and bade him drive to Craven Street, and on the way removed his wig and beard, which he placed in a concealed pocket.

But it seemed as if the fates were bent on exasperating him this day, for he had only the time to wash his face in his rooms, when Inspector Martin entered abruptly, and told him the chief was fuming with impatience, and that he – Martin – was to accompany Plummer in person to the Charing Cross Station, where the chief was waiting to take the 7.10 to Sevenoaks.

Plummer, cursing his luck and his chief's fussiness, but unable to refuse, threw a few things into a bag, and accompanied by Martin, hurried on to the station.

'I thought you were on to Blake's affair,' he said, as they turned into the station-yard.

'That's good from you,' growled Martin, 'seeing that I owe it to your cursed funniness being shelved to make room for you tomorrow.'

Plummer, whose question had been dictated by a sudden suspicion, laughed up his sleeve, his good humour returning on the instant. He did not care now if he kept Small & Fry waiting. He could do in the afternoon what was missed in the morning. He did not know – how should he? – that the 'drowned' boy Tinker, had at ten that morning, sought and obtained, in Sexton Blake's name, an interview with the Home Secretary, and exposed to that astounded gentleman the whole of the case. The result of that interview had been a note in the Home Secretary's own writing to the chief at Scotland Yard, bidding him to personally take Plummer to Sevenoaks that same day, not to let him out of his sight, and, above all, to let him feel assured that the Sexton Blake affair would be entrusted to him on his return next day from Sevenoaks. The note was marked private and confidential, and Tinker had felt no little satisfaction in evading the curiosity of the chief by a plea of State secrecy.

But Plummer knew none of these things, and he went on his way to Sevenoaks, basking in the added sense of security given him by his chief's unvarying urbanity.

Thus it was that when Sexton Blake, being released from his bonds by the feverish knife of Tinker, suggested the advisability of a reconnoitre, Tinker was able to reassure him that they had No. 13 Rail Street entirely to themselves.

Blake listened to the youngster's account of himself with growing admiration.

'I dared not go near Baker Street,' Tinker had explained. 'I was afraid Plummer might be rummaging there. It was one o'clock in the morning, too, and no place opened. I was stuck for a minute to get a change, till I thought of that old marine store down in Blackfriars. I got a set-out there that fairly made the porter at the Home Office take me for a "looney", when I told him who I wanted to see.

'Clothes do go for a lot, guv'nor, don't they? Even the Home Secretary thought I was lying, 'cos I wasn't in Shetland wool and a choker. Yet he ought to know that broad-cloth covers lots of limbs that ought to be under the broad arrow.

'But he couldn't get out of it. It took a lot of convincing, and it was only when I mentioned one or two little private matters only he and you and I and Pedro know of, that he began to take the squint out of his eye. Then we sailed in a fair wind; and, now, all's fixed up, and all we've got to do, guv'nor, is to crack this blessed crib.

'You see, guv'nor,' he wound up simply, 'I thought you were really done; so I'd nothing to do but to avenge you.'

Sexton Blake was very moved.

'My boy,' he said, 'I'm very proud to have you as a friend!'

For a moment they gripped hands, holding each other's eyes.

'We might do the larder first, sir,' said Tinker, with a grin. 'It's true it's his larder,' he added; 'but, all the same –'

'Oh, food is food, wherever it is!' said Blake easily. 'Moreover, I'm very hungry!'

Sexton Blake had none of the squeamishness that is inseparable from false sentiment.

They made an excellent and a happy meal off a plentiful store of cold provisions, and a couple of bottles of Pilsener.

Then, reposed and refreshed, and indescribably invigorated with the sense of their reunion, they fell to work on the 'crib'.

They cracked it thoroughly and methodically, and the more they progressed, the more their admiration grew for George

Marsden Plummer. There was absolutely nothing from roof to cellar in the slightest degree compromising. It might have been the house of a retired greengrocer, for all the evidence it contained.

Save Tinker's few possessions, which he recovered with joy, not a scrap of paper even rewarded their efforts.

'There's this dead bluebottle!' laughed Tinker. 'Look at him, guv'nor! Nipped clean in two! That's a bit of George Marsden Plummer's work, I'll bet!'

But Sexton Blake had found the safe. It was a find, for it was let into the wall and papered over, and nothing but the keen, abnormally keen eyes of Sexton Blake could have discovered the delicate change in pattern-work that concealed the lock.

'It's a combination letter-lock,' said Blake, after a short scrutiny. 'It's your lucky day, Tinker. Make a guess for it.'

Tinker, gazing at the dead bluebottle, gave a sudden bright grin.

'Well, seeing the dead bluebottle,' said Tinker, 'I should say he had plunged for success, and planked for Plummer.'

' "Plummer" we'll try, then,' said Blake.

'Plummer' it was, and though their search was ended, their admiration was not diminished.

Everything was there that was wanting to their case – three or four men with black hair and short, pointed beards, three or four with golden dittos, three or four benevolent Mr Frobishers. The bludgeon was there, the waterproof, the boots with the broken third nail on the left foot. Tinker's memorandum-book was there, too, and the papers proving Horace Jenkins's title, enclosed with various letters from Mrs Jenkins.

'After all,' said Tinker, as he viewed the mass of damnatory evidence, 'he must have known that he might be some day trapped. Why did he keep this lot, when he thought his work was done?'

Blake had fallen into a brown study, his face very pale, his eyes strangely shining.

'What a detective he might have made!' he muttered to himself. 'He's a great man, Tinker,' he said slowly, at last. 'Plummer kept these in order to convict Marsden, who would have taken fright, and forever have remained condemned but unfindable.'

'My eye!' said Tinker.

There was a long pause.

'We have done all, here,' said Blake, at last. 'Make these things into a parcel, my boy, and then we'll drive round to Mr Small's private house.'

'How is he in it?' asked Tinker.

'I want to verify my theory.' said Blake. 'Plummer could never convict Marsden unless he could prove that Marsden had tried to blackmail the family solicitors. If Marsden has tried, then our case is complete. Small lives near here, in St. John's Wood.'

Sexton Blake verified his theory, and the two, with their valuable packet, drove home to Baker Street. Their work, however, was not yet finished; and it was two o'clock in the morning before, everything being completed, they snatched a few hours' sleep.

It was ten o'clock the following morning.

The magistrate's court had been open two minutes, and all the neighbourhood was thronged in the stifling atmosphere.

The prisoner, Henry Jostle, was in the dock, and Detective-Sergeant Plummer was in the box, recounting to the court how he had first come to suspect the prisoner.

'But,' said the presiding magistrate, 'I understand that you do not own him to be a principal in the actual murder?'

'That is so,' answered Detective-Sergeant Plummer.

'But you know that there is a principal?' asked the magistrate.

'I do,' was the answer.

'Do you know who he is?' asked the magistrate.

'It is not convenient to state it at the moment,' answered Detective-Sergeant Plummer.

'I disagree with you,' said the cold, incisive voice of the Scotland Yard chief.

Plummer looked at him in amazement, as did everyone else. In the general confusion, no one noticed a tall man, followed by a lad and a frock-coated square-set figure, who thrust their way insidiously to the side of the witness-box.

Plummer's eyes, drifting suspiciously from the eyes of his chief, suddenly fell on the form of Sexton Blake, who was standing unobtrusively at his side. The sergeant's face paled. He recovered himself, and stared coolly at the great detective, who, moving a little, revealed the face of Tinker.

Then Plummer faltered. His face went livid, and for a moment he seemed about to fall.

The hush in the court was intense.

It was broken by a sharp 'click' of steel snapping steel.

Sexton Blake had steadied Plummer from falling by braceleting his wrists.

'George Marsden Plummer,' he said, in a quiet, unmoved tone, 'I arrest you for the murder of Allan Audley, Earl of Sevenoaks.'

'I congratulate you! You are the better man!' said George Marsden Plummer, coolly and unabashed.

Plummer was sent to his cell.

He looked round it, saw how white it was, and resolved he simply would not stay in it.

A week later, Sexton Blake and Tinker assisted in the Sevenoaks Parish Church as witnesses in the marriage of Horace Audley, fourteenth Earl of Sevenoaks, with Helen Lennox.

If the bridegroom was still somewhat pale, the bride had roses for both; but Tinker never forget that she had once taken him by the scruff of his neck, and had her way of him – and destiny.

THE LAW OF THE SEA

William Murray Graydon

THE PROLOGUE

I

'You have made a wise choice, my boy, a very wise one.'

'I am sure I have, father. Dulcie is the best and sweetest girl in all the world.'

'I don't doubt it, Dick. You are a lucky dog. It was a foregone conclusion that you would win her, though, for we Champneys have always made love as we made war. The motto on our coat-of-arms should have been that pithy saying: "Only the brave deserve the fair." '

'And everything else, eh? That is your creed, I know.'

'It is the family creed, Dick. It is born and bred in the bone. There has never been a coward in our family, and I trust there never will be.'

'Certainly not until after our time, father.'

The scent of lilac and the droning of bees floated through the open window into the dining-room at Broadlands, which was an old Elizabethan mansion situated in a wooded part of Hampshire, not many miles from the town of Winchester.

Father and son had finished luncheon, and were sitting idly at the table, the one toying with his glass of golden hock, while the other was enjoying the fragrance of his cigar.

General Horace Champney was an old soldier with a brilliant record behind him; a hale, stalwart man of sixty, with a florid complexion and a white moustache, and the clean-cut, aristocratic features of his race. He was proud of his ancient lineage, and none the less proud because he was a commoner: for he held that to be a mark of distinction for a country gentleman in these degenerate days, when the value of a title had been tarnished by the wholesale creation of a mushroom aristocracy.

Richard Champney, the second son, was what his father had been at the same age: tall and handsome, with fair hair and blue eyes, and a blonde moustache that drooped over a firm mouth. From boyhood the voice of the sea had whispered at his ear, and he had thrown up a military career to follow the calling that most appealed to him. He loved the great Atlantic leviathans, and was interested in their mechanism.

For several years he had been second officer in the service of the Green Star Line, and he had recently been transferred from one of the less important vessels of that line to the mightiest ocean greyhound that had ever been launched.

'We were speaking of Dulcie Romanis,' continued the old general, after a pause. 'I am heartily glad, my dear boy, that you are going to marry her, the daughter of my old friend and neighbour. Bless me, how the news would please him if he were alive today! She is a charming girl, and she will have a pot of money. And you will have a tidy little fortune yourself for that matter, though it will not be so much as your brother will have. But you won't mind that. The eldest son of the Champneys has more responsibilities and obligations than the others. And it is right that it should be so. The head of a family like ours must carry on the traditions that –'

General Champney interrupted the sentence to empty his glass, and then, rising from the table, he linked arms with his son, and drew him from the room.

'Come, I want to show you something,' he murmured.

A smile hovered on the young man's lips, but it was a tender and sympathetic one. He knew well enough where he was going. He was led straight to the long picture-gallery, where many painted portraits of Champneys, some in doublet and trunk-hose, and some in modern attire, looked down from their gilded frames.

The general pointed to them with a stick that he had taken from the hall. Often before, in this sacred apartment, he had spoken of his ancestors; but never had he expatiated so eloquently on their virtues as on the present occasion. He moved slowly from one to another, his voice quivering with pride as he uttered a few words concerning each.

'There are some missing, my boy,' he said. 'They never had a place here. In those early days, I dare say, they were too busy fighting to have their portraits painted. We'll begin with Harold Champney. There is a warrior for you. He met his end at Agincourt, and was carried from the field with a dozen archers' bolts in his mail. The next one is Malcourt Champney, who led his regiment in the Normandy wars. Here is Arthur, who lost an arm at Naseby; and this is Admiral James Champney, who thrashed the Dutch in the Thames during the reign of Charles II.

'Now look at Rupert. He went through the Peninsular campaigns with Wellington, and subsequently refused a title. This is my grandfather, a hero of the Mahratta War of '48. Here we have my father, who fell in the Indian Mutiny after distinguishing himself in the Crimea.

'And now there is your brother Mervyn out in the Soudan,' he went on. 'His portrait must hang here one of these days. He has won the Victoria Cross already, and I don't doubt that there are further honours in store for him. But one soldier in the family is enough, I dare say. I have been reconciled to your giving up the army, Dick. You have chosen the sea, and that often brings out a man's courage as fully as does the field of battle. The ocean has its perils, its code of honour, as well as the land.'

'Always remember that you belong to a race of warriors. Keep the gallant deeds of your ancestors before your mind. They were no milk-and-water, claret-led babes; no prinking, strutting coxcombs; no simpering, drawling Pall Mall loungers. They were men, every inch of them; men of grit and backbone! They were heroes, by gad, heroes! And the blood of heroes flows in your veins! You are bound in honour, by the bond of race, to hold fast to what you have inherited from the dead! If ever you were to falter in the hour of danger –'

'You surely don't think that I would, father?' broke in the young man with flushed cheeks.

'No, no, certainly not! Forgive me, my boy! I was talking nonsense! I hardly knew what I was saying! Come, let us go!'

Slowly, still arm-in-arm, they left the hall of heroes, and passed down the staircase and into the oak-panelled library.

'I'll slip over and see Dulcie for a few minutes,' said Richard Champney.

And as he strode across the lawn the old general watched him with dim eyes.

'He is a fine lad!' he reflected. 'A fine lad! And I am just as fond of him as I am of his brother!'

2

At Broadlands, on the eve of their parting for a week or so, General Champney and his son were sitting at the table enjoying their port and cigars; and in the drawing-room of the Grange, a thousand yards away, Dulcie Romanis was singing.

The nightingale at the upper end of the garden, which had been trilling melodiously, had stopped from sheer envy and chagrin. And there had also stopped, at the edge of the drive, a good-looking young man with dark eyes and hair, and a black moustache that was carefully curled. He listened for a moment, then went thoughtfully on towards the house.

'I should not have waited so long,' he said to himself, 'but I am sure that I stand as much of a chance as anybody else, and perhaps a better one. We have always been good friends, and I don't believe she will refuse me.'

Dulcie Romanis was singing! You would have had to know her to realise what that meant, and had you known her you would have been, figuratively speaking, at her feet. There was not a prettier girl in all of Hampshire, and as she had a large fortune, in addition to her beauty, she had been wooed more than once. But all of her suitors, with one exception, had wooed in vain.

As she sat at the piano, with her slim fingers running over the keys, the light from a shaded lamp caressed her velvety brown hair, and was reflected in her violet-hued eyes, and showed the exquisite curves of her witching lips. She was singing an old English ballad, and her very soul was in the words. Her rich, sweet voice, as clear as a silver bell, floated through the open window into the sultry night:

In woodland glade, at eventide,
Young Strephon sighed, young Strephon sighed,
For love of –

The music ceased, and the voice broke off abruptly. Dulcie rose from the stool, and came round from behind the piano.

'Mr Nairne, miss!' announced a little maidservant, and withdrew as the visitor entered.

Handsome and well-groomed, twisting his moustache, Hildred Nairne stepped into the drawing-room. He shook hands with the girl, whose greeting was a trifle less cordial than it had been wont to be; and when he had fidgeted on a chair for a little time, and uttered a few commonplace remarks, he rose impulsively and put his fate to the test.

'You can guess what I have come for,' he said. 'I – I love you, Dulcie, and I want you to be my wife.'

There was silence for a moment. Dulcie Romanis' cheeks were flushed, and a look of pain crept into her violet eyes. She edged away from the young man as he moved nearer to her.

'I am very sorry,' she faltered. 'I wish you had not spoken.'

'Don't tell me that there is no hope,' begged Hildred Nairne, 'I love you so dearly.'

'I never dreamed that you did. I do not care for you in that way.'

'But you can learn, Dulcie. It will not be hard. I am rich, as you know, and I am sure you will believe that I love you for yourself alone.'

'I don't doubt that, but – but I cannot marry you.'

'Are you going to refuse me?'

'I must, Hildred.'

'Then you care for someone else? I am too late. Is that it?'

'Yes, that is one reason. I love Richard Champney, and I promised yesterday to be his wife.'

'That fellow!'

The word burst angrily from Hildred Nairne's lips, and the colour ebbed from his face. A sinister gleam flashed to his eyes, and lingered there.

'I suppose there is no chance for me at all?' he muttered.

'No, none at all,' the girl replied. 'And there never was, Hildred. I have liked you only as a friend.'

There was nothing more to be said. The young man knew that. In sullen silence, without a word of farewell, he left the room, and picked up his hat and stick in the hall. He passed out of the house, and strode down the gravelled drive, switching viciously at the shrubbery.

At the gate he stopped for a moment. The nightingale was trilling at the end of the garden, but it suddenly ceased. Dulcie Romanis was singing again, and her voice was a torture to the suitor she had rejected.

'It was my last chance, and I have lost,' he reflected. 'It means ruin and flight.'

Hildred Nairne had been hard hit. The rich heiress, to whom he had pinned his hopes, was engaged to his cousin; for he was related, through his mother, to General Champney. He had lied to the girl. It was true that he loved her passionately, but he had desired her wealth as well as her hand. He was on the rocks, and only the marriage that he had contemplated could have saved him. The large fortune that he had inherited from his father was all gone, squandered at cards, and in fast and reckless living. He owed hundreds of pounds to tradesmen, and was deep in the clutches of moneylenders. And a far worse peril threatened him, one that now struck terror to his heart as he walked along the quiet country road.

'Only another month,' he said to himself with an oath. 'In five weeks that forged bill will fall due, and there is not the remotest hope of my being able to meet it. I had better disappear at once, so that I shall have plenty of time to cover my tracks. By heavens, how hard it will be to give up everything that makes life worth living, to join the army of those who have gone under! What a fool I have been!'

He had walked for some hundreds of yards, and now he saw to one side of him, between the trees, the lighted windows of Broadlands. He paused, and shook his fist at the old mansion.

'Curse you!' he snarled. 'Curse you, Richard Champney! I'll be even with you one of these days if I ever get the chance!'

He went on through the starry night, tramping along the dusty road, nursing evil and revengeful thoughts. The lovely face of Dulcie Romanis haunted him, and fed the burning hatred he felt for the man who had won such a prize.

3

The voice of mighty London, the subdued roar of the traffic that was gliding along Piccadilly, penetrated to a room in Ryder Street, where Hildred Nairne was standing before his dressing-table with a razor in his hand.

He had finished shaving. With the growth of beard on his cheeks and chin had gone the black moustache of which he had been so proud, and the face that he saw in the mirror was a face that could not have been easily recognised by his friends and acquaintances.

He put on his collar and tied his cravat, and got into the jacket of a tweed suit much the worse for wear. He reached for his hat, and glanced at the bag that was resting on a chair; then be touched an electric bell, and the summons was promptly answered by his valet.

'I am ready,' said Hildred Nairne.

'Yes, sir,' assented the man.

'You have served me well and faithfully, Hume.'

'Thank you, sir. I have always tried to do my duty, and our relations have been pleasant ones. I am sorry that we must part.'

'It may be for only a short time, my good fellow. Perhaps it will not be necessary for you to find another place. There is no telling what Fortune's wheel may do for me, what may happen in a month.' He laughed grimly, and went on! 'You mustn't take me seriously. I don't know what has put such an idea into my head. The chances are a million to one that I will never come back, and that you will never hear of me again.'

'I hope you will come back, sir.'

'I believe you, Hume. At all events, the rent for the flat is paid in advance, and so are your wages. I want you to remain here for a few weeks, and stave off those of my creditors who may call.'

'I will do my best, sir,' said the valet. 'What explanation shall I give them!'

'You can tell them,' Hildred Nairne replied, 'that I am at a fashionable German watering-place, paying court to an American heiress who is lending a favourable ear to my suit, and will almost certainly bestow upon me her hand and her millions.'

'Yes, sir.'

'As for any writs and summonses that may come, you will burn them.'

'With pleasure, sir. And if you should not come back!'

'You will forget me, Hume.'

'I – I will try to, sir.'

'Then it only remains for me to say goodbye.'

'Goodbye, sir, and good luck to you.'

Thus they parted, after three years of loyal service on the one hand, and of complete satisfaction on the other. There was a lump in Hume's throat. He was the one person who knew what his master really was, and, knowing the worst, was yet devoted to him.

Perhaps Hildred Nairne knew this and appreciated the fact, for his throat also felt queer as he left his snug chambers and descended the staircase. Carrying his bag, and looking wistfully at the lights of London, he walked down Duke Street to King Street, and got into a taxi-cab.

'Waterloo,' he said to the chauffeur as he pulled his hat over his brow.

He was going to Southampton, and from there, on the morrow, he meant to sail in the steerage for America. It was a vessel of the Green Star Line that he had chosen, but he had no idea that it was the one to which his cousin, Richard Champney, had recently been transferred. Had he been aware of that, he might have foreseen that the twist of Fortune's wheel of which he had spoken was not so remote a possibility, after all.

THE FIRST CHAPTER

The Shadow of Danger – The Jewel Thief

The steamship *Paleta*, the largest and most luxurious liner that had over been launched, was between three and four days out from Southampton on its voyage across the Atlantic. She carried more than three thousand souls, including the crew, and among the passengers were British noblemen, American millionaires and railway magnates, and many other persons of note and distinction. Most of them were returning to their native land after pleasure jaunts in Europe, and others were going to the New World as strangers, on pleasure bent.

It was drawing near to eleven o'clock at night, and the air was bitterly cold, which was a sign that there were icebergs in the vicinity. But the sea was calm, and the stars were shining, and a watch was posted in the crow's-nest. There was not a man on board but would have scouted the idea of danger, though the tremendous speed at which the vessel was travelling had not been decreased by the fraction of a knot.

A large proportion of the first-class passengers had retired to their berths. A few were strolling on deck, and several convivial little parties were assembled in the smoking room, where they were engaged in playing cards.

Others were idly watching them, and among the number was Sexton Blake, the famous detective, who was seated in a big, saddlebag chair, enjoying his inevitable pipe. A suspicious character, believed to be an Englishman who had committed a murder in America some years ago and escaped to his own country, had recently been arrested in New York, and Blake, who was the only man who could identify the prisoner to a certainty, was going over for that purpose at the request of his friend Fenlock Fawn, the American detective.

His young assistant was travelling with him, but he was not in the smoking-room at the time. He was in some sequestered nook, paying ardent courtship to a girl from Kalamazoo who chewed gum, and had a complete vocabulary of Yankee slang on the tip of her tongue.

Sexton Blake was talking to an acquaintance, and in the midst of a sentence he stopped abruptly. A slight jar, gentle and stealthy, had just been felt. It was nothing to cause any alarm. There had been no crash, no rending noise.

'There goes an iceberg!' said one of the company, pointing to the window.

'We must have grazed it just now,' remarked another.

'Darned risky, that sort of thing!' observed a third. 'What sort of watch are they keeping aloft?'

Cards were dropped, left unshuffled. Mild curiosity was expressed, and vague inquiries were made. The engines were presently stopped, but nobody took the trouble to go out to ascertain what had happened. The playing was resumed, and for twenty minutes it went on, to a running accompaniment of laughter and jesting. Then Tinker entered the room and stepped over to his master.

'You had better come up, guv'nor,' he said. 'I don't know what is wrong, but I believe we have run against something or other.'

Blake rose from his chair, and he and the lad went above, followed by several others. The vessel was resting motionless on the water. There were plenty of people about, some in evening dress and some wearing the first garments they had laid their hands on when roused from sleep. All were asking questions that nobody seemed to be able to answer.

No direct information could be obtained. The *Paleta's* officers and crew avoided inquiries. There was one thing, however, that was perceived by a few persons, among them

Tinker and the detective. The ship was slanting. There was an unmistakable list from the stern towards the bows.

'The water is pouring in,' said one of the two gentlemen standing near. 'Some of her plates must have been ripped off.'

'She can't sink,' his companion replied: 'that is certain.'

'No doubt some of the forward compartments have filled,' murmured Sexton Blake, as he saw the anxious look on the lad's face. 'The rest will keep us afloat.'

More people joined the throng, and stood in groups, gazing at the smooth, starlit sea. Some uneasily questioned Blake, who sought to reassure them, and did so in all sincerity. The *Paleta* sink? It was impossible, of course, no matter what damage might have been done by the iceberg. No one could seriously contemplate such a catastrophe. Suddenly an order was loudly shouted.

'All the passengers on deck with lifebelts on!'

Still there was no panic, no alarm even. The command, which was supposed to be only a wise precaution, was quietly obeyed. Up from their cabins, with lifebelts around their waists, the passengers poured in a slow, steady procession.

But the ship's list was increasing, and Blake and Tinker began to feel disturbed as they saw that the covers were being lifted from the boats, and that the crews allotted to them were standing by and uncoiling the ropes by which they were to be lowered.

The tide of passengers continued to ascend, many of them wrapped in blankets. Sexton Blake procured two lifebelts, and gave one to the lad. And now another order rang out.

'Men, stand back from the boats! Women and children first!'

Women and children first! It was the awaking call to the chivalry of those who knew what chivalry was, a reminder of the law of the sea to those who might be tempted to break that inexorable law. But there was no cowardice. As yet none could conceive that the great liner might actually be in danger of going to the bottom of the ocean. There was still, for a time, the strange amazing calm, the stupor of ignorance. And even when the truth made itself felt, when it began to be realised that a disaster was impending, there was no terror. There was still a widespread conviction that the *Paleta* could not sink.

There were parting scenes witnessed now, but with a few exceptions they were marked more by cheerfulness than by pathos. The boats were swinging out and down, and women and children were getting into them from the level of the deck, across a yawning gap. Most of the women got in willingly, while others obstinately refused to leave their husbands, and were allowed to remain with them.

'I will see you in the morning, little girlie!' said a youth, as he waved his hand to the young wife who had reluctantly obeyed the order.

'It will be all right, dear!' called another husband. 'Don't worry about me!'

They were never to meet again in this world, and Blake had a premonition that they would not. One boat had slipped away, and others were being lowered, with creaking of blocks and pulleys, through ninety feet of gloom. The vessel's list was increasing with every minute, as none could fail to see.

Yet for the most part the passengers were still calm. Some were pacing to and fro, others leaning against the railings. A young officer, pale but cool, hastened by. He nodded to the detective, and was recognised by the latter as Richard Champney, whom he had met at his father's house in Hampshire.

'It begins to look bad,' Tinker said huskily.

'I am afraid it does,' Sexton Blake replied. 'The captain knows what he is doing, we may be sure. I am going below for some money and papers,' he added. 'Remain just where you are, my boy, so that I shall have no trouble in finding you.'

'Right you are, guv'nor!' the lad assented.

By some means several of the steerage passengers had succeeded in reaching the upper deck, as Blake observed as he made his way to the staircase, which was now deserted. He hurriedly descended, and as he was walking along one of the empty corridors, within half a dozen yards of his cabin, he beheld a sight that stirred him to fiery indignation.

To one side of him, within the open door of a luxurious stateroom, a roughly-dressed man was standing, staring raptly at a magnificent string of pearls that he was holding in his hand. He had no right to be there. He looked as if he belonged to the steerage, and he must have taken advantage of the prevailing confusion to prowl about for the purpose of robbery.

'Drop that, you scoundrel!' cried Sexton Blake.

The man swung round, and there was a glimpse of his face – a handsome, clean-shaved one – as he slipped the jewels into his pocket, and leapt with an oath at the detective, who was scarcely prepared for the swift and sudden attack. He received a blow that staggered him. He struck back, and another blow landed on his jaw. He evaded a third one, and seized his assailant by the throat.

The next instant they were down, rolling over the floor, and after a short struggle Blake hit his head against the wall with such force that his senses swam. He was not unconscious, but for a brief space of time he lay there in the corridor half dazed; and when he rose to his feet, and looked about him, he was alone. The man had disappeared, and had doubtless taken the pearls with him.

Under the circumstances, when there was so much else to be thought of, the detective did not greatly concern himself about the robbery. The solitude below, and the still increasing tilt of the vessel, preyed on his nerves. He went to his cabin and got his money and papers; and then, returning to the deck, he joined Tinker at the spot where he had left him, and gave him a brief account of his adventure.

'It is one of the most contemptible things that can be imagined,' he concluded. 'Fortunately, I had a good look at the miscreant, and I should know him again. It is quite likely that I shall run across him some day.'

'If we survive, guv'nor,' said the lad, in a husky tone.

'Yes; if we survive,' Blake echoed.

And as he spoke his stout courage faltered for an instant. But it was of Tinker that he was thinking, not of himself.

THE SECOND CHAPTER

The Increasing Peril – Two Miles Deep

The law of the sea still ruled on the *Paleta*, which all now knew to be inevitably doomed, though the nature of the impending catastrophe was not yet fully realised. The men were still holding back, calm and self-possessed.

Women and children first! They were still parting from their dear ones, and taking their seats, and swinging load by load down the towering side of the liner.

'Level!' 'Aft!' 'Stern!' 'Both together!'

So rang the voices, clear and sharp, of those who were in charge of lowering the boats. The second officer again drew near to Blake and the lad. He was in a hurry, but he stopped when the detective tapped him on the shoulder.

'I can't talk to you now,' he murmured.

'Just a moment,' said Sexton Blake. 'Will you tell me something?'

'What is it?' asked Richard Champney.

'I want the exact truth.'

'Very well; you shall have it, if you insist. The bottom has been ripped off the ship, and she is sinking fast.'

'I knew that much. How long can she keep afloat?'

'Perhaps for half an hour, certainly not more.'

'Are there sufficient boats?' inquired Blake.

'Sufficient?' echoed the young officer, shrugging his shoulders. 'There are as many as the law requires, and that is just enough to carry one-third of the three thousand souls on board.'

'Only one-third? And what of the rest?'

'They must rely on their lifebelts. They must take their chances in the sea, in these icy waters.'

With that Richard Champney passed on, but an instant later he turned and stepped back. 'Our wireless operator has been in communication with the steamer *Florida*,' he said, 'and she is steaming towards us.'

'How far away is she?' Blake asked.

'Something like one hundred miles.'

'Then she can't get here before –'

'Not before daybreak at the earliest. Now you know the worst, Mr Blake.'

The young man disappeared, and for several minutes Sexton Blake and the lad stood in silence, neither looking at the other. They had learned the worst, and their minds were trying to grasp the meaning of it. Though they had known that the situation was more than serious, it had not occurred to them that it might be quite so bad as this. They knew now that there would be no place for them, or for hundreds of others, in the lifeboats that were being so hurriedly lowered. They must take their chance with the sinking vessel, fight for their lives after she had gone to the bottom. Tinker's hand stole into his master's hand, and he glanced up at him bravely.

'I understand,' he said. 'There is no hope for us.'

'None, it would seem,' Blake replied. 'Remember that we are Britons, that we belong to a race of heroes.'

'I won't forget,' vowed the lad.

That was all. In those few words they accepted the inevitable, and then, thinking less of themselves than of others, they lent what assistance they could to the work of embarking. And while thus engaged they saw Richard Champney quietly, nobly, doing his duty; separating wives from their husbands, lifting women and children into the boats, and giving instructions to the crews.

Meanwhile, the ghastly truth had spread. The *Paleta* was sinking! This monster leviathan going to the bottom of the Atlantic! All realised that it was so, and that two-thirds of those on board must be left to their fate. But still there was no panic on the upper decks. None of the passengers or crew showed a spark of cowardice. Rich and poor, purse-proud millionaires, and those to whom life had less to offer – all faced the prospect with calm, steadfast heroism.

In other parts of the great vessel, however, there were dramatic scenes to be witnessed, and isolated instances of wild terror. Clamouring steerage-passengers, many of them foreigners, were being held at bay by drawn revolvers; and now and again was heard the sharp report of pistols as frenzied men tried to leap into the boats that were passing the lower decks, and were ruthlessly shot down by the ship's officers.

Women and children first! Here and there the call rang out, and the Law of Chivalry must be obeyed, even at the price of bloodshed.

The last boat had gone, the last of the rafts had been lowered. Out there in the darkness the crews were bending to the oars, pulling hard away from the doomed vessel to save the sobbing little ones and the hysterical women who had been confided to their care. Sexton Blake and Tinker had not seen Richard Champney for some little time, nor did they know what had become of him. They had moved to the stern, where they were surrounded by many others who had been left behind, and were waiting quietly for the end.

This calm and starlit night, the gentle heave of the ocean, lent a sense of unreality to the impending catastrophe. It was still difficult to believe that the *Paleta* was sinking. Yet she had been slowly, surely bending to her last long home; and now, at two o'clock in the morning, she was settling rapidly with her bows and the bridge completely under water.

Deeper, still deeper, she crept. Higher and higher mounted the lapping tide. To those out in the boats, looking back as people might look in a trance, she presented a beautiful sight, for the electric lights were blazing from every saloon and porthole that had not been submerged. That this ocean palace, replete with luxury that included even a Parisian cafe, should be doomed to such a fate! It was almost incredible! It staggered imagination!

'How much longer, do you think?' the lad asked hoarsely.

'A minute or so, not more,' Blake replied.

'And what then, guv'nor? Will we have a chance to keep afloat?'

'I can't tell, my boy. We must put our trust in Providence. But I fear there is no hope of – ah, look!'

The ship had quivered as she settled still deeper, and a wave was rolling aft. Sexton Blake and Tinker involuntarily gripped the brass railing by which they were standing, and clung to it with might and main; and they were still clinging to it, drenched to the skin, when the wave had swept over them. They glanced at each other in a dazed way. They had expected to go to the bottom, and it was a surprise to find that the vessel had survived the swirl of foaming waters. But it was only for a moment.

'By Heavens, here we go!' gasped the lad, as the deck slanted to a dizzy angle.

'Hold tight!' bade Blake, hardly conscious of what he was saying. 'Hold tight, my boy!'

It was the beginning of the end; the dread, colossal prelude to this unparalleled, tragical drama of the ocean. Swiftly forward dived the *Paleta*, until she was tilted almost vertically upwards, and at the same instant her machinery went groaning, rattling, crashing from stern to bow. For some seconds she hung thus, with her lights still blazing, with nearly two hundred feet of her huge bulk reared stark like a tower against the starlit sky. There was a muffled explosion in the engine-room, followed by a dying roar that might have been heard for miles around. And then, of a sudden, the monstrous liner shot downwards with a slant, and vanished forever into the hungry maw of the Atlantic, into the awful abyss twelve thousand feet deep.

'Guv'nor! Oh, guv'nor!'

It was Tinker's voice, and it was the last thing that Blake heard as he plunged with the ship. Down, down he went in the vortex, spinning madly round and round, with a giddy roaring in his ears. He had been torn from the railing, but it seemed like an eternity before the suction loosened its grip and he felt that he was ascending. Slowly he mounted through the darkness, holding his breath as best he could. His head rose above the surface, and he gulped the fresh air deep into his lungs.

'Tinker!' he called. 'Tinker, where are you?'

THE THIRD CHAPTER

Adrift – The Raft – The Rescuing Ship

The *Paleta* had disappeared, and was whirling down through two miles of ocean; and Sexton Blake, drifting on the gentle swell above, was calling to the lad he loved so dearly.

But he got no answer, nor would it have been possible for him to have distinguished Tinker's voice. There was ringing in his ears the most appalling medley of sounds that was ever heard: the cries of hundreds and hundreds of people who were struggling for their lives on all sides of the detective, whose horror was intense. Believing that the lad had already perished, indifferent to his own fate, he drifted for a time with the tide.

He could not see a single boat, nor any light of a vessel, and therefore it would have been useless for him to have tried to assist the people around him: nor could he safely have ventured near any of them, so frenzied were their struggles.

Supported by his lifebelt, he slid on and on, witnessing ghastly scenes, and listening to the futile appeals of the poor wretches who were scattered over the surface of the sea. One by one they vanished from his sight, while the pitiful clamour, which at first had been shrill and strident, sank to a confused chorus of groaning and moaning, and then faded to silence.

Blake's constitution was in his favour. He was as hard as nails, and he had been shipwrecked more than once. He had survived the others, and his strength was equal to a prolonged fight. He did not care whether he lived or died, however, since he had no doubt that his young assistant had gone to the bottom with the *Paleta*. Yet the impulse of self-preservation bade him hold out as long as he could, and he mechanically obeyed that impulse. He had now been afloat for some minutes, and as he was thinking of the great catastrophe, trying to grasp the stupendous nature of it, a voice uttered his name, and his heart gave a throb of joy.

'Tinker!' he exclaimed. 'Is that you?'

'Right you are, guv'nor!' the lad replied. 'Here I am!'

Yes, there he was within half a dozen yards, clinging to a wooden grating. Sexton Blake swam quickly to it, but he had no more than rested his weight upon it when it dipped and went under. He released his hold, and let it rise.

'This won't support both of us!' he said hoarsely.

'Then you take it,' begged Tinker. 'Your life is more important than mine.'

'No; you are the youngest. Hold on as long as you can. If you survive until morning, you will be picked up by the steamer that is approaching.'

'I won't live without you, guv'nor.'

'I may be spared as well, my boy. We may meet again. At all events, you must keep this support.'

'If you leave me I will –'

'Goodbye, Tinker May Heaven care for you!'

With that, his eyes dim with tears, Blake nobly turned and swam away. He presently looked round, and saw that the lad was swimming after him.

'Go back!' he said, as sternly as he could.

'I won't!' vowed Tinker. 'I am coming with you!'

'I forbid you to, my boy.'

'I can't help it, guv'nor. Don't be so cruel!'

'You must live for Pedro's sake,' urged Blake. 'The poor dog will pine from grief if he loses both of us.'

'He would rather have you than me,' replied the lad.

'I tell you again to go back, and I mean it. Will you refuse to obey what may be my last command?'

'If you put it like that, I – I suppose I shall have to obey. But it is awfully hard to –'

Tinker's voice choked. He reluctantly turned, and began to struggle back towards the wooden grating, which was within easy reach.

'Goodbye, guv'nor!' he faltered.

'Goodbye, my dear boy!' the detective answered.

Thus they parted, neither believing that they would ever meet again. The lad was weeping, and Sexton Blake's anguish of mind was such as cannot be described. Not once did he look round. He swam steadily on and on, scanning the wide waste of the ocean, until the icy water begun to numb his limbs.

But for fully an hour he retained consciousness, while he was carried here and there on the gentle swell, and at last, when his senses were slipping from him, and he was resigned to his fate, a shout rang on his ears.

He was barely able to frame a husky reply. He was half-blind, for his eyelids were crusted with salt, but he could perceive a vague object not far off, and by a desperate effort he struggled towards it. His arms were grasped, and he heard a low murmur of voices. Then he was raised from the water, and dragged into one of the *Paleta's* rafts, on which were twenty other men, who had mostly been picked up after the vessel's plunge to the bottom.

'It is Mr Blake, the detective,' somebody said.

'Here is my flask,' said somebody else. 'Give him some brandy.'

Blake's teeth were chattering, and he could not speak until the flask had been put to his lips, and he had swallowed a quantity of the fiery spirit, which recruited his strength, and enabled him to endure the ordeal that awaited him. He was in a half-dazed state, as were his companions.

For hour after hour, thinking constantly of the lad, he stood with the others knee-deep in water on the frail raft, which was so heavily-laden that the least movement would be likely to overturn it. Thus the long, bitter night wore by. At length the grey light of dawn began to flush above the horizon, and a little later, as the detective was yielding to drowsiness, a joyous shout rang in his ears.

'We are saved. The *Florida* is coming!'

It was true. To the south, within a couple of miles, was visible a big liner that was swiftly approaching, belching smoke from her funnels. And in all directions, scattered over the heaving ocean, were the lifeboats that had pulled away from the doomed *Paleta*. They had been hovering ever since near the scene of the disaster, waiting for the expected rescue.

The raft was the first to reach the *Florida*, and Sexton Blake, who was less exhausted than his companions, refused to go to bed. He went below, where he drank a cup of steaming coffee, and got into dry clothing; and when he ascended to the deck, with a heavy heart, the work of rescue was in full progress.

It was a pitiful and harrowing sight. Some of the lifeboats were alongside of the liner, and others were drawing near. Many of the passengers had already been brought aboard, some in evening dress, and some wrapped in blankets. Scarcely a sob was heard from any of them.

All appeared to be stunned by the stupendous disaster, by the loss of their dear ones, as they were hurriedly led to the saloon for a hot breakfast. There were husbands without wives, and wives bereft of their husbands; parents without their children, and children whom the cruel sea had robbed of their parents.

'It is almost too much for the mind to grasp,' Blake said to himself. 'The *Paleta* two miles down, and fifteen hundred victims of the catastrophe. It is the greatest tragedy of its kind.'

He stood looking on, wondering why he had been spared rather than the lad he had loved so dearly. In silence the shivering passengers were hauled aboard, the adults by means of ropes tied round their waists, while the children and babes were hoisted in bags. One by one they ascended, from boat after boat. Presently up came the slim figure of a youth, and when the rope about his waist had been untied, and he had taken a couple of faltering steps, Sexton Blake caught sight of him, and stared in breathless amazement.

'Tinker!' he gasped, as he sprang forward. 'Tinker!'

'Guv'nor!' cried the lad. 'Dear old guv'nor! Oh, thank Heaven that you are alive!'

The next instant they were in each other's arms, not ashamed of the tears that coursed down their cheeks. They clung together, uttering incoherent words, overcome by joy and gratitude; and when they had partly recovered from their emotion, the detective spoke briefly of his rescue, and Tinker told in a few words how he had been picked up by one of the boats after he had held to the grating for an hour.

'I never expected to see you again,' he concluded.

'Nor I you, my boy,' Blake answered fervently. 'Heaven has indeed been merciful to us!'

Meanwhile most of the passengers had been disembarked. Some of the sailors of the *Florida* were preparing to drag up the empty lifeboats by means of the tackle, and the last of the little fleet of fifteen, laden to completion, was swinging alongside of the big liner.

Sexton Blake and the lad watched the scene from the rail. All of the passengers in this boat were women and children; there was not a male amongst them. As quickly as possible they were hauled up, by ropes and in sacks. Three seamen followed, and last came a young man who wore the gold-braided uniform of the *Paleta's* officers.

'There is Champney!' said the detective, with an odd expression on his face.

'It is rather queer that he should have been with that lot, isn't it?' murmured Tinker, in a low tone.

Richard Champney had not moved since he had reached the deck. He was standing there with his hand pressed to his brow, gazing about him as if dazed. He saw Sexton Blake, but did not even nod to him. At length he turned away, and at that instant he was confronted by one of the sailors who had been in the boat with him.

'You coward!' the man loudly exclaimed. 'You pitiful coward! I'm going to denounce you for what you are!'

'Don't do it, Messiter!' pleaded the young officer. 'Don't do it! What I told you was true! Give me a chance to clear myself!'

'You can never do that, sir!' declared the sailor. 'There's no use in trying to lie out of it. I'm in no mind to spare you, when I think of all the lives that have been lost. Look at this fellow,' he went on, raising his voice for the benefit of those around him. 'He is the second officer of the *Paleta*, and he ought to have gone down with his ship.

'But instead of doing his duty, he jumped into my boat at the last minute, down among the women and children, who were so tightly packed that the presence of one more person meant danger to all. I should have had him hauled up where he belonged, but there was no chance of that. We were lying close under the exhaust of the condensers, and we had to pull away at once, or be swamped. That's what Mr Champney did, ladies and gentlemen, and he can't deny it. There are plenty of others who will support my story.'

A profound hush followed the denunciation, which had been listened to by many of the rescued people, and by most of the passengers of the *Florida*. Richard Champney averted his eyes, conscious of the glances of scorn and contempt that were bent upon him. His face flushed hotly, then turned to the hue of ashes. With faltering steps he approached the detective, and looked at him appealingly.

'I hope you don't believe what you have heard, Mr Blake,' he said, almost in a whisper. 'Surely you know that I could never have been a coward.'

'It would be difficult for me to think that,' Blake replied, in no very hearty tone.

'I was not one! You can take my word for it!'

'Then you must have an explanation, Champney. What is it?'

'I was thrown into the lifeboat. I had helped women and children in, and was looking down, waiting to see it start, when somebody grasped me by the legs, and gave me a sudden heave that flung me over the rail. It was a big drop, and the fall rendered me unconscious. And when I came to my senses, and realised the terrible position I was in, we were half a mile away from the –'

'Don't you believe him, sir!' interrupted the sailor Messiter. 'I was looking up at the time, and I plainly saw him take the jump.'

'That is a lie, Mr Blake!' vowed the young officer. 'I have told you the truth, and I beg that you will do your best to clear me of this awful charge. I would rather be dead than rest under such a cloud.'

'Your explanation is a curious one, you must admit,' the detective said coldly. 'Had you an enemy on board the *Paleta?* Was there any person who had a grudge against you?'

'No; I am sure there was none.'

'Then what motive could anybody have had for throwing you into the boat? It could not have been meant for a friendly service. Who could have done such a stupid thing?'

'I cannot imagine, unless it was a man whom I observed standing behind me just before I was heaved over the rail. He was tall, and dark, and clean-shaved. He was roughly dressed, and was probably one of the steerage passengers.'

'You do not know who he was, Champney?'

'No; he was a stranger to me. I have no recollection of ever having seen him before. He was the only person who was near me at the time, and it would seem that he must have –'

Richard Champney broke off, and again a wave of colour flushed his pallid cheeks as he met Blake's searching gaze.

'You doubt my word!' he cried hoarsely. 'You do not believe me! Yes, I can read it in your face! I swear that I have told you the truth, but if you won't believe me, who will? By heavens, why am I alive! How can I face the world? My poor father! What will he say when he learns that I have been branded as a –'

His voice choked, and tears of shame filled his eyes. One of the officers of the *Florida* tapped him on the shoulder, and led him away. The two disappeared, the crowd parting in contemptuous silence to let them go by.

The work of rescue had been completed, and the *Paleta's* empty boats were being raised to the deck. In the saloon children were weeping for their parents, and wives were bemoaning the loss of their husbands. The great disaster had been marked by deeds of heroism worthy to be inscribed on the rolls of fame, but it would seem that there had been one glaring instance of cowardice where it should have been least expected.

The law of the sea had been broken by one whose paramount duty it had been to uphold it. The white flower of chivalry had been stained with dishonour.

'Do you think he did it?' asked Tinker.

'I am afraid there is no doubt of it,' Sexton Blake replied. 'The tale that young Champney told is absurdly unnatural. He could not have got into that boat unless he jumped in. His courage must have failed him at the last moment, as is sometimes the case with the bravest of men.'

'I suppose his career is ruined, guv'nor?'

'Yes; utterly ruined. The brand of the coward is on him. His shame will be blazoned to every part of the civilised world, and he will be cut dead wherever he goes. I cannot help feeling sorry for him, but I am more sorry for his father, who has high ideals of courage, and is intensely proud of his –'

Blake paused and shook his head sadly.

'Come, my boy,' be added. 'I am forgetting what you are in need of, after a night of exposure. How much we have to be thankful for, and how deeply we should sympathise with those who have been bereaved! Truly the ways of Providence are inscrutable!'

They went below, and when Tinker had drunk some hot coffee, and put on dry clothes, the two joined the other rescued passengers, and sat down to breakfast. The detective finished first, and returned to the deck, leaving the hungry lad at the table. The sun was above the horizon, and the *Florida* was resting almost motionless on the gentle swell. It was difficult to believe, as one gazed at the calm, blue sea, that there had been such a mighty catastrophe a few hours ago. Yet there in the distance, not many miles off, was a dread reminder of it: a glittering iceberg that towered high above the surface of the Atlantic.

And somewhere in the vicinity, with nothing to mark it, was the spot where the *Paleta* had plunged to her last, long home. And down with her to their doom, in twelve thousand feet of water, had gone the captains of industry, and the lords of money, the men of letters, and the weather-beaten seamen, that perchance the women and children whose lives were in their keeping might come to a haven of safety.

It was of the heroes that Sexton Blake was thinking, not of the wretched young officer who was wishing that he too had been among the victims. A few lines of a poem came into his mind, and he quoted them aloud:

> 'Women and children first!'
> That is the Law of the Sea,
> The labourer's wife in the steerage,
> The lady of high degree.
>
> That is the privilege granted
> To man – that he stand aside;

Nor has the blood proved lacking
Wherever the test be tried.

Thus they have died together,
Men of the Saxon breed,
All of them standing equal
In the light of a golden deed.'

For a little time Blake stood there, and then, with a heavy heart, he went below again, and attended a divine service that was being held in the saloon.

THE FOURTH CHAPTER

Home Again – Blow After Blow

Several weeks had elapsed since the foundering of the *Paleta*, and the people of two continents were still mourning for their brave dead.

On the arrival of the steamer *Florida* at New York, with the survivors of the tragedy on board, many of them had been summoned before a court of inquiry that had been promptly convened at Washington; and amongst the number was Richard Champney, who had tried hard to clear himself, but without avail.

His story had been picked to shreds by a clever cross-examiner, and he had returned to New York, and from there crossed the Atlantic on an insignificant vessel, under a false name.

The summer night had fallen, and the air was fragrant with the perfume of June roses, when the young officer opened the door of a compartment of the London train, and stepped on to the platform of the little Hampshire railway-station. He had seen nobody on the train whom he knew, and he was so altered by the blow that had ruined his career, his face was so drawn and haggard, that he need not have much fear of being recognised at all. But it was with rapid steps, with his hat pulled over his brow, that he passed out of the station.

Once in the road he breathed more freely. He was alone. There had been other passengers, but he had left them behind. He went on for a short distance to a stile, over which he climbed: and when he had crossed a field he entered a large plantation, and struck into a footpath that led for a mile and a quarter to Broadlands. He shrank from the thought of going home, and yet a stronger impulse urged him on, bidding him face the ordeal that he dreaded.

'It would look cowardly to stay away,' he said to himself. 'It will be much better to go. I am innocent. I have a clear conscience. But will my father believe me? Will I be able to convince him that I am still worthy to be called his son!'

It was dark and cool in the woods, which were a part of the Broadlands estate, and were associated with many memories of Richard Champney's boyhood days. The trilling of a nightingale floated to his ears, and reminded him of the one he had often heard singing at the top of the garden of Dulcie Romanis' house.

He quivered with anguish, and drew a deep breath; for greater than his dread of his father, far greater, was the fear that the girl he loved so passionately, his promised bride, might condemn him as the world had done. Yet he could hardly believe that to be possible. His faith in Dulcie was the one star that shone in the black firmament of his sorrow and shame. She, at least, would not doubt that he had been unjustly accused.

'Dear little girl!' he murmured, as he banished his apprehensions from his mind. 'She will be sure to stand by me!'

The plantation ended, and a gate set in a brick wall gave the young man access to the private grounds of Broadlands. Another footpath brought him to the ancient mansion, and his rap at the door was answered by the butler, who had always been devoted to his young master.

But he had no hearty greeting for him now. His expression was cold and forbidding, and there was a gleam of contempt in his eyes. And his first words were as chilling as his manner.

'Your father is at dinner,' he said, 'but I dare say he will see you.'

A lump rose in Richard Champney's throat. His father might consent to see him! The irony of it! Was he already regarded as a parlah in his own home?

'Tell him that I am here, Joseph,' he bade.

'Very good, sir,' the butler replied.

He walked for a few paces along the hall and threw open the door of the library as he might have opened it for an ordinary visitor. The young officer flushed as he entered the room, where a light was burning.

On the big, carved-oak table was a little pile of letters, and he perceived that they were addressed to him. He opened the top one, which had been sent from his favourite club in London, and ran thus.

DEAR SIR, –

In view of circumstances which you will understand, you are requested to tender your resignation, and thus avoid –'

Richard Champney had read enough. His cheeks were burning as he flung the letter down. He opened another which was also from a club, and was to the same effect. And now, as he was beginning to realise what his shame must mean to him in the future, footsteps approached, and he looked up to see his father.

For a moment they gazed at each other in silence. General Champney appeared to have aged since the two had parted several weeks ago. His face was dark with anger, and in his eyes was the steely glitter that had been wont to terrify the culprits who had been haled before him in his days of active military service.

'So you have had the audacity to come here?' he blurted out.

'Why should I not have come?' said the young officer.

'You dare to ask that? Could you not have spared me this infliction, since you have sullied yourself with perpetual dishonour?'

'I stand before you with a clear conscience, father.'

'A clear conscience, indeed! Do you suppose I have not read the finding of the American court of inquiry? Are you not aware that all England is ringing with your shame?'

'I am innocent,' vowed Richard Champney. 'The charge was utterly false.'

'It could not have been!' cried his father. 'Out of your own mouth you were convicted! Your explanation was improbable and absurd! With what motive could any person have thrown you over the rail of the *Paleta*? You yielded to a cowardly impulse, and jumped into that boat!'

'I swear that I did not!'

'I have not the slightest doubt that you did. Nothing could persuade me to the contrary. You are a liar as well as a coward, Richard!'

'I have never told you a lie in my life, father, and I am not lying now! I have told you the truth! I repeat that I am innocent! I was flung into the boat, but I do not know why it was done, or who did it. The affair is a deep mystery!'

'Enough, Richard! Let me hear no more falsehoods!'

The old soldier's eyes blazed with withering contempt. He struck his fist on the table, and then paced to and fro, tugging at his moustache. His outraged feelings, the blow to his pride, had stifled all the kindliness of his nature.

'Is it possible that you will refuse to believe me?' the young man asked hoarsely.

'Yes, I refuse!' declared General Champney, in a voice that was thick with passion. 'That question is settled, and I decline to reopen it. You shall hear what I think of you, however. You have broken my heart, shattered all my interest in life. You have been false to your trust. You have betrayed the confidence that was reposed in you. Forgetting the obligations of heredity, the claims of blood, you have brought disgrace on the name that you bear, and no less disgrace and dishonour on the name of British seamanship.

'You should have died at your post, should have gone to the bottom of the Atlantic with your captain and your ship. How you could have purchased your life at such a price passes my comprehension. Only a short time ago, before you sailed on that ill-fated voyage, you stood with me in the picture-gallery, in the presence of the portraits of dead and gone Champneys, while I told you of the heroic deeds of your ancestors and exhorted you to tread in their footsteps. And this is how you heeded my advice. By gad, sir, I wonder that you have had the courage to show your face to me!'

'Father, I beg you once more to believe that –'

'I will believe nothing. You are as dead to me as you are socially dead to the world. Nothing can purge your shame. You are no longer a son of mine. I disown you, cast you out. And if ever you attempt to put foot in this house again, I will have my servants –'

'I beg your pardon, sir.'

It was the voice of the butler, who had just entered the library with a long, yellow envelope. He handed it to his master, and when the latter had taken the enclosure from it, and glanced at it briefly, a swift change came over him. The passion died out of his eyes, and the florid colour faded from his cheeks, leaving them almost as white as marble. The paper fluttered from his limp grasp, and for a moment he did not move or speak.

The butler left the room, and when the door had swung shut behind him General Champney staggered against the table, and dropped heavily into a chair. His head sank on his breast. His limbs trembled, and his features twitched painfully.

'I had one son left!' he muttered. 'One boy to comfort me in my old age! But – but I have none now!'

The young man picked up the paper from the floor, and read what it contained. It was a short and formal message from the War Office in London, to the effect that Captain Mervyn Champney had been killed in action in the Soudan, near the military post of Gondoro, while leading his men against the hostile tribe of Anakas.

'By heavens!' gasped Richard Champney. 'Poor Mervyn!'

His eyes filled with tears, and a storm of grief surged up in his heart. It was a heavy blow, for he had dearly loved his elder brother, the handsome, gallant soldier who had won military glory with his sword. He stopped over to his father and touched him on the arm.

'On my honour,' he said softly, 'I am still worthy to be your son. Let me comfort you in your sorrow. Let us try to comfort each other, for we have both been bereaved.'

General Champney shook off his son's hand, and rose from his chair. His face was very cold and stern, and his emotion was under control.

'Go!' he bade harshly. 'Go, Richard! And never let me see you again! From this night I have no son!'

Against that sentence of banishment there was no appeal, and the young man knew it. Pride sealed his lips, and left him no alternative but to obey the command. He glanced at the unopened letters on the table, and perceived one that was addressed to him in Dulcie Romanis' handwriting. He slipped it into his pocket, and then, in silence, he left the room.

The butler opened the hall-door for him, and he passed out into the summer night.

With the consciousness of innocence, hoping that there was at least one person who had retained faith in him against the world, he held his head high as he strode down the gravelled drive to the gateway, over which was burning a lamp. Here he stopped, and took the letter from his pocket.

For a few seconds he hesitated, and then, mustering courage, he tore the envelope open, and with trembling fingers drew from it a folded sheet of paper. The sheet was blank; it contained not a word of writing. But on the creamy surface lay something that was more eloquent, more harrowing, than any words could possibly have been – a tiny white feather. A white feather! The emblem of cowardice! Richard Champney let that and the paper drop, and crushed them under his heel.

'By heavens, this is too much!' he cried aloud. 'So she, too, believes me to be a coward! She, too, has deserted me in my darkest hour! I have not a friend in the world to turn to for comfort!'

This last blow was the hardest and most crushing of all, and the more so because it had been less anticipated. Not only had Dulcie Romanis lost faith in her lover, but she had inflicted on him the most cruel humiliation that can be conceived. In sending him the white feather she had indeed expressed a degree of contempt that she could not have put into words. She must have wanted him to suffer, wanted him to know how much she loathed and despised him.

'By heavens, it is too much!' the young man repeated.

He had been asked to resign from his clubs, and had been turned out of doors by his father, and now the girl he loved had stabbed him to the heart. He stood there with his hands clenched, staring into vacancy with eyes that saw nothing. A tempest of passion, a mad sense of rebellion against the injustice of Fate, surged within him. They slowly abated, leaving him a prey to dull misery and despair.

Black and hopeless was the prospect that stretched before him, but he was a Champney, and he must bear his burden as any of his brave ancestors would have borne it. In that thought he took some slight comfort, and foresaw what he must do. It would be impossible for him to live in England. He must go into exile, and hide his identity.

'I'll enlist,' he said to himself. 'That will be the best plan. There are half a dozen parts of the globe where there is always fighting. I might join the Turkish forces in Tripoli, or become a member of the Foreign Legion. No, I'll do better than that. I'll fight under the British flag, in an assumed name. I know how one gets into the Indian Mounted Police, and that is the corps

I shall join. In some frontier war a spear or a bullet will put an end to my misery. But first I will distinguish myself by some deed of valour, so that I can let Dulcie know that I was not a coward, after all. Yes, I will do something that will justify me in returning to her the badge of shame she has sent me, and when I am dead she will –'

He remembered the white feather, and sought for it; he picked it up from the ground, and smoothed it out, and put it carefully in his pocket. And then, as he was about to bend his steps in the direction of the railway-station, he was assailed by a temptation that was too strong for him to resist. He yielded to it, though he knew that it would only intensify his suffering. He bore along the road for a short distance, and turned in at a gate, and as he crept up the garden-path, drawing nearer to the house where his lost sweetheart lived, he heard a voice singing to the strains of a piano.

'It will be a torture,' he muttered, 'but I must have one last look at her, a memory to carry into exile.'

In the drawing-room of the Grange, under the soft light, Dulcie Romanis was seated at the instrument. She, too, had suffered. All the brightness had gone from her lovely face, and it was a sad and mournful song – a ballad of a tragic love – that she was singing. The words were in accord with her feelings. The liquid notes, now low and plaintive, now rising to a sobbing melody, floated through the open window to the terrace where Richard Champney was concealed by the shrubbery, gazing into the room as one might gaze into a paradise from which he had been barred by a flaming sword.

The rain beats hard on lattice pane,
And still I wait and wait in vain,
For him who never more will –

The girl's voice faltered and broke. Her fingers slipped from the ivory keys, and her arms dropped listlessly to her sides. With a sigh she rose from the stool, and tears were streaming down her cheeks as she stepped to the window, and stretched out her hands towards Broadlands.

'Dick!' she sobbed. 'Oh, Dick, you have broken my heart! I have nothing left to live for!'

She was leaning from the window now, and the young man was sorely tempted to spring forward and throw his arms around her, and beg her to believe that he was innocent. But he hesitated, and it was well that he did so. Dulcie's tender mood suddenly passed. Her face hardened, and her lip curled in scorn.

'The coward!' she said aloud. 'He is not worth caring for! I could never forgive him for what he has done! Never, never! I will forget him!'

She closed the window, and turned from it. The light in the room was extinguished. Out in the darkness, through the shrubbery, Richard Champney was stealing noiselessly away. He was half-blinded by tears, and racked with anguish.

'I have tasted the cup of bitterness to the very dregs,' he reflected, as he passed from the garden into the road. 'There can be no worse suffering in store for me in the future.'

THE FIFTH CHAPTER

Trouble Brewing – A Way Out

The world was going very well with Mr Hildred Nairne. A few weeks ago he had returned from the German watering place – where his friends and acquaintances had been led to believe he had been – to his comfortable chambers in London, and to his faithful valet. He had gone away burdened with debts, and he had come back to shake off that incubus. He had lifted the bill that he had forged, and he had paid something on account to each of his creditors.

And he had done much more than that. He had succeeded in wriggling into his uncle's good favour, he was on the point of being made the latter's heir, and he was nursing the hope that he would in time win the hand and fortune of Miss Dulcie Romanis, since the frost of scorn had blighted that young lady's engagement to Richard Champney.

Dressed like a butterfly of fashion, Hildred Nairne emerged from his flat in Ryder Street into the bright sunshine of the summer morning, and stood on the step for a moment while he lighted a cigarette. Now twirling his stick in a lavender-gloved hand, and now stroking the silky moustache that was growing to its former proportions, he crossed Piccadilly, and sauntered slowly up Bond Street to the premises of Mr William Tourmalin, the well-known jeweller. That individual was alone in the shop, and at sight of the young man, who was an old customer, an odd expression crept into his eyes.

'Goodmorning,' said Hildred Nairne, with an affable nod. 'I want to see some bracelets, Tourmalin. Nothing very expensive, though. Ten pounds is about my mark.'

'Yes, sir,' replied the jeweller. 'I have some very choice ones at that price.'

The bracelets were shown and inspected, and when one had been chosen and paid for, and Mr Tourmalin had jotted down the address to which it was to be sent – the recipient was to be Miss Dulcie Romanis – he broached the subject that had been on his mind.

'By the way,' he said, 'there is a matter I wish to speak of. You remember that string of pearls you sold to me not long ago. You stated, I think, that it was a family heirloom that had come into your possession?'

'Yes, that's quite right,' assented Hildred Nairne. 'What of it?'

'Well, sir, a very curious thing has happened. I had a visit this morning from an American lady, a Mrs Bigelow of New York, who informed me that she was in a box at the opera at Covent Garden last night with a party of friends and that one of them – Lady Rathmore – was wearing a necklace of pearls which she identified as having belonged to her. And the strangest part of it is that she had the pearls with her on the last voyage of the ill-fated *Paleta*, that she left them in her state-room, and that she had fully believed they had gone to the bottom of the Atlantic'

'You are talking in riddles, Tourmalin. What do you mean?'

'It is the same necklace, you will understand, that I purchased from you, and subsequently sold to Lady Rathmore. How do you account for it, sir?'

Not a muscle of Hildred Nairne's face stirred, not in the slightest degree did he change colour. But for a moment he was silent. Then he laughed easily.

'It is a coincidence, of course,' he said, 'What did this Mrs Bigelow do? Did she try to get possession of the pearls under the impression that they were hers?'

'No, she did not try that,' the jeweller replied. 'But she questioned Lady Rathmore, who naturally sent her to me. And I told Mrs Bigelow that I had bought the necklace from you, and that she must have made a mistake.'

'Did that satisfy her?'

'No, far from it. She declared that it was the necklace she had left on board the *Paleta*, that she could not possibly be mistaken. She was so positive, she explained, because she had the jewels reset in New York within the last year.'

'And she fancied she recognised the setting, eh?'

'She was sure she did, Mr Nairne.'

'Well, Tourmalin, she is wrong. The necklace has been in the possession of a deceased relative of mine for the last seven years, and therefore it obviously could not have been stolen from the lady's state-room, or disposed of by the thief to me or to anyone else. As for myself, I was in Germany during the last voyage of the *Paleta*?

'I am quite willing to take your word for all that sir.'

'The fact simply is that there must have been an accidental duplicate of the necklace that went to the bottom of the Atlantic'

'Yes, that must be it.'

'But the truth must be made clear to Mrs Bigelow. Does she propose to call on me? Did you give her my address?'

'No, she did not want it. I told her that you were a gentleman of the highest reputation, and well known socially, and all that sort of thing. But she was in rather a nasty temper, and – and she left here with the intention of going to Mr Sexton Blake, and putting the matter into his hands.'

This time Hildred Nairne could not entirely keep his feelings under control. He gave a slight start, and his hand shook a trifle as he took a cigarette-case from his pocket.

'Sexton Blake, eh?' he murmured.

'Yes, Mrs Bigelow made his acquaintance on the *Paleta*,' the jeweller answered.

'She is going to a lot of trouble for nothing. I had better look her up. How long ago was she here, Tourmalin?'

'Less than a quarter of an hour ago, sir.'

'And she was going straight to the detective?'

'I believe she was.'

'By the way, where is she staying in London.'

'At the Cumberland Hotel, in Dover Street.'

'She is a very silly woman, Tourmalin.'

'And a very obstinate one, sir.'

'Yes, she must be.'

Hildred Nairne shrugged his shoulders, and smilingly looked the jeweller in the eyes as he lighted a cigarette.

'I am sorry you have had this annoyance,' he drawled, 'It is a nuisance for both of us. I will see Mrs Bigelow, and prove to her that I had every right to the pearls. About that bracelet – kindly send it off today.'

'I will, sir.'

'That's all, then. Goodmorning, Tourmalin!'

'Goodmorning, Mr Nairne!'

Mr Tourmalin had been apparently satisfied, but there was a puzzled expression on his face, and it remained there after the young man had left the shop.

'I wonder?' he reflected. 'I wonder?'

Hildred Nairne was also wondering, and his thoughts were of a most disturbing nature. As he walked down Bond Street, there was a sickening fear in his heart – fear of the clever man whom criminals dreaded more than they did any of the sleuth-hounds of Scotland Yard. He could not keep the pallor from his cheeks, or the look of haunting anxiety from his eyes. He turned into a side-street, and entered the saloon bar of a quiet public-house, where he sat drinking brandy, and thinking of what he had learned.

'Confound the luck!' he said to himself. 'Sexton Blake, of all persons! And I have believed that I was perfectly safe! I am quite capable, I am sure, of dealing with Tourmalin and Lady Rathmore and Mrs Bigelow. But it is different with this clever detective, who can ferret out anything and everything. He would suspect that I had been on the *Paleta*, would discover that I had been, and would jump to the conclusion that I was the man with whom he struggled in the corridor on the night of the disaster. And he might even recognise me, though my moustache has grown again. By heavens, I shall have to get rid of him somehow! It will be worth the risk when there is so much at stake! But how am I to do it? That is the question.'

His uncle's fortune was the stake that Hildred Nairne had referred to. And he was also passionately in love with Dulcie Romanis. Once more he had to face the prospect of certain ruin, unless he could remove from his path the man he feared. An idea had occurred to him, and from that, by the aid of his fertile brain, he worked out a diabolical plan that promised to be attended with little or no risk to himself. Should it succeed, he would have disposed of Sexton Blake in such a way that the latter would appear to have met with an accidental death.

'I'll do it!' he reflected, as he left the public-house. 'It is not likely that there will be any hitch. After hearing Mrs Bigelow's story, Blake will recall the affair of the *Paleta*. He will want to question me, and to ascertain if I am the man he saw with the pearls. He will call at my chambers in the course of the day, and when he learns where I have gone, he will follow me, and will take the footpath from the railway station. He probably won't arrive until evening, but I will be ready for him before that. When I have set the trap I will pack a bag, and travel as far as Winchester, and walk over by the wooded hills without being observed. Yes, I'll risk it. And I had better not waste any time.'

Hildred Nairne had shaken off the apprehensions that had gripped him. There was murder in his soul, but no one could have suspected that from his looks. With a jaunty air, now and again raising his hat to a lady of his acquaintance, he strolled on towards Ryder Street.

Sexton Blake had been absent in the City when Mrs Bigelow called at his house that morning, but when she called again during the afternoon, she found the famous detective at home. He remembered her at once, though he had only met her casually while on his eventful voyage across the Atlantic.

She briefly related the circumstances that had brought her to him, and when she had finished her narrative Blake surprised her by telling of the episode that had occurred on the ship on the night of the catastrophe.

'I knew it!' exclaimed Mrs Bigelow. 'I was sure that there could not have been another string of pearls set exactly like mine. And so you really saw the thief that night, and fought with him! But he was not Mr Nairne, of course? The jeweller gave him the highest character.'

'I am afraid it was not deserved,' murmured the detective. 'I am not acquainted with Hildred Nairne, nor have I ever seen him, to the best of my knowledge, though his uncle is an old friend of mine. But I happen to know that he has been leading rather a fast life, and that he has been concerned in several disreputable transactions.'

'That may be, Mr Blake. I am certain, however, that Mr Nairne could not have been the thief. There was no such name on the passenger list of the *Paleta*, for I inquired at the offices of the company after I first called here this morning.'

'You are a very businesslike woman, Mrs Bigelow.'

'Yes, I have managed my own affairs since the death of my husband. He gave the pearls to me, and that is why I am so anxious to recover them. I can't afford to buy them back from Lady Rathmore, so I have come to you. Since they were stolen property, the jeweller is liable for their value.'

'Yes, that is quite right.'

'As for Mr Nairne, I don't suspect him of having any guilty knowledge of the matter. But he may have got the necklace from the thief.'

'Have you no reason to suspect him, madam? Why did he tell Mr Tourmalin that he had inherited the necklace from a relative?'

'Oh, I never thought of that!' said Mrs Bigelow. 'How stupid I have been! Mr Nairne has made a false statement. I can positively assure you that those pearls are mine! I hope you don't doubt me?'

'No, I am disposed to believe you,' the detective replied, 'and I will do all that I can for you. Leave the affair to me. I shall look into it without delay, and you will hear from me in the course of a day or so.'

He rose to indicate that the interview was ended. The lady departed, and Blake, having lighted a pipe, sat down, and gave his thoughts to the case he had undertaken. He knew where Hildred Nairne lived, General Champney having not long ago mentioned the address to him.

'It is fairly obvious,' he said to himself, 'that Nairne is guilty. Otherwise the pearls could not have come into his possession. They would have been disposed of through some regular channel. For some reason he must have sailed on the *Paleta* under an assumed name. Perhaps he was in flight from his creditors, and the theft of the necklace enabled him to return and pay off his –'

An idea suddenly occurred to him with such force that he jumped out of his chair.

It was a startling theory that he had conceived. General Champney was an old man, and his soldier son, who had been killed in action since the foundering of the *Paleta*, was at the time of the tragedy in a warlike land where his life was in danger. Hildred Nairne was the general's nephew, and, therefore, could he have contrived to have the second son disinherited, he would have had a fair chance of one day succeeding to the estate.

Had he thrown Richard Champney into the boat on that fatal night, with a view to getting him into indelible disgrace? It was to be assumed that Nairne had been on the *Paleta*, and that he had stolen the pearl necklace. And the appearance of the thief – as the detective now remembered – tallied with the description given by the young officer of the man who had been standing behind him on the deck.

'I believe I am right,' Sexton Blake muttered. 'Yes, it certainly looks as if poor Champney had been wrongfully branded as a coward! By heavens, what a terrible thing!'

He put on his hat, and left the house, and hailed a taxicab. It was his intention to question Hildred Nairne, and see if he could recognise him as the man who had stolen the pearls. He drove to Ryder Street, and the door of the flat was opened by Hume, the valet, who stated that his master was not in town.

'He has gone down to his uncle's place in Hampshire, sir,' he continued.

'When will he be back!' asked the detective.

'Not for two or three days. Will you leave your card, sir?'

'No, I haven't one with me. By the way, was your master in America this spring?'

'No, sir. He has never been there. But he was abroad for some weeks – at a German watering-place.'

'What was the name of it?'

'I – I can't remember, sir,' was the stammering reply, 'not at the moment. It was a very queer name.'

Blake did not put any more questions. He descended the stairs, and passed out to the street.

'The valet is trying to shield his master,' he said to himself. 'Hildred Nairne was a steerage passenger on the *Paleta* beyond a doubt. And now for Broadlands. I will go down by the first train.'

THE SIXTH CHAPTER

The Trap in the Wood – Fortune in Sight

Hildred Nairne had calculated his plans with shrewd foresight, and with a knowledge of the fact that the detective had paid more than one visit to Broadlands. There was no vehicle to be had at the isolated little railway station that was nearest to General Champney's residence, and it was, therefore, only natural that when Sexton Blake arrived there, shortly after the sun had set, he should decide to go to his destination by the footpath instead of by the road, which was considerably farther round.

He was in no particular hurry. He had not been out of London for weeks, and the beauty of the country appealed to him. He climbed over the stile, and slowly crossed the field that led to the path. Twilight was falling, and when he had struck into the deep plantation he was shrouded in purple gloom. He could see the way clearly enough, however. He strolled leisurely on, wondering if his theory in regard to Richard Champney was correct, until he had put half a mile behind him.

Then he stopped, and took a cigar from his pocket, and set it alight. Just as he had finished, he heard a faint, rustling noise, and at the same instant, by the glow from the flaming match that he was still holding, he saw a twig drop from the leafy bough of a tree that was two or three yards in front of him.

As it was a calm night, without a breath of air stirring, the fall of the twig, and the faint noise, were not easily to be accounted for. The detective's suspicions were at once aroused. He could hear nothing now, nor could he see anybody in the tree. He tossed the match from him, and for a moment stood listening; and then, as he prudently moved a pace or so backward, something was thrown at him from the mass of foliage. It was a large stone, and it was hurled with such good aim that it grazed Blake's head, and struck him with no little force on the shoulder.

He was dizzy with pain, and hardly conscious of what he was doing. Staggering to one side of the path, he reeled through a screen of bushes, and swayed against some obstruction that yielded to his weight. He lurched away from it, and as he did so, he heard a muffled crashing and rattling that continued for several seconds before it faded to silence.

Sexton Blake shivered. Half-stunned though he was by the blow from the stone, he was aware that he had narrowly escaped death. He remembered that there was an old well in this vicinity, and he knew that he must have dislodged a portion of the crumbling masonry that surrounded it, and sent it toppling to the bottom. He stood there for a few seconds, afraid to move; and then, as he heard a dull, heavy sound from the path, he realised that the mysterious person who had hurled the stone at him had dropped from the tree, and that he was in peril of his life.

He had no revolver with him, not even a walking-stick. He was still dizzy and in pain, and had he taken to his heels, he must have drawn pursuit after him, and been soon overhauled, since he could not have run fast. For a moment he hesitated, aware of his danger. Then he dropped to his hands and knees, and crawled noiselessly into a copse of bushes until he came to a tree, behind which he crouched.

Footsteps were now approaching. They stopped, drew nearer, and stopped again. The next instant a match flared in the darkness, and the light revealed to the detective a man who was within three or four yards of him: a young man, well dressed, with dark hair and a black moustache. He was standing close to the well by the ragged gap in the masonry. He leaned over the parapet, and peered down into the yawning abyss. The match burnt out, and when he had struck another one, he held it above him, and looked sharply into the surrounding thickets.

'It is all right,' he said to himself, half-aloud. 'Sexton Blake has saved me the trouble of finishing him off. He is at the bottom of the well, no doubt of it. He has gone to his death, and I have nothing to fear. No suspicion will fall on me.'

He tossed the match from him, and turned away. His footsteps faded to silence along the path and a little later Blake crept out from his hiding-place. His head still pained him, and his shoulder had been severely bruised, but otherwise he was none the worse for his injury. The whole truth had flashed upon him, and it was with hot anger that he thought of the dastardly trap which had so nearly ended his life.

'The man was Hildred Nairne, of course,' he reflected. 'He must have learned this morning, from the jeweller, that Mrs Bigelow had gone to put the case of the pearl necklace in my hands. He determined to get rid of me because he felt sure that I would be able to fasten the theft on him, and he shrewdly judged that I would call at his chambers during the day, learn from the valet that he had gone to Broadlands, and follow him down here. His intention was to kill or stun me with that stone, drag me to the old well, and drop me into it. The coldblooded scoundrel! He fully believes that I am at the bottom of the well, but he will discover his mistake before he is much older.'

The detective had by now retraced his steps to the footpath, and turned in the direction of Broadlands. By then Hildred Nairne was some distance away. Not doubting that the man he feared was dead, he had taken his bag from the thicket where it had been concealed, and hastened on through the woods.

He was expected at his uncle's residence, as it happened. He had meant to come down from London late that afternoon, and when he arrived at the house, to find that dinner was about to be served, he did not wait to get into evening-dress. He went up to his bedchamber for a few moments, and then, having removed from his clothes all traces of his climb into the tree, he joined the old soldier in the dining-room.

The death of his eldest son in the Soudan, and the disgrace that had banished the younger son from home, had aged General Champney. He scarcely spoke during the meal, and almost ignored the presence of his nephew, for whom he had never had much of a liking. More than once his eyes grew dim with tears, but Hildred Nairne felt no pity for him. He had contrived to worm himself into his uncle's favour, and his hopes for the future were bright. Moreover, he believed that he knew why he had been invited to Broadlands on this occasion.

The two did not linger long over their port and cigars. The old general rose, and led the way to the library. It was a warm evening, and one of the windows that looked on to the terrace was open. Hildred Nairne sat down on a couch, and his uncle dropped into the big chair by his roll-top desk.

'I have something particular to say to you,' he began.

'Yes, sir,' murmured the young man, trying to hide the satisfaction that he felt.

'I have seen very little of you in past years,' General Champney continued. 'I have heard nothing in your favour, and nothing to your disadvantage. But I do not know what kind of a life you have been leading. I have no intimate knowledge of your character.'

'I have a clear conscience, sir. My tastes have been simple, and I have not indulged in any dissipations. I do not drink or gamble.'

'You inherited a considerable fortune from your father. Do you still possess it!'

'I do, sir,' lied Hildred Nairne, without turning a hair. 'I have spent the income, but have not touched the principal.'

'Well, I will take your word for it,' said the old man. 'Hitherto you have had no reason to expect anything from me. I have given you scarcely a thought, for your mother married against my wishes, and I never entirely forgave her. But blood is thicker than water, and the blood of the Champneys flows in your veins, though you do not bear my ancient name. My estate is a large one, and I am not inclined to dispose of it to charitable institutions. I have no sons now. The one is dead, and the other, as you know, has –'

General Champney paused. His features softened for an instant, then grew harsh and cold again.

'We won't speak of Richard,' he went on, when he had recovered from his emotion. 'He is as dead to me as Mervyn is, and I am trying to forget that he exists. You are the only relative I have, and I have decided, after careful consideration, to regard you as my future heir.'

'I thank you, sir,' said Hildred Nairne. 'It is very kind of you.'

'It is my duty. I cannot ignore the claims of kinship. But there is an obligation on your side as well – to keep unsullied the honour of the family to which your mother belonged.'

'I can assure you, sir, that I will always be worthy of your trust and confidence.'

'It will be a comfort to me to believe that. I do trust you, else I should not dream of –'

General Champney paused again. He swung round to his desk, and unlocked it, and raised the lid. He picked up a thick packet of banknotes that were lying in plain view, and tucked them into a pigeon-hole; and then, opening a drawer, he took from it a long, narrow document.

'I have destroyed my former will,' he said, 'and this is a rough draft of a new one. In the course of a day or so my solicitor will make a copy of it, and it will be properly signed and witnessed. My son Richard will have nothing. I am leaving everything to you, Hildred, with the exception of certain bequests to charities, and legacies to some old friends. After my decease you will live in this house, and you will have entire control of –'

He left the sentence unfinished, for at that instant Sexton Blake vaulted lightly through the open window into the room. His face was pale and haggard, and his clothing was soiled and dishevelled.

THE SEVENTH CHAPTER

A *Crushing Blow – Suspicions*

For a few seconds there was utter silence. General Champney was speechless with surprise, and Hildred Nairne was staring in dumb horror, as one might stare at an apparition that has crept from the grave. The detective stepped quickly and quietly forward to the desk, opened one of the lower drawers, and took from it a revolver that he knew was kept there.

'Remain where you are, Nairne,' he said. 'Don't move, or it will be the worse for you. I am going to denounce you in the presence of your uncle. You have grown a moustache since you returned from America, but that does not prevent me from recognising you as the man with whom I fought on the night the *Paleta* went to the bottom. And I saw you no less distinctly an hour ago, when you stood by the old well with a lighted match in your hand.'

'What – what does all this mean?' gasped General Champney.

'It means that your nephew is one of the greatest villains on earth,' Blake replied. 'I have been listening to your conversation from outside the window, and I am very glad to have the opportunity of preventing you from leaving your property to a man who ought to be in prison.'

'It is a lie,' faltered Hildred Nairne, who was white with fear and consternation. 'You can't prove anything against me.'

'I can prove everything, and you know it,' declared the detective. 'Denials will be useless. Look at him, general,' he continued. 'See how he is trembling. He cannot hide his guilt. For some reason, a couple of months ago, this scoundrel sailed for America under an assumed name, in the steerage of the *Paleta*. On the night of the disaster, an hour before the great liner foundered, he took advantage of the prevailing confusion to enter the state-room of one of the lady passengers, where I disturbed him in the act of stealing a valuable pearl necklace. He got away from me after a short struggle, and I did not see him again. But subsequently, by some means, he escaped from the vessel with those who were picked up the next morning. He returned to England with the necklace, and sold it to a Bond Street jeweller, who in turn disposed of it to a London lady of title, the widow of Sir John Rathmore. She went to the Covent Garden opera last night with a friend, and that friend, who was the American lady from whom the pearls had been stolen, recognised them on Lady Rathmore's neck. The result was – to cut the tale short – that inquiries were made of the jeweller, and the case was promptly put into my hands.'

'How can I believe this?' exclaimed the old soldier.

'You will have to believe it.' said Sexton Blake. 'And you have not heard the worst yet. Your nephew tried to murder me tonight, so that he might cover up his other crime and retain your confidence.'

'He – he tried to kill you, Blake?'

'Yes, and he very near succeeded.'

Continuing, the detective told of his thrilling adventure in the plantation, and his narrow escape from death; and when the narrative had been finished, there was a brief silence. The sight of the revolver had kept Hildred Nairne in his chair, and he was now dumb with terror, realising that he was now fast in the toils. General Champney had been convinced. He gazed in horror at the trembling, cowering figure of his nephew, not doubting that he was guilty of all that he had been accused of

'This is the last blow,' he said hoarsely. 'I have suffered one affliction after another.'

'I know that,' Blake told him. 'I am very sorry for you.'

'You have done me a service, though, and I am grateful. But how do you propose to deal with this scoundrel? Would – would it be possible to let him off?'

'It would be a great mistake to do so.'

'Yes, I admit that. He richly deserves to be punished, Blake. But spare him for my sake, because he is my dead sister's son. I have suffered enough. Don't bring more shame and disgrace upon us.'

'I really ought not to consent, general. He has tried to commit murder. And there is the charge of theft –'

'That can be hushed up,' interrupted the old soldier. 'My nephew is wealthy, and he can be made to refund the money he received for the pearl necklace.'

'He has nothing at all,' replied Blake. 'He squandered all his money long ago, and has been living on his wits.'

'Then he deceived me. He told me only tonight that he has been spending only the interest of the fortune he inherited from his father.'

'That was untrue. He has run through the whole of his fortune.'

'Well, no matter. Spare him. Blake. I beg you not to refuse my request. As for the pearls, I will buy them back from Lady Rathmore, and present them to the lady from whom they were stolen.'

The detective hesitated for a moment, and then reluctantly nodded assent.

'For your uncle's sake I will let you off, Nairne,' he said sternly. 'Be thankful to him, not to me. And now go. If you will heed my advice you will leave England as soon as possible, and try to lead an honest life in some foreign country.'

Hildred Nairne felt no gratitude for the mercy that had been shown to him. He had escaped a long sentence of imprisonment, but all his bright prospects had been shattered – his uncle's wealth, the chance of winning the girl he loved, a life of ease and luxury. And he was almost at the end of his resources; he had no means of subsistence.

He rose slowly from his chair, and with a gleam of venomous hatred in his eyes, with a muttered curse on his lips, he slunk from the room. His footsteps echoed along the half, and the door slammed behind him as he passed out into the night. General Champney had been sitting with bowed head. He looked up with an expression that was pitiful.

'It is too much,' he said. 'What have I done to deserve all this? I have given the best years of my life to my country's service, and I had a right to expect a peaceful and happy old age. The afflictions of Job could hardly have been worse than mine. First Richard's disgrace, and then the death of my elder son, and now this last crushing blow. My spirit is broken. I cannot live much longer. Soon my wealth will be distributed amongst charities, and strangers will dwell in this ancestral cradle of my race.'

'Don't talk like that,' replied Blake. 'I trust that there are many years of happiness before you.'

'It is impossible.'

'Don't be too sure of that. There is hope for the future.'

'What do you mean?'

'I am thinking of your younger son.'

'I forbid you to mention his name. I have disowned him, and he is as dead to me as if –'

'But what if he had not been guilty of cowardice, general? Suppose the explanation that he gave was true?'

'You – you surely don't think that he told the truth?'

'Yes; I am practically certain that he did. I have every reason to believe that he was thrown into the boat by Hildred Nairne.'

'By heavens! by my nephew?'

Sexton Blake nodded. He had been reluctant to speak of the matter before, because he had no proof to offer, but his friend's distress had opened his lips. He went on to state the reasons for his belief, laying stress on the probable motive for the deed, and on the fact that the man standing behind the young officer on the deck had answered in every way to the appearance of Hildred Nairne when the detective had seen him in Mrs Bigelow's state-room. The old soldier had risen from his chair, and was pacing to and fro as he listened.

'You have convinced me!' he exclaimed. 'Yes, Hildred did that wicked thing! But you are wrong about his motive! It was revenge, I am sure! He and Richard were rivals, as I have lately learned, for the hand of Dulcie Romanis, whom you have met. My boy won the girl's love, and thus incurred Nairne's hatred.'

'Ah, that is a more plausible theory!' declared Blake. 'It would appear that you are right. At all events, Hildred Nairne must have thrown your son into the boat.'

'And we have let him go!' raved General Champney. 'We may not be able to find him again! Why did you not accuse him of his villainy, and force him to confess?'

'It would have been useless. He would have stubbornly denied his guilt, from sheer malice.'

'Yes, that is true. He could not have been induced to confess. But I am satisfied, from what you have told me, that Richard is indeed innocent of that vile charge. Can you understand what this means to me, Blake? Can you realise what my feelings are? By heavens, this will break my heart! My poor boy! His friends, his own father, the girl he loved – all against him! And I stabbed him with the most cruel words I could think of, sneered at his vows of innocence! I disowned him, turned him out of doors, told him that if ever he dared to show his face here again I would have my servant –'

The old general's voice choked. He was intensely agitated. The recollection of the parting scene brought tears of remorse to his eyes, and his features twitched with anguish as he sank into his chair again.

'I may never have the chance to beg his forgiveness,' he groaned. 'It may be too late to make reparation. My son has been gone for weeks, and I have no idea where he is.'

'Have you heard nothing of him?' asked Sexton Blake.

'No, nothing whatever. He has taken me at my word, and disappeared. He has probably gone to some foreign country, to hide his unmerited shame. Or – or he may even have killed himself in his despair.'

'I don't believe that. He was no coward. I am sure that he is alive.'

'Then search for him,' begged General Champney. 'Spare no expense. Devote your whole time to it. Find my poor boy, and bring him back to me.'

Blake was deeply moved. He bent over his friend, and rested a hand on his shoulder.

'I will do what you wish, and gladly,' he said. 'If your son is in England, I will find him and bring him to you. And if he should have gone to a foreign land, I will go there after him.'

'And will you be sure to bring him back? He may refuse to forgive me.'

'Nonsense, Champney! He will be only too ready to throw himself into your arms.'

'I hope so.' sighed the general. 'I would go down on my knees to him if he were here now. But you are not going, are you?' he added, as Blake offered him a hand to shake. 'You must at least spend the night here.'

'No, thanks, I had better get back to town,' was the reply, 'I will begin my quest without delay, and will let you know what progress I make.'

'Heaven bless you, Blake! You are a true friend. But wait. I will go with you to the door.'

'No, I will leave as I entered. The servants do not know that I am in the house, and it would rouse curious speculations if they were to see me.'

'Yes, you are right. I don't want them to know what has occurred, if it can be helped.'

General Champney sighed again. Blake spoke a word of farewell, and then, with a backward glance at the pathetic figure of the old man, he vanished through the open window. But a little later, as he was crossing the garden with the intention of going to the railway station, a disturbed thought flashed to his mind, and he suddenly stopped.

'I mistrust that fellow,' he said to himself. 'There is no telling what he may do.'

The detective had witnessed and overheard everything during his vigil outside of the open window. While crouching on the terrace, and gazing into the library, he had seen the lid of the desk raised, and had observed that Hildred Nairne's eyes had rested on a sheaf of banknotes that his uncle had picked up and tucked into a pigeon-hole. The young man was desperate, and probably in an impecunious condition. The exposure meant utter ruin to him. He would find it advisable to leave the country, and he would require money to do so. Was it not extremely likely, therefore, that he would make an attempt to steal the banknotes he had seen?

Such was the train of deductions that Sexton Blake's mind quickly conceived, and as quickly he decided that he would not return to London just yet. While in the library he had slipped General Champney's revolver into his pocket, and it was still there. He was glad that he did it, for he felt that he might have need of it weapon before the night was over.

'I will search for the scoundrel,' he murmured. 'I dare say he is lurking about somewhere in the vicinity, waiting for his uncle and the servants to go to bed.'

The sky was overcast with clouds, and there was no moon. For an hour, as stealthily and noiselessly as an Indian scout. Blake moved here and there through the large garden that surrounded the house. He left no spot unsearched. He looked behind every tree, and into every clump of shrubbery, until he was at length satisfied that Hildred Nairne was not anywhere in the private grounds. What had become of him? Was he hiding further off, or had he gone back to town? The detective did not believe that he had. His theory had taken a strong grip of him, and he could not shake it off. He was wondering what he had better do, when an inspiration occurred to him. If the young man was meditating another crime, he would probably have sought the nearest public house, there to fortify his courage and dull his sorrows as well.

'I think I know where I shall find him,' reflected Blake.

Though the railway station was a couple of miles distant, there was a tiny village within half a mile of Broadlands. Thither the detective bent his steps, keeping in shadow as much as possible as he went along the road: and when he had reached the Maypole Inn, which was on the edge of the village, he crept up to the window that was at one side of the door, and peered warily through it into the humble tap-room. At a glance he saw that his deductions had been correct. An elderly woman was reading a newspaper behind the bar, and on a bench in a corner of the room, sat Hildred Nairne. He was the only customer at this late hour. He was staring into vacancy with a sullen, ugly expression on his flushed face, and on the rough table in front of him were a bottle of brandy and a glass. For a few moments Blake stood furtively gazing within, and then, not doubting that the young man had resolved to commit a robbery, he stole quietly away, and sought for a hiding place near the inn.

'I will set a watch on the fellow,' he said to himself. 'I would like to send him to prison, but for Champney's sake I must be content with frustrating his object. I will first make sure that it is his intention to steal the money, and then I will give him a sound lecture, and offer to assist him to leave the country.'

THE EIGHTH CHAPTER

Blake is Tricked – A Far Quest

It had been near to closing time when the detective reached the inn, and twenty minutes later Hildred Nairne emerged from it. His gait was perfectly steady, though he had drunk a considerable amount of brandy. It looked at first as if he meant to return to London, for he bore away from the village by the road that led to the railway station. But when he had gone for a quarter of a mile he turned into a cross road, and from that he presently entered a plantation that belonged to the Broadlands estate.

Meanwhile Sexton Blake had been on the young man's track, and was not far behind him. He now lost sight of his quarry, but he was guided by the latter's rustling steps, to which he stopped to listen at intervals. For a quarter of an hour the two slowly threaded the plantation, and then passed through a gate into General Champney's private grounds. They crept on until they were within twenty yards of the old mansion, when Hildred Nairne slipped into a dense copse of shrubbery. The detective, who was no more than five or six yards in the rear, at once stopped in the black shadow of a tree, and strained his ears. He could hear nothing now, not the faintest sound. There could be no doubt, it would seem, that the young man had also stopped, and was lurking in the shrubbery.

It was barely eleven o'clock, and he evidently meant to wait until the time was ripe for his evil purpose. It was likely that the servants had retired for the night, but their master would not have gone to bed so early. He was probably still in the library, which was round on the further side of the house. No lighted windows were visible on the near side, which was almost entirely concealed from view by masses of foliage.

'I must have patience,' thought Blake. 'It will be an hour, I dare say, before the fellow makes a move.'

Not doubting that a waiting game was to be played, he stood there by the tree for a long time, meanwhile hearing no sound whatever. And he might have remained there through half the night without any sense of uneasiness but for an incident that was trifling in itself, and yet was full of significance. A rabbit hopped slowly and calmly from the clump of shrubbery, and began to nibble the grass in the open space that stretched over to the detective. It was not in the least frightened, and that fact, and the fact that it had obviously not been startled out of the cover, sharply suggested that Hildred Nairne was no longer there.

'By Jove, I believe I have been had!' muttered the detective. 'It looks as if the fellow had departed noiselessly. I can't be certain of that, though.'

He moved a pace or two, and at once the rabbit scurried off with a whisk of its tail. Blake took the revolver from his pocket, dropped to his hands and knees, and wriggled warily across the open to the clump of bushes. Having crept about for a little time, and made sure that the thicket was deserted, he emerged on the further side, and rose to his feet. He had been tricked, and mingled with his chagrin was a keen sense of alarm. What had happened, he asked himself, while he had been waiting by the tree.

Fearing lest the general's nephew had already stolen the money and made good his escape, he hastened over to the house, and was about to move round to the other side of it, when he observed a French window that was partly opened. A brief inspection showed him that it had been forced. He slipped through into the dining-room, and groped from there into the hall, which was dimly lit. And as he stood there listening he heard a scuffling noise, and then the sound of a dull fall.

'By heavens, that may be murder!' he reflected.

In half a dozen strides he reached the library door, and as he threw it open a startling sight met his gaze. General Champney was prostrate on the floor by the fireplace, apparently dead, and Hildred Nairne was standing by the desk in the act of thrusting the packet of banknotes into his pocket. As the door creaked he swung round and saw the detective, and at once, with a savage imprecation, he sprang towards him.

'None of that, you scoundrel!' cried Sexton Blake. 'I've got you!'

But he was wrong. Though he had levelled his weapon as he spoke, the attack was so swift that he had no chance to fire. His arm was struck up, and the revolver was knocked from his grasp. A hand fastened on his throat, and the next instant he was at grips with Hildred Nairne, who, in his rage, had not hesitated to run the risk of being shot.

'I'll fix you this time!' he snarled. 'You won't get another chance to meddle with my affairs.'

'I shan't want another chance!' panted the detective. 'I'll show you which of us is the better man!'

He had broken the clutch on his throat, but in his excitement it did not occur to him to shout for assistance, nor did he feel that he would need it. The two tripped over a rug and fell, and for a short interval – it seemed longer than it really was – they rolled about the floor, fighting desperately.

Hildred Nairne had now abandoned his murderous intentions, and was bent solely on escape. But he had caught a Tartar, and his efforts were futile. In vain he pitted his wiry strength against Sexton Blake, who was every bit as strong, and was winning by dogged willpower. He was determined that the man should not get away from him. He held to him like grim death, striving hard to overcome his frenzied struggles, and he was beginning to do so when the two collided with a table and upset it. Down it toppled, and with it a heavy bronze statuette, which struck Blake on the arm with such force as to instantly render the limb numb.

His grip relaxed, and gave to Hildred Nairne an advantage that he was prompt to seize. He wrenched himself partly free, gave the detective a smashing blow on the jaw with his clenched fist; and by another wrench gained his feet. In a trice he had snatched a chair and dashed across the library to the window, which he burst open with one stroke that shattered glass and woodwork. Out he leapt into the darkness, and with him went the packet of banknotes, which were in his pocket.

By then Blake had scrambled up, but as he was exhausted by his strenuous efforts and dizzy from the blow on the jaw, it would have been useless for him to give chase to the fugitive. With anger and chagrin he realised that he had lost his man. He staggered to the window, and looked out for a moment; and then, as he turned away, the butler hastened, half dressed, into the library, having been roused by the noise of the flight.

Oh, my poor master!' he cried, at sight of the prostrate form. 'He is dead! He has been murdered!'

But General Champney was not dead, nor was he seriously injured. He had been stunned by striking the back of his head on the floor. The detective called for brandy, and when the servant had fetched it and a few drops had been forced between the old soldier's lips, he stirred, and opened his eyes. He was placed on a couch, and very soon he was able to speak coherently, though he was suffering from the shock.

'It was my nephew, Blake,' he said, in a low tone. 'He – he did it.'

'Yes, I know that,' Sexton Blake assented; and in a few words he explained how he had happened to come on the scene. 'You had not gone to bed, I suppose!' he added.

'No: I was sitting here in my chair half asleep,' the general replied. 'I heard a suspicious noise and jumped up, and found myself face to face with Hildred Nairne. I grappled with him, and we struggled for a little time. Then he struck me to the floor, and as I fell everything seemed to grow dark. By heavens, what a villain my nephew is! I believe he meant to murder me.'

'It was not so bad as that. His object was robbery, and it has succeeded. He has carried off the packet of banknotes that were in your desk.'

'Well, it is no great loss. Only one hundred pounds.'

'Have you the numbers of the notes, Champney?'

'No, unfortunately I have not. It will be difficult to trace them.'

'But not to trace the man, perhaps.'

There was silence for a few seconds. The old soldier's face was very cold and stern, and there was a hard glitter in his eyes that pleased Blake, who foresaw that he was going to have his own way. He mixed some brandy and water, and drank it at a gulp.

'It is after twelve o'clock' he said, as he looked at his watch, 'and the last train left the station at ten-fifty.'

'What do you mean?' inquired General Champney.

'I am thinking of Hildred Nairne,' the detective answered. 'He cannot get up to London by rail tonight. Will you let me deal with him? Surely you will not ask me again to spare him after this last crime that might have resulted in your death. You must see that it is impossible.'

'I know that it is. You are quite right. My nephew deserves no mercy, and he shall have none. I must do my duty at any cost. Yes, Blake. I will leave the scoundrel to you. Let the law take its course with him.'

'It won't be my fault if it does not. I shall make every effort to find him, and I don't think he will be at liberty very long.'

'But don't forget your promise to look for my son.'

'I won't forget that. Hildred Nairne is to be thought of first, however. By the way, you must lend me your motor car.'

'Certainly,' replied the general. 'It is at your disposal.'

'Then I will have it at once,' said Blake. 'I want to go up to town before your nephew can reach there, and it would be advisable not to waste any time.'

'Very well,' assented General Champney. 'I should like to accompany you, but I am in no fit condition to travel. Go out to the garage, Joseph,' he continued, turning to the butler, 'and waken the chauffeur, and tell him to bring the car around as quickly as possible.'

In twenty minutes the car was at the door, and when Sexton Blake had shaken hands with his old friend and spoken a few words of comfort to him, he stepped into the vehicle, and was whirled away towards London, there to seek for the man he was so anxious to being to justice. But he was by no means confident of success.

'I have my work cut out for me,' he said to himself. 'The fellow will be too shrewd to venture near his chambers, and he may not even go back to town. His first thought will probably be to leave the country, since he has money for present needs.'

Blake's apprehensions had been only too well founded. The man he had hoped to catch had proved to be no less cunning than himself. Though the chambers in Ryder Street had been watched night and day, Hildred Nairne had not returned there; nor, it was certain, was anything known of him by his faithful valet, who was greatly distressed by the disappearance of his master and the troubles that had compelled him to flee from the law. In vain had London been dragged by the police net, and descriptions of the missing man sent broadcast through the provinces, and a close surveillance kept on all persons sailing from British ports. A week had elapsed since the night of the robbery at Broadlands, and not the slightest trace of the fugitive had been discovered. It was believed by the detective, and by the police as well, that he had left the country before the hue and cry was raised.

Meanwhile, General Champney had bought the pearl necklace from Lady Rathmore at the price she had paid for it, and Mrs Bigelow had gratefully accepted it from the old soldier after she had been informed that it was his nephew who had been the thief. And Mr Tourmalin, it may be said, had good reason to congratulate himself; for though he had acted innocently in the matter in one sense of the word, he had legally been a receiver of stolen property, and could have been held liable for the amount that General Champney had paid to Lady Rathmore.

Sexton Blake had taken an active part in the search for Hildred Nairne, and when at length he abandoned it, satisfied that it would be a waste of time to seek any further, he gave his attention to the case he had promised to undertake on behalf of his old friend, and tried to find Richard Champney. It was a quest that strongly appealed to him, since he was convinced, or very nearly so, that the young man was innocent of the charge that had blasted his career and held him up to public scorn and contempt.

He set to work with wholehearted zeal, employing all the resources at his command. For more than a week his patient efforts led to nothing, and then, one afternoon, he let himself into his house in Baker Street and walked into his consulting-room with such a cheerful expression on his face that Tinker guessed at once what it meant.

'Well, have you found him?' he asked.

'I haven't exactly found him.' Blake replied, 'but I have learned where he is.'

'Where, guv'nor?'

'He is far away from England, my boy. He is out in India.'

'Soldiering. I'll bet.'

'Yes; that is quite right.'

The detective sat down with a sigh of relief, for he was tired. He set his pipe alight, and watched the smoke wreathing upward from the bowl.

'It struck me that the heartbroken young fellow might have enlisted,' he went on, 'and that idea led to success. I have been making inquiries on those lines, and I have learned to my complete satisfaction, that Richard Champney, under the name of Rupert Dare, applied at the London recruiting-office for admission to the ranks of the Indian Mounted Police. It is not an easy matter to get into that corps, but he pulled through somehow by the skin of his teeth. I have a shrewd suspicion – I won't put it into words – that the recruiting-officer recognised him, and was disposed to give him a chance of dying in action or redeeming his lost honour. At all events, young Champney was accepted, and was shortly afterwards shipped off to the East with a draft of new recruits.'

'He has been out there for some time, then?' said Tinker.

'Yes! for several weeks.'

'And how will you get him back?'

'We shall have to fetch him back, my boy.'

'You are going to India after him?'

'That is what I intend to do.' Sexton Blake replied. 'Two reasons urge me to that step. In the first place, it might be difficult for a letter to find the young man; and, again, I feel sure that only a personal interview with him would overcome his pride and induce him to return home.'

'You are not going alone, are you?' the lad anxiously inquired.

'No: I shall take you with me. You and Pedro.'

'That will be ripping, guv'nor! I should have been wretched if you had left me behind. But do you know just where Richard Champney is?'

'Not yet. We will ascertain that when we get to Calcutta.'

'And when do we start?'

'In two days,' Blake answered. 'A boat sails on Thursday, and we can be ready by then. I don't want to lose any time, for a little war is brewing in India. One of the frontier tribes has rebelled against British authority, and if young Champney should happen to be ordered up there, as is quite likely, his reckless mood would urge him to seek a soldier's death or to hazard his life in the hope of –' The detective broke off, and looked at his watch. 'Ring for the landlady, Tinker,' he added. 'We will have tea, and then I shall write to the old general. I shall merely tell him, however, that I have learned that his son is in a foreign land, and that I am going out to find him. It would not be advisable, under the circumstances, to give him more explicit information.'

THE NINTH CHAPTER

In a Tropical Land – The Camp – Private Dare

The long, sultry day was drawing to a close, and the air had turned cool. Colonel Renfrew was seated on a folding-stool outside his tent, studying a map; and by his side, holding a pair of field-glasses to his eyes, was a subordinate officer. The slanting rays of the sun, which was sinking in the west, shone on a wild and picturesque scene. Here in the open, on the sloping stretch of sward, was the camp of the expeditionary force: a small detachment that comprised one hundred men of the Indian Mounted Police, five hundred of the Third Native Rifles, a number of coolies, two machine-guns, and half a dozen transport mules. In front of the camp, to the north, rolled a dense, trackless region of jungle and swamp; and beyond that, at a considerable distance, was the blue range of the Darjeeng Hills. Slowly the sun dipped below the horizon, and the mellow glow faded. The younger officer lowered his glasses, through which he had been gazing steadily at a pass that cleft the distant hills. The colonel put his map aside, and looked up.

'No smoke yet?' he asked.

'No; not a sign of it,' replied Captain Trent.

'There won't be, I fear.'

'I am afraid not, sir.'

'Either the messenger has been killed, Trent, or he has found it to be impossible for him to get back.'

'It must be one or the other, sir, I have no doubt.'

There is always trouble of some kind in India, and on this occasion the Nagas, a savage tribe dwelling on the Assam frontier, were in open revolt. Having swept down the hills, and burnt several plantations, they had been attacked and repulsed; and they had then retreated to the north and invested the remote outpost of Paragong, which was held by a Major Errol and a small native garrison. This had occurred three or four weeks back; and meanwhile, news of the investment having been received by the Government, Colonel Renfrew and his command had been sent to the rescue. Three days ago, on reaching the spot where he was now encamped, the colonel had been met by a native courier bearing a letter from Major Errol. It was to the effect that the besieged officer had sufficient food and ammunition for another week, and that he was confident of being able to hold out for that length of time. But he also stated that the enemy were in very strong force, and that he believed it to be impossible to relieve the post except by a stratagem.

Within an hour after the arrival of the courier – who had since died from a sharp attack of fever – a member of the Mounted Police had set forth from the camp on foot, in the hope that he might succeed in getting through to the outpost. His instructions were to make a certain arrangement with Major Errol and then to return as far as the pass in the Darjeeng Hills, and there send up a column of smoke, which would be a signal for the command to advance. As it was no more than a day's march to the hills, and as the post was only two or three miles on the other side of them, the smoke should have been seen within a day and a half from the start. But three days had now elapsed without the appearance of the signal, and it was evident that the messenger had either met with his death in going or coming, or that he was cooped up with the beleaguered garrison.

'The situation is getting critical,' said the younger officer, after a pause. 'The time that Errol mentioned will soon expire.'

'Yes, in another three or four days,' assented Colonel Renfrew, shaking his head gloomily.

'What is to be done!'

'That is the question. I ought to send another man, but I hesitate to risk his life.'

'And it would mean further delay, sir, unless we were to push on to the base of the hills, and wait there for the signal.'

'I should not care to do that, Trent. If we were to camp so near to the post it would probably result in our being discovered by Naga scouts. It is to be assumed that the enemy are as yet ignorant of our approach, and if they are to be taken by surprise it must be by a rapid and uninterrupted march. I am strongly inclined to advance in the morning, and take the chances of a repulse.'

'Perhaps it would be the wiser plan, sir, to make another attempt to get into communication with Errol.'

'I had given up that idea. I feel that you are right, however. And there is still time to spare. Though one man has failed, it is possible that another might succeed in –'

Colonel Renfrew paused abruptly, and glanced at a trooper of the Mounted Police who was drawing near to the tent. He was a tall, good-looking fellow, with bronzed features and a heavy, fair moustache. He stopped, and raised his hand in salute to his commanding officer.

'I beg your pardon, sir,' he said, 'but may I have a few words with you!'

'Certainly,' replied the colonel. 'What is it, Dare?'

'I wish to offer my services, should you have need of them. It is generally believed, sir, that your messenger is either dead or that he is unable to carry out his orders.'

'Yes; it must be one or the other.'

'Then send me, colonel. I will try to accomplish what you want.'

'Do you realise what you are offering to do? The risk will be very great.'

'I am quite willing to face it.'

'In all probability you will be shot or speared by the Nagas,' said Colonel Renfrew.

'I am not afraid, sir,' the trooper calmly answered.

'Do you think that you are fitted for this task?'

'I don't know about that, colonel, but I can assure you that I will make every effort to get through to Paragong.'

'Ah, that is the right spirit! Have you any knowledge of the way?'

'I have studied a survey-map that my lieutenant let me have.'

'Very well,' said the colonel, after a moment of reflection. 'You are a brave fellow, Dare, and I shall accept your offer. You will start at dawn tomorrow. Come back in a couple of hours, and I will give you full instructions and a compass.'

'Thank you, sir. And there is something else I would like to speak of, if I may. There is a letter addressed to you in my kit, and if anything should happen to me I wish you would –'

'I understand, Dare. If this errand should cost you your life, I will open the letter.'

'I thank you, sir,' Private Dare repeated.

He saluted again, then turned and strode off. The two officers gazed after him, and looked at each other.

'I have thought from the first that there was a mystery about that fellow,' said Colonel Renfrew, shrugging his shoulders.

'So have I,' declared Captain Trent. 'He is a gentleman ranker, I am sure.'

'I wonder what his real name is?'

'It is not Dare, I'll wager. He must have got into a scrape of some kind, and enlisted in an assumed name.'

'Yes, he is no doubt one of the legion of those who have gone under,' assented the colonel, with a sigh. 'Poor devil! the fault may not have been his. At all events. I hope the man won't try to throw his life away,' he added, as he rose from his stool. 'It is most important that he should get through, and fix things up with Errol.'

'We can't count on that,' said Captain Trent. 'He has about a chance in a thousand of doing what poor Lumley has failed to do.'

They separated, the colonel going into his tent. Twilight was falling, and the distant peaks of the Darjeeng Hills were veiled in shadow. Slowly they melted into the darkness of the night; while Private Rupert Dare, standing apart from his comrades, gazed towards them with an inscrutable expression on his face, thinking of the little garrison that was in a state of siege behind that range.

'I'll do my best,' he told himself. 'I have my chance, and I'll make the most of it, for success ought at least to mean honourable mention in the colonel's despatches. And if Fate should be kind to me afterwards, and let me die a soldier's death, that letter will reveal my identity.'

THE TENTH CHAPTER

The Way of Peril – Fresh Orders

The day was nearly over, and Rupert Dare, who had once been Richard Champney, had not as yet met with any peril, though his courage had been sorely tried in other ways. He had left the camp that morning with a rifle on his shoulder and a brace of revolvers in his belt, with a flagon of water along at his side, and a handful of biscuits in his pocket. For hour after hour, guided by his compass and by the memory of the chart he had studied, he had traversed the wild jungle, now floundering with difficulty through dense thickets of bamboos and tangled vegetation, and now fording swampy streams where lurked venomous reptiles. The heat had been terrible, and he had felt at times that he must drop from fatigue; but his will power had sustained him, and he had held doggedly to his course, little accustomed though he was to the Indian climate.

He had threaded the high pass between the Darjeeng Hills, and was now, as nearly as he could judge, within a couple of miles of the beleaguered outpost of Paragong. All was quiet, There was no fighting in progress, else he could have heard the shots. But he was within the zone of danger, and must be prepared to come in touch before long with the bloodthirsty horde of Nagas who were investing the British officer and his native garrison. How he was to get through he did not know, yet he had a premonition that he was going to succeed.

'It is a curious coincidence,' he said to himself, 'that Major Errol should be the son of my father's oldest and dearest friend. For that reason I am the more anxious to save him.'

But there was a stronger motive back of it all, stronger than the young trooper's sincere and natural desire to be the means of relieving the post. It was the primary object that had induced him to enlist for active service. He wanted to wipe out, as far as possible, the unjust stigma that had sullied his honour and blackened his name; he wanted his father and his lost sweetheart, his friends and the world, to know that he was capable of a brave deed. Beyond that he had no hope. He did not wish to live after he had done that one thing, had no intention of ever going back to home and England, since the brand of cowardice, the false charge of breaking the Law of the Sea under the most shameful circumstances must still hang over him. His innocence of that charge could not be proved, and therefore he felt that it would be better for him to die.

'My father and Dulcie!' he reflected. 'Only so they will think of me a little less harshly, perhaps with a twinge of remorse at times, when they remember that I did at least one brave deed! This is the most I can expect. The past is dead, and I shall be fortunate if a spear or a bullet sends me shortly to a soldier's grave. That will be the crowning mercy. And yet – and yet –'

A choking lump rose in Richard Champney's throat. Though he knew that death would be best for him, and wanted it to come, the memories of the past had not lost their power to torture him. He could not forget the sweetness of life, and the joys it had once held for him. It was hard for him to relinquish all hope. He thought, with bitter, stabbing regrets, of his ruined career, and of the pleasant associations of his clubs; of the cruel words with which his father had driven him from home; and of the lovely girl who was to have been his wife; and of the white feather – the emblem of cowardice – that she had sent to him. He had carefully kept it. It was in the envelope that he had addressed to his colonel, and some day it would be sent to Dulcie Romanis.

Thus he went on, blinded by tears, until he emerged in a shallow glade, and stopped abruptly by a dead man. It was the lifeless body of Trooper Lumley, of his own company. He had been hacked with spears, and his face, which was the only part of him not mutilated, was upturned to the sky. He had been attacked while on the way to Paragong, for the sealed despatch that had been given to him for delivery to Major Errol was still in his pocket; and the empty cartridge shells that were scattered around him showed that he had made a hard fight for his life. Here and there were crimson stains on the trampled grass, but the Nagas who had been slain had been carried off.

'Poor fellow!' muttered Richard Champney. 'I was afraid he had been killed.'

He would have liked to bury the dead messenger, or to have covered him with bushes, but he dared not stop to do either. He glanced at his compass and pressed fleetly on, yet with stealth and caution. For another half-hour he threaded the jungle, pausing frequently to listen. He was drawing near to the outpost now, and every nerve tingled with excitement. He knew that a girdle of peril lay between him and his goal, and he knew also that his life would presently hang by a thread.

But his courage did not falter, not even when a chorus of bloodcurdling yells dinned in his ears. A spear grazed his head, and a matchlock roared at him, the charge narrowly missing his arm. On all sides were dusky faces, and brown, half-naked bodies. He had blundered into the midst of the foe, and they were swarming around him. He did not bother about his rifle, which was strapped to his back. At once he whipped his revolvers from his belt, one in each hand, and as he took to his heels he let fly at the bronzed figures that were closing in on him. Crack, crack, crack – crack! He heard shrieks of agony and crashing sounds. Two savages barred his way, and he shot them both.

'I've got to get through somehow,' the young trooper told himself. 'By heavens, I must! I'll lose my chance if I don't!'

He forgot his fatigue, forgot all but the duty that he must perform. Firing to right and left, firing in front and behind, he plunged through the tangled bush as fast as he could. Spears and bullets showered about him, but left him unscathed. Still he blazed away, whirling to this side and that. He splashed into a marshy pool, and floundered across it submerged to the waist. On the farther side he stopped to reload his pistols, and then resumed his flight, for the enemy were close in the rear. He had cleft his way between the cordon; but the Nagas were gaining on him, and now and again he had to pause to hold them in check, which he did by rapid volleys. A slug whistled by his ear, and another tore a furrow in the fleshy part of his left arm. He ran on, not feeling the warm blood that was trickling down his sleeve.

'They'll get me in the end,' he thought, as he poured a raking fire into a bunch of the foe. 'I can't keep this up much longer.'

He had but a short distance to go yet, however. Ahead of him the purple shade of the jungle was faintly illumined, and presently, when the screeching Nagas were almost at his heels, he burst from cover into a clearing, and saw within twenty yards of him a high stockade made of sharpened bamboos. He staggered towards it, panting hard; and now, as he felt that his strength was failing him, a gate in the stockade was flung open, and he saw brown-skinned soldiers in khaki uniforms.

'Down!' a voice shouted. 'Down, for your life!'

The command was not needed, for Richard Champney had at that instant dropped from exhaustion; and as he lay there on the ground, half-dazed, two spluttering volleys were fired over his head. The shooting ceased, and he heard the yells of the baffled Nagas fade to silence. Somebody helped him to his feet and gave him a strong arm to lean on, and led him through the gateway into a compound, where he saw the British flag fluttering above him. He entered a blockhouse, and now, as he found himself in the presence of a handsome officer with a fair moustache, he suddenly realised that he had got through. He pulled his wits together and saluted, then took a sealed envelope from his pocket and handed it to the officer.

'From Colonel Renfrew, sir,' he said huskily.

'How far off is he?' asked Major Errol.

'A short day's march, sir,' the young trooper replied. 'He is on the farther side of the jungle.'

'And you have come through alone?'

'Yes, sir. I started at daybreak.'

Major Errol was silent for a moment, and there was an odd expression on his face as he closely scrutinised the features of the messenger.

'What is your name?' he inquired.

'It is Dare, sir,' the trooper answered promptly – 'Rupert Dare.'

'You have done well, Dare. You are a brave man.'

'Thank you, sir.'

'But what's this, eh? Blood on your sleeve! My good fellow, you have been wounded!'

'I – I didn't know I had been, sir. I remember feeling a sort of a prick, but – but –'

Private Dare's head was swimming, and the next instant he was on the floor in a swoon. He was quickly revived, and meanwhile his wound, which was trifling, had been bathed and bandaged. He was taken to another room, and given food and drink; and then, looking and feeling a different man, he was shown again into the presence of the commander of the post, who drew from him a full account of his journey, and of the tragic fate of the first messenger. The narrative finished, Major Errol picked up from his writing-table the despatch that had been sent to him.

'Do you know what this contains?' he asked.

'Yes, sir. The colonel told me every word of it.' Private Dare replied.

'And your instructions, I believe, are to consult with me in regard to the sortie, and then to return as far as the top of the pass in the Darjeeng Hills, and there light a signal-fire?'

'That is right, sir.'

'Well, it is not to be thought of,' declared Major Errol. 'You cannot leave here. I am not yet in extremities. I have sufficient supplies and ammunition for another four or five days. Colonel Renfrew's force will have to advance at their leisure and take their chances with the enemy, who will probably give them a warm time of it.'

'But – but the colonel was particularly anxious that I should carry out my instructions,' stammered the trooper.

'It is impossible, my good man. You will have to remain here where you are for the present. The Nagas are on all sides of us, and they will be more than ever on the alert. It would be fatal for you to attempt to get through them.'

'I would like to try, sir, if you don't mind. There might be a chance for me.'

'Do you want to lose your life, my good man?'

'I wish to do my duty, major. I beg that you will let me go.'

'You are a very obstinate fellow, Dare. Is your heart set on this foolhardy act?'

'It is, sir. And it will be for your own good, if you will pardon me for saying so. It might be impossible to relieve you, except by the arrangement that Colonel Renfrew has suggested.'

'Yes, that is true.'

The young commandant pondered the question. He was in a tight place, and he wanted to get out of it for the sake of his wife and child, who were down in Calcutta.

'You may go,' he said. 'I give you my consent.'

'Thank you, sir,' the trooper replied.

'You need not thank me for letting you go on such a mad venture. It will be suicidal, I fear. If by any possibility you should succeed in getting through, however, you will not light the signal-fire on the pass.'

'Why not, sir?'

'For one thing, because it might be interpreted by the enemy, who would thus be put on their guard. Moreover, I don't want the relief column to advance with reckless and undue haste. The signal, if shown tonight, would convey to Colonel Renfrew that the sortie was to be tomorrow night. You will therefore, in the event of your success, press on to your camp without stopping. And you will say to your colonel that I will expect him to march at dawn on the day after tomorrow. He will be near to my post by sunset of that same day, and two hours after midnight I will create a diversion, draw the Nagas in force to the north of the stockade, and keep them there as long as I can.'

'And the relief column will then enter from the south, sir?' Private Dare inquired.

'Yes, that is the idea,' the major answered.

'Very good, sir. I quite understand.'

'That is all, then. I will give you some food to take with you, and a fresh supply of cartridges. By the way, you – you talk like a gentleman, Dare.'

'I was one once, sir.'

'I beg your pardon. If I can be of service to you in any –'

'You can do nothing more for me than you have already done, sir, unless it will be to mention my name in your report.'

'That will not be omitted, you may be sure.'

'Thank you, sir.'

With that the trooper saluted, and left the room. He was well pleased with what he had accomplished, and with the further prospect that was before him. He had already distinguished himself, and he would have an opportunity of doing so again. His courage was equal to the second ordeal. He knew how important it was that he should get back to camp, and he felt that he was going to succeed. And then let come what might. He would have shown to the world that he was capable of brave deeds, and would be ready for his soldier's grave.

'There will likely be some stiff fighting before the post is relieved,' he reflected. 'It may not be long until the white feather is sent back to Dulcie.'

It was advisable that the start should be made as soon as darkness permitted. The sun had now set, and half an hour later, when night had fallen, Major Errol and the messenger left the blockhouse together, and crossed the enclosure to the stockade, where brown-skinned soldiers were watching alertly by the loopholes and on the platforms.

'You are a plucky fellow, Dare,' said the major, as he shook hands with him. 'I wish you luck, for your sake and mine.'

'I will do my very best, sir,' the trooper replied.

Thus they parted. The gate was noiselessly opened, and Rupert Dare slipped out. The gate was at once locked behind him, and the commandant waited in the enclosure, listening with keen apprehensions. For five minutes all was quiet, and then was heard the crack of a revolver, followed by a rattling volley, and by a burst of shrill yells. The firing and the clamour soon ceased. Hushed silence again fell on the jungle.

'Just as I feared,' said Major Errol to his native orderly. 'That is the last of the messenger, and heaven only knows what will become of us. Poor fellow!' he added to himself. 'I wonder what his history is? He reminded me of somebody I know.'

THE ELEVENTH CHAPTER

Visitors to Camp – Back from the Grave

The night had passed, and another day was nearly over. The sun was low on the horizon, and a cool breeze was rousing the camp from its siesta. Colonel Renfrew and Captain Trent were standing in front of the former's tent, and the younger officer had just lowered the glasses through which he had been gazing at the pass in the distant Darjeeng Hills.

'I am afraid there is no hope,' he murmured.

'None at all,' assented the colonel. 'Had the man been able to reach the outpost, he would have got there last evening, and the signal fires should have been lighted during the night, or early this morning.'

'It is not likely that he got through, sir?'

'No, he was probably killed on the way. I should not have sent the poor follow, and I shall certainly not send another.'

'Then what is to be done?'

'We will move without further delay, Trent. We have waited too long as it is, and now I shall –'

The sentence was interrupted by a huge bloodhound that rushed at Colonel Renfrew with a joyous bark, and leapt upon him so impetuously that he was thrown to the ground, where a wct tongue licked his face as he was struggling to rise. He scrambled to his feet, scarlet with anger.

'What the deuce!' he spluttered. 'Where did that vicious brute come from? Shoot it, Trent! No, no, don't! The dog knows me, and I am sure I have seen it before. By Jove, it cannot be possible – yes, it must be Sexton Blake's hound!'

'Right you are!' a hearty voice exclaimed. 'That is the very dog, and here is the owner of it. Pedro's welcome was rather too exuberant, Renfrew, but you must remember that he has not seen you for a couple of years.'

It was the voice of Sexton Blake. With his young assistant, Tinker, at his heels, he had just emerged from the forest that was close behind the tent. Both were bronzed, and in the pink of condition. They wore sun-helmets, and high hoots, and suits of grey linen, and each was armed with a rifle and a brace of revolvers. The colonel stared at them in utter bewilderment.

'You here, Blake!' he gasped. 'Have you dropped from the sky? What on earth does it mean?'

'Suppose I should tell you,' replied the detective, 'that we were a couple of soldiers of fortune, and that we had come to offer our services to you.'

Colonel Renfrew, having no sense of humour, took the remark quite seriously.

'It is impossible,' he said angrily. 'You had no business to come up here, to this wild country. There is to be some stiff fighting, and you can't come with me. I should be held responsible if you were to be killed. No, you must go back. I positively refuse to –'

'I was only joking,' Blake interrupted, with a smile.

'You might have said so,' snapped the colonel. 'What have you come for, then?'

'On a matter of private business, Renfrew.'

'I can't imagine what it can be. But you shall tell me after you have had something to eat.'

'Thank you. We are both tired and hungry, for we have been tramping over the hills since daybreak, following the trail of your column. And this is the fourth day of our march.'

The visitors were introduced to Captain Trent, who had not the pleasure of their acquaintance; and not long afterwards, the colonel's native servant having been summoned, Tinker and the detective and the two officers sat down to the evening meal at a camp-table in front of the tent.

Sexton Blake was in no hurry to offer explanations. He waited until he had finished his supper, and then, cigars having been produced and lighted, he casually opened the subject.

'Of course you know all about the loss of the *Paleta*, Renfrew?' he said.

'Certainly I do,' the colonel answered. 'Do you suppose we don't get the news out in India! By the way, I think you and your young assistant were on the ill-fated vessel.'

'Yes, that is right. And there was also among the passengers the son of an old friend of mine. I refer to Richard Champney, the second officer of the ship.'

'I remember reading of him. He saved his life by jumping into a boat among a lot of women and children, and the American court of inquiry held him to have been guilty of rank cowardice.'

'Yes, his career was ruined. He was blackened with shame. Having been disowned by his father and spurned by the girl he was to have married, he disappeared. At first I had no doubt of his guilt, but I was subsequently convinced, owing to certain facts that cropped up, that he was entirely innocent. He declared that he had been thrown into the boat, and I believe that statement to have been correct. His father is of the same opinion now, and at his request I undertook to find the young man. And that is why I am here, Renfrew.'

'That is why you are here! What do you mean?'

'Richard Champney enlisted in London in the Indian Mounted Police, and I was informed in Calcutta that he was with your column.'

'You are wrong,' declared the colonel. 'There is no such man in my force, I am sure.'

'He does not bear that name,' Blake replied. 'He is known as Rupert Dare.'

'As Rupert Dare!'

'Yes, that is the man.'

'By heavens!'

The words burst sharply from Colonel Renfrew's lips, and there was an odd expression on his face as he glanced at Captain Trent, who was no less startled. Sexton Blake perceived that something was wrong, and when the story of the hazardous errand had been briefly told to him, and he had realised that the young man he had come so far to find was probably dead, he shook his head sadly.

'I half-expected this,' he said. 'I was afraid that the poor fellow would try to throw his life away.'

'I don't think he meant to do that,' the colonel answered. 'No, it is more likely that he wanted to distinguish himself, and partly redeem his honour. At all events he was no coward, or he would not have volunteered for such perilous work.'

'He was a brave man,' put in Captain Trent. 'I have had my eye on him since we started, and there was no one who endured the hardships of the march with more courage than he did.'

'Is it certain that he has been killed?' asked Blake.

'It would seem so,' replied Colonel Renfrew. 'Otherwise he would have returned to the pass, and lighted the signal fire.'

'Perhaps he was unable to return. He may be shut up with the besieged force.'

'That is possible. There is at least a chance of it, I will admit.'

'Then I shall not abandon hope. I will try to believe that he is still alive. But I want to learn for myself whether he is or not. You must let me accompany the column.'

'Very well. Blake. Under the circumstances, I will not refuse my consent. I warn you, however, that there will be hard fighting, and loss of life.'

'I am not in the least afraid, my dear Renfrew. I am prepared to face any risk in order to get through to Paragong.'

But there was very little ground for the hope that Richard Champney might be safe at the outpost. The chances were that he had met with his death on the way. Sexton Blake was in low spirits, troubled by doubts; and the colonel, observing this, turned the conversation into a different channel.

'Have you over heard of a Hindoo named Aga Khan?' he inquired.

'Yes; I have heard a great deal about him,' Blake answered, in a dull tone, 'and I have met him in London. He took a degree at the University of Cambridge, and afterwards lived in England for some months before returning to India. He is a firebrand, is he not?'

'He is a revolutionary, to put it plainly,' replied Colonel Renfrew, with a frown. 'He is a wealthy man, and he has been using his money to harass the Indian Government. He has instigated the rising of the Nagas, if report be true, and it is feared that he will persuade other tribes to break into rebellion. He disappeared from Calcutta some weeks ago, and he is said to be now amongst the Nagas, helping them to fight. And it is also said that he has an Englishman with him, a man with whom he was intimate at Cambridge and in London. I can hardly believe that tale, and yet it may be –'

The colonel paused abruptly, and the next instant he and his companions had leapt to their feet. They looked at one another in surprise and alarm. The report of a revolver had just been heard in the jungle, at no great distance. There was a shrill yell, a shout, and then half a dozen more shots were fired in rapid succession.

'What can that mean?' exclaimed the detective.

'It must be Dare,' said Colonel Renfrew.

'Do you think so?'

'I can't imagine who else it could be.'

'He is fighting for his life. Come, we must save him!'

The camp was in a turmoil of excitement. Men were seizing their arms, some fearing that the enemy were about to make an attack. A bugle was pealing, and the machine-guns were being planted in position. More shots rang out, but the firing had ceased, and all was quiet by the time Sexton Blake and his companions had got to the edge of the jungle. They stopped here for a moment, and then, as they were on the point of plunging into the cover, they perceived the dusky figure of a man approaching them. On he came, slowly and wearily, through the tangled undergrowth; and when at length he emerged in the open, a burst of cheers greeted him, and scores of voices shouted his name.

'It is Dare! He has come back! Hurrah for Dare!'

Yes, it was Private Rupert Dare, looking like a ghost of himself. His face was haggard, his eyes sunken; he was wet to the middle, and coated with mud. One arm was bandaged, and tied around his head was a strip that he had torn from his shirt. He at once saw and recognised Blake and the lad, and for a moment, as a flush dyed his cheeks, he gazed at them in consternation. Then, satisfied that his heavy moustache was sufficient to hide his identity, he staggered towards the colonel, and raised a shaking hand in salute.

'I have returned, sir!' he faltered. 'I – I had orders to –'

He swayed dizzily, and would have fallen had he not been caught by Captain Trent, who supported him, and put a flask of brandy to his lips. The detective touched Colonel Renfrew on the shoulder, and drew him aside.

'The man has recognised me,' he said, in a low tone, 'but he is not aware that I know who he is. I shall not tell him yet why I am here. I will ignore him for the present, until we get through to Paragong.'

'Very well,' assented the colonel. 'Just as you like.'

'You will not withdraw your permission for us to accompany the column, I trust.'

'No, that will be all right,' was the reply. 'You may come with me, Blake.'

The excitement had calmed down, and all were waiting for news. The fiery spirit that Private Dare had swallowed was recruiting his strength, putting new life into him. He did not glance at Sexton Blake or Tinker again. He squared his shoulders, and stood at attention before his commanding officer.

'I have done it, sir,' he said quietly. 'I reached the outpost after some desperate fighting with the Nagas, and found all well there. And on the way I came across the dead body of Private Lumley, who had been killed and mutilated. Major Errol has been hard pressed, but he can hold out for another four days, at the least. I remained with him for a short time, and then started back. He ordered me not to light the signal fire, because he was afraid that the enemy would see it and understand what it would mean, and also because he did not want you to advance today. His instructions were that I should return to the camp, and tell you to march early tomorrow morning. And tomorrow night, at two o'clock, he will make a sortie from the north side of the stockade, and engage the Nagas while you approach from the south.'

'Very good,' said the colonel. 'That is just the arrangement I desired to effect. But did not Major Errol wish to keep you at the post, after your perilous experience?'

'Yes, sir, he refused to let me go at first,' replied Private Dare. 'But I insisted, and he yielded. I pointed out to him the necessity of communicating with you either by signal or otherwise.'

'And did you have any more trouble?'

'Plenty of it, sir. I had a brush with the enemy before I had got a hundred yards from the post. I squeezed through somehow, in the darkness, and thought that I was safe. But they hung on to me doggedly, though I made several wide detours. I never quite got rid of them. I had to keep up a running fight for hour after hour, and at the last, when I was close to the camp, I was attacked by five of the rascals, who must have been tracking me. I shot three of them, and the other two fled.'

'I perceive that you have been wounded, Dare.'

'They are only trifling injuries, sir.'

'When did you leave the post?'

'Just after dark last night, sir.'

'Then you have been traversing the jungle, in peril of your life, all of yesterday, and all through the night, and all of today.'

'Yes, sir, I have had a long stretch.'

'You have done well, my brave fellow,' declared Colonel Renfrew. 'By gad, you are a hero! I am proud of you. I shall certainly recommend you for the Victoria Cross. You fully deserve it.'

'Thank you, sir,' said Private Dare.

As he spoke his face flushed with joy, and he shot a furtive glance at Sexton Blake.

'You need rest,' continued the colonel. 'Get something to eat, Dare, and then go to bed. Let all be in readiness for an early start, Trent,' he added, turning to his subordinate officer. 'We will advance at daybreak tomorrow.'

There was more cheering as the gallant young trooper walked off to his tent. The sun was now below the horizon, and darkness was falling.

'Well, what is your opinion, Renfrew?' asked the detective. 'Do you believe that the man was innocent of that charge of cowardice?'

'Do I believe it?' replied Colonel Renfrew. 'If anybody should tell me that Private Dare was a coward, or had ever been one, I should be tempted to knock him down.'

'Same here,' murmured Tinker, under his breath.

A tent was provided for Blake and the lad, and they slept until they were roused by a bugle call. It was not yet daylight, but the camp was astir; and half an hour later, as the first streak of dawn was finishing the sky, the march was begun. The horses of the Indian Police were left behind in charge of a small detachment, and the rest of the column, including the transport mules and the machine guns, filed into the jungle and disappeared. All that day they pressed on through the dense fastnesses, crossing nullahs and fording streams.

Late in the afternoon they emerged on the farther side of the pass in the Darjeeng Hills, and a couple of hours after sunset they halted within a mile of the military station of Paragong, and threw out scouts. There the force waited in darkness and silence, and at two o'clock in the morning, when the crackling of rifles was heard in front, the command for a rapid advance was given.

THE TWELFTH CHAPTER

Private Dare Decides – To the Rescue

All had gone well, though it might have been otherwise but for the messages that had been carried between the two commanders by Rupert Dare, since the Nagas were in great strength. But most of them had been drawn to the north by the sortie made by Major Errol, and while the engagement was in progress Colonel Renfrew's column had entered the post from the south, after encountering some slight resistance.

And then, in the grey light of the dawn, the garrison and the relief-force had delivered a combined attack on the enemy, who fought with desperate valour until the machine guns were brought into action. That was more than they could stand, and they soon fled in panic and confusion, leaving many dead behind them.

A number of the British force had been killed and wounded, and there had been some conspicuous instances of gallantry, Sexton Blake and Tinker having distinguished themselves amongst others. Pedro had clung to his master's heels, but fortunately he had not been injured, though he had been in the thick of the struggle.

It was now the middle of the morning, and the flying column that had pursued the routed Nagas had returned. Silence had settled on the post. In the large enclosure the soldiers, native and British, were resting after their exertions, under the flag for which they had fought.

A message had been brought to Private Dare, and he was standing in a room in the blockhouse, in the presence of Blake and the lad and several officers. The trooper was one of those who had shown marked gallantry in action, and he felt that he had done far more to redeem his honour than he had ever expected to do.

'I want to thank you, Dare,' said Major Errol. 'I have had a splendid report of you from Colonel Renfrew, and have learned that your return journey was accomplished under far greater difficulties than those you met with in coming.'

'I only did my duty, sir,' murmured the young man.

'You did more than your duty,' replied the major. 'You have proved yourself to be a hero. You have saved the post, and we have inflicted on the enemy a blow that will probably induce them to sue for peace. Your colonel tells me that he intends to recommend you for the Victoria Cross, and I can assure you that I shall gladly join my recommendation to his.'

Private Dare's face flushed with pride, and it was evident that he was deeply moved. He expressed his gratitude in a few words, and then, as he turned to go, Sexton Blake barred the way.

'May I too congratulate you, Champney?' he said.

For a few seconds a pin might have been heard to fall. The trooper drew a deep breath, and the colour ebbed from his cheeks, leaving them very white, as he stared in dismay at the detective. The mention of his real name, the unmasking of his identity, had been a startling and unpleasant surprise to him.

'Champney!' muttered Major Errol. 'Ah, that accounts for the resemblance that puzzled me so! I know you now, my dear fellow, in spite of your moustache. Your father was my father's oldest friend, and I have met you on several occasions at your home in Hampshire. But how does it come that – !'

He broke off abruptly, covered with confusion. The news of the world had penetrated to him even in this isolated corner of India, and he had suddenly remembered the loss of the *Paleta*, and the finding of the American court of inquiry. Blake, who was watching him, read what was in his mind.

'You will he glad to hear, major,' he said tactfully, 'that I have every reason to believe that Richard Champney was innocent of the charge that ruined his career, and drove him to enlist under an assumed name in the Indian Mounted Police.'

'I am more than willing to believe that,' declared Major Errol. 'Nothing could convince me that this brave fellow had ever been guilty of cowardice.'

'And it would be no less difficult to convince me,' put in Colonel Renfrew, 'no matter how strong a ease had been made out against him.'

Richard Champney stepped towards the detective, and in his excitement grasped him by the arm.

'I – I don't understand,' he said hoarsely. 'What do you mean? You doubted my word when I told you the truth on the steamer *Florida* that morning. Why do you now believe that I was innocent?'

'Because of certain things that have since come to my knowledge.' Sexton Blake answered. 'I did doubt your word, I admit. But I now feel that I was wrong.'

He briefly and clearly related the whole story, and the young man, listening in silence, learned that his cousin had been a steerage passenger on the *Paleta*; and learned also, with astonishment, of the strong motive that had presumably induced Hildred Nairne to hurl him into the boat.

'You are right, of course,' he said. 'If my cousin wanted to break off my engagement to Miss Romanis – I had no idea that he had been my rival – that would account for it. I remember now that the man who was standing behind me was not unlike Hildred Nairne. Yes, it must have been he who flung me over the rail.'

'I am sure of that, and so is your father,' replied the detective. 'He is stricken with remorse, and at his request I have come all the way to India to find you and fetch you buck.'

'It is not enough that you and my father should have faith in me,' said Richard Champney, 'Can you restore the confidence of my friends? Can you remove every shadow of doubt from the mind of the girl I loved? Can you entirely clear my name of dishonour? Can you prove to the world, by substantial evidence, that I was not a coward?'

'No, I am afraid I cannot do that. For one thing, Hildred Nairne is a fugitive from the law. And even if he could be found it would probably be impossible to get a confession from him.'

'Then I cannot return home, Mr Blake.'

'I do not see that anything stands in the way of your doing so. Is not your father's faith enough? Why not go back to him, and forgive the wrong he did you, and comfort his declining years?'

'No, it is impossible.'

'I ask you to be reasonable, Champney.'

'You are asking me to return to an existence that would be unbearable to me,' said the young man. 'I should be a prisoner in my father's house. If I stirred abroad I should be regarded with scorn and contempt by all who knew me. The labourers on the estate, the village people, the girl who was to have been my wife – all would cut me dead. The past is over and done with. I enlisted with a definite object, and to that object I shall adhere. I made up my mind to show the world that I was capable of a brave deed, and I have done so.

'My one wish now is to fall in action, and lie in a soldier's grave. I have nothing else to hope for, since there is no chance of my innocence being established by evidence that would win back for me all that I have lost. Nothing less would content me. I repeat that I cannot –'

His voice faltered, and he paused for a moment.

'I feel that you will agree with me, gentlemen,' he added, 'And I beg that you let the name of Dare continue to hide, as long as I live, the identity of one who has been broken on the wheel of Fate. That is all.'

For a few seconds there was silence. Nobody spoke. Private Rupert Dare hesitated, and then, his face very pale, he saluted, turned on his heel, and walked out of the room. He left behind him aching hearts and dim eyes. Those who had listened to him were conscious of a supreme tragedy, of a great sorrow that they were powerless to alleviate.

'Poor fellow!' murmured Colonel Renfrew. 'I am afraid you will not be able to break down his obstinacy.'

'He is right,' Sexton Blake said sadly. 'I should feel as he does if I were in his place. But what a pity it is! Ah, what a pity!'

Another night had passed, and the morning sun was beating fiercely down on the little military station that had been relieved in the nick of time. There was no intention of evacuating the post, or of attempting at present to deal another blow at the enemy, who had doubtless left the neighbourhood. A larger column of troops was on its way up-country, and when they had arrived, the combined forces would advance against the Nagas, and teach them a salutary lesson by destroying their villages.

In a room in the blockhouse, which was kept cool by damp mats at the windows, the two officers were chatting with Blake and the lad, who had been persuaded to remain until the arrival of the expected column, when they would be provided with an escort to take them through the jungle. Outside the soldiers were lounging under shelters of boughs, save those who, for precaution's sake, were watching from the platforms.

'I can't help thinking of young Champney – or rather, of Private Dare, as he prefers to be called,' said Major Errol, during a lull in the conversation.

'And he is constantly on my mind,' said the colonel, as he put a match to a cigar. 'I shall never forget that little speech he made yesterday. What are you going to do about it. Blake? Will you make further efforts to persuade him to go home to his father?'

'I am pretty sure that it would be useless to do so,' the detective replied. 'The poor fellow knows what is best for himself. For his father's sake, however, I shall try again to –'

He broke off abruptly, and listened. Pedro, who had been lying at his master's feet, had just jumped up and growled. Now a faint shout was heard, and the next instant there was a confused clamour of voices. Colonel Renfrew dashed from the room, followed by his companions; and when they reached the enclosure, fully believing that the enemy were advancing to attack, they saw that several of the men were undoing the heavy fastenings of the gate, while the rest were crowded around the loopholes or looking over the stockade.

'What is it?' exclaimed Major Errol. 'What is the matter?'

'A messenger, sir,' answered a native sergeant. 'He is not a Naga.'

'There he is, guv'nor,' said Tinker.

The bars had clattered to the ground. The gate had been pulled open, and, a moment later, it had swung shut behind a man who had staggered through it into the enclosure. The sight of him was a surprise to all, for he was a strange figure to be seen in this wild and remote part of India. He was obviously a pure-blooded Hindoo.

He had lost his turban, and his tunic and drawers were hanging in shreds, and were soiled by blood and water. He would have dropped from exhaustion had not two of the native soldiers taken hold of him, and as he hung in their arms, he looked appealingly at Colonel Renfrew, and made several futile attempts to speak.

'I – I have come for help, sahib!' he managed to ejaculate, at last. 'I am Moultan, the servant of Aga Khan!'

'Of Aga Khan?' gasped the colonel.

'By Jove! The servant of that scoundrel!' muttered Major Errol. 'I wonder what's up? What can this mean?'

'I can make a pretty shrewd guess, major,' Sexton Blake told him. 'We'll see whether I am right or not.'

He had jumped at a theory that proved to be correct. He and Tinker and the officers gathered about the Hindoo, who drained a pannikin of water that had been brought to him, and was then able to tell his story rapidly and coherently. It appeared that the rumours that had been circulated in regard to Aga Khan had been quite true.

That political firebrand, the implacable foe of British rule in India, had come up to the territory of the Nagas, and distributed gold amongst them, and induced them to break out in revolt. And the report had also been true that he had been accompanied by an English friend of his.

The two had made all the trouble they could, and had actually been with the large force of Nagas who had besieged the post; and now, it seemed, they were likely to pay for their folly with their lives. They had incurred the wrath of the savage tribesmen, who had blamed them for their defeat, and for the heavy losses they had sustained.

'It happened last night,' continued Aga Khan's servant, who could speak perfect English. 'After the fight, the Nagas retreated to a wild place by a stream. All of yesterday they held a palaver there, and when they had finished, towards evening, they seized my master and Cameron sahib, and threatened to put them to death.

'They would have seized me also, but I escaped from them, and fled to the jungle, where I lay hidden while they searched for me. In the night, when all was quiet, I crept back to the edge of the camp, where I could see and hear. My master and the Englishmen were lying, bound, on the grass, and Yalmak, the chief, and his leading men were sitting nearby talking. And by listening to them I learned what they mean to do.

'Today, most of the Nagas will march to their villages, and fortify them against attack; and the others, with the chief, will take the two prisoners to the cave where dwell the sacred serpents, and there offer them as a sacrifice to the reptiles. So much I overheard, sahibs, and then I crept away, and hastened here as quickly as I could. The day was dawning when I started, and now it is –'

The Hindoo paused, his voice choked with emotion. He stretched out his hand to the colonel, of whose rank he was aware.

'My master has always been kind to me, and I am devoted to him,' he went on. 'I would not have him die. Go to his rescue, sahib! Save him and the Feringhee, I beg of you!'

'They don't deserve to be saved!' replied Colonel Renfrew. 'If they fall into my hands. Aga Khan will be exiled for life to the Andaman Islands, and I should be tempted to shoot the renegade Englishman, for whose crime there is less excuse. By gad, the thought of a man inciting savages to make war on his own countrymen makes my blood boil! But you have probably been deceived, my good fellow,' he added. 'I can hardly believe this tale of the cave of the sacred serpents!'

'I have told you what came to my ears, sahib,' vowed the servant.

'It is true, Renfrew,' declared Major Errol. 'There is such a place. I know it to be a fact.'

'Save him!' pleaded the Hindoo, throwing himself at the officer's feet. 'Save my poor master from so terrible a death!'

'I will do what I can,' said the colonel, 'though I have no great liking for the task. How far is it from here to the enemy's camp?'

'It is three hours' march,' the servant answered.

'And at what time of the day were the chief and his party to have set off with their prisoners?'

'I cannot tell you that, sahib; but I will guide you to the camp.'

'And suppose we should find it deserted when we get there? What then? Do you know where the cave of the serpents lies?'

'Alas! I have no knowledge of it!'

The question was put to others, and put in vain. Not a man in the enclosure, Major Errol included, could give the desired information. And now, after a moment of silence, an idea occurred to Sexton Blake.

'If the camp should he deserted,' he said to the colonel, 'my bloodhound will no doubt be able to follow the scent of Aga Khan and the Englishman. Tinker and I will gladly accompany you.'

'And I shall be glad to have you,' said Colonel Renfrew. 'Your suggestion seems to solve the difficulty, for I know what Pedro can do. He will show us the way, but can we overtake the party in time to save the lives of the prisoners? That is the question, and I doubt if –'

He paused, and looked at Private Dare, who had just stepped forward, and was standing in front of him with his hand raised in salute.

'I want to go with you, sir, if you will let me,' he said.

'Don't you think you have distinguished yourself sufficiently?' asked the colonel.

'It is not that, sir. I don't want to be idle.'

'And I don't propose that you shall throw your life away.'

'I will do no more than my duty, colonel.'

It was no business of Blake's to interfere, nor did he venture to do so, but he hoped that permission would not be granted. Colonel Renfrew hesitated for a moment, and then nodded assent.

'You may come with me, Dare,' he said. 'It is not good for you to be moping about doing nothing. But there must be no foolhardy recklessness. Bear this in mind.'

'Very well, sir,' replied the trooper, as he turned away.

A responsible officer had to be left in charge of the post, and that duty fall to Major Errol. Orders were issued by the colonel, and in a short space of time, the Hindoo servant having meanwhile recruited his strength by a hearty meal, a little force of sixty men, including both British and native soldiers, set off to the rescue of Aga Khan and the renegade Englishman. And with them went Sexton Blake and Tinker, the bloodhound, and Private Rupert Dare.

'I hope we shall be able to save those scoundrels,' Colonel Renfrew said to the detective. 'I want them to be tried and punished by the Government as a warning to other seditionists.'

THE THIRTEENTH CHAPTER

The Twin Serpents – The Confession

It was now about the middle of the morning. The sun was beating down fiercely, but its heat was tempered by the dense foliage of the jungle. Moultan led the way, retracing the course by which he had come. Though he had not recovered from the fatigue of his journey to the post, he set a good pace, and held to it.

No sympathy could be felt for Aga Khan, who had instigated the revolt; but it was impossible not to admire the servant's devotion to his master, not to be moved by his distress. Again and again, as his straining efforts took him ahead of his companions, he urged them to hasten.

For more than three hours the column pressed steadily on, and at length, Moultan having stated that the camping-place of the Nagas was nearby, a halt was called by the colonel.

'I shall have to send a scout forward to reconnoitre the ground,' he said.

'Let me go, sahib!' begged the Hindoo. 'That will be best.'

He did not wait for permission, but disappeared at once in the thickets. He was absent for only a few minutes, and when he returned, his face showed that he was the bearer of bad news.

'They are gone!' he cried, in despair. 'They are all gone! Not one is left, sahib!'

The word to advance was given. For two or three hundred yards more the little force pressed on through the deep cover, and then emerged from it in the wide, open space where the Nagas had stopped after their flight. The clearing was silent and deserted; there was nobody there now.

It was soon perceived, on investigation, that the enemy had indeed split into two parties, a large one having obviously gone towards the west, while a smaller one had departed in a northerly direction.

It was to be taken for granted that the prisoners were with the smaller party, and that fact was indisputably proved by Pedro; for when the spot where Aga Khan and the Englishman had been lying had been indicated to the dog, and he had sniffed at the trampled grass, he looked intelligently at his master, and then trotted straight to the northern edge of the camp.

'That's all right,' said Tinker. 'He has the scent.'

'How long a start have the Nagas got?' inquired Colonel Renfrew. 'Can you tell me that, Blake?'

The detective, who was scarcely inferior to a redskin in his knowledge of woodcraft, dropped to his knees, and closely studied the trail for a few seconds.

'As nearly as I can judge,' he said as he rose, 'they have been gone for less than an hour. Certainly not more than that.'

'Then we have a chance of overtaking them,' declared the colonel.

'And a chance of a fight,' replied Blake, 'for it would appear that there are three or four score in the party.'

'Do not delay, sahib,' urged Moultan, appealing to Colonel Renfrew. 'Let us be quick. My master's life is in peril, and my heart is heavy with grief.'

There was some hope of effecting a rescue, but it was a slim one. Everything depended on whether or not the cave of the sacred serpents was within a short march, and there was nobody who could answer that question. No further time was wasted.

The bugle sounded the advance, and the khaki-clad column filed across the open space and into the jungle that stretched to the north. The bloodhound now clearly led the way, and Sexton Blake came next, holding him in leash.

The trail was clearly visible to the naked eye, and there was therefore no need for Pedro to follow it by scent; but it was as well that he should be in front, since his keen hearing would enable him to give timely warning of danger.

'If we only have a short way to go, guv'nor,' said the lad, 'it will be all up with the prisoners before we get there.'

'They are hardly worth saving,' Blake replied; 'but we must do our best for humanity's sake.'

'And for the sake of this poor Hindoo.'

'Yes, I am sorry for him. He is a noble fellow, my boy.'

It was rugged travelling, and much of it up hill and down, amidst tangled undergrowth. There was no path from this direction to the place of sacrifice, though one probably led to it from the Naga villages that lay to the west. Mile after mile slipped behind. Hour succeeded hour, until the sun was low and the day was drawing to a close. There was now more ground for hope, for the rescue-party had been moving rapidly, and there was reason to believe that they had been gaining on the band of savages.

When another mile had been covered the bloodhound growled, and bristled his neck. It was evident that he had heard or scented the enemy, though nothing was audible to human ears. But shortly afterwards there suddenly rose, from no great distance in front, a shrill clamour of voices mingled with a hollow sound that was like the roll of drums.

'There they are!' exclaimed the colonel. 'They are at their devilish work!'

'No doubt of it,' said Blake. 'But there may be still time to prevent the sacrifice.'

'Be quick!' begged Moultan. 'Oh, sahibs, be quick!'

The formation of the column was at once changed. The men were thrown out to right and left, and like skirmishers going into action, in two parallel lines that were several yards apart, they pressed on as fast as they could, their approach drowned by the noise that guided them.

Colonel Renfrew and the detective were in advance, with Tinker and the Hindoo at their heels. For a short distance they fleetly traversed the jungle, drawing nearer and nearer to the shrill tumult; and then, having halted the two lines of soldiers, they stopped in a fringe of cover, and saw beyond it a weird and thrilling scene.

At a sweeping glance they took in every detail of the picture. They were almost on the verge of an open glade that was surrounded on three sides by a dense vegetation and bamboos, and here a horde of Nagas, to the number of a hundred, were dancing wildly about, and yelling at the tops of their voices, and pounding on tom-toms. On the opposite side of the glade was a rocky hill.

At the base of this was the wide mouth of a cavern, and immediately in front of it, each tied to a stake that had been planted in the earth, were Aga Khan and his English friend. Their features could not be seen, for their backs were towards their captors.

'There they are,' Moultan whispered eagerly; 'they have not yet been sacrificed.'

'No, we have come in time to save them,' said the colonel. 'But what are these scoundrels doing?' he added, in a puzzled tone.

'I have no doubt,' Sexton Blake replied, 'that they are screeching and drumming in order to draw out the serpents. They have been at it for some minutes, and so far they have not succeeded. But there is no telling how soon the noise will –'

'Look!' interrupted Tinker. 'By heavens, look!'

Two fiery eyes were shining amidst the gloom of the cavern. A huge serpent appeared, and after it came another. They were hamadryads, or king cobras, the most venomous and dreaded reptiles in India. Side by side, with hooded heads erect, they glided towards the hapless men who were bound to the stakes. They could be plainly seen by the little group who were watching from the shelter of the bushes.

For a moment they stared in dazed, numbing horror, while the fiendish clamour rang louder in their ears. Then Colonel Renfrew turned, and uttered a loud word of command, and the next instant, as he and his companions dashed into the open, a bugle sounded the charge, and the two lines of soldiers swept impetuously from cover.

'Have courage, my master!' cried the Hindoo. 'Have courage!'

It was a startling surprise for the Nagas, but instead of taking to flight they offered a furious resistance, so determined were they that their victims should not be rescued. Yells of rage blended with the lusty shouts of the attacking force, and the roar of matchlocks mingled with the crackle of rifles and pistols.

Having given the bloodhound in charge of Tinker, and bade him keep out of danger, Sexton Blake had promptly attempted to reach the threatened captives. But he had been forestalled. Heedless of his promise to the colonel, Private Dare had plunged into the thick of the fight, and was displaying the utmost heroism.

It might have been supposed that he bore a charmed life. With a revolver in each hand, firing as rapidly as he could, he cleft a way through the swarm of Nagas, trampling the dead under heel, while spears grazed him and bullets whistled around him. On he went, until at last he got clear of the foe. By then Blake had overtaken him, and a few more yards brought them to the space by the mouth of the cavern, where the situation was critical in the extreme.

One of the hamadryads had wrapped itself around the body of the Englishman, and was apparently about to strike at him. It was hissing viciously, and its hideous, spotted head, puffed out like a bladder, was hovering above the horror-struck man.

And Aga Khan was in no less danger, for the second reptile was coiled within a yard of him, and was in the act of springing upon its prey.

'Be quick, Dare, or they are lost!' cried the detective.

Crack! Crack! Two shots rang out. Sexton Blake and Private Dare had fired almost together, and the latter had blown to fragments the head of the great serpent that had been threatening the Englishman.

As for Blake, his bullet had severed the spinal-cord of the other snake, but in its frenzied convulsions it leapt upon Aga Khan, and darted its poisoned fangs into him.

By a second shot the detective finished the reptile, and a brief and tragic scene followed.

Blake drew a knife, and slashed at the fetters that bound Aga Khan, who had no sooner been released from the stake than he dropped to the ground, gasping and speechless.

Nothing could be done for him. The fangs had struck him twice, and the fleet, terrible poison was coursing through his veins, paralysing his mental and physical faculties. His skin turned to a greenish hue, and his eyes seemed to be bursting from his head. He writhed in anguish, sank into a stupor, and was dead in three minutes.

Meanwhile, Private Dare had cut the other prisoner free, and finding that he had swooned from horror, had placed him against the rocky base of the hill in a sitting position.

He called to Sexton Blake, who came over to him, and forced some brandy from his flask between the lips of the unconscious man, who almost immediately revived.

He had a dark moustache, and his beard had been allowed to grow for a week or two. He looked up with a dazed expression at his rescuers, and as they gazed at him closely they made a startling and bewildering discovery.

'By heavens, it is my cousin!' cried Rupert Dare.

'Yes, you are right,' declared Blake. 'It is Hildred Nairne! This is the last place in the world in which I should have expected to find him!'

The two great serpents had been slain, and Aga Khan had perished. The fight was over, and the Nagas had fled in all directions into the jungle, leaving half a score of dead behind them.

Six of the attacking party had also been killed, and amongst these was the Hindoo servant Moultan. He had tried hard to save the master to whom he was so devoted, and in death they were not divided.

The victors were cheering, and Colonel Renfrew, and Tinker and the bloodhound, had crossed the glade to the mouth of the cavern. But Private Dare and the detective paid no heed to them; they were still gazing down at Hildred Nairne, who had recognised both of them. He muttered their names, in a voice that was barely audible, as they assisted him to rise.

'You and Dare have certainly distinguished yourselves, Blake,' exclaimed the colonel. 'It is a great pity that you were not able to save Aga Khan. I am glad that you have rescued this renegade Englishman, however. I should like to know who he is. I cannot imagine what induced him to throw in his lot with that –'

'We know who he is,' Sexton Blake interrupted quietly. 'He is Dare's cousin – of whom you heard me speak.'

At that instant a small party of the Nagas, who had daringly ventured back to the scene of their defeat, discharged their matchlocks from the edge of the cover. Two of the colonel's men were wounded, and another was killed; while one of the slugs whistled past Blake's ear, and penetrated Hildred Nairne's breast.

The fire of the enemy was at once answered by a volley from the soldiers, who then dashed into the jungle, thirsting for vengeance. In the midst of the excitement the stricken man, who was insensible, was carried to a grassy spot by Private Dare and the detective, and was there examined by a surgeon who was with the force.

'It is a mortal wound,' he said, shaking his head. 'There is no hope for him.'

'How long is he likely to live?' asked Sexton Blake.

'Perhaps for two or three hours,' was the reply.

'And will he recover consciousness?'

'Yes, I have no doubt that he will.'

'It is most important that he should.'

'Very well. I will try to pull him round, and I dare say I shall succeed. I have my medicine-case with me.'

Rupert Dare had been listening to the conversation in silence. He now touched the detective's arm, and drew him to one side.

'I know what is in your mind,' he said. 'I have been thinking of the same thing. Do – do you believe that my cousin will –'

'Do I believe that he will confess?' Blake broke in.

'Yes, that is what I mean.'

'Well, Dare, you may hope for the best,' was the answer. 'Nothing is certain, but the fact that you saved your cousin from the serpent, and the knowledge that he has but a short time to live, may soften his heart, and persuade him to clear your name.'

'It will never be cleared, Mr Blake, if he does not do it.'

'I am afraid that is true, my dear fellow,' the detective reluctantly admitted. 'This is your one and only chance.'

'I am afraid it is a very slim one.'

'I don't think so. No, Dare, I feel that your innocence is going to be fully established.'

The Nagas had been widely dispersed, and those of the soldiers who had gone in pursuit of them had returned. The sun was now setting, and half an hour later, when night had fallen, and sentries had been posted to guard against a surprise, Sexton Blake and the young trooper were summoned to the side of Hildred Nairne, who was lying under a rude shelter that had been made of boughs. Tinker followed his master, and stood a little distance in the rear.

'How long?' Blake asked in a whisper of the surgeon.

'His strength will hold out for half an hour, perhaps,' was the reply.

The dying man was quite conscious, and able to speak. Drugs had numbed his pain, and he was also under the influence of stimulants. He nodded to the detective, and bent on his cousin a gaze that was inscrutable, void of any emotion.

'They told me that you would like to see me,' he said. 'I am glad that you have come, though I don't know as it will make any difference. There was never much affection between us, and there isn't now. Things might have gone on well with both of us, however, if we hadn't fallen in love with the same girl.

'Dulcie Romanis chose you, and that made me reckless, and dragged me down from one step to another, until England was too hot for me. And it was the same with you, Dick. I mean the affair of the *Paleta*.

'It was that, of course, that urged you to hide your identity in the Mounted Police. But I was talking of my own troubles, not of yours. After I found it necessary to disappear – no doubt Mr Blake has told you all about it – I came out to India, and looked up my old chum, Aga Khan, who had been at Cambridge with me. I knew that he was rich, and that he would be a friend in need to me. But I turned up at a bad time.

'He was just about to start on this daredevil, harebrained scheme for inciting the hill-tribes to rebel, and he persuaded me to accompany him. What a fool I was! It was the adventure that appealed to me. I didn't care a hang for the rights or the wrongs of the matter. I got the adventure, and more of it than I wanted. I wish now that I hadn't –'

Hildred Nairne paused, and shook his head wearily. He had been talking rapidly and lightly, in feverish haste, as if anxious to prevent a conversation that might lead to a distasteful subject. Private Dare, the man who was Richard Champney, had not yet uttered a word. He had kept quiet at a sign from the detective, who had begun to fear that his hopes might not be realised.

'I want to talk to you seriously, Nairne,' he said, as he stepped closer to him. 'For your life is nearly over. You are dying, and you must answer for your sins before a higher tribunal than any on earth. You are paying a just penalty, while your cousin has suffered unjustly. He has everything to live for.

'I have come out here at his father's request, to take him home, but he will not go as long as any shadow rests on his name. Will you not clear his honour, remove the stigma of cowardice? It is in your power to prove his innocence of the charge that drove him into exile.'

'In my power?' murmured Hildred Nairne, with an ironical smile on his lips. 'How can that be?'

'Don't trifle with me,' said Blake. 'I know all. I am absolutely certain that it was you who flung your cousin into the boat on the night the *Paleta* was lost. General Champney believes that, but the world will not believe it without proof.'

'Why should I have done such a stupid thing? What object had I to gain?'

'You had a very strong object. You hoped that by getting your cousin into indelible disgrace you might ultimately win the hand of Miss Romanis. That is why you did it, I have no doubt.'

There was silence for a few seconds. The smile was still on the dying man's lips, and there was a gleam of sinister triumph in his dark eyes. It looked as if he was going to be obstinate.

'Be merciful, Hildred,' begged Private Dare. 'My future rests with you. Give me back what I have lost. Why should you not? I have never done you any wrong. You have no reason to hate me.'

'Cannot gratitude melt your heart, Nairne?' put in the detective. 'Have you forgotten what your cousin did for you? There was no selfish thought in his mind when he fought his way through the Nagas to your side, and killed the great serpent that was threatening you. It was simply because you were in peril that he risked his own life to come to your assistance. Will you not requite the debt you owe to him? Are you willing to die with such an unconfessed crime on your soul? There is mercy at the bar of Heaven for all repentant sinners, remember.'

Hildred Nairne's face had softened while he listened, and the evil, mocking gleam now faded from his eyes.

'Yes, you are right, Mr Blake,' he said. 'Dick saved me at the risk of his own life. It was a plucky thing to do. I am not a coward myself, and I can admire bravery in any man. I will tell the truth, and clear his honour, though I had meant to let him suffer for robbing me of the girl I loved. I threw him into the boat that night, and I am sorry for it now. I will make a full confession. Get paper and pencil, and I will dictate to you.'

Colonel Renfrew had what was required, and in the course of a quarter of an hour, the confession had been taken down by Blake, and signed by the dying man, and witnessed by the colonel and the detective. And then, overcome by his exertions, Hildred Nairne closed his eyes and sank into a stupor.

'He will not speak again,' murmured the surgeon. 'He will remain unconscious until he dies.'

There were tears in Private Dare's eyes, and his cheeks were flushed with joy, as he gripped Blake's hand.

'I don't know how to thank you,' he said. 'My entreaties would have failed, I am sure. It is you who have done this, and I shall never forget it. My innocence has been established, I shall be ashamed to look no man in the face. I can go back to the world, back to my father and my friends, back to Dulcie –'

His voice faltered and broke, and he turned away to hide his intense emotion. Tinker and his master exchanged glances.

'And now for home and England, I suppose,' said the lad.

'Yes, as soon as possible,' Sexton Blake replied. 'Our work is finished.'

'And Mr Champney? Will he –?'

'He will go with us, my boy, of course.'

And Blake stooped down to caress the bloodhound, who wagged his tail as if he had understood what had been said.

At daybreak, Hildred Nairne breathed his last, and several hours later, after all the dead had been buried, the little column set off on their return to Paragong. They safely reached the military-station, and on the following day; the colonel having given permission, and provided an escort, Private Dare started down-country with those who had come so far to seek for him.

THE FOURTEENTH CHAPTER

At Raglan Barracks – The White Feather

A month had elapsed since the defeat of the Nagas, who, realising that they had been misled by Aga Khan, had promptly sued for peace. The rising was at an end, and Colonel Renfrew had without delay gone down to Calcutta, obtained leave of absence, and travelled across to Bombay, where he had overtaken the detective and his companions, and sailed with them for England.

One sunny morning, shortly after Sexton Blake and Tinker had finished their breakfast, a hansom stopped before the house in Baker Street, and from it stepped General Champney. The landlady admitted him, and led him up to the consulting-room, where he arrived heated and breathless. He offered one hand to Blake, and clapped him on the shoulder with the other.

'Glad to see you!' he exclaimed. 'I have been wondering what had become of you! But – but where is my boy?' he went on, gazing about the room. 'I felt sure that he would be here. Isn't that why you sent for me?'

'He is in London, Champney. That is all I will tell you at present.'

'What the deuce do you mean? Confound it, Blake, why are you so mysterious? Have you no consideration for a father's feelings? You have been absent for many weeks, looking for my son, and now you obstinately refuse to tell me –'

'You must be patient, and let me have my own way,' interrupted the detective. 'I expect to have some information about your son in the course of the day, and he will probably accompany you back to Broadlands.'

'It will be hard for me to wait,' declared General Champney.

'I can suggest a means of passing the time. Suppose you come with me to witness an interesting little ceremony.'

'What is it, Blake?'

'It is a military affair. The Victoria Cross is to be presented to a trooper of the Indian Mounted Police, at Raglan Barracks.'

'A friend of yours, eh?'

'I am acquainted with the man, Champney. He is Private Rupert Dare.'

'Ah, I might have guessed that!' said General Champney. 'I shall be glad to go with you. I was reading about the brave fellow the other day. It was due to his courage that the military post of Paragong, up in the Assam Hills, was relieved in time. It was besieged by the Nagas, and the commander of the garrison was Major Errol, the son of an old friend of mine.'

'Yes, that is quite right,' assented Blake. 'The man displayed the utmost heroism going and coming. We will be off at once,' he added, as he looked at his watch. 'We have not many minutes to spare.'

Without delay, Sexton Blake and the old soldier left the house, accompanied by Tinker, and a taxicab whirled them across the heart of London to Raglan Barracks, where they did not have long to wait. The detective was expected, and he and his companions were at once taken to the barrack-yard. Here a number of other spectators were standing in a group, and opposite to them, along one side of the enclosure, a little column of troops was drawn up.

All was in readiness, and when two or three minutes had passed, Colonel Renfrew appeared, walking with a Royal prince, who represented the King in the latter's absence from London. They moved slowly down the line, and stopped at the middle of it; and then, at a word of command, a bronzed trooper stepped out from the ranks and saluted. The impressive ceremony, which has not its like for importance the world over, now began. Having spoken a few appreciative words, Prince

Victor pinned the bronze cross, the reward of valour, to Private Rupert Dare's breast. The young soldier saluted again, and stepped back, feeling this to be the proudest moment of his life; and the next instant, as a burst of cheers rang out, General Champney rushed forward with a flushed and agitated face.

'It is my boy!' he cried. 'It is my boy Dick!'

'Father!' burst from the trooper's lips.

And with that he threw himself into the arms of his parent, who had not recognised him until the ceremony was over. With tears in their eyes, too thrilled for speech, they clung together. Thus they had met again, after that bitter parting many months ago. The spectators cheered lustily, and Sexton Blake and Tinker were deeply moved as they looked on

'I can hardly realise it,' the old general said hoarsely. 'It was a complete surprise. I never dreamed that you were Private Dare, that you were the hero of Paragong. And – and to think that I believed you to have been a coward!'

'Hush, father,' bade Richard Champney. 'Don't talk like that. The past is dead. Let us try to forget it. My innocence has been proved. I have the written confession of the man who threw me into the boat that night.'

'It was Hildred, of course?'

'Yes, it was my cousin. Fate brought us together out in India, where he –'

'I want to congratulate you both,' interrupted Colonel Renfrew. 'I never knew a finer example of heroism and endurance. You have a son to be proud of, Champney. And now come into the barracks, and you shall hear all. Come along, Blake,' he added, 'and bring that young assistant with you.'

The colonel led the way to the officers' mess, and there the whole story, from beginning to end, was related by the detective to General Champney, who was at times moved to tears as he listened to the stirring narrative. When it had been concluded, he thanked Sexton Blake in a voice that shook with emotion, vowing that he would never forget what he owed him; and then, turning to his son, he rested a hand on his shoulder.

'I know what you are thinking of, Dick,' he said. 'I can guess what is in your mind. Come, we will go to Dulcie.'

'It would be best to wait, Champney,' broke in Blake, addressing the general. 'I would suggest that you run down to Hampshire at once, and prepare the young lady for a visit from your son.'

'Very well,' assented General Champney. 'I will do as you suggest, and will be off without delay. Goodbye for the present, Dick,' he added, as he rose. 'I shall expect you and Mr Blake by the train that arrives at five o'clock, so don't miss it.'

Dick's return to his native heath was a veritable triumph. A small crowd was at the station to see the train come in, and there was a burst of applause as the young trooper appeared, wearing the uniform he was so proud of.

In an open carriage, seated opposite to his father and Sexton Blake, he rolled along the country road, and passed through the village, and so on to the stately old mansion of Broadlands.

'Here we are,' said Blake, as the vehicle stopped.

'Home again, my dear boy!' exclaimed General Champney, rising from his seat. 'Home again, thank Heaven!'

'Yes, thank Heaven!' echoed the young soldier.

But he did not long remain at home, glad though he was to be there. Ten minutes after he had entered the house he left it, his heart beating fast with a thrilling sense of anticipation.

Slowly he struck across the grounds of Broadlands, and out by a gap in the hedge, and along the road for a short distance. Then he glided over to the gateway that led to the Grange, and as he was approaching the house, walking quietly on the strip of grass that bordered the gravelled drive, he heard a low sound of sobbing. It came to his ears from the left, and when he had gone for a dozen yards in that direction, stealing through the trees and shrubbery, he paused by a rustic bench that was overhung by foliage.

Dulcie Romanis was sitting there, weeping softly, with her head bowed on her hands. She looked up with a start, and saw before her the man she had so deeply wronged in her thoughts, the bronzed hero who had suffered more from the loss of her faith than from anything else. Every trace of colour ebbed from her cheeks. She sat speechless, dumb with emotion. Slowly Richard Champney drew an envelope from his pocket, and took from it a white feather, and dropped it into the girl's lap. She gazed at it for an instant, and then her tears flowed afresh.

'How cruel!' she sobbed. 'Oh, how cruel of you! I hate myself, Dick! When I remember what I thought of you, what I believed, I wish that I was dead! I have heard all! I know what an injustice I did you! But you need not have made my burden harder to bear than it was! You cannot forgive me, or you would have spared me this bitter humiliation!'

'I do forgive you!' cried the young soldier, as he clasped her in his arms, and kissed her quivering lips. 'I love you, and you will soon be my wife, and we will forget the past!'

And needless to say they did!

THE BROTHERHOOD OF THE YELLOW BEETLE

G. H. Teed

THE FIRST CHAPTER

What Came Out of the Mist – The Vengeance of the Yellow Beetle – Sir George Halliday is Marked Down

The heavy evening mist was closing down with an almost sinister stealth over the yellow waters of Pe-chili Strait. Through the passage which is guarded on the one side by Port Arthur, and on the other by Wai-hai-wei, it came creeping from the Corea Bay and the Yellow Sea.

Instinct with all the mystery, the stealth, the cunning, and the deep inscrutable purpose of the teeming and changeless East it came, throwing, as it were, a protective blanket over the purposes and intentions of its children.

Into its capacious maw empty many rivers and streams – rivers which, like the long and winding Hwang-ho, pass through many different peoples and dissipate in their sweeping torrents the whisperings of night-born plots and deep Oriental passions.

Tiny and insignificant, in comparison, are the coast streams which hurry onward to the sea, but no less eloquent are they of mystery and stealth.

Why it is that the Celestial is so fond of the rivers and harbours for the conception of his plans and the pursuit of his purposes is a mystery; but so it is, from the water worshippers of the Ganges to the almost extinct swarthy pirates of the Malay Archipelago.

On the night in question, when the creeping mist had done its work, and only the lapping of the yellow water broke the stillness, there might have been seen stealing phantom-like through the night the form of a Chinese junk.

The guiding hand on the tiller evidently knew his way through the invisible waters as well as when they were lit by the orb of day, for straight and unhesitatingly she went, her sail barely bellied out by the dying breeze.

She had come from the direction of the Hwang-ho, and was heading south; not even when the wash of water on the shore became audible did she change her course. Rather, the helmsman guided her dead on the shore as the sound grew louder and louder, until suddenly it faded away into a distant murmur, and even through the mist could be seen the dark bulk of a river's bank, and below could be made out the placid waters of a river, indicating that, like the men who existed about it, they ran deep.

A hundred yards or more after he had left the waters of the gulf, and entered the river, the helmsman headed the junk for the bank. As though he had known the exact moment when the last puff of the fitful breeze would die out, he put the nose of the boat gently into the bank, just as the sail flapped slackly, and then hung still.

Until now, the man at the helm had been the only occupant of the deck of the junk; but, as though the slight jar of the boat against the bank had been a signal, another Chinaman suddenly appeared and leaped nimbly over the rail to the bank, a mooring-line in his hand.

Once the bow had been made fast, he turned his attention to the stern, and when that had also been secured, he squatted on his heels and silently rolled a cigarette.

The man at the helm hung as silently over the stern, watching, with impassive features, the waters beneath.

For half an hour the two sat thus before movement of any kind occurred. Then a shadowy figure loomed up out of the mist, and after exchanging a few muttered words with the man on the bank, stepped aboard and descended to the cabin below.

Hard on his heels another figure appeared. Again the low-toned colloquy took place, and he, like the other, silently stepped aboard and went below.

Another and another appeared, all stopping for a few words, and then disappearing after the others. Ten had come, and still the silent guard on the bank smoked on; still the man in the stern moved not.

Suddenly, however, thc guard stirred slightly, and, throwing away his cigarette, got to his feet.

Simultaneously with his action came another figure through the mist – tall, cloaked, and with bent head. The guard bent himself with respectful submission, and as the last comer raised his head to speak in low tones, even through the mist one could feel, though not see, the power of his deep-set, inscrutable almond eyes.

He passed on and went below where the other ten were already seated. They stood up respectfully as he entered, and waited until he passed up to the other end, and squatted on the floor.

Then they followed his example, and waited for him to speak.

The so-called cabin was not a cabin in the strict sense of the word. What its original disposition had been, it would be hard to say; but now it was a long, low compartment, without table and without chairs.

The floor itself was covered with a thick grass carpet on which were carelessly thrown thick, vivid-toned rugs. Along the floor, close to the walls, were heaps of silken cushions, rivalling in their gorgeous tints the rugs beyond.

Overhead, the rough beams of the deck of the junk contrasted in dark-toned bulk with the colour below, while, if there ever had been windows, they were obscured by the heavy silken hangings of rich, blazing yellow, which covered every inch of the walls.

Seated down each side on the cushions were the ten men who had first arrived.

Alone, at the other end, and squatting on a yellow cushion, was the man who had entered last. A big, swinging lamp lit up the scene below, and by its light could be seen the power of the eyes which above could only be felt.

His head was close-cropped like that of the European, and by its shape and poise, the head was that of the thinker and student, while the thin, yellow hands and square, slightly bulging lines of the jaw indicated the practical and determined.

The brow was high and broad, and though in repose, the face might have been earnest, cruel, or what not, for all one could read in its expression. He had neither beard nor moustache, and on his hands wore no jewellery of any description, with the exception of a blazing yellow topaz on the little finger of his left. His clothes were rich, and a blend of blue and yellow, while gleaming against his tunic was a glittering, jewelled order.

Before him was set a low, desk-like affair, containing modern pens, with a supply of thin parchment-paper, and a pot of ink. Before speaking, he bent over and inspected them, and then, lifting his head, he glanced slowly and piercingly at each man who sat there.

They were, by their dress, of all stations in life – some wearing the rich costume of the wealthy mandarin, while one, at the far end, wore a coarse suit of blue cotton.

It seemed not to affect the man at the other end, however, for as his eyes passed over the cheap garments, his expression altered not a whit. For the tiniest fraction of a second, his glance lingered on a stout, richly-dressed mandarin sitting near him, then it passed on, finally to come to rest again on the low desk in front of him.

Suddenly he raised his head, and, looking at the stout mandarin, spoke, his tone coming in soft, liquid accents, pregnant with force.

'A week ago, we, the Brethren of the Yellow Beetle, met here. Then we deputed you, Foo Loo, to carry out the decision of the council which was a step in our great campaign. Tonight you were to bring us news of your success. Speak!'

The stout mandarin listened, as though fascinated, to the slow words of the other. His brow showed first a tiny bead of sweat, then another and another, until there were a host of them. He struggled to speak, but seemed held by the fascination of the other's gaze.

'Does Wu Ling, the head of the Yellow Beetle, need to order twice?' asked the man at the upper end, as the mandarin failed to open his lips.

As though the menacing quiet of the words had unlocked his jaws, Foo Loo, the mandarin, rose and walked up between his seated companions until he stood before the desk. Then, dropping to his knees, he bowed his head and spoke.

'Oh, illustrious one, head of the most favoured and exalted Yellow Beetle, your unworthy and not-to-be-mentioned creature craves your indulgence.'

'Away with such preamble!' replied Wu Ling impassively. 'Speak!'

'Oh, Excellency, I went as the council ordered. I spent money as water in an effort to carry out the purposes of the council against the English pig. I failed, however, for he got away and is even now on his way to England!'

For a moment Wu Ling's eyes closed as though to conceal the hidden fire which blazed forth at the news he had heard. Then he slowly opened them, and his voice was toneless as ever as he spoke.

'So, Foo Loo, you have failed to carry out the orders of the council?'

'Yes, Excellency, and I beg for the leniency of the council. If given more time I can achieve the purpose.'

Wu Ling seemed not to have heard him, for he gazed over his head at the others.

'Brethren of the Yellow Beetle,' he said slowly, 'there are three men – English pigs, if you will – who know the great purpose of the council. Two left China and made their way to England before we knew of their knowledge. The third, however, Sir George Halliday, was still here. By the method of the council we drew lots to see who should put him out of the way. It was too important a matter to trust to a mere agent. It was imperative that it should be done. Foo Loo drew the straw which appointed him to do our will. He has failed. He comes to us and begs for leniency, while the man who possesses our secret is on his way to England.'

'But, Excellency,' broke in Foo Loo, 'I looked for him as a passenger, nor did I know until late that he had escaped by disguising as a stoker.'

'The council is not dealing in excuses, Foo Loo,' replied Wu Ling impassively. Then, looking at the others, he continued: 'Brethren, what is your verdict?'

A low rumble sounded as the answer came: 'The Beetle.'

Wu Ling turned back to the kneeling mandarin.

'You hear?' he asked softly.

The mandarin bowed his head in silence. Then Wu Ling thrust his hand into the folds of his rich tunic, and when he drew it out it held a tiny metal case.

Silently he held it out. Foo Loo, with fascinated gaze and trembling hand, reached out and took it.

For a moment he gazed at it fearfully and turned appealingly to the assembled council. Only impassive countenances met him on every side, however, and with trembling knees he rose.

Slowly he made his way down the centre of the cabin until he reached the farther end where the heavy silken curtain hid the entrance to the companion-way. Then he turned and once more dropped to his knees.

His yellow face worked convulsively as his trembling fingers forced the cover off the metal case. Inside was a piece of cotton wool, from which came the odour of a heavy, pungent perfume. Setting the box on the carpet in front of him Foo Loo bared his throat and, lifting the saturated bit of cotton-wool, wiped it over the throat from chin to chest. Then he replaced it in the box and closed the cover. Once more he looked appealingly at Wu Ling, who made no sign.

With a choking gurgle Foo Loo again lifted the box and in the bottom pressed an invisible spring.

The first sign of expression passed over the faces of the watchers as the bottom flew open and there dropped on the carpet a small shining beetle of pure, brilliant yellow. Its vivid tones were those of the silken curtains and cushions, the yellow of Wu Ling's tunic and the deep tone of the topaz which blazed on his hand.

For a moment the tiny beetle seemed dazed by its sudden entry into the lighted room, but as the pungent odour of the perfume smeared on Foo Loo's throat caught its senses, it slowly turned and lifted its pin-like head from which projected a needle-like point fully a quarter of an inch in length.

The mandarin gazed in speechless horror, and shuddered as the beetle waved the needle-like point slowly about; then, as it began moving forward with a soft, metallic rustle of its scales, he closed his eyes and waited with clutched hands.

Foo Loo opened his eyes, saw it coming, and gave a stifled shriek as he dropped forward on his face and lay still.

For a few moments the watchers sat there, waiting for a sign from Wu Ling. Finally he raised his hand, and pointed at the coolie who sat near the fallen, crumpled figure of Foo Loo.

There was no need for him to speak. The man knew only too well what was required of him. Rising quickly, he moved noiselessly across to the body, and with a deft movement threw Foo Loo back on his shoulders.

It was hard to believe that the still face had been working so convulsively a moment before, and that one touch of the needle-like point of the Yellow Beetle had killed him so suddenly. Against his throat was a dark point, sole proof that he had died other than a normal death.

As for the beetle, it had dropped to the carpet and was running about blindly, drunkenly, drugged into harmlessness by the pungent perfume, but not until it had achieved its intended purpose.

Drawing the metal box to him the coolie pressed the spring in the bottom. Then, picking up the dazed beetle, he dropped it in the opening, its scales rattling harshly as it flapped feebly against the steel sides.

With a click he closed the box and walked up to Wu Ling, who took it in silence and returned it to his tunic.

The coolie moved noiselessly back to the hangings over the companion-way. There he drew them aside and sent a guttural hail up to the deck.

A moment later the man who had been there on guard and the helmsman appeared.

The coolie spoke not, but pointed to the body.

Silently they bent and lifted it up, and when they had gained the deck a soft splash in the mist-laden waters was the last act in the evening's brief drama.

When the deck-hands had disappeared with Foo Loo, the coolie dropped the hangings, and, after bowing to Wu Ling, squatted once more in his place by the wall.

All eyes sought the features of Wu Ling, and it is safe to say that, inscrutable as were their features outwardly, inwardly they were consumed with curiosity as to what he had to say.

Not without a full knowledge of the rules of the Brotherhood of the Yellow Beetle had those men of every class gained the Inner Council. Not without being prepared unhesitatingly to fulfil their self-inflicted doom should they fail to carry out any of the decrees of the man who wielded a power many kings might envy.

One and all, they would stop at nothing to obey orders, and in the pursuance of such even should father, brother, or friend be an obstruction, they would swiftly be removed.

After a silence of some moments Wu Ling opened his eyes and began speaking in his low tones, which, for all their liquid softness, reached every man there.

'Brethren,' he said, 'you have seen the reward of failure. Foo Loo was my friend, and now that he is gone I send him my blessing. But, were he my brother, were he my father, were he myself, the penalty for failure must be paid. In our great purpose no man, no thing, must stop us. We have set ourselves a purpose, and with the aid of the blessed and all-wise Confucius, will we be victorious.

'Our illustrious race, which has rested for centuries in the reflected glory of Confucius, shall now by the guiding of Wu Ling, most unworthy though I be, go on until the white races, who have in their vanity spurned us and oppressed us, are under the heel of the East.

'I, Wu Ling, say it shall be so. I have spent years in their cities and houses of learning, preparing for the great day, and now the day is at hand. First must we find and crush by the Yellow Beetle the three men who have escaped to England with a knowledge of our secrets and purposes.

'The man who betrayed us has met with a just punishment, as has Foo Loo tonight, but those men must be removed. I myself – I, Wu Ling, the head of the illustrious Brotherhood of the Yellow Beetle, will lead the campaign in person. And you, my brethren, will follow me. That is all. If you would ask anything of me, speak!'

A dead silence rested for some moment over the assembled men, but finally a man in rich garb rose, and bowed low.

'Most illustrious one,' he said, 'your unworthy servant would ask a question.'

'Speak!' said Wu Ling.

'Is it of thy purpose, O illustrious one, to tell us more of your plans?'

Wu Ling waved his hand.

'Be seated, I will tell you. I go to London, and you, my brethren, come also. There, we first remove the men who bear our secret, and if others have gained possession of it we will remove them also. Then, my brethren, will we create a reign of terror throughout the land of the white pigs until they meet our demands. And may Confucius bless our efforts by the blessing of the Three Lakes and the Four Moons.'

All heads bowed again as Wu Ling finished, and then he rose. Celestial though he was, he was the highest expression of dignity and majesty as he passed down between the bowed heads and drew aside the yellow silken hangings over the entrance to the companion-way. There he turned, and spoke in soft, guttural accents.

'Brethren, remember the Yellow Beetle!'

A moment later he was gone, and with his departure the remaining nine lifted their heads and rose. One by one they passed out silently behind him, until last of all the man in coolie garb dropped the curtain and disappeared.

In blazing yellow silence was the cabin left, the stillness only broken a few minutes later by the gentle waving to and fro of the wall-hangings, as the crew of two got out long sweeps and propelled the little junk along with the current to try and catch some of the night breeze in the open sea beyond.

In silence – yes, for half-an-hour the cabin showed no signs of movement except the curtains. Suddenly, however, up at the far end, directly behind where Wu Ling had sat, the yellow hanging was pushed aside stealthily, one eye appeared, and then a tousled black head.

Slowly, and peering about cautiously the while, the head came further and further into view until it was entirely clear of the curtains – the head, the eyes, the skin of a white man – an Englishman.

His hair was tangled, his face smutted with soot and grease, and his clothes consisted only of greasy black overalls and jumper, but the prominent nose, clean-cut chin, and independent poise of the head betokened the ruler and law-maker.

Clever as the now departed Foo Loo had thought himself, and in spite of the money he had spent in order to remove Sir George Halliday before he got out of China, his efforts had been fruitless, and he had paid the penalty.

But when he said Sir George had disguised himself as a stoker he was only partly right. True, Sir George had disguised himself as a stoker, but had only remained on board the steamer during her stay in port. Foo Loo's men, hot on his trail, had driven him at the last moment to throw up his intention.

In a situation where he could not seek assistance, and with half a dozen bloodthirsty Chinamen at his heels, he had taken to the docks. From there the chase had led across the decks of a tangled mass of junks until the pursuers had been baffled by the sudden disappearance of their quarry.

As the spot where he had disappeared was near the liner, and as at that moment the big steamer had slipped her mooring, they concluded he had in some way regained her deck, and was on his way to England.

Not so, however, for Sir George had tumbled down the first open companion-way he saw. On his arrival at the bottom he had turned, expecting every moment would bring the yellow fiends down after him, but as minute succeeded minute, and still they did not come, he began to breathe more freely. Had he, after all, shaken them off, or had they with true diabolical cunning set themselves to wait there, knowing he could not escape?

He had been surprised to find a soft curtain hung before the entrance to the cabin. From the feel of it he knew it was silk, and it was not usual for coastal junks to go about with silken-hung cabins. Passing his hands along the walls in his search for a window or porthole of some description through which he might find an avenue of escape, he marvelled still more at the continuation clear around of the silk.

Once he stumbled, and, finding the object which he had struck, whistled softly at feeling a pile of soft, luxurious cushions.

'Gad!' he muttered. 'It seems as though I'd struck some sort of a portable harem. I'll be worse off than ever if I'm caught nosing about in here, for it certainly is not an ordinary junk. I wonder what the deuce it is used for.'

At that moment the noise of a soft slushing step on the staircase caught his ear, and grabbing at the silken hangings he slipped behind, and stood close against the wall.

Lucky was it for him that a heavy supporting stanchion passed down there, and by standing stiff and straight he did not bulge the curtain at all.

A moment later a dim yellow gleam came through the hangings, but what the new arrival was doing he could not guess. Then he had put out the light, and departed, leaving Sir George once more alone.

He dared not move, however, for fear of discovery, and cramped as was the position, he was compelled to keep it all through the night.

Dawn found him stiff, sore, and haggard, but disregarding his physical discomfort, he drew aside the hangings and peered out.

The cabin was still shadowy and dim, but the curtain over the entrance to the companion-way had been thrust aside, and some daylight filtered in. He was too astonished for words as he found himself gazing out on the luxurious cabin where Wu Ling met the council of the Yellow Beetle, and which was that coming night to witness the self-inflicted death of Foo Loo.

Steps on the deck overhead warned Sir George that people were about, and soon the moving of the junk told him it was under way. Such a physical strain had he gone through the past few days during his strenuous attempts to escape from the vendetta which had been proclaimed against him that, dangerous as was his position now, it was impossible for him to remain awake any longer.

He surreptitiously pushed aside the hangings, drew a pile of cushions in nearer, in order to hide the bulge, and then, casting himself down as close to the wall as he could, in less than a minute he was sound asleep. What providence watched over him during that long day it is hard to say, but when he awoke it was evening.

The junk still held on her way, as he knew from the gentle rolling; but whither they were bound he had no idea. He was ravenously hungry, but ruefully decided that for the moment the question of food must be put aside. The junk might come to an anchor during the evening, and then he might find some means of escape.

Cautiously he pushed the curtains back where they had been, and once more took up his position close to the wall. Then his hopes had been raised by feeling the motion of the junk almost cease, and he had lost no time in making his preparations.

Just as he was about to push aside the hangings and investigate matters a shuffling footstep sounded, and once more the cabin was flooded with light. Then the footsteps departed, the junk stopped entirely, and Sir George knew from the faint noise overhead that she was being moored.

Once more he was about to make a bid for freedom, when another interruption occurred. It was the first of the council to arrive, and the man in hiding puzzled his mind in futile conjecture as Chinaman after Chinaman arrived. It was the gathering of the council whose doings that night have already been related.

Sir George Halliday was a man who knew China better than most white men, and who spoke the language like a native. Like the intrepid Sven Hedin he had traversed Tibet and the Himalayas, looking for the elusive source of the Brahmaputra. He had followed the brave and gallant Bruce on that long, tortuous journey from Leh overland to Peking, crossing on his way the extreme north-west corner of Tibet.

Qualities which made such hazardous trips possible had been, however, coalesced into a single aim by the incentive of his desire to become an authority on the hidden, mysterious country and peoples through which he passed.

There he had heard faint whisperings of a force – a mighty, all-powerful force – which eventually was to sweep Christendom from the face of the globe. Once, and once only, had he heard used the expression, 'Yellow Beetle', but more than that all his diplomacy, all his knowledge of the language, and all his offers of gold failed to tell him.

In Peking, however, he had gained more knowledge of the secrets of the mysterious organisation, but before he could follow it up his informant had met the vengeance of the Yellow Beetle. Then had started the persistent attempts to put him out of the way before he could reach the comparative safety of England.

These efforts he had so far, however, eluded, until the wheel of Fate had so strangely cast him behind the silken curtains of the very cabin in which a meeting of the Brotherhood was being held – a night on which Wu Ling himself, the very source of the organisation which had spread its tentacles around the world, had outlined to the council his plans for the future.

He had seen too many horrors in China to be much affected by Foo Loo's death, but the sinister rustle of the beetle's scales had sent a cold shiver up his spine. Had any of that inscrutable council known of his presence in the very heart of the organisation, his death would have been slow and lingering, but none the less certain.

However, by an almost superhuman effort to stand motionless, we have seen how he succeeded. Now, after peering cautiously about, he stepped forth, and stood beside where the powerful Wu Ling had just been sitting. If he could only get out of his present position he was in possession of information which no other white man had.

The two others spoken of by Wu Ling would possess no more than he had had, if as much. But now he knew the colossal and gigantic plan of the organisation which had been so carefully built up, and it behoved him to get to England as quickly as possible. His thoughts were interrupted by the sound of a shuffling footstep, but this time, instead of slipping back behind the curtain, he sped quickly down to the other end, and concealed himself there just as the curtain over the door was thrust aside, and the deck hand entered. He walked straight up to the hanging lamp, and, lowering it by a cord, turned it out. Then he drew it up again, and turned to find his way out.

As his shuffling steps drew nearer and nearer, the man in hiding quickly formed a plan. It would require swift, sure action, but that must be risked. He was determined to escape at all costs, and could hardly risk more than he had already done, he thought grimly.

Nearer and nearer drew the steps until the silken hangings behind which he stood fluttered slightly from contact with the passing Chinaman's sleeve.

Then Sir George acted, and acted quickly. Without pausing to thrust aside the hangings, he leaped forward, a ripping, tearing sound following as the hangings gave. Heedless of this he hurled himself blindly at the startled Chinaman, who had gasped sharply at the noise.

Rather than a hindrance the curtain was of use to Sir George, for it fell over the head of the Celestial, hindering his movements materially. As Sir George's hands felt the other's throat, he closed them convulsively, and then began a silent, deadly struggle in the darkness, neither man being able to see his opponent.

Up the full length of the cabin the fight raged, and then back again. Weak though he was for want of food, Sir George was fighting with the strength of desperation.

As for the Celestial, he knew every trick which was used from Batavia to Shanghai, and he made use of them. The Englishman, however, relaxed his grip not an atom, and as for the second time they reached the upper end of the cabin the Chinaman yielded to the pressure.

There was an ominous crack in his arm as Sir George hurled him to the floor, but the victor spent no time in finding out the cause. Quickly he stripped the clothes from the unconscious Celestial, and after taking off his own greasy overalls, put the others on.

The overalls he put on the Celestial, and then, with strips of the yellow curtain, bound him. The same material served as a ball for a gag, and after sticking the Chinaman's kris in his waistband, he moved cautiously towards the companion-way, and ascended to the deck.

The mist was gone, the stars hung low and large in a purple sky; the moon beat down in cold unconcern, her disc as yellow as the curtains back in the cabin. Leaning indolently over the tiller was the helmsman, and forward the sail flapped in the growing breeze.

On each side Sir George could see the banks of a river, but even as he looked the current swept them out into the open gulf, the sail bellied out, and the helmsman put her head for the north.

All this he saw in a moment, and then, adopting the shuffling step of the Celestial, he made his way towards the stern. The helmsman took no notice of his approach until Sir George was close upon him. It was then he saw the difference between his fellow and the newcomer.

Without hesitating the fraction of a second, or inquiring as to the why and the wherefore, he dropped the tiller, drew his crooked-bladed knife, and sprang forward.

Sir George expected a struggle, but had hardly looked for such a sudden onslaught as this. He thanked his stars in that moment that he had brought the other's knife with him. Springing back, he drew it, and jabbed it up to the guard, while the junk, free of control, brought up dangerously before the wind and headed for the shore.

The helmsman was shrewd enough to know that a stranger dressed in the garb of his shipmate and in possession of his knife was of a dangerous calibre, and as the pale light of the moon flashed from the knife-blade to Sir George's face the Celestial's eyes narrowed as he saw his antagonist was a white man.

Hurling himself forward, he slashed viciously at the other's guard, a dripping flow of vivid red showing where the point of his blade got home.

The Englishman, however, had been waiting for just such a move, and barely had the other's knife ripped his arm than he had an iron hold on the wrist. Then, struggling and straining, he threw his injured arm up and down with lightning rapidity in an endeavour to escape the attempted clutch of the Chinaman.

Back and forth across the deck they went until a vicious roll of the junk hurled them both half senseless against the side. Driven on by the shock, the helmsman's guard drove back, weighted by Sir George's grip; the crooked blade turned sharply, and as they crashed together, by his own hand was the Chinaman's knife driven to his heart.

Another violent roll sent them reeling backwards, and as Sir George pushed free, the return of the junk threw the Celestial against the low rail, and with a slanting somersault he tumbled over the rail.

Shaken by the accidental result of the fight, Sir George dropped his own blade and leaped for the tiller. As he sent the junk's head round and the sail slowly filled he held his breath.

The shore was barely ten yards away, and he expected every moment to feel her go bumping on the rocks. Indeed, as she came round, he felt an ominous quiver run along her hull as she grazed a hidden boulder; but the sail filled out, and, carried by the breeze, she swung clear.

How he ever made his way out of the gulf past Wei-hai-wei and down through the Yellow Sea to Shanghai Sir George never knew. He was crew, captain, and cook all in one, and small as the junk was, it was no sinecure.

Had the weather been rough he would never have made it, but several days later he floated in through a tangled conglomeration of steamers, junks, and sampans, and after recklessly tying up the junk, made his way, more dead than alive, to a big liner about to sail for England, realising full well the strength of the sinister power which was on his heels.

THE SECOND CHAPTER

Blake Hears an Exciting Story – Blake takes up the Case – Sir George's Last Letters – Another Problem

'Going out, guv'nor?'

Tinker asked the question and looked up as his master emerged from his dressing-room clad in evening-clothes.

'Yes, my lad,' replied Blake thoughtfully. 'I'm going round to Sir George Halliday's for dinner, and I am afraid my writing has kept me late. However, I'll get a taxi, and will not be long reaching there.'

'Not a case, is it, guv'nor?'

'I don't know yet,' said Blake absently, as he selected a cigar and lit it. 'Sir George wrote me a note asking me to drop round to dinner, and saying, incidentally, that he had something of interest to tell me. It may not be anything but some inside information regarding developments in the East. He has just arrived from China, you know.'

'Oh, yes; I remember, guv'nor. Isn't he the man who has done so much exploration work out there?'

'Yes, indeed!' answered Blake warmly. 'He has added much to our knowledge of Tibet and Turkestan, as well as Central China; and if, as I think, he has some fresh notes, I look forward keenly to reading them. However, I must be getting along. Hallo! I wonder who that is?'

This, as an agitated ringing came at the street door.

'Just see who it is, my lad,' added Blake, with a frown of irritation. 'I hope it isn't a professional call.'

Tinker slipped out of his chair and left the consulting-room to answer the door. From where he stood Blake heard the hurried question of an excited voice, and then hasty steps came down the passage. A moment later the door opened, and there dashed in a tall, well-dressed young man in an evident state of great agitation.

'Mr Blake?' he asked excitedly, almost chopping off Tinker's nose as he unthinkingly banged the door after him.

'Yes,' replied Blake calmly. 'But might I ask –'

'Yes, yes!' cried the newcomer, sinking into a chair. 'I'll tell you everything as we go along! Can you come at once?'

'Look here!' remarked Blake. 'Get a grip on yourself, man, and speak more definitely. You rush in here like a wild man, and ask me to go to some place with you, neither saying where nor on what business. You are taking my consent for granted, which is not yet given. Now, if you will favour me with your name and try and tell me the cause of your excitement, perhaps I can be of assistance to you. If not' – and Blake shrugged – 'I am afraid I must ask you to excuse me, for I am on my way to fulfil a dinner engagement.'

As though suddenly sobered by the cold douche of Blake's remarks, the other straightened up, and passed his hand across his brow.

'Yes, yes,' he muttered; 'you are right, Mr Blake. I apologise, but for a moment the awful thing that has happened drove everything else from my mind.'

'Well,' interrupted Blake curtly, 'please get to the point.'

'It is this,' responded the other. 'First, I will tell you my name is Carslake – Godfrey Carslake. I – I am the affianced husband of Miss Halliday – Sir George Halliday's only daughter. Oh, it is too terrible!' he muttered, breaking off.

'Ah!' remarked Blake quickly. 'Sir George Halliday, you say? Is the trouble connected with him?'

The other nodded.

'Yes – he – is – dead!'

'What!' snapped Blake, leaning forward tensely. 'Sir George Halliday, the Asiatic explorer, dead?'

'Yes,' responded Carslake; 'dead. He died less than an hour ago, and the doctor whom we called pronounced it heart-failure. But – but both Miss Halliday and myself think that in some way there has been foul play.'

'Wait!' interrupted Blake. 'Tell me the details in the taxi. Tinker, get my hat and coat. Bring Pedro. Look alive!' Then, turning to Carslake, he said: 'It is a very strange coincidence. I was just on my way to dine with him.'

Carslake nodded.

'Yes, I know; the butler told me. I had forgotten before to mention that that was the reason of my coming to you at once. I thought Sir George might have intended consulting you about matters.'

'About matters!' jerked Blake, remembering Sir George had said in his note he desired to tell him something. 'What matters?'

Carslake shook his head.

'That's it,' he replied. 'I don't know what; but of this I am convinced. There has been foul play, although the doctor scouts any such idea.'

At that moment Tinker returned with Blake's hat and coat, and five minutes later the whole party, with Pedro, were in a taxi heading at a smart pace for Sir George's house.

'Now then,' said Blake, as the driver turned out of Baker Street. 'I think you said you were engaged to Miss Halliday?'

'Yes; only since last evening, though. You see, while Sir George was in China his daughter stayed with her aunt, and although there was an understanding between us there was nothing definite. We were waiting for her father's return. As you know, he arrived last week, and in order to let him get over the fatigue of the journey I didn't speak to him until last night.

'He was very nice about it, and said he had no objection, but before permitting an announcement he said he felt in duty bound to tell me of a peril which was hanging over him, and which he was afraid might hang over his daughter unless he were able to change conditions soon. Of course I thought he might be exaggerating, and told him I didn't care what the peril was, and that as my wife, Gertrude his daughter would be entitled to my protection.

'After leaving him, however, I saw Gertrude and told her what he had said. Instead of looking at it as I did, she grew very frightened and told me that ever since her father's return he had been very oppressed and worried. The upshot was that he arranged to tell me what it was tonight after dinner, and I can only think now he intended to tell you as well.'

Blake nodded.

'Yes; I have no doubt of it. However, go on, please.'

'There is not much more to tell,' went on Carslake. 'Sir George was in his study, writing before dinner, while Gertrude and I were in the drawing-room. We didn't know then that you were coming to dinner. It seems, however, that the butler went to the study to inquire of his master as to when he expected you to arrive.

'The next thing, he had come tearing into the drawing room, his face as white as chalk, and his eyes wide with horror. I saw at once there was something wrong, and hurried out to the study. The moment I entered I saw what it was.'

Carslake again passed his hand over his brow, and then continued: 'Sir George was sitting at his desk just as though he had fallen asleep. His right hand still grasped the pen, while his left was clenched tightly and lay curled up under his head, which rested on it as though in sleep. Two letters were sealed and addressed, while the sheet of paper before him contained only the date written on it.

'I sent for a doctor at once, but it was plain to be seen he was dead. The doctor called it heart failure, and said the very fact that he was in the act of writing a letter precluded all possibility of the suicide theory. Besides, he said his lips gave off not the slightest odour of any drug or poison. Foul play he scouted at once, saying everything pointed to that as being impossible; but, in view of what he told me, both Gertrude and myself feel we would like you to make an examination.'

'She is, of course, very much broken up?' remarked Blake.

'Completely prostrated,' replied Carslake. 'She and her father were very fond of one another.'

'You say there were no signs of violence?' said Blake, after a short pause.

'Not the faintest. Certainly, everything points to a natural death, and now that I am calmer I am beginning to wonder myself if perhaps, after all, Gertrude and I have not built too quickly on our fears.'

'That remains to be seen,' answered Blake, as the taxi stopped. 'However, here we are. I'll make an examination at once.'

Carslake led the way up the steps and pressed the button of the electric-bell. The door was opened almost at once by the butler, whose face still bore traces of the shock through which he had passed. Miss Halliday was not to be seen, and the butler, in answer to Carslake's question, informed him in a whisper that, before leaving, the doctor had given her an opiate, and that now she was sleeping.

'This is Mr Blake,' went on Carslake. 'He desires to make an examination.

'Yes, sir,' replied the old servant, looking with respect at the brilliant criminologist. 'Shall I go with you, sir, or do you prefer to go alone?'

'Has the room been disturbed?' asked Blake, speaking for the first time since entering the house.

'No, sir. Only Sir George' – and the old butler's voice broke – 'has been moved, sir. The doctor ordered us to lay him on the couch.'

'Very well,' replied Blake. 'If you will lead the way, Carslake, we will lose no time. You, Tinker, keep Pedro here in the hall for the present.'

Tinker pulled Pedro back and sat down on a big oak seat, while Carslake led the way to Sir George's study.

It was more of an elaborate library than a study, its tones being a restful shade of deep crimson. Around the walls were bookcases packed with what Blake knew was one of the finest collections of books in London.

At one end was a huge open fireplace, and to the right of this stood a massive, flat-topped mahogany desk – the one at which the ill-fated baronet had been writing when he was so suddenly struck down. Against the wall, to the left of the door on entering, was a big leather couch, on which lay the man, calm and peaceful, who a bare hour before had been full of vigorous life.

For a moment Blake stood on the threshold of the room and cast his keen eyes rapidly about. Then they lingered on the deep alcove straight across, where long French windows opened on to a wide balcony which overlooked a series of terraces leading to a garden, and thence to the high stone wall which separated Sir George's grounds from the lane at the rear.

Then Blake turned his attention to the man whose guest he had started out to be. Reverently lifting the hands, he made a close examination of the palms and nails, but even with the aid of the powerful pocket-glass he had brought, they were perfectly normal in appearance. From the hands he transferred his attention to the head, running his long, sensitive fingers over the thinly-covered scalp. No bump, no abrasion could he find.

Then slowly, and with the utmost care, he again picked up the glass and began a most minute examination of the features. Over brow and eyes he worked slowly and patiently until he had covered every particle. Then he shifted the glass to the cheeks and lips. From ear to ear he turned his gaze, but as he passed the glass along the rim of the lower lip, he suddenly paused and leaned forward intently.

Magnified by the glass, he saw a tiny yellow spot, which was so small that it would be almost certain to escape the naked eye.

But it was not the tiny yellow spot only which caused him to lean forward, but what he saw in the very centre of it. There, rimmed by the yellow, was an infinitesimal black puncture, which for all the world looked as though the point of the finest of fine needles had touched the lip.

There was nothing remarkable in a man having a tiny puncture in his skin, but such a minute hole would, in the ordinary course of events, heal up very quickly in a normally healthy man, and Sir George Halliday had been more than that – he had been robust.

Even as he looked, Blake knew the puncture, from its appearance, must be less than half a dozen hours old; but whether such an innocent-looking mark had anything to do with Sir George's death he had no idea. It seemed highly improbable; but, true to his capacity for details, Blake stored the point in his mind and turned his attention to the throat.

For fully an hour he worked ceaselessly, examining the dead man minutely; but, when he finally straightened up, he had to confess to himself that, beyond the tiny, almost invisible mark on the lip, he had found nothing, and that the doctor's conclusions didn't seem hastily formed. He merely grunted in answer to Carslake's anxious questions, and waving him curtly aside, turned his attention to the desk.

It had very little on it. A heavy silver inkstand, several pens in a tray, a large blue pencil, and square blotting-pad, the top sheet of which had been only slightly used.

To the left of where the writer would sit were two letters, while lying on the blotting-pad, just as it had been when death so suddenly overtook the writer, was a sheet of heavy paper containing only the date – or, to be more correct, nearly all the date, for at the very last figure the writing trailed off in a shaky, blotted line where the pen had faltered.

Beside the sheet of paper was the pen with which Sir George had been writing, but beyond that neither desk nor chair showed anything else, and least of all anything of a suspicious nature. Blake sank into the chair and leaned his elbows on the desk.

For some time he sat in deep thought, his eyes closed, his chest barely rising and falling as he breathed lightly. Then he opened his eyes, picked up the pen, and took – as far as he could judge – the position which would have been assumed by Sir George. Placing the point of the pen at the last number of the date on the paper, he began a slow scrutiny of the room. First the desk before him, then the walls, the ceiling, and the floor on either side.

From that his eyes wandered to the huge fireplace, and thence to the deep embrasure of the window. Carslake followed each movement with puzzled and expectant eyes, but looked still more so when Blake laid down the pen and stood up.

'I presume Miss Halliday would not object to my reading the addresses of these two letters?' asked Blake in low tones.

Oh, no, indeed!' replied Carslake: 'She would be glad to have you do anything which will clear up matters. But tell me, Mr Blake, do you consider Sir George's death was after all a natural one?'

Blake shrugged.

'My dear fellow, what impossible questions you do ask! The doctor scouts any such idea, while the only suggestion of foul play emanates from you and Miss Halliday, and is based on Sir George's harassed manner since his return, as well as by some mysterious peril which he told you was hanging over him, and which, by the way, he would have confided to you tonight had death not intervened. The point is, Carslake, was this peril real or supposed, of a physical, mental, or momentary nature? What was its cause – its cause – do you understand?

'Sir George no doubt had something of moment to tell, for, as well as confiding in you, his future son-in-law, he thought it wise to confide in me as well. Does that pre-suppose a peril of a physical nature and of such severity as to cause his death? At present there is just one point, Carslake, which could possibly be attributed to an outside source, but it is so infinitesimal that I hesitate to base much upon it.

'With your leave, however, I shall now proceed to make a minute examination of everything in the room, and beg of you to touch nothing, least of all anything on the desk. If any outside agent was the cause of Sir George's death, it must, by the very nature of things, have come into the vicinity of the desk, and perhaps has still left some trail – who knows? It is a pity we do not know the peril to which Sir George referred, for, knowing that, we would sooner or later be able to put our fingers on the motive – the motive, Carslake, which generated the cause and leaves its mark in the effect which we see before us in the form of my old friend.

'Now let us see to whom Sir George was writing. Ah! as I thought, he has come home with some fresh notes on China, for this one is addressed to "The Chinese and Tibetan Research Society", of which I believe he was a fellow, and at one time its president. The other, I see, is to the publishing firm of Dobbs, Milne & Co., who, as you know, specialise in scientific publications.

'If you will send for the butler, Carslake, we will have these letters posted at once, and in the morning I shall go around to both places and ask to be shown the contents. By one of those hidden elements of chance, that on which Sir George was occupied when death came may serve to throw some light on our investigations.'

With this, Blake picked up his pocket-glass, and shifting the light to the required angle, dropped to his knees. Those who have followed Sexton Blake's methods will be familiar with his mode of procedure on this occasion. With his usual care for detail, he mapped out the zone for examination in a series of imaginary squares. In this way every detail of the carpeted floor was brought under the glass, and did the tiniest bit of the map show any discoloration or other sign out of the ordinary, the keen eyes of the detective would pick it out at once and dissect it.

Floor, chairs, tables, and walls gave no indication of any extraordinary condition, however, and Blake, with a muttered remark, turned and contemplated the big fireplace. On the dogs lay three immense logs which by force of their heat precluded, in Blake's mind, any chance of a hostile entry from that source.

There was nothing left now but the window, and signing to Carslake to throw the light around, Blake entered the deep recess and began to examine the catch. Barely had he focused the glass on it, however, when he leaned forward quickly and drew a sharp breath.

To the ordinary observer there was nothing in its appearance to cause comment. Its composition was of brass-finished metal, and consisted of two parts, the catch being on one sash and the bolt on the other. The bolt was of the spring variety, and when the windows were closed it automatically locked where the two sashes joined in the centre.

Up at the top and down at the bottom, respectively, there were bolts on the half of the window containing the catch, and these were at present pressed home. Thus for safety the window depended in reality on the one middle spring-catch, trusting to the bolting of the other sash to prevent the window being forced without considerable trouble.

What had caught Blake's eye, however, was the tiniest shred of cotton-wool hanging to the edge of the brass. So small was it that he held his breath lest it might be blown away, and quickly drawing a pair of fine tweezers from his pocket, he nipped it off and took it over to the desk.

There he laid it down and returned to the window.

Up and down the sash he worked on the inside until every particle had been covered. This finished and nothing else being discovered, he pressed back the bolt and stepped out on to the balcony.

'Ask the butler to bring a hand-light of some sort,' he called to Carslake, who had followed him.

'Or, stay! Tinker, I believe, has his electric-torch with him. Just slip out into the hall and get it.'

Carslake hurried away, and returned a moment later with Tinker's torch. Then Blake went to work on the low sill, which was almost flush with the balcony floor.

It was almost in the very middle of its edge that he once more bent, and a dry, hard glitter came into his eyes as he saw, caught in a splinter, another minute piece of cotton-wool. Again bringing the tweezers into requisition, he carefully disengaged it and re-entered the room. Laying it on the desk beside the other, he returned to the balcony.

Further along was a broad flight of steps leading to the terrace, but Blake disregarded these. Instead, he leaped lightly over the railing opposite the study window, landing on his toes on the soft turf below. Swinging the torch downwards, he dropped to his knees, and, like a human bloodhound, began nosing and working over the ground.

Owing to the thick carpet of grass, he had not many hopes of picking up a footprint, for grass has a habit of working back to the vertical after a foot has pressed it. However, he sought patiently for some part where the grass might be less thick, and near a supporting-post he found it.

In close against the edge of the balcony, and immediately under a spot where the rain-drip continually fell, the grass had not grown as thickly as elsewhere, and here he found the faint, curved edge of what could only be the impression of a foot.

True, it was more likely to be that of one of the gardeners than of anyone else; but since he had been searching for anything in the shape of a mark, and had finally found it, he would naturally follow it up.

Passing the torch up to the waiting Carslake, who stood leaning over, pulling nervously at his thin, light moustache, Blake nimbly vaulted back over the railing and landed softly.

'What's the next move?' inquired Carslake, following Blake through the French window into the study.

'I am going to try an experiment,' replied Blake shortly. 'Just wait where you are, please, until I call my assistant.'

Going to the door and throwing it open, Blake called softly up the hall to Tinker, and signed for him to bring Pedro along to the study. A moment later the lad was at the door, whispering: 'Found anything suspicious, guv'nor?'

Blake vouchsafed no answer, but taking Pedro's leash from Tinker, drew the lad inside and closed the door. Carslake meanwhile had partially closed the windows, and stood waiting with the torch in his hand for Blake's next move.

Whatever that was he was not to find out for a few moments, for barely had Pedro entered than Blake and Tinker watched with puzzled brows the dog's strange actions, while Carslake drew back startled. And well he might!

Pedro, one of the best-trained and most sagacious of bloodhounds, stood stock still where he had paused when Blake closed the door. But his appearance underwent a startling change. Suddenly, and without the slightest warning, every hair on his body stood out stiff and straight as a multitude of needles, his great ears went back angrily, his great jaws dropped threateningly, and he grew rigid as though cast in granite.

At first Blake thought it might be caused by the still, draped figure on the couch; but this he scouted almost at once, for Pedro had been in the presence of death too often to make such a to-do over it.

He bent forward and looked at the bloodhound's eyes, and gave a startled exclamation as he saw them. Like two fixed, blazing coals they returned his look unseeingly and without recognition.

If it is possible for animals to feel horror, then the expression in Pedro's eyes could only be described as that. Once in South America, Blake had seen a horse in mortal fear, and never to his dying day would he forget the look in the beast's eyes. They had held the same expression as Pedro's now held, together with the same fixed and rigid pose.

He began to straighten up, with the intent to speak sharply to the dog, when his words broke off, and all three were startled by a long, blood-freezing bay from the great hound.

Tinker, in a fever of anxiety as to what could be affecting Pedro so, dropped to one knee and endeavoured to pass an arm about the dog's neck; but Blake, suddenly springing forward, grasped him and dragged him back unceremoniously.

'Don't!' he whispered sharply. 'Can't you see the dog is under a spell of horror? Carslake, come behind here where he can't see you – quick! Have the door open ready; and you, Tinker, stand near it. He is in such a state that he is not responsible. Quick!' he snapped; and Carslake barely reached safety as Pedro dashed madly forward as though filled with all the demons of the underworld.

Round and round the room he dashed, with Blake hanging desperately on to his collar. Then suddenly, as they passed close to the desk, Pedro pulled up suddenly, his lips bared, his teeth in an angry snarl, and with great red, dripping jaws, he launched himself straight at a large painting which hung over the desk.

Blake, strong as he was, had found it impossible to restrain him, and relaxed his hold as Pedro cleared the desk.

With a crash the big painting tumbled to the floor as Pedro struck it, and Blake leaped back as the dog turned.

A second later, however, he leaped forward and grasped the end of the leash as something shot past his head with a peculiar metallic rustle. A momentary silence had caused Pedro to hear that metallic sound, and, straight as an arrow, he shot after it. Blake, hanging on to the leash, went after him, but pulled hard as he saw the dog making for the window.

A moment later something struck the glass, rebounded, struck the sashes at the point where they were parted slightly owing to Carslake not having closed them tightly; then it disappeared.

So quickly had the whole thing happened that it was impossible for Blake to get an idea of the form of the thing which had flashed past him. That it was no larger than the end of his finger he felt positive, but that was all. With its disappearance Pedro tried to dash through the window after it, but Blake dragged hard on the leash and held him back.

As suddenly as he had apparently gone mad, did Pedro regain his usual condition. His hair grew flat, his eyes assumed their old expression, and his ears hung slackly; but no man there would ever forget the haunting sound of his blood-freezing bay of a few moments before. As for Carslake, he stood, white as chalk, where Blake had placed him, and Tinker hastened across to the dog.

Between them, Blake and the lad made a hurried examination of him, but he was as normal as ever, and, beyond a few flecks of foam on his jaws, showed no signs of the hurricane rage which had just possessed him.

Passing the leash to Tinker, Blake hastened across to the desk, and, moving around it, made an examination of the fallen picture. Suddenly he gave a muttered exclamation, and bent forward.

When he straightened up, he held in his hand a tiny ball of cottonwool of a similar texture and colour to the two pieces he had found at the window. But one thing he noticed about it which he had failed to detect in the others, and that was a very faint perfume.

With a very thoughtful manner, Blake placed the piece of cottonwool on the desk beside the other pieces, and then signing to Carslake to bring the torch, he took Pedro's leash from Tinker and led the way outside.

This time he passed along the balcony and down the steps, keeping along in the thick turf until he had reached the footprint which he had seen before. There he put Pedro at the impression, and after waiting patiently until the bloodhound had thoroughly got the scent, he eased the leash, and gave Pedro his head.

Close against the balcony hung Pedro until he reached the steps. There he turned, and crossed the gravelled path, taking again to the turf on the other side, and once more hugging the balcony.

Suddenly at the very end of the balcony, and at the base of a supporting pillar, he paused and sniffed upwards. In a moment Blake had signed to Tinker.

'Up you go, my lad!' he rapped. 'Our quarry has gone up the post. I'll pass Pedro up to you.'

As nimbly as a monkey, Tinker wrapped his legs about the post, and, given a starting boost from Carslake, he was soon drawing himself over the edge. As he knelt on his knees and leaned over, Blake picked Pedro up in his arms. Heaving the dog upwards, he held him while Tinker caught his collar. Then, with Pedro bracing his hind feet against the pillar, he drew up while Blake pushed, and, with a spring, Pedro landed safely.

'Let him follow it up there, and see where he goes,' jerked Blake.

'All right, guv'nor,' replied Tinker. 'He's on it now!'

It was true Pedro was on it, but he took barely three steps before he stopped, worried.

'What's the trouble?' asked Blake irritably.

'I don't know, guv'nor. He has stopped about six inches from the end, and doesn't seem able to pick it up again.'

'Walk about the top of the balcony, and see if he can get it again,' ordered Blake.

With an 'All right!' Tinker drew on the leash and began methodically pacing the length and breadth of the balcony. His efforts were of no avail, however, for beyond the one spot at the end of the balcony, Pedro seemed unable to get the scent. Tinker finally desisted, and returned to the edge.

'It's no use, guv'nor,' he said. 'He can't pick it up. It seems to have vanished into the air.

Blake grunted.

'Very well. Pass him down, and then come down yourself.'

Tinker did so, and when they had landed safely, Blake took the electric-torch and extinguished it. With a muttered remark to the others to remain where they were, the detective moved back and gazed upwards.

Before him was the rear of Sir George's house, with the balcony running the full width. Behind him stretched the terraces and garden, while on either side rose high walls, separating the grounds where he stood from the adjoining gardens of the next-door houses.

Between each side of Sir George's house and the dividing walls there was a space of fully twenty feet, which, after a further glance round, Blake verified by pacing the distance.

It would have been easier to work by the assistance of the torch, but in view of the remarkable seizure which Pedro had had, and the finding of the third bit of cotton-wool, Blake was beginning to suspect that after all, there might be something very sinister behind everything.

Consequently, when the trail he had discovered ended so mysteriously, he preferred to be on the safe side by working in the light cast by the stars, rather than run the risk of having his movements watched by some unseen person.

Carslake watched him curiously, while even Tinker was puzzled by seeing his master pacing the distance between each side of the house and the dividing wall.

After he had paced out the distance, Blake stood back in the shadow of the balcony, under the spot where the trail had ended. For some moments he made no move, the while he searched with his eyes the shadowy bulk of the house on the other side of the wall. Not a single light gleamed in any of the rooms, and, turning to Carslake, he asked briefly: 'Do you know if that house is occupied?'

'I don't know,' responded the other. 'You see, I don't know very much about the neighbourhood. Sir George only returned a week ago, and previous to that Miss Halliday was staying with her aunt.'

'I see. However, it doesn't matter now. We will return to the library. But before doing so let me say a few words to you, to which I want you to pay the closest attention.

'In the first place, my discoveries, though very vague and very slight so far, have been sufficient to convince me that there is a strong probability – note, please, I only say probability – that Sir George did not die naturally, nor by his own hand. That being so, it is essential that his enemies, if such exist, must be kept in ignorance of the fact that foul play is suspected.

'To attain that end it will, in my opinion, be of the utmost importance to keep our suspicions secret for the time being. Until I feel more certain of my ground I don't care to make any explicit statements, and since he is dead, I think it best to permit things to go ahead for the present as though the death had been a natural one. Not even the old butler must know that we suspect anything.'

'All right, Mr Blake,' replied Carslake. 'I'll do exactly as you suggest. But how about Miss Halliday?'

'It would serve no useful purpose at present to tell her anything,' replied Blake. 'On the contrary, she is sufficiently upset already by the shock, and should it be necessary for me to gain any details by questioning her later, I will then tell her myself.'

Carslake heaved a sigh of relief.

'I'll be jolly glad for you to take the responsibility.' he said. 'In the meantime, if there is anything I can do, command me. As for funds' – and he laughed apologetically – 'well, I'm not exactly a pauper. If there has been any foul play I'd spend my last penny in order to run Sir George's murderers to earth.'

'We will discuss that later,' replied Blake. 'For the present I will look after that part of it myself.'

With that he turned and led the way back to the house where they found the doctor who had returned.

'Ah, Mr Carslake,' he said, 'I was just looking for you.'

'What can I do, doctor?' asked Carslake. 'By the way, permit me to introduce you to a friend of mine, Mr Smith.'

He had just caught Blake's warning nudge in time, and stammered slightly as he mumbled over the name; but the fussy little doctor was too much taken up with his own importance to notice Carslake's momentary embarrassment.

'How do you do, sir?' he said hurriedly, as Blake bowed. Then, turning to Carslake, he went on: 'I have made out the certificate – called it heart failure. I waited to see you though. I suppose you will look after the arrangements for the family?'

'Yes,' replied Carslake gravely. 'I have already sent for Miss Halliday's aunt, and will see about everything else for them.'

'Then I will hurry along,' answered the doctor. 'Goodnight! Goodnight, Mr Smith.'

With a bow to Tinker, who stood just inside the window, he was gone.

At that moment the old butler entered to inform Carslake that by the doctor's orders they had removed Sir George to his bedroom upstairs, and then he informed them that he had prepared a meal, if they cared for it.

Carslake was too upset to eat anything, but Blake and Tinker had been through too many scenes of a similar nature to be affected in that manner. Consequently, both the lad and his master did justice to the food the old butler had prepared, while Carslake drank sparingly of a glass of wine.

Then, informing Carslake he would communicate with him on the morrow, Blake signed to Tinker, and, with Pedro following, the famous Baker Street trio took their departure.

They walked along for some distance before a taxi came in sight. Hailing it, they climbed in, and giving the address, Blake sank back and closed his eyes, while Tinker pulled Pedro's ears, and puzzled over the events of the evening, not least of which was the attack which had seized Pedro in the library.

The lad started slightly as Blake's voice suddenly broke the silence.

'Did you see the thing which went past me, and escaped through the narrow opening between the windows?' asked Blake.

'No, guv'nor,' replied Tinker. 'I heard it, though. It sounded like scales rubbing together, and made me creep.'

'Quite so, my lad; but doesn't it occur to you to wonder at Pedro's attack?'

'Indeed, yes, guv'nor. I can't make it out.'

'Nor can I, my lad; but this much is certain. While we were in the room there was something there of a sinister nature. We couldn't detect it, but in that mysterious way only known to animals, Pedro's canine intelligence detected it at once, and, my lad, he felt the horror of it. That is proof conclusive. Then, although he was rigid with fear, his natural bravery overcame that, and he attempted to locate it, and stamp it out. That was when I drew you back, for he could not recognise either you or myself. I had seen that in his eyes, and I never want to see them look that way again.

'With the escape of the thing, however, he immediately regained his usual condition; but, my lad – and mark well what I say – that thing which was so sinister as to upset Pedro, as it did, had some bearing on Sir George Halliday's death. I have seen many things tonight which, I must confess, puzzle me as much as I have ever been puzzled, but I feel positive the thing which escaped had some bearing on the cause of his death, and had it not been for Pedro we would hardly have seen it; or else, by some means, we may have followed in the footsteps of Sir George. But we will bring deduction to bear on it, my lad, and if I am not mistaken, it will need all our resources to ferret the thing out.'

With this Blake closed his eyes again, and silence reigned once more until the taxi drew in to the kerb in Baker Street.

A moment later they were back in the consulting-room, and Blake was spreading out on the desk the varied assortment of articles which he had brought from Sir George's house, and which consisted of the following.

The blotting-pad, the sheet of paper on which Sir George had been writing, the pen he had used, together with the rest of the pens in the tray, a small bottle full of the ink from the stand, the blue pencil, a few plain envelopes and sheets of paper similar to that which the dead baronet had been using, and lastly the two tiny shreds and the larger piece of cotton wool which he had found.

Little did Blake know as he bent over the articles, that outside stood a dark figure which had followed them the whole way from Sir George's house. And even had they known it, they would not have known that the figure had slipped forth after them from the front gate of the house adjoining Sir George's.

'Now, my lad, here is your programme for this morning.'

It was the morning after the evening on which occurred the events related above. After their arrival at Baker Street, Blake had sent Tinker to bed, and with only Pedro keeping him company, he had spent many long hours examining the articles he had brought from Sir George Halliday's.

It was daylight when he retired, but after only a couple of hours' rest he was up again and at work. They had breakfasted in silence, for Tinker, reading the signs, offered no comments of any sort until Blake chose to speak. He had done so only when they had adjourned to the consulting room, and Tinker waited for him to go on.

'I want you,' continued Blake, stuffing his pipe full of black tobacco, 'I want you to disguise in something, and go along to where we were last night. Just walk past, and find out if the houses on either side are occupied. It will be easy enough to tell. If not, find out who the agents are. It is unlikely that both will be empty, if either, but I wish to know. If they are occupied, get into conversation with the policeman on the beat, and find out what you can about the tenants. They are large places, and require people with a fairish income to keep them up. Consequently, the officer should be able to tell you what you wish to know. As soon as you have found out what you can, return here at once.'

'Very well, guv'nor,' replied Tinker, making for his room in order to change. 'I'll find out all I can. Will you be here when I return?'

'If I am not, wait until I come,' replied Blake briefly; and with that he sank into the big chair, and began thoughtfully smoking.

At nine o'clock punctually, however, he stirred and rose. Tinker had been gone some time, but Blake evidently didn't propose to await his return, for he entered his dressing room, and emerged a moment later, wearing his hat and coat. Then speaking to Pedro, and telling him to look after things, Blake made his way to the street, and hailed a passing taxi.

Giving the address, 'The Chinese and Tibetan Research Society', Blake stepped into the cab, and leaned back with puckered brows. Twenty minutes later he was asking for the curator, Professor Somers, and when shown into that gentleman's office found him seated before a littered desk, an open letter in one hand, a crumpled newspaper in the other, and a blank look of startled amazement on his face.

'Ah, Professor Somers,' remarked Blake, as he seated himself, and returned the professor's rather flurried greeting.

'I see you have read the sad news coincident with your receipt of Sir George's letter.'

'Why, bless my soul!' gasped the bespectacled little man. 'You are positively uncanny, Mr Blake. How on earth did you know? What a very terrible thing it is!'

'It was very simple,' replied Blake, smiling slightly. 'I myself instructed the butler to post that letter, professor. It was written just a few minutes before his death. You are right. It is a very sad and very sudden affair.'

'To think,' cried the professor, 'that Halliday of all men should die of heart failure. Why, hang it, he struck me as being as strong and vigorous as an ox. I can hardly believe it, for think of the altitudes to which he went in the Himalayas, Mr Blake. No man with a weak heart could stand the cold and the rarity of that atmosphere. But perhaps it was the strain which really weakened his heart. Ah, yes, very sad – very sad! To think that I received a letter, too, written just before his death.'

'Yes, it brings the thing home rather forcibly to you, professor,' remarked Blake gravely; 'but I took it upon myself to have that letter posted for a certain reason.'

'Eh – what – er – I don't understand, Mr Blake.'

'For reasons sufficiently weighty, professor, I desire to read its contents. I realise my request is distinctly out of the ordinary, but I think you know me well enough to be aware that I would not make such a request unless I had a very strong motive.'

'Why, as far as I know, Mr Blake, I see no reason why you shouldn't read it. As you say, it is a bit irregular, but as we are – er – fellow scientists in a way, I have no objection. In fact, now I think of it, I am rather glad.

'I knew Sir George very intimately, but, to say the least, his letter struck me as rather peculiar. And then this awful shock of his death. Oh, dear – oh, dear, you really must excuse me, Mr Blake.'

The warm-hearted little professor blew his nose violently, and handed the letter to Blake, who walked with it to the window in order to give the professor time to recover from his emotion. There he read the letter, which ran as follows.

MY DEAR PROFESSOR SOMERS, – I am seizing the first opportunity since my return in order to write to you, knowing you will be keenly interested to hear what knowledge I have acquired on the subjects dear to your heart as well as to mine during my last trip.

Rest easy, old friend. I have a fund of notes with me which will satisfy even your insatiable appetite, and I foresee many interesting hours in the discussion and cataloguing of them. I will bring them with me at three in the afternoon on Friday, when you can arrange a schedule of days for their investigation.

In the meantime, professor, I should be greatly obliged if you would look carefully through your records and endeavour to find some trace of the following insect – or beetle – which I believe exists in China, and which I also have reason to believe is a mud borer. I have searched every book and record I have, but can discover no trace of it. Unfortunately I have no specimen, and can only give you a vague description. However, here it is.

In size I have an idea it is about that of the common bluebottle fly. Its colour, I think, is yellow or yellowish. When flying and crawling, its wings make a peculiar metallic sound – not unlike scales being rubbed together – and in addition, I have strong reason to believe it has in front of its head a horn, or borer. Of the length of this I have no idea, and, in fact, am not certain that it really exists. Lastly, professor, it is of a deadly poisonous nature. This fact I am thoroughly certain of, and furthermore, know that its poison kills within a few seconds. I might add that it is very partial to a perfume of some description, but as to its nature I am ignorant.

You must pardon my speaking of this matter in my letter, and you will probably think it could have waited until I came myself. It is, however, of an urgent nature, and I trust you will be able to find some record of the insect I have described.

Sincerely,

George Halliday

Blake read the letter with great care, memorising in every detail the description of the beetle mentioned by Sir George. Then he turned and walked very thoughtfully back to the desk.

'Well, Mr Blake,' asked the professor, 'what do you think of it?'

'I must confess that although I was not so intimately acquainted with Sir George as were you, professor, still I knew him fairly well, and must say I agree with you. I think it is a bit – er – peculiar, shall I say?'

'That was exactly my impression!' assented the professor.

'By the way,' went on Blake casually, 'might I ask if you have any knowledge, professor, of any such bug or beetle as he describes?'

The professor placed the tips of his fingers together and pursed up his lips.

'Well, Mr Blake, off-hand, I can't say I do. There are of course, a good many mud-borers, and, from what I remember, several would fulfil his description in one, or perhaps two, ways. At the moment, however, I have no recollection of any such as he describes. Of course, the list of poisonous beetles is not large, and unless it is of a species unknown so far, it shouldn't be hard to discover its identity. I have in mind a beetle which, so far, has only been found along the head waters of the Magdalena in Colombia; but, if my memory serves me correctly, it is black –

inky-black – and consequently would not comply with the points mentioned by Sir George, which demand that it should be yellow or of that shade.'

'Might it be possible that it would acquire that shade when shedding its skin?' suggested Blake.

'H'm – yes – possible!' replied the professor, with a rising inflection. 'Yes, on consideration, Mr Blake, that is a point worth looking into, and I will bear it in mind. It is, however, not probable!'

'I suppose, in any event, you will endeavour to look up such a beetle, won't you?' asked Blake.

'Certainly! Since it was an urgent wish of my poor friend, I shall do so at once. In fact, this very day I shall start, although the information will be of no use to him now.'

'I'm not so sure, professor!' said Blake softly.

'Eh – ah! What?' asked the old man, starting up. 'What do you mean, Mr Blake?'

'Listen, professor,' said Blake earnestly. 'If I ask you to trust me for a few days, will you do so? All I can say at present is that any information you can give me on the subject of the beetle Sir George describes, may be of great use. If he could speak, I can assure you he would say so himself. Will you trust me, and for the present ask no questions?'

As he finished, Blake looked at the professor with his rare, winning smile, and the old man nodded.

'Yes, Mr Blake!' he said huskily. 'I will. What do you wish me to do?'

'This, professor. I want you to start as soon as possible and look up what you can about this beetle. Everything, you understand? Its habits, its characteristics, and, in fact, all that pertains to it. Will you do this?'

'I will begin at once,' answered the professor.

'Thank you!' said Blake. 'If you find anything, will you send me a wire at once?'

And even as Blake opened the door, the old man was already beginning his search.

'He'll be a willing worker,' muttered Blake, as he reached the street. 'He is working for love of his friend, and no inspiration could be stronger.'

Re-entering the taxi, Blake told the driver to proceed to the offices of Dodds, Milne & Co.

There he found the manager had received Sir George's letter, and although he demurred slightly at first, when Blake asked permission to read it, he finally capitulated.

It was merely an order for half a dozen books which Sir George requested should be sent at once, but, of course, the manager explained, on reading in the papers of his sudden death, he had naturally not sent them.

'Have you all these books in stock now?' asked Blake.

'Yes, certainly! We always carry a supply of every book in our catalogue.'

Blake made no reply, but drew out his cheque-book and opened it. Then he spoke.

'I will take a copy of each,' he said quietly. 'I am under the impression I already have two of them in my library, but that doesn't matter.'

The manager was unable to refrain from showing the astonishment he felt, but, as they were all exceptionally expensive books, he lost no time in giving orders for them to be packed up.

Twenty minutes later Blake entered the taxi bearing a parcel in his arms, which contained six books of a highly scientific nature, and with the following titles:

Insects, Flies and Beetles of India.

Insects of Japan.

Mud-boring Beetles of the World.

Tree-boring Beetles of the World.

Insects and Beetles of China and Tibet – (translated from the original).

Poisonous Beetles of the World – (a complete treatise, translated from the original).

Rather a formidable array; but Blake was nothing if not thorough, and hard as he knew the professor would work, he was determined to apply his own knowledge to the research.

On his arrival at Baker Street, he expected to find Tinker had returned. The lad, however, was nowhere to be seen, and instead, sitting nervously on the edge of a seat, was a poorly-clad woman with wan features, whose whole appearance spoke of poverty and the East End.

She rose and curtseyed to Blake as he entered, and then spoke in trembling tones. 'Please, sir, are you Mr Blake?'

Blake nodded.

'Yes,' he said kindly, 'I am Mr Blake. Are you in trouble? If so, what can I do for you?'

'Oh, please, sir, I am sorry to take up your time, but I have been to two other men, sir, and they refuse to help me unless I pay them a lot of money, and, sir, I haven't a penny. I wouldn't have come to you, sir, with my troubles, but my married daughter insisted. She says as how you often help poor people who can't afford to pay.'

'You are quite right, Mrs – '

'Green, sir!'

'Thank you! As I was saying, Mrs Green, you are quite right. Rich or poor, it makes no difference to me, but in order that my help be received free of charge, three things are necessary.'

'What are they, please, sir?' asked the woman fearfully.

'One is, they must be worthy; the second that the trouble must be serious enough to demand my assistance; and the third, that they must be perfectly frank with me in every way. Do you think you can fulfil all those conditions?'

'Oh, yes, sir!' cried the poor soul. 'I can indeed!'

'Very well,' replied Blake, laying his books down with a regretful sigh. 'Tell me what is the trouble!'

'Please, sir, it is' – and her voice trembled – 'like the end of the world to me. My son – my only son Tom – him as was stoker on a ship between here and Chiney is dead, sir, and I can't believe it is heart failure, which the doctor says it is. He was so hale and hearty, sir, and I haven't liked the looks of those foreign devils – begging your pardon, sir – as has been hanging around the neighbourhood ever since he arrived home three weeks ago.'

'Just what do you mean by "foreign devils"?' asked Blake quietly.

'Heathen, sir – Chinamen; but not like the laundryman at the corner, sir.'

'And you think your son's death is due to them?' asked Blake quickly, as he rose and began walking up and down.

'Yes, sir; I do. I can't believe my Tom's heart was weak.'

'Wait, wait, Mrs Green!' said Blake suddenly, and holding up his hand. 'I wish to scribble a note, and then I will come with you to your home.'

Five minutes later, after writing a note to Tinker, Blake was in a taxi with Mrs Green beside him, speeding eastwards on a mission which was to increase the mystery of the baffling maze in which he seemed to be entering.

THE THIRD CHAPTER

Tinker Reconnoitres – The Trap that Failed – The Struggle at Baker Street – Pedro on Guard

When Tinker was sent by Blake to disguise himself and proceed to make investigations in the neighbourhood of the late Sir George Halliday's house, he chose, as he had often done before, the suit which gave him the appearance of a ragged Italian boy. When he had donned this and brought into play his knowledge of the language, he made such a perfect representation of the part that more than once he had befooled native Italians themselves.

It came in particularly useful in the crowded precincts of Soho, but experience had taught him it was equally useful in the West End. Consequently, when he slipped quietly through the consulting-room and gained the street, he thought, as he breathed in a deep breath of the fresh morning air, that he was thoroughly safe from discovery, should any risk arise.

Although Blake was beginning to feel vaguely the force of a mysterious and sinister power behind the cause of Sir George's death, he was as yet in a maze of threads, each one of which seemed to be inextricably tangled up with the others.

His deductions from an analysis of the strange occurrences which had taken place, plus the mystifying letter written by Sir George to Professor Somers, made him certain that the baronet had not died by natural means.

Still, that was as yet only a tentative hypothesis, all he had on which to build it being an extremely minute mark on Sir George's lower lip, and the thing which had caused Pedro's strange actions in the library.

Part of this, however, he only found out during the morning when he went to see the professor, and with his master still knowing so little, Tinker knew even less, for Blake had confided nothing to him since the conversation in the cab the previous night on their way home.

Consequently, neither he nor Blake had been aware of the figure which had followed them home, and had stood on guard throughout the night. Nor did they know that, when Tinker issued forth, the same figure swung along after him at a safe distance.

Tinker hailed the first taxi he saw, and, grinning to himself as the driver seemed inclined to doubt his ability to pay for it, he climbed in and spoke in extremely plain English.

'Look alive, fathead!' he said pleasantly. 'Haven't you learned yet that things are not always what they seem?'

'What in blazes do you mean by talking first in a Dago lingo that I can't understand?' grumbled the driver. 'What are you masquerading in them things for?'

'Would you really like to know?' asked Tinker. 'Because if you would, I don't mind telling you. But first I must swear you not to breathe it to a soul. The fact is the German Emperor is arriving today, and I am on the reception committee. And now send me along Piccadilly, fathead!'

Tinker slammed the door as the driver turned back to his wheel with a sheepish smile.

The short colloquy was an unfortunate delay for Tinker, however, for it gave the man following him sufficient time to secure a taxi and continue his surveillance of Tinker's movements.

Had the lad been able to see the narrow, deep-set, almond eyes which followed his course, he would have felt something akin to the sensation which had caused Pedro to fly into such a rage the previous night. He knew it not, however, and whistled blithely to himself as the cab threaded its way up Piccadilly.

At Hyde Park Corner Tinker descended, and, after some further chaff with the driver, sauntered along until he reached the street where Sir George's house was situated.

It was in the form of a crescent, and completely lined with big houses, thus making it impossible to see very far along it before the curve cut off the view. Half way along, and just as he was approaching Sir George's house, he caught sight of a policeman coming towards him.

As he drew near he glanced suspiciously at Tinker, and made as though to question him.

Tinker, however, greeted the officer familiarly.

'Hallo, Kelly!' he said cheerily. 'You are the very man I'm looking for.'

'Well, I'm blest!' grinned the big officer, as he recognised Tinker's voice. 'I was just debating whether or not to ask what a ragged individual like you wanted up here. What's on? Nothing wrong in this neighbourhood, is there?'

'Oh, no,' replied Tinker. 'I'm just out after a little information which perhaps you can give me.'

'Well?' inquired Kelly. 'Go ahead! If it's anything on my beat I can probably tell you what you want to know.'

'Thanks!' said Tinker. 'You see that house over there – Sir George Halliday's?'

'Yes; but why do you ask? He died last night.'

'I know, Kelly. I don't want to know anything about it, but I do want to know what you can tell me about the tenants of the houses on either side of it. I see they are both occupied.'

'Well, I'm afraid I can't tell you very much,' replied Kelly, sweeping the street with his eyes, and thrusting his thumbs in his belt. 'Mr Fordham, the financier, lives in one of them, but the other has only been occupied for about a fortnight. Foreigners have taken it. Chinese they are, and I imagine from their looks they are mighty high caste. They have all Chinese servants, too, so I haven't found out much about them.'

'You say they have only been there for about a fortnight?' remarked Tinker thoughtfully.

'Yes. They arrived on a Saturday, for I remember it was wet. They have leased the place furnished, and must have paid a pretty figure, for it really belongs to Colonel Porter, who himself returned about the same time. He is gone to a private hotel to live, and you can bet he wouldn't do that unless they made it worth his while. However, Tinker, if I'm not mistaken, you will have a chance to see one of them now. See that big limousine coming up the street?'

Tinker nodded.

'They keep that in a garage in the rear, and it's not the only one they have got. You will see one of them come out in a few minutes.'

'Crikey!' muttered Tinker. 'I wonder what I'd better do. I'll wager the guv'nor never expected the house was occupied by Chinamen, and that they had only been in it a fortnight. It's a toss-up whether to go back and report at once, or to follow that limousine.'

His musings were interrupted by a nudge from Kelly.

'Look! Quick, Tinker! There is the chap who lives there! Isn't he swell stuff?'

Tinker looked up, and saw descending the steps a tall, grave-looking Chinaman. He knew enough of that race to know that the man was a pure Manchu, and from his undoubted wealth and the dignity of his carriage, evidently an important personage.

The man driving the limousine, as well as the footman, were also Celestials, and the marked obsequiousness of their manner only convinced Tinker all the more that the master was a personage.

'You don't know his name, do you?' he asked of Kelly.

'No. I did hear it, but those Chinese names are such jaw-breakers. I call them all "John"!'

At that moment the man across the street entered the limousine, and very slowly it began moving along.

Tinker, with a muttered word to Kelly, swung round and started after it, keeping a sharp eye open the while for a taxi.

Had he known of the man who had followed him, and had he also known that as soon as he saw Tinker enter the crescent he had hurried along the lane at the back of Sir George's house and then into the house in which Tinker was interested, and furthermore that the departure from the house of the man in the limousine was firstly and lastly solely on Tinker's account, the lad would have thought twice before he started after the slowly-moving motor. On the contrary, he would have gone as fast as a taxi could take him to Baker Street, and there reported to his master what he had seen, for of a surety it would need a Blake, and all the subtlety of a Blake, to combat the force which was beginning its work of terror in England.

Ignorant of this fact, and keen to acquire as much knowledge as he could regarding the inhabitants of the house next to Sir George's, Tinker hailed the first taxi he saw, and told the driver to follow the limousine ahead.

There was certainly no trouble in keeping it in sight, for it continued to move at only a moderate pace. When they had been winding through the traffic for some time, Tinker finally saw that the car ahead was going steadily towards the East End of the City, and, like a flash, he muttered 'Limehouse!'

Although the almond-eyed man following Tinker had for many hours successfully kept up his surveillance without being discovered, it was not an easy matter to keep either Blake or Tinker shadowed continually without their dropping to it.

Like the criminals they hunt, a detective must keep his eyes open to each side, and behind as well as in front, and although stress of matters had kept Tinker completely engaged in watching the car ahead, as they entered the purlieus of Limehouse, he cast his eyes through the little window at the back of the taxi.

Catching sight of the taxi behind, it for the moment created no suspicion in his mind; but when after taking many devious turns, it still followed at the same distance, it suddenly dawned to Tinker that he was being followed.

'Well, crikey!' he muttered. 'I wonder how long that taxi has been following me? It must have been on my trail ever since I started after the heathen ahead, and, perhaps, even longer. There's more in the thing than I thought; but I'll bet even the guv'nor didn't know we were being watched. I'd give something to know where that limousine is going; but it's no use. I'll have to shake off this chap behind, and get back to Baker Street.'

With that Tinker picked up the speaking-tube which, for a wonder, was in working order, and as soon as he had attracted the driver's attention, gave him his instructions.

The man nodded, and kept on until they reached a corner. There, taking advantage of the extra space, he suddenly turned in a sharp swing, and headed back exactly as he had come.

Just as they were getting up speed again the other taxi swept by them, and Tinker got a fleeting glimpse of a pair of dark, sinister-looking eyes. He hurriedly looked back, but instead of following him the other taxi put on more speed, and Tinker's brow clouded.

'That means,' he muttered, 'that the man in the taxi following me is putting on speed in order to get in touch with the man in the limousine; but my shadow was a Chinese, too. I wonder what their game was? Anyway, I'll not run any chances. I'll have my driver take me by a roundabout way in order to be sure I have shaken them off, and then I'll get back and report to the guv'nor.'

Following out this decision Tinker once more got in touch with the driver, who put on all the speed he dared, and began a series of bewildering spurts and turnings which would have shaken off Sexton Blake himself.

Then, after half an hour of this, he swung back Citywards and headed for Baker Street.

Tinker paid him, and hurriedly ran up the steps in order to lose no time in making a report to his master; but even as he turned the handle of the consulting-room door he heard a scuffling noise within, accompanied by Pedro's angry growl.

Hastily throwing open the door Tinker stood on the threshold, and looked in amazement at the scene which presented itself.

Standing before the door opening into Blake's dressing-room was Pedro, his lips drawn back in an angry snarl, while crawling before him with a crooked-bladed knife in his hand was the immaculately-dressed high-caste Chinaman whom Tinker had followed to Limehouse.

How on earth he had managed to reach Baker Street so soon was a mystery to Tinker, nor did he have any time to wonder.

With a pantherlike spring the crouching Celestial gained his feet and swung on Tinker. Without the slightest warning he followed up this spring by rushing precipitately at the lad.

Tinker had no time in which to pick up a weapon of defence. He reproached himself for having gone out without his revolver, which oversight now left him weaponless. He ducked sharply, however, as the Chinaman lunged fiercely, and, as the sharp point stuck in the door, Tinker dived for his assailant's knees. Tackling them in a strong grip, he heaved just as Pedro landed heavily on top of the Chinaman from a magnificent spring which had carricd him clear over from the dressing-room door.

The Celestial, who was really Wu Ling himself, although Tinker did not then know it, began cursing rapidly in Chinese as Pedro landed. The sudden turn of events, however, seemed to endow him with the force of three men. With a violent wrench he threw Tinker free, ramming his head sharply between the lad's eyes as he did so.

Then he swung on Pedro, and, regardless of the dog's gaping jaws and powerful legs, he grappled with him. His strong, supple hands sank into Pedro's neck, and with a knowledge born of much experience, he insinuated his fingers around Pedro's windpipe.

Nobly as he struggled the dog was no match for Wu Ling, master of every subtlety of the East. Slowly the great bloodhound's head went back until Wu Ling was able to get an arm-lock under his jaw.

Tinker was lying helplessly dazed on the floor, and for the moment was *hors-de-combat*.

Wu Ling took no chance of his recovery, however, for, as soon as he had secured a powerful lock under Pedro's jaw he bent quickly, seized the dog by the hind legs, heaved upwards, and swung with all his strength, sending Pedro crashing through the half-open door of the dressing-room.

Then, glancing hurriedly at Tinker, Wu Ling pulled the knife from where it stuck in the door. He raised it, and made as though to hurl it at the prostrate lad; but a grey flash came flying from the dressing-room, and he turned sharply. Leaping for the door he slipped through and slammed it, just as Pedro, mad with rage, landed heavily against it.

Tinker stirred and sat up, and the first sound which met his awakening senses was the sharp slamming of the front door. The noise brought him to his feet, still dazed, but with a full realisation of what had happened.

Throwing open the door of the consulting-room he dashed along, and out to the street. His late antagonist, however, was nowhere to be seen, and even as he stood on the kerb Tinker saw the luxurious limousine swing into Baker Street from a side street and disappear rapidly in the distance.

He slowly made his way back to the consulting-room, and there rapidly ran his hands over Pedro. The big fellow was tough and strong, however, and beyond the shock of his fall had not suffered materially from his aerial journey through the door of the dressing-room.

To say the least, Tinker was savage, and he grew still more so when he thought over the events of the morning.

'I'll bet anything,' he muttered, as he surveyed the disordered room, 'that that bunch of Chinese had me shadowed while I was talking to Kelly. What a fathead I was not to be more careful! And then after spending half an hour in an elaborate attempt to shake off the taxi which was following me, I got home here just in time to find the Chinaman of the limousine in here.

'I wonder just what the guv'nor's idea was in sending me to find out who lived there. It's a dead cert. that they are on to me anyway; but have they any connection with Sir George Halliday's death, and if so, does the guv'nor suspect that? It beats me what that fellow wanted here. I'll just ferret around and see if he has touched anything; but I guess old Pedro prevented that. Crikey, he did go for me like a whirlwind!'

Tinker proceeded at once to make a hurried examination of the consulting-room, but nothing had been disturbed, and he concluded his thought had been correct. Pedro had prevented the visitor from carrying out his purpose, whatever that was.

During his examination, however, Tinker saw Blake's note which told the lad his master was gone to the East End, and expected to return by four or five in the afternoon. It was now past one, and as he stood holding Blake's note in his hand, Tinker decided he would utilise the remaining time which would ensue before Blake's return, in an effort to find out more of the mysterious occupants of the house next to Sir George's.

But first, in case he should be late, he would write a report of what had happened, and leave it for Blake. He seated himself at the desk, and began writing quickly.

'Guv'nor,' he wrote, 'am giving below my report, and am off again to make further investigations.'

Then followed a minute description of his movements during the morning, ending with the surprise attack he had received on his arrival home.

> I'm sorry the Chinaman got away [he then wrote], but I can describe him to you. Anyway, there is a piece of his jacket left, which came away in Pedro's jaws. What he wanted here I don't know, but hope to be able to report more when I return.
>
> You may know the reason of his visit. This much is certain. Whoever is living in that house they are a hot bunch, and for some reason they have it in for us.
>
> TINKER

Folding the note and sealing it, the lad stuck it in the interior of an odd-looking Japanese idol which was on the mantel. Then, turning the idol's face to the wall, in order to indicate to Blake that there was a note for him, Tinker rapidly changed his ragged disguise for one of a fashionable description, and, calling Pedro, snapped the leash on him and started out.

He moved with a greater degree of caution this time, and, in case he were being shadowed, he had cooked up a plan which he thought would fool anyone who was following him.

He hailed a taxi, and telling the chauffeur to drive first to Soho, he stopped at a disreputable-looking dwelling-house.

Then he descended, and with Pedro at his heels, entered the house.

A tired-looking woman was fashioning paper flowers at a table, while a boy of about Tinker's size was arranging the finished flowers in several baskets preparatory to going out with them on the streets.

They greeted Tinker cordially, for more than once had the lad befriended them.

'I see you are going out, Tim,' he said, after greeting the woman.

'Yes, sir!' replied the boy. 'I did pretty well this morning, and thought I'd try the West End this afternoon. But can I do anything for you, sir?'

'Yes, Tim,' smiled Tinker. 'It won't take you long, I want you to take Pedro and enter that taxi outside. Tell the driver to take you to Baker Street, and get out there. Here is my key. Open the door and go into the consulting room. You remember how to get there?'

'Oh, yes, sir!'

'Very well! All you have to do is to sit there for half-an-hour. Then leave Pedro, put my key on the desk, and return home. Will you do that?'

'With pleasure, sir. I'll do everything exactly as you have told me.'

'Good!' replied Tinker, laying a half-sovereign on the table. 'You can keep that for your trouble, Tim. There may be people shadowing my movements, and when you go out with Pedro they will think it is I, and that I only stopped here in order to disguise myself.'

'I understand, sir. I'll keep my head down and go right along.'

A moment later, leading Pedro, Tim had disappeared, and Tinker turned to Mrs Williams, Tim's mother.

'There is a back way out of here, isn't there?' he asked.

'Oh, yes, sir. It takes you out into a narrow alley, and if you go along to the end of it, then turn to the left, it brings you out into the Tottenham Court Road.'

'Good! I'll go that way,' replied Tinker.

Mrs Williams showed him the way, and once he had gained the alley he swung along at a brisk pace.

In Tottenham Court Road Tinker caught the first taxi he saw, and giving as the address the crescent on which was situated Sir George Halliday's house, he lay back.

As the cab drew in before the house, which had the blinds drawn, Tinker knew his call would not cause any comment, for since the baronet's sudden death the night before many old friends had called to offer their condolences to his daughter.

Just before leaving the cab Tinker took the precaution to fix a jaunty little moustache on his upper lip, and after dismissing the taxi, walked with sober dignity up the steps.

The sorrowing old butler opened the door, and without any preamble Tinker stepped inside.

'You remember me, don't you?' he said, removing the moustache.

'Oh, yes, sir!' replied the butler, 'now I do. Did you wish to make any further examination of the study, sir?'

'No! But what I wish is to pass through the house into the garden at the rear. I want to make an examination of the grounds by daylight. Do you mind?'

'Certainly not, sir. Miss Halliday is lying down, but I know she wouldn't mind. Tell me, please, sir, do you suspect anything unnatural about the master's death?'

Tinker, remembering Blake's caution to Carslake of the previous night, shook his head.

'I know absolutely nothing,' he replied, and with a sorrowful shake of the head the old butler led the way through the hall to the study, wondering why, if nothing were wrong, his caller desired to make an inspection of the garden.

However, he was too well-trained to ask any further question when Tinker had shown so plainly that he had nothing to tell him. The faithful old fellow would worry his mind and wonder, but for the present Tinker knew Blake's orders on that score must be obeyed.

He stood on the terrace and surveyed the tangled garden before him until the butler had gone back to the house. Far down against the wall dividing the garden from that of the house occupied by the Chinese was a small tool-house, the flat, sloping roof of which was a few inches below the top of the dividing wall. At one end, and almost covering the roof with its branches, was a thickly-leaved tree, and as soon as he cast his eyes on it Tinker gave a grunt of satisfaction.

'Couldn't be better,' he muttered. 'I'll lose no time in getting up there. It ought to overlook the whole place!'

Quickly he dived along the terrace until he reached the wall, and then, keeping in its shelter he made his way down the garden until he reached the tool-house.

He reconnoitred a bit, looking for a method of ascent. Nothing presented itself but the sill of the window, and he discovered that by gripping the edge of the roof he could just make it.

A spring carried him up, and pulling himself over the edge, he lay flat, squirming along slowly in order not to make any noise on the galvanised material of which the roof was composed. A disappointment met him when he reached the wall and lifted himself to peer over.

As he had thought, from his position he could overlook every inch of the next garden, but the branches screened him far less than he had imagined they would when looking at them from the ground.

Dropping back, he gazed up at the tangled branches overhead, some of which hung over the wall into the next garden.

Suiting the action to the word, Tinker raised himself cautiously and caught hold of an overhanging branch. Then he swung clear of the roof and landed with his feet on a branch lower down.

To a lad of Tinker's activity and training the ascent was child's play, and when he had gained a higher position he settled himself and breathed a sigh of satisfaction.

'This is splendid,' he said to himself. 'Couldn't be better. Now, Mr Chinaman, we'll keep a watch on your place until five o'clock.'

Tinker hardly hoped for anything of a decisive nature to occur, particularly during the afternoon, but he was more keen than ever to know all he could about the curious people who lived in the house on the other side of the wall, and at the same time to discover, if possible, the reason of the mysterious occurrence in the consulting-room a little before.

For over an hour he sat motionless, watching intently, but nothing of the slightest description occurred.

At the end of that time, however, the gate at the end of the garden which gave on to the lane, flew open, and the big limousine he had seen earlier in the day rolled in and entered the garage.

A minute later he saw the Chinaman with whom he had had the struggle in the consulting-room come out of the garage and walk slowly up a garden path towards the house. Almost simultaneously a rear door in the house opened, and another Chinaman, dressed in Oriental fashion, hurried down the path, and Tinker saw with a quiver of joy that the two Celestials would meet almost under the tree in which he sat.

He held his breath as the two Chinamen drew nearer and nearer, and finally met not ten feet from him.

He noticed at once the obsequiousness of the greeting which the man from the house gave the newcomer, but as to what they were saying Tinker could not distinguish. He knew some Chinese words, but so rapidly and earnestly was the conversation being carried on that he could glean nothing which sounded familiar.

The pantomime of the man who had arrived in the limousine, however, told him as plainly as could any words what was the subject of their conversation. He went through a vivid reproduction of what Tinker knew was the fight in the consulting-room, all the time keeping up a guttural flow of words.

Suddenly one word in English, spoken by the man who was obviously the master, caught Tinker's ears.

It was 'Blake', and it took little deduction to know that the fierce tones which accompanied the name boded ill for the detective.

Tinker bent eagerly forward in order not to miss anything, and to stamp indelibly on his mind the appearance of the two Celestials, when an awful thing occurred.

In his eagerness he leaned too far for the support of the branch on which he was resting. As his full weight came on the weak part it bent dangerously, and Tinker, with a smothered gasp, reached wildly for a branch above.

His efforts were too late, however, and with a slithering, slipping scramble he dived headlong, falling with a heavy thud at the feet of the two men standing beneath.

THE FOURTH CHAPTER

The Plot Thickens – The Puzzling Sketches – The Night of Horror – Another Bolt from the Blue

On his arrival at Mrs Green's modest home, which he discovered was on the outskirts of Limehouse, Blake wasted no time in beginning his investigations. In the course of his long career he had had hundreds of people – yes, thousands – come to him with their troubles. No matter whether they could defray his expenses or not, Blake never refused a needy man or woman; but, as he told Mrs Green, they must first prove that his assistance was really essential.

He had read honest trouble, and the sorrow of a heart-broken mother, in the poor woman's eyes, and even had she not mentioned her belief that her son had in some way fallen foul of some Celestials, Blake would have lent his aid.

He would, however, have delayed his trip until the evening, and instead, spent the afternoon poring over the books which he had procured from the publishers, Milne, Dodds & Co. For out of the class of facts which investigation had grudgingly supplied, and which his own brilliant analytical capacity had added to and elaborated, he was beginning to evolve a few concrete facts.

It was plain to him after his perusal of Sir George's letter to Professor Somers, that the peril of which the dead man had spoken to Carslake had been no chimera. Every word, every letter of the communication had breathed – in view of what had ultimately occurred – the urgent desire of a brave man to know exactly what he had to fight against. Much as Sir George knew – and Blake felt a very great deal of knowledge had gone with him – he had not been able to estimate at its full value the force which was working against him, and which had so well succeeded in striking him down. Putting two and two together, Blake decided that the beetle, regarding which Sir George had written to the professor, had played a leading part in the ultimate end of the drama.

He thought grimly of the description in the letter. Sir George had been vague and uncertain about most of the particulars regarding it, but of one thing he had been positive – deadly positive. He had known the sting of the beetle was fatal, and instantly so. That argued a definite knowledge of the beetle's power, but also proved that he had not been permitted to investigate the matter thoroughly.

And then again, his letter had been written to the professor on Tuesday evening. He had made a definite appointment to see the professor on Friday afternoon. Why, then, had he asked the professor so urgently to look up such a beetle as he described, unless he felt himself in deadly peril?

Then again he had refused to permit the announcement of an engagement between his daughter and Carslake, until he had told Carslake of some peril which was hanging over him. Blake had known Sir George intimately enough to know that he was no panic-monger. On the contrary, the man's whole life had been one of dignity and quiet bravery.

'No!' he concluded. 'If Sir George felt the peril was real, it must have been real, and in fact the baronet's death routed any doubt on that point.'

Blake felt that his death had not been a natural one, and, moreover, though tentatively he felt convinced that the mysterious beetle of which Sir George had written had been the chosen instrument of his death, Blake did not yet go so far as to conclude the repulsive thing which had stirred Pedro to such depths, and which had escaped through the window, was the beetle, or being, that was the one chosen as the instrument.

Knowing so little of the mysterious insect, he took into account the fact that several might have been necessary in order that the blow should be certain. He had hoped for much from his examination of the bits of cotton-wool he had found, but before he had been able definitely to classify the perfume with which they had been saturated, it had all evaporated. Another proof that traces would not be plentiful.

The question first to be solved was, supposing Sir George to have met with foul play, and again, supposing the mysterious beetle to be part of the whole of the cause, who were behind it? Blake had not reached the definite point even yet, where he felt certain Celestials were engineering matters; but certainly Sir George had just returned from China, and everything so far pointed to the genesis of his peril in China.

The only connection which seemed to exist between the sudden death of a poor stoker in the East End, and the equally sudden death of a wealthy and distinguished baronet in the West End was, to Blake's mind, comprised in three facts. One was that both men had apparently died of heart failure while in perfect health; the second was that both men had just returned from the East; and the third, that vaguely in one, and positively in the other, native Chinese had apparently been connected.

Little enough to go upon truly, but Blake was beginning to realise that he was feeling the first shafts of a very powerful, a very subtle, and a very far-reaching power, and it behoved him to leave no stone unturned, in order to discover definitely just what that power was. Knowing that fact, he could fight it, but, not knowing it, like the ill-fated baronet, he might fall a victim within its toils.

It is unnecessary to give a detailed description of Blake's examination of Tom Green, who lay in the little room upstairs. Those who have followed the methods of Sexton Blake will be familiar with his mode of procedure. Sufficient is it to say that when he returned to the little kitchen where Mrs Green sat weeping silently – the truly sorrowing are usually silent in their grief – he wore a very grave expression on his face. Above all, the hard, dry glitter of his eyes was particularly marked.

Only when greatly disturbed, or when coming to grips with one of his numerous foes, did that glitter assume a place in the detective's eyes. For the net result of his examination had coincided with the doctor's decree of heart failure, except in one thing. That one thing was a tiny spot on Tom Green's throat just where he buttoned his shirt.

The spot was of yellow, and rimmed by the yellow was a tiny black puncture in the very centre. That was all, but to Blake it held an immensity of meaning. Size for size, point for point, colour for colour, it was the fellow in every way of the spot he had seen on Sir George's lower lip.

Stepping gravely across the narrow width of the kitchen, Blake laid his hand on the sorrowing mother's shoulder.

'I fully realise you have much to sorrow for, Mrs Green,' he said gently, as for a moment the glitter disappeared from his eyes. 'But what is done is done, and we poor mortals must accept the decree. It is, however' – and Blake's face looked strangely gaunt in the afternoon light, while the glitter returned once more to the deep-set eyes – 'it is, however, in our power to justly avenge the wrongs done to us.'

The poor woman lifted her tear-stained face, and looked up at him.

'Then – then, Mr Blake, you think they have done my Tom foul?'

'Mrs Green,' said Blake, in the same gentle tones, 'why did you come to me to help you?'

'Because I trusted you as a true, honourable gentleman, sir.'

'Then I want you to trust me still further,' replied Blake. 'All I can tell you at present is that your son, Tom – and I doubt not that he was a good son – is the victim of some force which as yet I have not defined. You are not the only sufferer, Mrs Green. At this very moment at the other end of the city there is a poor, motherless girl, brought up in the lap of luxury, who is lying with an aching heart because, through the same fiendish mechanism, she has lost that which is dear to her – her father.'

'I know I must accept what comes, Mr Blake,' answered the poor woman chokingly; 'but it is hard. Tom was my all.'

'You must try to bear up, Mrs Green,' said Blake; 'and in the meantime, help me as much as you can in discovering the truth.'

'I will, sir – I will!' she cried, her eyes flashing. 'If you can discover them as has done for my Tom I'll do anything to help.'

'It will only be necessary for you to answer me a few questions,' answered Blake. 'Tell me, first, how long was your son home?'

'Going on three weeks, sir!'

'Ah! And he was stoker in a ship which came from – '

'Chiney, sir. I don't just remember the name of the port.'

'That is immaterial,' replied Blake. 'He came from China. Another question, Mrs Green. Did he show any signs of worry since he arrived, or did he act quite as usual?'

'It's funny you ask me that, sir, because he was as glum as you please, sir, ever since he got home. I often thinks, sir, he felt something hanging over him.'

'He was glum,' repeated Blake. And then to himself, 'Fact two.' Aloud he said: 'I am sorry to touch on this, Mrs Green, but believe me, it is essential. Did he leave any papers of any particular description?'

'Only his insurance, sir. He was a good son, and as regards money, sir, I never need worry as long as I live. He spent a good deal of his earnings in that. But in there is something which might be of interest to you, though I don't think so.'

'What is that?' asked Blake.

'Well, sir, Tom, he never showed any leaning, as it were, to drawing. Since he come home, though, sir, he drawed and drawed almost continually. I never seen him do that before.'

'What were the subjects of his drawings?' asked Blake.

'They was all the same thing, sir – a spidery-looking animal what made me creep.'

For once in his life, Blake's composure almost deserted him. Leaning forward tensely, he said: 'Are there any of his drawings left?'

'Oh, yes, sir! The drawer in the kitchen table over there is half full of them.'

'May I see them?'

'Yes, sir, of course.'

With that, Mrs Green rose, and walked over to the table. Pulling out the drawer she drew out a pile of papers, and walking back to Blake, handed them to him.

Without comment Blake took them, and spread them out on the table before him. For a moment the most prominent thing in his face was the hard glitter of the eyes. Then his lids fell as he leaned over the papers, and silence reigned.

One paper was the same as the other. Each and every one of them had a crude, rough drawing upon it, and it is not surprising that, to Mrs Green, they were only 'spidery things'. To Blake, however, they were of the utmost importance. Some were large, some were small, but all were roughly alike, and conspicuous about all was the crude attempt to make them assume a beetle-like shape.

There were the bent, fragile legs, the flat head, a rough attempt to show the scaly wings; but, chief of all, on every one of them was a horn or needle-like point protruding from the head. By the aid of a cheap yellow crayon the drawings had been shaded yellow, and even as he looked at them Blake kept muttering to himself: 'The Yellow Beetle! The Yellow Beetle!'

Finally, he raised his head and said: 'Do you mind if I keep these, Mrs Green?'

'No, sir. As I said, anything I can do I will do. If those are of use to you keep them. Though, please, sir, when you finish with them, can I have them back? They were the last things he did, sir.'

'Certainly,' answered Blake. 'I promise you I will take care of them and return them, I hope, soon. Now, another question or two, Mrs Green. Where did your son have his laundry done, or did you do it for him?'

'I did his collars, sir, but his boiled shirts he had done at the laundry down the road.'

'Ah, what kind of a laundry is it?'

'A Chinese laundry, sir. It's just two blocks down.'

'He always had it done there, did he?'

'Oh, yes, sir! Though those laundry-men are always changing, sir.'

'H'm! When did he receive his shirts home?'

'Well, sir, he always called for them Saturday night, but last Saturday I was late doing the shopping, and he left it till Monday, sir.'

'Who unwrapped it?'

'I did, sir. I always do.'

'Did you notice anything out of the ordinary?'

'No, sir; leastwise, now I think of it, I did, sir. It was a peculiar smell about them, but I put it down to some stuff they had been using in the wash, sir.'

'Ah!' breathed Blake. 'I don't imagine you are anything of an expert in perfumes, Mrs Green, but try to remember what the smell was like. Have you ever smelt a poppy?'

'Oh, yes, sir! I have some Shirleys in the back garden.'

Blake smiled slightly.

'I didn't mean those exactly. Wait, though! Did you ever smell opium?'

'Yes, sir, I have!' cried the woman excitedly. 'And, now I come to think of it, sir, the smell on Tom's shirts was something like it.'

Blake rose, and again placed his hand on her shoulder.

'That's all I intend asking you tonight, Mrs Green. I will, as I said, take these drawings with me. Meanwhile, do nothing, say nothing. I know you will find it hard without him, but try to bear up. On my part, I will let you know just what conclusions I have reached as soon as possible.'

'Oh, you are very good, sir, and may Heaven bless you!'

Escaping from her trembling thanks, Blake stuffed the drawings in his pocket and departed.

Instead of making his way at once in order to find a taxi, however, he sauntered slowly along the street until he had passed the Chinese laundry two blocks farther down. In one glance he got the name at one side of the door, the number, and a mental photograph of its appearance and those of the adjoining buildings. Then he kept on in the same casual way until he caught a stray taxi.

It was nearly five when he reached Baker Street, and on opening the consulting-room door he stood in amazement at the disordered scene which presented itself.

Several small chairs were overturned, a tabouret, on which had stood his smoking paraphernalia, was upended, and the general appearance gave every evidence of having been the scene of a struggle.

As he entered Pedro emerged from the dressing-room and greeted him affectionately, but of Tinker there was no sign.

Instinctively Blake glanced at the Japanese idol on the mantel, and, reading the signal of its face to the wall, he crossed the room and pressed a spring in the bottom.

The top half of the idol swung slowly around, and thrusting in his hand he drew out Tinker's note. Rapidly tearing open the flap of the envelope, he read, and as he did so an irritated frown creased his brow.

'Why didn't he remain here until I arrived?' he muttered. 'The fact that the force I am working against has shown its hand in the visit of the man of whom Tinker speaks in his note, puts the seal to my conclusions. He was altogether too reckless in returning there to investigate, for as yet he has no idea of whom he is up against. However, he may be all right, and pick up some useful information.'

Carefully tearing Tinker's letter to shreds, he touched a match to the pieces and tossed them in the grate.

Afterwards he walked to the desk, whereon lay the piece of the jacket which Pedro had torn from Wu Ling during the struggle. It was of the ordinary black material used in morning-coats, and, picking it up, Blake held it to Pedro's muzzle. An angry growl followed as the dog stiffened slightly and looked at his master.

'Good boy!' smiled Blake, pulling his ears. 'You evidently recognise the scent, and have no love for the owner. That point may come in useful yet. But now to investigate the drawings. I have to see if there is anything resembling them in the books I got from Milne, Dodds & Co.'

He drew out his knife, and cut the string of the parcel of books, and then, piling them on the floor beside the big chair, set to work.

Hour after hour went by, and still Blake pored over technical descriptions, making notes, underlining in a methodical manner, picking out every point which by any chance at all might have a bearing on the matter he was investigating.

When he had finished the last book and laid it down, he began to re-examine the points he had marked, in an endeavour to ferret out one which, by making the necessary allowances, might fit in a general way at least the vague description of the beetle as written by the late Sir George Halliday.

It was nearly midnight when the telephone rang, and at the other end he heard Professor Somers' voice.

'Hallo! Is that you, Mr Blake?' he said.

'Yes,' answered Blake. 'I'm glad you called up. I was just about to try to get you.' 'Ah! Have you discovered anything?'

'No,' replied Blake; 'nothing definite. I have, however, come across a remarkable coincidence in the shape of some drawings, and if possible will drop down and show them to you tomorrow. Have you discovered anything?'

'Not exactly, although I have hopes,' replied the professor. 'My records showed nothing, but this evening I got in touch with Dr Moore. He made the trip from Leh, overland, to Peking, you remember. Well, I gave him a general description of the beetle, and he says that on his last journey he heard several things which seemed to indicate the existence of such a beetle. He also said that by some of the tribes it was regarded with awe. He knew nothing, however, of its poisonous attributes, and seemed keen on learning if that were so.'

'Well,' remarked Blake, 'I can tell you this much, professor. The beetle does exist. How far it coincides with the description Sir George gave I can't say yet, but of three facts I am almost certain. One is that it is yellow; the second that it has the needle-like horn in front; and the third that it is deadly poisonous, as Sir George said. Furthermore, I am of the opinion that it does not sting without provocation, and that in order to ensure its doing so it is lured on by a drug or perfume. That is, as yet, but a tentative theory which has to be proved, but I have discovered some very strong facts in support of it.'

'Well, well,' came back the professor's voice. 'You are a remarkable man, Mr Blake. How did you discover all that?'

'I cannot tell you over the 'phone, professor,' laughed Blake, 'but will do so when we meet. Goodnight!'

With that Blake rang off, but even as he hung up the receiver he sat in tense silence, watching Pedro.

The big fellow had risen, and was standing, rigid and intent, before the dressing-room door. Something, Blake knew, had disturbed him, and, getting softly to his feet, Blake stepped stealthily across the floor.

Then he swiftly turned the handle of the dressing-room door, but no one was there. Hastening through into the bedroom, he switched on the lights and made an examination. There was nothing to be seen, however, and he turned to Pedro with puzzled brows.

'It is not like you to get suspicious over nothing, old chap,' he muttered; 'but I'm blest if there seems to have been anybody in here. The window is only open a couple of inches, and I surely would have heard it if anyone had opened or closed it.'

Walking over to the window, Blake threw it up and leaned out. The street was silent and deserted, and from the distance came a measured tread which he knew was that of the policeman on the beat.

'You're developing nerves, old chap,' he said, closing the window to within its two inches of the sill.

Had Blake dashed through while he was still talking with the professor, however, he would have seen that Pedro's instincts had not betrayed him, even though the dressing-room had been between him and the bedroom. For, during the telephone conversation, a stealthy, almond-eyed figure had softly raised the sash, crept through the window, and stolen across to the bed.

There the intruder had thrust his hand under the pillow-slip of one of the pillows, and hastily retreating, had barely drawn down the window again, and slipping down a silken ladder gained the security of a dark area-way as Blake threw up the window.

Ignorant of this, Blake returned to the consulting-room, and, gathering up his notes, laid them on the desk. Then he sat down and began puzzling over Tinker's non-appearance.

By all odds the lad should have returned during the evening. If his second investigation of the place adjoining Sir George's had revealed anything which he had thought worth following up, he should have wired. 'Still,' thought Blake, 'he may not have had the opportunity to do so. At any rate, I wish I knew just where he is. He has no idea of the depths of cunning against which we are fighting. That they are Celestials there is now no shadow of a doubt, but the question is, what is their identity, and above all, what is their motive?

'I confess it baffles me to connect the death of Sir George Halliday and Tom Green with one and the same motive, but I feel certain that is so. People, even Celestials, don't take such elaborate precautions to ensure the death of a poor stoker unless they have a powerful motive.

'Is it possible that Sir George in a scientific way, and Tom Green in a casual way, stumbled on something in China which brought upon them the deadly enmity of powerful interests? I must confess it seems so, and another link is the fact that both men had but just returned from China.

'Again, it is not a usual occupation for a stoker on shore leave to spend his time in covering sheets of paper with crude drawings, and all of one thing. The mentality which was forced to do that was, without the shadow of a doubt, driven on by some vague, intangible fear, but nevertheless real, as events have proved.

'Almost to the last degree the method of death was the same, and mathematically it is impossible that the perpetrators should not be the same in each case, and that the motive should be different.

'But why – why? Until I know that it is impossible to connect up the threads which, though gradually being untangled, are still too weak to bear the strain of a definite theory. However, tomorrow may bring forth something further, and I myself will make an examination of the house adjoining Sir George's, which seems to have such remarkable tenants.

'It seems evident that in some way they have gained the knowledge that Sir George's death has not taken place without suspicion being aroused, and that I have been looking into matters. That argues that my identity is known, and explains the reason of the Chinaman visiting my rooms today, but with what purpose it is hard to say.

'At any rate, Tinker and Pedro baulked that move, but it behoves us to tread warily. I wish the lad had returned, but morning may bring him.'

With this conclusion Blake rose and prepared to retire. First he wrote a note to Tinker against his return, telling the lad if he had discovered anything to wake him at once. This he put in the idol and turned the face to the wall.

Then, pulling Pedro's ears, he made his way into the bedroom.

With only his two hours' rest of the night before, and an extremely wearying day and evening, Blake was distinctly tired. He had found very early in his career as a detective that if he were to keep himself fit for business he must cultivate the faculty of being able to sleep in any place and at any time. In addition to this, it was a creed with him never to take worries or business to rest with him, and consequently, as soon as he had retired, he composed himself for sleep.

In five minutes he was breathing evenly, in half an hour he was completely wrapped in slumber. A full hour passed, however, before any sound or movement impinged on the regularity of his breathing.

At the end of that time, however, it came in the form of a stealthy hand creeping slowly over the sill through the two inches of space under the sash. First the fingers appeared, then the wrist and part of a yellow arm, but with that it stopped.

Slowly and silently the fingers unclosed, and a tiny metal case came into view. Then the wrinkled fingers moved cautiously about the smooth side, there was a soft click, the bottom of the case flew open, and as the hand holding it hastily withdrew, something dropped to the floor with a soft, metallic thud.

A moment later two hands appeared on the sill, the sash was gently lowered, the stealthy figure stole away into the night, and Sexton Blake was left alone in the dark room with a something on the floor under the window gazing forth with two tiny, sinister, beady eyes.

For another long hour it sat there motionless, while the man in the bed slept on, but as he turned over on his side with a deep sigh, suddenly a pungent perfume began filling the room.

The pin-like head of the thing under the window began suddenly waving about, a long needle-like horn in front quivering in an endeavour to locate the position of the odour which, like a magnet, would draw it.

Then, with a rustling of scaly wings, it began creeping rapidly across the floor until it reached the bed. There the clothes hung over, and, gripping them with its fly-like legs, the sinister thing crawled up and up until it reached the top. There the pungent odour met it with all its force, and straight as an arrow the awful thing crept up the bed towards Sexton Blake's face.

It had reached the clothes over Blake's chest, when suddenly something of a startling nature occurred. The door leading to the dressing-room, which had been almost closed, flew open with a terrific bang, and through the darkness shot a terrifying streak with hair on end, eyes fixed and blazing, and great red jaws foaming.

Its terrific spring carried it with crushing force on to Blake's chest, and with a startled exclamation the detective leaped up to find himself in a whirlwind tangle of legs and bedclothes.

Ferocious and straight as had been Pedro's mad spring, it had not been in time to prevent the thing from stinging, but it had been in time to alter the object of its sting, for just as Blake leaped up the beetle struck again and again, its horn burying itself in the drug-soaked pillow.

Throwing himself free, Blake sprang from the bed and switched on the light. Then he turned to witness a remarkable sight. Pedro, with every hair on his body still on end, was pawing and tearing at the bedclothes and pillows in a frenzied attempt to locate the thing, the presence of which he could feel.

Suddenly as Blake looked, he saw something of a vivid yellow colour flop from the edge of the bed and fall to the floor, where it lay still. Like a flash Pedro was after it, but Blake dashed forward, and just as the bloodhound's jaws came together with a terrific snap, Blake pulled him away. Then, pulling him to the door of the dressing-room, he thrust him out and closed the door.

His first thought was that the yellow thing on the floor had been killed by Pedro's frenzied attack, but then, Blake did not know of the power of the drug over the beetle, which, after luring it on, sent it almost at once into a state of coma.

On more closely investigating it, however, Blake saw that it was not injured, and, hastening through the door leading to the laboratory, he picked up a specimen bottle and returned to the bedroom. Picking up the beetle with a pair of fine tweezers, he popped it into the bottle and replaced the cork.

Then, putting the bottle away for the time being, he opened the door and called to Pedro, who had recovered from his frenzy. Blake bent down and laid his hand on the dog's head.

'Faithful, brave old chap!' he said huskily. 'If it hadn't been for your instinct and bravery I would not have been here now. You have rendered me many services, old fellow, but never before have you saved me from a tighter shave than that of tonight. In your canine way you understood the menace of that yellow beetle, but I don't think even your animal instinct told you just how deadly it was. But now, Pedro, we will investigate and find out how that perfume came on my pillow.'

As he spoke, Blake straightened up and approached the bed. Rearranging the tumbled clothes, he lifted up the pillow and made an examination of the part which was still saturated where the liquid had been poured on it.

'If that had been there when I went to bed,' he muttered, 'I must have noticed it immediately. The smell is too distinct to pass. That means that it was put there while I was asleep, and – Ah, what's this?'

His hand had come into contact with something hard in the pillow itself, and thrusting his hand down, he drew off the slip. There, in almost the very spot where his head would lie was a small slit, and thrusting in his fingers, he drew forth a tiny bottle. The feathers surrounding it were saturated like the slip, but there was still some liquid left in the bottle, and as he held it up, Blake saw how the trick had been worked.

'Very clever!' he muttered. 'They get in here before I come to bed and put the bottle in the pillow. Instead of using a cork they pack the neck with cotton wool, and make it just tight enough to ensure a period of two or three hours before the liquid soaks through and saturates the pillow.

'But how about the beetle – ah!'

This as he swung around and saw the window closed tight.

'So Pedro was right, after all,' he muttered; 'and there was somebody in here while I was speaking on the 'phone. It was then, I presume, that they secreted the bottle, and then – now I see it all.

'After I had retired they returned and threw the beetle into the room, and then closed the window. The liquid may even then have worked through, or, on the other hand, the beetle may have been here alone with me in the room for some time. In any event it was well thought out, and stood little chance of failure.

'If the door leading to the dressing-room had been tightly closed as well as the one leading into the consulting-room, I would never have known what happened to me. But I think the subtlety and persistence of my unknown enemies is sufficient to convince me of their nationality, and I have at last a perfect live specimen of the Yellow Beetle.'

Smiling with grim satisfaction. Blake picked up the phial containing the liquid, and the specimen bottle in which he had placed the beetle. After locking them carefully in the safe he sent Pedro to sleep on a rug under the window, and once more retiring, was soon asleep.

Blake was not fated to sleep in peace that night, however, for barely had daylight come when he was awakened by a violent ringing at the street door-bell.

Pedro growled and got to his feet, and Blake, slipping out of bed, put on his slippers and dressing-gown, and made his way through to the front door. On opening it, he glanced with surprise at Godfrey Carslake, who stood there looking half-demented.

'What is the trouble?' asked Blake quickly.

'Gertrude – Miss Halliday – has disappeared!' gasped Carslake.

'Come in!' said Blake grimly, and dragging him in, closed the door.

THE FIFTH CHAPTER

Wu Ling Tries a Bold Move – Tinker in the "Room of Madness"

When Tinker landed heavily at the feet of Wu Ling and his companion, he was half stunned by the fall, which would have been serious but for the soft turf. As the two Chinamen, startled for once out of their native calm, glanced at the lad who had apparently tumbled from nowhere, Tinker got to his feet.

Without any attempt at bluffing he turned like lightning, and made a running leap for the wall, grasping as he did so one of the overhanging branches of the trees, which it will be remembered had formed his hiding-place.

Startled though he was, Wu Ling was as quick as the lad, and as Tinker's legs drew upwards Wu Ling made a flying leap and clutched him by the ankles. He then rapped out a guttural command, and his companion, leaping also, caught Tinker around the waist.

Then, cling as he would, the lad was forced to relax his hold, for it was impossible to sustain the weight which was dragging at him. Slowly and painfully his hands slipped along the rough branch until finally he released his hold entirely and tumbled back into the arms of his captors. While the man who had grabbed him by the waist threw him over with a deft twist, and held his arm in a grip which forbade the slightest movement, Wu Ling bent and gazed for some moments into the lad's face.

'Why have you come here?' he asked suddenly, in perfect English. 'Didn't you get enough before?'

'I might ask why you came to Baker Street and set on me with a knife as soon as I got inside the door,' replied Tinker, who knew Wu Ling had recognised him, and that bluff was out of the question.

'It is my place to ask, and yours to answer,' rejoined Wu Ling haughtily.

Then, turning to his companion, he said: 'Take him inside, I will speak with him there. If he refuses, we will use methods which will make him do our bidding.'

With an obsequious 'Yes, Excellency', and a vicious twist of Tinker's arm the lad's captor dragged him to his feet and hurried him along in the shelter of the wall, until he reached the house. Then, opening the door, he hustled him through into a well-furnished library, followed at a more dignified pace by Wu Ling.

'Now then, my young friend,' remarked Wu Ling gutturally, 'you will be good enough to answer my questions.'

'I might as well tell you at the start,' replied Tinker, 'that I don't know anything, and even if I did, I wouldn't tell you.'

'Oh!' remarked Wu Ling pleasantly, as he raised his brows. 'Just give his arm a preliminary twist, San.'

The Chinaman who held Tinker brought the lad's arm behind him, and jerked it up his back until it rested at the back of the neck. Tinker stiffened under the excruciating pain which it caused, but eyed Wu Ling in silent defiance.

'Let it go now,' ordered his inquisitor, and Tinker heaved an involuntary gasp of relief as the hold was relaxed.

'Now, my lad,' went on Wu Ling, his accent remarkably free from slurring, 'you have had the very slightest taste of what you will get if you refuse to answer my questions. Firstly, what connection have you with Mr Sexton Blake, and what were both of you doing at the residence of Sir George Halliday last evening?'

'You seem to know more than I do,' jerked Tinker.

'San,' said Wu Ling imperturbably, as he lit a cigarette, 'give him just a shade more this time – slowly, San, it is so much more effective.'

Tinker's breath left him in the sudden pain of the torturing twist, but he was game, and closed his lips in a thin straight line.

'Easy now, San,' remarked Wu Ling, and once more the pressure was relaxed. 'We will pass that for the moment,' went on Wu Ling. 'If you refuse utterly to tell me what I wish to know, my lad, I have a method which will make you very glad to talk, and of which you cannot even imagine the torture. Come now, what do you say?'

'You can do what you will,' muttered Tinker. 'I've told you I know nothing.'

Wu Ling waved his hand.

'Take him away, San, and see that he is kept secure. Tonight I shall give him a taste of the glass-room, and if he retains his sanity, he will be only too pleased to speak. Go! Return here, I have things to say.'

'Yes, Excellency,' replied San; and, unceremoniously dragging Tinker after him, he descended to the cellar and thrust the lad into a dark stone-walled cellar and slammed the door, locking it after him.

Then he returned to the library where Wu Ling sat, and stood submissively waiting for his chief to speak.

'There is much to be done,' began Wu Ling slowly.

'Yes, Excellency.'

'In some way,' went on Wu Ling, 'suspicion has been roused as to the death of Halliday. I have looked up everything about this man Sexton Blake, and find he has the reputation of being the cleverest investigator of crime in Europe – probably in the world.'

'Yes, Excellency.'

'He was not at Halliday's last night by accident, and if there was any doubt about it, the fact that this lad came here this morning settles it.

'I went as fast as I could in the limousine from Limehouse to where this man Blake lives, in order to search the place and find out what I could. There was, as I told you, in the garden a cursed dog there, however, which blocked every move I attempted to make, and when I tried to knife him he jumped clear like a cat.

'Then, as I explained, this brat of a lad arrived, and we had a struggle. I considered it wiser for the moment to get clear, and make the attempt later; but it shows the persistency with which they are on the scent when this lad follows back here and conceals himself in the tree.'

'Yes, Excellency.'

'Now, we can't run any risk of having our great purpose spoiled by this man Blake. And he must be stopped. I will think over how we shall do it. Tonight, after he has had a taste of the glass-room, the lad will talk, and then we shall give him the Beetle. You should not have failed to get the papers from Halliday's library; but since you accomplished the decree of his death successfully, I pass that over for the present. But we must have every note and record he made regarding what he discovered in China. And, if the deck-hand on the junk is to be believed, it was Halliday who must have been present during our last meeting on it, where Foo Loo paid the penalty.'

'He swore by the Beetle, Excellency.'

'Yes, I know. Besides, we have other proof which makes it seem probable. At any rate, he has been swept away before he had an opportunity to disclose anything. But he must have notes still in existence.

'For a day or two, until he is buried, the house will be too full to make any attempt to secure them. But after that these English always have what they call "the reading of the will", and then all papers are gone over. We must have them before that. And I have a plan.'

'May your unworthy servant ask what it is, Excellency?'

'Yes, San, for you are to carry it out. The funeral is to take place the day after tomorrow.'

'Yes, Excellency.'

'Therefore, we must act quickly. Tonight will be best. This is what you will do: At midnight get someone to assist you. Lay the board from the dividing-wall to the top of the balcony on the Halliday house, as you did before. Halliday's bedroom overlooks it, and he is no doubt there. Lift the window, and make your way into his room.

'Miss Halliday will be up and dressed, for I shall send a telegram to her saying an old friend is calling, and can only come at midnight, and will she wait up to see him? She will do so, and you are almost sure to find her up and dressed.

'Study your plan of the house well, and don't make any mistakes. Get her quickly, and bring over the plank at once. Then we can all get away, and by morning they are welcome to search here all they wish.'

'And then, Excellency?'

'Then,' smiled Wu Ling softly, 'Miss Halliday is no doubt a dutiful daughter, and will pay any price in order to be set free in time for her father's funeral. That price, San, is the handing over of all her father's notes and records before she is freed, and I think the plan will be successful in achieving its purpose. Now go! I would think.'

San bowed, and left to make his plans for the carrying out of his master's orders, and Wu Ling, once alone, settled back and closed his eyes.

Celestial though he was, with no trace of white blood in him, he looked as he lay back there a man accustomed to command and to be obeyed. His brow was broad and intelligent, his features reposeful and inscrutable, his head carried with dignity. And, far apart as the poles though they were, he had an indefinable air of power about him which reminded one of Sexton Blake.

What was passing behind those lowered lids no man knew, nor ever would. He might some day feel the effects, but of the intricacies of that deep Oriental mind probably the man who would read its mazes more than any other was the man who was destined to be his greatest foe – Sexton Blake.

And likewise Wu Ling was to discover, when he came to grips with the man who was called a mathematical machine, that another mind than his was a maze of intricate thoughts.

He had sat for some time in motionless silence, when a low, hurried knock came at the door, and a Chinaman in native attire entered. Bowing low, he approached Wu Ling, and stood, with bent head, waiting for permission to speak. Wu Ling slowly opened his eyes and gazed at the man before him, who was one of the thousands who obeyed his slightest command.

'What is it?' he asked, after a pause.

'Oh, Excellency, I have news which your unworthy servant would tell you.'

'Speak!' commanded Wu Ling. 'Speak! And be brief.'

'Oh, Excellency, this day I have followed from his home the man whom I shadowed last night. He left with a woman, and the woman, Excellency, was the mother of the man on whom I carried out the decree of the Beetle. This man Blake, Excellency, went to the woman's home, and remained some time. Then he left, Excellency, and walked past Looey Sing's laundry, and entered a taxi.'

'Did he look at the laundry as he passed?' asked Wu Ling, in even tones.

'I think not, Excellency.'

'Do you know what this means?' asked Wu Ling.

'Yes, Excellency. It means danger.'

'Then you know what must be done?'

'Yes, Excellency. He must go.'

'Yes, Sexton Blake must go at once. I will tell you how.'

Thereupon Wu Ling ordered the man to bring him paper and pencil from the desk. A moment later he was sketching a rough plan of Blake's rooms; and then, speaking in low, earnest tones, he was instructing the man to carry out the Beetle decree against Blake – which, as we have seen, would have succeeded only too well but for Pedro's timely interference.

Sharp on the stroke of midnight two shadowy figures stole out of the back entrance of Wu Ling's temporary residence, and, hastening down the garden to the garage, they entered. A moment later they emerged, carrying a long plank, which had it been daylight, might have been seen to be padded with leather on one end.

Carrying it along beside the dividing-wall, they laid it down, and San – the man in the lead – pulled himself up and peered over the wall.

All was silent on the Halliday side. A few dim lights shone in the windows, but that was all.

Softly San signalled to the other to push up the plank, while he sat astride the wall and steadied it. Up it went until over half was above the wall. San held it while the other gained a place beside him. It needed all their strength then to hoist the plank the rest of the way; but they had done it before, and knew exactly what to do. Bracing it, they lowered it slowly until, with a soft thud, the padded end rested on the edge of the Halliday balcony, where Pedro had found the mysterious finish of the scent the night before.

Without hesitation, San stood up and noiselessly crossed. On reaching the top of the balcony he paused a moment, and then crept stealthily up until he was crouching under the window of Sir George's room.

Under his expert fingers the sash presented few difficulties, and after lifting it softly, he crept through. Pausing inside, he drew out a bottle, and, saturating a handkerchief, thrust the bottle back, and stole towards the door.

Now was the ticklish time, and he knew it. But Wu Ling had decreed, and it never crossed San's mind to disobey. If disaster overtook him, he must suffer it – that was all.

But as he settled a long, crooked-bladed knife in his belt, it was evident he did not intend to have disaster overtake him without putting up a struggle.

He knew Wu Ling had sent a telegram under an assumed name, and it was probable that Miss Halliday would remain up to see the man who said he was an old friend of her father. But she might remain downstairs, and if so, it meant a risky wait until she came up.

On the other hand, being ill from the shock of her father's death, Wu Ling calculated that Miss Halliday would rest on the couch in her room until the visitor arrived. And later events proved him to be correct.

The Celestial had left nothing to chance in his plans for vengeance on Sir George. In the quiet hours of the night he had, bit by bit, visited, and made a plan of the main part of the house, and by the study of this plan San knew exactly where Miss Halliday's room was.

Softly opening the door of Sir George's room, he stepped into the dark hall, and moved silently along the thick carpet until he reached the door of Miss Halliday's room. It was closed, and for a bare moment the Celestial's eyes clouded.

He made his decision suddenly, however, for without hesitation he raised his hand and knocked softly. A soft rustle, and then steps in the next room told him the occupant evidently thought it was a servant to tell her her father's old friend had arrived. A moment later the door opened, and against the dim light of the room could be seen the wan figure of a girl dressed in black.

'Has he arrived?' she began, unable to see for a moment who was at the door.

Before she could say more, however, San leaped forward and held her in a grip of iron while he pressed the drug-saturated handkerchief against her face. She struggled vainly for a few moments, and then relaxed, falling back with closed eyes. The drug had worked quickly on her worn-out system.

Picking her up in his arms, San closed the door and sped silently along until he reached the door of Sir George's room. He passed through quickly, closing the door carefully and then the window.

With perfect coolness he shouldered his burden, and walked across the narrow plank until he reached the wall, where he silently handed his captive to the other man who had descended to the ground. He in his turn laid her down, then pulled himself up beside San.

With a sudden heave, they drew the plank back and bore down on it in order that the length on the Halliday side might not touch the ground.

Again they heaved and slid it softly back. Then, leaping to the ground, they picked it up, carried it to the garage, locked the door, and hastened to the prostrate girl who still lay on the ground.

Tinker had been dozing, and had no idea what time it was when the door of his prison was unlocked and he was dragged forth. Without speaking, his captors tied his hands behind him and gagged him with a soft ball of silk.

Then he was led upstairs, through the garden, and into the garage where two motors were standing. As he passed the limousine, he thought he caught sight of the black-garbed figure of a woman, but wasn't sure.

He had no opportunity to look again, however, for his captors led him to the second car – a big touring car.

There they tossed him like a sack of meal on the floor of the tonneau, and he could see nothing but the ceiling and the interior of the car.

He knew a trip of some sort was being contemplated, for he had seen several Chinamen in the garage. He little dreamed, however, that Wu Ling and his men were making a general exodus, and that the house adjoining Sir George's would see them no more.

Soon he felt the car moving, the lights of the garage were extinguished, a pause while he listened to the creaking of a gate, another pause during which he heard the other car drive through, and the gate closed, then they moved again, travelling at a rapid pace.

Tinker judged it to be about half an hour later when the car he was in came to a stop. Three Chinamen had been sitting in the tonneau, but with one accord they descended, and the lad knew they had reached the end of their journey for that night, at least.

Had there been any doubt in his mind, it was swept away as he was dragged forth, and found himself standing in a rough-looking shed, which was evidently being used as a temporary garage. The limousine had arrived first, for it was standing silent in the corner, while its former occupants were nowhere to be seen.

Up a rickety flight of stairs Tinker was pushed, until at the top one of his captors pressed aside a panel through which they stepped.

The room in which he found himself was certainly an improvement on the rough place below, for although not as luxurious as the study where he had seen Wu Ling in the afternoon, it was comfortably furnished.

Squatting on a pile of vivid yellow cushions, and garbed in rich Chinese garments, was a man whom at first he did not recognise, but after a moment he saw it was Wu Ling. The men who led him bowed in silence, and Tinker grudgingly admitted that the man certainly exhaled a certain power.

He had little time to make conjectures, however, for Wu Ling looked up and said evenly: 'Have you decided to answer my questions?'

Tinker shook his head. He felt a sinister menace in the expression of the eyes into which he gazed, and for the first time since he had fallen into their hands, he felt that he was in a grip which would not easily let go. He was determined not to give in, however, and defiantly gazed back at Wu Ling.

If he expected Wu Ling to command his men to torture him, as he had been tortured in the afternoon, he was mistaken, for the Celestial did no such thing. On the contrary, he smiled pleasantly, and waved his hand.

'Take him to the glass-room,' he said, and without another word Tinker was dragged out

Thc house had evidently been well arranged for its purpose, for Tinker found they passed through two more secret panels before they stood in a small, dark passage. Then one of his captors pressed a hidden button, the end of the passage seemed to slide away, and he blinked his eyes at the dazzling brilliance of what he saw.

One moment it looked like a huge apartment, and the next it looked like a tiny box. It was mirrored all over, with the exception of the floor; but the mirrors had been so arranged that it would be a very clever man indeed who could tell the size of the room. Blazing from dozens of points were brilliant electric bulbs, and as Tinker was thrust in, he saw the floor was of steel.

A moment later the panel had been snapped close, and he swung around; but to save his life he could not tell through which one he had come. There seemed to be hundreds of them, and he grew faint and giddy with the reeling mass.

He lowered his eyes to the floor in order to overcome his dizziness, when a panel behind him opened, and a hand stretched out.

He was dragged back, while a piece of cotton-wool, saturated with some pungent stuff, was fastened at his neck.

Then a low voice spoke in perfect English.

'This is the glass-room – the room of madness. Look about, and you will see where the floor ends. From here it looks as though it covered the room. But not so. Go to the edge and look over. What you see there is deadly poisonous. One is instant death. Hundreds will make your brain reel with madness. The glass which separates you from them is very thin. You can save yourself by calling out when you will speak. The perfume you smell will draw them to your throat as the magnet draws the needle. That is all!'

The grip was released. The panel slammed, and the amazed Tinker was left alone.

'What on earth did the voice mean about the floor ending?' he muttered. 'What were the things it said I would see by looking over the edge? And what did he mean when he said the perfume would draw them? Probably all bluff. Well, they aren't going to frighten me with their silly mirrors.'

Trying to convince himself that he felt no misgivings, Tinker slowly advanced, step by step, until he saw, with a start that the voice was right. The floor curved over, and ended abruptly.

Dropping to his knees, he peered over, but gave a gasp of horror, and drew back, sickened from what he saw.

Below him, and seemingly protected by a very thin barrier of glass, he had seen hundreds and hundreds of repulsive-looking yellow beetles crawling about with ghastly needle-like points waving madly about.

He turned his face away, but gasped again as they became suddenly mirrored on every side of him. He never knew that a hand outside the room had pressed a lever which cunningly altered the angle of the mirrors so that walls and ceilings reflected the awful mass of crawling things on every side.

The glare of the reflected light was painful, and Tinker crawled back from the edge and lay down with closed eyes. The silent fascination of what he had seen, however, conquered his resolve not to open them, and time and again he lifted his lids to gaze in sickening horror at the vistas of crawling yellow beetles which seemed everywhere.

Then he moved suddenly, and gasped again. The floor on which he had sat was quite cool when he entered. He was positive of that. Now, however, it was quite warm, and growing hotter every minute.

He remembered with a twinge that his shoes had been removed in the garage, and then in a flash he recalled something Blake had told him.

White as chalk he rose, and stood up, and his eyes filled with despair as he saw what Blake's story had suddenly caused him to expect.

Slowly – very slowly – the steel floor began to move, passing over the edge where it was curved like an endless belt. Blake had told him of the torture, and now he knew the meaning of the glass room. The floor would grow steadily hotter and hotter until he was compelled to keep dancing in order not to burn his feet.

The floor would move slowly for an hour, perhaps hours, but gradually, at stated intervals, it would increase its speed, until where at first he must walk to keep from going over the edge, he finally would be compelled to run.

If his torturers proposed to let him go mad or go over the edge, to fall crashing through the frail glass barrier into that crawling deadly mass below, he knew there was no hope for him.

However, he would not go over until every once of strength was gone. He shuddered again at the reflected horrors about him, but at that moment the floor grew unbearably hot, and ever so slightly increased its speed, and Tinker, who had been making only an occasional step, was now compelled to walk briskly, and lift his feet quickly from the hot floor in his awful race against death.

THE SIXTH CHAPTER

Inspector Thomas Receives a Surprise Summons – Blake in the Camp of the Enemy – Escape of Wu Ling – Conclusion

To say that Carslake was upset when he rushed around to Blake with the news that Gertrude Halliday had disappeared, was, to say the least, putting it mildly. On the night Sir George had so suddenly died he had been, on account of his connection with the family, greatly agitated; but Gertrude's disappearance had struck still nearer him, and Blake was forced to give him a strong drink of spirits before he could gain any sense from the incoherent tale which Carslake poured out.

'Now then,' said Blake, 'pull yourself together, and tell me just what has happened. You say Miss Halliday has disappeared. When did you find out? How did you discover it? Tell me everything.'

'Well,' replied Carslake, licking his dry lips, 'it's this way. I was at the house last evening in order to finish the funeral arrangements. I was also endeavouring to cheer her up. About ten o'clock, her aunt, who has been there all day, brought in a telegram addressed to Gertrude. When she opened it she found that it apparently came from an old friend of her father, and –'

'Wait!' interrupted Blake. 'Do you remember the wording of it?'

'Yes, I think so.'

'Then repeat it.'

'It went this way, I think: "Just heard sad news. Am passing through city at midnight. Beg of you remain up, as am very anxious to call on way through. Your poor father and I were very old friends."'

'And the signature?' asked Blake.

'Simeon Jones.'

'H'm! That tells nothing! Go on!'

'Naturally,'continued Carslake, 'Gertrude at once decided to remain up, and meet her father's old friend, and consequently, instead of leaving at ten-thirty, as I had intended, it was about half-past eleven when I got away.'

'Yes, yes, go on, man!' jerked Blake impatiently. 'If things are as I think, every moment is precious.'

'The next thing that happened,' said Carslake, 'was about two o'clock, when the telephone in my apartments began ringing like mad. On answering it I discovered it was Miss Halliday's aunt. She asked me to come round at once. I dressed as quickly as possible and while doing so, sent the night porter out for a taxi. When I arrived at the house I found everything in a terrible state of commotion. As far as I could gather this is what occurred.

'Gertrude's aunt, being very tired, had gone to her room. The servants had also retired with the exception of the old butler, who remained up in order to be on hand when Sir George's old friend arrived.

'Gertrude herself was lying down in her room fully dressed, and when the visitor came the butler was to call her. Well, when midnight came, and the expected caller did not arrive, the butler thought nothing of it, for many causes may have kept him late.

'It pulled around to one o'clock, and when the bell rang the butler went to the door, thinking it was he. Instead it was a messenger boy, with a message which he handed in, and then departed. It was addressed to Gertrude, and the butler went up at once with it.

'He knocked at the door of the room, but there was no answer. Thinking she had fallen asleep on the couch, he knocked louder, but still no reply. A third summons failed to rouse her, so he went along to her aunt's room. She answered his knock at once, and on hearing why he had roused her she went at once to Gertrude's room.

'Like the butler's, her knock received no reply, and she at once opened the door. A dim nightlight was burning, but of Gertrude there was no sign. She at once turned on the lights, but the room was empty.

'Mrs Foulsham, her aunt, was not anxious even then, but the first thing she did was to tear open the message. It was signed "Simeon Jones", and merely said: "Regret unable after all to come." '

'Of course – of course!' muttered Blake quickly. 'However, go on!'

'Well, Mrs Foulsham sent the butler downstairs to look for Gertrude, thinking she might have left her room to be down in the library. She herself made a hasty search upstairs, but there was no sign of her.

'When the butler came back and said she wasn't downstairs either, her aunt began to get worried. The servants were at once roused, and the house searched from top to bottom. They could not find the slightest trace of her, however, and then 'phoned to me.

'When I got there I made a search of the grounds as well, but it is as though she had simply vanished into the air.'

'Were any of her hats or jackets missing?' asked Blake sharply.

'No. that's the peculiar thing. Her aunt has gone through her entire wardrobe, but beyond the black frock she was wearing, nothing else has been touched.'

'Where was the butler between half-past eleven and one o'clock, when the messenger boy came?'

'He was on a seat in the front hall every moment of the time. He says he did not doze for a single moment, and that he can swear no one entered by the door, or ascended the front stairs.'

'And the windows?' asked Blake.

'He himself locked every window as he always does, and when he examined them they were just as he had left them.'

'I think I will make an examination as well,' replied Blake drily. 'With all due respect to the old butler I think I could spring a catch and fasten it again, without his being able to detect that it had occurred. However, Carslake, you seem to have told as much as you can, and now I will dress at once.

'It will be necessary for me to make an examination personally, but I think I have an idea as to the direction in which Miss Halliday has apparently so mysteriously disappeared.'

'My heavens! Tell me, then!' cried Carslake hoarsely.

'One moment,' said Blake, holding up his hand. 'I said I had an idea, but until I know my theory to be correct you must be patient. Keep cool, Carslake, for if I am not very much mistaken, you are in for one of the most strenuous days you have ever experienced.'

'I'll try,' answered the harassed Carslake; 'but it's jolly hard, believe me.'

'I know – I know,' replied Blake dreamily, as he turned and entered his dressing room.

Had Carslake been able to overhear what Blake said as he dressed, he would have been still more puzzled. In effect it would have told him nothing, but the latest development in the case had made for Blake a concrete fact of what had previously been but a tentative theory.

'I wondered, when I was examining the grounds,' he muttered, 'if the trail ended at the edge of the balcony, for the reason that a plank had bridged the space between it and the wall. Then, however, that theory rested principally on the character of the tenants occupying the adjoining place. Tinker's discoveries, and now Miss Halliday's disappearance, convince me that must be so. But I must tread warily, for their latest move proves the calibre of the other side.

'What on earth is their identity, and what is the motive? By the way, that reminds me: why hasn't Tinker returned? I trust he hasn't fallen into their hands. It will go desperately hard with him if he has.'

Little did Blake realise as he went along to Tinker's room to make sure he hadn't returned, that at that very moment the lad was beginning his ghastly race against death on the hot floor of the mirrored room – truly, as the voice had said, 'the room of madness'.

When he returned to the consulting-room fully dressed, Blake wore a savage frown, and to Carslake's questions, he answered not at all.

'Have you a revolver?' he asked curtly.

'No, why?'

Without replying, Blake went to his desk, and drew out two, tossing one to Carslake.

'Put that in your pocket, your coat pocket,' he ordered. 'You may need it, and if you do you will need it urgently. Now come on!'

A moment later, with Pedro on the leash, and the fragment of Wu Ling's coat in his pocket, Blake led the way out, and hailed a taxi.

Silence reigned during the drive to Sir George's house, for Carslake was diffident about breaking through the other's cold reserve, and Blake was untangling a mass of threads, endeavouring to find the exact motive connecting up two certainties and one probability.

The certainties were the practically simultaneous attack on himself and Miss Halliday's disappearance. The probability was Tinker's having fallen into the hands of the enemy, and as he thought matters over, he grimly decided that was also more of a certainty than a probability.

On their arrival Blake went at once to the library, where Mrs Foulsham sat in agitated anxiety. Most of the servants were gathered in the hall, and from their ranks Blake beckoned to the old butler.

'Come in,' he said briefly. 'I wish to ask you a few questions.'

The man obeyed, and Blake, turning to him, said: 'Do you remember the appearance of the lad who was with me last evening?'

'Oh, yes, sir!' cried the old man excitedly. 'And I clean forgot about it until this minute. There has been so much happening, sir,' he added apologetically.

'Forgot about what?' asked Blake curtly.

'Why, sir, he came here this afternoon and asked permission to go through to the garden, sir.'

'Ah! and how long did he remain there?'

'I – I don't know, sir. I led him through the library and left him on the terrace. He never came back through the house, sir. He must have gone out by the lane in the rear.'

'Very well, that will do,' jerked Blake, who knew only too well now that the lad had not gone out by the lane.

As the old butler retired, Blake turned to Mrs Foulsham, who was preparing to launch upon him an avalanche of questions.

'I can tell you nothing yet, Mrs Foulsham,' he said quietly. 'I have several theories which require that no time should be lost. Try to bear up until we know something definite.'

As she began weeping silently, Blake turned to Carslake. 'Take me upstairs,' he said. 'I wish to examine Miss Halliday's room.'

Carslake turned and led the way along the hall and up the broad staircase. Pausing at Gertrude's door, he turned the handle and stood aside. Blake walked at once to the window which looked out on the garden, and then turned.

'What room looks out over the end of the balcony where the dog lost the trail the other night?' he asked sharply, for he had expected Miss Halliday's room to be that one.

'Oh, Sir George's,' replied Carslake. 'Until this morning he was there, but he is now in the drawing-room.'

'I wish to see it,' said Blake, and, guided by Carslake, he went along the hall until they reached it.

Crossing to the window, Blake looked out, and his lips compressed in a thin, straight line as he saw it overlooked the spot on the roof of the balcony where Pedro had lost the scent.

The sill was a bare foot above it, and Blake was about to make an examination of the catch when Pedro, whose leash Carslake had been holding, dropped his muzzle and began pulling.

'I say, what does he mean?' asked Carslake.

Blake turned and watched the bloodhound.

'He has merely saved me some time,' he replied grimly. 'He recognises the scent on which he was before. It must be fairly strong. Let me see. It is now eight, and Miss Halliday disappeared between midnight and one o'clock. I think we shall find Pedro will lead us to the very spot at the end of the balcony where he stopped before.'

Pedro had by now reached the window-sill, and throwing back the catch, Blake lifted the sash and stepped out. Then taking the leash from Carslake, he held it while Pedro leaped over the sill, and, with muzzle down, headed straight for the end of the balcony, finally stopping in almost the identical spot where the scent had ended before.

While he was worrying about endeavouring to follow it up, Blake, knowing his efforts would be useless, held the leash slackly, and stood gazing over the dividing wall before him.

From where he stood he could see almost the full stretch of the garden on the other side, and far down near the lane entrance a garage. Suddenly he pulled Pedro back and turned to Carslake.

'Here, hold the leash! I wish to make an examination of the window-catch.'

The wondering Carslake took the leash, while Blake stepped back through the window and drew down the sash. Then, with his powerful pocket-glass, he made a minute examination of the catch, the hard, dry glitter appearing in his eyes as he saw two faint scratches on the brass which told him, as plainly as though he had been there when it happened, exactly how the window had been forced.

Then, lifting the sash again, he took the leash and motioned Carslake to follow him.

Down the stairs went Blake, and pausing only long enough to pick up their hats, he led the way out to the front door.

As he gained the street he saw in the distance Kelly, the policeman on the beat, and, with a muttered word to Carslake, hurried along.

'Goodmorning, Mr Blake!' exclaimed Kelly, as Blake came up. 'You and Tinker seem to be spending a lot of time around here lately.'

Blake smiled and went straight to the point.

'See here, Kelly!' he said. 'I want you to come along with me. 'I'm going to make a call at that house next to Sir George Halliday's, and I want you with me.'

'Why, that was the one Tinker was interested in,' said Kelly, in surprise. 'What! have the Chinese been up to anything?'

'You'll know later,' replied Blake. 'Come along, and let's lose no time.'

With Kelly added to their number, Blake led the way up the steps of the big house and pressed the bell. For a few moments they waited, but as no answer came he pressed it again and again. Still only silence met them, and after several minutes of this Blake turned to the others.

'Wait here,' he said. 'I'll take Pedro and step through Sir George's house to the garden. From there I can get over the wall and try the back door. I'm afraid, however, the birds have flown.'

Without waiting for their reply, Blake dashed down the steps and back through Sir George's house. Then, telling one of the servants to bring a ladder, he kept on until he reached the dividing wall. In a few moments the servant came running up with a small ladder, and hoisting Pedro up, Blake tumbled over after him.

Still running, he made for the back door, but found when he reached it that it was wide open. Inside all was silent, and without pausing to make an examination, he hurried along and unlocked the front door.

'I was right,' he jerked, as Kelly and Carslake entered. 'They are gone. Kelly, go into the library and see if there is a 'phone. If there is, ring up Inspcctor Thomas at Scotland Yard and tell him I wish to speak to him. You, Carslake, go upstairs and make a search there. I don't imagine you will find anything, but make sure. Have your revolver handy in case of emergencies. I will take the rooms on this floor.

As Kelly hastened to the library and Carslake leaped up the stairs, Blake took Pedro and started through the drawing-room. As he feared, however, both his search and Carslake's were abortive of result, and when they arrived at the library Kelly seemed the only one to have had any success, for he had found a 'phone, and Inspector Thomas was on the wire.

Blake picked up the receiver and bent down: 'Hallo, inspector! This is Blake speaking.'

'Yes?' came back the inspector's voice.

'Can you manage to come to Baker Street inside half an hour?' went on Blake.

'What is it?' asked the inspector.

'It's something big,' jerked Blake. 'I haven't any time for explanations now. Will you come?'

'Surely. I'll be there to the minute.'

'All right,' and Blake rang off.

'Now for the garden,' he said, turning to Kelly. 'Keep your eyes open for a plank of a good length. I'm anxious to know if there is one about. Carslake, you come with me. We will look through the garage.'

'Oh, by the way!' broke in Kelly. 'When I relieved at six this morning, the man on night-duty told me two motor-cars – one a limousine and the other a big touring-car – had come from the lane about one o'clock in the night.'

'Why didn't you say so?' asked Blake irritably. 'That gives us the exact hour when they cleared out, and means more than ever that we have no time to lose.'

He turned as he spoke and led the way through the back door.

While Kelly began an examination of the garden, Blake and Carslake walked down and entered the garage. Almost the first thing Blake saw was a long, narrow plank, one end of which was padded with leather. After the briefest of examinations he turned and hastened out, with Carslake following and looking at Blake as though the detective had suddenly lost his senses.

Blake called to Kelly, who was across at the other side of the garden: 'Lock the door of that garage,' he ordered, 'and put a seal on it. Then you had better keep your eye on the place, Kelly, until you hear from Inspector Thomas. Meanwhile, if any Chinamen of any description whatsoever approach the place, arrest them on sight. I'll guarantee sufficient cause.'

'All right, Mr Blake,' replied the policeman. 'I don't know what the game is, but I'll do as you say, pending instructions.'

Blake nodded, and, signing to Carslake, hurried back through the empty house to the street.

'Do you wish to see this thing through?' he asked, turning to his companion.

'Rather!' replied the other savagely. 'But – '

'Then ask no questions,' rapped Blake. 'We have no time for anything but action. Come; we will take this taxi.'

Blake held up his hand to a passing cab, and, giving the Baker Street address, motioned Carslake to enter. On their arrival at Baker Street, Blake told the driver to wait, and, hurrying in, he waved Carslake into a chair.

'Wait here,' he said. 'If Inspector Thomas comes tell him I won't be many minutes.'

He hastened on through into the dressing-room, and there began rapidly to disrobe. From his exhaustive stock of disguises he chose that of a Chinaman, the disguise which several times before had proved so valuable in Limehouse, in half the Chinese quarters through the world, as well as in China itself.

Taken all in all, it was one of the most difficult of disguises to assume, for in order to pass muster it must be correct to the last detail. The eyes which would search him from head to foot were not eyes which saw only the surface, but which analysed and dissected. Consequently, it was only Blake's masterly capacity for detail, his perfect adaptability to the disguise, and his flawless command of the language which lent to his disguise the necessary value.

When he had completed his work he gazed at himself in the glass, and smiled a grim smile of satisfaction. Then he assumed once more the look which by pigments he had created, and, throwing open the door, stalked out.

Inspector Thomas had arrived while Blake was changing, and as the sleek-looking Celestial advanced into the consulting-room both he and Carslake leaped to their feet in consternation.

Blake smiled, and waved his hand: 'Be seated, gentlemen. I see my efforts have proved successful.'

'Well, by heavens, Blake, you are the limit!' gasped the inspector. 'But why did you wish to see me?'

'Good, inspector,' remarked Blake, seating himself at the desk. 'I like to see your anxiety to come to the point. How soon can you get together a dozen men and motor them through to Limehouse?'

'I don't understand,' replied the inspector.

Rapidly Blake sketched as much as he himself knew of the case he was on, omitting all details. Then as he finished he said: 'So you see, inspector, although I haven't the faintest idea where the gang is, I am positive it is in Limehouse, and I think I can find them. Now, how soon can you get your men together?'

'Twenty minutes,' answered the inspector promptly.

'Very well,' went on Blake. 'I wouldn't bring less than ten, for I am under the impression the gang is of no small proportions, and, from what I have seen of their methods, I think the lengths to which they are prepared to go are equally formidable. As I told you, inspector, I don't know who they are or what their motive is; but, in view of the facts I have succeeded in gathering, I think a prompt raid is essential. Now this is my plan.

'Carslake will take Pedro and go with you. Get your men together, and pile them into a motor. Then, if you proceed straight to Limehouse and turn down Limehill Lane which runs parallel to Belmere Road, you will come to the widow Green's house, which is the fifth from the further end.

'Go in the back way, and get her to place you where you can see me pass. I will saunter down Belmere Road until I reach the Chinese laundry two blocks down. Watch me when I go in, and if I come out with another Celestial, follow us. On your success in doing this the whole thing depends, for if you fail I have no doubt I shall never escape alive.

'As soon as you see me enter a house have your men surround it on all sides, and then do nothing until something happens inside. If you hear a revolver-shot you will know that is a signal to raid, and when you do, lose no time. Everything will depend on it. And don't forget, inspector, if, as I think, Sir George Halliday's murderer is there as well as his daughter, the capture will be a great feather in your cap.'

'I certainly appreciate your letting me in on this, Mr Blake,' answered the inspector. 'You can bank on my carrying out my end of it in every point,' he added fervently.

'Very well,' said Blake. 'If you will go now, and take Carslake, I will get away after you. Oh, by the way, Carslake, if I do gain admittance to the house which I think exists, and if a raid should take place, keep Pedro on the leash until you find me and then free him. He will do as good work as a man if necessary.'

Carslake promised he would do so, and, gratefully shaking hands, followed the inspector.

When they had gone Blake sat in deep thought for some time. Then he rose, and got the piece of coat which he had taken with him earlier in the morning. For some moments he contemplated it, then he stuck it in his jacket.

'I don't think it will be of any use now!' he muttered; 'but it won't do to neglect a single thread.'

Slowly he walked over and opened the safe. Lifting out the specimen bottle in which he had placed the Beetle the night before, he carried it to the window and held it up.

The Beetle had quite recovered from the state of coma into which the drug had cast it, and though he was accustomed to many strange things a thrill went up Blake's spine as for the first time the sinister creature and himself were face to face.

'I'm just as well pleased that you are safely in there,' he muttered. 'But, gad, what a creature you are!'

In the glint of morning sun the beetle's scaly wings shone like burnished gold. Its beady eyes glared malevolently through the glass at him, and the needle-like horn waved about angrily.

Blake gazed at it curiously for some moments; then, seeing that the cork was secure, he thrust the bottle in his jacket.

After that he slipped an extra clip of cartridges in beside his automatic, swung round, and made for the door.

Blake sat well back in the taxi until he reached the very fringe of Limehouse. There he directed the driver to continue on to the end of Belmere Road, when he descended.

A moment later there sauntered down through Belmere Road a well-dressed Celestial, with sleepy-looking almond eyes, and a yellow cigarette in his lips. The coolie class who passed him gazed at him respectfully, for his dress was of the superior caste, and his manner truly typical of that degree.

He kept on for several blocks, and had anyone been closely watching the front window of a certain small house, they might have seen a stealthy hand part the curtains, and a peak-capped, blue-uniformed man peer through. For a bare moment his eyes met the sleepy ones of the Celestial, then the Chinaman sauntered on, and the curtains fell into place again.

For two blocks more the Chinaman walked on until he reached a laundry, at one side of the door of which was the sign 'Looey Sing'. Here he turned, and, pushing open the door, which jangled a harsh bell as he did so, he shuffled in, and stood at the counter. Looey Sing himself happened to be industriously ironing collars, but as he looked up and saw the class of his visitor he hastily dropped the iron and advanced.

Contrary to the usual custom, the Celestial who had just entered did not speak, but after casting his sleepy eyes about he thrust his hand inside his jacket and drew out a small bottle. Keeping it covered by his hand, he pushed it forward until it was directly under Looey Sing's nose. Then he lifted his hand, and as Looey Sing saw the yellow, scaly beetle which it contained he bent over in an attitude of submission.

'What would you command your servant to do, Excellency?' he asked, in low, guttural tones, as the other thrust the bottle back in his jacket.

'You have already done well,' answered the newcomer slowly; 'but I have great and urgent news for the master. I have hurried on to London to the address he gave me. He had left, however, and I would go to him.'

'He left last night, Excellency,' answered Looey Sing; 'and is even now near.'

'Ah,' remarked the other slowly, 'I must see him at once! By the Beetle, I must see him! You will conduct me to him!'

'I obey, Excellency. Will you grant your servant a moment?'

Blake – for it was he – nodded. 'Be quick! My mission is urgent.'

And so by his masterly knowledge of the Celestial nature, plus his correct estimate of the power of the beetle, and his command of the language, did Blake enlist Looey Sing's innocent aid.

A moment later, with Blake beside him, Looey Sing shuffled out and turned to the left. Then he swung to the right, and headed towards the river. As he did so several blue-garbed men slipped into Belmere Road, and hastened cautiously after.

For less than five minutes Looey Sing shuffled on until he came to a rickety-looking building. There he turned down a narrow odorous alley beside it until he reached a low door.

Pressing a hidden button the door flew open, and he stood aside while his companion entered. Although the man Looey Sing called 'Excellency' gazed about him with the same sleepy eyes, the laundry-man never knew that his companion's pulse had gone the barest trifle quicker as on entering he had seen a limousine and a big touring-car. His manner betrayed no sign that the sight meant anything to him as he impassively waited for Looey Sing to close the door.

After he had snapped it to, the laundryman turned, and with a 'This way, Excellency!' led the way up a rickety flight of stairs. At the top he paused, and rapped on a panel. A low voice came from inside, bidding them in Chinese to enter.

Looey Sing pressed the secret button which released the panel, and as Blake entered he closed it and retreated down the stairs, to fall at once into the arms of Inspector Thomas and his men, who had lost no time in surrounding the building.

As soon as Blake entered the room he saw, sitting on a pile of vivid yellow cushions, a grave, dignified-looking Chinaman, who, he felt instinctively, was the man he sought.

His pulses hammered as he realised the fact, and he asked himself, had he, by the result of his mathematical analysis and deduction, coupled with pure audacity, finally reached the very source of the mysterious and deadly power which, as far as he knew, was but beginning to make itself felt in England? Had he by chance placed his hand on something big, something gigantic, which later would prove to have a bigger menace than any man knew? And by the same token could he, after all, capture them and nip the whole thing in the bud?'

These and a dozen other questions chased through Blake's mind in the brief second in which his eyes met those of the man on the cushions. Then, in pursuance of his plan, he bowed his head submissively as Looey Sing had done to him, and waited for the other to speak.

Wu Ling studied the bent head thoughtfully. In the Brotherhood of the Yellow Beetle there were thousands – yes, millions whom he had never seen. The man before him must be one of the number, but his evident high caste caused the subtle mind of the Celestial to wonder for a moment. But, as the other's head remained bent and he made no move, Wu Ling spoke.

'The sign!' he said briefly.

For answer Blake thrust his hand inside his jacket, and drew out the bottle which had had such an instantaneous effect upon Looey Sing. Still keeping his head bent submissively, he held it out, and as Wu Ling saw it he said: 'It is enough. Be seated. I will speak with you later.'

Blake moved over to the pile of cushions indicated by Wu Ling, and, squatting down, half closed his eyes, looking for all the world like a carved image of Buddha.

Then Wu Ling clapped his hands, and for the third time Blake's pulse quickened as another Celestial entered, holding by the arm a white girl garbed in black, and, with an angry constriction of the heart, Blake recognised Gertrude Halliday.

For a moment his fingers ached to grip his automatic, and then and there bring things to a head. But he wished to know more, and besides, a delay might tell him whether Tinker had also fallen into their hands, whereas a precipitate move might cause the instant death of all three of them.

He watched, therefore, with lowered lids, while Gertrude Halliday was led before Wu Ling, and the poor, terrified, sorrowing girl never dreamed that the sleek-looking Celestial on the cushions at one side was the only man in London at the moment who could combat the power of the web in which she had become entangled, and rescue her, if such a thing were possible.

As she was brought up before Wu Ling he gazed at her impassively.

'I trust you have rested well,' he said, in his unaccented English.

Gertrude made no reply, but waited.

'You, of course, realise, my dear young lady,' went on Wu Ling, 'that you have been brought here for a purpose.'

Gertrude bowed, and still waited.

'That purpose, like every other purpose, has a cause, my friend, and the cause has a price – a price which will purchase your freedom.'

'What is the price?' asked Gertrude, her lips trembling and her voice very low.

'I have reason to think,' replied Wu Ling, 'that your late father returned from the East with certain notes and memoranda to which he had no right. If he did, they are bound to be with his other papers, and the price of your freedom is as follows.

'You are to write a note requesting that all his papers be handed to the man who shall bear it. They will be brought here, and I myself will go over them. I pledge you my word that beyond retaining the notes I wish, I will hand you back all the others. It is now ten-thirty. If you despatch a note at once they can be here by noon, and your release will immediately follow. What is your answer?'

'My answer is "No! Decidedly no!"' replied Gertrude, in quivering tones.

'Ah,' remarked Wu Ling, in his deadly pleasant voice, 'then I take it you have no desire to attend your father's funeral?'

'Oh,' gasped Gertrude, 'you couldn't – you wouldn't dare to do such a thing!'

'My dear young lady, the sooner you learn that I can and do intend doing exactly that, the sooner we shall come to terms!'

'You mean you – would – keep me a prisoner here like that?' she gasped.

'Your sense of perception is marvellous!' murmured Wu Ling.

'I can't purchase my freedom at such a price!' wailed Gertrude, breaking down. 'Oh, won't you listen and set me free?'

Wu Ling's expression never altered.

'That sort of thing will do you no good,' he said. 'Come, answer at once! If you don't consent, I will not only keep you here until after the funeral, but send you secretly to China. That and nothing but that will I do. Now, what is your answer?'

'Then – I – con – ' began Gertrude, terrified at the threat; but she broke off as the sleek-looking Chinaman at the side got slowly to his feet and swung round.

Then as the other gazed at him his sleepy eyes opened wide, and his indolent manner dropped from him like lightning. His hand dropped, and when it reappeared it held unshakingly a businesslike looking automatic of heavy calibre.

'Her answer is – no!' he said suavely. 'Miss Halliday, you will not worry any more. I am a friend, and there are a dozen more outside.'

Turning to Wu Ling, he said, in the same suave tones: 'Since you are so emphatic about what you can and will do, let me inform you that I am equally so. It is my intention to make a clean hole in the very centre of your forehead if you so much as move a finger. In addition to that' – he jerked over his shoulder at the man holding Gertrude, who happened to be San – 'I will end your career very suddenly if you try to leave.'

Wu Ling, to do him justice, never changed expression in the faintest degree. Instead, he smiled his pleasant smile and said smoothly: 'You are a brave man, and I think I can guess your identity – Sexton Blake. Am I right?'

Blake bowed ironically as Wu Ling continued: 'It is evident that things were badly bungled last night. I was under the impression that long ere this you had paid the penalty.'

'Instead, I gained admittance to you by using the instrument which I succeeded in capturing,' murmured Blake, secretly admiring the quality of his foe.

'Ah, yes; the beetle!' replied Wu Ling. 'Really, I think you are the only man living who has achieved such a thing. It is a pity, therefore, that you are fated to be dropped into several hundreds of them.'

'Indeed!' replied Blake. 'I think you are mistaken. I forgot to mention at this moment the house is entirely surrounded, and that by a prearranged signal my men will in a very few moments be coming up.'

'I am glad you told me,' replied Wu Ling. Then, in a sharp tone, he said: 'San!'

Blake, knowing from the tone that some move was intended, swung sharply but the wily San was not to be caught. Grasping

Gertrude firmly by the arms, he held her forcibly in front of him, and, using her thus as a shield began backing towards the silken yellow draperies through which he had come.

Blake's jaws snapped like a steel trap as he saw what was happening, and for the moment disregarding San's move, he turned back to Wu Ling.

The cunning Celestial, however, had not wasted any time in taking advantage of Blake's turning. Momentary as it was, it gave him the opportunity he desired, and, even as Blake turned, Wu Ling's lithe, yellow-clad body shot upward and forward, with the force of a catapult.

Blake braced his legs and took the shock on his hip, then, as San vanished through the draperies with the terrified Gertrude, he pulled the trigger of his automatic.

A moment later the revolver went flying to the floor, while he and Wu Ling whirled about the room in a mad tangle of straining limbs and heaving chests, Blake trying to bring things to a sudden finish by a throat-hold, while Wu Ling strained every nerve to get at his knife.

Then, in the very midst of the struggle, both combatants fell apart in one of those unintentional mutual movements, and Blake's eyes gleamed as he saw Wu Ling suddenly assume a correct boxing attitude.

The detective was, for the moment, surprised at such an attitude in a Celestial, for it is by no means the Oriental method of fighting. He did not know then, however, that with his insatiable desire to learn every detail of the lives of the Occidentals, whom he hated, Wu Ling had trained long and hard, and was no mean exponent of the 'noble art'.

Blake was not slow to assume a like position, and once more the two Oriental-clad figures went at it – their methods strangely at variance with their garb.

Blake dropped his head in a cautious crouch, and took Wu Ling's hail of blows on his forearm. Then suddenly his right came up and his left shot out in a clean hook to the jaw.

As Wu Ling shuddered from the shock, Blake swayed back easily, and slid a vicious jab off his arm. Then his right shot out, catching Wu Ling on the shoulder, while his left fell a trifle short.

Barely had he swung back, when Wu Ling rushed to a clinch, hailing a stream of blows over Blake's shoulder, in an endeavour to use the unsportsmanlike kidney punch.

Blake blocked with his fists against Wu Ling's chest, and, as he gradually worked free from the clinch, he insinuated his right fist up and up until it was in a perfect line with his opponent's chin.

Then, as he finally pushed free, he whipped it up like a steel piston-rod, catching Wu Ling fair on the point. The impetus of the blow lifted the Celestial clean off his feet, and as he feebly dropped his hand to his knife, Blake drove a straight left to the face, which sent him like a bundle of broken chips into the corner, where he lay still.

Panting, but grimly pleased, Blake bent quickly and picked up his revolver.

At that moment the draperies parted, and a horde of Celestials, led by San, dashed in, just as a furious pounding came from outside.

Inspector Thomas and his men had heard the shot, but were unable to locate the secret panel which gave entrance into the room.

Blake knew he must reach that spot at all costs, and, unless he acted quickly, the horde of crazy Chinamen would block his way. Levelling his revolver, he dashed forward, but San and his men were not to be baulked. The sight of the illustrious Wu Ling lying crumpled up against the wall filled them with a frenzy, and with a low, ominous mutter, they drew their knives, and rushed forward.

Blake saw that unless he acted rapidly he was done for. Once before he had stood in a tight corner under a hail of knives thrown by the unerring aim of the Celestial, but then he had a companion to hurl them back.

He had no more time to think, however, for a knife shot straight through the air and cut the silken jacket where it touched his shoulder.

Dashing forward, he began firing the automatic, while a terrific hubbub broke out from the inspector and his men on the other side of the panel.

Then pandemonium reigned. To the accompaniment of curses, howls, poundings, flying knives, and the vicious spitting of the automatic, Blake rushed the gang and gained the panel. Risking a crooked blade in the back, he turned, and kicked on the panel, just as the assault from outside succeeded, and the inspector and his men tumbled in head over heels.

As they did so, a startling change took place. San and his men, instead of putting up any resistance, fled through the draperies, and Blake leaped to his feet.

'Quick!' he gasped, pushing two men towards Wu Ling. 'Tie him up and take him out. He is the chief one.'

Then, leaping forward, he cried: 'Come on, inspector, with your men.'

Something at that moment shot over the heads of all and landed beside Blake. It was Pedro, who had broken free from Carslake's hold, and side by side master and dog led the way.

Tearing the draperies aside Blake rushed on through a narrow corridor. At the end was a flight of stairs, and crowded together were the Celestials, evidently prepared for a last stand before fleeing. At this point Pedro left Blake and dashed down a side corridor, and Blake, pointing to the massed Chinamen, shouted: 'On! on! don't let one escape.'

A momentary hush followed, before the rush took place, and in the lull Blake heard a far-away voice shouting: 'Help, guv'nor – help! I can't hold out!'

Blake's eyes blazed as he recognised Tinker's voice, and shouting to the inspector to lead the charge, he dashed down the corridor where Pedro had disappeared, knowing instinctively that the bloodhound had scented his young master. His brows knit in puzzlement as he reached the end, and found Pedro tearing and growling apparently at the bare wall. Knowing sufficient of the Oriental nature, however, to know that it was undoubtedly a panel, he rapped on it sharply, and was rewarded by a hollow sound. Then, from the other side, came Tinker's voice in weak accents: 'Guv'nor! Guv'nor! I can't hold out. Miss Halliday is here, too.'

'Hang on, Tinker,' shouted Blake. 'I'll be through in a minute.'

Feverishly Blake searched the wall for the secret button which would open the panel. Each moment seemed like an eternity, but he gasped with relief as a point in the wall yielded to his fingers, and what was apparently the end of the corridor flew open.

He caught his breath and leaped forward, however, as the blazing light of the mirrored room flashed out at him. For a moment the horror of the sight shook him with tempestuous anger, but, as Pedro leaped forward, Blake grasped his collar and pulled him back. Then he dashed through the panel.

The sight which had met his eyes had told Blake in a flash what had happened. A hot dry wave came from the steel floor, which was now moving swiftly.

Although she had only been thrust into the mirrored room when San had escaped by using her as a shield, Gertrude was nearly exhausted in her endeavour to keep on the floor and not be swept over the curved edge into the mass of deadly beetles below.

Tinker had for hours and hours been a victim of its exquisite torture. First having had to walk briskly in order to keep on it, as its speed gradually increased, and as the steel grew hotter, he had been compelled to break into a dog-trot, and from that into a brisk run.

It was for all the world like a heated treadmill, and Blake knew only too well the horror and the torture of it. Mirrored on every side were the horrible crawling beetles, while at his throat was the saturated piece of cotton wool, which would, did he go over the edge through the thin glass, bring upon him the whole horde of deadly creatures. Even now, as Blake reached the room, he was perilously near the edge, but his master lost not a moment.

Grasping Gertrude, he unceremoniously dragged her clear into the passage, and then dashed in to Tinker's assistance. It seemed, however, that he would be too late, for, with a choking gasp, Tinker reeled, and slid towards the edge, carried onwards by the swiftly-moving floor.

Blake gasped and reached out, and just as the lad went over, he grasped him by the arm. For a bare moment there was a maddening suspense. Then Blake heaved, and as Tinker's toes scraped the fragile glass which was the only barrier between him and death, Blake swung him clear.

Truly, it was the 'room of madness'. Once over the edge, Blake trod the swiftly-moving floor until he got to the panel. As he did so, the flying figure of a Chinaman tore down the passage, and leaped for the button which would close the panel. Had he been possessed of the speed and strength of a dozen men, however, it would have been impossible for Blake to prevent the threatened calamity. But Pedro, with teeth bared, sprang forward straight as an arrow, his jaws coming together like a steel trap in the throat of the Chinaman.

Blake gained the safety of the corridor in the momentary respite and dragged Pedro free. As he did so, however, the Chinaman with a crimson stain on his jacket staggered to the other side of the corridor apparently to lean against it for support.

Blake saw all too late what he was really doing. He leaped forward, but not soon enough to prevent the Chinaman pressing another button.

Something inside the mirrored room dropped. A sudden wave of pungent perfume swept along the corridor and through the whole house, and then, as a splintering crash of glass followed, there came an angry rattle of scaly wings as the thin glass barrier imprisoning the beetles was broken and the whole mass sailed upwards.

With a lightning-like spring Blake picked up Gertrude and shouted: 'Rip that wool from your throat, Tinker, and follow me. Our lives depend on it. Quick!'

Placing Gertrude over his shoulder, he dashed forward, followed by Tinker dragging Pedro, who seemed to freeze stiff as the horrible rustle of scaly wings met his ears.

When they reached the end of the corridor the other Celestials and the inspector's men were nowhere to be seen. Only Carslake was wandering about vainly searching for Gertrude, and as he saw Blake he dashed forward.

'Quick! Come on!' panted Blake, and Carslake had perforce to follow.

Through the room where he had fought with Wu Ling dashed Blake, and thrust Gertrude through the open panel. Then he pushed the others through and banged the panel, just as the angry whirring beetles flapped madly against it.

'Come on! Take Miss Halliday, Carslake. The brutes will be through that panel unless the odour in the house is strong enough to drug them first into insensibility.'

He led the way down the rickety stairs, and as he turned into the temporary garage he saw on the floor the two men who had taken charge of Wu Ling, while only the limousine remained. The touring car had disappeared.

Vaguely apprehensive, Blake dragged them out into the yard, and as he did so, heard the sound of firing near the front.

Hastening around with Tinker and Pedro, he was just in time to see the inspector and his men firing a fusillade of bullets at several Chinamen in the windows above, who in turn were firing back and keeping up a deadly hail of flashing knives.

Then, as though by a prearranged signal, every head disappeared, and Blake shouted: 'Around to the back, inspector!'

Drawing his revolver, and slipping in a fresh clip he had brought, he tore round, while Tinker stopped only long enough to snatch a couple of knives from the ground.

What had become of Wu Ling Blake had no idea, nor had he time to wonder, for as he reached the rear alley from one end, and the inspector and his men from the other, the whole horde of Celestials poured out through the door armed to the teeth.

Then began a fight in the narrow alley which will go down forever in the annals of Limehouse. Up and down it raged, the Chinamen fighting with the desperation born of a forlorn hope, while the Scotland Yard men were filled with a savage determination to bring things to a head quickly.

Then, in the very midst of the struggle, while bullets were zipping and knives flying, there came a sudden interruption. A ragged Celestial stumbled out of the garage, waved his arms weakly, and collapsed just as a terrific explosion shook the ground beneath their feet and sent the roof and walls crashing inwards.

In the hail of flying debris the Celestials made a concerted rush to break the barrier, but the inspector's men roped them in, and ten minutes later wounded and unwounded alike were lying bound, just as the flames spurted upwards from the wrecked building.

Blake and Tinker, who had been holding their end of the alley from being rushed, and covering the rear of the Celestials, were mopping their brows as the inspector hurried up.

'Gad! we got 'em,' he said breathlessly. 'This is a great haul, Blake. I thought once they were going to get clear.'

'How?' asked Blake.

'Well! when you left us up in the corridor the fiends disappeared through some panel in the wall before we could reach them. I thought it was a secret way out and made for the alley, but they were nowhere to be seen. On getting around to the other side, though, we saw a ladder hanging from the window, and one of them was just preparing to descend. They drew back, however, and we opened fire. Then you rushed up. But what happened to you?'

'I'll tell you later,' replied Blake. 'What became of the fellow your two men were to look after?'

'I don't know,' answered the inspector. 'They were lying over there wounded. Come over, and we'll ask them.'

Blake did so, but could get nothing from either of the men but a rambling tale. It seems that they picked Wu Ling up and carried him down the stairs into the garage, intending to bind him there.

At the head of the stairs, however, he seemed to suddenly come to life. One of the men he kicked viciously, sending him headlong to the bottom. Then, drawing his knife, he turned on the other. Over and over they rolled to the bottom, but Wu Ling landed on top, and, leaving his knife in the other's shoulder, he had leaped into the touring-car.

While the fight was raging up above he had started the car and apparently got clean away. The inspector's joy over the capture received a shock when Blake muttered savagely on hearing the news and turned curtly.

His brow cleared, however, as Carslake came up with Gertrude, who had recovered, and as the fire brigade rolled up at that moment the little party moved clear while the inspector and his men hastened to get their prisoners into the patrol-waggon, which had also arrived.

Blake and Tinker looked after Gertrude while Carslake procured a cab, and, piling in the whole party, left the scene.

'I'll see you later,' said Blake to the inspector as he departed, and sinking back, closed his eyes.

On their arrival at the Halliday home Gertrude's aunt met them with a look of fright on her face.

Oh!' she cried, 'I am so glad you have come. But why have you brought this Chinaman? What does he want?'

Blake smiled grimly as Carslake explained that it was a disguise.

'But what has happened?' he asked.

'Not half an hour ago,' she said, 'a big motor stopped out in front. The butler answered the door, and a Chinaman rushed in. He went at once to the library and forced open the safe with something. We didn't dare go near for he threatened to shoot us. I sent the butler for a policeman, and when he came in he rushed straight through.'

'The Chinaman, however, got away by the French window, and climbed over the wall. The policeman followed him, but the other was too quick. He ran through Colonel Porter's house, and coming out of the front door, jumped into the car and drove off at once. The policeman has gone to report it.'

'And you have discovered that he took some of Sir George's papers, I presume?' remarked Blake grimly.

'Oh, yes, but how did you know?'

Blake made no reply, but he and Gertrude exchanged glances of understanding.

Then, turning, he said: 'Come, Tinker, let us be going.'

On Blake's evidence San got the limit of the law for kidnapping Gertrude, but so persistently did the doctors hammer any suggestion of foul play in the death of Sir George and Tom Green, that Blake kept silent. In the absence of Sir George's notes, he really had only his own facts to go on, but as he thought of the reality of the Yellow Beetle, he vowed the future should bring him again face to face with the elusive Wu Ling. The rest of the captured gang were deported, but all trace seemed to have been lost of Wu Ling.

The only consolation Blake felt was three months later when he and Tinker attended the quiet wedding of Carslake and Gertrude, for the pallor of her drawn features had given place to a healthier flush, and Carslake looked manfully determined to make her happy.

Thus ended Sexton Blake's first struggle with Wu Ling, once prince of the realm, and now head of the movement which had evolved from the chaotic condition of affairs during the fall of the Manchu dynasty, and of whose purpose Sexton Blake was at present only dimly aware.

A CASE OF ARSON

Robert Murray Graydon

THE PROLOGUE

1

The solitary occupant of the taxicab that was bowling smoothly down North Audley Street leaned forward in his seat and tapped sharply on the window. In obedience to the summons, the driver applied his feet to the clutch and the brake, and drew his vehicle up alongside the kerb.

'You're one of the few honest cabbies I've ever had the good fortune to meet,' drawled the young man in the opera hat and the evening-dress, as he stepped out on to the pavement and slipped a hand in his pocket, 'I've come here dozens of times before, and you're the first man for months who's brought me by the shortest and quickest route.'

He dropped a couple of half-crowns into the chauffeur's ready palm, and, swinging his gold-mounted cane, strolled leisurely away.

By the light of the street-lamps one could have seen that he was good-looking, well-set-up, and immaculately dressed. His clothes fitted him to perfection, and he carried them with that unmistakable air of good breeding that is typical of le *haute-monde*.

The cigar-case, from which he halted to extract a fragrant Corona Corona, was composed of the same precious metal that adorned the top of his ebony stick, as was the matchbox from which he produced a light.

Not one of the prime attributes of life was lacking – health glowed in his ruddy cheeks and clear eyes, wealth was obviously marked by his habiliment and possessions, and happiness must have been there; if not happiness, at least self-satisfaction, to judge by the light air that he was humming.

For about a hundred yards from the spot where he had left the taxi he continued on his way, and then turned off sharply to the left down a street that was lined on either side with big, five-storeyed mansions that would not have been out of place in Park Lane.

Brilliant lights shone from the majority of them, gaudily-bedecked footmen lounged in the imposing pillared porticos, and there were at least half a dozen luxurious private cars drawn up alongside the pavement.

From a distance came the haunting sob of a violin, the bow wielded by a master-hand, and the liquid notes of Covent Garden opera's latest prima donna, evidently the lion – or rather, lioness – of some aristocratic assembly.

The young man in the evening-dress suddenly flung away his partially-consumed cigar, and skipped lightly up the broad steps of one of the houses that was not so brightly illuminated as were the others. Save for a crimson glow shining from the fanlight above the big double doors, the place was in darkness.

Slipping his fingers through the letter-box, he found and pressed a tiny knob, which he knew from past experience to be there. Three times he pressed it, the last time keeping his finger on it for a space of several seconds.

Almost at once the door swung silently open, and closed quickly behind him as he slipped past the thickset manservant in the sober-hued livery into the luxuriously-furnished but dimly-lighted hall.

'Evening, Carfax!' said the young man lightly. 'Many here tonight?'

'About the usual, sir,' replied the manservant stolidly, as he took the newcomer's hat and coat and gave him a numbered slip. 'You will go straight down?'

The young man nodded carelessly, and, smoothing his fair hair back, lounged off down the corridor. At the end was a flight of stairs, which he descended, and at the foot of which stood another manservant – a muscular, pugilistic-looking individual, clad in the same sober-hued livery.

Pausing for a moment, the newcomer drew a tiny gold badge from his pocket and fastened it in the lapel of his coat. Enamelled upon it in red letters was the number '36'.

The manservant was standing before what was evidently and apparently a blank wall; but, after casting one glance at the gold badge, he pressed a certain spot, and a cunningly-concealed door slid silently open, revealing another passage beyond.

From within, in striking contrast to the dead silence that had previously reigned, came the hum of many voices, masculine and feminine, the clink of glasses, the popping of corks, and a clicking noise.

Extracting another cigar from his case and lighting up, the young man passed quickly along the passage, and, drawing aside a heavy curtain, stepped through.

It was a strange and bizarre scene that lay before him. A vast saloon, luxuriously carpeted and brilliantly illuminated by a hundred delicately-shaded electric-lights. In the centre were three long, green-baize-covered tables. The first was marked out for roulette, and it was the skipping of the ivory ball on the revolving wheel that made the clicking sound.

The second table was laid out like a miniature racecourse, with starting-gate and winning-post complete, and with tiny miniature racehorses, moving each in its separate groove.

The third table was spread for *trente-et-quarante.*

It was nothing less than a miniature Monte Carlo into which the young man had stepped, and the company was just as select. The big room was crowded with men in evening dress, and gorgeously-gowned women, whose white necks, dainty ears, and slender fingers were a-shimmer with sparkling jewels.

But all were similar in one respect. In the glittering eyes and on the flushed cheeks of each one was indelibly stamped the feverish spirit of lust and greed as they clustered around the tables, casting various coloured counters on the roulette-board, backing their fancy at the *petits chevaux*, or trusting to the luck of the cards at *trente-et-quarante.*

In one corner of the room was a marble-countered buffet. At one end were set out plates of dainty sandwiches, portions of cold meats and salads, and baskets of choice fruits. The other end was fitted up as an American bar, and a lantern-jawed man in a white drill coat, backed by a heterogeneous array of bottles, was busy mixing drinks by the aid of a silver shaker and a swizzle-stick.

In another corner, safely ensconced behind a steel grille, sat a Jewish-looking gentleman with a vast expanse of snowy shirt-front, who was busily and obligingly selling counters, giving change, and cashing cheques.

Everyone present in the swell gambling-hell – for such it was – was evidently like Caesar's wife, above suspicion.

The scene was evidently no new one to the young man who had just entered. He suppressed a yawn with a slightly bored air as he lounged across the big saloon to the marble bar and ordered a champagne cocktail, which he consumed at one gulp.

'Alone tonight, Chester?' drawled an insipid-looking youth with no chin, and evidently more money than brains, as he hurried past on his way to the roulette-table, counting over a sheaf of rustling notes as he went. 'My luck's clean out, confound it. I've just dropped a monkey straight off the reel!'

Dirk Dolland, alias Derek Chester, and known to the criminal world and the police of three continents as the Bat – the most impertinent, audacious, cunning, unprincipled, elusive, and polished gentleman crook and cracksman who had wormed his way into select circles – set his empty glass down and fingered his closely-cropped moustache.

As Derek Chester – the latest name that he had taken to conceal his identity – he had worked up a reputation as being a young man of good family, large means, and extravagant and profligate habits – the beau ideal man about town, who could gamble away five hundred pounds in one night without turning a hair, and win ten times that amount with a bored air, as though it was too much trouble to take the money.

As Dirk Dolland, the Bat – an identity that he had successfully sunk since Sexton Blake, the famous private detective, of Baker Street, had so nearly brought his nefarious career to a close – he was known as one of the cleverest criminals of modern times, a master of disguise and elusiveness, and the man who had so far triumphantly evaded all the human bloodhounds and picked brains of Mulberry Street, New York, the Préfecture in Paris, and Scotland Yard, London.

And yet, as Derek Chester, the Bat still pursued his unchecked career of crime, and Samuel Otzmann's – a name well known as that of a respectable Argentine millionaire – gambling-hell, in which he now stood, was one of his most profitable hunting-grounds.

There he found many birds to pluck – birds with golden feathers, who, though they occasionally found themselves robbed of much of their plumage, never for one instant allowed their suspicions to turn in his direction.

Derek Chester was one of the best! Derek Chester was a good sport, and as straight as a die! And meanwhile Derek Chester laughed up his sleeve at the blindness of the guileless fools whom he had so completely duped.

As a gentleman cracksman he was schooled to the highest state of perfection. His personal equipment was complete in every detail. At any time, had he so chosen, he could have commanded a princely salary on the variety stage as a quick-change artist, a mimic, or a conjurer. But it was utterly foreign to the Bat's nature to run straight. It was as impossible as for an Ethiopian to change his skin or a leopard its spots.

He was a born criminal, and what was in the blood could not be eradicated. A grant of a million a year for life would not have altered his mode of life. It was not a love of gain or necessity that made a criminal of him, but sheer spirit and love of adventure.

Ordering and consuming another cocktail, the Bat strolled across to the Semitic individual behind the iron grille, and, exchanging a sheaf of banknotes for a handful of various-coloured ivory counters, he made his way across to the roulette-table, and slipped quietly into a vacant place.

Many people nodded to him, and opposite stood the insipid youth who had lately addressed him, and whose luck, to judge by his expression, was still out.

Casually the Bat threw a crimson counter – the value of which was five pounds – upon the number 13, in direct defiance to its reputed evil reputation. The croupier spun the wheel that set the little ivory ball clicking and skipping on its journey until it lodged silently into one of the tiny compartments.

'Black – thirteen,' said the croupier, picking up his long-handled rake; and envious glances were cast at the Bat as he lazily scooped up the pile of crimson counters that was pushed towards him.

Five of them he placed on red. Red won, and the Bat left his winnings where they were. Four times in succession the red turned up ere he removed the growing pile of counters to his pocket.

'Mr Chester, your luck is supernatural,' gushed a stout, diamond-bedecked woman in a daring emerald-green gown, and with hair of the latest fashionable colour. 'You never seem to lose. I only wish I had followed you! Do tell me! What do you think will win this time?'

The Bat shrugged his shoulders, and there was a curious little smile in his blue eyes.

'Take your age, Lady Beaker, and see if that will bring you luck,' he said politely.

Lady Beaker looked a trifle nonplussed, and then, without a blush, deliberately placed a couple of red counters on the number thirty.

The croupier spun the wheels again, and after a mad dance of defiance the little ivory ball slid meekly to rest.

'Number Forty-five wins!'

Lord Beaker, a choleric-looking, red-faced man, with pouchy eyes, who was seated at the other side of the table, uttered a snort of annoyance.

'Lydia, you're a confounded idiot!' he snapped, with more heat than politeness, as he glared across at his wife. 'Why didn't you do as Chester told you? You'll never get a chance like that again.'

A little titter of laughter ran round the table, and, slipping his counters into his pocket, the Bat strolled away. And as he went the gorgeous, diamond-encrusted comb that had a moment before shimmered in Lady Beaker's auburn tresses became conspicuous by its absence.

'Worth three hundred at least,' muttered the Bat appraisingly, as he fingered it in his pocket. 'I think my luck must be in tonight.'

There was no doubt that the Bat's luck was in that night. In ten minutes he had won another fifty pounds at the *trente-et-quarante* table, when, tired of the game, he flung himself down in an armchair in one of the numerous alcoves that surrounded the big room, and gave himself up to the enjoyment of a cigar.

He had a pleasurable sense that he had not come to Otzmann's for nothing that night. He had won just on two hundred pounds at the tables, and the diamond hair-comb – which Lady Beaker would probably be advertising for the next morning as having been lost in a taxi – would bring him in at least another three hundred.

For several minutes he sat idly scanning the crowded room before he became cognisant of the sound of voices in the next alcove to his. One voice was familiar to him, and, cautiously lifting the curtain a trifle, he peered through. Nothing was too slight to attract the attention of the Bat. His eyes and ears were always on the alert.

The broad-shouldered, elderly man, with the bristling grey moustache, he knew for Colonel Eustace Boden, a retired Army officer, with a short temper, a long purse, and an insatiable mania for gambling. He generally lost, and it was evident from his expression and bearing that that had proved no exception to the rule.

The man who was addressing him was a tall, lean individual, with a sallow, hatchet face, and a pair of shrewd grey eyes.

He was quietly garbed, and wore a magnificent solitaire diamond in his tie, that at once excited the Bat's professional instincts.

'I believe I have the pleasure of addressing Colonel Eustace Boden?' drawled the tall man, in unmistakable American accents.

'The pleasure is indeed yours!' snapped the colonel irritably.

The tall man was in no way nonplussed by the frigidness of his reception.

'Allow me to introduce myself,' he said coolly, extracting a slip of pasteboard from a gold cardcase, and laying it on the small copper-topped table. 'My name is Cyrus C. Crag, of New York.'

The Bat gave a slight start, and a light of renewed interest crept into his blue eyes. Cyrus C. Crag was a name to conjure with. Who had not heard of the famous American Railroad King, whose fortune was reputed to run into twelve million sterling?

But the name seemed to make no impression on Colonel Eustace Boden.

'I haven't the pleasure!' he said stiffly, paying no attention to the proffered card.

'That is why I am taking the liberty of introducing myself,' drawled the American, calmly sinking into a chair, and flinging one leg over the other. 'I shan't take up more than a couple of minutes of your time, Colonel Boden, and I will come straight to the point. I believe you are fortunate enough to be the possessor of that world-famous old master, the Corottzi "Venus"?'

Colonel Boden knitted his bushy brows, and his moustache seemed to positively bristle.

'I am, sir!' he snapped curtly.

'Wal, I reckon I want to buy it, colonel. I understand it's valued at fifty thousand pounds. I'll give you seventy thousand.'

Colonel Boden positively jumped out of his chair, his broad shoulders quivering with indignation.

'I'll have you understand, sir,' he rapped fiercely, 'that the Corottzi "Venus" is not for sale – not to you or any other jumped-up, swollen-headed Yankee who thinks that he can get the whole earth with his almighty dollars! The Corottzi "Venus" belongs to me. And when I have no further use for it, it will go to the British nation! I consider your offer an insult!'

'But I consider it a plain, business proposition,' replied Cyrus C. Crag blandly. 'Come, colonel, I'm dead-set on having that there little painting in my collection. I'll give you a hundred thousand pounds for it.'

'Not for five hundred thousand!' barked the colonel. 'You have had my answer, sir. Further conversation is unnecessary and undesirable!'

The American millionaire shrugged his square shoulders.

' "*Nil desperandum*" is my motto, colonel,' he said slowly. 'Don't think me rude, put it down to persistency – obstinacy, what you like. That Corottzi of yours has drawn me across the Herring-pond like a magnet. You may change your mind later on. If you should, I am staying at the Ritz. You can name your own price.'

Colonel Eustace Boden's reply was to turn his back deliberately on the American and stride pompously away.

'Stiff-necked old cuss!' muttered Cyrus C. Crag, jamming his hands in his trousers-pockets, and staring quizzically after the ex-Army man. 'Reckon that's what they call British insularity! Never mind! I guess he's dropped a bit tonight, and that's what's put him out of sorts! I'll have another shot at him tomorrow, for, by gum, I don't mean to go back home without that there "Venus"! Not yours truly!'

He wandered off leisurely, and no sooner had he been swallowed up in the gay throng than the Bat had sprung to his feet, and, lifting the curtain, slipped quietly into the next alcove.

Cyrus C. Crag's card was still on the table where he had placed it, and, picking it up, he put it carefully in his pocket, and sank into the chair recently occupied by Colonel Eustace Boden.

'Phew! One hundred thousand pounds for a scrap of canvas, with a few daubs of paint on it!' he muttered, under his breath. 'That's a fancy price for an old master, if you like. I only wish the Barottzi "Venus" was mine to dispose of. I'd soon have Mr Cyrus C. Crag's cheque in my pocket. As it is he'll never get it, unless he steals it. Colonel Boden means what he says.'

One hundred thousand pounds! The Bat's mouth watered at the thought of such a sum. He had brought off some big coups in his time, but nothing approaching such an enormous amount.

'Now, I wonder if I can make anything of this?' mused the gentleman cracksman, lighting another cigar and leaning back in his chair. 'I'm glad I was in that next alcove, for it seems to me that what I have overheard tonight opens up a prospect of something that is worth serious consideration. Nothing so orthodox and crude as stealing the colonel's "Venus" – which I have no doubt I could easily do. From what I know of Cyrus C. Crag he is not the sort of man to buy stolen property. H'm! This is decidedly interesting!'

For over half an hour the Bat sat, puffing steadily at his cigar, and, though there was a placid expression on his boyish countenance, his clear, finely-balanced brain was working at high pressure. Put to a better use it would rapidly have elevated him to the topmost pinnacle of any profession he might have taken up.

Gradually a strange glint crept into his blue eyes, and, with startling impetuosity, he suddenly sprang to his feet, and gave vent to a sharp exclamation of satisfaction.

'By the Lord Harry,' he muttered, in awed tones, 'I believe I've hit it – I believe I've struck the right idea! If only it can be carried out, it'll be the greatest coup of the century! Dirk, my boy, you're improving in your old age! If this doesn't give Scotland Yard and Sexton Blake something to think about – well, call me a fool!'

Suppressing his excitement, and assuming his usual expression of chronic boredom, he lounged across to the American bar, and, ordering a drink, asked for the *London Directory*, which he knew was kept there.

Hastily he flipped over the pages, and as he found that which he sought he gave a visible start of amazement, and a faint flush of colour crept into his pale cheeks.

'Of all the luck,' he muttered to himself – 'of all the colossal luck! Gee! would you have believed it? Dirk, my boy, here's luck!'

Tossing off his drink, he shot a keen glance around the room until his eyes came to rest upon the upright figure of Colonel Eustace Boden, who had apparently succumbed to the fascinations of the roulette-board in an attempt to retrieve his losses.

Casually the Bat took up his stand within a few feet of the man, and for a space of five minutes his keen scrutiny never left the colonel's face. Every lineament of his features, every little natural action was indelibly engraven upon his memory ere he suddenly swung round on his heel, and left Samuel Otzmann's swell gambling-hell in the semi-secret way in which he had entered it.

He was fortunate enough to find a taxi a few doors up the street, and attracted the driver's attention with a wave of his stick.

'Linden Lodge, Beech Avenue, Roehampton,' he said to the man, as he stepped inside. 'It's a bit off the map; but I'll make it worth your while, especially if you hustle.'

It was not often that the Bat allowed himself to get into such a state of excitement as had gripped him that night.

The rich haul he had made at Otzmann's that evening paled into insignificance in comparison with the possibilities of the scheme that his fertile brain had evolved.

He could scarce repress his feelings as the taxi bowled past Hyde Park Corner and on through High Street, Kensington, to Hammersmith Broadway. With scarcely a check it hummed over the suspension bridge, and up Castlenau to Barnes Common. At the farther side of the common the cab turned into Roehampton Lane, and close to the village it turned down a road, where one might almost have imagined they were in the country.

'First turning on the right,' said the Bat, sticking his head out of the window.

There was an air of placid prosperity about the big, stately houses – one might almost have called them mansions – in Beech Avenue. In appearance and construction they were almost identical, each standing in its own spacious grounds, with a broad, horseshoe-shaped carriage-drive sweeping up from the double pair of gates.

The driver drew up before the one on which was painted in white letters the name 'The Lindens', and, jumping out, the Bat handed him a pound note and bade him a curt goodnight.

He stood for a moment watching the cab drive off, and then, making no attempt to enter the gate behind him, walked quickly down the road. Three other houses he passed, and then halted outside the fourth.

Painted across the top bar of the gate in Gothic letters was the name 'Delhi Lodge'. The Bat studied it critically, with his head on one side, and then swiftly retraced his footsteps to the Lindens, strode up the drive to the house, and let himself in with a latch-key.

There was a light in the tastefully-furnished hall, but the front rooms on either side were in darkness. Hanging his hat and coat up on the stand, he made his way down the passage and pushed open a door at the end. A blaze of light and a flood of fragrant tobacco-smoke greeted him as he entered the room.

Three men were lounging in comfortable easy-chairs before the roaring fire in the grate, and a Moorish table, with a silver tray bearing a tantalus, syphons and glass, stood between them.

'Hallo! Here's the night-bird returned! Any luck, my youth paragon of all the virtues?'

The Bat closed the door behind him, and took up his stand with his back to the crackling logs.

Had Scotland Yard cast its net over the Lindens at that moment, it would have made such a haul as would have sent Sir Henry Fairfax and all his satellites almost delirious with joy.

Upon the right of the fireplace sat a little, narrow-chested man, with a wizened face lit by a pair of remarkably alert and birdlike eyes. His name was Nicholas Mark – sometimes known as 'Nick the Nib' – and he was one of the cleverest forgers who had ever laid pen to paper in his nefarious trade. No signature was beyond his skill, no bank balance safe whilst he remained outside prison walls.

Opposite him sat a tall, immaculately-dressed man with raven-black hair, and a carefully-trimmed beard and moustache of the same colour. His eyes were hard and cold, and had he been walking anywhere in the vicinity of the Law Courts or Chancery Lane anyone would have pointed him out and named him as Brandon Delmas, one of the foremost criminal lawyers of modern times. A man above suspicion, but at heart a thousand times worse than the unfortunate souls whom he daily defended or prosecuted, as the case might be. Jonathan Wild, the thief-taker, was but a tyro to him.

The third person was bulky, bald, and gravely owl-like in countenance. He was slovenly in dress, and his long fingers were stained purple with nicotine.

Dr Stephen Stone had at one time commanded an extensive practice in the West End of London, but an addiction to drugs had sapped his morals and integrity and turned his mind into criminal channels. A bogus death certificate – the granting of which would have brought him in more money than he could have earned in the ordinary way in a year had he not been discovered – found him struck off the medical register, and a wonderful knowledge of subtle poisons, science, and chemistry made him a valuable ally to the evilly-disposed.

The Bat picked his company with a shrewd and calculating eye, and the roof of the Lindens sheltered four of the greatest rogues who had ever taken advantage of the gullibility of a long-suffering public.

'There's something in the wind. Our young friend is on the war-path,' said Brandon Delmas, noting the gleam in the Bat's eyes as he squirted a stream of soda-water into his glass. 'I knew he would break out again before long. What is it this time, Bat? Something big?'

'The biggest thing we've ever done if it comes off,' said the Bat tensely; and his three companions sat up interestedly, for they had brought off some pretty big coups since they had amalgamated under the leadership of Dirk Dolland, alias Derek Chester.

'You know the decision we came to the other day,' went on the Bat, sweeping a swift glance around at his three companions. 'One more big haul, and then a removal to fresh fields and pastures new – either the Continent or South America.'

'Perfectly,' said Brandon Delmas, answering for the others. 'But we decided that it must be a very big haul to induce us to give up these comfortable quarters and burn our boats behind us.'

'It will be a big haul.'

'Approximately, what?'

'Three hundred thousand pounds, or thereabouts.'

'Nicholas Mark sat bolt upright in his chair, and Dr Stephen Stone's fingers trembled more than ever as he lit a fresh cigarette.'

'Three hundred thousand pounds.' echoed Brandon Delmas musingly. 'Yes, that is quite a nice little amount to split up amongst us, my friend. May we hear more?'

The Bat wasted no time on words. In a few brief sentences he related all that had transpired at Samuel Otzmann's gambling hell that night, and gave the gist of the conversation that he had overheard between Colonel Eustace Boden and Cyrus C. Crag, the American millionaire.

'I'm afraid I don't quite follow your meaning,' said Brandon Delmas, leaning back in his chair and caressing his neatly-trimmed moustache. 'I can see that your scheme is largely centred on the Corottzi "Venus"; but that is only worth – to Cyrus C. Crag – one hundred thousand pounds.'

'Three hundred thousand to us,' said the Bat mysteriously, 'as I will explain to you in a few minutes. In the meantime, have you any idea where Colonel Eustace Boden lives?'

'Not the vaguest.'

'Nor had I until I looked it up in the Directory. He lives four houses from here – Delhi Lodge.'

Nicholas Mark gave a low whistle of surprise.

'That is bound to simplify whatever scheme you may have hit upon,' he said slowly. 'Come, Dolland, don't keep us in anticipation any longer! I am eager to hear all about this three hundred thousand pounds. The sooner we get our hands on it the better. I would like a change of air, especially as I learn that Sexton Blake has been called in over that last little affair I brought off. He's a nuisance, that man!'

The Bat poured himself out a stiff drink, and, drawing a chair up to the fire, gave his three companions full details of one of the most cunning and audacious schemes that human brain had ever devised. It was a master-stroke of criminal genius that was to set all England and Scotland agog with amazement and bewilderment before many days had passed.

2

Colonel Eustace Boden was not a particularly sweet-tempered man at the best of times – forty years of service had seen to that – and, to judge by the fluent manner in which he swore at the taxi-driver for having drawn him up six inches short of his house, and the vicious manner in which he slammed the gate and stamped up the drive, it was obvious that he was less amiable – or more unamiable – than usual.

He had dropped a trifle over two hundred pounds during his nightly visit to Samuel Otzmann's gambling-hell, all during the last half-hour of his stay, previous to which he had been on the right side to the tune of almost five hundred; and on top of that Cyrus C. Crag, the American millionaire, had once again been pestering him to sell his Corottzi 'Venus', despite his continued refusals.

'Confound the luck! Confound everything!' snarled the old soldier, as he crunched heavily over the gravel and ascended the broad steps to the front door. 'Why the deuce didn't I come away at the right time? That's almost a thousand in one week! I must pull up, or else chuck the game altogether!'

He beat a strenuous tattoo with the heavy brass knocker. There was a sound of shuffling footsteps within, and the door was opened by a grey-haired old man attired in a faded suit of livery.

That he, too, was an old Army man was obvious by the way in which he raised his hand to the salute as the colonel stepped over the threshold.

'Anything to eat, Rooney?' snapped the latter brusquely as he slipped off his overcoat and hat and handed them to his manservant.

'I've laid you some supper, sir, in case you should want it. A little cold chicken and some salad.'

'That'll do!' grunted the colonel. 'Open me a half-bottle of Beaune and bring it in.'

He turned through a door on his left, switching on the electric light as he went. The spacious room in which he took his lonely meals – for Colonel Boden was a bachelor – was comfortably and lavishly furnished. His feet sank deep into the costly carpet, and everything was of solid English oak, exquisitely carved, and black and shimmering with age. The big Jacobean sideboard positively winked with silverware –

the genuine Georgian stuff – and the walls were hung with portentous gold-framed paintings, out of which stared the features of past generations of Bodens.

One end of the long dining-table was set for a solitary meal – spotless linen, glittering cutlery, and exquisite cut-glass. Colonel Boden passed along the length of the room to the fireplace, on the brass dogs of which crackled a glowing pine-log, and stood staring up at the painting that hung over the mantelpiece.

It was the gem of his collection, the Corottzi 'Venus', for which Cyrus C. Crag had only that night renewed his offer of £100,000. And as a specimen of its kind it was well worth the price. The sight of it in no way soothed the colonel's irritable state of mind.

'Confounded impudence!' he snorted to himself. 'I'd die in the gutter before I'd allow that to leave the country to be stuck up in that upstart Yankee's garish home in New York! I'll show him that the almighty dollar's not so almighty as he and his kidney think it is!'

He plumped himself down in his chair at the head of his table just as Rooney, the manservant, stole noiselessly in and carefully filled his glass.

It was apparent that Colonel Boden's run of bad luck that night had not impaired his appetite or thirst. The better part of a cold chicken speedily vanished, and nothing remained of the Beaune save the empty bottle.

Pushing his chair back, he poured himself out a glass of green Chartreuse, and lit up a fat cigar. Even as he did so the whir of an electric bell rang through the silent house.

Colonel Boden struck a fresh match, with a gesture of annoyance.

'Now, who the dickens can that be at this time of night?' he snapped. 'I'm not in to anyone, Rooney, no matter who it is!'

'I understand, sir,' said the old manservant, shuffling out of the room and closing the door behind him.

Colonel Boden replenished his liqueur-glass and gazed musingly at the end of the cigar.

'I wonder if that system of Vincent's is any good?' he muttered, as his mind wandered back to the roulette-table that he had lately left. 'He seemed to be winning tonight. I saw him bring off a succession of six coups on the red, and double the lot on the odd numbers. Let me see, what was the sequence?'

He drew out a pencil and jotted something down on the spotless tablecloth. It must have been at least five minutes later that he suddenly realised that Rooney had not returned, and that there was not a sound to he heard from the direction of the front door.

'Where the dickens is the man?' he muttered irritably. 'What can be keeping him? Rooney! Rooney!' he went on, raising his voice.

'Rooney is otherwise engaged, colonel.'

Colonel Boden started as though he had been shot. He was seated with his back to the door, and as he spun round in his chair his jaw dropped and his eyes bulged in amazement at the strange sight that met his gaze.

Standing behind him in the doorway were four men. Each wore a long overcoat closely buttoned up to the throat, each wore a black velvet mask that completely screened his features, and each had his eyes fixed upon the colonel in a most disconcerting manner.

Colonel Boden was no coward. His temper always had the upper hand of his other emotions.

'What the dickens does this mean?' he barked, half rising in his chair. 'Who are you? What are you doing here? What is the meaning of this intrusion and tomfoolery Where is Rooney? Rooney – Rooney, how dare you admit these – these men?'

'Rooney had no choice in the matter,' said one of the masked men suavely. 'We admitted ourselves. And it is useless you calling Rooney. He could not come if he wanted to.'

Colonel Boden's normally crimson countenance turned purple with fury, and his grey moustache positively bristled.

'Kindly leave this house at once, you impudent scoundrels!' he roared, springing to his feet. 'If you're not gone in two seconds I'll call the police! If this is meant for a practical joke, allow me to inform you that you've got hold of the wrong person!'

'Nasty temper he's got,' said one of the strange men musingly. 'I'm afraid he's going to give more trouble than we expected.'

'I regret that we cannot fall in with your wishes, colonel,' drawled another of the four calmly. 'We have come to stay for some time. It is necessary that we should be your guests for a space of several days.'

'It strikes me that I am dealing with a collection of lunatics,' said Colonel Eustace Boden grimly. 'I have given you your chance to go quietly, and I will stand no further nonsense. This is obviously a case for the police.'

He strode quickly over to the big writing desk that stood in the window, and jerked open a drawer which he knew to contain both a police-whistle and a loaded revolver.

But he had scarcely laid hands on either of the articles when there was a concerted rush at him, and a pair of muscular arms dragged him backwards and pinioned his limbs to his sides.

But the fighting blood still ran sluggishly in Colonel Boden's veins, and anger gave him fresh strength as he fought and struggled to wrench himself free. Backwards the five of them reeled, overturning a chair with a crash, and almost capsizing the big dining-table against which they staggered.

'Help! Help! Police!' bawled the colonel at the top of his voice; and then a heavy hand was clapped over his mouth, cutting short his cries for assistance.

'Out with the rope!' panted one of the masked men sharply. 'It's the best way! Hurry up!'

The shortest of his companions whipped out what looked to be an ordinary scent-spray from his pocket, and squirted a fine spray of some pungent-smelling liquid full in the colonel's face.

The effect was instantaneous. Colonel Boden's frenzied struggles ceased like magic, and without a sound he collapsed limply into his captors' arms and lay huddled up in the big chair in which they placed him.

'Phew! I never thought he would be such a troublesome customer!' muttered the taller of the masked men, coolly helping himself to one of the colonel's expensive cigars. 'He's a regular old firebrand!

'Well, so far so good.' he went on, casting a swift glance around the room. 'The next thing to do is to find safe quarters for our military friend and his faithful henchman. I should imagine that the top of the house would be the best place.'

Stooping down, he picked up the senseless form of the colonel and flung it over his shoulder as though it had been the merest featherweight. He led the way out into the hall, where, propped up against the wall, with his head lolling over his knees and his arms hanging limply by his sides, sat Rooney in a similar state to his master.

Two of the masked men lifted him up between them, and coolly and methodically the strange procession filed up the broad staircase towards the top of the house.

3

Mr Henry Bargrove, head-manager of that gigantic concern, the Impregnable Insurance Company, leaned back in his comfortably-sprung armchair, and, adjusting his gold-rimmed pince-nez, gazed quizzically at the card that the obsequious, mild-mannered clerk had just handed him.

'Mr Bernard Mellish,' he muttered to himself. 'The Lindens, Beech Avenue, Roehampton. Does this gentleman want to see me, Smith? Won't Mr Rawdon do?'

'No, sir. He asked specially to see you.'

'Very well. Show him in.'

Mr Bargrove carefully straightened his ink-stand, adjusted the little array of pens and pencils, and approvingly studied his long, white fingers and well-manicured nails, by which time his visitor had been ushered in.

Mr Bernard Mellish was an elderly gentleman, with a square-cut white beard, a florid complexion, and an air of sober prosperity about him. He plumped down in the chair that was offered him, and clasped his gloved hands on the top of his gold-mounted umbrella.

'Good afternoon, Mr – er' – Mr Bargrove referred to the card again – 'Mr Mellish! What can I have the pleasure of doing for you? I presume this is a business call?'

'Most decidedly – most decidedly!' replied the visitor briskly. 'Yes, I have a little business to transact with you, Mr Bargrove.'

'You wish to take out a policy, or policies, of some kind? Burglary? Fire? Life – '

Mr Bargrove uttered the last word a trifle dubiously. Mr Mellish was somewhat advanced in years to think of insuring what remained of his life.

'Burglary and fire. I wish to insure my house and its contents against both those risks.'

Mr Bargrove looked a trifle annoyed. He was a busy man, and this affair could easily have been transacted by one of his trusted subordinates.

'That is easily managed, Mr Mellish,' he said stiffly. 'I will send an assessor along to – '

His visitor checked him with a little wave of his hand.

'Excuse me, Mr Bargrove!' he said seriously. 'I should be more than obliged if you would give this matter your personal attention. The transaction must be completed as quickly as possible, as I am leaving town. Hitherto I have been foolish in not having my property insured, and it is acting on the advice of my lawyers that I have come here today. It is a large sum that I wish to insure for – my property is of great value – and I am willing to pay a high premium. But I wish to deal entirely with you, as the head of your firm.'

Mr Bargrove looked flattered. 'It is very unusual, Mr Mellish,' he said tentatively. 'May I ask what is the amount you wish to insure for?'

'One hundred and ten thousand pounds.'

Mr Bargrove gave a little gasp of surprise. It was certainly a somewhat large transaction that he was called upon to engineer.

'One hundred and ten thousand pounds!' he echoed. 'Your property must indeed be of considerable value, Mr Mellish!'

'It is, as you will see. I take it that you will fall in with my wishes?'

'As you press the point, and as the business is on such a large scale, I will,' said Mr Bargrove, with the air of one conferring a great favour. 'I will come personally to your place tomorrow, Mr Mellish.'

'Tomorrow will not do, Mr Bargrove. As I told you before, I want the whole affair fixed up as quickly as possible, as I am called out of town. I will trespass still further upon your kindness. My car is waiting outside. Put your hat and coat on, and I will run you up to my place now, so that you can assess it and put the policy through tomorrow.'

Mr Bargrove shook his head decisively. It was impossible. He was too busy. It was utterly out of the question. It was too late in the day. It was only when Mr Mellish rose, and apologised for having taken up so much of his valuable time, and murmured something about the Integrity Insurance Company, that he gracefully capitulated. It was too big a bit of business to lose.

'If you wait a moment, Mr Mellish, I will give a few instructions to my head-clerk, and will then be ready to accompany you.'

Mr Bargrove not only interviewed his head-clerk, but he also flipped hurriedly over the pages of the *London Directory* and satisfied himself on the point that Mr Bernard Mellish did indeed reside at the address on his card – The Lindens, Beech Avenue, Roehampton.

Five minutes later he was seated in a small private car speeding through the City in the direction of Barnes. Mr Bernard Mellish was an interesting conversationalist, and obviously a widely-travelled man, to judge by the places in various parts of the globe that he dilated upon in comparison to London. He was also an excellent judge of a good cigar, if the one that he offered Mr Bargrove from his case was a sample of those he generally smoked.

Under the circumstances the time passed quickly, though it was already dusk when the car turned into Beech Avenue, and Mr Mellish poked his head out of the window.

'The twelfth house on the right, driver,' he called. 'This is a hired car,' he said almost apologetically to Mr Bargrove. 'My own has met with an accident, and is being repaired.'

Had Mr Bargrove been on the alert, he would have noticed that when his travelling companion stuck his head out of the window he made a peculiar signal with one hand, and in answer to that signal a man who had been standing further up the road, as though waiting, waved his hand back and strolled leisurely away.

The car came to a halt, and Mr Bargrove stepped out and gazed appraisingly at the big house standing back in its own grounds, and though it was rapidly getting dark his eyes did not fail to notice the name, upon the big drive-gate.

A wizened-faced man in a faded suit of livery opened the door in answer to Mr Mellish's ring, and Mr Bargrove was ushered into a room on the right, where he removed his hat and coat, and accepted the offer of a whisky-and-soda.

The place was certainly luxuriously furnished, and all his business instincts were to the fore as he took in the magnificent old oak furniture, the solid silverware, and the valuable pictures and curios that hung upon the walls. And in every other room was the same air of prosperity and comfort.

'A very fine place, and exquisitely furnished, Mr Mellish,' said Mr Bargrove, as they came back to the ground floor, after their tour of the entire house. 'You have some very valuable possessions, but, really, you were joking when you mentioned the sum of a hundred and ten thousand pounds. I could not place a higher value than the odd ten.'

'I said a hundred and ten, and I meant it,' replied Mr Mellish mysteriously. 'And I will show you why.'

He ushered the insurance manager into a little room at the back of the house, that was furnished as a study and library. Three of the walls were lined from top to bottom with books, and on the fourth hung a painting in a faded gold frame.

'The famous Corottzi "Venus", Mr Bargrove,' said Mr Mellish, with a sweep of his hand. 'You have no doubt heard of it, and therefore would know its value. That is the chief reason why I am taking out this policy.'

'Yes, it is certainly the Corottzi "Venus", Mr Mellish,' he said slowly. 'But I was under the impression that this picture was the property of – let me see – er – Colonel Eustace Boden?'

'It was until lately,' replied his companion candidly. 'I purchased it from Colonel Boden three days ago for the sum of one hundred thousand pounds. I trust you will not let this go any further, Mr Bargrove. The sale was made in private, and Colonel Boden does not wish it to be known just yet that he has parted with the picture. A severe financial loss compelled him to sell. With that in my possession, you can realise why I am so anxious to insure against all risks.'

'I can indeed,' murmured Mr Bargrove as they returned to the front room. 'You are wise in doing so, sir.'

There was a slightly dubious expression on his face, and, going across to the writing-desk that stood in the window, Mr Mellish pulled open a drawer and drew out a sheaf of papers.

'Here, Mr Bargrove,' he said, handing across one document, 'is Colonel Boden's receipt for the hundred thousand I paid him for his "Venus". And here are the title-deeds of this house made out in my name. If you require any further credentials, I must refer you to my lawyer, Mr Brandon Delmas, of 36a, Chancery Lane.'

'Quite unnecessary, my dear sir – quite unnecessary,' said Mr Bargrove, his face clearing as if by magic at the mention of the famous lawyer's name, 'I have seen all that I want to see, and have quite satisfied myself as to the *bona fides* of your application. Your policy shall be put through at once. If you will call at my office tomorrow morning at about twelve I will have everything ready for you.'

'Ah, that is how I like to see business done!' declared Mr Mellish gravely, as he helped the insurance manager on with his coat and accompanied him to the door. 'My car is at your disposal, and my chauffeur will drive you wherever you wish to go. I will see you tomorrow punctually at twelve.'

The strange man previously mentioned was still hanging about in the near vicinity as Mr Bargrove drove off, rubbing his hands gleefully together at the thought of the big stroke of business he had done.

He stood for a moment watching the car till it was out of sight, and then, ripping something away from the gate, placed it under his coat, and, striding up the path, entered the house in company with Mr Bernard Mellish.

The gorgeous blue-uniformed and gold-braided commissionaire bowed deferentially as he held open the big door, and Cyrus C.

Crag, of New York, stepped briskly down the marble entrance-steps of the Hotel Britz and into his luxurious Rolls-Royce.

'Delhi Lodge, Beech Avenue, Roehampton!' he said curtly to the dapper, neatly-dressed chauffeur, who stood awaiting his orders. 'And hustle! Guess I'm in a hurry!'

There was a strange gleam of satisfaction in the American millionaire's grey eyes as he flung himself back on the soft-cushioned seat and, for at least the tenth time, drew a letter from his pocket, and scanned it through. It had only reached him a few minutes before, and the intelligence it contained was obviously of great interest.

'I knew the stiff-necked old cuss would give in in the end!' he muttered triumphantly, under his breath. 'I reckon he was only temporising, to try and get me to shove up the price. Despite all his talk about the almighty dollar, it seems even he can't resist it. Gee! I'm glad things are going to be fixed up at last. I shall be able to catch the *Megantic* now.'

Cyrus C. Crag lit one of the long black cigars that he specially favoured, and, propping his neatly-shod feet up on the opposite seat, gazed listlessly out of the window. He was hungering for a sight of the Statue of Liberty and the skyscrapers of New York.

The American's high-powered car made short work of the journey to Roehampton, and, the gate being open, swept up the drive to the door of Delhi Lodge.

A wizened-faced man, with a pair of remarkably alert eyes, and clad in a suit of faded livery, answered his sharp ring at the bell.

'I want to see Colonel Boden,' drawled the millionaire. 'My name's Crag – Cyrus C. Crag, of Noo York, and I guess he's expecting me!'

'Yes, sir, he is. Will you come this way?'

The American stepped into the wide, antler-hung hall, and allowed the manservant to usher him into a room on the right.

Colonel Eustace Boden was seated at a writing-desk by the window, and he rose quickly to his feet, and stepped forward as his visitor entered.

'You have wasted no time in coming, Mr Crag,' he said quietly.

'I never waste time,' replied the American cheerfully, as he extended his hand in greeting. 'I guess I must have been born on an express train. So you've altered your mind after all, colonel – you've decided to sell the Corottzi "Venus"?'

Colonel Boden shrugged his square, military shoulders, and there was a strange look on his lined countenance.

'I am compelled to!' he replied shortly.

'Compelled to!' echoed Cyrus C. Crag. 'Say, that's rather a strange way of putting it, colonel!'

'It is none the less true. Circumstances alter cases, Mr Crag, and my circumstances have suffered a big change since I last saw you, and gave you my last refusal.'

Colonel Boden took a quick turn up and down the long room, his hands clasped behind his back and his head bowed.

'I will be quite candid with you, Mr Crag,' he went on. 'I have experienced a severe financial reverse, owing to some rash speculations I made, and it is necessary for me to lay my hands on a big sum of ready money. That is the reason why I am parting with the Corottzi "Venus". Otherwise I would not dream of allowing the picture to leave my possession.'

'Gee, I'm real sorry to hear that, colonel!' cried the American millionaire sincerely. 'And yet, you'll excuse me, but I can't help feeling glad in another way. I'd set my mind on taking that Corottzi back to the States with me, and it seems your ill fortune is my good fortune. I'm just aching to get my eyes on it!'

'You won't have to look far,' said Colonel Boden. And he swung round and pointed to the oil-painting in the faded gilt frame that hung over the fireplace.

Cyrus C. Crag stepped forward with a little exclamation of delight, and for a space of a couple of minutes he literally devoured the beautiful oil painting with his gaze. He was no mean judge of old masters, and he knew a genuine one when he saw it.

'It's great! Gee, it's fine!' he muttered admiringly. 'I don't wonder you didn't want to part with it, colonel. And the price – one hundred thousand pounds, eh?'

'Guineas,' said the colonel stoutly. 'I can't part with it for less.'

'Oh, wal, I guess another five thousand won't break me!' drawled the American whimsically. 'It's a big price though.'

'There's one stipulation you must agree to, Mr Crag,' went on Colonel Boden, twisting nervously at his bristling moustache. 'This transaction must be kept a secret for the present. I don't want it publicly known that financial circumstances have compelled me to part with the Corottzi. I don't want you to say anything about the matter until you have to produce the picture before the New York Customs.'

'I'd like to have told a few friends of mine who bet me I wouldn't get it,' muttered the American ruefully. 'But, there, that don't matter. Yes, I'll agree to that, colonel. I must tell you that I'm sailing tomorrow by the *Megantic* now that I've fixed this up.'

Colonel Boden stepped forward and almost reverently lifted the Corottzi down from its hook, and laid it out on the big dining-table.

'You won't take it away in the frame, of course, Mr Crag?' he said quietly. 'That would be too noticeable. I will get my man to strip it off and pack it up in a neat roll for you. Don't be alarmed. He will not damage it in the slightest. Rooney knows how to deal with such matters.'

Rooney evidently did. Cyrus Crag stood over the old manservant with an eagle eye as he carefully removed the priceless picture from its faded gilt setting, and one by one gently removed the nails that held the canvas to the framework.

Then in a truly professional manner he rolled it up, faced by a strip of soft material, and, with much protective padding, bound it securely and neatly in brown paper.

'Well, you've done your part, and now it's up to me to do mine,' said Cyrus C. Crag, drawing out his cheque-book as the finished parcel was laid on the table. 'Would you like it open or crossed, colonel?'

'Open, if you don't mind,' replied the colonel. 'It will save time in passing it through my bank.'

The American millionaire seated himself at the writing-table in the window, and, drawing the ink towards him, made out a cheque for the enormous sum for which the famous Corottzi 'Venus' had changed hands.

Colonel Boden took the pink slip of paper almost regretfully, and Cyrus C. Crag's lean facc was all smiles as he took the brown-paper roll that the manservant held out to him.

'Wal, colonel, that's done,' he said as he shook hands. 'I hope that you're satisfied with your part of the transaction?'

'Quite,' replied the colonel quietly. 'I sincerely trust that you will be.'

A couple of minutes later Cyrus C. Crag drove off in his luxurious car.

Had he been in a position to waft himself back to the room that he had just left he would have witnessed the extraordinary spectacle of the dignified Colonel Eustace Boden and his withered-faced old manservant holding hands and dancing frenziedly around the big dining-table.

THE FIRST CHAPTER

Sexton Blake Takes up a Case for Mr Bargrove – Swindled by an Impostor!

'Well, I've often heard of a man escaping death by the skin of his teeth, but never by a hair of his head!' said Tinker, flinging himself back in his comfortable armchair in Sexton Blake's consulting-room and gazing ruminatively into the glowing embers of the fire. 'Yes I have, though! Deadwood Dick and Blackbird the Pirate usually dodge death by a hair's-breadth, don't they? At least, in all the yarns I've read they do.'

Sexton Blake carefully tilted the reflector of his microscope and gazed keenly through the eyepiece before replying.

'You've got a lot to learn yet, my boy,' he said, briskly polishing the powerful lens with his silk handkerchief and taking a tentative puff at his cigar. 'There is as much valuable knowledge to be gained from a study of the human hair as there is from a ten-volume history of the progress of civilisation. I'll tell you something now that I don't suppose you know. Take a European's hair and examine it beneath a microscope, you will find that it is round; take an Asiatic's, it is oval; then take a hair from one of the Negroid race, and you will find that it is flat, with a distinct kink in it.

'The hair that I have got here is of the Negroid variety, which proves almost conclusively that it was not young James Willoughby who murdered his uncle.'

'But how do you make that out, guv'nor?' asked Tinker as he rose and took a peep through the microscope. 'This ain't a negro's hair – it's quite fair!'

'There again you display your ignorance,' smiled Sexton Blake, rising and stretching his arms wearily above his head. 'There are plenty of full-blooded negroes in this world with hair as fair as flax, and white-skinned, too. You can tell them by the half-moons on their nails, and the whites of their eyes, which aren't white.

'Old Sir Peter Willoughby's manservant is a negro, though you wouldn't think it, and he's the scoundrel who struck the poor old fellow down. Coutts has been on the wrong scent again. I think I'll just run down to the Yard and – confound it, there goes the bell, and I thought I was going to have a day to myself! Perhaps it is Coutts.'

But it was not the burly detective-inspector who had called. A moment later Mrs Bardell came stumping up the stairs, wiping her hands on her apron, and handed the detective a slip of pasteboard.

'Gennelman – see you – hurgent!' she panted.

Sexton Blake propped himself up against the mantelpiece and glanced irritably at the card.

'Mr Henry Bargrove,' he read out slowly. 'General manager, the Impregnable Insurance Company. Now, what the dickens does he want to see me about? Is he touting to get me to insure my life, or is it a professional matter? Does he appear to be an itinerant individual, Mrs Bardell?'

'Ho, no, sir. 'E's a Henglishman,' replied the detective's housekeeper decisively. 'An' in a very hexaggerated state of mind, too.'

Sexton Blake hesitated.

'All right; show him up!' he said, with a hopeless gesture. 'I might as well see what the fellow wants.'

The moment Mr Henry Bargrove entered the room it was plainly to be seen that he had not called to canvas for life-insurance policies. Sexton Blake had seldom seen a man in a more acute state of agitation. The hands that held his hat and stick were trembling so that he could scarcely hold those two articles, and his face was drawn and haggard with worry.

He sank gratefully into the chair that the Baker Street detective pushed forward for him, and, drawing out his handkerchief, mopped his forehead unsteadily.

Sexton Blake made no attempt to draw him into conversation. He relapsed into his own favourite seat and carefully lit a fresh cigar. But all the time he was studying his visitor keenly beneath his lowered eyelids.

'Mr Blake,' gasped the man at length, leaning forward and laying an almost imploring hand on the detective's sleeve, 'I have come to crave your assistance! I am in great trouble!'

'It is a personal matter, then,' said the detective quietly – 'nothing to do with your firm?'

'It has to do with both myself and my firm,' replied Mr Henry Bargrove agitatedly. 'Through me I have every reason to believe that my firm has been swindled out of a sum of one hundred and ten thousand pounds.'

Sexton Blake allowed himself to exhibit as much surprise as could be conveyed in a slight elevation of his eyebrows.

'One hundred and ten thousand pounds!' he said musingly. 'That is certainly a very large sum of money! And yet you speak with a manner of uncertainty, Mr Bargrove. You say that you have every reason to believe that you have been swindled out of that amount. Why cannot you be positive on the point?'

'I will explain, Mr Blake. I will tell you everything,' cried Henry Bargrove, leaning forward with his elbows resting on his knees and his chin cupped in his palms. 'As you can see from my card, my name is Henry Bargrove, and I am the general manager of the Impregnable Insurance Company. It is a position of trust and great responsibility, and most of the business of the firm passes through my hands.

'Some days ago I received a visit from a certain Mr Bernard Mellish, who resides at The Lindens, Beech Avenue, Roehampton. He told me that he was anxious to take out a policy to insure his property against the risks of fire and burglary, and named a very high sum – one hundred and ten thousand pounds, to be exact. I expressed surprise at the amount, but he said that he had some very valuable property, and requested that I should give my personal attention to the matter.

'More to humour him than anything else, I assented, and it ended in him driving me there and then over to his place, that I might assess it and put the policy through with all expediency. He wanted it done quickly, as he told me that he was being called out of town on business.

'His house, with its contents, was certainly a very valuable property; but ten thousand pounds was the highest value that I could put upon it until he drew me into a room and showed me a genuine old master hanging there – the Corottzi "Venus", to be exact.'

'The Corottzi "Venus"!' broke in Sexton Blake, with a slight start of interest. 'I was under the impression that that valuable painting was the property of Colonel Eustace Boden.'

'As was I,' went on Henry Bargrove, 'until Mr Mellish informed me that he had recently, and privately, purchased it from the colonel for the sum of one hundred thousand pounds. He even showed me the receipt. It was only natural that with such a valuable possession in the house he was anxious to insure against all risks. Everything was in order. He showed me the title-deeds relating to his property, and referred me to the famous lawyer, Mr Brandon Delmas, for any further credentials should I require them.

'I saw nothing to prevent my issuing a policy for the amount he desired, and promised to have it ready for him by twelve o'clock the following day. To make sure on every little point, I rang up Mr Brandon Delmas on the 'phone the next morning, and was informed that he certainly represented Mr Bernard Mellish from a legal point of view, and that I was perfectly safe in dealing with him. The business was completed, the premium paid, and the policy issued.'

Mr Bargrove broke off and mopped his forehead again.

'That is the first part of my story, Mr Blake,' he went on. 'And now for the second. Five days later I picked up an evening paper, and read of a disastrous fire in Roehampton. Imagine my horror to learn that it was none other than Mr Bernard Mellish's house that had been burnt down and completely gutted. It was one of the heaviest blows that my firm had suffered for a long while. I hurried to Roehampton as quickly as possible, to find that things could not have been worse. The old house had gone up like a torch, and nothing but the four bare walls remained standing. The salvage corps were on the scene, and the decision that they had arrived at was that the fire had been caused by burglars who had broken in, for they had discovered the remains of a dark-lantern and a jemmy.

'There was no one in the house at the time, for Mr Mellish was away in Scotland. The Corottzi "Venus", representing one hundred thousand pounds sterling, had gone up in smoke. A portion of the gilt frame with the name-plate on it, was discovered among the debris.

'That policy I had issued to Mr Bernard Mellish was one of the most unfortunate investments I have ever made on behalf of my firm, and I felt that I was personally responsible for the gigantic loss we should suffer, and there is no doubt that my directors looked upon it in the same light.

'The following morning Mr Brandon Delmas paid me a call, and put forward his client's claim for one hundred and ten thousand pounds. He told me that Mr Bernard Mellish was completely prostrated with grief at the loss of his home, and that he was under medical attention at a certain hotel in London.

'There was no disputing the claim for the insurance money. To have done so would have done the firm more harm than good, especially as we should have had such a famous man as Brandon Delmas against us. Without argument, a cheque was drawn and the claim settled. That is the second part of my story, Mr Blake. Now for the third.'

Mr Bargrove polished his gold-rimmed pince-nez excitedly, and adjusted them on his nose again.

'Yesterday, Mr Blake, one of our directors who had been transacting some business abroad landed in England, and came to the office post-haste. He had read an account of the big fire at Roehampton coming up in the train from Southampton, and he was in a terrible state of excitement over it, especially when he learned that we had already settled the claim.

'He declared that he knew Bernard Mellish personally, that he had met him at an hotel in New York, and that he had left him there when he had sailed for England! If that was so, how could Mellish have called at my office, and taken out a policy on his property? There was something radically wrong somewhere. He was positive that it was *the* Mr Bernard Mellish, for he had mentioned that he had a house at Roehampton.

'You can imagine the effect this information had on my firm! If Mr Bernard Mellish, the owner of The Lindens, Beech Avenue, Roehampton, was in New York, then I had been visited by an impostor, and we had been swindled to the tune of over a hundred thousand pounds.

'Caution is the watchword of the Impregnable, and before taking any steps my directors despatched a cablegram to Bernard Mellish, care of Supreme Hotel, New York. We received a reply this morning. Here it is, Mr Blake!'

Sexton Blake, who had been an interested listener, took the flimsy sheet of paper that was proffered him, and gave a little whistle of surprise as he read it through.

KNOW NOTHING ABOUT OTHER MELLISH. IMPOSTOR. DETAIN HIM. AM CATCHING NEXT BOAT. – BERNARD MELLISH

'That's decisive enough,' he said quietly. 'What action did you take on the face of it?'

'Myself and two other directors called at the hotel where Bernard Mellish was supposed to be lying under medical attention. We were informed that he had left the previous evening, and that they had no idea where he had gone. We immediately paid a visit to Brandon Delmas's office, and were told that he was out of town on business, and would be back some time in the afternoon. Our first intention was to immediately communicate with Scotland Yard, but the last thing the firm desired was publicity of the manner in which it had ostensibly been duped, and it was decided to put the matter in your hands, Mr Blake. That is why I am here – to ask you to take up the case, at any fee you may care to name.'

Sexton Blake leaned back in his chair, his eyes half-closed, and the tips of his fingers pressed together. He remained so for several minutes without speaking.

'What you have told me, Mr Bargrove,' he said at last, speaking slowly and distinctly, 'ostensibly amounts to a case of imposture, arson, and barefaced swindling. Did I think it merely that, I should decline the case, and advise you to put it in the hands of the police. But I see interesting points standing out. For one thing, Brandon Delmas is a big man, with a big and sound reputation. One can hardly imagine him implicated in an affair of this kind.'

'We are not for one moment hinting that he is,' put in Mr Bargrove hastily. 'I have not the slightest doubt that Mr Delmas has been completely taken in and duped, as we have been.'

'You do not often find such a clever exponent of the law so easily duped,' said Sexton Blake drily. 'And now, another point. That Corottzi "Venus". You are sure it was the genuine one?'

'I am positive!' cried the insurance manager vehemently. 'I am considered an expert in such matters.'

'Humph! Well, that makes another interesting point,' went on the Baker Street detective. 'If your Mr Bernard Mellish was an impostor, the question is – was he the rightful owner of the Corottzi? Did he, indeed, purchase it from Colonel Boden?'

'I saw the receipt. And how was he to know that I would not make inquiries of the colonel? He lives within four or five houses of the Lindens.'

Sexton Blake sat up with an expression of enhanced interest.

'That's true enough,' he said puzzledly. 'But what on earth is the object of a man paying a hundred thousand pounds for a picture, then insure it for a like amount, deliberately destroying it, and drawing his money back again? If he had insured it for double the amount he had paid for it, there might be something in it. You might go even further, and say he stole the Corottzi, and forged a receipt. But then the colonel would have been bound to have reported his loss.

'There is even a third line to go on. Perhaps the picture was not destroyed at all.'

'We found part of the frame, with the charred remnants of canvas still adhering to it,' said Henry Bargrove stoutly.

Sexton Blake's firm lips parted in a slight smile as he rose to his feet and flung the remains of his cigar in the grate.

'I think I will look into this case, Mr Bargrove,' he said quietly; 'it interests me. If you will give me a few minutes to dress I should like you to accompany me.'

'Accompany you? Where?' echoed Henry Bargrove, puzzled.

'To Roehampton,' Sexton Blake flung back over his shoulder, as he passed into the next room. 'We will see if we can learn anything from Colonel Eustace Boden.'

THE SECOND CHAPTER

Telling How Blake Met Inspector Coutts at Roehampton – And What Happened

'If that was, as you say, the genuine Corottzi "Venus",' murmured Sexton Blake, as he hunched his lean form back in one corner of the taxi, 'then I feel certain that we shall learn something from Colonel Boden regarding this mysterious Mr Bernard Mellish – whether he did indeed purchase the picture from him, and the receipt he showed you was genuine.'

'I see no reason to doubt it,' said Mr Henry Bargrove gloomily. 'I would stake my life that it was the genuine Corottzi. Whether or no he purchased it legitimately from Colonel Boden is another matter. What a fool I was not to have made further inquiries at the time, before issuing that policy!'

'You were,' said Sexton Blake candidly. And Tinker, seated opposite him, adroitly changed a snort of laughter into a particularly hacking cough.

Little did Sexton Blake realise that he was embarking upon one of the most amazing and baffling cases that had ever taxed his skill as a private detective. Little did he dream of the dramatic events that the next few hours were to produce.

There was a distinct smell of charred wood and water-sodden ash as the taxi turned into Beech Avenue, and Sexton Blake stopped it for a moment to gaze interestedly at all that remained of what had once been the Lindens.

The fire had certainly done its work well, and the big house was absolutely gutted. Nothing remained standing save the four gaunt, scorched and blackened walls, with the empty, frameless windows, yawning like hungry mouths. The roof had fallen in, and what had once been the interior of the house was piled high with debris. The neat garden had been trampled down by many feet, and pools of dirty water had collected everywhere.

'It'll be a long time before the Lindens is habitable again,' muttered the detective, as he resumed his seat. 'It'll be rather an unpleasant homecoming for Mr Bernard Mellish – if it is the real Bernard Mellish who is sailing from New York by the next boat. Here you are, cabby!'

The taxi pulled up outside the gates of Delhi Lodge, and the three occupants jumped out and made their way up the neatly-kept drive to the front door.

There was no sign of life about the place, and Sexton Blake seized the heavy brass knocker, and beat a thunderous rat-a-tat-tat on the door.

Several minutes passed, and there was not a sound from the big house.

'It strikes me there's nobody at home,' he muttered; 'unless they're all as deaf as posts. Tinker, run round to the back and see if you can see anybody about there.'

His young assistant hastened off around the side of the house, whilst Sexton Blake resumed his futile hammering.

'I fear it is useless,' said Mr Henry Bargrove ruefully. 'It is obvious that all the occupants are out.'

'You'd think there would be somebody in to look after a big place like this,' mused Sexton Blake, lifting the letter-box, and peering through. 'I have heard that Colonel Boden is a bit of a recluse, and a crabbed and confirmed old bachelor; but he must have a servant or servants of some kind – hallo! what's Tinker discovered?'

It was obvious that Tinker had made a discovery of some kind. His face was flushed and his eyes were shining with excitement as he came dashing up.

'Guv'nor, there's something wrong inside there!' he panted. 'There's nobody to be seen round at the back; but you come and listen to the funny noises!'

'Noises!' echoed Sexton Blake. 'What do you mean, my boy? What kind of noises?'

'I can't explain. You come and hear for yourself.'

Sexton Blake lost no time in accepting the invitation. With Mr Henry Bargrove trotting at his heels he strode briskly around to the back of the house.

The spacious stone-flagged courtyard, surrounded by high brick walls, was utterly deserted, save for a dilapidated-looking black cat that was perched on the zinc dustbin, busily engaged in removing the traces of the previous night's sanguinary engagement.

'I tried the door and hammered on it,' Tinker explained eagerly. 'And then I noticed that little window leading into the pantry was ajar, so I struck my head in and shouted.'

'The kind of liberty your colossal impertinence would lead you to take!' said Sexton Blake stiffly.

'And when I shouted someone answered me.'

'Answered you?' echoed the detective. 'Then there is someone in. What did they say?'

'I don't know. It seemed to come from a long way off. You listen for yourself.'

Sexton Blake stepped forward, and, pulling the tiny square window open, poked his head in. For several minutes he stood, straining his ears in vain, and then, just as he was about to upbraid Tinker for a chuckle-headed, imaginative young idiot, from afar off in the depths of the big house came a muffled, pounding noise and the faint sound of a human voice.

Sexton Blake jumped back as though he had been shot, and his face was a picture of amazement.

'By Jove, Tinker, you're right!' he exclaimed. 'There's something funny going on inside there. Someone either ill or in trouble.'

'Goodness gracious!' gasped Mr Bargrove. 'Extraordinary! What shall we do, Mr Blake?'

'We must find a way in,' replied the detective, without hesitation. 'But first we must get a constable, so that we shall be on the right side of the law. I've no desire to be run in for housebreaking. We're sure to find one somewhere in the vicinity.'

In a rising state of excitement the three of them hastened back to the front of the house, and even as they strode down the drive the gate was pushed open and two men entered.

Sexton Blake could scarcely believe his own eyes. It was almost supernatural. It was just as though some magic power had granted him that which he sought. One of the newcomers was a police-constable in uniform, and the other was none other than Detective-Inspector Coutts of the Criminal Investigation Department.

'Well, I'll be hanged!' said Sexton Blake, stopping short and rubbing his chin bewilderedly. 'What the dickens are you doing here, Coutts?'

Inspector Coutts looked no less surprised, and a trifle irritable.

'I've come to water the flowers and give the worms their canary-seed!' he snapped irascibly. 'And may I ask what the Blue Alsatian Band you are doing here, Blake? I suppose you've got one as well?'

'One what? A worm?' echoed the Baker Street detective puzzledly. 'Or a Blue Alsatian Band? I give you my word of honour that I have not got such a thing in my possession. I have a distinct abhorrence of –'

'Don't be a confounded idiot, Blake!' snorted the C.I.D. man. 'A telegram, I mean! Was it a telegram that brought you here?'

'No,' replied the detective curiously. 'It was a taxi, to be precise. I came along to have an interview with Colonel Boden. What do you mean by telegram? Perhaps I can help you.'

'It's deuced funny!' muttered the inspector. 'What do you make of that?'

He handed Sexton Blake a telegram as he spoke. It was addressed to Coutts at Scotland Yard, and ran as follows.

> GO TO DELHI LODGE, BEECH AVENUE, ROEHAMPTON, AND SEARCH THE HOUSE.

Sexton Blake gave a low whistle of surprise. It seemed to him that a net of mystery was gradually closing around him.

'There's a lot in this telegram, Coutts,' he said slowly, 'and I should advise you to do as it says. It was just what I was about to do. There's something wrong in this place.'

And in a few brief words he told the inspector of the muffled, pounding noise, and the faint cries for assistance that they had heard through the back window.

'Well, I'm hanged! I thought I was coming on a wild goose chase at first!' gasped the C.I.D. man. 'I thought someone was trying to pull my leg, but I decided to come and make certain. Phew! we'd better make an investigation. How are we going to get in?'

'I'll soon manage that, so long as you give me permission,' smiled Sexton Blake, as he drew a bunch of skeleton-keys from his pocket.

Sexton Blake was no vain boaster. With that bunch of keys he could have opened almost any street door in London. In less than a minute he had slipped the catch back, and they filed into the hall.

And now, plainer than ever, from the upper regions of the house came that muffled, pounding noise, and the faint sound of a human voice!

Mr Henry Bargrove was the last man to enter the house, and as he did so an extraordinary change seemed to come over the man. His eyes positively bulged in his head as he gazed around, and his hands trembled with amazement. He made a dart into the room on the right of the hall, and then came staggering out again in a dazed and bewildered manner.

Sexton Blake made a dart back, and flung an arm around him, fearing that the man was going to fall.

'What's the matter, Mr Bargrove?' he asked puzzledly. 'Aren't you feeling well? Is anything wrong?'

'Wrong? Yes, there must be something wrong!' stammered the insurance manager excitedly. 'Where are we, Mr Blake? What is the name of this house?'

'Why, Delhi Lodge, of course!' replied the detective, beginning to think that the man's reason had failed him.

'Delhi Lodge? Delhi Lodge? Are – are you sure it's not the Lindens?'

Sexton Blake's suspicions became almost a certainty.

'The Lindens!' he echoed. 'What do you mean, Mr Bargrove? You know that the Lindens has been burnt down. How could this be the place?'

Henry Bargrove passed a hand wearily over his forehead, and swept another glance around thc hall.

'Mr Blake, I can't make this out. This is most extraordinary!' he faltered. 'You will understand what I mean when I tell you that this is the house that I came to the other night to assess for insurance. And yet it was the Lindens. I saw the name on the gate!'

Sexton Blake drew a deep breath, and glanced almost pityingly at his companion.

'You must have made a mistake, Mr Bargrove,' he said soothingly. 'This affair is preying on your mind. You have been deceived by a chance resemblance. All the houses in this road are alike; they are all built on the same lines.'

'But it's not the house; it's the furniture!' cried the insurance manager excitedly. 'There's the very peg on which I hung my hat and coat. That's the room where I sat with Bernard Mellish;

I could tell you every bit of furniture in it. Could even tell you how every room in the house is furnished.'

A strange light crept into Sexton Blake's hard, grey eyes, and a thrill of wonderment ran through him. Henry Bargrove spoke in tones of the deepest conviction, and he felt certain that there must be some foundation for the extraordinary statement that the man was making.

He began to realise instinctively that when he had agreed to take up the case for the Impregnable Insurance Company he had unknowingly involved himself in what was to turn out a veritable maze of mystery – one of the most bewildering cases that he had ever tackled.

'There's no one on the ground floor, Blake,' broke in the gruff voice of Inspector Coutts, as he came stamping out of one of the back rooms. 'We'd better get straight up and see what's wrong upstairs.'

'We'll discuss this matter later, Mr Bargrove,' whispered Sexton Blake, as he followed the inspector up the broad flight of stairs. 'I feel that we are even now on the eve of a discovery of some kind.'

There were five storeys to Delhi Lodge, and as the little party filed higher and higher the pounding noise and the sound of the human voice – or, rather, voices it was now – grew nearer and nearer and louder and louder.

At length they reached the top landing of all, and it was clear that all the turmoil came from the other side of the door of one of the back rooms. The key was turned in the lock on the outside, and a heavy padlock had been fitted as well. In that the key had also obligingly been left.

'All right! All right! We're coming!' called Inspector Coutts gruffly.

He turned the two keys, wrenched off the padlock, and then, putting his shoulder to the door, sent it crashing open.

THE THIRD CHAPTER

Cyrus C. Crag Returns

It was an extraordinary sight that met the gaze of the five people as they surged forward and peered excitedly through the open door.

The room beyond was barely furnished. There were two single beds, a table, a couple of armchairs, and a bookcase. On the table was the remains of a meal, and seated in the armchairs, and securely bound to them with stout cords, were two men.

Both were elderly. One was clean-shaven, and the other had a bristling, grey moustache, and a complexion the colour of a beetroot. He was also possessed of a remarkably powerful voice, which he made good use of in a flow of language that betokened a past acquaintance with the Army.

For a full minute Sexton Blake and his companions stood staring in speechless amazement. What on earth did it mean? What fresh mystery lay behind this peculiar situation?

'How much longer are you going to stand gaping there, you confounded idiots?' suddenly bellowed the man with the bristling moustache. 'Come and undo these cords at once!'

Inspector Coutts was on his dignity at once.

'Now then, what's the meaning of all this?' he said ponderously, as he strode into the room. 'What are you doing here, and what's your name?'

The gentleman with the moustache seemed almost on the verge of an attack of apoplexy.

'Doing here!' he raved. 'I'll have you understand that this is my house! My name is Boden – Colonel Eustace Boden!'

'What are you sitting up here, making all that noise for?' put in the local constable, with a brilliant flash of inspiration, and gazing at Inspector Coutts in expectation of what he considered due appraisement.

It was Sexton Blake who stepped forward, and, drawing out his pocket-knife, severed the cords that bound Colonel Boden and his companion to their chairs.

The colonel bounded to his feet like an indiarubber ball, and waved his arms high and frenziedly in the air.

'Where are they? Where are the scoundrels?' he bellowed. 'Have you arrested the lot of them? By Jingo, just let me get anywhere near them!'

Inspector Coutts jumped out of the way just in time to avoid one of the colonel's circling fists, and it was Sexton Blake who stepped into the breach again.

'Who do you mean, colonel?' he asked soothingly. 'I think you'd better tell us all that's happened. My name is Sexton Blake.'

'Sexton Blake!' gulped Colonel Boden, with a stare. 'What, *the* Sexton Blake? The detective? What are you doing here? Were you after the fellows?'

'I can't say until you tell me what fellows you are referring to,' said the detective, with a smile. 'My real motive in being here is to have a chat with you. Perhaps you will tell us how you got into this extraordinary predicament.'

'Tell you! By thunder, I'll soon tell you!' puffed the colonel, waxing wroth again at the bare recollection of what he had gone through. 'I've been the victim of the most dastardly outrage that was ever perpetrated upon a respectable British citizen, and, by heavens, someone's going to suffer for it! I was having my supper when four scoundrels wearing black masks forced their way into my house and flung themselves on me, after having overpowered my servant.

'I put up a tough fight; but the hounds drugged me, and the next thing I knew I found myself tied up in this room, with Rooney beside me. And here I've been ever since, with one of the black-faced ruffians coming up every day to feed us like convicts.'

Inspector Coutts stroked his fat chin puzzledly, and he and Sexton Blake shot a blank glance at one another. It was a wild and woolly story on the face of it that the colonel had told, but they had not the slightest doubt that it was true.

But what on earth could it all mean? Who were the four men in the black masks, and what nefarious work were they up to?

'How long ago was this, colonel?' asked Sexton Blake suddenly.

'Well, it seemed about six months, but it was really about ten days ago.'

'And you've been here ever since a prisoner in your own house? Great Scott! There's something funny behind this!' grunted Inspector Coutts. 'A good thing I paid serious attention to that telegram!'

'Telegram! Did they send you a telegram, the impudent scoundrels?' snorted Colonel Boden. 'When they went off this morning they said they'd communicate with somebody to come and set us free. So that's what brought you here, inspector? And you, Mr Blake? I am puzzled as to what it is you wished to see me about.'

Sexton Blake looked up suddenly. He had been lost in thought. The two separate little receptacles in his brain which he had reserved – one for the insurance case that Henry Bargrove had put into his hands, and the other, just lately, for the extraordinary story that Colonel Boden had related – had suddenly amalgamated one into the other, and given him the idea that there was a strong connection between the two separate mysteries.

'What I wished to see you about, colonel?' he echoed. 'Oh, of course! I came here today to ask you if it was a fact that you just lately sold your Corottzi "Venus" to Mr Bernard Mellish for a hundred thousand pounds?'

Colonel Boden's eyes positively bulged in his head, and his moustache bristled ferociously.

'Sold! My Corottzi "Venus"!' he gulped spasmodically. 'Who's been circulating that confounded lie? My Corottzi "Venus"? I wouldn't sell that picture for all the money in the world! Sell it, indeed! You'll find it hanging up downstairs, unless – unless – '

Colonel Boden broke off short, and a look of horror crept across his face. Then with one bound he was out of the room and tearing down the stairs like a madman.

'The man's not in his right senses!' declared Inspector Coutts decidedly, and then almost jumped out of his skin as, an instant later, such a bellow of fury came echoing up from below as set every window in the house rattling.

'As I thought!' muttered Sexton Blake under his breath. 'This case is developing very quickly.'

He hurried down the stairs, followed by Inspector Coutts and the others, to find Colonel Eustace Boden standing in the hall, his whole frame positively quivering with rage.

'My Corottzi – gone – stolen!' he raved. 'Scoundrels – those villains! They must have taken it away with them! By heavens, I'll set the whole of Scotland Yard after them! I'll have them hung, drawn and quartered!'

Sexton Blake and Henry Bargrove shot a strange glance at one another.

'So the Corottzi was stolen!' gasped the insurance manager. 'This is a most extraordinary affair, Mr Blake. I am getting quite out of my depth.'

'What's this? Your Corottzi stolen?' asked Inspector Coutts, whipping out his notebook. 'What's that? A bit of jewellery, or some sort of a stuffed animal?'

'It's a painting – a valuable old master!' puffed the colonel scathingly. 'And worth a hundred thousand pounds!'

'Phew!' whistled the inspector, making copious notes and a laudable but unfortunate attempt to spell Corottzi. 'This looks like being a big case, Blake,' he went on, throwing a superior glance over his shoulder.

'Yes, I've already got it in hand,' said the Baker Street detective blandly.

'You've already what?' barked Inspector Coutts.

'I said that I'd already got the case in hand – have had since this morning.'

Coutts positively, glared.

'Do you mean to say you knew all along that this here – er – Carrotsea had been stolen?'

'By no means,' said Sexton Blake. 'I had my suspicions, though. I will tell you everything later on, when we are alone, Coutts, if Mr Bargrove here has no objection.'

Inspector Coutts looked somewhat mollified.

'The whole affair is confoundedly rummy!' he said as he proceeded to glean all the information that Colonel Boden's agitated state of mind would allow him to give. 'If those four men came here to steal that Car – oil-painting, why didn't they hop off with it at once, instead of staying on for ten days?'

'I dare say I shall be able to enlighten you on that point later on,' said Sexton Blake in a low voice. 'This is a far bigger case than you imagine, Coutts. It seems to be the work of a gang, and a very clever gang, too – hallo! Who the dickens have we here?'

There was the crunch of wheels on the gravel path outside, and the throbbing of a powerful motor. Hurried footsteps ascended the entrance steps, and someone gave the bell a tug that set it clattering and jangling fit to awaken the dead.

Rooney, Colonel Boden's manservant, who had soon slid back into his natural groove, after having spent ten whole days imprisoned in the same room with his short-tempered master, shuffled forward and swung the door open.

Drawn up outside was a long, grey, limousine-bodied motor-car, with a neatly-uniformed chauffeur seated at the wheel.

And standing on the threshold of the doorway a tall, thin, hatchet-faced man, clad in a travelling-ulster and a tweed cap. He carried a lengthy roll of brown paper in one hand, and there was a hard light of anger in his blue eyes as he allowed them to rove over the little group of men standing in the hall before him.

And then, as his gaze finally rested upon Colonel Eustace Boden, a faint flash of colour leapt up into his sallow cheeks, and he took a quick step forward.

'So there you are, you swindling old ruffian!' he rasped, with a strong American accent. 'And the police have nabbed you, have they – eh? About time, too! Where's my money? Hully gee! Guess I'll learn you to palm your imitation old masters off on me!'

And, with a snort of indignation, he flung his brown-paper roll down at the colonel's feet.

'Now kick in your nut before I make you!'

THE FOURTH CHAPTER

The Mystery Deepens

Had a bombshell burst in the centre of the little group standing in the entrance-hall of Delhi Lodge, it could not have caused a greater sensation than did the sudden arrival and dramatic denunciation of the tall, thin man in the travelling ulster.

There was an almost comical expression of surprise on Inspector Coutts's heavy features, as he stood, his pencil poised in one hand, his notebook in the other.

Sexton Blake's face was as expressionless as usual, and Tinker looked thoroughly interested.

Colonel Boden's bearing conveyed nothing but the most profound amazement and bewilderment. For quite a minute he stood staring blankly at the newcomer, and then he positively bristled with fury like an enraged hedgehog.

'May I ask what you mean by this most unwarrantable intrusion and your peculiar language, Mr Crag?' he snapped, in freezing tones. 'Have you taken leave of your senses, or have you an explanation to offer for your conduct? If not, I will bid you good afternoon! As you can see, I am busy with these gentlemen.'

'And you'll be a durn sight busier with 'em before I'm finished with you, colonel!' drawled Cyrus C. Crag meaningly. 'Goin to try and bluff it out, are you? You'll find that game won't pay! Come on! Either dub up my hundred thousand pounds, or hand over the genuine Corottzi, and I'll say no more about the dirty trick you tried to play on me! Good job I had another look at it before I got aboard the boat at Liverpool!'

A thrill of excitement ran through the assembly. What could it mean? What fresh mystery was this that had been sprung upon them at the eleventh hour?

If ever a man looked dazed and bewildered it was Colonel Eustace, and the keen glance that Sexton Blake shot at him showed him that he was not feigning.

'Still more developments!' he muttered, under his breath. 'When are we going to hear the last of this Corottzi "Venus", I wonder, and how many more people are implicated in it?'

'Mr Crag, I haven't the remotest idea what you are talking about,' said Colonel Boden at last, in steady tones. 'I can't understand your reference to my Corottzi, or to the large sum of money you mention.

'My Corottzi has been stolen. Ah, perhaps you know something about the thief, as you were so anxious to get it into your possession!'

Cyrus C. Crag passed his hand across his forehead, and uttered a long, low whistle of wonderment.

'Waal, if this don't beat the band!' he drawled. 'It won't do, colonel, you can't kid me! Your Corottzi stolen! What's the game? Why, you sold it to me – at least, you took the money for it, and then palmed off an imitation on me! Deny it if you can!'

'Deny it! By heavens, of course I deny it!' burst out Colonel Boden vehemently. 'You're either mad, or else I am!'

'Yes, I'm mad right enough – I'm as mad as a hornet over the way you tried to diddle me!'

Sexton Blake suddenly stepped forward between the two men. An inkling of the truth was beginning to filter into his brain.

'There's a big mistake here somewhere,' he said quietly; 'and the best thing to do is to get it cleared up as quickly as possible. Mr Crag – I think I recognise you as Mr Cyrus C. Crag, of New York – my name is Sexton Blake. Perhaps you have heard of me. If not, I may tell you I am a detective. You have made some remarkable accusations against Colonel Boden – perhaps on very good grounds, but perhaps erroneous ones. Perhaps you would kindly let me hear your story?'

'You can have it with pleasure!' said the American briskly. 'There ain't much of it, but what there is is to the point. I'll begin at the beginning. I've been over here in this country three weeks, and I came over for one special reason, and that was to make Colonel Boden an offer for his Corottzi "Venus", which I was dead-set on getting for my collection.

'But it weren't a bit of use. The colonel wouldn't sell, even though I ran the price up to a hundred thousand pounds, Is that correct, colonel?'

'Quite correct!' snapped the colonel icily, and all the time dreading that the millionaire would make a slip and mention Samuel Otzmann's gambling hell.

'I had almost given up hope of ever getting him to dub up,' went on Cyrus C. Crag, 'when, at what you might call the eleventh hour – that was yesterday – I received this letter from the colonel.'

'You what?' burst out Colonel Boden excitedly. 'A letter from me! I have never written you a letter in my life, sir!'

The American shrugged his shoulders, and passed the letter across to Sexton Blake.

The sheet of fine linen paper was stamped with the address, 'Delhi Lodge, Beech Avenue, Roehampton', and the missive ran as follows.

> Dear Sir, – If you are still of the same mind as regards your often-expressed desire to purchase my Corottzi 'Venus', I should be glad if you would give me a call at your earliest convenience. Circumstances have compelled me to alter my previous decision.
> – Faithfully yours,
>
> Eustace G. Boden, Colonel H.M.F.

Sexton Blake studied the letter quizzically – Inspector Coutts leaning interestedly over his shoulder – and then handed it across to the owner of the much discussed and now vanished Corottzi.

'Is that your writing, colonel?' he asked.

Colonel Boden's eyes almost popped out of his head, and he turned as white as a sheet as he glared at the sheet of paper.

'Great heavens! What does this mean?' he gasped. 'It's my writing, and yet it's not my writing, for I never penned this letter. It's forgery, and a particularly audacious forgery! And on my notepaper, too!'

Cyrus G. Crag still smiled sceptically as he continued his story.

'I answered that letter in person,' he went one. 'I called here yesterday afternoon, and saw Colonel Boden – '

'By Jupiter, this is too much!' roared Colonel Boden. 'You confounded liar – '

'One moment, colonel. You will be able to say all you want to say afterwards,' said Sexton Blake, laying a conciliatory hand on the old man's arm.

'I repeat that I saw Colonel Boden,' continued Cyrus C. Crag defiantly. 'We conversed in that room there, and he informed me that he was compelled to part with the Corottzi, as he had suffered a severe financial reverse. I renewed my offer of one hundred thousand pounds, and he told me that he would accept if I made it guineas. Guineas it was. With his own hands the colonel took the Corottzi down from where it hung over the fireplace, and his servant – Rooney, I think he called him – '

'There is my servant Rooney!' cut in Colonel Boden sharply, pointing to the old man in the faded livery.

'Not the one I saw!' declared Cyrus C. Crag curtly, after one keen glance. 'As I was saying, the servant removed the picture from the frame, took out the nails and stripped off the canvas, and packed it up like that.'

He pointed to the lengthy roll of brown paper that still lay where he had thrown it on the floor.

'Without further ado I made the colonel out an open cheque for one hundred thousand guineas. He asked me to do him a special favour, and that was not to make it known that he had sold me the Corottzi until I reached the other side of the water. It was a cunning wheeze, but it didn't work. He thought that I wouldn't unpack the picture until then; but I had another look at it at my hotel in Liverpool, just before I was due to sail on the *Megantic*. What did I find, but that it wasn't the genuine Corottzi at all, but a dud copy that had been palmed off on me. He must have had another parcel made up just like the one I saw him prepare, and changed them while I was writing out the cheque.

"That's why I'm here now. Cyrus C. Crag wasn't going to be made a fool of like that! I gave up the idea of catching the *Megantic*, and came straight back to London. I had already wired my bank to stop the cheque, but it was too late. And now that have you got to say, Colonel? Where's that one hundred and five thousand pounds?'

Colonel Boden's jaw was set like a vice.

'What I've got to say is that I've never heard such an outrageous piece of fiction in my life!' he said vehemently. 'Either you are guilty of having composed it, Mr Crag, or else there is a bigger mystery behind all this than I can fathom. For the past ten days I have been kept a prisoner in a room at the top of this house by four unprincipled scoundrels, who broke in and overpowered me. These gentlemen will vouch for that.'

A puzzled look crept into Cyrus C. Crag's grey eyes.

'Say, is that so?' he said slowly. 'But how can it be, when I saw you yesterday, colonel?'

'You did not see me yesterday!' declared Colonel Boden. 'I don't know how you can stick to such a ridiculous assertion!'

'I think I can offer an explanation,' said Sexton Blake quietly. 'Both of you are correct in the versions you stick to. It appears to me, Colonel Boden and Mr Crag, that the two of you have been the victims of one of the cleverest swindles that was ever evolved or carried out. I am not going into details at present; but allow me to inform you, Mr Crag, that it was not Colonel Boden whom you interviewed here yesterday.'

'Say, do you think I can't trust my own eyes?'

'To a certain extent, yes,' replied the detective, with a smile. 'But they deceived you yesterday. The person you saw then was, without doubt, a man cleverly made up as Colonel Boden. It was he who so obligingly took your cheque for the Corottzi, and palmed a copy off on you. At that moment Colonel Boden was a prisoner at the top of the house, as was his servant. It was only a bare hour ago that they were released.'

'But this letter?'

'A clever forgery. If you will allow me, I will take charge of that. It may prove a valuable clue.'

'Waal, I'll be durned!' said Cyrus C. Crag, slowly and with much emphasis. 'If this don't beat the band! Colonel, if what Mr Blake says is right – and I'd rather trust his opinion than mine – then I owe you an almighty apology. Will you shake?'

'With the greatest of pleasure!' replied Colonel Boden, throwing back his square shoulders. 'We are both losers in the trick that has been played on us. You have lost your hundred thousand guineas, and I've lost the Corottzi that I would not have parted with for ten times that amount!'

'But we're going to get it all back again!' declared Cyrus C. Crag with a confident shake of his head. 'I feel certain of that now that I know it's Mr Sexton Blake, the famous private detective, who's on the job! Get the bracelets on the chap who diddled me out of that hundred thousand guineas and who snaffled the colonel's Corottzi, and I'll give you an open cheque to draw what you like, Mr Blake!'

'I should advise you to be a little more careful with your cheques, Mr Crag,' smiled Sexton Blake. 'And I fancy there is more than one chap. There must be four at least. And that reminds me. Coutts, with Colonel Boden's permission, I think we will have a look round. After having resided here as uninvited guests for at least ten days, it is extremely possible that our birds may have left some clue as to their identity behind. If you don't mind waiting, Mr Bargrove, we will drive back to town together.'

THE FIFTH CHAPTER

What Blake Discovered at the Estate Agents'

Sexton Blake was nothing if not thorough. He had the nose of a bloodhound and the sight of a hawk, and it was an object-lesson in doing a thing and doing it in the right way to watch him examining a room in search of some infinitesimal something that might serve as a clue.

A single hair, a grain of sand, a fragment of bootlace – all received their due scrutiny and mental valuation.

'What do you make of this case, Blake?' muttered Inspector Coutts as he followed the Baker Street detective about from room to room, somewhat in the manner of a clumsy retriever following a graceful greyhound. 'I little dreamed what it was going to lead to when I got that telegram this morning.'

'It's one of the biggest cases that I've ever struck,' replied Sexton Blake, sniffing at a tumbler he had picked off the mantel-piece of the room he was in. 'H'm! morphine! One of our men is evidently addicted to drugs. I don't think there's anything more to learn here, Coutts. If you're going my way I'll give you a lift in our taxi.'

'Just suit me!' grunted the inspector as he led the way out of the room.

Sexton Blake halted on the threshold and suddenly turned back. His observant eye had caught sight of a strip of something hanging down in the fireplace as though it had been stuffed hurriedly up the chimney.

With a quick jerk he pulled it free. It was an oblong piece of green canvas, about two feet long by about a foot wide, and as the detective turned it over and examined it a gasp of excitement passed his lips, and a strange sparkle crept into his eyes.

'Well, I'll be hanged!' he muttered under his breath. 'So that is how it was done! Henry Bargrove is right! There's some brains behind this gang, or my name's not Sexton Blake!'

He stood for a moment gazing ruminatively at what he had found, and then, placing it carefully in his pocket, followed Inspector Coutts out into the hall.

'Run those scoundrels down and get my Corottzi back for me, and you're on a reward of two thousand pounds, inspector!' Colonel Eustace Boden was saying excitedly.

'And I guess I'll duplicate that offer!' drawled Cyrus C. Crag. 'See, what gets my goat is to think that I was so easily roped in – and for a hundred and five thousand pounds clean off the reel! Now I look at you, colonel, I can see that you're not the same man who sold me the dud Corottzi. But, by thunder, it was a darned good make-up! Who do you reckon it was, Mr Blake?'

Sexton Blake shrugged his shoulders.

'I haven't the remotest idea, Mr Crag,' he said candidly; 'but I think and trust that I soon shall. Such superlatively clever scoundrels ought to be easily traced, for there are not many about capable of having carried out such a cunning scheme.'

A few minutes later the four of them – Sexton Blake, Henry Bargrove, Inspector Coutts, and Tinker – had entered the taxi that was still waiting outside for them. Cyrus C. Crag and Colonel Eustace Boden had found something in common in their mutual loss, and the American millionaire remained behind to talk the matter over with the late owner of the Corottzi 'Venus'.

'Now then, Blake, what the dickens does all this mean?' asked Inspector Coutts curiously as he leaned back in his seat and helped himself from the detective's cigar-case. 'What is it that you have to tell me? What brought you over to see Colonel Boden today? What gave you the idea that the Corottzi "Venus" had been stolen?'

'One question at a time, my dear Coutts,' said Sexton Blake queerly. 'I'm not a human gramophone. And before I satisfy your curiosity I must ask Mr Bargrove's permission, and you must give your promise of secrecy.'

'Mr Bargrove's permission!' echoed the C.I.D. man, staring blankly at the insurance manager. 'What in the name of sense has the Corottzi "Venus" got to do with Mr Bargrove?'

Sexton Blake lifted his eyebrows interrogatively, and Henry Bargrove gave a nod of his head.

'Yes, you can tell Inspector Coutts, so long as he does not allow it to go any further,' he assented wearily.

Sexton Blake flicked the ash neatly from his cigar, and then in a few brief sentences he related everything that Henry Bargrove had told him that morning. He told of the visit that Mr Bernard Mellish had paid to the Impregnable Insurance Company, of his desire to insure his property against fire and burglary, and of Mr Bargrove's trip to the Lindens in the vogue of assessor.

Inspector Coutts's eyes positively bulged in his head as the detective went on to tell of the Corottzi 'Venus' that Mellish declared he had purchased from Colonel Boden, of the receipt he showed, on the face of which Henry Bargrove unsuspectingly issued him a policy for £100,000.

By the time he had heard the rest of the narrative, dealing with the fire, the payment of the insurance, and the cablegram from the real Bernard Mellish in New York, Inspector Coutts was in a state of utter bewilderment.

'Great Scott, Blake, what in the name of goodness does it all mean?' he gasped, pulling out an enormous handkerchief and mopping his forehead perplexedly. 'This makes things about a hundred times worse. How could the Corottzi "Venus" have been at the Lindens, and been destroyed in the fire? The fire took place several days ago, and it was only yesterday that that

American fellow, Cyrus C. Crag, saw it at the colonel's house, palmed off on him instead of the original.'

'But it was not at the Lindens that I first saw the Corottzi "Venus",' broke in Henry Bargrove. 'I'm positive of that. The house that we have just left – Delhi Lodge – is the house that Bernard Mellish took me to. And – and yet I saw the name on the gate with my own eyes. I can't make it out! I can't understand it at all!'

'I can,' said Sexton Blake calmly. 'If I am not much mistaken, I fancy I know exactly how the whole affair worked.'

The three other occupants of the taxi turned to him in mingled wonder and amazement.

'If you'll listen for a few minutes, and don't interrupt, I'll try and reconstruct the whole business,' went on the detective as he lighted a fresh cigar. 'It's one of the biggest swindles that's been carried out. I think we are safe in the assumption that the supposed Bernard Mellish and his three accomplices – from Colonel Boden's story it is obvious that he had three accomplices, if not more – resided at the Lindens. No doubt the real Bernard Mellish let the place furnished when he went to New York – probably placed it in the hands of an agent. That we must inquire into.

'In some way or other the gang, as we will refer to them, learned of Colonel Boden's valuable Corottzi, and also of Cyrus C. Crag's anxiety to buy it. Working on this knowledge, they formulated the following scheme.

'Some ten or more days ago the four of them made their way to Delhi Lodge, overpowered both Colonel Boden and his manservant, and took possession of the place. The following day one of the rogues, without doubt disguised, called at the Impregnable Insurance Company's office, and under the name of Bernard Mellish interviewed Mr Bargrove with reference to insuring his place, the Lindens. By pleading urgency, he prevailed upon Mr Bargrove to accompany him to assess the property he wanted to insure. Instead of driving Mr Bargrove to the Lindens, he drove him to Delhi Lodge – '

Henry Bargrove sat up in his seat and shook his head bewilderedly.

'But – but how can that have been, Mr Blake?' he broke in. 'I am positive that I was driven to the Lindens. I saw the name on the gate. And yet it was the same house we have just left. Oh, I can't make it out at all!'

'I'll explain to you,' went on Sexton Blake, with a quiet smile. 'Perhaps you noticed, Mr Bargrove, that all the houses in Beech Avenue are built in the same style? Outwardly you can scarcely tell one from the other, save by the name on the gate.

'It was the first time you had ever been to Beech Avenue. I don't suppose you paid particular attention to the house you were taken to. You didn't notice its exact position?'

Henry Bargrove shook his head blankly, and Sexton Blake drew something from his pocket. It was the strip of green canvas that he had found poked up the chimney of one of the rooms of Delhi Lodge, and as he smoothed it out on his knee, and his companions bent their gaze on it, they saw that printed upon it in large white letters was the name, 'The Lindens'.

'You were driven to Delhi Lodge, Mr Bargrove!' cried the Baker Street detective triumphantly. 'When your car turned into Beech Avenue one of the gang, who must have been on the watch, fastened this piece of canvas over the name on the gate. There you saw it, and naturally did not dream but that you were entering the Lindens.'

Henry Bargrove uttered a sharp cry of amazement, and Inspector Coutts sucked in a deep breath and puffed out his crimson cheeks.

'Well, I'll be hanged!' gasped the C.I.D. man, almost admiringly. 'That's a deuced clever wheeze! When did you get hold of that, Blake?'

'I found it stuffed up one of the chimneys at Delhi Lodge,' explained Sexton Blake, 'and I at once guessed what it had been intended and used for. So you see, Mr Bargrove, that is how you were deceived into thinking you were visiting the Lindens.'

The insurance manager nodded mutely. He was too flabbergasted for words.

'Small wonder, when you examined the house and were shown the Corottzi, that you consented to issue the supposed Mr Bernard Mellish the policy he required. The receipt he showed you was obviously a forgery, but the title-deeds of the Lindens were probably genuine. I have no doubt they fell into the rogues' hands when they took the place furnished.

'So far, so good. Now came the riskiest part of the whole affair. Mr Bernard Mellish ostensibly left town, and a few days later the Lindens was deliberately set on fire, and a jemmy left behind to give thc impression that burglars had broken in and accidentally started a conflagration. Meanwhile, the gang still remained in residence at Delhi Lodge. They probably gleefully watched the Lindens burning from its very windows.'

'The dastardly scoundrels!' muttered Henry Bargrove under his breath. 'And we were fools enough to pay the insurance!'

'You were,' said Sexton Blake candidly. 'But then, of course, you were not to know. The rogues now entered upon the second part of their scheme,' he went on. 'They were not satisfied with the hundred and ten thousand pounds they had already netted. They saw a simple way of doubling it, and they didn't hesitate to carry it out. Another forgery was perpetrated in the shape of that letter to Cyrus C. Crag, purporting to come from Colonel Boden, and expressing his willingness to sell his Corottzi.

'Crag was easy game. He never dreamed for one moment that it was not Colonel Boden, but an impostor, whom he was dealing with. He was shown the Corottzi, and saw it carefully removed from its frame and packed up. And then, while he was making out his cheque, the parcel was adroitly changed for one that had been specially made up previous to his arrival; and Cyrus C. Crag went off with a spoof picture.

'That leaves the gang with a profit of a clear two hundred and fifteen thousand pounds, and the genuine Corottzi still in their possession. No doubt they will be able to get another hundred thousand pounds on it. Not a bad haul – eh, Coutts?'

Inspector Coutts lay back in his seat and gave vent to a long, low whistle of blank stupefaction.

'By heavens, Blake, it's one of the most diabolically clever swindles I've ever heard of!' he gasped at last. 'And what a combination of crimes – false pretences, arson, forgery, imposture! You're right, Blake; it must be the work of a particularly clever gang. But who? We haven't got the slightest clue to their identity.'

Sexton Blake pursed his thin lips as he threw the butt of his cigar out of the window.

'I'm not so certain,' he said slowly. 'I fancy that I could name one – if not two – of them. Take this, for instance.'

He put his hand in his pocket, and drew out the letter that Cyrus C. Crag had received, and which Colonel Boden had condemned as a particularly audacious and clever forgery.

'There's only one man could have written this,' he said grimly. 'Do you know who I mean, Coutts?'

Inspector Coutts took the letter, studied it, rubbed his heavy chin, and then gave a slight start of enlightenment.

'By James, I know who you mean, Blake! Nicholas Mark – Nick the Nib!'

'Just what I was going to say!' cut in Tinker eagerly.

Sexton Blake nodded his head.

'I don't think there's the slightest doubt about it,' he said quietly. 'There are not many expert forgers outside of prison in England at the present time. But Nick Mark is one of them, and I'll wager anything that he also is one of the gang who have stolen the Corottzi "Venus". Have you any idea what Mark's movements have been of late, Coutts?'

The C.I.D. man shook his head.

'I haven't,' he admitted frankly. 'He only came out of prison a couple of months ago, and since then he seems to have vanished into thin air. I thought he'd gone abroad. I'll make inquiries up at the Yard. One of my men may have seen him lately. But – hallo! what the dickens are we stopping here for?'

The cab had suddenly pulled up in the Hammersmith Road, just the other side of the Broadway, and directly outside a shop, on the facade of which was the name, 'Ray & Snows, Auctioneers and Estate Agents'.

'I told the driver to stop here,' said Sexton Blake, as he opened the cab door. 'I noticed several "To Let" boards bearing this firm's name in Beech Avenue, and I thought they might know something about the letting of the Lindens. I shan't keep you a minute.'

The detective crossed the pavement and entered the shop, where a fair-haired young man came forward with a polite bow.

'Goodmorning!' said Sexton Blake. 'I understand that you are the agents for a considerable amount of property in Beech Avenue, Roehampton?'

'Yes; we have several houses there on our books,' replied the young man. 'In what way can we serve you, sir?'

'Was the Lindens amongst those on your books?'

'The Lindens – you mean the house that was lately burnt down? No. That was the sole property of Mr Bernard Mellish. We did act for him some years ago, when he desired to let it furnished. But I understand that he always leaves it in the hands of his lawyer now.'

'His lawyer?' echoed Sexton Blake keenly. 'Could you oblige me with the name of the gentleman in question?'

'I don't know it myself, but I will ask Mr Snow!' said the clerk, a little puzzledly.

He hurried away into another room, and reappeared an instant later.

'Mr Mellish's lawyer is Brandon Delmas, of 36a, Chancery Lane.' Sexton Blake gave a slight start, and a strange gleam crept into his steely blue eyes.

Brandon Delmas! So he was the real Bernard Mellish's lawyer? And yet he was also the man who vouched for the impostor who had defrauded the Impregnable, and who had put in the claim and drawn the insurance money!

'H'm! This is getting interesting!' muttered the Baker Street detective. 'I think I am getting on the right track.'

He thanked the estate agents' clerk, and hastened back to his companion in the waiting taxi.

'Ah! I can see you have learned something, guv'nor!' said Tinker curiously. 'What's in the wind?'

'Yes, I have learned something,' replied the detective, as he lit a fresh cigar. 'Mr Bargrove, would it surprise you to know that I have just been informed that the real Mr Bernard Mellish's lawyer is none other than Brandon Delmas?'

'Brandon Delmas!' echoed the insurance agent. 'But how can that be? This is very strange, Mr Blake! If Delmas acted for the real Bernard Mellish, how came he to be also acting for the impostor who deceived me?'

'There is only one explanation to it,' said Sexton Blake convincedly. 'Delmas is one of the gang. He was implicated in the whole scheme to defraud you and steal the Corottzi "Venus".'

Inspector Coutts's jaw dropped, and he stared blankly.

'Preposterous! Ridiculous, Blake!' he jerked almost indignantly. 'Brandon Delmas, one of the most famous criminal lawyers we've got in England, mixed up with a gang of swindlers! There's a big mistake somewhere!'

'There would be if I were to be so cocksure of Delmas's innocence as you are,' replied Sexton Blake blandly. 'The man is obviously a criminal lawyer in more senses of the word than one. I suggest that you arrest him at once – if you can find him. I have always had an idea in my head that the man was not straight.'

THE SIXTH CHAPTER

Getting on the Track

Inspector Coutts was loud in scornful ridicule of Sexton Blake's suspicions of Brandon Delmas, and even Mr Henry Bargrove seemed doubtful on the point. It seemed incredible that the famous lawyer – the man whose name was a household word almost – should be the accomplice of rogues and vagabonds.

But Sexton Blake paid no attention to their arguments. He was convinced in his own mind that Brandon Delmas had been deeply implicated in the case of the Corottzi 'Venus'.

Without doubt, he reasoned, Delmas had let the real Bernard Mellish's house, furnished, to the gang of cracksmen, and had supplied them with the title-deeds that had been used to convince Henry Bargrove of their authenticity.

Again, he had vouched for the pseudo-Bernard Mellish, and had even drawn the cheque for the one hundred and ten thousand pounds insurance money.

'No; the man's an arrant scoundrel!' muttered Sexton Blake. 'And goodness knows how many other thefts and swindles he hasn't been mixed up with under the guise of a lawyer. This is evidently his last coup. He must realise that he is bound to be found out, and I shouldn't be surprised if he has not already left the country. I wonder who the dickens the other two members of the gang are, and who was the clever ruffian who impersonated Colonel Boden?'

He had given the cabman instructions to drive to 36a, Chancery Lane, but he had not the slightest hope that he would find Brandon Delmas there.

And he was correct in this supposition. The lawyer's head clerk volunteered the information that Mr Delmas had gone out of town on business the previous day, and had not as yet returned.

'Have you any idea where he has gone?' asked Sexton Blake.

'No, sir. He did not say.'

'Could you give me his private address?'

The clerk drew himself up stiffly. 'No, sir; I cannot!' he said coldly.

Sexton Blake drew a card from his pocket, and planked it down on the counter before him.

'That is my name – Sexton Blake!' he said curtly. 'I am a detective, and I must insist that you give me the information that I require. This gentleman here is Detective-Inspector Coutts of Scotland Yard.'

The mention of two such well-known names had a remarkable effect on the lawyer's clerk. He crumpled up like a sheet of tissue-paper, and showed himself only too willing to answer any questions.

'Mr Delmas has no real private address, sir,' he stammered, obviously bewildered by the proceedings. 'He has been staying at the Waldemar Hotel as far back as I can remember.'

'The Waldemar!' whispered Mr Henry Bargrove. 'Why, that is where I went to see the man who posed as Bernard Mellish, when he was supposed to be laid up with the shock of the loss of his home!'

Sexton Blake nodded, and turned to the clerk again.

'Just one more question,' he said curtly. 'Where does Mr Delmas bank?'

'The West Central United Bank, in Kingsway.'

Sexton Blake had gained all the information that he required.

'What the dickens is the game now, Blake?' grunted Inspector Coutts, as they returned to the taxi. 'I tell you straight, you're making a big mistake. What did you want to know Delmas's bank for?'

'I'll show you when we get there,' replied the detective blandly. 'If I am not in error, we shall learn something that will compel you to alter your opinions.'

The West Central United Bank in Kingsway was but a stone's-throw from the office in Chancery Lane, and, leaving Tinker and Henry Bargrove in the cab, Sexton Blake and the C.I.D. man entered the imposing premises, and the detective sent his card in to the manager.

A moment later they were ushered into a comfortably furnished office, and a stout, bald-headed man, with gold-rimmed glasses, rose from behind the flat-topped desk to greet them.

'This is an unexpected pleasure, Mr Blake!' he smiled. 'What can I do for you?'

'I have come to you for a little information regarding one of your clients, Mr Hebstone. This is Detective-Inspector Coutts, of Scotland Yard!'

The bank manager stared puzzledly, as he shook hands with the C.I.D. man.

'One of my clients?' he echoed uneasily. 'Who do you mean, Mr Blake?'

'Mr Brandon Delmas. I believe he has an account with you?'

Mr Hebstone looked more bewildered than ever.

'Mr Delmas! Yes, he banks with us. But surely there is nothing wrong? Mr Delmas, of all people! Why –'

'I only want to ask you one question,' said Sexton Blake quietly. 'How does Mr Delmas's account stand at present? Has he drawn any large sum out within the last couple of days?'

The bank manager drew out a voluminous silk handkerchief, and mopped his bald head.

'Why, yes – yes! As a matter of fact, he has. Mr Delmas called here yesterday, and drew practically everything he had out of the bank. He said that he had a big investment to make, and just left enough money behind to keep his account running. Just over two hundred thousand pounds he took away.'

Sexton Blake gave a sharp exclamation of satisfaction, and Inspector Coutts's jaw dropped.

'By James, Blake, I believe you're right after all!' the detective gasped. 'Brandon Delmas must have been in with the gang! And he's hopped it with them! That's why he drew all the money out of the bank.'

'Exactly! I told you I should get you to alter you opinion, Coutts,' said Sexton Blake blandly. 'Don't be alarmed, Mr Hebstone. Brandon Delmas has done nothing that can reflect upon your bank. I can't explain anything to you now; but I want you to let me have a list of the numbers of all the notes that you handed over to Mr Delmas yesterday.'

Five minutes later the two men left the bank premises with the required list in their possession.

'But where now, Blake?' asked Inspector Coutts eagerly.

Now that he was convinced of Brandon Delmas's villainy he was all on tenterhooks to get on the man's track.

'The Waldemar Hotel,' replied the Baker Street detective. 'We will see what we can learn there.'

The Waldemar was a palatial new hotel that had been but lately erected on one of the vacant Kingsway sites, and the manager was a courteous person, who willingly placed his services at the detective's disposal, meanwhile expressing great amazement that their inquiries should deal with the famous Mr Brandon Delmas.

'Oh, yes, Mr Delmas has been stopping here, on and off, for the past twelve months! His rooms are always reserved for him; but he does not always sleep here.'

'You had another gentleman, a Mr Bernard Mellish, staying here?' asked Sexton Blake, as he nipped the end off a cigar, and lit up.

'Mr Bernard Mellish! Ah, yes; he was a friend of Mr Delmas's! He only stopped for a couple of days. He was confined to his room with a nervous breakdown,' replied the manager. 'He left yesterday morning.'

Sexton Blake's lids dropped over his eyes as he gazed thoughtfully at the glowing end of his Havana.

'Did Mr Mellish leave with Mr Delmas?' he inquired.

'Oh, no! Mr Delmas left later in the day.'

'You have no idea where either of them was bound for?'

'Not the vaguest. Mr Delmas often goes away for a few days at a time.'

'Did he take any more luggage than usual away with him on this occasion?'

'You seem to know everything, Mr Blake,' said the hotel manager puzzledly. 'As a matter of fact, I remarked at the time that Mr Delmas was carrying a lot of luggage for a few days' trip. He took his two gladstone-bags, a dressing-case, and, let me see – ah, a golf-bag and clubs!'

'A golf-bag and clubs!' echoed Sexton Blake musingly. 'Quite new, Mr Auckland – eh? Only bought yesterday, perhaps?'

'Why ask me those questions when you already know the answer, Mr Blake?' said the manager, with a bewildered gesture of his hands. 'Yes, the golf-bag was quite new. It was delivered only yesterday from Ramages.'

'What the deuce are you driving at, Blake?' muttered Inspector Coutts querulously.

'A roll of canvas is an awkward thing to carry about, Coutts,' said Sexton Blake, in a low voice, and with a meaning glance at his companion. 'Now, I wouldn't mind wagering that, besides the clubs, the new golf-bag also contained the Corottzi "Venus"!'

Inspector Coutts opened his mouth, and shut it again with a snap.

'You're a blessed wonder, Blake!' he breathed admiringly. 'It never struck me. Of course, you're right again! Where do you think Delmas and his fellow-scoundrels have gone to with the Corottzi?'

'That is what we must endeavour to ascertain,' said the detective thoughtfully. 'Ah, I have an idea! One moment, Coutts!'

There was a bureau de change situated in the entrance-hall of the big hotel, and Sexton Blake stepped quickly over to it, and engaged in a brisk conversation with the young clerk behind the steel grille.

He returned a couple of minutes later, and there was a faint flush of excitement in his pale cheeks and a keen glint of triumph in his eyes.

'Coutts,' he said calmly, 'Brandon Delmas and his fellow crooks have gone to France.'

Inspector Coutts gasped like a floundering codfish as he stared bewilderedly at his friend.

'France!' he spluttered. 'What the deuce do you mean, Blake? How do you know? What makes you think that?'

'For the simple reason,' said Sexton Blake, almost gaily, 'that before Brandon Delmas left the hotel yesterday he was foolish enough to change two hundred-pound Bank of England notes into French money. The clerk at the bureau de change has just told me. For what other reason would Delmas want French money unless he were going to France? Besides, French notes are almost impossible to trace, as they bear no numbers!'

THE SEVENTH CHAPTER

In Paris

Inspector Coutts plumped himself down on one of the comfortable lounge-seats, and blew his nose vigorously.

'Now, why the dickens didn't I think of that?' he said, almost pathetically. 'I feel like a child in long-clothes when I'm out with you, Blake! But France is a confoundedly big place. What part do you think they have gone to?'

Sexton Blake shrugged his shoulders as he carefully placed the remains of his cigar in one of the silver ash-trays.

'When one speaks of France one immediately thinks of Paris,' he said quietly. 'And to a man with plenty of money in his pockets Paris is an irresistible magnet. It is also an excellent hiding-place for the criminal genius, and a place where illegitimately-obtained old masters can occasionally be disposed of without a great deal of trouble. Yes, Coutts, I think we can safely say that our birds have flown to Paris.'

'And what do you mean to do?' asked the C.I.D. man eagerly.

'Why, follow them, of course. I am anxious to know the composition of this superlatively clever gang who have got away with, approximately, three hundred thousand pounds. We will endeavour to find out how much of that sum they changed into French money. Tinker.'

He beckoned to his young assistant, who was standing outside by the waiting cab.

'I want you to get another taxi, and run down to the head office of Cook's. See the manager, and ask him to find out from his various branches, by telephone, if, during the last few days, there has been an inordinate desire for French notes. When you have done that, come straight back to Baker Street. We are catching the night-boat to Paris.'

'To Paris!' echoed Tinker delightedly. 'You've got a clue, then, guv'nor? You know where the gang have gone?'

'I have a pretty good idea. I'll tell you when you come back.'

Tinker was off like a shot out of a gun, and, bidding the puzzled hotel manager good-day, Sexton Blake returned to his cab, and briefly gave Mr Henry Bargrove the result of his investigations.

'Get back to your business, and leave everything in mine and Inspector Coutts's hands,' he said meaningly. 'And tell your directors to sit tight and do the same. If I am not very much in error, we shall have the rogues by the heels in a very short time, and we will have recovered at least the greater part of the money of which your firm have been defrauded.'

Henry Bargrove departed in a happier frame of mind than he had enjoyed for the past forty-eight hours, and Sexton Blake and Inspector Coutts went off different ways in different taxis – Blake back to his rooms in Baker Street, and the C.I.D. man to make arrangements with headquarters.

There was at least a couple of hours to spare before the boat-train left Charing Cross, and Sexton Blake leisurely devoured the tea that Mrs Bardell brought him, and then proceeded to fling a change of linen and his toilet and shaving utensils into a well-worn leather dressing-case.

By the time he had finished his packing there was the sound of a taxi outside, and a few minutes later Tinker came bounding up the stairs into the room.

'I've been as quick as I could, guv'nor!' he panted, as he flung himself into a chair. 'But the manager at the head office kept me waiting some time whilst he rang up the branch offices. He seemed surprised that you should know that there was such a large demand for French notes yesterday. He said it exceeded anything that he had known for a long while. Over a hundred thousand pounds' worth was passed over the counters yesterday!'

'Not all at the same branch, of course?'

'Oh, no! Split up amongst the lot.'

Sexton Blake nodded his head, as he carefully filled his largest cigar-case, and in a few sentences he told Tinker of the discovery that he had made at the Waldemar Hotel, which had put him on the track of Brandon Delmas and his fellow cracksmen and swindlers.

'What you have told me absolutely clinches it,' he said decisively. "They are a cunning lot to change their proceeds into French notes, for, having no numbers on them, they are not easily traced. Members of the gang must have gone all over London getting rid of English banknotes; but by so doing they have betrayed their intentions. Hurry up and get a few things together, Tinker! We have got to get to Charing Cross to meet Coutts and catch the boat-train to Dover!'

Inspector Coutts was pacing impatiently up and down the entrance-hall of the station twenty minutes later, when Sexton Blake and his young assistant, accompanied by Pedro the bloodhound, arrived upon the scene. The Baker Street detective had special permission from those in high quarters to take his famous animal out of the country and bring it back again whenever he so chose without submitting to the quarantine restrictions.

'Saw Sir Henry Fairfax – fixed up everything,' jerked the C.I.D. man, with one eye on the clock. 'And I've got the necessary warrants and credentials for the French Préfecture. Let's hope it won't turn out to be a wild goose chase, Blake!'

'I fancy not,' said Sexton Blake quietly as they strolled towards the waiting train; and he told of the result of his inquiries at Cook's.

The run to Dover was uneventful. All had travelled the same route dozens of times before, and the journey had no interest for them. Sexton Blake buried his head in the great pile of newspapers and periodicals that he had purchased, whilst Inspector Coutts pulled his cap down over his eyes and proceeded to drown the rumble of the wheels with his snores. Tinker also dozed, with Pedro's head resting in his lap.

A salt, bracing breeze was blowing as they left the train at Dover and passed into the cross-Channel boat. After a hearty meal, during which time the vessel had cast off, they returned to the deck, and paced briskly up and down to the throbbing tune of the churning propellers.

'Delmas and his gang have got exactly twenty-four hours' start of us,' said Sexton Blake, shielding the flame with his palm as he set a light to his favourite briar. 'They must have travelled over on this very boat last night, and probably trod this very deck where we tread it now. I have made inquiries in the bar. The man there has vague recollections of a party of four gentlemen who spent most of their time either there or in the smoke-room playing cards; but he is unable to give any definite description, save that one was very tall and dark, one was very young in appearance, one was a very heavy drinker, and the fourth one was in a particularly good-humour. That is not much to go on.'

Inspector Coutts was not a very good sailor. Suddenly experiencing unpleasant qualms, he went downstairs, where he remained in a state of suspended animation until the boat put into Calais harbour.

From then onwards all three of them slept as the train carried them on through the darkness over the French countryside towards its great capital.

And the first flush of dawn was tingeing the sky as they rolled into the Gare du Nord, and a horde of chattering porters and officials swept down upon them.

Paris in the early dawn is a Paris rubbing its eyes drowsily and going to bed, whereas in London that is the hour when the City awakes and the wheels of labour are set in motion. No one ever seems to work in Paris – at least, you apparently see no visible signs of toil. I don't know whether it is because the industrial quarters are so securely hidden away, or whether it is that the Parisian takes such a cheery pleasure in his work that it is not recognisable in that guise.

After Pedro had made a vain attempt to masticate a burly ruffian in a blue blouse who pounced on the new arrivals' luggage like a cat on a mouse, the whole lot of them squeezed into a taxi, and were driven to a quiet hotel situated in the locality of the Place de l'Opéra.

THE EIGHTH CHAPTER

On the Track at Last – What Blake Saw in the Cafe de Vivre

'Blake, I'm beginning to think that we've come on a wild goose chase after all. I shall have the chief wiring for me to come back if something doesn't turn up soon.'

Inspector Coutts spoke moodily as he sat at the little table on the pavement outside the Café de la Paix.

'You always were an impatient old grumbler, Coutts!' said Sexton Blake quietly as he fondled Pedro's silky ears and gazed at the ever-moving stream of varied humanity that passed before him. 'You surely didn't expect us to run our quarry to earth within a couple of hours? You forget the difficulties we have to combat. Paris is a big city for one thing; and for another Delmas and his companions are bound to be disguised, and not likely to advertise their presence too conspicuously, even though they are unaware that they are being sought for.'

Three days had elapsed since they had set foot in Paris, and so far no trace or sign of Brandon Delmas, his three accomplices, or the Corottzi 'Venus' had been seen or found.

And Sexton Blake had not let the grass grow under his feet. The Paris police had been made fully aware of the reason of their presence in the French capital, and, working on the all too meagre description that they had been supplied with, were doing their best to run the gang of swindlers to earth.

There was not a quarter of the city that Sexton Blake and Coutts had not visited, scarcely a place of amusement that they had not attended, or an hotel that had not had its visitors' list keenly scanned, and up to now without success.

'I say again that I think we're on a wild goose chase!' grunted Inspector Coutts irritably as he crumbled up a piece of his roll and flung it to an itinerant sparrow. 'To start with, we've got no definite proof that Delmas and his gang are in Paris, and – hallo! what do you want?'

An alert-looking boy in uniform and a gold-braided cap had suddenly approached the table at which they sat, and, ignoring the inspector's truculent query, held out an envelope to Sexton Blake.

'Are you Mr Blake, sir?'

The Baker Street detective nodded as he took the missive and hastily tore it open. A strange, eager expression crossed his face as he read it through.

'What was that last remark you made, Coutts?' he said slowly, turning to his companion.

'I said that we have no definite proof that Delmas and his gang are in Paris,' repeated the C.I.D. man grumpily.

'That's just where you're wrong. We have got proof,' cried Sexton Blake triumphantly. 'So kindly retract your words and eat humble pie, Coutts! This note is from the manager of the Paris branch of Cooks. As you will remember, we gave him the numbers of all the English notes that were paid over to Delmas by the West Central Bank, and told him to advise us if any of them were presented to him to be changed into French money. This morning one of them was presented by a man who, on being questioned, said that he was a waiter from the Café de Vivre, and that he had cashed the note for one of his customers who had come in the previous evening. Delmas is in Paris – I don't think that there is any doubt of that now.'

Inspector Coutts positively gaped with excitement.

'By Jingo, Blake, that's great news!' he exclaimed. 'Yes, I'll admit that I was wrong again. The Café de Vivre – where is that?'

'Over in the Latin Quarter – the Boulevard St Michel.'

Inspector Coutts sprang to his feet and clapped his hard-felt hat on his head.

'We'd better get there!' he said decisively. 'If Delmas has been there once he's bound to go again.'

Sexton Blake shook his head and motioned his companion back to his seat.

'Impetuous as usual, Coutts,' he said quietly. 'No; I don't think it advisable for you to go. Excuse me saying so, old friend, but no manner of disguise could make you look anything else but what you are – a British detective. They say that environment alters a man – that a groom grows to look like the horses he tends. You are the living embodiment of Scotland Yard, and Delmas would spot you at once.'

'What do you suggest, then?' snapped the C.I.D. man grumpily, though he realised the truth of his companion's words.

With a quick movement Sexton Blake suddenly pulled down the brim of his soft-felt hat in front, and tilted it up at the back. Then he swept one hand across his face, and where before he had been cleanshaven he was now adorned with a neatly-waxed black moustache and a tiny imperial of the same colour.

He looked a typical Frenchman, and even Coutts was visibly impressed, whilst Tinker uttered a little exclamation of surprise. The change had taken place with such lightning rapidity.

'I scarcely think Delmas would recognise me,' said Sexton Blake, with a quiet smile. 'You leave me to spy out the land at the Café de Vivre, Coutts. Should I spot our man I shall endeavour to discover where he and his gang are hanging out, and then I'll communicate with you so that you can be in at the death. *Au revoir*!'

And rising from his seat, he strode away with a cheery wave of his hand, Pedro staring after him with a look of canine amazement at the extraordinary change that had taken place in his master's face.

Sexton Blake's step was light as he made his way briskly towards that part of Paris known as the Latin Quarter. The unexpected news conveyed in the letter he had just received had buoyed his spirits wonderfully. Previously, though he had not admitted it, even he had been beginning to wonder if he had not been following up a false trail.

But now there could be no shadow of doubt that Brandon Delmas and his fellow-swindlers were in Paris – or, at least, they had been there. Sexton Blake did not allow himself to believe that they had left since the previous evening.

Not a single countenance escaped the keen scrutiny of his grey eyes as he sauntered along the Boulevard St Michel and ultimately arrived at the Café de Vivre.

Selecting a table that served as a good point of vantage, he ordered a grenadine from the portly garçon who approached him, and lighting a cigar, ostensibly gave himself up to the perusal of a copy of *Le Matin* that he had purchased from a news-stand.

The Café de Vivre was evidently a regular resort of the young students and bohemians who resided in the vicinity, and the majority of the little tables set out on the pavement were occupied by them. They presented a picturesque spectacle in their baggy trousers and velveteen jackets, and with their flowing ties and unkempt hair, as they sat chatting merrily together.

The time dragged almost painfully. At the end of two hours Sexton Blake was still apparently scanning *Le Matin*, several cigar-stumps lay at his feet, and there were three little saucers piled up in front of him by which the waiter checked the amount of drinks he had had.

But still no sign of anybody resembling Delmas in the faintest degree, and the Baker Street detective grew almost pessimistic.

'Probably it was not Delmas at all who changed that note last night!' he muttered irritably to himself. 'Perhaps it was one of the other members of the gang – one of those whom I don't know. He may have been and gone, may be sitting within a few feet of me now.'

Another hour winged its weary way. Sexton Blake purchased another paper from a passing newsvendor, and slowly sipped his *café au lait*. Dusk was beginning to fall, and the gay lights of Paris sprang up like a million fairy-lamps. A string band inside the café suddenly struck up one of the latest waltzes.

Sexton Blake stared quizzically at the portly waiter. No doubt he was the man who had taken the note to Cook's to change it. He felt half inclined to ask him if this were so, and whether he could point out to him the person who had given it to him; but in the nick of time he realised the foolishness of such a procedure.

'What an ass I am to dream of doing such a thing! I –'

Sexton Blake suddenly broke off short, and his whole body stiffened as though he had been struck with paralysis. For a moment his cup remained poised midway between the table and his mouth, and then he set it down shakily, and, to cover his momentary confusion, drew out his cigar-case and lit up afresh.

His visit to the Café de Vivre had not been in vain! He had sighted his quarry!

Four men had suddenly entered the café and seated themselves at a table scarcely a dozen feet away. All were attired in the garb of the Paris student, and three of them were speaking volubly in French as they ordered their aperitifs and puffed at their Caporal cigarettes.

One was a tall man, clean-shaven, and with piercing black eyes. His cheeks were blue, showing that he had recently been accustomed to a heavy growth of beard and moustache, and his fingers were long and white.

Sexton Blake drew a sharp breath in between his teeth. He had seen Brandon Delmas too often to fail to recognise him, even though he had made good use of a razor and scissors.

And the man next to him, the little, narrow-shouldered man with the bright, bird-like eyes and the nervous jerk of the head – Nicholas Mark – Nick the Nib – master-forger!

Sexton Blake stealthily turned his eyes on the third and fourth men. Both he failed to recognise, though there was something vaguely familiar about the one who was muffled up to the ears in a white muffler, and who wore tinted spectacles that concealed his eyes.

The detective's brain was in a positive whirl as he gazed unseeingly at the paper he held in his hands, and a fierce thrill of triumph ran through him.

He had triumphed! He had tracked his men down, and in a very short time, if all went well, he would have the whole gang of them under lock and key!

Stealthily Sexton Blake watched the four of them out of the corner of his eyes. They had dropped their voices now, and were conversing in whispers. For several minutes they kept their heads together, and then, with surprising suddenness, they swallowed down their drinks and sauntered out of the café.

Sexton Blake noted which way they had gone, waited a few brief seconds, and then, flinging down a few coins that more than doubly paid his score, rose to his feet and dived into the passing throng.

Twenty yards ahead he caught sight of his quarry sauntering along arm-in-arm in the manner of the typical Paris student. They halted for a second to chaff and throw a coin to an old apple-woman by the kerb, and then continued their way.

'They're certainly acting their part very well,' muttered Sexton Blake under his breath, never for one instant removing his glance. 'They'll soon find out that that hasn't availed them much. Once let me know where they live, and in half an hour I'll have the whole place surrounded with police.'

Straight along the Boulevard St Michel he followed, and then into the Boulevard St Germain. As the crowds thinned Sexton Blake dropped further and further behind, in case it should be seen that he was following, and then quickened his footsteps, and almost broke into a run as he saw the four figures vanish round a turning by the Quai St Bernard.

Just in time he reached the corner of the street, and out of the corners of his eyes, as he sauntered past, glimpsed his quarry entering the doorway of the fourth house down. He could hear the clatter of their feet as they ascended the wooden stairs, and then the bang of a door.

Quivering with excitement, Sexton Blake turned back to the house, and crept up to the open doorway. Tentatively he stepped over the threshold to see what could be seen by the feeble light of a solitary flickering gas-jet in the hall.

And then, with startling suddenness, something struck him a crushing blow on the head, and his senses left him in a blaze of flame, followed by a wave of darkness!

THE LAST CHAPTER

How Blake was Rescued – And 'the Bat' earned his freedom

Sexton Blake drifted back to consciousness with a growing realisation of an almost unbearable throbbing pain in his head. His throat was as dry as a lime-kiln, and when he opened his eyes, it was to find that he was enveloped in Stygian darkness.

It was only when he tried to raise a hand to his aching head that he discovered that he was trussed up like a fowl, with stout cords drawn tight around his arms and legs.

Realisation of what had occurred slowly dawned upon him, and he ground his teeth in bitter chagrin at the thought of the lamblike way that he had walked into the trap that had obviously been laid for him.

'The cunning scoundrels! They must have known all along that I was following them,' he muttered to himself. 'Though how they found it out Heaven only knows! Two of them must have purposely made that noise going upstairs, whilst the other two waited in the shadows, and struck me down the moment I poked my stupid head through the door!'

Sexton Blake's thoughts were indeed bitter ones. He had spoilt everything by his carelessness. Why, even Coutts would not have allowed himself to be so easily duped, and –

There was the sound of a key turning in a lock, the creaking of a door on its hinges, and then a glare of light momentarily dazzled Sexton Blake's vision. When he could see properly, it was to find the dark, cruel face of Brandon Delmas peering down at him, with Nicholas Mark and the stout, owl-like man, who was a stranger to him, standing behind him.

'Well, Mr Sexton Blake,' jeered Brandon Delmas, with a harsh laugh, 'how do you fancy yourself now? Not quite so clever as you thought you were – eh? You must be a fool, to think you could get the better of us so easily, and with that childish disguise!'

Sexton Blake set his lips grimly, and stared boldly back.

'The game's not played out yet, Brandon Delmas,' he said calmly. 'There are others on your trail besides myself, and you're not likely to escape from them!'

Brandon Delmas gave a start, and shot a glance of alarm at his companion.

'Bluff! He's bluffing you!' croaked the owl-like man. 'There's no one else! He was alone when he came to the Café de Vivre. Take my advice, and don't waste any time over the hound. The sooner he's out of the way for good and all the better!'

'Them's my sentiments!' said Nick the Nib callously. 'I haven't forgotten the five years' living hell you got me, Sexton Blake. Call yourself a detective? Pah! Do you think I wouldn't recognise that cigar-case of yours?'

Sexton Blake gave a slight start, and bit his lip with chagrin. So that is how they had recognised him when he had been seated in the Café de Vivre – by his cigar-case with the gold monogram on it; the case that more than one criminal, including Nick the Nib, had had their last smoke from. Yes, he certainly was a fool to have produced it!

'You're right, Nick,' said Brandon Delmas suddenly. 'The sooner he's swept out of our path the better and safer it will be for us. I'll defy any other detective to track us down once he's dead. Bring him along!'

In a trice Mark and the owl-like man had lifted Sexton Blake up – one by the shoulders, and one by the arms – and borne him out of the bare room in which he had lain. Down a flight of cold stone steps he was carried, and then along a hollow, echoing passage that smelt cold and musty.

Brandon Delmas unfastened what was apparently a solid steel door at the end, and flung it open, exposing a narrow, cell-like chamber, the walls of which were dripping with moisture and green slime.

'Not a very pleasant spot to spend your last few moments on earth, Mr Blake,' rasped the criminal lawyer brutally; 'but we couldn't do any better at such short notice. Do you know where you are? Under the Seine – and under the Seine your rotting carcase will remain until the crack of doom!'

Sexton Blake's head reeled, and his heart gave a great throb of horror as he was dumped down with his head against one of the slimy walls.

'What do you mean to do with me, you scoundrels?' he cried hoarsely. 'You wouldn't dare murder me?'

'Wouldn't I?' sneered Brandon Delmas. 'You've brought it on yourself. You shouldn't have come sticking your nose into our affairs! You'll never leave this place alive, if ever at all. Do you see this plug in the wall? I simply unscrew it, and the River Seine proceeds to empty a part of its contents into this comfortable little apartment. The door is quite watertight, and, once it is closed, you can reckon that you've got about ten minutes to live. This is how it is done!'

Delmas strode across to a rusty iron plug that was set in the brick wall of the cell, and, with a mighty wrench, unscrewed it. With terrific force a solid jet of water spurted out, splashing against the opposite wall, and drenching Sexton Blake in its spray.

'You black-hearted scoundrel! Have you no sense of mercy or humanity?' gasped the detective appealingly.

'Not an atom!' replied Brandon Delmas, with an evil grin. 'Goodbye, Mr Blake! We shall all be basking in the warm sunlight of Monte Carlo by this time tomorrow, while you will be where your friends will never find you!'

The door closed with a hollow clang, and Sexton Blake was alone in the pitch darkness, with the water bubbling and gurgling around him, and a terrible death staring him in the face.

For one brief moment his saner senses left him, and he screamed and shouted like a madman as he wrenched at his bonds and strove to struggle to his feet. To be drowned like a rat in a trap was a prospect that was enough to appal the stoutest heart.

He was doomed – he was beyond all human aid, save that of the dastardly scoundrels who had placed him where he was. Already the water was lapping around his waist and rising steadily towards his chin.

Now it was up to his shoulders, now forming an icy circle around his neck. Higher – higher –

Again Sexton Blake shouted – shouted vainly, wildly: 'Help! Help!'

What was that? The shooting of a bolt – the creaking of rusty hinges? Was it a hallucination of his maddened brain? No, merciful Heavens! The big iron door was slowly opening against the pressure of the water. A beam of light showed through the ever-widening aperture, and now the water dropped swiftly as it gushed out into the corridor beyond.

The figure of a man with an electric torch in one hand came wading forward, and, kneeling down, deftly severed Sexton Blake's bonds.

'Thank Heaven I was in time!' he muttered audibly. 'Another minute, and it would have been too late!'

Sexton Blake staggered limply to his feet and stared wonderingly at his rescuer.

It was none other than the fourth member of Brandon Delmas's gang – the man who had worn the white muffler and the tinted spectacles!

The muffler was still there, but the tinted spectacles had vanished, and Sexton Blake uttered a great cry of amazement as the truth flashed upon him.

'The Bat!'

'Yes, it's me, Sexton Blake,' replied Dirk Dolland simply. 'But we've no time to waste on words now. If my partners knew what I'd done, they'd shoot me like a yellow dog. There's one thing I draw the line at, and that's murder. They did this to you without my knowledge. I never dreamed that Delmas was such a darned villain!

'See here, Mr Blake, I've done you a good turn, and now you've got to make me a promise! You've got to promise to wait here where you are for the next ten minutes, and then go straight back to where you're stopping, and make no attempt to follow us until tomorrow morning. Is that on?'

Sexton Blake hesitated for a fraction of a second, and then shot out his hand.

'It's on, Dolland!' he said, a trifle huskily. 'You're a white man, and I owe my life to you! I shan't forget it! Perhaps I shall be able to pay you back in kind one of these days!'

'Let's hope so,' said the Bat, with a whimsical smile. 'I'll wait till the time when they've got the noose around my neck, and then I'll send for you.'

For one instant their palms met in a grip that spoke more eloquently than words, then the Bat spun round on his heels and vanished.

There was a strange lump in Sexton Blake's throat as the Bat dropped his hand and vanished through the door of the underground cellar that, but for his timely arrival, would have constituted the famous detective's tomb.

'Good luck to him! He deserves to get clean away!' he muttered hoarsely, under his breath. 'I owe him my life, and I shan't forget it! The next – '

Sexton Blake broke off short. There was the sound of a scuffle in the passage without, and then a boyish voice, that he knew only too well, rang out in clear tones: 'Hands up there, whoever you are! I've got the drop on you! If you move an inch I'll drill a hole through you! What have you done with my guv'nor? Speak up! I know he's down here somewhere!'

'It's Tinker!' exclaimed Sexton Blake amazedly. And, without further ado, he darted out into the passage.

It was a strange sight that met his gaze. Half-way up the steep flight of stone steps stood the Bat, his hands raised above his head, and a whimsical smile on his youthful face. Just above him stood Tinker, a revolver levelled in one hand, and the other grasping the leash of Pedro, who was straining and panting to break away.

'Guv'nor! Thank Heaven!' cried the lad, as he caught sight of his master. 'I thought something had happened to you! I feared that the scoundrels had done you some harm! I've got one of them! Collar the beggar whilst I keep him covered!'

'I guess this is where I kick in!' said the Bat regretfully. 'I suppose the arrangement between us doesn't hold good with your assistant, Mr Blake? It's his capture.'

'It holds good so far as you're concerned, Dolland,' replied Sexton Blake quietly. And, moving up the steps past him, he took the revolver from Tinker's hand and shoved it in his pocket. 'Don't you see who it is, my boy?' he asked.

'Jumping Jehoshaphat!' he gasped. 'It – it's the Bat!'

'Yes, it's the Bat,' said Sexton Blake. 'And he has just been the means of saving my life, in return for which he is to have his freedom. I'll tell you about it later, Tinker. Off you go, Dolland, while there's time!'

The Bat made another movement towards the head of the stairs, and at the same instant the sounds of a fierce struggle, hoarse cries of mingled rage and triumph, and a few scattered revolver-shots rang out from the upper part of the house.'

'It's Coutts and the French police – the gendarmes,' said Tinker, in reply to Sexton Blake's blank look of inquiry. 'I reckon they've roped in Brandon Delmas and his precious gang. The whole house is surrounded!'

'But how did you know this place? How did you find your way here?' asked the detective perplexedly.

Tinker pointed mutely to Pedro.

'As you were so long gone Coutts and I decided to walk to the Café de Vivre. You weren't there; but when we described you to the waiters, one of them recollected you, and said you had gone off an hour before, and left your gloves behind on the tables. The gloves were all that Pedro needed. He dragged us along here like a house on fire, and the moment we knew you were inside we guessed Delmas and Co. were here as well. Coutts switched straight on to the police, and in less than ten minutes we had the whole place surrounded.

'They all forced their way upstairs, but Pedro insisted on dragging me down here.'

Sexton Blake bent down and patted the sagacious bloodhound's head, and then turned to the Bat.

'How are you going to get out of this now, Dolland?' he said gravely. 'It's impossible for you to go out the front way. Once Coutts catches sight of you nothing that I can do could save you.'

'If I can't get out the front way, then I reckon I can go via the underground,' said the Bat, pointing back down the steps. 'These cellars run right along to the other end of the road, and I've got an electric torch. Mr Blake, I'll bid you *au revoir*, and you, too, Tinker! I feel that we shall all meet again!'

The next instant he had gone, darting down, seemingly, into the very bowels of the earth. And not a moment too soon, for scarcely had his muffled footsteps died away in the distance when Inspector Coutts and a group of French gendarmes appeared at the head of the stairs.

The Scotland Yard man's face lit up like a full moon as he caught sight of Sexton Blake, and the next instant he was pumping his hand and patting him excitedly on the back.

'We've got 'em, Blake – three of 'em, at any rate!' he cried. 'Brandon Delmas, Nick Mark, and that old scoundrel Dr Stephen Stone.

'They put up a stiff fight; but they're all in irons now and on the way to the Préfecture. And we've retrieved Colonel Boden's Corottzi. It was rolled up in a golf-bag, as you guessed it would be. And we've got all the stolen money back except about ten thousand francs.'

'And the fourth member of the gang?' said Sexton Blake, with a strange little smile.

'Never set eyes on him!' grunted Inspector Coutts, with a shrug of his shoulders. 'He must have got wind of our coming, and got clean away. Never mind! We'll get him in the end! He'll never manage to get out of Paris!'

'Won't he?' muttered Sexton Blake grimly, under his breath. 'If you only knew who the fourth man was, Coutts, my boy, you wouldn't make such a cocksure assertion!'

THE BLACK EAGLE

G.H.Teed

THE FIRST CHAPTER

The Cabinet-maker of Seven Sisters Road

Those who have ever made the journey from London out to Finsbury Park to the Manor House Corner, will readily recall the vast number of small tradesmen who have their shops on both sides of the Seven Sisters Road all the way down the long hill and right along to the very fringe of the park itself.

Among these scores of small enterprises is represented every conceivable type that can find any possibility of trade among the class of residents of the Stoke Newington and Finsbury Park districts.

There are greengrocers and fruiterers, fishmongers and butchers, ironmongers and drapers, milliners and modistes, confectioners and pastrycooks, second-hand furniture shops and stationers – all displaying their wares at moderate prices, for the average resident of that part of North London is a cash buyer and a close buyer, and he has no money to waste on West End prices.

They are an industrious, sober, and usually cheerful lot, those tradesmen, each with a keen eye for the advancement of his own business, but with a generous sympathy for a neighbour who is in bad luck. They are not too inquisitive, which means they mostly have about as much as they can do to attend to their own affairs without prying too closely into those of their neighbours.

Of late years, with business generally in a depressed condition and money 'tight', even for small enterprises, shops change hands much more frequently than formerly, owing to the fact that persons with too little experience, and far too little capital, will persist in believing that the sure road to independence is through the portals of a little shop.

Nevertheless, there is usually a new tenant to be found moving into the Seven Sisters Road, and it is certainly frequent enough to hold the attention of the neighbours for a day or so at the most.

In that long road there was one little shop which was not governed by the regular conditions. This was a small cabinet-maker's shop, behind the dust-begrimed windows of which there had stood for years what were apparently the same few sticks of furniture. It had been occupied for a matter of twenty years or so by an old man who had seemed satisfied to do just enough pottering about to keep the rent of his shop paid up, and himself supplied with simple food and a regular supply of tobacco.

Now and then he would make a sale, and would then set to work to duplicate the piece he had sold, his skill being confined, apparently, to just about six different models.

When he died quietly, with as little ostentation as he had lived, a few of his neighbours got together to make arrangements for the funeral. But it seemed that the old man had anticipated the coming of the grim Reaper, for before the funeral arrangements had been completed a nephew had appeared from the North and had taken charge of things.

It was understood that sufficient money had been put away to secure a decent burial and leave a few pounds over for the benefit of the nephew who had been sent for. Following the funeral, the nephew lost no time in winding up the estate, and, somewhat to the surprise of the neighbours, he had scarcely any difficulty in finding a purchaser for the furniture and tools and lathes in the shop.

This purchaser also took over the lease of the shop, and within three days of his arrival the neighbours, finding him a tall, sombre-looking individual, extraordinarily sparing in his words, soon accepted him as a younger counterpart of the old man who had died, and left him to himself.

They felt vaguely that there must be something about the cabinet-making business that caused a man to grow dour, and left it at that.

But it was not long before the street discovered that there was a very great difference in the work of the two men.

Where the former tenant had exhausted his art in the making of some six different models of furniture of extreme simplicity, the newcomer was soon displaying some very beautiful pieces, carved and turned and finished by a master hand. The rubbish in the windows was swept away. The dirt-laden panes were thoroughly scoured and kept polished. The new pieces were displayed with a real touch of art, and soon more and more persons began to pause in front of the shop to admire them.

And when people pause to admire, it is not long before they enter to buy – a secret which the retail trade was a long time discovering.

The old, half-obliterated sign over the door was removed and a new one in neat gilt letters on a dark blue board was put up. It read as follows.

A. LONG, CABINET-MAKER

Special Designs Prepared Free of Charge

And 'A. Long' soon demonstrated himself as industrious as he was expert at his trade. Where he had learned was not exactly known, but it somehow came to be understood that he had worked in the north of England and abroad. Perhaps the fact that the previous tenant's nephew came from the north gave rise to this impression.

At any rate, at any time of the day, from seven o'clock in the morning to midday, and from one o'clock to six, if one entered the shop one could hear in the work room at the back the sound of hammer on chisel, the slide of the plane, or the low hum of the lathe as the cabinet-maker pursued his art.

The shop itself was a small, self-contained building, consisting of the ground floor and one floor above. On one side it abutted on the adjoining shop, but on the other it formed the corner of a narrow street leading out of Seven Sisters Road. On this street the lower wall of the building was blank brick, with two windows above. Then at the back, and shut off from the side street by a brick wall and heavy twin gates of green painted wood, was a small yard containing several small stacks of either seasoned cabinet wood, or wood in the process of seasoning.

From the rear of the shop a door gave on to this yard, and in one of the double gates was a small wicket-gate by which the elderly woman who looked after the newcomer, as she had his predecessor, entered each morning and left each evening.

On the upper floor there was a bedroom, a sitting-room and a small kitchenette. The sitting-room was also used as a dining-room.

That made up the modest establishment of A. Long, cabinet-maker, and by the time a month had gone by he was as much an established institution in the street as any of his neighbours.

He was a satisfactory customer, too, to the various shops surrounding him. He did not live elaborately, but the old woman purchased liberally of plain, wholesome food, paying cash for everything.

During the evenings the cabinet-maker was seldom seen abroad. Sometimes, dressed in neat and inconspicuous black or dark blue serge, with a black bowler hat on his head, he would go for a stroll in the park. As he passed he would bid a courteous 'good evening' to those of his neighbours whose acquaintance he had made, but he never stopped to gossip.

He would usually return from his stroll about ten o'clock, and for an hour or so, after, the gleam of a light might have been seen in the front room above the shop. But by eleven it was usually extinguished, and for a short time the light in the back side window would be seen as the cabinet-maker prepared for bed. Then darkness and silence reigned on the premises until the shop was opened for business in the morning.

As a quiet, law-abiding industrious citizen the newcomer could not be criticised.

During the second month, had anyone taken the trouble to pry into his movements they would have discovered that on each Saturday evening he left the shop a little after dusk and walked towards the park. Even if this had been particularly noticed, it would have been thought that he was just off for one of his usual strolls. During the other nights of the week this would have been the case. But on each Saturday evening he might have been seen to enter the Underground at the Finsbury Park Station, and book through to the Marble Arch.

And on a certain Saturday evening towards the middle of the third month his subsequent actions would have amazed his fellow tradesmen in the Seven Sisters Road – as a detailed relation of them will show.

THE SECOND CHAPTER

Strange Proceedings

On the particular night in question the cabinet-maker of the Seven Sisters Road left his shop, and, after carefully locking the door, proceeded to walk leisurely towards the railway bridge which crosses the road just before one comes to the Underground station.

Dusk had fallen, and, as Saturday evening was the busiest one of the week among the tradesmen along the street, all the shops were brilliantly lighted. The footpaths were crowded with shoppers who jostled their way along good-naturedly, and as he passed no one took any particular notice of the tall, spare figure of the cabinet-maker who, among all the tenants of the street, had no inducement to keep his shop open in the evening.

He kept on his way steadily until he passed under the bridge, when he turned towards the Underground station. He entered and purchased his ticket, after which he made his way to his train, which had just swung round the loop.

He took a seat in the rear coach, which was also a smoking carriage, and carefully filled a well-seasoned briar pipe with a heavy, strong-looking tobacco. He took some care in lighting the pipe, then he drew from his pocket a copy of an evening paper, and settled back in his seat to read.

He changed on to another line once, and again selected a rear smoking carriage, where he continued his perusal of the paper. On arriving at Marble Arch he dropped the paper to the floor and joined the crowd in forcing a way out of the station. Emerging into the street, he walked to the Edgware Road, into which he turned, and continued along it until he came to a side street leading into a very secluded crescent. He walked half-way round this crescent until he came to a corner, where he turned off.

On that corner was a narrow, old-fashioned house, which residents of the crescent remembered as having once belonged to a famous but eccentric artist. He had built it according to some fantastic idea of his own away back in the sixties, and, owing to its bizarre interior plan, it lay empty for several years after his death.

Unlike the other houses in the crescent, it had no front door. Where that useful portal should have been was just a blank wall, and, just above, a wide, bowed glass front that gave light to a vast studio. The only entrance was in the side wall round the corner, and those who had ever entered the house knew that from this entrance a staircase led to the living apartments on the first floor back of the studio.

On the ground floor was an extraordinary sort of apartment, which in the old days had been fitted up as a Shanghai poppy den, and rumour had it that the young bucks of the sixties and seventies staged some weird orgies there.

Back of that were domestic offices and a kitchen, and at the back a small garden shut off from the view of its neighbours by a very high wall which had once been the subject of litigation. The living quarters in the back on the first floor were extremely luxurious, and the place had never been furnished more sumptuously than at the present time.

Bizarre as the plan of the building was, it was an ideal place for a bachelor who was also an artist, and the present tenant appeared to be both. He had purchased the lease, and it was understood vaguely that he was a wealthy gentleman who had returned to England after spending many years abroad pursuing his art.

No one had entered the house to inspect whatever examples of his art he may have brought back with him, but had they done so they would have found some extremely well-executed paintings in the studio and hanging on the walls of the various rooms. And each painting was signed with the name of the present tenant – David Stone.

A detailed examination of the pictures would have caused one to conclude that the artist must have followed in the footsteps of R. L. Stevenson, for there were some really beautiful examples of tropical subjects, in which the artist had seemed to catch the very spirit of the white surf, the green palms, and the blue, blue sea.

And on the Saturday night in question the cabinet-maker of Seven Sisters Road fitted a key into the side door of this strange house, and let himself in.

As he closed the door after him he stood just inside for a few seconds, gazing about him at the beautifully furnished hall. On the floor were rich Eastern rugs, while luxurious silk-covered divans had been placed in two corners. From the ceiling was suspended a magnificent copper filigree brazier, in which a softened light was burning. The walls were lined with rare old tapestries and silks.

When he had finished his inspection, the man drew a deep breath, like one who has been under water a considerable time. Then he walked across to a small rosewood tabouret, and picked up a silver bell. He rang it gently and set it down. Almost immediately there came a sound from the direction of the staircase, and a moment later there appeared a very strange figure.

He was dressed in the regulation black of the servant, but his walk was more the roll of an old sailor than of the landsman. His face was literally pitted with smallpox, and his colour, accentuated in that subdued light, was of a deep coppery hue. His eyes were a queer shade of yellow and absolutely expressionless. His nose was twisted and flattened as if it had been smashed half a dozen times. His hair grew low on his forehead, and was beginning to show streaks of grey against the black. One of his ears held a big gold ear-ring in the lobe. The other was badly cauliflowered, and, at one time, the ear-ring worn in it had evidently been dragged out by force, for the lobe was torn and hung loose. His body was heavy and squat, his shoulders broad, and the 'barrel' of his body enormous. His arms were long, and swung ape-like. In brute strength he was obviously far above the ordinary; in mental capacity he would scarcely have passed the twelve-year-old test.

The man who had entered stood by the tabouret waiting for the other to approach. As he reached him he did a strange thing for one who was so obviously the master. He lifted his arm and laid it across the heavy shoulders of the servant; then he patted his arm in an affectionate manner. But the words which he spoke were even more strange.

'Well, brother mine,' he said in tones that were almost as tender as those of a woman, 'is all well with thee?'

The dull eyes of the misshapen creature lightened at the touch and the tone. His mouth opened in what was evidently meant for a smile, exhibiting big, crooked, yellow teeth. There was not one feature about that poor bit of humanity that Nature had not mocked – except one thing, and that was his voice. It was the purest, sweetest voice that ever issued from the throat of man – vibrant and clear as a bell, flexible as the 'voice' of a Stradivarius under the touch of the maestro.

'It is long since thou hast come, dear brother,' he said, fondling the thin, supple hand of the one who was such a physical contrast to himself. 'What hast thou brought me?'

'Ah, *mon petit*, see what I have fashioned for thee this time!'

With that the cabinet-maker thrust a hand inside his coat and drew out a small packet wrapped in tissue paper. He gave it to his brother – for the term used between them was no formal term of affection, but indicated their actual relationship, children of the same mother – and stood back while the other opened it. A few moments later there was revealed a small bit of plain wood, carved in the form of a bird – a simple enough thing, though the carving was truly exquisite.

The great hairy hands of the misshapen one came up, and he devoured it with his eyes. His voice came in a cry of utter joy, and he pressed the little bit of carved wood to his lips. His strange eyes burned with an extraordinary light as they flashed at his brother, then he turned and sped up the staircase, to disappear from view.

The man by the tabouret watched him disappear. Then, with a heavy sigh, he strode forward and began also to mount to the floor above.

THE THIRD CHAPTER

David Stone goes out for the Night

David Stone – for the tenant of that strange house and the cabinet maker of Seven Sisters Road were one and the same – entered a luxuriously furnished sitting-room and passed through to a big bedroom beyond. Through a half-open door one could glimpse the gleaming white tiles of a bath-room, and at the moment the pleasant sound of running water could be heard.

Stone proceeded to undress. His movements were abrupt and precise, like those of one who had done a certain thing at a certain time each day for many years. Muscular habit is the hardest thing in the world to break.

When he had stripped he threw on a silk Oriental dressing-gown and entered the bath-room. It was a magnificent apartment, built by the eccentric artist, but modernised by the present tenant.

It had a huge sunken bath, the fittings of which were solid silver, as were those of the hand-basin. The mirrors almost covered two walls, while in one corner there was a wide basin set in the floor, and, above, a complicated-looking array of taps for a shower. Close to the edge of the bath was a low chair, on which lay several big Turkish towels, and bending over the bath testing the water with a thermometer, was the misshapen creature whom David Stone called 'brother'.

Stone walked to the hand-basin, which had already been half-filled in readiness. On a glass shelf above were all the implements for shaving, and the man made a quick but efficient job of that part of his toilet. He finished at just about the moment his brother rose from the bath with a brief remark that it was ready.

Then the other plunged in and for a quarter of an hour revelled in the hot, soothing water. From that he went to the cold shower, after which he took a brisk rub down.

By the time he re-entered the bedroom his brother had laid out his clothes, and when he had finished dressing he stood before the mirror, with a critical frown on his face. In full evening-dress he looked little indeed like the cabinet-maker who had left the shop in Seven Sisters Road earlier in the evening.

On the dressing-table had been laid ready a gold cigarette-case, a small gold pencil, a silk notecase which bulged as if it had been stuffed to its capacity with notes – which it had – a very thin platinum watch to which was attached a black silk fob, a small gold matchbox, a bunch of keys, a crocodile cigar-case, a thin gold-edged tablet containing a small memorandum-pad, and a bit of folded black silk which looked as if it might be a mask – which it was.

David Stone distributed these articles among various pockets, then he picked up a cigarette and bent over towards the flame of the match which his brother held out to him. Then he turned and led the way through the sitting-room and down the stairs to the hall below. There his brother brought him a silk-lined wrap-coat and an opera hat, which he donned. They walked to the door together and paused.

'What time?' asked the misshapen one in his soft, musical tones.

'About as usual, brother mine,' answered Stone. 'If thou should grow tired, do not wait.'

'I shall wait for thee,' answered the other simply.

Stone laid an affectionate hand on his brother's shoulder, then he opened the door and stepped into the street. Somewhere in the distance a clock was just chiming the hour of eleven, and at that same moment a big, dark-coloured limousine drove silently round the corner. It stopped at the kerb beside which

David Stone was standing. He opened the door and stepped in, and without waiting for instructions the chauffeur drove off.

From that quiet crescent off the Edgware Road the man drove past the Marble Arch and down Park Lane until he came to Brook Street, into which he turned. He kept on to Grosvenor Square, thence to Berkeley Square, and up Hay Hill to Grafton Street. There he turned to the left and drew up at a house near the bend. It appeared to be in complete darkness, for not a light was visible, but David Stone did not hesitate.

Stepping out of the car, he made a curt gesture with his hand, and the vehicle at once drove off towards Bond Street.

The man in evening clothes mounted the steps to the lobby of the house. Inside the lobby he drew out the folded silk mask which he had placed in his pocket, then he pressed a button. The inner door opened almost immediately, disclosing a small, richly-furnished hall lighted by a single shaded bulb.

Holding the door was a man in servant's livery, who stood waiting for the man in the lobby to speak. The latter uttered a single word, and as he heard it the servant stood aside, permitting Stone to enter.

Closing the door, the servant took the hat and coat which the visitor handed him and disappeared towards a cloak-room at the end of the hall, while the other strode to the staircase and went up briskly. At the top he came to a heavy green baize door, at which he knocked lightly. A small wicket in the baize swung open, and a masked face appeared.

Again Stone uttered a single word, which appeared to be an Open Sesame to the place. The green-baize-covered door swung open, and he stepped into a small ante-room. He crossed this, and a servant opened another baize-covered door, permitting him to pass through.

David Stone found himself in a brilliantly-lighted lounge in which several other gentlemen in evening-dress and also masked were moving about, smoking, or chatting in low tones.

At one side was a well-loaded buffet, at which stood a serving-man in white jacket ready to oblige any of the guests with what they might choose. Close at hand was a smaller buffet, behind which stood another white-jacketed servant dispensing drinks, and on the floor were a dozen or more buckets containing champagne and ice.

The newcomer did not speak to any of the others. Nor did he pause to patronise the buffet. He crossed the room and pushed aside a pair of heavy curtains. Beyond he found a large room containing all the paraphernalia for roulette, and a dozen men playing. But Stone did not pause here. He kept on past the table and swung to the right, passing through another doorway into a smaller apartment where baccarat was in progress.

And the limited number of persons who were permitted to pass the portals of that exclusive gambling-club knew that in this inner room the game ran to enormous sums, so large that among the members it had been dubbed the 'diamond-room'.

As in the other rooms, every man was masked, for that was a privilege of membership; and, while one might suspect the identity of another player, one never questioned. The right of entry was all the proof needed that one was 'safe', and that right was only secured through unimpeachable introductions.

David Stone stood just inside the door watching the game for a few moments. His gaze then fell for a brief space on each player, and as he scrutinised one figure about half-way down the table his hand, which was still holding the curtain, dropped to his side. Then he went forward, and after a formal bow which included all the players he drew out a chair and began to play, waiting until the 'shoe' should pass to him.

THE FOURTH CHAPTER

In the Diamond-Room

The 'pukka' baccarat game played in that secret gambling-club in Dover Street was a much higher game than the ordinary run of *chemin de fer* which was in progress in one of the outer rooms. It was for that reason, perhaps, the inner chamber had been dubbed the diamond-room.

The minimum amount of each turn was five hundred pounds, and at that figure the evening's game always commenced. But it was optional to raise the limit as often as desired during the evening, and it was very rarely that by the time the game broke up the figure had not reached a thousand pounds, or more.

On this evening, when the man from the strange house in the quiet crescent off the Edgware Road entered the diamond-room, it was evident that play had already been in progress for some time, for on the little card which stood in a brass stand on a side table the figure of eight hundred pounds could be seen, which meant that was the figure for each turn of the shoe. The amount apparently held little interest for the newcomer, for he gave it the briefest of glances, then he took out a thick roll of notes and placed it in front of him.

At the moment the shoe was being held by a player seated four places away from David Stone, and it was plain that he had been having a run of very bad luck, for both sides of the table were cashing in against him. He made one more turn after Stone's advent, then he gave a low exclamation of disgust and passed the shoe to his neighbour.

This player made a couple of lucky turns and passed it again, being apparently a believer in the maxim of cautious play.

For the next half-hour the play went with varying luck, and as the holder passed it someone on the other side of the table turned round and covered the eight hundred pound card with one marked a thousand pounds.

It was the player next to Stone who now held the shoe, but at the new limit he passed, and the shoe came to Stone. He at once made the turn, showing a nine as against a table average of eight. He gathered in the stakes and made the turn again. For the second time he showed the nine, and followed that up for the third and fourth turns – a very rare run to make it four times consecutively.

In those few minutes he had gathered in several thousands in winnings, and when he had completed the fourth turn he pushed the shoe to the man on his left. Then without a word he gathered up the pile of notes in front of him, stuffed them into his pockets, and rose.

With a formal bow, which included the whole table, he made his way back towards the outer room, and as he went there was one player at that table who gave an almost imperceptible nod of approval, for the method of play used by Stone was exactly the one he himself would have followed had he made four consecutive turns.

Passing through the chemin and roulette rooms, David Stone made his way to the buffet, where he helped himself to a sandwich and signed to the attendant to open him a half-bottle of champagne. In that establishment the annual income from percentages collected was so enormous that all refreshments were free, although it was permissible for a member to give a *pourboire* if he wished.

It was David Stone's custom, whether he won or lost, to drop a hundred-pound note on the buffet when he had finished his light repast, and this night he followed his usual custom. Although his features had never been seen by the attendants, there were other ways of marking a man, and it is safe to say that there was not a member, masked though he might be, who was not set down in some way in the minds of the servants and whose idiosyncrasies were well known.

But the only thing that marked David Stone was that habit of his dropping a hundred-pound note on the buffet. He never spoke, merely thanking the attendant with a slight inclination of the head. But no member was ever better served than he, and not altogether was that because of the handsome *pourboire* he invariably gave.

David Stone set his bottle and glass on a small side table. In doing so he found it necessary to push aside a heap of used playing cards which had been tossed there.

In absent-minded fashion he gathered the heap together into a pack, and, in the same absent-minded way, tore the whole lot in half in one single twist of the hands that gave him apparently not the slightest effort, although there were no fewer than three packs in the pile. Then he dropped the pieces into a waste-basket and proceeded munching his sandwich as if the act of super-strength was not at all extraordinary.

But the action did not go entirely unobserved, for the same man who had been seated at the baccarat-table, and who had nodded his approval of Stone's method of play, was at that very moment entering the buffet lounge from the roulette-room, and his eye had noted the nonchalant manner in which the cards had been halved.

'That gentleman appears to be not only an extremely well-balanced baccarat player, but possessed of other talents as well,' he mused as he strolled across to the buffet. 'It is no easy task to tear a single pack of cards in half, and I am certain there must have been fully three packs in that pile which he halved as easily as he might have torn a single sheet of writing-paper. I do not think I should care to be entirely at his mercy with his hands about my throat. I have an idea it might be interesting to discover his identity. Up to six months ago he did not appear here, but since then he has been a regular visitor.'

While the second gentleman helped himself to a sandwich his thoughts continued to run on the individual who had attracted his notice twice within the hour, but he made no attempt to approach the object of his curiosity, for the simple reason that one person never entered into conversation with another in that club unless a request were made through the director.

It was an inviolable rule which no one dreamed of breaking, but it is safe to say that had the identity of the gentleman who then stood at the buffet been known to several members there would have been a slight feeling of nervousness, for it was none other than Mr Sexton Blake, the well-known criminologist.

That secret gaming club was but one of many queer haunts to which Sexton Blake had the entrée, and he was usually to be found from time to time at one or another, for the simple reason that to keep in touch with the habitués of such places was part and parcel of his profession.

More than once his knowledge of the inner workings of the secret haunts of London and other great cities had proved invaluable to him in an inquiry, and it goes to show in what estimation he was held that never for a single moment did the directors of those places feel the slightest doubt of Blake.

It was not Blake's province to act as a 'nark' for the police, and, indeed, he would have been sorry in many ways to see those various haunts wiped out, for in their passing they would break an important link between him and the secret night life of the great capitals.

His interest in the man who had refused to 'ride' his bank after four consecutive turns, and who again had so nonchalantly torn a thick pile of playing cards in half, had been merely abstract, and when he had finished his sandwich and a glass of wine he tossed a *pourboire* on the buffet and continued his way to the cloak-room.

Had Blake been a little more observing he might have noticed that the stranger was seated where he could command, through a large mirror, a view of more than half of the roulette and *chemin de fer* rooms, as well as of the curtained doorway that gave access to the diamond-room. But through the eye-slits of the mask it would have been impossible for him to see that the stranger was undoubtedly keeping a surveillance on that curtained doorway.

But Blake saw nothing of this, and after leaving the anteroom he was permitted to pass the heavy green baize door that gave on to the main staircase. He walked leisurely down this and along to the cloakroom, where an attendant handed him his opera hat and coat.

Blake donned them, and, dropping another note in the plate, made his way to the front entrance, where another attendant was waiting to let him out. Just as the door was opened he noticed a figure descending the stairs, and, glancing up, saw that it was the same masked stranger who had previously attracted his attention. He gave a courteous salute, which the other returned, and then Blake passed out and the door closed softly behind him.

While he was still in the lobby Blake slipped off his silk mask and thrust it into the side pocket of his coat; then, with his opera hat at a jaunty angle, he passed down the steps to the pavement, reaching it just as a constable came along.

Glancing at the constable, Blake saw that he was one he knew, so he wished him a cheery goodnight, which the officer returned, adding Blake's name as he recognised him. When Blake had passed the constable continued his beat towards Bond Street, but not before he had cast a glance in the direction of the dark building from which Blake had just emerged.

'Must be all right,' he muttered to himself. 'Mr Blake goes there, and it seems to be popular with a lot of gentlemen, but it is queer why they always keep the blinds closed so tight.' And little did that conscientious constable dream, as he turned into Bond Street, that at that same moment the limit in the diamond-room was being raised from a thousand pounds to twelve hundred pounds, making it as stiff a game as one could find anywhere on the Continent.

As for Blake, he walked on slowly towards Hay Hill, but as soon as the turn of Dover Street hid the constable from view he did a very strange thing. He slipped quietly into a dark doorway, and in the twinkling of an eye had removed his opera hat. Closing this, he thrust it inside his overcoat and drew out a folded cap, which he dragged well down over his eyes.

Then he turned up his coat collar and drew well back just as the door of the club closed again and a second member, whom Blake knew must be the man who had excited his interest, came along.

Like Blake, he had removed his mask, and as he passed under the street-light on the corner of Hay Hill Blake had a fairly good view of his features. But as he turned the corner and proceeded down Hay Hill Blake shook his head.

'Don't know him,' he muttered. 'And never saw his face before. I wonder who he is? However, it's none of my affair, only I thought I had nearly every member of the club placed.'

With that he resumed his opera hat and also took his way down Hay Hill. At the bottom he could see the figure of the other man as he crossed the road, and a few seconds later he had disappeared into the small passage that runs from there across to Curzon Street. It occurred to Blake that the stranger probably lived either in Curzon Street or Half Moon Street, or one of the streets in that quarter, and as he turned into Berkeley Square he dismissed the matter from his mind.

But he would have been vastly interested had he been a witness of what look place during the next twenty minutes, shortly after another gentleman who had been playing in the diamond-room came down Hay Hill, and likewise disappeared into the passage leading to Curzon Street.

On entering the passage, David Stone had tossed away the cigarette he had been smoking and strode on, looking neither to right nor left, until he went up the few steps that brought him out into Curzon Street. He kept to the right-hand side and walked along until he came to the entrance to a well-known building of flats, the lower door of which was worked by pressing an electric button. There was no light in the lower hall, but all the tenants of the building knew that just inside the door was another button, which would illuminate the whole staircase, and which was worked by an automatic cutoff that kept it effective until even the slowest of persons could walk to the third floor, which was the top, for there was no lift.

David Stone pressed the outer button, and as the door clicked open he stepped inside. He did not press the inside button, however, but, instead, he stepped softly to one side until, with his coat-collar turned up to hide the white of his shirt and collar, he blended completely with the shadow.

He stood there until he heard the sound of a footfall outside, when he shifted his position ever so little. A moment later the door clicked open again, and a man stepped into the hall. He began to feel for the inside button before he closed the door; but before his groping fingers discovered it a pair of hands had gripped him about the throat.

A sharp twist to the left, another to the right, an almost imperceptible click, a faint gasping sigh, and the man who had entered last collapsed in a limp heap, his neck broken as clean and as instantaneously as if a gallows had been sprung beneath him.

That faint click and that soft escaping whisper of death were the only sounds that had accompanied the murder. And it was in the same silent manner that the killer, still gripping his victim by the throat, lifted him off his feet and carried him across to the foot of the stairs, where he allowed him to slip to the floor.

Then he recrossed the hall, stepped through the half-open door out into Curzon Street, and drew the door after him. A swift look he gave up and down, then, with long purposeful strides, he made for the opening of the passage that would allow him to reach Berkeley Square.

THE FIFTH CHAPTER

A News Item – and an Appeal

The following Monday the London papers carried the following paragraph.

TRAGEDY IN CURZON STREET
Fatal Accident to Mr Geoffrey Howland

At six o'clock yesterday morning the porter of a block of flats at No. 154a Curzon Street, found the body of one of the tenants, Mr Geoffrey Howland, lying in the lower hall at the foot of the staircase. Mr Howland had apparently been dead for some hours.

It is surmised that on returning home Saturday night, and on reaching the first landing. Mr Howland in some way overbalanced and fell down the stairs to the tiled floor beneath, breaking his neck.

One of the other tenants states that he returned home about half-past one, and that the body was not there then. It appears, therefore, that the accident occurred some time after that. Mr Howland's manservant, who was asleep in the flat on the second floor, states that it was not unusual for his master to return in the early hours of the morning, and that on going out on Saturday evening he said he would probably be late.

Mr Geoffrey Howland is supposed to have been a man of considerable private fortune, and spent most of his time between London and the French Riviera. He was a well-known clubman, and popular in club circles. He was a bachelor, and had one brother, Mr James Howland, who, we understand, resides on the Riviera. So far, inquiries at the three clubs to which he belonged, and among

> several of his friends, have failed to reveal where he spent Saturday evening, although it is expected this information will be forthcoming at the inquest which will be held.

Among the many thousands of persons who read that article was Sexton Blake, who scanned it while seated at his desk in the consulting-room at Baker Street. As Tinker, his assistant, was out at the time, Blake took up a pair of scissors and carefully cut it out. Then he rose and laid it on Tinker's desk, to be pasted in the famous 'Index' in due course. That done, Blake reseated himself and gazed out of the window.

'Sudden – very sudden!' he muttered. 'Howland was at the table in the diamond-room on Saturday night, and I left him there when I came away; so the statement of the tenant that the body was not lying in the hall when he returned home at about half-past one is quite correct, for I did not leave Dover Street until past two. Let me see! Who else was at the table in the diamond-room?'

Blake drummed on the desk with the tips of his fingers while he went over in his mind just who had been at the baccarat-table two evenings before. Although his own identity had been entirely unsuspected, he knew every man who had been at the table, with the exception of one – the individual who had left the club immediately after himself. And as the name of a man whom he knew in the City flashed into his recollection, he turned towards the telephone and drew the instrument towards him.

Opening the 'Telephone Directory', he gave a number, and in a few moments heard a voice at the other end of the wire. It appeared that the gentleman he was calling had not yet gone out to lunch, and, after giving his name, Blake waited. He was put through, and as soon as he had confirmed the identity of the other he said: 'I want to ask you a question, Mr Morgan. You were at a place the night before last which I shall call by the simple letter "X". I speak of a table in a certain room which has been named after a precious stone. I – '

'Here, hold on!' came the voice of the man Blake had addressed as Mr Morgan. 'Did you say you were Sexton Blake speaking?'

'Yes. There is no need to feel nervous, Mr Morgan. I, too, was at that same table that evening. I will recall myself to you. Do you recall being handed something just after the player on your right made a coup of a considerable amount?'

'Y-yes.'

'Well, I was the person on your right. You will remember, perhaps, that I left the table almost immediately after. I do not want to say too much on the telephone, but I will put it so you can understand. On your left was another player, whose identity I also know. That gentleman was Mr Geoffrey Howland, who, it seems, was accidentally killed by falling downstairs on returning to his flat in Curzon Street Saturday night. Now, what I want to ask is this. Can you remember just when he left the table?'

There was a brief silence. Then: 'Why, yes, Mr Blake! If I remember rightly, it was almost immediately after you got up – or, at least, not many minutes after.'

'Thank you, Mr Morgan. That is all I wanted to know. I have been a member there for several years, and there is no cause to feel uneasy.'

There was a nervous laugh at the other end of the wire.

'That's all right, Mr Blake. You gave me a bit of a shock at first. I didn't know just what was up. I read about Howland's death. I didn't know him personally, and I hadn't the faintest idea it was he who sat on my left that night.'

'Well, it was,' said Blake. 'And if he went straight home, the accident couldn't have been due to overindulgence in alcohol, for I know that he drank sparingly all evening. I am very much obliged to you, Mr Morgan.'

And with that Blake hung up the receiver.

'Just as well to ascertain the time,' he muttered. 'It will probably be up to me to make either a private or public statement at the inquest as to where Howland was last night. The name of the club mustn't be dragged in, and I think I shall be able to arrange that it isn't. If it is, the police will want to know quite a lot about it, and it won't suit my purpose to have them prying about. So I'll ring up Phillips and tell him that I will fix things.'

With that Blake again lifted the receiver and gave another number. A few moments later he was carrying on a guarded conversation with the man he had referred to as 'Phillips', who was, in fact, the director of the secret gaming club in Dover Street.

When he had put that gentleman's fears at rest – and the director had been feeling distinctly nervous since reading of the death of Geoffrey Howland – he rehung the receiver, and made a note in his appointments-book to attend the inquest. Then he settled down to work, but before he had accomplished very much there was a knock at the door, and Mrs Bardell, the housekeeper, entered, bearing a tray on which reposed a piece of pasteboard. Blake took the card and read the name.

MR BRAMWELL CHESTER

Voyagers' Club, Pall Mall

'Show him in,' he said briefly.

Mrs Bardell departed, but soon returned to usher in the visitor. Blake glanced up to see a well-dressed man of about forty-five years of age enter, holding a silk hat in one hand, while he pulled nervously at a close-cropped moustache with the other.

'Mr Sexton Blake?' he asked abruptly.

Blake nodded. 'Yes, I am Sexton Blake,' he answered. 'Will you be seated, Mr Chester.'

The visitor dropped into a chair by the desk, and laid his hat on the floor. Then he drew out a monocle and screwed it into his eye. He regarded Blake for some seconds.

'I have heard a great deal about you, Mr Blake,' he said finally. 'In fact, only yesterday I heard you being discussed at lunch at my club. It was that really that caused me to come to you today to ask your advice.'

'During my hours of consultation I am usually available,' returned Blake suavely. 'You appear to be in some mental distress, Mr Chester.'

'I am – I am. Have you read today's papers, Mr Blake?'

'I have.'

'Have you noticed a report of the accidental death of Mr Geoffrey Howland?'

'Yes.'

'Well, that is why I have come to see you. The paper says he fell downstairs and broke his neck. It is put down as an accident. I know better. It was no accident. It was murder! And the same fate hangs over me!'

'Ah! What causes you to think it was murder, Mr Chester?'

'Because I know who did it!'

'Then it isn't here you should be, but at Scotland Yard. Your evidence should be available at the inquest.'

The other gave vent to an irritable exclamation.

'Don't think I haven't considered all that. But that would do no good. Scotland Yard will never catch the man who murdered Geoffrey Howland. As far as that goes, I don't care if they do. It is protection for myself I am seeking.'

'What makes you think I can protect you against a similar fate which you say threatens you? Isn't it just possible that you just fancy this? If Mr Howland was a friend of yours, perhaps the shock of his death has given rise to this thought in your mind?'

'Nothing of the sort! Don't run away with the idea that I am crazy or a monomaniac. I know Howland all right – used to be intimate with him at one time, but I have scarcely set eyes on him for years. But I tell you I know who killed him, and I know that the murderer will kill me, too, if he can!'

'In that case, it would be better if you were a little more explicit,' remarked Blake, a trifle coldly. 'I am not a mind-reader, Mr Chester.'

'That is just what I am going to do. I am going to tell you something that has not passed my lips for more than twenty years – something that affects me as it affected Howland and several others. And I beg you to remember that this is in the strictest confidence.'

'Every word spoken in this consulting-room is sacred,' said Blake curtly.

'I don't doubt that, but I don't want any misunderstanding.'

As the visitor paused Blake opened a silver cigarette cabinet and pushed it across the desk. The other took one, after which Blake chose one for himself. He was leisurely in his movements, for he wanted to give his client time to pull himself together. It had been plain to Blake that the man was labouring under some strong emotion, and for that reason he overlooked the almost rude tone of some of the remarks.

His treatment was a good deal like that of a mind specialist would have been, but because he was ready to hear the tale was by no means any indication that he would do as the other wished. Presently his visitor, who seemed to find the mellow Turkish tobacco soothing, leant forward.

'Yes; more than twenty years, Mr Blake,' he went on. 'At that time I was a young fellow with more money than was good for me, and a dabbler in painting. Like a lot of other youngsters, I thought I had the makings of a great artist in me. I went to Paris to study, and in the Quartier Latin there I soon made friends among other students, some of whom were serious, but most of whom were just wild blades.

'I have heard enough about you to know that you have some acquaintance yourself with the life of the Latin Quarter, so you will understand what I mean. That is where it all began – the incident that culminated in the murder of Geoffrey Howland last night.

'I had been in Paris a year or so when this incident occurred. I was mixed up in a pretty wild crowd, of whom Howland was one. There were others, some of whose names I have forgotten, but a few with whom I have kept in touch ever since.

'It was one night after we had been through a solid week of debauch that things reached a climax. I can't tell you – no one can tell you exactly what happened that night. I don't suppose any of us really knew what we were doing. We had had supper in one of the cafés on the Boul' Mich', and afterwards we went to the rooms of one of the gang to play cards. He had dug up a faro outfit somewhere, and at that time the game was the craze in the Latin Quarter.

'I don't know how long we played – probably until the early hours of the morning. We were drinking steadily, too, you understand. Then a row started. Everyone took a hand in it, the girls as well as the men. The place was smashed up pretty badly, and when things finally calmed down several of the crowd cleared off.

'A few of us remained – five men, of whom Howland and myself were in the number, and a couple of girls. We began to play again, but before long another row started, and that broke up the play entirely. When this second row was over the rest of us departed, leaving our host to himself.

'I went to my rooms and threw myself on the bed without undressing. I fell asleep at once, and woke up to find Howland shaking me by the shoulder. It was broad daylight, past noon. I sat up, and, as soon as I was fully awake, he told me that Paul Hasford, who had been our host the previous night, had been arrested two hours before for the murder of a model, one Heléne Merchardier, who was one of the girls who had been present at the party, and, in fact, about whom both rows had started.

'She had been Hasford's model for some time, and it was rumoured that they were to be married. What started the row I can't tell you, as I have already explained, but it seems that the concierge of the building entered Hasford's rooms about ten o'clock in the morning and found him lying asleep across the table among the cards and bottles and glasses, and on the floor near him was Helene Merchardier.

'She was dead, had been shot through the heart, and just underneath Hasford's right hand was a nickel-plated revolver which was his own property.

'The concierge informed the police, and Hasford was arrested at once. Howland had gone round to the building to get a pipe which he had left there the night before, and discovered on his arrival what had occurred. As my diggings were nearer than those of any of the others who had been at the party he came to me first.

'As soon as I understood what he was driving at, I fell into a cold bath and dressed. We went round to see each of the others who was present during the second row, for, of course, Hasford must have killed the girl after that. We – '

'Just a moment, please,' broke in Sexton Blake. 'One question. When you and your friends left after the second altercation, did the girl who was found dead leave with you or remain?'

'She remained with Hasford.'

'Very well. Proceed, please.'

'As I was saying, we went to see the others, Howland and I. There were three of them – Joe Thurlston, the son of an American millionaire who had been playing about the quarter like myself, Ricardo Gispert, a wealthy Cuban, and the Hon. Freddie Buckford, who is the present Lord Baymore. Those three, with Geoffrey Howland and myself, made up the five who had remained after the first row.'

'You spoke of another girl. Was she a model?'

'Yes.'

'Can you remember her name?'

'Yes; it was Camille Desmoulins. I remember it, because it was the same as that of the famous character in French history.'

'Go on, please.'

'Howland and I dug out the other three, and told them what had happened. All five of us went round to Camille's flat and had a confab there. It was decided that we should go on to the Sureté and see if we could get an interview with Hasford. It was refused, so we went to one of the leading lawyers of the Paris bar, and retained him to defend Hasford.

'Well, Mr Blake, the trial created quite a sensation at the time. Hasford denied absolutely any knowledge of the shooting. His defence was that he had no reason to kill Heléne Merchardier, as there had been no trouble between them, and they were to be married the following month.

'The rest of us had to give evidence, but the result was that Hasford was found guilty. The French were "off" the guillotine at that time, although they have gone back to it of recent years. So Hasford was sentenced to a life term on Devil's Island, the

French penal settlement off the coast of French Guiana, in South America.

'The affair brought us all up with a round turn, and most of us left Paris soon after. It dropped into the past as the years went on, but about six months ago I had good reason to recall it again, for I received a letter from Joe Thurlston, who had inherited his father's banking business in New York, saying that he had received information that Hasford had escaped from Devil's Island.

'He followed that letter with another about two weeks later, in which he said that Ricardo Gispert, who had returned to Cuba after the affair, had been found shot in his office in Havana. He also enclosed a slip of paper on which had been written just the words: "H is free – the guilty shall pay." He was convinced that Hasford had sent this to him, and also that, after his escape from Devil's Island, Hasford had made his way to Cuba and had killed Gispert.'

'But why?'

'Because, at the time of his trial, he accused the five of us of having created the evidence against him. He swore that the pistol had been fired during the second row, and that one of us had shot Heléne Merchardier. He also swore that he had been struck down unconscious, and that, when he was discovered with the pistol under his hand he had not been asleep but had not recovered consciousness.

'At the time he was sentenced he swore in court that he would be revenged upon each of us for what he accused us of doing, and it seems that since his escape he has begun to fulfil his vow, for, about four months ago, I read in the papers that Joe Thurlston had fallen from the window of his private office at his bank and had been picked up dead. His neck had been broken.

'Following that, I had a letter at my club. It had been posted in London, and in it was a slip of paper bearing the same words which had been received by Thurlston. I got in touch with Howland, and found that he had received a similar letter, although he had heard nothing from Thurlston. We went to see Lord Baymore, who had also received a letter. We discussed things, and agreed that the death of Gispert and that of Thurlston, could only be the work of Hasford, the escaped convict.

'And now Howland is gone in the same way. As soon as I read the news I tried to get in touch with Lord Baymore, but found he had gone to Scotland. I have telegraphed him, asking him to come, if possible, to London. In the meantime I determined to come to you, Mr Blake, and seek your protection, for I know that Hasford is the murderer and that Baymore and I will be his next victims. That is the story. Can you help me?'

'Was this man Hasford guilty, Mr Chester?' asked Blake quietly.

'Yes – or I suppose so, unless the girl committed suicide.'

'She couldn't kill herself and afterwards put the gun under his hand.'

'No; that is true.'

'At the trial, you say that Hasford swore he had been struck down unconscious, and was still in that condition when discovered.'

'Yes.'

'Was he struck during the row?'

'I imagine so. Everything loose was used as a weapon. I was battered considerably, and so were most of the others.'

'If Hasford had been knocked unconscious there must have been a bruise on his head. Didn't the counsel for the defence have an examination made?'

'Yes; they found a bruise all right.'

'Ah! You say he was to be married to the girl, Heléne.'

'So he swore in court.'

'But you said it had been rumoured in the quarter.'

'Yes, it had.'

'Was Hasford a rich man?'

'No; he was poor. He lived mostly on what he made out of his work.'

'From what you have said, I take it the rest of you were more or less well supplied with money.'

'Yes.'

'And Hasford was the only poor man among you?'

'Of those who were immediately concerned with the affair, yes.'

'What were the two rows about? What started them?'

'I don't know what began the first one – some dispute over the game, I think. The second was begun between the two models, and the men took sides.'

'Who did the other girl usually pose for?'

'Myself, and sometimes Thurlston.'

'Had she ever posed for Hasford?'

'Yes; before he discovered the other one.'

'What, roughly, was the gist of the evidence you five and the other girl gave at the trial?'

'Why – er – just what happened – that we had all left except Heléne Merchardier. We had to admit that she and Hasford had quarrelled, and that they were still quarrelling when we left. That is about all.'

'Then he was not unconscious when you came away?'

'No.'

'So your evidence would brand his as false?'

'That is the way the court looked at it.'

'In his defence he swore that a gun had been used during the second row, and that it was then the girl must have been shot. Was a gun used?'

'Not to my knowledge.'

'You believed that he shot the girl?'

'Why, yes, he must have.'

'And now you believe him to be in London, and that it was he who killed Geoffrey Howland.'

'I do.'

'But what do you expect me to do to protect you? I have never seen the man. I have nothing to go on to find him. In the long years he was on Devil's Island he must have changed greatly. I doubt if even your description of him as he was twenty years or so ago would assist me. And if danger really threatens you he would probably succeed in his purpose before I could prevent him.'

The other wiped a damp brow. He was in a bad funk, and showed it.

'But – but they said you were a wizard,' he muttered.

Blake smiled.

'I am afraid someone was romancing about me, Mr Chester. The death of your friend in New York has started you imagining things. I doubt if you are in any real danger.'

'But he has escaped, and he has threatened!' cried Chester.

'Yes, that is so,' admitted Blake. 'But suppose I did find him, what could you do? It would be extremely difficult to prove that he killed Howland, and it is practically certain the coroner's jury will bring in a verdict of accidental death.'

'We could notify the French authorities, and have them extradite him and send him back to Devil's Island.'

'That might be done. But don't forget they failed to extradite the notorious Eddie Guerin, who also escaped from Devil's Island. Besides, I don't know that I should want to be a party to sending any poor devil back to that hell-hole after he had had twenty years of it.'

'But can't you help me? Won't you help me? I'll pay anything you ask. I go in fear every moment. I can't stand the suspense much longer!'

'I haven't said I wouldn't. You put this fear away from you, Mr Chester. You have given me one or two things to work on, and I will see what I can do. Keep your nerve, and if I can come on anything that makes me believe Geoffrey Howland's death was not an accident, then I shall take vigorous steps to discover the whereabouts of this man Hasford. That is all I can say now.'

And with that his visitor had to be content.

THE SIXTH CHAPTER

Deduction and Investigation

Scarcely had his client departed than Sexton Blake once more had recourse to the telephone. But this time it was 'trunks' he asked for.

On inquiring how long it would take him to get through to Paris, he was informed that it would not be under two hours. He gave two numbers, one being that of the Prefect of Police at the Sureté, and the other the office of a well-known Paris newspaper, the editor of which was personally known to him.

Next he called up the nearby garage where the Grey Panther was kept and gave instructions for it to be sent round. By the time it was at the kerb he was ready to go out, and as Tinker had not yet turned up, he took the wheel himself.

He drove to Oxford Street and down as far as Oxford Circus, where he turned into Regent Street. In Regent Street he drew up before a block of buildings, which he entered. He mounted to the second floor and rapped lightly on a door which bore no name. But Sexton Blake, like a few other persons, knew that office was one of the places where he would probably find Jack Phillips, the director of the secret gaming club in Dover Street.

On the door being opened he passed through an outer room, where a single clerk was at work, and opened the door leading to a private room. As he had hoped, the director was seated at his desk checking up some accounts. He shook hands with Blake, and as the latter sat down said: 'I can tell you, Blake, you took a load off my mind when you phoned me about Howland. I had the breeze up – thought it would all have to come out at the inquest.'

'I think I can fix things so the club won't come into it,' said Blake. 'But that isn't what I came to see you about exactly. I have been thinking that affair over. Now, I was playing in the diamond-room on Saturday night while Howland was there. I left before he did, but, from what I have learned since, he must have left the club soon after.'

'Well, I have been making some inquiries about that myself. While the servants are not supposed to know any of the members, I have been able to discover that he left shortly after two.'

'That coincides with what I have found out. If we take it that he went straight home, then the accident must have taken place twenty minutes or so later.'

'I should think around half-past two.'

'I agree. Well now, Jack, I left, as I said, just before then. I knew, too, that another man left immediately after, but it wasn't Howland. This man went down Hay Hill and entered the passage leading to Curzon Street. I am a little curious about him, for he is, I believe, the only member of the club I can't place, masked or unmasked. And I saw him unmasked.'

The gambler smiled faintly at Blake's words, for he knew only too well why Blake was a regular attendant at the gaming-room.

'What was he like? Must be a new member if you don't know him.'

'He has been about the club for several months to my knowledge. He only plays in the diamond-room, and nothing is too high for him. He plays an excellent game – never rides his shoe, and I have never seen him quit a loser. He played there Saturday night, and was at the table less than an hour altogether. Have you had many new members lately?'

'No, not many. Describe your man. Perhaps I can place him.'

Blake gave a minute description of the man who had attracted his attention on Saturday night, knowing that as he subjected every applicant for membership to a minute scrutiny, even though each was invariably vouched for by another member, he ought to be able to place the man. When he had finished

Phillips mentioned one or two names, but at each Blake shook his head, for they were names of men he knew.

'Well, I never forget a face,' remarked Phillips. 'It is my business to remember them. I'll get out the list and run through it. I might get an idea.'

He rose and unlocked a safe, taking out a thin morocco leather book and returning to his desk. He opened this, and, beginning at the last page which contained names, he began going back over those he knew had belonged to the club for a year or less. He was engaged thus for some little time, during which Blake smoked in silence; then he glanced up, his finger resting on a name.

'Your description fits this man, more or less,' he said. 'Name is Stone – David Stone.'

'What does he do? Is he independent?'

'I don't know what he does exactly, but it seems to me something was said about him being a painter. I don't know his address either. You know our rule about not asking a member for his private address. His sponsor is supposed to cover that.'

'Yes, I know. Do you mind telling me, Jack, who sponsored him?'

'Wait a second. Let's see. Card index number four hundred and nine.'

He rose again, and took from the safe a small polished oak box containing cards such as are used in card index filing. He ran his fingers through these until he came to the letter 'S', and a few seconds later he turned his head sharply.

'What the dickens made you think of that?' he asked.

'Why?'

'Because his sponsor was Geoffrey Howland.'

Sexton Blake had come up against a good many surprises during his long career, but even he could scarcely repress a start as he heard the gambler's words. He made no comment, however, but, with a nod, rose.

'I just wanted as many particulars as possible,' he said. 'I think with what I have now I can manage all right, and you needn't worry about the name of the club being dragged in.'

'You will make me your debtor if you can fix that, Blake,' said the other gratefully. 'I don't mind admitting to you that I don't want the police searchlight turned on that club.'

'Nor do I,' admitted Blake, with a laugh. And the two shook hands.

From Phillips's office Blake drove the Grey Panther through to Chelsea, where he drew up in front of a house occupied by a certain well-known painter.

On ringing the bell, he was admitted by a neat maidservant, who took his card and asked him to wait. She returned a few minutes later, to announce that her master would see him, and forthwith ushered Blake upstairs to a large studio, where the painter was at work.

When the greetings were over Blake said: 'I haven't come to ask you to paint my portrait, but to make use of you, if you wish to put it that way.'

'You needn't hesitate to ask, Blake,' returned the other. 'I haven't forgotten that you bought the first picture I exhibited. And it was you who sent my earliest clients to me.'

'Your work was first-class, or I shouldn't have done it,' responded Blake. 'Do you know a painter of the name of Stone – David Stone?'

'No, but I know some of his work.'

'What do you know about him?'

'Practically nothing. I saw some of his pictures at a private exhibition, that is all. If you wish, I shall make inquiries among some of my friends.'

'I should be grateful if you would. I want all the particulars about him I can get – where he comes from, how long he has been in London, his address, and so on.'

'Is it urgent?'

'Not urgent, but the earlier I have the information the better.'

'I'll start inquiries today, and communicate with you just as soon as I have anything to tell you.'

'Thanks awfully! I shan't forget it.'

From Chelsea Blake drove back to Baker Street, and while he was waiting for his Paris connection he consulted several directories, but in none of them could he find any record of a David Stone. He was still so engaged when Tinker came in, and after he had listened to the lad's report Blake said: 'Get in touch with our agents in London, my lad. Give them the name of David Stone, supposed to be a painter. I want any particulars they can gather; but chiefly I want to learn where he is living – if he is living in London. Ah, that will be Paris now!'

The telephone had interrupted Blake, and on lifting the receiver he was informed that he was through to his first call.

A few seconds later he recognised the voice of Monsieur Dupuis, the Prefect of Police in Paris, and, after announcing his identity. Blake said: 'Some twenty years or more ago a man of the name of Hasford was sentenced in Paris to a life term on Devil's Island, M. Dupuis. I am given to understand that this prisoner escaped not long ago. Can you tell me if that is correct?'

'In a way it is, M. Blake. He served a full twenty years, the normal life term, and, as his record was a good one, he was released on licence and allowed to cross to Cayenne on the mainland and take up work there. It was from Cayenne he escaped, not from Devil's Island.'

'Do you know where he went, *monsieur*' ?

'We picked up his tracks in British Guiana, and lost them there. The docket which I received from Devil's Island states that it was reported he had joined a diamond prospecting party in British Guiana and had gone up the Essequibo. Have you any news of him?'

'No. His name came up in a case of mine, and I am anxious to know about him. If he were located, would you want to extradite him?'

'We are not anxious to get him back. He has served a full twenty years, and if he keeps away from French territory I doubt if we shall worry him.'

'You have received the last of his docket from Devil's Island?'

'Yes, M. Blake.'

'Could you manage to send it across to me by registered post, in order that I may read the full history of the case? I should keep it only a day or so, and would return it safely.'

'Certainly, *monsieur*, I shall be happy to do so. Shall I send the whole docket?'

'If you will be so kind.'

'I shall forward it by tonight's post without fail.'

'*Merci, monsieur!* You are very amiable.'

'At your service, *monsieur*, always.'

Blake had scarcely hung up when he was rung up again and informed that his second call was through. His conversation this time was somewhat longer; but when he had finished he had succeeded in arranging with the editor in Paris, whom he had called, that the old issues of the journal dealing with the tragedy of more than twenty years before should be forwarded to him by post that night.

He had had what purported to be the full story of the affair from his client of the morning, but he wanted to read just what the papers had recorded at the time, since he knew a man's memory is not always to be relied on after the passage of years.

Following that, Sexton Blake called up Detective-Inspector Thomas at Scotland Yard, and gave that efficient official a mild surprise at the request he had to make – for that request was: 'Will you please arrange that an X-ray photograph be taken of the neck vertebrae of Geoffrey Howland, the man who was found dead in Curzon Street?'

THE SEVENTH CHAPTER

A Remnant of the Past

Two registered packages arrived from Paris the following morning.

The first was the complete docket from the Paris Sureté of one John Hasford, from the time he had been convicted, more than twenty years before, for the murder of Heléne Merchardier, until he had escaped from Cayenne, the seaport of French Guiana into British Guiana.

The second was a big batch of newspapers, published at the time of Hasford's trial, and giving, over a period of some weeks, a complete report of the case, and of all those who had had any connection with it. That it had created no small sensation was plain, for in those days far less space was given to a *cause celébre* than in these days of keen journalistic competition, and the old journals which had been sent to Blake contained an exceptionally full report.

Sexton Blake gave his attention to the newspapers first. From the first paragraph, announcing the arrest of John Hasford, to the last day of the trial, on which he was sentenced to Devil's Island for life, he missed not a single word.

When he had finished he took down the very first volume of the 'Index', which he had begun compiling when he had commenced practice as a criminologist, and there he found that he had cut out and pasted in a small clipping referring to the affair. But that was back in the early days of his career, and Blake had been giving all his attention then to developing his practice in London. It was not until later that it grew to become a vast international network, such as no other investigator of crime has built up.

From the papers he turned his attention to the police docket, and was deeply engrossed over that almost up to the time when he had to leave for the inquest on Geoffrey Howland.

At the inquest Blake volunteered a written statement to the coroner, in which he stated that the dead man had been in the company of himself and others until a few minutes past two the night of the tragedy, and that he had departed for home alone shortly after two. In view of Sexton Blake's standing, this statement was accepted without a cross-examination, and, as he had promised, Blake was able to keep the name of the gambling-club from being brought up.

As he had expected, the jury brought in a verdict of 'Accidental death', and immediately after Blake and Tinker returned to Baker Street. So far Blake had said little to the lad about the private investigations he had been making.

At the time Tinker was engaged on digging up some records of a fraudulent transaction that had taken place about two years before, and which were necessary for Blake to have in his possession before he went ahead on another case in which he had been retained.

Moreover, there was just a nebulous theory taking form in his mind, and he was by no means ready to come out with a definite hypothesis. At the same time, he had found more than a little food for thought in the reading of those newspapers and that police docket from Paris, and, if he agreed with Mr Bramwell Chester in little that gentleman had said, he certainly did believe that Geoffrey Howland had been murdered.

For the whole of that evening Sexton Blake continued his study of the docket from the Sureté. It was a most comprehensive affair, giving a minute Bertillon description of the convict – for in those days the fingerprint system was not in use at the Paris Sureté – and after his arrival at Devil's Island a detailed account of his life as a prisoner there.

Later on, when the fingerprint system had been introduced, all the prisoners at Devil's Island had had their prints taken, and a set of Hasford's was attached near the end of the report.

Sexton Blake went into his laboratory and spent some time in making a very careful record of these prints, then he completed his study of the remainder of the docket; and when he had finished he knew as much about the intimate daily life of John Hasford for the past twenty years as was known to the governor of the prison on Devil's Island. He knew what the man's behaviour had been; he knew what hobbies he had taken up when this indulgence was granted after ten years; he knew in what he was most proficient; he knew in what physical way the man was most marked; and he knew, too, why the other convicts had dubbed Hasford the 'Black Eagle'.

The system of espionage on prisoners at Devil's Island is one of the most thorough of any prison in the world, and in Hasford's case apparently not a single item was overlooked.

When he had finished the docket Blake returned once more to the newspapers and carefully wrote down all the names of those who had given evidence in the case. One of these names he wrote on a separate slip of paper, and underneath it the address at which the person in question had lived when the killing of Heléne Merchardier had taken place. Then he re-wrapped the newspapers and docket very carefully and locked them away in his safe. That was on Tuesday night.

On Wednesday morning Sexton Blake informed his assistant, Tinker, that he proposed running over to Paris for a day or two, and that he – Tinker – would have to look after things at Baker Street until his return. That same morning he had another visit from Mr Bramwell Chester, who was accompanied by Lord Baymore, who had returned from Scotland.

The noble peer seemed to be in as great a funk as his friend; and, just because he wanted to get the peer's version of certain phases of the tragedy of the past, Blake listened patiently to what he had to say. He asked a few questions, which, apparently, had little bearing on the matter; then he eased their anxiety to a certain extent by promising to arrange that very day that a confidential agent of his would shadow them wherever they went.

He kept his word, too, for before he got away for Paris on the evening train he had detailed two of his regular agents to this work.

Sexton Blake arrived in Paris early the following morning. He drove at once to the Carlitz Hotel, in the Rue de Rivoli, where he booked his usual suite. After a bath he changed and went down to *petit déjeuner*, after which he telephoned to the Sureté for an appointment with the Prefect of Police. When he had fixed this he took a taxi and drove to the Boulevard des Italiens, where he handed back the bundle of old newspapers which his editor friend had sent him.

He spent half an hour or so in conversation there, after which he proceeded to the Sureté, arriving sharp on the minute for his interview with M. Dupuis, the Prefect.

Blake's first duty was to hand over the docket referring to the convict, John Hasford, then he drew from his wallet the slip of paper on which he had written a name and address the previous evening in Baker Street.

'Here is the name and address of a person who was rather prominently connected with that old affair,' he said. 'Of course, I know that in the passage of years this person may be dead. But as your records probably contain any information known about the individual in question, I should be grateful if you would have a search made.'

The Prefect took the slip of paper and glanced at the name. Then he read the address.

'This person, if alive, would not be at that address now,' he remarked. 'The buildings in that street were pulled down more than ten years ago, and modern flats erected in their stead. However, *monsieur*, I shall have a search made. Will you wait?'

'No, thanks. It will probably take some time, and you are busy. I shall return to the Carlitz. Perhaps you will be good enough to communicate with me there?'

'Certainly, *monsieur*, with pleasure.'

So, after a few more words, Blake took his departure and returned to his hotel, where he wrote letters until it was time to go down to the grill-room.

He had just finished lunch and had returned to the lounge, when a messenger came from the Sureté with a note from M. Dupuis. The note informed Blake that the special man who had been put on the job had got track of the person desired, but had not yet exactly located the individual. It added that as soon as this was accomplished the special would report personally to Blake at the hotel, and that he had instructions to place himself entirely at Blake's orders.

Blake stuck close to the hotel the whole afternoon, but it was not until nearly seven o'clock that the special turned up. He had succeeded in locating the person at last, and had taken the precaution of putting another man on watch, so that there should be no difficulty if Blake wished to go along. The report was a very detailed one on the lines along which the Paris Sureté trains its men, and when Blake had finished it he made his decision quickly.

'We will go along,' he said, rising, and with no thought of the dinner which he would miss. 'I want an interview with this person, and it is likely to be a difficult one. In one section of your report I notice something, however, which may enable me to achieve what I want; so before we go I want to go along to a *pharmacie* and buy something. As the stuff I want is not permitted to be sold indiscriminately, I shall be glad if you will come with me and inform the pharmacist that it is all right.'

As the special had received instructions from the Prefect himself that he was to do exactly as M. Blake said he made no objection; so a few minutes later they walked into a pharmacie in the Rue de Rivoli, where Sexton Blake purchased a pill-box full of a certain white powder. He thrust that in his pocket, and, on emerging, hailed a taxi. He left it to the man from the Sureté to give the address, although he knew well enough where they were bound for.

It was about half an hour later that the taxi, after having passed through the Belleville quarter, past the dingy shacks which skirt that unlovely part of Paris, drew up just at the old fortifications. Here Blake and the special descended, bidding the taxi wait for them.

The special led the way past the fortifications, and then suddenly they plunged into a filthy quarter of hovels and dug-outs that beggar description.

Sexton Blake knew it only too well as the haunt of all the thieves, beggars, ragpickers, and human vermin of Paris – and in no city in the world can that quarter be exceeded for utter horror, unless perhaps it is in the 'trenches' of Shanghai, or the Thieves' Market of Canton.

There is scarcely a denizen of that ghastly place who would not commit a dozen murders for a few sous.

But they went ahead as if it were as safe as the grand boulevards, and, after stumbling along past a scattered confusion of old tin and wood huts for some minutes, they came suddenly upon a roughly-clad person who was leaning against the rickety door of a dug-out or what was simply a hole dug into the rising slope of the old fortifications.

It was the man who had been left on guard, and as Blake and his companion came up he uttered a few words in a low tone to the special.

The latter turned to Blake.

'The bird is still in the cage,' he whispered. 'Are you sure you want to go ahead? It is less dangerous now than it will be when the vermin comes back at midnight or later, but there is plenty of trouble waiting even now.'

'I'll go in,' said Blake curtly. 'If any trouble starts, please call me at once.'

The special uttered an affirmative, and his companion dragged open the rickety planks that formed a door. Sexton Blake bent half double and stumbled through, then he managed to straighten up as he found himself in one of the worst pits of filth and squalor he had ever encountered.

It was practically devoid of even rough sticks of furniture. In one corner was a heap of rags, on which an old hag was lying. On the mud floor beside her was a battered tin plate, containing a bit of cold grease with a lump of mildewed meat marooned in the middle of it. Stuck in a broken bottle was a candle, the flame of which was burning almost without flicker in that mephitic hole.

That was all – the very last dregs of horror to which that which might once have been human could descend.

As he entered the old woman dragged herself to a sitting posture. She pulled a vile rag about her withered body, and from beneath her tangled, discoloured grey hair two rat-like eyes glared at him. Then she began, and for a full five minutes she cursed him in an unceasing stream.

Sexton Blake stood close to the door, staring at her calmly, quite unmoved by the torrent. He waited until she wore herself out by sheer exhaustion, then slowly, while her eyes watched him, he took from his pocket first the small pillbox he had purchased at the *pharmacie*, then from another pocket a note for a thousand francs. He held both these out close to the candle flame, so that she must see the denomination of the note. That he thrust back into his pocket, and then gently twisted off the lid of the box. From the box he took a tiny pinch of the white powder, which he held out towards her.

Her eyes darted from his face to the pinch of white powder and back again. Blake did not speak. He just waited, and slowly, ever so slowly, her claw-like fingers came out and plucked at the powder. She scraped every last atom from his hand, and he shivered at the touch of those sin-twisted fingers. But otherwise he stood motionless until she had finished.

Then he watched her while she dropped the powder on the back of her own hand and lifted the hand to her nostrils. She sniffed once, twice, then she gave a cry and fell to her knees.

If before she had reviled him by the most terrible words man ever listened to, now she fawned upon him like some ghastly, maudlin, mewling gnome of the night. In that mud-hole, by the light of the dying candle, she brought to her lips every word of cajolement and endearment she could drag from what had been her past.

She cried and sobbed and maundered. She essayed to embrace him by the knees, but Sexton Blake drew back just enough to avoid her touch. He had had enough of that.

And then, when for the second time she paused, he bent low, and his voice came in a slow, deadly hiss.

'Coke,' he said, 'coke that you live for, coke that you would do anything to get, coke that you can't live without, coke that you must have, or you will die! Here in this box there is enough for many, many days. In my pocket there is money to buy you all you need for many months. And it is yours, if you want it, Camille Desmoulins.'

'Cam – Camille Desmoulins!' she stammered. 'Who are you? Why do you call me that?'

'Because you are Camille Desmoulins. You are slave to the power of this drug. You will die if you do not get it. You take the scraps which others throw you, and you live but to snatch a grain of the drug which makes you forget. Think! Look at this box – enough for days and days. And money – plenty for you to buy all you wish. And it is yours, Camille Desmoulins, for the speaking of two words.'

'Who are you? What do you want of me?'

'Go back into the years of the past, Camille Desmoulins, when you were a model in the Quartier Latin. Go back to the days when you were young and pretty, and knew the love of youth. Go back, I say, to those days when you knew John Hasford. Go back to the days when you knew Joe Thurlston and Ricardo Gispert, Geoffrey Howland, Bramwell Chester, and Freddie Buckford. Go back to the night when you were all together in John Hasford's rooms, and Heléne Merchardier was killed! Go back to that night, I say, and – tell – me – who – killed – Heléne – Merchardier!'

As he hammered out the last words the woman gave a scream and tried to rise. Sexton Blake drew back again near the door and stood waiting. He knew from the report the special had brought him that for years this hag, who had once been the pretty model of the Latin Quarter, was an inveterate slave to the terrible drug cocaine.

He knew she managed somehow to drag along in that terrible pit, existing on the few grains she could beg from time to time. Without it she would die. With it she could prolong her terrible existence a little longer. That one pinch he had given her would, he knew, only serve to give her new life for a short time.

Soon, very soon, she would be begging for the box which she had glimpsed, and which meant heaven to her.

It was a terrible sight. Twenty years before she had been young, and, by the accounts in the papers of the time, extremely pretty.

Today she could have been scarcely past forty, and yet she looked seventy. It was one of the most horrible human wrecks Sexton Blake had ever gazed upon, but he did not flinch. He was determined that before he left that mudhole he should drag from her the truth of that night of long ago, for he was convinced that the truth had not been spoken at the trial.

So he waited until her paroxysm of fury wore itself out. She fell back on the rags and sat staring at him through the tangled masses of grey hair. Blake again drew out the box and held it up. She lurched forward, but he avoided her, and again she began to call him by names of endearment. But he was inflexible.

'Answer my question,' he kept reiterating. 'Who killed Heléne Merchardier?'

At last the words seemed to penetrate into her mind. She looked at him cunningly and smiled, showing toothless gums.

'And if I tell you, will you give me the box?' she wheedled.

'Yes, if you tell me the truth.'

'It was John Hasford!' she screamed. 'John Hasford killed her, and he went to Devil's Island! Curse him for what he was! But he was paid – oh, yes, he was paid! Now, dearie, I've told you! Give me the lovely little box!'

Blake shook his head.

'No. You have not told me the truth. John Hasford did not kill Heléne Merchardier. If you lie to me I will go, and take the box and the money with me. I give you a last chance. Tell me, who killed Heléne Merchardier?'

There was another space, during which she reviled him with all her dying strength; then she fell back once more and began panting with exhaustion. It was a terrible sight – a sight that would have made almost any man waver.

But Sexton Blake never moved – just waited.

And when she began to moan and crawl towards him he knew he had won.

'Who killed Heléne Merchardier?' he could hear her muttering. 'Wasn't it John Hasford? No, no, no! You want to know who killed her? It was I, Camille Desmoulins, who killed her! Ah, I was cunning that night. John Hasford – curse him in his prison till he rots! – had thrown me aside for that vain wench. I waited and I watched, for I knew my chance would come. It did come, and I killed her! I killed her in front of him! But he did not see, for he was lying unconscious on the table! Ah, we worked it well that night! And John Hasford went to Devil's Island!'

'We! You say "we"!' broke in Blake sharply. 'Who helped you to plan it?'

'Joe Thurlston! He hated John Hasford because Heléne loved Hasford. I hated Heléne because she had taken Hasford from me. We arranged it. It was Joe Thurlston who struck down Hasford, while I shot Heléne! Now, my pretty one, give me the box and leave me!'

'Soon! Soon!' said Blake, trying desperately hard to keep her wavering mind on the subject. 'Tell me first about the others. What had they to do with it?'

'The others! Freddie Buckford loved me, and would do as I wished. He and Joe Thurlston persuaded Gispert and Chester and Howland to keep silent and give evidence that would convict Hasford. And we did – ha, ha! We sent him to Devil's Island, and I am here! Now, dearie, give me the box!'

Sexton Blake took the box from his pocket and dropped it into her outstretched hand. Then he thrust the thousand-franc note after it and, turning, stumbled out of the place. As he emerged he turned and panted: 'Come on, let's get out of here! I've got what I wanted!'

And with that he literally fled from that place of sin and misery.

THE EIGHTH CHAPTER

A Visitor to Baker Street – Unauthorised

Sexton Blake returned to London the following day, arriving at Baker Street early in the evening. On his desk he found a parcel which Inspector Thomas had left, and which, on being opened, proved to contain three large X-ray photographs of the neck vertebrae of the late Geoffrey Howland.

Sexton Blake studied these three photographs long and carefully, and, since they had been taken on Wellington plates, 14 ins. by 19 ins., the detail was remarkably good. Then he locked them away.

He dined early with Tinker, after which he held a brief telephone conversation with Jack Phillips, the gambler.

Tinker had received regular reports from the two men who had been set to shadow Lord Baymore and Bramwell Chester; but Blake scarcely glanced at them. Then for the next few days he confined himself to routine work and to making a résumé of the material regarding the other case, which Tinker had succeeded in gathering together.

To see him at work, one would have thought that he had entirely dismissed from his mind all thought of the other affair which had engrossed him earlier in the week.

But on Saturday evening Blake slipped into formal evening-dress, and, after giving some careful instructions to Tinker, took his way on foot to the gaming club in Dover Street.

On entering the club, he made his way at once to the diamond-room, which was already nearly filled with players. And, as his eyes swept over the masked countenances, Sexton Blake knew that the unknown who had roused his curiosity a week before and whose identity he now suspected, was already in his place, playing.

Blake selected a chair, and placed a thick roll of notes before him. Then he settled down to the game, which was running at a minimum of six hundred pounds to the turn, as if nothing else whatsoever occupied his mind. He knew that this was the first night in a week that the unknown had appeared at the club, for he had had Phillips on the lookout since the night he had telephoned him, and if the unknown had showed up the gambler would have let him know.

For some time the game progressed until at last the 'shoe' came to the man on whom Blake's attention was fixed. Blake watched the play, noting that this night luck was going strongly against him. He could not help but admire the cool power of control exhibited by the other, and he mentally applauded when he pushed the shoe along and rose from his chair.

'Follows the same system for losses and winnings,' thought Blake.

He waited a few moments after the unknown had disappeared behind the heavy velvet curtains, then he, too, rose. He strolled out through the chemin-de-fer and roulette rooms and into the buffet, where he saw his man eating a sandwich and drinking a glass of wine. Blake also selected a sandwich and took a glass of wine.

He strolled to the other side of the room, and remained, apparently engrossed in his own thoughts, until the masked unknown rose. When he had passed out of the buffet towards the ante-room, Blake gave him sufficient time to get downstairs to the cloak-room.

Then he, too, left the buffet; but, instead of going downstairs, he went along a hall and into a small private room, which looked out on to Dover Street. It was dark and deserted, but Blake did not turn on the lights. He crossed the room and lifted the heavy curtains until he could look down to the street.

Then he raised the window a trifle, after which he took out a small pocket torch.

He stood thus until he heard the soft closing of a door just beneath, followed by the footfall of someone walking towards Hay Hill. Blake waited about another five seconds, then he lifted the torch to the window, and flashed it just once.

He kept peering out until he saw a figure slip away from a shadowy doorway on the opposite side of the street, then he dropped the curtain, and made his way back to the buffet, knowing that Tinker was on the trail. And it seemed to Blake that to shadow the man was his only way of finding out where he lived, for his own inquiries had revealed nothing, nor had his agents or his artist friend been able to tell him anything whatsoever about the address of an artist known as David Stone.

Blake finished his light supper, then he strolled into the roulette-room, and began to play very moderate stakes. With Sexton Blake it was always the game itself and not the amount at risk that held his interest, and, while his winnings or losses at the roulette meant absolutely nothing to him, he was quite as keenly engrossed in the click of the little ivory ball as he had been in the turn of the 'shoe' in the diamond-room.

Hence, at the end of a winning streak, when he felt his throat growing dry, and ambled along to the buffet to get a glass of wine, he was astounded, on glancing at a clock, to note that it was nearly four o'clock in the morning.

When he had watched Tinker start shadowing the unknown from the club it had been just after midnight. Tinker's instructions had been short, but to the point.

'Follow the man who leaves the club when you see me flash a signal from the window of the room over the door,' Blake had said. 'Find out where he goes, and return at once to the club to report. You know the password which Phillips gave you to use whenever you wished to speak to me when I was there. That is all. Don't make a single move on your own initiative.'

That was all, and, unless it had been necessary for the lad to follow his quarry a considerable distance out of London, then he should have been back long since.

Blake began to grow uneasy. If the lad had failed, he would have come back to report the fact. There could have been no misunderstanding with the servant on duty at the door, for Tinker would not muddle things there.

However, just to make sure, Blake descended into the lower hall and interviewed the doorman.

It was as he had expected. It was certain that Tinker had not been at the club since leaving the doorway opposite. Blake knew that the only other alternative was, if no mishap had overtaken the lad, that he would go straight on to Baker Street, thinking, perhaps, if he had been longer than he expected, that Blake would be waiting there.

Thinking this must be what had happened, Blake donned his overcoat and opera hat, and stepped into the lobby, removing his black silk mask as he did so. Then he started off at a brisk pace for Baker Street.

With long legs, and being a naturally good walker, it was not long before he had reached home. As he went up the steps and felt for his latchkey, he noticed that the whole house seemed to be in darkness, which would hardly be the case if Tinker were waiting for him. He decided, however, that it would scarcely be worth while returning to the club, so he opened the door and stepped into the hall.

Blake closed the door gently, and walked along to the consulting-room door, not taking the trouble to turn on the hall light, for he knew every inch of the way blindfold. He fumbled for a second, until his fingers encountered the handle of the consulting-room door, then he turned it, and stepped inside. His hand slid up along the wall to the switch, and as his fingers came in contact with it he pressed it over.

At once the room was flooded with light, and Blake pushed the door closed as he turned to walk towards his desk.

It was at that moment that he suddenly became aware that a masked man, in evening dress, was seated in one of his low, saddlebag chairs, facing the door, with an automatic pistol in his hand, the barrel of which was in a straight line with Blake's heart.

THE NINTH CHAPTER

Expiation – and Renunciation

'Stand just where you are, Mr Sexton Blake!' came a command.

Sexton Blake stood motionless for the space of perhaps three seconds. Then: 'Why not remove the mask, Mr Hasford? I know your features quite well. And besides, we have already been in each other's company tonight.' With that Blake turned, and coolly began walking towards his desk, but as he went along he shot over his shoulder: 'Nor do I think you will shoot, Mr Hasford. The Black Eagle might break a man's neck, but I don't believe he would shoot one in the back.'

Blake could not see now what his visitor was doing. Himself, he paused by the desk, his back still turned, and laid his silk hat down. Then he leisurely removed his silk-lined coat and threw it on a chair. Quite coolly he pulled the big box of Turkish cigarettes towards him, and carefully selected one, which he lit.

Then, and only then, did he drop into the seat in front of the desk and turn to face his visitor. The silk mask had been removed; the revolver was no longer in sight.

'That, I think, is better,' remarked Blake. 'And now, Mr Hasford, perhaps you will tell me why you have come to see me tonight; also, how you got in, for I am under the impression that my housekeeper is spending the night with relatives on the other side of London.'

David Stone, his face as lean and as immobile as Sexton Blake's, was regarding the detective queerly. So sure was he that he had not overlooked a single point that he was entirely at sea as to how Sexton Blake had come to utter that name which he had not heard another person speak for more than twenty years. At last he spoke.

'Have you in your service a young man known as Tinker?' he asked abruptly.

'I have. And an extremely efficient assistant he is, too.'

'Did you set him to spy on me tonight?'

'His instructions were to follow you from a certain club in Grafton Street to your home – if it should be possible.'

'He obeyed your instructions. But you forgot that I, too, might have a watchdog. Your spy was seen, and as he passed the door of my house he was drawn inside. For your information, Mr Blake, I may say that his position is most precarious. His life depends on the result of my visit here tonight. In his pockets I found letters which contained your name. I also found keys, one of which admitted me to this house.'

'I fancied something of the sort had happened,' remarked Blake. 'What can I do for you, Mr Hasford? Do you wish to discuss the death of Ricardo Gispert, in Havana? Or would you prefer to talk of the death of Joseph Thurlston, in New York? Or, again, perhaps the "accident" to Mr Geoffrey Howland would prove of more interest. And, by the way, I have something here in my desk which, I am sure, will interest you. One moment, please.'

With that, Blake drew open the drawer in which he had placed the three X-ray photographs which Inspector Thomas had left with him. He glanced at them for a moment, then he handed them to the other. Without a word John Hasford took them, and sat gazing at them, while Blake continued: 'Excellent results, Mr Hasford. As you will see, they are of the neck vertebrae of a human being. Look at them carefully, I beg you. You will see that the column has been broken from being jerked from side to side, and not as it would have been broken if one had just fallen downstairs, for example. There were two motions – one which strained the cushions between the vertebrae, but did not quite break it, the other which snapped it clean. A very quick and very efficient bit of work, Mr Hasford.

It needed a pair of powerful hands to do that, a pair of hands strong enough, shall we say, to tear in half two or three packs of playing-cards at a single stroke.'

John Hasford's eyes met Blake's.

'You have said too much – or too little, Sexton Blake,' he said, in tones of ice. 'You may banter if you wish, but, believe me, before I leave here this night there is going to be a showdown, or one of us will not be alive in the morning. I think you are judge enough of human nature to realise that I mean what I say.'

'Yes, I believe you,' admitted Blake quietly. 'But don't you think, Mr Hasford, that you have already taken toll enough of human life, considering that not one of the three men you have killed was guilty of shooting Heléne Merchardier?'

'By—!' The startled oath shot from between John Hasford's teeth, and he half started up. But Blake held up his hand.

'Wait!' he said curtly.

'Just to enlighten you, Mr Hasford, I will tell you that I have been unearthing quite a lot about you ever since last Monday. In fact, it was entirely due to this that I travelled to Paris on Wednesday and returned on Thursday. And ever since Thursday I have been waiting for you to appear at the club in Grafton Street. I was anxious to discover where the artist David Stone lived. Apparently, my assistant succeeded only too well.

'I have had quite an interesting time in reading the complete docket of one John Hasford, who spent some twenty years on Devil's Island, and who escaped from Cayenne after he had been allowed to go there on licence. I may say here that I am assured by the Prefect of Police in Paris that as long as John Hasford does not return to French territory he will not be worried by the French police. That may interest you.

'I have also read in the newspapers of the time the history of the trial of John Hasford for the murder of Heléne Merchardier.

I know, too, all about the party in Hasford's room that night more than twenty years ago, when Heléne Merchardier was found shot through the heart and John Hasford was found lying asleep – or shall I say unconscious? – across the table. The evidence was damning, and he was convicted.

'In the docket of the convict, John Hasford, I read all about his daily life, and the hobbies he followed when he was permitted to do so after ten years' confinement. I know that he displayed no little talent as a painter, and became very efficient indeed as a cabinetmaker and wood-carver. Also, I know that he practised such exercises as developed his wrists and arms to an extraordinary degree, so much so, in fact, that, owing to his feats of strength from great heights, he was christened by the other convicts the Black Eagle.

'I also saw a member of a certain club in Grafton Street gather up a large bundle of playing-cards and tear them in half with scarcely an effort. That took extraordinary strength, Mr Hasford, and, considering that the same man walked through the passage from Berkeley Square to Curzon Street just a short time before Geoffrey Howland passed the same way, it seemed a trifle curious to me. I suppose it is because my detective faculties have been developed that I remarked these apparently unimportant things.

'But to return to Paris. While I was there I succeeded in getting track of another person who had been at that party years ago. This was a woman known as Camille Desmoulins. In those days, I understand, she was a pretty and popular model. Today she is – well, she has reached the dregs of human wretchedness. But I knew that if anyone could tell the truth of the killing that night, she was the one. I found her, and I made her talk – never mind how.

'You have suffered terribly. You have given twenty years out of the best part of your life for a crime which someone else committed. I can understand and sympathise with the bitterness you feel. You were betrayed, and everyone at that party that night had a hand in your betrayal. But this unlicensed vengeance of yours cannot be permitted to continue. If you could see Camille Desmoulins today you would not ask for further vengeance. The five men all betrayed you. Thurlston was the most culpable of the lot, while Howland was next. The others were persuaded into it in some way, and that was how you were shunted off to Devil's Island.

'But the person who killed Heléne Merchardier was not one of the five. It was a woman maddened by jealousy. It was Camille Desmoulins who shot her after Thurlston knocked you on the back of the head. Now, what are you going to do about it, Mr Hasford?'

John Hasford began. He told of the horror he had felt at the discovery of Heléne Merchardier lying dead beside him. He told of his love for her, and how they were to be married the following month. He explained that he was so deep in the grip of misery that he scarcely knew what was happening at the trial, and yet how he had felt vaguely that in some way he was being betrayed.

Then he went on to speak of the long years on that hell's-hole, Devil's Island, and how, over the years, he lived but for one thing – to get free and be revenged; for in the solitude of his cell understanding had come to him, although he never dreamed that Camille Desmoulins had done the killing.

He told how he had planned each step from the moment he should be free; how he had struck it rich in the diamond diggings on the Essequibo, and how, afterwards, he had gone to Havana to find Ricardo Gispert. Blake knew the rest, but he allowed his confession to run its course. When the man grew silent he said: 'And now, what are you going to do?'

'It is rather what are you going to do? I killed Geoffrey Howland – I don't deny it.'

'I am not a watchdog for the police. Nor am I judge and jury. I believe in the law of order, and I uphold it. I do not believe any man will gain ease of spirit by taking the law into his own hands. There is much to be considered in your case, for you have suffered grievously. Your ideas, fixed on one thing all those years, have become warped. You will never find true vengeance by continuing to break one of the commandments which have been laid upon us.

'But, for me, you may go and search your own mind, on the promise that you will leave the remaining two men who took part in that betrayal in peace. You must take your own chances with the law. But if I were you I would make that inner searching a long and patient one, and I think you will find that I am right. That is all.'

'You – you mean you are not going to inform the police?'

'That is what I mean.'

John Hasford stood up.

'Then, Mr Blake, I will go and meditate as you suggest. I can promise nothing, except that Bramwell Chester and Baymore may go in peace, so far as I am concerned. And Camille Desmoulins is her own punishment. What I shall do in the future I do not know. If I change, it will be because of what you have said and done this night. If I move in the shadows, it will be because I cannot find the light. But if I fail, you will always know that I shall carry with me one spark of belief that there is at least one loyal and upright man in this world of misery. Now I go.'

'I shall walk with you.' said Blake simply. 'I wish to bring my assistant back with me.'

And a few minutes later those two men, so alike in strength of body and character, so unlike in the spiritual cosmos in which each dwelt, passed out into the night, and took their way to that strange house in that quiet crescent off the Edgware Road, where a grotesque human caricature was keeping guard over Tinker.

That same night David Stone dropped completely out of sight, but there was to come a time in the future when his paths and Blake's were again to cross.

As for A. Long, the cabinet-maker of the Seven Sisters Road, he returned to his little shop in the early hours of Sunday morning, and the following day was busily at work in the workroom at the back of the shop.